Wicked Company

"This isn't one of those 'male tricks' you told me by the river you wouldn't employ?" she demanded with a weak smile.

"I fear that it is," he admitted, the ghost of a grin pulling at the corners of his mouth. "But I also said then that I would wait for you to come to me, if you so desire—and it appears you have. And you do. Desire, I mean. I can *feel* it, Sophie."

Her heart was beginning to thud so strongly, she wondered if Hunter could hear it. He raised her hand off the table and slowly, deliberately inserted her forefinger an inch into his mouth, his lips tugging on it sensuously.

"A-another trick?" she whispered, feeling as if she were about to fling herself off a cliff.

"Just one of many I have up my sleeve—*if* you so desire," he divulged quietly, his dark blue eyes riveted on hers.

"Oh, Hunter," she said in a breath. " 'Tis so unfair . . . you know so much of . . . these . . . matters . . . and I'm a—"

"Novice?"

"Virgin," she corrected him faintly. "I am completely untutored in this subject, I assure you. . . ."

Praise for Ciji Ware's first novel,
Island of the Swans

"A richly imagined tapestry . . ."

—Publishers Weekly

*"An enthralling tale of a splendid era
and an amazing woman."*

—Judith McNaught

Wicked Company

*a Novel of the
Eighteenth Century*

Ciji Ware

BANTAM BOOKS

New York   Toronto   London   Sydney   Auckland

WICKED COMPANY

A Bantam Fanfare Book / November 1992

ISBN 0-553-29518-7

Published simultaneously in the United States and Canada

Bantam Books are published by Bantam Books, a division of Bantam
Doubleday Dell Publishing Group, Inc. Its trademark, consisting of the
words "Bantam Books" and the portrayal of a rooster, is Registered in
U.S. Patent and Trademark Office and in other countries. Marca
Registrada. Bantam Books, 666 Fifth Avenue, New York, New York
10103.

PRINTED IN THE UNITED STATES OF AMERICA

RAD   0 9 8 7 6 5 4 3 2 1

For
Catherine Turney
playwright, screenwriter, novelist, friend

and for
Aphra Behn (1640–1689)
playwright, novelist, and
the first English woman to earn her
living by writing

Author's Note

One of the reassuring aspects about writing historical novels is that the seeds of one's next book are often to be found in the book preceding it. This is certainly the case with *Wicked Company*.

When I was researching *Island of the Swans*, a biographical novel based on the life of Jane Maxwell, the Duchess of Gordon (1749–1812), I discovered that her "eccentric" sister Eglantine, Lady Wallace, was the author of several plays, one of which was produced (and failed miserably after a three-night run) at Covent Garden. As I sat in the rare-book room at the Huntington Library in San Marino, California, leafing through the dusty copy of Eglantine's play, *The Ton, or Follies of Fashion* (1788), I exclaimed aloud, (a great sin in any library), "I didn't think women *wrote* plays in the eighteenth century!" Certainly I never dreamed that a number of women had their works produced at the most celebrated theaters in the kingdom.

That moment in my life as an historical novelist led me to the astounding discovery that some *ninety-eight* women wrote plays that were either staged, published, or survived in manuscript in Britain between 1660 and 1800. A significant number of these writers were extraordinarily prolific dramatists, with fifteen to twenty plays mounted in professional theaters during their lifetimes. Some were among the most successful writers in their day. For example, Aphra Behn (1640–1689) and Susannah Centlivre (d. 1723) wrote comedies that were still being produced a hundred years after their deaths.

Even the casual theater buff is familiar with Sheridan's *The School for Scandal* and *The Rivals*, or Goldsmith's *She Stoops to Conquer*. Yet most students of English literature know virtually nothing about these dramatists' female contemporaries—their lives, their careers, or even the plays themselves. What is even more remarkable, the works written by these professional women playwrights were enormously popular in their day and, as in the case of Elizabeth Inchbald (1753–1821), their efforts as dramatists made some of them rich.

Without delving into the reasons *why* a serious examination of these women dramatists is generally not found in most survey courses on eighteenth-century British theater, my goal has been to bring this glittering, talented, competitive, hardworking coterie of women artists back to life in novel form.

Details of the theater world during this period were garnered from texts, letters, contemporary periodicals, maps, memoirs, and primary sources relating to the major figures in and around London's competing theaters, Drury Lane and Covent Garden—as well as Sadler's Wells, Bath's Orchard Street Theater, Edinburgh's Canongate Playhouse, the Shakespeare Jubilee of 1769 in Stratford, and the fledgling theater in Annapolis, Maryland, in the 1770s. With the exception of the heroine's own plays, the productions mentioned throughout the novel consist of plays that were actually presented on the specific dates given and featuring cast members recorded on contemporary playbills.

In this work of fiction, I have had the pleasure of delving into the lives of many luminaries of the day, including theater managers David Garrick, Richard Sheridan, and George Colman; barrister-writer James Boswell, lexicographer Dr. Samuel Johnson, Lord Hertford (the Lord Chamberlain from 1766 to 1783); the Deputy Examiner of Plays Edward Capell; the actors, actresses, and "stage servants," and, of course, the playwrights—both male and female. Great effort has been invested in accurately weaving biographical details concerning the lives of these historical figures into the story of fictional characters whose search for love, glory, and freedom of expression strikes a contemporary chord.

I have included a map of the tightly knit London theater community known as the Covent Garden District during the period the novel takes place (1761–1779), as well as a list that differentiates the fictional characters from the historical figures. These, I trust, will serve as guideposts on the reader's journey into the bawdy, rollicking world of eighteenth-century British and American theater—where women took center stage, along with the men.

                                        Ciji Ware
                                        Beverly Hills, California

. . . when ladies, fearful lest their poetic offspring should crawl through life unheeded, publicly expose themselves to the world . . . who does not wish they had occupied their time with a needle instead of a pen?

—CHARLES DIBDIN

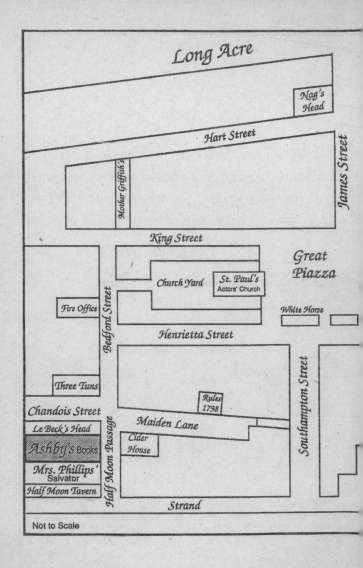

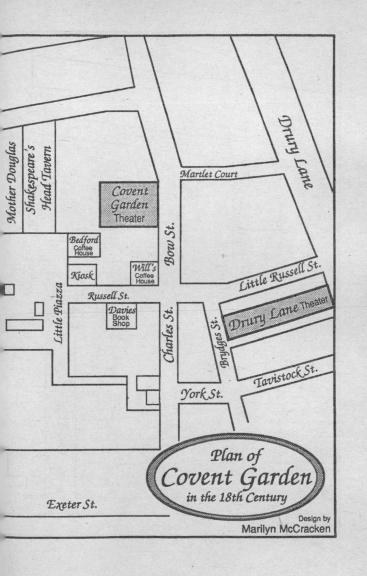

Mother Douglas

Shakespeare's Head Tavern

Drury Lane

Martlet Court

Covent Garden Theater

Bow St.

Bedford Coffee House

Kiosk

Will's Coffee House

Little Russell St.

Little Piazza

Russell St.

Davies Book Shop

Charles St.

Drury Lane Theater

Bridges St.

Tavistock St.

York St.

Plan of
Covent Garden
in the 18th Century

Exeter St.

Design by
Marilyn McCracken

Fictional Characters

(In order of appearance)

DANIEL McGANN
bookseller-printer

SOPHIE HAMILTON
McGANN
dramatist-printer

LORD LEMORE

REVEREND MR.
MEEKER

HUNTER ROBERTSON
juggler-dance master-actor-manager

JEAN HUNTER
ROBERTSON
singer

RORY ROBERTSON
harpist

HARRIET McGANN
ASHBY
bookseller-printer

LORNA BLOUNT
dancer

MARY ANN SKENE
prostitute

MAVIS PIGGOTT
actress-dramatist

RODERICK DARNLY
(later VISCOUNT GLYN
and EARL OF
LLEWELYN)

SIR PETER LINDSAY-
HOYT, BARONET

MRS. HOOD
housekeeper

TREVOR BEDLOE
estate factor

VAUGHN DARNLY,
VISCOUNT GLYN

ROWENA DARNLY,
COUNTESS OF
LLEWELYN

BASIL DARNLY, EARL
OF LLEWELYN

MR. BEEZLE
barrister

CAPTAIN MARSHALL
sea captain

MR. LASLEY
barrister

Historical Figures

MRS. FRANCES
   ABINGTON 1737–1815
actress

DOMINICO ANGELO
   c. 1760s
*Drury Lane special effects
   director*

JOHN ARTHUR 1708?–
   1772
*Orchard St. theater
   manager-actor*

WILLIAM BATTIE 1703–
   1776
physician

JOHN BEARD 1716–1791
Covent Garden manager

DAVID BEATT c. 1760s
playhouse manager

APHRA BEHN 1640–1689
novelist-dramatist

JAMES BOSWELL 1740–
   1795
*journalist-barrister-
   biographer*

MR. BRYAN c. 1760s
Orchard St. prompter

EDMUND BURKE 1729–
   1797
Irish statesman-philosopher

EDWARD CAPELL 1713–
   1781
*deputy examiner of plays-
   Shakespeare scholar*

DOROTHEA CELESIA
   1738–1790
dramatist

SUSANNAH
   CENTLIVRE c. 1667–c.
   1723
dramatist

KITTY CLIVE 1711–1785
actress-dramatist

MR. COLLINS d. 1783
Drury Lane doorkeeper

**GEORGE COLMAN
1732–1794**
theater manager-dramatist

**WILLIAM CREECH
1745–1815**
publisher

TOM DAVIES 1712–1785
actor-bookseller-printer

**SAMUEL DERRICK
1724–1769**
*author-master of
ceremonies, Bath*

**CHARLES DIBDIN 1745–
1814**
songwriter-dramatist

**DAVID DOUGLASS c.
1770s**
*American Company
manager*

**THADDEUS
FITZPATRICK c. 1760s**
rioter

**SAMUEL FOOTE 1720–
1777**
dramatist-actor-manager

DR. FORD c. 1770s
Drury Lane Patentee

**DAVID GARRICK 1717–
1779**
*actor-manager-dramatist-
Patentee*

**EVA-MARIA GARRICK
1724–1822**
dancer

**GEORGE GARRICK
1723–1779**
theater servant

**KING GEORGE III 1738–
1820**
*king of England, Ireland,
Scotland, and Wales*

**ANNE CATHERINE
GREEN c. 1767–1777**
printer-publisher

**ELIZABETH GRIFFITH
1727–1793**
dramatist

**THOMAS HARRIS d.
1820**
*Covent Garden manager-
Patentee*

**ELIZA HAYWOOD c.
1693–1756**
novelist-dramatist

JOHN HENRY c. 1770s
*American Company
manager*

WILLIAM HOPKINS d.
1780
Drury Lane prompter

WILLIAM HUNT c. 1760s
Stratford town clerk

MR. JACKSON c. 1760s
Tavistock Street costumer

DR. SAMUEL JOHNSON
1709–1784
lexicographer-writer-critic

JAMES LACY 1696–1774
*Drury Lane theater
manager*

WILLOUGHBY LACY
1749–1822
actor-Drury Lane Patentee

MR. LATIMORE c. 1760s
Stratford Jubilee architect

ELIZABETH LINLEY
1754–1792
*singer (later Mrs. Richard
Sheridan)*

THOMAS LINLEY 1732–
1795
*composer-Drury Lane
Patentee*

JAMES LOVE 1721–1774
actor

MRS. JAMES LOVE c.
1719–1807
actress

SALLY LUNN c. 1680
Bath baker

SIR JAMES MANSFIELD
1733–1821
*Chief Justice, Court of
Common Pleas*

DR. JOHN MONRO
1715–1791
Bethlehem Hospital director

HANNAH MORE 1745–
1833
dramatist-essayist

CONSTABLE MUNRO c.
1760s
city of Edinburgh

RICHARD ("BEAU")
NASH 1674–1762
master of ceremonies, Bath

JOHN PAYTON c.1760s
Stratford innkeeper

MRS. (PERKINS)
PHILLIPS c. 1760–1780
Green Canister apothecary

HANNAH PRITCHARD
1709–1768
actress

MR. & MRS. REYNOLDS
c. 1770s
Annapolis tavern keepers

THOMAS ROSOMAN c.
1746–1772
Sadlers' Wells owner

FRANCES SHERIDAN
1724–1766
novelist-dramatist

RICHARD BRINSLEY
SHERIDAN 1751–1816
dramatist-manager-
Parliamentarian

THOMAS SHERIDAN
1719–1788
actor-manager-educator

PEG WOFFINGTON
1720–1760
actress

Book 1

1761–1762

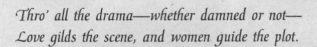

Thro' all the drama—whether damned or not—
Love gilds the scene, and women guide the plot.

—RICHARD BRINSLEY SHERIDAN,
"EPILOGUE," *THE RIVALS*

Chapter 1

Edinburgh, May 1761

"Sophie, lass! Quickly! Hide your book!" Daniel McGann urged his daughter, as he peered anxiously through the square windowpanes at the front of his small book shop. Outside, a group of dour, somberly attired men were striding like avenging angels along Edinburgh's High Street. "'Tis the Kirk elders!" he confirmed, wringing his ink-stained hands. "They're coming this way!"

Sophie sprang from her stool in front of the diminutive hearth that was the shop's only source of heat. She quickly shoved her copy of Fielding's *Tom Jones,* along with Rousseau's novel *La Nouvelle Heloise,* beneath a pile of pungent chunks of peat stored in a wooden box next to the fire. Without further instructions, she grabbed several other books that she, even at the age of sixteen, knew would be judged "ungodly" by the gaggle of religious fanatics bearing down on her father's book-and-printing establishment. Swiftly she stashed the offending volumes behind a row of Bibles displayed prominently on one of the front shelves and reserved precisely for just such an emergency.

Daniel McGann, his gray periwig slightly askew and his upper lip sheened with sweat, was greatly alarmed that for the second time in scarcely a month his shop was the apparent target of the wrath of Calvinist churchmen from nearby St. Giles Cathedral. The local Presbyterian clergy had long voiced disapproval of the novels, plays, and engravings that had made McGann's one of the most popular gathering places for the *literati* in Edinburgh. From the angry looks on their faces today, the zealots seemed determined to drive McGann's out of business.

Somber bells in the church tower overhead tolled the noon hour as Daniel McGann reached beneath a counter and pushed several parcels wrapped in outdated theater playbills into Sophie's hands.

"Out the back portal with you!" he croaked over the tolling bells. "Deliver the thin packet to Lord Lemore and the thick one to the Canongate Playhouse." As his daughter bolted toward the rear exit, he called after her, "Hurry, now! And mind that you collect the siller for 'em! We've scarcely two Scots pennies in the till."

Making her escape, Sophie heard the sound of the front door opening as the imperious men in black once again invaded her father's domain. She sped through the back room that housed the small wooden hand press and a variety of implements that comprised their modest printing business. Several sheets from a recently completed order hung drying on lengths of cord stretched across the back of the low-ceilinged chamber. As she rushed through the squat door at the rear of the press room that was permeated with a perpetual smell of carbon black and linseed oil, she prayed—blasphemously, she supposed—that no offending political broadside, pamphlet, or chapbook would be inadvertently discovered by the raiding churchmen. Pausing to listen, she heard a chorus of angry voices fill the front chamber.

"Vile works! *Abominations!*" a voice thundered from inside the shop. "You, sir, traffic in the Devil's commerce!"

Those squawking black vultures should leave us alone! Sophie thought defiantly as she darted down the narrow alleyway shadowed by St. Giles's bell tower looming overhead.

Inside her father's book shop, the churchmen were systematically pulling books from the shelves and flinging them onto the flagstones beneath their feet.

"We've given you ample warning, McGann," the Reverend Mr. Meeker pronounced, "yet *still* you trade in the works of Satan!"

Daniel McGann stared with growing dismay at the pile of

volumes by the likes of Defoe, Molière, and the dramatist William Congreve, heaped on the floor next to his desk.

"Surely you don't consider Shakespeare—" Daniel began to protest, as he watched several of the bard's comedies join the pile.

"'Tis bawdry!" Reverend Meeker retorted. "Full of jesters and fools mouthing blasphemy. 'Tis intolerable!"

Briefly, Daniel imagined how his wife, Margaret, would have responded to such an invasion, such absurd pronouncements. When Margaret was alive, her dark head bent over her weekly correspondence with the best book agents in London, he had boldly challenged the arguments and actions of these Kirk zealots and had been a leader in local efforts to beat back the meddling churchmen's attempts to dictate cultural and religious standards to the entire city.

But that was before the bleak winter when the tumor had first appeared on his wife's neck, the malignancy that had squeezed the breath and life out of the poor woman by the time nearby Whinny Hill was splashed with autumn heather. These days, he could barely summon the energy to peruse his stock of books, much less battle the fanatics holding forth from the pulpit next door. Many buyers had stayed away and sales were dwindling. When he was forced to sack his clerk, Sophie, bless her, had taken over minding the accounts and had acquired a working knowledge of the shop's inventory. She had even learned the skills necessary to run the small printing press in the back chamber where broadsides, chapbooks, and playbills earned them much needed extra income.

"Have you been struck *dumb*, McGann?" demanded the rotund Reverend Meeker. "I'm asking you to forswear selling such ungodly texts in future, or stand ready to accept the dire consequences that God shall mete out! What *say* you?"

"I say you are blinded, bigoted fools," Daniel replied without rancor, "and ignorant ones as well, if you don't delight in Shakespeare," he added, staring sorrowfully at the books that Meeker's henchmen would probably burn to cinders.

Reverend Meeker glared at Daniel McGann with speechless indignation. At last he turned and strode toward the front door, followed by the others. Upon reaching the threshold, he turned to impart a final threat, his bulbous nose crimson with fury.

"If you persist in leading the public down such paths of wickedness, McGann, you shall find yourself brought up on charges of libel and blasphemy!"

Sophie was scarcely aware of the cobbles digging into the bottoms of her leather brogues as she sped down the dank passageway behind her father's shop. With her mind on the drama taking place there, she nearly collided with Duncan McClellan. The fishmonger was just emerging from the back door of his tiny establishment, one of the numerous Luckenbooths—or "locked booths"—built adjacent to St. Giles Cathedral where the public purchased everything from meat to ribbons to first editions at McGann's.

"Whoa, there, lassie," the grizzled old man exclaimed. "And where might you be headed in such a tear? Not making mischief with those pig-riding Maxwell sisters?" he teased, referring to a pair of hoydenish neighbors who had a penchant for racing sows down the center of the High Street during the city's busiest hours.

"N-no," Sophie said, panting, anxious to be on her way without undue explanations. "I've placards for the new *Macbeth* to deliver to the playhouse. The manager's been skirlin' for them day and night. Pardon, but I must be off!"

"Aye, there's a good lass," Duncan said fondly, stepping aside and saluting with his basket of plaice, salmon, and sole in a mock bow. He was about to set out on the second of his morning rounds, treading up and down the Royal Mile calling out enticing names of the day's bounty pulled from nearby Leith Harbor. "Your da's a lucky man to have such a fine assistant, and that's a fact—even if you be a mere girl," he said with a wink.

A mere girl! Sophie thought with some annoyance, but she didn't have time to engage in a battle of wits with her good-hearted neighbor. Instead, to prove she bore him no ill will, she tossed her auburn curls in a show of mild reproof, grinned at him saucily, and continued swiftly on her way.

Sophie's breathing became labored as she veered away from the last of the Luckenbooths and entered Parliament Square. A crowd was milling in front of the old Mercat Cross where royal proclamations had been read to the populace for centuries. As Sophie pushed through the knot of people clogging the square, she heard a strange, rhythmic melody nearby and caught a glimpse of an old man whose gnarled fingers plucked gamely at a small harp. Seated on a low stool, surrounded by spectators, the ancient musician strummed a wild, compelling sound on the Celtic instrument's metal strings. His hunched shoulders were swathed in moth-eaten red and navy tartan wool. A buxom woman of indeterminate age, clad in a ragged skirt and blouse with a square of similar plaid tossed over one arm, clapped in time with the hypnotic music, encouraging someone or something moving within the circle of bystanders.

Suddenly, a slender wooden cylinder soared above the heads of the crowd, accompanied by a chorus of oohs and aahs. An instant later, another wooden pin flashed overhead, and then a third and a fourth. The gaily colored shapes danced in a blur against the clear May sky. Despite her eagerness to do her father's bidding, Sophie paused to stare as quite the handsomest young man she'd ever seen flung oblong wooden pins into the air with an agility that took her breath away.

The street juggler stood a head and a half taller than anyone in the admiring throng, a fact that only served to emphasize his startling height and broad shoulders. Every few seconds, he tilted his dark blond head skyward to trace the route of the juggling pins, displaying a profile enhanced by a straight nose and high cheekbones. It was a visage that betrayed in his ancestry some strapping Viking in search of plunder who had no doubt landed on a mist-shrouded Scottish coast a thousand years before this sun-splashed spring morning.

Grinning broadly at his appreciative audience like some Highland incarnation of Tom Jones himself, the juggler jauntily threw the pins into the air in time to the throbbing Scottish tune played by the old harpist. Sophie gazed openmouthed at the strolling player's rakish smile, the appealing cleft in his chin, physical attributes that would have earned him notice even if his juggling talent had not.

The splendid-looking street performer slung his pins higher and higher until it seemed to Sophie that they soared above the hammer beam roof of Parliament Hall. Without warning, he snatched the pins from the air in rapid succession and held them at arms length like a bouquet. Then he proffered the throng a deep bow and quickly exchanged the pins for a tambourine held by the woman with dirty blond hair who stood next to the harpist.

"And now, lads and lassies . . ." the juggler called to the crowd, "I'll sing for ye a joyful tune taught me by the Highland fairies and guaranteed to bring the listener the best o' Scottish luck, if only ye'll favor us with a wee bit o' siller . . ." He spied several people edging away from the crowd. "Aye . . . *ye* there! Dinna slink away like that or the fairies will do ye mischief," he warned mockingly, his distinctive Highland burr rolling richly off his clever tongue. "And that's as sure as I am that m'name's Hunter Robertson and this here's m'mother, Jean, and m'blind grandfather, Rory Robertson—the proud harpist to the chief of the Clan Robertson, faithful to the end to Bonnie Charlie!"

A murmur of sympathy rose from certain members of the crowd and the pair attempting to escape remained frozen with embarrassment. Hunter Robertson spoke quickly to his grandfather, who commenced playing the song. Despite Sophie's conscience prompting her to be on her way, she watched admiringly as the good-looking juggler-musician boldly approached the pair who had tried to make their escape. He began singing in a warm, full baritone to the spirited, staccato tune his grandfather played:

> 'Tis time, my dears, with all good cheer
> To Pay the Piper well . . .
> You've had your show, and you should know
> The Highland Fairies tell
> On those who play at thrift and say
> They cannot spare a pence
> 'Tis good to see you'll pay our fee
> So, show us your good sense!

One of the men reluctantly dug into his pocket and placed a small coin in the tambourine Hunter held out to him. The crowd applauded. Hunter's deep blue eyes scanned the assembly with a mischievous twinkle. He brazenly swung his tambourine in a slow wide arc, shaking the little metal disks attached to its circumference in a not-so-subtle reminder to the crowd that he sought more donations.

"*'Tis time, my dear, with all good cheer to Pay the Piper well. . . .*" he repeated in a soft, caressing voice, and Sophie found herself taking the measure of his enormous height, broad shoulders, tapering waist, and well-shaped thighs clad in tight red and navy tartan trews buckled at the knee. The performer's raw charm and boldness were impressive, as was his ability to wheedle a farthing out of the onlookers without the slightest chagrin that what he was doing was one notch above simple begging. He executed a little jig for each person kind enough to put a penny in his tambourine and, for good measure, intoned with exaggerated politeness, "A thousand Highland thank yous, m'lord. May the blessings of St. Ninian be yours, m'lady."

When the charmer stopped in front of Sophie, their eyes locked and she found herself unable to pull away from his riveting gaze. He surveyed her slender frame and gave his tambourine a sharp, demanding thump. Shyly, she shook her head, indicating she had no penny to donate to his cause. She feared he might embarrass her with some bit of tomfoolery. Instead, he glanced at her worn indigo skirt and threadbare linen stomacher and an endearingly sweet smile spread slowly across his handsome face. With a faint nod of understanding—accompanied by a roguish wink—he moved on to his next victim.

Sophie felt oddly bereft as the dashing man bestowed his winning grin on the spectator standing next to her. She glanced down at the packets destined for Lord Lemore and the playhouse that she held tightly against her chest. Guiltily, she thought of the clerics pestering her poor father and bolted through the juggler's admirers, heading toward the Old Tolbooth. The loathsome stone prison shared a common granite wall with the wigmaker's emporium, the last in the line of Luckenbooths situated at the far end of the square.

A red-coated town guardsman glanced suspiciously at Sophie's swift pace as she trotted past the rear of the massive turreted structure. The western end of the forbidding fortress—home to debtors, thieves, and murderers—supported a porchlike two-story extension that had been added a century earlier. The flat roof of the second story was ringed by a wooden railing that framed an area on which a permanent scaffold stood: the very spot where convicted criminals were hung by the neck until dead.

Sophie shuddered, recalling how, on execution days, she would retreat to the deserted book shop and block out the noise and barbarity by escaping in an engrossing novel like Richardson's *Pamela* or Mary Davys' *The Reform'd Coquette*. Having learned her alphabet at the age of seven from an unsold primer published for young masters at the Edinburgh High School, Sophie had found the world of books a refuge from life's tribulations.

Sophie gave a nod of greeting to a second hard-faced guardsman posted at another entrance to the gloomy prison. She received no response. Most town guardsmen were aging remnants of disbanded government regiments who had fought for the king against the troops of Bonnie Prince Charlie. The year Sophie was born, the "Prince from O'er the Water" had landed in the Highlands to launch a bloody but unsuccessful attempt to overthrow the Hanovarian Georges and restore the Stuart dynasty to the British throne. He had failed, of course, as the previous autumn's coronation of the twenty-two-year-old George III had attested. As a result, these battle-scarred veterans serving as prison guards were unpopular among those Scots who had lingering sympathy for the Stuarts.

With a growing sense of foreboding, Sophie picked up speed as she entered the chaotic stream of High Street traffic that stretched from Castle Hill at one end of what was called the Royal Mile to Holyrood Palace at the other. She threaded her way past the sedan chairs transporting their single passengers. These small carriages without wheels were attached to long poles and their passengers were conveyed all over the city by pairs of burly men.

At a propitious moment she darted between two coaches that were rolling down the cobbled pavement of Edinburgh's grandest thoroughfare. The aptly named High Street bisected the four-hundred-foot mound of volcanic rock that served for centuries as the foundation of the ancient walled city. It was this mammoth chunk of granite, with its labyrinth of alleyways, narrow lanes and wynds, that had protected Scotland's capital from marauding enemies for a thousand years. Today within its stone confines, the momentary gaiety spawned by the self-assured street juggler faded and Sophie felt vulnerable and afraid.

"The most dangerous enemies are the ones who pose as friends," her father once told her solemnly during a reading of the saga of the famous Trojan Horse one quiet rainy afternoon. *'Twas true,* thought Sophie glumly, considering the marauding clerics from next door. She scanned the entrances to the four- and five-story buildings lining both sides of the road and ducked into a gloomy passageway that led to Chessel's Court.

Despite the increasing warmth of the May morning, Sophie shivered slightly as she crossed the small sun-dappled courtyard of the secluded square. Pausing to confirm which town house was Lord Lemore's, Sophie wondered how her retiring bookworm-of-a-father would defend himself if the men in black tried to have him evicted, as well they might.

At length she identified the heavy oak door belonging to the home of her father's aristocratic patron, praying the nobleman would somehow intervene with the authorities. If many of Daniel McGann's books had been confiscated this morning, their future would be bleak indeed. Soon, there would be no new books for her to read, nothing to sell, and no way to pay the rent.

Hoping for the best, she raised Lemore's heavy brass knocker and rapped sharply. She heard footsteps approaching. If only her father's best client would double his order of the special editions of engravings regularly procured for him from London, Sophie thought anxiously, McGann's Printers and Booksellers might survive this latest assault from the clergy.

"I'm Sophie McGann," she explained to the liveried servant who opened the front door. "I've come with the engravings m'lord has ordered from my father's book agent in London."

A window curtain stirred to her left, and Sophie spied a gold signet ring winking on the smallest finger of a well-manicured hand whose wrist was wreathed in lace and a bottle green velvet cuff.

"I'll see that his lordship receives these," the manservant answered, barely deigning to acknowledge her presence as he reached for the packets clutched in Sophie's arms.

She resisted his attempt to take her packages from her.

"Only *one* of these is for Lord Lemore," she replied sharply. Recalling her father's instructions, she took a deep breath and added, "And my father has asked for monies in full upon his lordship's receiving the merchandise."

"You may settle accounts when his lordship agrees to purchase the material," the servant said loftily.

When Sophie made no move to hand over the packet, the servant shrugged and began to close the door. Quickly, she reached out to prevent its being shut in her face.

"Lord Lemore has *already* agreed to purchase these drawings," Sophie said heatedly. "I am merely to deliver this special purchase from London and collect the fees owing."

"God's wounds, Laribee, shut that door!" a voice bellowed from what Sophie assumed to be a front sitting room off the foyer. "The draft's blowing the coals all over the Turkey carpet!"

"Enter and wait here," the butler said irritably. He indicated that Sophie should remain in the chilly entrance hall. "I shall see if his lordship will receive you."

Within minutes, Sophie was ushered not into a parlor, as she had anticipated, but a spacious, well-proportioned room fitted with a pair of massive glass-fronted mahogany bookcases carved in the same, beautiful Queen Anne style as the table she'd glimpsed in the hallway. The walls behind the crowded bookshelves were painted a delicate shade of green and trimmed with elegant but restrained cornices of creamy white. Carpets in rich hues of deep garnet and blue warmed the room that otherwise might have seemed wintry despite the fire glowing in the grate.

Lord Lemore was seated in a leather wing-backed chair positioned beside a walnut keyhole desk. Upon the desk's leather-tooled surface rested a scattering of pictures that had tumbled out of a large portfolio. A brass-ringed magnifying glass lay nearby.

"Ah . . . Mistress McGann . . . from the book shop," he said, his cool gray eyes flitting from the tip of her shoes to the curve of her modest neckline.

Lord Lemore appeared to Sophie to be a man of about her father's age, fifty-five. Edinburgh's most celebrated book and engraving collector was tall and slender, except for a slight paunch emphasized by sloping shoulders—the result, perhaps, of hours spent hunched over his desk, peering at rare images. As a young man in his early twenties, Lemore had made the acquisition of drawings by William Hogarth fashionable among his set and was among the first to subscribe to the rather risqué series issued in 1733 titled *A Rake's Progress*.

Sophie offered a respectful curtsy and extended the wrapped packet to the aristocrat's outstretched hands. His gaze settled on her face, and his short-sighted squint lent him an even more imperious demeanor.

"You work with your father in the book shop, do you not?" he inquired, looking at her steadily.

"Aye, m'lord," Sophie answered, unnerved by his piercing stare.

"And you're familiar with the engraving trade as well?"

"I am learning the business of *selling* them . . . yes, sir."

"Ah . . . *learning*," he echoed her words softly. "And how *old* might this comely student of art and commerce be?" he asked sardonically, as his bony fingers untied the string around the packet Sophie had handed him.

"I'm nearly seventeen," she lied, hoping that adding nine months to her age might supply her with the degree of dignity she felt was sorely lacking during this rather strange interview.

"Hmm . . . seventeen," he murmured, carefully removing the recycled playbill encasing his new purchases. "In the Highlands, lassies of your age are often betrothed. Have you a sweetheart, my dear?" he asked, examining the first engraving of the pile of four he held in his pallid hands.

"N-n-no," Sophie stuttered, perturbed by the suggestive nature of the gentleman's inquiries. She knew of girls hardly older than she living in the adjoining squalor of Edinburgh's poorest wynds and closes whose "sweethearts" had gotten them in the family way—to their endless misery. She cast a nervous glance at the door to the chamber, which the disdainful butler had discreetly closed when leaving them alone.

The trace of a smile creased Lord Lemore's thin lips. He breathed deeply and pleasurably as his eyes drank in the contents of the image he held in his hands. Then he abruptly tossed it on the desktop and, reaching for his magnifying glass, gave the next new engraving his full attention. Seemingly oblivious, now, to her presence in his library, he took several paces toward the window, angled the picture toward the shafts of spring sunshine streaming through the panes, and surveyed his purchase through the thick examining lens.

Observing his rapt concentration, Sophie clasped her hands around her remaining packet and glanced furtively about the room. She compared the library's airy spaciousness with the cramped, low-ceilinged, stuffy chambers she and her father maintained above the book shop.

During the lengthy silence, Sophie's gaze fell on the engravings that were spread on top of the desk. The picture tossed nearest her view was the one from the packet she had just delivered. Her amber eyes widened in shock as she began to scrutinize this particular black-and-white drawing. Printed in frilly script at the bottom were the words *Le Religieux, 1740,* and above the title were depicted three women and a cowl-robed priest.

Sophie's generous mouth sagged open slightly as she gazed down at the engraved image of a disheveled woman sitting at a table, clutching a joint of beef in her fist. A second female held out a glass of wine in the direction of a lecherous-looking monk who was sexually assaulting a half-naked woman stretched out on a couch. Little wonder Sophie's father had practically shoved her out the back door of the book shop with this delivery when the clerics were about to invade his domain! If images like these had been found on the premises, Daniel McGann would have been hauled off to the Tolbooth prison forthwith!

Suddenly, Sophie felt Lord Lemore's gaze fasten on her face. Flushing scarlet, she raised her glance and their eyes met.

"Your father has done well," he said on a low breath, taking a step toward her and gently placing the three other engravings beside the one that had riveted Sophie's attention. "At first, he seemed reluctant to fulfill my request," he continued, setting the magnifying glass on top of the desk as well, "but I see that even though he scorns such works as prurient, the man has his price."

Sophie's chin jutted defiantly in the air, despite her utter shock at learning that her father sold such erotica. He had never displayed this type of engraving in the shop. Indeed, her father must have been in desperate financial straits to be fulfilling such requests from the likes of Lord Lemore.

Sophie clutched the package she was to deliver to the Canongate Playhouse manager and made movement as if to depart.

"At your service, m'lord," she murmured, nodding her head respectfully. "I fear I must beg your leave to return to my father." She bit her lip uncertainly and then plunged ahead with the request she knew she had to tender. "He asks that I secure payment for this special order from London."

"Ah . . . yes," Lord Lemore replied, seizing her hand familiarly with his own. "I must pay for my pleasures, must I not? Have your father send me an accounting," he said, and he raised her right hand to his lips and laid a lingering kiss against her flesh. Suddenly, he pulled her hard against his concave chest and the packet destined for the playhouse was crushed between them. She could smell the brandy on his breath and the stench of musky perfume masking odors far less pleasant. A strange mound pressed against her thigh and she could hear Lemore breathing heavily next to her ear.

"Did that picture arouse your senses, my sweet?" he murmured into her hair, his grip tightening around her shoulders with suffocating strength. "Did that monk's obscene pose put ideas in your pretty head?"

"*No!*" Sophie hissed, at once confused and repelled by the aristocrat's rough fondling. She pushed against his narrow chest with all her strength, but despite Lemore's slender frame, he held her with unyielding force, his thin fingers biting into her flesh. "Let me *go!*" she cried desperately, twisting side to side in a frantic attempt to escape his steely grip.

A sudden upward motion of her pinioned arm slapped Sophie's playbills sharply against his chin, pushing him off balance. Lord Lemore emitted a low grunt and Sophie felt him lose his footing. The two of them fell awkwardly against the wing-backed chair, pushing its upholstered bulk into the desk. Having managed to yank a hand free, Sophie grabbed the heavy magnifying glass off the desk top and held it up threateningly over her head like a weapon.

"Now, now! No need for head bashing," Lord Lemore protested, stepping back.

Panting from exertion, Sophie watched, dumbfounded, as the nobleman adjusted the waistband of his breeches, shaking first one bony leg and then the other in the oddest fashion imaginable.

"You *do* look rather young," he conceded, scrutinizing her slender form and small stature as if she were a yearling at a horse auction. "Not that youth cannot pique one's fancy." His eyes narrowed and his thin lips pursed. "Pray, tell me not that you're merely a lass of twelve or thirteen?"

"No . . . as I told you before . . . I am *nearly* seventeen," she said, her voice ragged despite a herculean attempt to regain her composure. She set the magnifying glass carefully on the desk, fighting the tears of fright and anger that suddenly welled up. She swallowed hard, and once more clasped the packet of playbills to her bosom. "But *nothing* gives you the right to say such things to me or take such liberties . . . *nothing!*"

"No right?" the aristocrat repeated, eyeing her coldly. "I suggest you remember what rights I do, indeed, possess—and curb your slattern's tongue. Otherwise, someone in authority shall have to curb it *for* you!" He waved his slender hand at her with a gesture of dismissal, the circlet of lace swaying from his coat cuff. "You may go."

"I would like payment for your order, if you please," Sophie said stiffly, conscious of a heavy thudding in her chest.

Lord Lemore took a menacing step toward her. His eyes glittered with malice.

"I will repeat this just once more," he said in a controlled voice. "I bid you have your father send me an accounting of what I owe and I will have my man of business consider his request and attend to it as he sees fit. Good day!"

Sophie stared at her father's best customer with a coil of black rage twisting inside her stomach. How *dare* he do this? How *dare* he act as if *he* were the one who had been insulted? How *dare* he order such material through her father's shop, put them all at risk from the authorities, and then have the audacity to refuse to pay! High-born nobles were infamous for ordering meat and port and all manner of luxuries "on account" from merchants throughout Edinburgh and then disregarding the obligation to the poor tradesman. In her father's situation, Daniel McGann would certainly not hazard bringing Lord Lemore legally to task for unpaid bills relating to bawdy drawings that were forbidden by the religious censors anyway. And if Sophie accused the man of making improper advances toward a lass of her age—an age at which, as he said, many young Scottish lasses became brides and even mothers—'twould only make the situation worse.

Lord Lemore retrieved his magnifying glass and continued studying the newest purchases in his collection of engravings while utterly ignoring her. A smug smile played across his narrow face. Sophie bobbed a perfunctory curtsy. "As you wish, m'lord," she said and made an unceremonious dash for the door.

In the distance she could hear St. Giles toll one hour after noon as she emerged, trembling from her ordeal, into the sunny square. Head high, back straight, she retraced her steps to the arched entrance to Chessel's Court, wondering if Lord Lemore's cold gray gaze was boring into her back.

Nonsense! she chided herself. The old rogue was probably slavering over the lewd details of his latest acquisitions, too absorbed to give her another thought.

The throng of carriages and sedan chairs had thinned out on the High Street as Sophie proceeded down the road toward the Canongate Playhouse, a virtual stone's throw away from Chessel's Court. She was more than a little disquieted by her discovery that her learned, high-minded father trafficked in such salacious merchandise, yet her young mind wrestled with the central precept he had always taught her: that neither church nor state had a right to control an individual's *words* or *thoughts*.

As he had often maintained, "You may heartily disagree, Sophie, with what a man may say or write, but you've *no* just cause to take away his right to express it!"

Sophie had always admired these brave words and had subscribed to his philosophy with all her heart and soul. Certainly freedom of speech applied when her father defended Fielding's *Tom Jones,* which critics had declared "indecent," or championed the newspapers and magazines censured by Parliament for printing the truth about some proceeding in the House of Commons or the House of Lords.

But those *engravings*! she thought, recalling their vile images. How could her own father defend such a thing?

Her internal debate was abruptly halted by the familiar sight of colored juggling pins arching against the buildings leading to Playhouse Close. The youthful street entertainer and his band had made their way down the Royal Mile and were performing for a small but enthusiastic throng at the entrance to the Canongate Playhouse itself. Edging closer, she smiled as she watched a toothless bawd grin broadly when the spirited conjurer caught his pins in one hand and kissed the doxy's grimy paw, addressing her as "m'lady." However, Sophie shrank back nervously when the cocky young man circled in her direction. With a look of recognition, he approached her for the second time this tumultuous day and bowed deeply from the waist.

"And now, m'friends . . . just to show ye we're all Scots lads and lassies here—not squabbling Highlanders and

Lowlanders—I'll ask this fair sweetling to join me in a fine old Scottish country dance."

Before Sophie could protest, the strolling player reached for her hand and pulled her into the circle of bystanders that fanned out around them. He pried the playbills from her clenched fingers and handed the packet, along with his tambourine full of coins, to the woman he had called his mother. The crowd was clapping hands and shouting encouragement as the wizened old harpist began to pluck a sprightly melody from his harp.

"Just follow me," the juggler whispered. He was a foot taller than she and was forced to bend sharply at the waist in order to instruct her, his warm breath blowing against her ear. And as the music grew faster, to Sophie's utter astonishment, she and the stranger named Hunter Robertson began to dance.

Chapter 2

Hunter clasped Sophie's hands and whirled her around in a dance of his own invention—a lively Highland fling blended with bits and pieces of a Scottish reel. Sophie quickly realized that the combination of steps made no sense, as she had observed proper reels, jigs, and strathspeys for years from the children's gallery at Miss Nicky's weekly Dancing Cotillion in Bell's Wynd.

Hunter's touch was firm and his gaze spellbinding. He spun his young partner faster and faster to the encouraging shouts of the onlookers. Sophie threw her head back, gamely imitating the simple heel-to-toe steps her handsome partner performed in front of her. To show her his appreciation, he flashed her another dazzling smile, which revealed his straight, even teeth and deepened the striking cleft in his chin.

All memories of carping black clerics were banished from her thoughts. Her anxiety over her father's financial woes faded from her consciousness, as did her new-minted fear of the menacing Lord Lemore and his drawings. All her senses were attuned to Hunter's extraordinarily tall stature and his palpable magnetism. Her only concern was that she be able to match the graceful movements of this exuberant young man who had chosen her as his dancing partner.

Presently, the old harpist played a long rolling trill, his clawlike nails skittering back and forth on the strings of his instrument to produce a crescendo of sound. Hunter whirled Sophie to his side and, holding her hand firmly, prompted her to perform an elegant curtsy. With that, the throng shouted their approval and tossed a few more coins in their direction. As Hunter nimbly bent over to scoop them up, the audience sensed the performance had concluded and began to drift off down the road and into the darkened closes and wynds.

"Since ye couldna give me a coin, here's one for ye, pet!" Hunter laughed, placing a penny in her hand. "'Twas a braw performance for such an unrehearsed team, wouldna ye say, wee one?"

Sophie could only nod her assent, breathless from their recent exertions and awed by his good looks and easy charm. She pocketed the money gratefully, relieved she'd have at least something to offer her father to offset the disappointment of Lord Lemore's refusal to pay his debts promptly.

Meanwhile, Jean Robertson was eagerly counting the coins in her tambourine and extended a hand to Hunter for the few he'd harvested among the cobblestones. Hunter's grandfather said nothing. He was leaning over his harp as if it were the only thing keeping him from tipping into the stone gutter.

"Da's a bit fagged," Jean Robertson remarked. "We can buy a bit o' mutton and ale at the tavern over there," she added, offering her arm to the frail old man. "Ye bring the pins and the stool when ye come, eh, lad?" The woman hardly gave Sophie a second glance, leaving Sophie to conclude that this was not the first time she had observed her son making friends with females from the audience.

At the mention of beer, the elder Robertson suddenly appeared strong enough to sling his small harp under his arm and walk slowly beside his daughter-in-law. However, he leaned heavily on her arm, his sightless eyes staring vacantly ahead, as they made their way to the Red Lion Inn on St. Mary's Wynd.

"I suspect ye're a mite too young to tipple ale," Hunter said, looking at Sophie's slight frame speculatively. "Could I offer ye a bit o' water from the well, here?"

"I drink ale," Sophie asserted, "that is, when my da can afford to give it to me."

"Well, ye look like a lass who still laps milk to me." Hunter's blue eyes bored into hers with renewed curiosity. "What's yer name and how old might ye be? Twelve? Not fourteen, surely?"

"My name's Sophie McGann and I'm nearly *seventeen!*" Sophie said with exasperation for the third time that morning. "Not much younger than *you,* I'll wager."

"No!" he replied mockingly. "Ye canna be such an old crone as *that!* I know ye canna be eighteen, like me."

"Well . . . I'm rather small for my age . . . barely five feet, in fact," she replied earnestly, so fascinated by the dark golden eyelashes framing Hunter's startling blue eyes that she totally disregarded his playful tone. "And the absolute truth is that I was sixteen last February, but da's customers can testify I know his stock of books well enough to be *twice* that age!"

"Oh, *do* ye now? And are those books ye had clutched to yer stomacher?"

"*Sink* me!" she cried with sudden alarm. "Where's the packet?"

"Not to worry," he soothed, pointing to the stool his grandfather had used during his performance on the harp. Sophie dashed to retrieve the parcel. "They must be most valuable," he murmured.

"These?" she replied, surprised at the solemn tone of Hunter's voice. "Oh, these are just playbills and actors' sides for *Macbeth* and *The Beggars' Opera.* We print the play notices in our shop . . . McGann's . . . among the Luckenbooths near St. Giles?" she explained. "Have you seen where we are?"

"No," Hunter said, his expression growing serious. "But I'd like to pay a visit . . . especially if ye stock printed plays. I'd dearly love to see what one looks like."

"Well, we do carry some. I can show you the copy of Shakespeare I worked from, if you like," she said shyly. "It actually belongs to Mr. Beatt," she added as she carefully unwrapped the package she was to deliver to the playhouse just a few yards away. "I copied these speeches myself from the printed version," she said proudly, pointing to a stack of papers with neat, even writing centered on the pages. "The prompter usually makes these copies for the actors, but he's been a mite boozy of late, so the manager, Mr. Beatt, hired me to copy a few of the smaller parts for some new players that are filling in." She smiled brightly, pleased to be able to impart a bit of backstage gossip. "When the theater's about to close for the summer months, players have a nasty habit of departing early if they've employment in Dublin, or Sadler's Wells, or such, and wrongly take their parts with them. At the end of a season they just stash them in their trunks. Mr. Beatt was furious to have to pay to have more copies made, but da was pleased I could earn a few extra shillings."

Hunter scarcely seemed to be listening. He was preoccupied with running his thumb down the spine of the bound volume of *Macbeth* that Sophie was carrying with her commissioned work. He turned the pages of the book slowly, his eyes scanning the print. Then he stared at the sheaves of rag paper that bore her handwritten copies of several scenes. Finally, he fingered the stack of playbills and their written announcement.

*The Beggars' Opera and Macbeth
will be performed successively
at the Canongate Playhouse through
May fifteenth, sixteenth, and seventeenth with
High Life Below Stairs
as an Afterpiece in which the
Finest Players in the Kingdom will appear!*

"Have you ever performed your juggling act in a theater?" Sophie asked tentatively, unnerved by the intensity of Hunter's concentration on the playscript.

"What?" he asked vaguely, reluctantly pulling his eyes away from the pages he held almost reverently in his hands. "Ah . . . no . . . I'm merely a strolling player . . . a clown, really. Not like a genuine actor. Not like the artists at the Canongate."

"Oh *them!*" Sophie said with a dismissive wave of her

hand. "Most of them are really comical . . . they hardly know their parts, and the women are forever squabbling as to who has the comeliest gown—even on stage, during the actual play *itself*! I expect the actors who perform in London at Drury Lane or Covent Garden would please you a great deal more. The ones who come to Edinburgh have usually been sacked from other theaters or run out of some place for bad debts or drunkenness. I wager *you'd* make a far better job of it than most of *them*!" she added stoutly.

"Me . . . on a real stage?" Hunter scoffed, "I dinna think so." The confidence that had so dazzled her during his juggling and dancing performances seemed to have evaporated. Swaggering Tom Jones had turned almost timid.

"Why ever not?" she demanded, staring at his dejected expression in utter amazement.

"Because . . ."

"*Because* is no reason," she said tartly. "My da says people who say *because* and don't finish their sentences are mental sloths."

By this time, Hunter's handsome features had taken on a scowl and he stared over the top of her head in sullen silence.

"From what I've seen of you," she teased, "you've enough boldness to prance upon any stage and speak your lines with the best of 'em!" she exclaimed, pointing at the pages, or "sides," she would soon deliver to the playhouse manager. "Give me *one* good reason you couldn't learn these speeches?"

"Because I canna *read*!" he said explosively, turning to face her, his blue eyes blazing. "I'm the grandson of the most famous living bard in the Highlands . . . the son of a man educated at the university in *this* city, and the grand-nephew of the chief of the Clan Robertson, but *I canna read*!"

Sophie flinched at the anguish she heard in his voice, the pain and regret and fury. Instinctively she laid her hand on his arm and stared up at him sympathetically.

"But surely, you read a *wee* bit?" she whispered.

"I can read nary a *word*!" he snapped, and then looked at her as if he regretted his harsh tone. "We've lived the wandering life since I was a bairn . . . m'grandfather's sight faded years ago and he canna teach me . . . and Mother's as doltishly illiterate as I," he said sadly. "Thanks to old Rory, though, I've memorized some Shakespeare and a bit of Milton, and I inherited a few books from m'father, until we had to sell 'em to keep from starving."

"Have you no home? Your da . . . ?" she asked in a low voice.

"Killed at the Battle of Culloden Moor, when I was a lad of two," he answered, all animation draining from his expressive face. "I never knew him. Like many who fought for the Bonnie Prince, we lost everything we had . . . our land . . . many members of our family. All m'life, I've traveled from town to town performing as a strolling player to earn a few coins." He shrugged. "Vagabonds though we are, we manage to keep body and soul alive most times—unless the constable or the kirk elders chase us out the city for vagrancy or disturbing the peace. 'Tis an interesting life," he finished wryly, his pleasant disposition and cockiness slowly returning.

The kirk elders! Sophie's heart ached with the injustices in life. Here was a stalwart well-born young man, desperate to learn to read and educate himself, without a farthing to spare, and just down the road lived that *toad* Lord Lemore, with enough money to buy books aplenty and an entire collection of repulsive drawings in the bargain! 'Twas *galling,* that's what it was!

"*I* could teach you to read," she said slowly. Hunter's penetrating blue eyes flitted across her face, but he did not respond. In fact, he didn't appear to have heard what she had said at all. "I'd be willing to teach you to read," she repeated while almost holding her breath.

Hunter cocked his head to one side and stared down at her, deep in thought. During the silence, Sophie found herself gazing at his luxuriant dark blond hair, which was pulled back smoothly and fastened with a leather thong in simple periwig style at the nape of his neck.

"Wee as ye are, I expect ye could," he said at length. He seemed to be studying her. "Sixteen, are ye?" he murmured. "M'sister Meg would have been about yer age now . . ."

Some half-buried memory seemed to be rekindled in his mind and he took a long breath. Sophie felt awkward under his scrutiny and made no reply. Then, in a sudden shift of mood, he flashed her the rakish grin that had so charmed his audience. "I'll be taking those," he ordered, extracting the playbills and actors' sides from her arms and placing the copy of *Macbeth* ceremoniously on top of the pile. "I've just had a grand idea for m'self!"

"And what might that be?" Sophie demanded with an excited giggle. When Hunter bestowed on her that engaging, mischievous grin, the world seemed full of marvelous possibilities.

"Ye'll see. Lead on, MacDuff!" Hunter cried in mock, stentorian tones, quoting a line Sophie had so recently copied from *Macbeth* in her commission for the manager of the Canongate Playhouse. Hunter laughed at her quizzical look.

"If an illiterate knave from Nairn—not a day's ride from Macbeth's castle—is going to know *anything* of Shakespeare, it's bound to be *that* play, wouldna ye suppose?"

Sophie could hardly suppress a smile, and Hunter took it as a signal that he was welcome to accompany her as she delivered her wares.

"Come, wee Sophie McGann," he said with a rascally chuckle. "Let us convey these placards and scripts to the renowned thespians of the Canongate Playhouse—and see what fate awaits!"

Sophie and Hunter made their way through an arched stone portal into Playhouse Close itself, a narrow alleyway that led off the High Street to the entrance of the theater. Once inside, they paused to get their bearings in the murky light that filtered through the auditorium. Their nostrils were assaulted by a pungent odor of tallow still hanging in the air, a remnant of the hundreds of candles placed in wall sconces, overhead chandeliers, and troughs at the front of the stage to illuminate the evening performances.

Sophie squinted in the gloom, searching for David Beatt, the theater's perpetually harried manager. Suddenly, a loud noise rumbled through the building and a trapdoor in the front of the stage popped up and then slammed down against the stage floor. A bald-headed gentleman pulled himself through the square opening to a sitting position, his legs dangling down into some unfathomable pit. It was the manager himself, minus his hairpiece.

"Halloo, Mr. Beatt," Sophie called loudly, advancing toward the stage. "'Tis I . . . Sophie McGann, with your playbills and sides."

"Lot of good 'twill do me now," the theater manager groused, shaking his head disgustedly. "That scoundrel West Digges took flight last week and this morning I find several more players have fled in the night with nary a fare-thee-well! Now, what shall I do for a leading man, I ask you?" he demanded. "As it seems I must cancel the rest of our playing schedule, those playbills won't be of much use to me, will they?" he demanded peevishly.

"But I've gone and *printed* them, as you requested," Sophie responded sharply, attempting to keep the dismay in her voice from turning into a whine. "We've used up considerable paper at the shop, not to mention our labor," she added, recalling only too vividly the exhausting hours she'd spent in the low-ceilinged room that housed their small printing press. Her back still ached from the exertion it required to ink the metal letters with a short-handled wooden cup covered by a large wool pad sheathed in sheepskin. Once she'd thoroughly saturated the type with the viscous black fluid, her slender arms had barely the strength to pull the bar of the wooden press, thus lowering the platen, and thereby pressing the paper into the inked type set in a wooden frame. All this effort produced but a single playbill, and David Beatt had ordered *fifty copies* to trumpet the playhouse's last two offerings of the season. "I've also penned the sides for *Macbeth*, just as you directed," she said dolefully, hoping her lament would shame him into settling accounts despite his own woes.

The manager wearily pulled himself to a standing position and slammed the trap door back into place.

"I'll pay . . . I'll pay," he said resignedly with a wave of his hand. "But you'll have to be patient, Sophie. I must get Rutledge up in the part of Macbeth and fill in with the remnants as best I can. Then we must sell tickets and fill the coffers. 'Twill take a bit more time before the fees are squared, that's all."

That's all! Sophie thought, her spirits sinking. She knew David Beatt would eventually meet his financial obligations to McGann's, but her father needed funds *now* to remain in business.

Hunter Robertson interrupted her gloomy thoughts by shifting his six-foot frame and poking Sophie gently with his elbow.

"Oh . . . yes . . ." she said, attempting to summon enthusiasm in the wake of such disappointing news. "Ah . . . Mr. Beatt . . . I-I'd like to introduce you to a splendid singer and jug—I mean, *performer*. This is Hunter Robertson. Hunter?" she said, turning to take the pile of playbills from his arms, "this is David Beatt, manager of the Canongate Playhouse."

Beatt's bushy gray eyebrows seemed to bristle.

"Weren't you the one tossing wooden clubs in the air in front of my playhouse?" he demanded irritably. "I'll not have you wheedling coins from the crowds on nights we play here, young man, I'll warrant you *that*!"

"Aye, sir, I am that very performer," Hunter said eagerly, as if Beatt's familiarity with his juggling act indicated the warmest of welcomes. He reached for one of Sophie's handwritten parts from *Macbeth*. "Since ye are short of players," he continued baldly, "perhaps I could take part in crowd scenes in yer new *Macbeth,* or even play a small part?" he added, waving the manuscript at Beatt.

"'Twould have to be a *small* part, to be sure," Beatt replied sarcastically, "with that unintelligible Highland burr of yours. I can barely understand you myself, and my mother was from Inverness!"

Sophie glanced at Hunter, but the insult seemed simply to bounce off him.

"'Tis m'plan to improve m'speech," Hunter retorted cheerfully. "And m'grandfather and I could provide musical interludes on stage, here, that might please yer patrons."

Beatt pulled on one of his bushy eyebrows as he apparently considered Hunter's proposition. Then he scratched

his bald head vigorously and seemed to come to some conclusion about the lad.

"Have you sufficient melodies to make up an evening's
concert? Enough *good*, lively fare?" Beatt asked, staring at
Hunter narrowly.

Hunter threw back his dark golden head and laughed.

"M'grandfather and I know airs enough to present *ten*
concerts!" he assured him. "We could perform for ye till
West Digges and all yer laggard actors *beg* to come back to
work!"

"Hmm . . ." said Beatt dourly. "I think a concert or
two would suffice until I can get Rutledge ready for *Macbeth*."

"And will ye hazard me an opportunity to try m'hand at
some small parts?" Hunter shot back, his swift glance in
Sophie's direction telling her that he fully expected her to
help him memorize the lines he could not read.

"I'll allow you some crowd scenes, and we'll leave it at
that. You may continue performing in front of the playhouse
—providing you'll pay half the siller to *me*. It might attract a
crowd."

Hunter nodded, albeit reluctantly.

"And . . . uh . . . let's plan one concert for . . . let
me think . . . May fifteenth," the manager continued.
"Half the profits will accrue to you, minus house expenses,
of course."

"And what might those run?" Hunter inquired casually.

"Oh, the usual," Beatt replied airily. "Candles, stage
crew, playbill costs, my management fee. If you half-fill the
playhouse, you'll not be in arrears."

"I see," Hunter said, with a doubtful look.

Noting Hunter's lack of enthusiasm, Beatt quickly assured him, "And, of course, if you *do* fill at least half this
barn, I'd definitely want you to perform musical fare during
the intervals between the main performance and the afterpieces, next season." Beatt pulled out a gold watch and chain
from a small pocket in his stained waistcoat. "And now,
pray excuse me," he said, smoothing his bald crown with his
stubby fingers. "Put the playbills and sides on the forestage,
Sophie, and please print up some new ones announcing this

young man's concert. You know what it needs—the usual
ruffles and flourishes to pull in the patrons. Now, if you'll
excuse me," he said, pointing to the trap door beneath his
feet. "The deuced stage machinery has gone a bit wobbly
and I must have at the repairs."

"I'll give ye a hand," Hunter volunteered, flashing a sly
wink at Sophie as David Beatt stooped to pull up the trap
door once again.

Sophie rolled her eyes at her new acquaintance's nerve.
She suspected Hunter knew as much about the winches and
pulley systems that created certain stage effects as he did
about acting Shakespeare.

"Well, I must be off," she announced, "and I shall count
on you to compensate McGann's for this new order—as
well as the other one—as soon as you're able, Mr. Beatt."

"Of course, my dear . . . of course," he pledged absently. "Just send me a complete accounting. Now Robertson, lad, if you can just have a quick look at the spindle that
threads through the turnkey down here . . ."

The pair disappeared into the subterranean maze beneath
the stage of the Canongate Playhouse, leaving Sophie no
choice but to make her way through the pit, past the lower
stalls and out into the narrow stone close that lead back to
the Royal Mile. As she trudged up the High Street and
caught sight of the imposing granite tower of St. Giles Cathedral piercing the afternoon sky, she worriedly began to
finger the single Scots penny that Hunter had given her as
payment for dancing with him.

When Sophie walked through the door to McGann's
book shop, her father was sitting at his desk staring morosely at the pilfered shelves that surrounded him.

"They've confiscated most of the novels, the volumes on
Eastern philosophies, the Shakespeare comedies, and virtually anything we had for sale that wasn't written in English,"
he reported dully.

Sophie stared dejectedly at the myriad gaps marking the
absence of many well-loved books. She dashed over to a row

of Bibles remaining on a lower shelf and investigated the space behind the tomes. Empty! The men of St. Giles had discovered her favorite hiding place for novels like *Miss Betsy Thoughtless* by Eliza Haywood and *Memoirs of Miss Sydney Biddulph* by Frances Sheridan whose recently published book had proved wildly popular with readers and irresistible to Sophie herself.

"Blast and bother!" Sophie cried. "They've practically put us out of business, the swine!"

"Now, Sophie . . ." Daniel cautioned, peering furtively out the shop's square-paned windows flanking the High Street, "you must watch what you say! That Reverend Meeker is full of threats. You mustn't let him hear you speak blasphemy." Her father heaved a sigh and shook his head in defeat. "I must admit, I wonder if we shouldn't just resign ourselves—"

"Da . . . no!" Sophie cried, rushing to his side. "We shall simply have to reorganize. I'll make an inventory of what they failed to steal in the name of driving out Satan," she added bitterly, "and we shall carry on as before."

"But Sophie . . . to keep our doors open we must buy foolscap and ink and stock items ordered from London . . ."

Items from London . . . those ghastly engravings!

Daniel McGann seemed so dispirited, Sophie hadn't the heart to report to him Lord Lemore's unseemly advances or that the aristocrat had not paid for the vile etchings he'd secured through McGann's. She also hesitated to reveal that she knew her father's financial woes had led him to traffic in such scurrilous material. Much as she despised the narrow-minded clerics who had wreaked havoc in their shop, still she found herself revolted by Lord Lemore's perverse taste and her father's catering to it. Unable to grapple with the conflicts the day's events had brought to pass, Sophie pushed the entire situation from her mind, fervently hoping that neither the clergymen of St. Giles nor Lord Lemore would do anything else to cause them further trouble. Meanwhile, she dutifully produced a small playbill announcing a concert presenting:

For the FIRST time in Edinburgh!
The CLAN ROBERTSON SINGERS
Presenting the famous Highland Bard
RORY ROBERTSON and his HARP
and his balladeer grandson
HUNTER ROBERTSON
and Mother Robertson
Singing Highland and Lowland Favorites!!!

When Sophie had set the type that listed the date and
admission prices, she prayed that her superlatives and exclamation points would be sufficient to draw a crowd large
enough for Hunter at least to cover his expenses. As she
trudged around the town posting her handiwork, she
thought about poor playwrights who, she'd heard actually
wound up *owing* money to the theater management, instead
of reaping profits for their efforts.

The next day, Daniel McGann drifted down the alley to
speak with another bookseller about his recent contretemps
with the local clergy. Alone in the shop, Sophie heard the
door open and the sound of masculine laughter. As she
emerged from the printing chamber wiping her ink-stained
hands on her apron, she felt her heart skip a beat at the sight
of Hunter Robertson pointing at the placard she'd put in her
window announcing his concert. He was flanked by two
young men, one of whom was rather stylishly attired.

"Aha!" Hunter exclaimed to his companions, flashing the
smile that had lingered in Sophie's memory. "Here's the
clever wee lassie whose broadsides have garnered me notice
all over Edinburgh! Not only does she *write* brilliantly at
the tender age of sixteen, but can set type as if she were *twice*
her age—as she informed me the day I met her. What's
more," he added gallantly, "she dances like an angel!" Sophie found herself blushing to her auburn roots. "Sophie
McGann," Hunter continued, "may I present Mr. James
Boswell and Mr. William Creech—longtime residents of this
fair city who have kindly befriended me."

Will Creech and Sophie exchanged smiles. They were

practically the same age and had known each other for ages. Creech was currently attending the University of Edinburgh and often browsed through the volumes in their shop.

"Will and I are two bookworms of long acquaintance, eh Willie?" she laughed. Her attention focused on the other, elegantly dressed visitor.

James Boswell's name was familiar to her not just because his father was a famous judge, but because she had heard rumors about the twenty-year-old heir to the Auchinleck estate south of Edinburgh. Boswell had engaged in a torrid affair with a Catholic actress ten years his senior and had subsequently run off to London in the midst of his law studies, much to the fury of his stiff-necked, kirk-going father. She had it from some local gossip that the wayward lad was now dutifully pursuing his legal education locally, under Lord Auchinleck's watchful paternal eye.

"I'm so pleased to make your acquaintance," Sophie nodded to Boswell, wondering that such a portly, round-faced law student had proved irresistible to the flamboyant actress, Anna Cowper. "Welcome to our shop," she added, ignoring as best she could the pillaged bookshelves surrounding her guests.

"Did the raiding clerics leave you your stock of printed plays?" Boswell asked, glancing at the plundered shelves.

"So you've heard about our recent visitors," Sophie replied stiffly. "Yes . . . a few."

She found herself comparing Creech's sharp features and Boswell's rather doughy countenance with Hunter's; his straight nose and high cheekbones recalled engravings she'd seen of Greek warriors. Then she remembered his look of anguish when he had acknowledged he could not read. In that painful moment of truth, Hunter's demeanor had been free of any effort to captivate, bewitch, or beguile. Today, however, the charmer who stood in the book shop with his two companions was completely self-assured and treated her like the little sister he had alluded to when first they met.

"Well, wee one . . . I've come to thank ye for telling the town so eloquently of my impending concert."

"How many tickets have you sold?" Sophie inquired.

Hunter erupted into laughter.

"Did I not tell ye the lass is a canny merchant?" he chortled to Boswell and Creech. "Bozzy, here, heard me sing at Fortune's Tavern last night and has promised to write a boast for me in the *Edinburgh Courant* the day before the concert."

"But have you *sold* any tickets yet?" Sophie persisted anxiously. "'Twould be disastrous if you find yourself *owing* David Beatt forty pounds, or so."

Her words seemed to give Hunter a moment's concern, but then he shrugged. "Creech tells me the lads will line up in droves on the day of the performance."

"Perhaps the young bucks who frequent the tavern will," she replied tartly, "but you must entice ladies of fashion as well. Otherwise you'll not get the necessary gentlemen to plunk down the siller for the entrance fees."

"The lass is probably correct in that," Boswell said thoughtfully, pulling a book from the shelf and thumbing its pages.

"We could always take him to Miss Nicky's cotillion tonight," Creech grinned at Sophie. "If the ladies saw him in satin breeches, they'd swarm to hear him sing."

"I've no satin breeches, I can tell ye that!" Hunter laughed.

"I could lend you a pair," Boswell said, looking up from the pages of the book he was scanning, his eyes alight with mischief. "With your height, they might be a wee bit tight," he added, "but that would be all to your advantage, I suspect!" At that, the three young men laughed heartily, exchanging knowing glances.

"He'll have to be able to do the minuet," Sophie said primly. "Miss Nicky insists any newcomer be sponsored by someone known to her, and that he be able to dance properly."

"Do you know the minuet, Robertson?" Boswell asked Hunter. His questioning look reflected his evident doubt that a rough Highlander could have acquired any drawing room refinements.

But before Hunter could admit that he knew nothing of that complicated confection imported from France, Sophie announced, "I can teach him."

"By *tonight*?" Creech said skeptically.

"God's bones, I think she *could*!" Hunter laughed. "She danced some flimflam with me the other day on the street without even knowing the steps."

Sophie was relieved to see that Hunter took seriously the advantages of making a public appearance at the cotillion to drum up a paying audience for his concert.

"Mr. Boswell," Sophie entreated, "would you sponsor Hunter at Miss Nicky's and lend him proper attire? And Willie, would you sing his praises to the ladies of the town?"

Boswell pulled his gaze from the book he had been skimming, a volume written by an English traveler to Italy. "I shall present him to the sister of the Earl of Mansfield *only* on condition that you can make him a presentable dancer of the minuet by six o'clock this evening," he replied. "I mean it, Robertson," he added slyly. "I'll never hear the end of it from my father if I sponsor some hairy Highlander who makes a fool of himself at Miss Nicky's Assembly. 'Twould destroy my reputation."

"And *your* reputation is so unblemished, Bozzy," Creech interjected sardonically, adding, "I'll champion the lad."

Boswell's soft, round cheeks took on a rosy hue and he swiftly returned his attention to examining an engraving of Roman ruins. Shortly thereafter, Hunter's new acquaintances departed, and between infrequent appearances of customers in the shop, Sophie drilled Hunter all afternoon in the basic steps of the minuet.

By five o'clock, Hunter, with his natural musical talent and innate dancing ability, appeared to have mastered a passable minuet. Boswell and Creech arrived, dressed handsomely, and Hunter donned his borrowed finery in the back chamber, hanging his tartan trousers on the handle of the printing press.

"Gadzooks, man!" Boswell exclaimed as Hunter entered the front of the shop, "Deuced if you don't look better in my clothes than *I* do!"

Sophie could hardly credit the extraordinary change in Hunter. Boswell had lent him a fine linen shirt, complete with cascading lace at collar and wrist, which contrasted nicely with his ivory satin breeches and a midnight blue velvet coat with deep cuffs and matching buttons. As she stared at the startling metamorphosis of the strolling player whose unvarnished good looks had been transformed into classic masculine beauty, her heart filled with pride and confidence.

Sophie dashed up to the second floor to change from her printer's apron and faded skirt into her only dress, a gown cut down from one her mother had worn. The cotton garment wasn't the least luxurious and the style was more than a decade out of date, but the skirt and bodice were of a pale peach color that set off Sophie's auburn hair.

She stared forlornly at the fabric bunched-up where her bosom should be. In spite of her sixteen years, her breasts had barely grown! Struck suddenly by an idea, Sophie scooped up her petticoat and rolled down her woolen stockings. Stuffing them into her bodice, she stared at the resulting hillocks. Unfortunately, the protuberances looked hard and artificial. With a sigh, she extracted the scratchy camouflage and headed toward the narrow stairs that led down to the first floor.

By the time Sophie reappeared in the shop, her father had returned and was conversing animatedly with Jamie Boswell about an island off Italy called Corsica. The younger man had seen it mentioned in the book he'd been perusing earlier that day.

"You've met Mr. Boswell," Sophie asked her father rhetorically, "and Mr. Robertson, whose playbills we printed?"

"Aye," her father said genially as the church bells somberly tolled the hour of six in the cathedral belfry above their heads.

Boswell handed Daniel the book on Italy.

"I'd like to purchase this, if you please," he said.

"That will be six shillings," Daniel replied, his eyes dancing with pleasure at the pending sale.

"Will four do for the moment?" Boswell inquired smoothly, "unless Creech will stand me for the other two?"

"Sorry, Bozzy, my lad," Creech said shaking his head. "A poor university student has barely the entrance fee to Miss Nicky's."

"Not to worry, Mr. Boswell," Daniel said abruptly. "Take the book and pay me the rest when you can."

"You're very kind," Boswell replied cheerfully, digging four shillings out of a small pocket in his white brocaded waistcoat. "I shall retrieve it when we escort your daughter home tonight."

"We'd best be off," Sophie said briskly, attempting to mask her annoyance that her father was so easily taken advantage of. Yet, four shillings was better than none, and perhaps young James Boswell was good for his debts. "I've left some bannocks and a bit of broth in the kettle for you, Da," she added.

"Thank you, my dear," her father answered vaguely, lost in the pages of the book Boswell had selected from their shelves. "Enjoy yourselves, laddies," he said, barely looking up.

"Do ye really think my attending tonight's assembly will help sell tickets to the concert?" Hunter asked quietly, falling into step beside Sophie as the quartet headed toward Bell's Wynd. "I perform on cobblestones, not in a ballroom of dandies and ladies in corsets," he added glumly.

"Just *smile* at those ladies when you speak, and when you're dancing, concentrate on the steps, not on their corsets. I know you can do it! You can't afford *not to*!"

Hunter shot her a rueful grin, but also seemed to gain confidence from her words.

"Don't expect *me* to stay by your side, laddie mine," Boswell announced bluntly. "Too many beauties will require our attention."

"I thought your heart was permanently broken by a certain lady of the theater," Creech heckled his friend.

"'Twas broken, to be sure," Boswell said with mock seriousness, "—but that was *last* year!"

Even Sophie laughed.

"To the lassies in our futures!" Hunter cheered, extending his velvet-cloaked arm heavenward in a high-spirited salute.

"To the *lassies!*" chorused Creech and Boswell.

Sophie remained silent at this, but none of her escorts appeared to notice. She could hear the sedate strains of a string orchestra playing a minuet as they entered the flow of pedestrians approaching Bell's Wynd. She was acutely aware of the whispering onlookers as their small group joined the throng entering the ballroom. Handsome young women, resplendent in satin and brocades, acknowledged their entrance from behind fluttering fans, their ornately powdered wigs nearly colliding as they craned their necks to get a look at the tall stranger with dark blond hair.

Hunter's skin-tight borrowed breeches showed off his muscular frame to seductive advantage, and Sophie could sense a palpable excitement stirring among the females in the ballroom, most of them wearing deep-cut bodices that barely restrained their rounded, opalescent flesh. Her own peach-colored gown felt grotesquely loose against the pathetically small mounds on her chest, and for the first time in her life, Sophie experienced a witch's brew of raw envy flowing through her veins.

The room had become insufferably stuffy, the cloying scents of the dancers masking not only the sweat produced by their exertions on the ballroom floor but odors of much baser origins. Hunter, Boswell, and Creech were already surrounded by a group of chattering young people their own age, including a bevy of beauties who clustered nearby, anxious to make Hunter's acquaintance.

As the orchestra struck up a sedate minuet, Sophie found herself all but abandoned by her three companions. Her fear that Hunter Robertson would be unable to sell tickets to his performance at the Canongate Playhouse melted into the packed ballroom, replaced by a bleakness that seemed to invade her bones. She watched as Hunter, by way of introduction, kissed the hand of one coquette who stared at him invitingly with large luminous eyes. At this flirtatious exchange, Sophie's pleasurable anticipation of the evening drained away entirely, leaving her wretchedly bereft and utterly ignored.

Chapter 3

The Canongate Playhouse was packed to the rafters on the evening of May 15. Sophie stood backstage, trembling with apprehension. It was all very well that Edinburgh's women of fashion had apparently adopted a new pet—the devilishly handsome Hunter Robertson—but would the theater patrons sitting restlessly out front tire of Scottish ditties and laments and the novelty of a blind old man playing the harp? And what if the kirk elders thundered from their pulpits on Sunday against theatergoers who indulged in such wicked amusements?

Sophie retreated from the spy hole and gazed nervously into the tiring-room. Hunter stood in front of the looking glass neatly securing his blond mane at the nape of his neck with a black ribbon. He had combined Boswell's blue velvet coat and laced-trimmed linen shirt to excellent effect with his Clan Robertson tartan trews woven of crimson, forest green and navy wool. He glanced at her standing in the door frame and grinned.

"What think you, Sophie lass? Will the ladies swoon—or throw rubbish?"

Before she could answer the obvious, the theater manager appeared in the doorway.

"Ready, lad?" Beatt asked. "I think we should begin."

The performers moved toward the wings. Sophie watched the old man settle painfully on the low stool placed stage right. His daughter-in-law Jean Robertson took her customary position next to him as Rory pulled his stringed instrument to his arthritic shoulder and prepared to begin the performance.

Without so much as a nod to his mother, Hunter took Sophie by the hand and crossed to the curtained flies, stage left. She was relieved to see that he seemed full of confidence, almost as if he couldn't wait to greet the potentially hostile audience.

"Can ye believe all these people paid good shillings for what they could have heard a week ago on the street for a farthing!" he said jovially.

"'Tis a lot bigger space here in the Canongate than performing on cobblestones," she warned. "Mind that you sing loudly, so the top galleries get their money's worth and don't hiss at you!"

"Always the till keeper, eh lass?" Hunter laughed, looking down at her fondly. "Dinna worry . . . I plan to sing my lungs out tonight."

"'Tis better you should *sing* than speak," she said anxiously. Some Lowlanders felt prejudiced against the Highland burr that was a hallmark of speech in the predominantly Catholic regions in northern Scotland.

"Aye," Hunter agreed, suddenly looking pensive. "I'll take yer suggestion to heart, pet."

And before she could wish him good luck, he bent down and kissed the top of her head like an affectionate brother. Then he nodded to David Beatt who gave the signal to the small orchestra he had hired for the occasion, at Hunter's expense, to commence playing the medley of Scottish melodies that served to preview the evening's entertainment.

At the sound of the music, the audience quieted. Through the peephole Sophie could see that their faces were turned attentively toward the stage.

Oh, please let him be good, she cried silently. *Please let them like him!*

Hunter stepped on stage and flashed his captivating smile. His rich, resonant baritone carried throughout the hall, dazzling even the patrons in the top gallery, who were delighted to be able to enjoy the words as well as the melody.

There was a wee cooper who lived in Fife
Nick-e-ty, nack-e-ty, noo, noo, noo
And he has gotten a gentle wife
Hey wil-ly wal-lack-y, noo, John Dougāl!
She wadna bake, nor she wadna brew
For the spoiling of her comely hue!

By the last verse of this musical jest, the audience was
smiling and clapping, the upper galleries boisterously joining
in on the chorus of *"Nickety, nackety, noo, noo, noo!"*

Sophie glanced over at David Beatt whose bald crown
was fashionably covered by a bagwig in honor of the evening's festivities. Sensing Sophie's gaze, Beatt turned to look
at her and vigorously bobbed his head in relief that everything was going well.

Sophie, the theater manager, and the audience had barely
caught their collective breath when Hunter broke into the
traditional "I'm a Rover," emphasizing the teasing lyrics
with his own special brand of rakish charm.

I'm a rover and seldom sober
I'm a rover o' high degree
It's when I'm drinking, I'm always thinking
How to gain my love's company!

Sophie returned to the peephole once again and stared at
the women in the audience, who gazed with languorous eyes
as Hunter swaggered back and forth across the stage. He
seemed to display an astounding talent for making each of
them believe that he sang only to her. Even Lord Lemore,
sitting in a choice box seat in the second tier, was no longer
surveying the crowd with his characteristic reptilian gaze
and, instead, was giving Hunter his complete attention.

Song after song—some solemn, some sprightly—issued
from the Clan Robertson Singers, as Sophie had dubbed
them, and the audience was enthralled with the sounds of a
bygone era.

Finally, as the candles burned low throughout the auditorium, the little orchestra eased into a quiet, melancholy refrain, and Hunter's demeanor changed dramatically from

that of a loveable rogue with an eye for the ladies to a heartsore lad whose musical lament told of tragedy and loss.

> *Flow gently, sweet Afton, among thy green braes,*
> *Flow gently, sweet river, the theme of my days;*
> *My Mary's asleep by the murmuring stream,*
> *Flow gently, sweet Afton, disturb not her dream.*

Hunter's deep tones spoke of a stinging, private grief
more eloquently than any keening cry. Sophie watched from
the wings and while the soft candlelight flickered across the
smooth planes of his features, her eyes suddenly filled with
tears. The shadows carved hollows beneath his cheekbones,
imprinting his classic profile in her memory.

Sophie watched while several powdered ladies fumbled
for their lace handkerchiefs. Their male companions looked
heavenward and blinked hard. As the orchestra's haunting
theme faded, the only sound in the hall was the last mourn-
ful cadence stroked by Rory Robertson, his gnarled fingers
caressing the harp strings in a Highland requiem for some
missing piece of Hunter's past.

In the dead silence that hung in the air, Hunter uttered
the only words he'd spoken during his entire performance.

"Will ye no come back ag'in?"

It was the traditional Highland farewell. He bowed
gravely and marched off stage, straight into Sophie's outstretched arms. She had to stand on her very tiptoes to hug
him properly, shouting her praise over the thunderous applause that rolled over the footcandles glowing at the lip of
the stage. Hunter picked Sophie up under her arms and spun
her around, emitting an ear-splitting Highland battle cry
that could almost be heard over the din out front. Without
warning, he leaned down and was within inches of kissing
her on the lips. Then, just as quickly, he thrust her away
from him with a look of chagrin. Before either could utter a
word, David Beatt was thumping his protégé on the shoulder, urging him to return to the stage to take another bow.
Hunter obliged, but regardless of how hard his newly won
admirers clapped their hands, he merely grinned what So-

phie now recognized was his performance smile and stead-fastly, but charmingly, refused to perform an encore.

"Let them pay to hear more," he declared as he headed toward the Greenroom, a chamber designed for accommodating actors and their admirers. The origins of the reception room's name were lost, although some actors claimed it derived from the village green where strolling players traditionally performed.

Hunter collapsed into a straight-backed chair, looking suddenly exhausted. Sophie poured him a cup of whiskey from a jug on a nearby table and he drank it down. For a moment it was eerily quiet, and Sophie was too tongue-tied by what had almost happened in the wings to break the silence.

"Sophie, I—" Hunter began, taking another draft of spirits. Then he set his cup down, and shook his head ruefully. "I'm an impulsive rogue when it comes to the fair sex, and that's a fact. I apologize for—"

"Oh, Hunter," she replied quickly, attempting to find a safer topic. "You've a beautiful voice and an amazing . . . talent for . . . *communing* with your audience."

"Communing, is it?" He laughed gruffly. "'Tis how angels speak with saints, is it not? That canna be what *I* do!"

"Truly," she insisted, not to be deterred from speaking what was in her heart. "'Twas most remarkable, what you did tonight. You *do* know that, don't you?"

"Why thank ye," he said, his handsome features animated by a gentleness far removed from the bold sensuality he had displayed on stage or his joyful abandon when he embraced her in the wings. "You've been a great friend, and 'tis *that* I treasure more than . . . all that hand-thumping out there."

Sophie gave him a wry smile.

"Oh, I'm certain you'll soon accustom yourself to the applause," she said, aware that their private moment would be interrupted any moment by an avalanche of well-wishers. "And I'll bet you your evening's wages tonight that Beatt will offer you a position in his company next season."

"I'll have to learn to read then," he answered with a tight smile. "Do ye think you could teach this lumpkin his ABC's by autumn?"

"Aye, Hunter Robertson, I could indeed," she replied happily.

No sooner had she said the words than a legion of admirers—most of them women, and not a few actress employed at the playhouse itself—burst into the Greenroom, all talking at once. Sophie slipped out of the chamber quickly to avoid a possible encounter with the unnerving Lord Lemore.

Hunter's concerts were the talk of Edinburgh—including a sermon by the chief minister at St. Giles, who denounced the "blasphemies sung by rogues and vagabonds in the playhouse where Satan's seat is and from whence He sends out Detachments of the Wicked to further his Campaign of Sin!"

"Goodness, did he say all *that*?" Sophie asked of Boswell, who had been required to attend the Kirk session by his father, Lord Auckinleck, now returned to Edinburgh from his temporary duties as a circuit judge.

"Aye, that and more," Boswell replied, thumbing through a copy of the *Edinburgh Courant* to see if several verses he'd written had been granted publication.

The young law student had stopped by the book shop to persuade Hunter to accompany him to the Netherbow Coffeehouse to while away the rest of the afternoon sipping the bitter Turkish brew for a penny or two in front of a fire. There they could read the latest pamphlet or London newspaper and enjoy the company of any number of intriguing companions. Fops, justices, lawyers, pickpockets, actors, nonconformist clergy—all sorts of people frequented these smoky dens where, Sophie realized, the only women present tended to be barmaids, actresses, and prostitutes. But at least Hunter now had the funds to pay for such outings. With the tidy sum his performances had garnered, the Robertsons had even been able to take lodgings in White Horse Close, the first real home they had shared since Hunter's childhood.

When Boswell appeared at the book shop's door, Hunter had quickly hidden the reading primer he'd been studying. Three or four times a week he would sit cross-legged on the floor beside Sophie's stool near the window and attempt to make sense of the letters on the page in front of him. Sophie desperately tried to remember how *she* had learned to read and gradually developed a method of linking each letter in the alphabet to the first word in a song Hunter knew.

"The letter *I*" she had demanded of Hunter before Boswell's interruption.

"*I . . . I,*" Hunter repeated, his brow furrowing. The cleft in his chin flattened as he grimaced, searching his memory for the song title that would help him identify the letter. " 'I'm a Rover'!" he exclaimed triumphantly. "*I* is for 'I'm a Rover'!"

"Yes!" Sophie had said enthusiastically, writing the song title on a little chalk board. "See . . . here's the *I* in 'I'm a Rover.' Now, what about *W*? First make the *sound* of the letter *W*."

"Blast!" Hunter replied in frustration. "How did I know ye'd ask me that one?" His eyes lit up. "Wha . . . wha . . . wha . . . *W* is for 'One Merry Day'!"

Sophie shook her head and smiled encouragingly. "*One* sounds like a *W* sounds . . . but, no, *W* is for 'Wee Cooper O' Fife,' or 'Will Ye No Come Back Again'?"

"Or 'Will This Sapskull Ever Learn His Alphabet'!" he said, disgusted. "Here *ye* are, not even eighteen, and ye've mastered every tome on these shelves. As for me, I'm near witless with my letters. 'Tis sheer folly for me to try to make them into *words*."

Sophie put her hand on his arm and said sympathetically, "You're making *good* progress, Hunter. But it takes time to make up for all those years when you were memorizing the songs by heart and learning your skill at juggling. You'll be reading like a professor before the year is out, I promise."

Hunter gazed at her for a long moment and then took her small hand, completely covering it with his own.

"Sophie, coming to know you and your da . . . 'tis like having part of my family again. A blockhead like me couldna ask for a better friend." Sophie's heart thudded against her chest and her eyes searched his, willing him to say more. "Ye so put me in mind of my sister, Megan," he added slowly. "She was such a sprite, like ye . . . a little elfin creature who made ye glad just to see her smile . . ."

"Where does she live?" Sophie ventured tentatively. A look of bitter sadness flooded his eyes.

"She died," he replied, retracting his hands from hers and balling them into fists, "when she was still a bairn."

Sophie waited patiently, but Hunter offered no more information on the subject. His gaze had taken on a faraway look, as if he were viewing a scene of absolute desolation.

The moment of closeness between them had ended even before Boswell sauntered through the front door of the book shop and issued his invitation for Hunter to join him at the Netherbow Coffeehouse. Hunter swiftly agreed.

"Farewell, pet," her pupil said with a breezy wave, his former cocksure demeanor reasserting itself. "Tell yer da I may want a new playbill printed if Comely Gardens will sponsor a concert in August."

"Aye . . . I'll see he gets your message," Sophie replied, falling in with the subterfuge. She was eager to specify their next appointment, but merely bid the two young men adieu, not wanting to reveal Hunter's secret intention to learn to read.

Hunter failed to return for another reading lesson for more than a week, although, a few days later, Sophie caught a glimpse of Hunter and Boswell entering the Pen and Feather across the road, accompanied by two voluptuous-looking actresses from the playhouse. In the days that followed, Sophie was filled with a sharp longing to see that cocky grin and experienced deepening anxiety over the deplorable state of their family finances. McGann's had received a few printing commissions but nothing that would earn them enough to order more books from London and abroad to replenish their woefully depleted shelves. Without the enticement of new wares, business had fallen off dramatically. Sophie's father grew even more disheartened as the week wore on. The only thing Sophie could suggest was that he seek the same diversion Hunter and Jamie Boswell had indulged in at the Netherbow Coffeehouse.

"'Tis like a tomb in here," she commented, glancing around the empty book shop. "I'll finish up the placards for the wigmaker and keep on the lookout for a book buyer with blood in his veins and a few coins in his pocket."

Daniel offered a wan smile in response to her attempted levity and drifted off to the coffeehouse.

Every time Sophie heard someone come in the shop, she raced past the wooden hand press to see if it was Hunter, but the few customers who did stop by were neither six feet tall nor blessed with a smile that could make Sophie forget everything but its engaging warmth.

She pulled the handle of the wooden press with an angry jerk. For some reason, Hunter seemed to regret having almost kissed her, and now he was keeping company with that doxy at the playhouse! Why, she wondered peevishly, did he continue to treat her as if she were a mere child? Lord Lemore was practically in his dotage, but even *he* had viewed her as an object of desire.

Before Sophie could ponder this riddle further, she heard the door open and a cane thump smartly three times on the floor, a signal that demanded immediate attention.

She jumped down from her composing stool and rushed into the other chamber, halting abruptly at the threshold. As if materializing from her thoughts, Lord Lemore stood leaning against a silver-headed walking stick, his thin-lidded eyes gazing at her like a lizard at a fly.

"Is your father available?" he asked. "I'd like to discuss ordering several new engravings from your agent in London."

He stated the request as if it were perfectly reasonable to discuss with his local bookseller's daughter his desire to add to his collection of obscenities. She assumed that his assortment of pictures stoked the fires of some warped craving in the man, and that now he must be in need of new stimulation.

"My father is not here, sir, and I'm afraid I don't know when he's expected," she said stiffly, rooted to the floor.

Lord Lemore strolled toward her, a sardonic smile tugging at his features.

"A happy accident, perhaps," he murmured, drawing near. "I'm sure that, young as you are, you have the experience to assist me in selecting some additions to my noteworthy collection."

He gazed at her steadily, carefully placing his cane on the desk where her father kept his accounts.

"I-I cannot help you, sir," she stammered, her heart quickening with apprehension. "The type of engravings I delivered to you two months ago are not what we normally stock, you understand."

"Oh, but I am confident they are *available* to you," he replied. "You are being too modest about your ability to locate what I want. I am told that you are wise beyond your years and know the book trade as well as your esteemed father."

"I don't know about *lewd etchings*!" she exclaimed with an unexpected flash of anger. Immediately, however, she regretted her outburst. Lord Lemore eyed her narrowly, but remained silent. "I'm terribly sorry I can't help you and I'm afraid, also, that you'll have to excuse me, m'lord," Sophie added with a politeness she certainly did not feel. "I have a printing order to complete."

"'Tis folly to speak so indiscreetly of lewdness, my dear," the nobleman said in a low, menacing voice. "'Twould be disastrous for McGann's, wouldn't it now, if the good churchmen next door were to hear of your pronouncing such blasphemies? If you cannot supply my needs, I shall seek elsewhere. Good day."

With that, he snatched his walking stick off the desk and turned on his heel. Heading for the door, he nearly collided with Hunter Robertson, who was just then sauntering across the threshold.

Sophie clung to the door frame of the printing chamber, her face drained of color as she watched Lord Lemore stride into the High Street without a backward glance.

"Hello, lass . . . have ye an hour to spare for a reading lesson?" He peered at her closely. "Are ye all right?" he inquired solicitously. "Ye look fashed, and that's a fact."

"Th-that man . . ." Sophie began, and then burst into tears.

"What man? The coxcomb who just left the shop?" Hunter sent a confused look over his shoulder at Lord

Lemore's figure, retreating down the road. He put a brotherly arm around Sophie's heaving shoulders.

"That *coxcomb*, as you just called him, is Lord Lemore!" Sophie blurted. She reached for a corner of her printer's apron and dried her eyes. "He's a man of great influence in Edinburgh and a good customer of my da."

"So?" Hunter asked practically. "Best to tug yer forelock and be polite to those aristos and leave 'em be," he advised.

"But he could do us dreadful *harm*!" Sophie wailed and found her eyes filling with tears once again.

"Why? How? Sweetling, whatever is the matter?" Hunter responded, folding his arms around her again protectively. "What can a coxcomb like him do to such a brave lass as ye, will ye tell me now?" he teased.

"H-he can h-hurt Da," she gulped. "He can tell th-those Kirk elders about the p-pictures!"

"Pictures?" Hunter asked, bewildered. "But ye sell *books* at McGann's. What would Lord Lemore be wanting with pictures?"

"I don't know why *anyone* would want those horrid engravings!" Sophie shuddered. "I suppose Da only sends for them from London when things are as wretched as they are now!"

Hunter sat her down on her stool where they usually had their reading lessons and took one of her hands in his.

"Ye better just tell me what this is all about, wee one."

"I'm *not* wee!" she cried, tears once again spilling over her eyelids despite her fierce efforts to hold them back. Just because Hunter had fallen into the arms of some jade at the playhouse didn't give him license to treat her like a doltish child!

Hunter looked abashed.

"*Wee* is just a word that seems to fit ye," he apologized. He smiled encouragingly. "Winna ye tell me now?"

Sophie took a deep breath and then, blushing furiously, told Hunter about the erotic engravings Daniel McGann had procured for Lord Lemore. When she described her encounter with the nobleman the day she delivered the last packet to his lodgings, Hunter looked aghast.

"God's bones!" he cursed. "Preying on such a bairn as ye!"

"Perhaps I seem a bairn to *you*, Hunter Robertson, but the filthy cad considered me woman enough to lay siege to my drawers!"

"But ye're only sixteen!" he exploded. "And ye look to be about twelve!"

"Sixteen and six months!" Sophie snapped. "Lord Lemore assured me *Highland* lasses were frequently wed at my age and, therefore, I should know perfectly well what happens between men and women in bed—marriage or no!"

It was Hunter's turn to flush scarlet, and for once he was unable to summon a suitable retort.

"When I didn't accept his order," Sophie continued anxiously, "Lemore hinted that he would call down those ranting clerics on us again! If that happens, Hunter, we're *finished*. Da will be evicted from the Luckenbooths and we'll have nowhere to go!"

"'Twas probably an idle threat, to keep ye from spreading tales that would call the elders down on *him*!"

"And they'd be believing a bookseller's lass against a nobleman!" she retorted sarcastically. "No, Hunter . . . I'm really frightened. Lord Lemore—"

"Lord Lemore's a twisted scoundrel, to be sure," agreed Hunter. "But, have faith, pet. He'll find another source of filth in this fair city, dinna ye fret. And then he'll forget about yer impetuous words." He smiled down at her reassuringly and gave her hand another squeeze. "And dinna be too hard on yer da," he added as if reading her thoughts. "He's only trying to look after ye as best he can. One man's filthy pictures is another man's art."

"I know," Sophie replied softly. Yet it disturbed her that a man with reverence for truth and beauty could bend to the base demands of a villain like Lemore. Despite what Hunter might think, she was no longer a child, and she suspected she was in the process of discovering just how difficult adulthood could be.

"How about a reading lesson to take yer mind off yer worries?" Hunter inquired, interrupting her reverie. "Since I saw ye last, I have signed articles with David Beatt officially joining the playhouse, and I *must* be able to learn my parts, small as I suspect they'll be. So, these days, *W* is one of my favorite letters," he grinned. "*W* is for 'With a Hundred Pipers'."

"Or 'Winna Ye Give Me a Smile, Laddie Mine?' " Sophie replied, her spirits sinking even lower as she recalled seeing the pretty actress clinging to Hunter's arm as he and Boswell repaired to the Pen and Feather. Her mood improved somewhat at the thought that permanent employment for Hunter meant that he could give up being a strolling player and remain in Edinburgh at least throughout the theatrical season. "Your mother and grandfather must be pleased about this stroke of good fortune," she commented.

" 'Tis sure that Rory's at the end of his traveling days," he noted somberly, "and Jean . . . well, Jean's a survivor. She's happy to have a clean bed and a roof over her head."

"Who isn't?" Sophie replied, wondering if Hunter would share a confidence because she had meted out so many this afternoon.

"Is Jean really your mother?" Sophie asked quietly.

"What a question!" Hunter replied, startled by her directness.

"You didn't answer. Is she?"

Hunter stared silently out the shop window for a long moment and then looked at Sophie and sighed.

"Sometimes I wish to St. Ninian she wasn't . . . but yes, Jean Hunter Robertson spawned me and kept me alive in the face of everything," he answered cryptically, his jaw clamped, as if to prevent himself from commenting further.

Just at that moment, William Creech and James Boswell burst into the shop. Gesturing at Hunter, Boswell gave his companion a sly wink. "If he's not at his lodgings, or in the feathers with Gwen, 'tis always a likely bet we'll find this lad lounging around these dusty tomes, eh, Creech?"

"Why, ye insolent swine!" Hunter responded with mock indignation, "I was just telling Sophie my bit o' good luck, getting a berth with Beatt's players for the new season."

Sophie had flushed at the mention of the name of

Hunter's apparent new *amour*, but no one seemed to notice her chagrin.

"We're going to change your life . . . or at least help you along in your new profession," Boswell proclaimed grandly. "The great god of elocution, Thomas Sheridan, has come to this fair city to offer lessons in the art of speaking the king's English, my lad!" Boswell pronounced. "He's being sponsored by the Select Society of Edinburgh to help us bumpkins purge Scottish colloquial speech from fashionable Edinburgh. *You*, Hunter, he will teach to *speak* English."

"'Tis a guinea a head for the series of lectures," confided Creech excitedly to Sophie, "and we've enrolled the three of us."

"'Tis a chance to speak our native tongue without being the subject of ridicule in London!" Boswell declared.

"Sheridan sounds like an Irish name," Hunter replied doubtfully.

"He's Irish, all right, but that makes what he teaches all the more remarkable," Boswell enthused.

"Tell me truly, lads," Hunter demanded, "who gives a newt's nose if some London knave dinna like the roll of yer *R*'s?"

"A theater manager gives a newt's nose," Sophie interjected sharply, her dismay concerning the unwelcome confirmation of Hunter's liaison with some actress named Gwen translating into a caustic tone. "Remember Mr. Beatt? He claimed he could hardly understand half your participles and his mother was from Inverness!"

"*Ye* three understand me well enough!" Hunter protested.

"Ah . . . but we're *used* to you!" she rejoined. "You may know every Scottish ditty ever invented, but when you speak, your accent is atrocious!"

Hunter shot her an injured look and then asked quietly, "When do Sheridan's classes begin?"

"In a week's time," Boswell answered, "and they run through August."

"I'm told his style gives the great Garrick pause," Creech chimed in, referring to David Garrick, the most famous actor-manager in all of Britain and the titan of the Theater Royal, Drury Lane, in London.

Sophie noted the stubborn expression that had invaded Hunter's features, and she sensed it had more to do with his being a Highlander than a Scot.

"Come ye now, Hunter," she coaxed, valiantly trying to regain her good humor by adopting the burr that made his speech unintelligible at times. "'Twould be excellent training for the stage. And ye kin speak yer barbaric tongue with me privately whenever ye fancy," she added, struck by the thought of how much *she* would enjoy attending such a series of lectures. To hear one of the finest actors in the land expound on a subject that fascinated her—

She sighed. The Select Society of Edinburgh was decidedly men only.

"Ye'll need *lessons* to speak *my* way, lassie," Hunter chided her, "so I suppose 'tis sensible for this fledgling player to learn his craft so he can challenge this Sheridan, or perhaps even that fellow David Garrick for parts in London someday."

"Then you'll do it?" Sophie asked earnestly, coming to the abrupt decision that she'd rather have Hunter as a friend, if nothing else.

"Aye . . . and I'll come after these two villains for the guinea if learning to prattle like some stiff-necked English fop doesn't someday fill my coffers!"

"Splendid!" Boswell exclaimed.

"I say, capital, old boy!" Creech said in a fair imitation of the speech they all hoped to mimic.

"This calls for a toast. Let's repair to the Pen and Feather, eh, lads?" Boswell proposed.

"What about—" Sophie stopped short of reminding Hunter they were about to have a reading lesson.

"I'll be back tomorrow or the day after," Hunter said blithely over his shoulder as the three young men headed out of the shop.

Sophie stared after them moodily. But gradually her face lit up with a private smile as a plan started to take shape. Perhaps, for *once* in her life, she could use her flat bosom to her advantage.

※

Daniel McGann nervously watched the last sheets of their paper stock disappear under the platen as Sophie gave the printing press handle a counterclockwise yank, moving the wooden form containing the metal letters to its proper position.

"And you're positive this Sheridan will pay?" he inquired anxiously.

A second push of the handle caused the type to impress its characters on the paper. What resulted was a placard ballyhooing Thomas Sheridan's distinguished acting career and exhorting fashionable Edinburgh to subscribe to his series of lectures, "The Elocutionary Arts."

"Aye, Da," Sophie assured him, breathing heavily from the exertion required to pull the heavy handlebar. "He promised to give full payment directly following his first program at the Royal Infirmary tonight."

"Well, that's a blessing," Daniel sighed.

"And did you know that he's the Sheridan married to *Frances* Sheridan?" Sophie added, brimming with enthusiasm. "The novelist who wrote *Memoirs of Miss Sydney Biddulph.*"

"Yes, I *did* know that," her father said with a trace of his former good humor. "But I didn't realize you'd read all three volumes when I wasn't looking," he teased, retreating through the door to the book shop itself.

Sophie hung the last of the placards to dry on lines strung across the low-ceilinged chamber. She gathered a stack she had printed the previous day and prepared to make another foray down the High Street to add them to the scores she had already affixed to walls and doorways all over the town. Thomas Sheridan himself had appeared at the threshold of McGann's earlier in the day to announce that his lecture series was nearly sold out. He offered bemused thanks to Sophie for her efforts, handing her a free ticket as part of the bargain they had struck when she had called at his lodgings in St. James's Court and first proposed printing his placards.

As soon as Sheridan left, Sophie had returned to the printing room to produce the last of the advertisements slated for distribution around the city. Gathering the broadsides in her arms, she paused when she heard the shop door open and the now too-familiar voice of Lord Lemore.

"I'm glad I spied you on the High Street, McGann," Sophie heard the nobleman address her father as he followed the proprietor into the shop and shut the door. Quietly setting the placards on top of the printing press, Sophie crept closer to the door to eavesdrop. "The last time I called at this establishment to place a special order from your agent in London, I was insulted by that little saucebox daughter of yours."

"Sophie?" Daniel replied, sounding bewildered by such a damning description of his beloved child. "Oh, I am most sorry to hear that, sir . . . h-how may I help you?"

"I'd like you to see about securing an illustrated copy of Curll's *Treatise on the Use of Flogging in Venereal Affairs*," he said blandly. "I understand the 1718 edition has been republished this year."

"It has?" Daniel replied uneasily.

"And if that is not available, please obtain a set of engravings from Cleland's *Fanny Hill, or Memoirs of a Woman of Pleasure*."

"But I'm afraid, m'lord, that book was published a good t-ten years ago, and the a-authorities—" Daniel stuttered nervously.

"A friend of mine has Drybutter's 1757 edition," Lemore snapped, "so if you *truly* wish to be of service to me, your sources in London can undoubtedly locate the engravings, if not the book itself."

"I shall try, m'lord . . . that's all I can promise," Sophie heard Daniel murmur.

"I suggest you try with special diligence, my man," Lemore retorted. "Certain circles might come to learn that this establishment has, in the past, been the provider of such —ah, ribald, some might say *irreligious,* material. 'Twould be most dangerous to you personally if that intelligence should reach the ears of our saintly clerics next door . . . do you not agree?"

"Would it not bode ill for you also if the men of St. Giles knew of the orders you'd placed for—" Daniel began.

"I would simply call you a liar," Lemore replied flatly.

"I shall write to my London agent," she heard her father say dully, "and notify you of the response."

"Very good," Lemore said pleasantly. "I bid you good day."

As soon as Sophie heard the door to the High Street close, she stormed into the book shop.

"I heard what Lord Lemore asked of you, Da," she exclaimed angrily. "'Tis an outrage! 'Tis *suicidal* for the shop to be dealing in such filth with St. Giles a stone's throw away! I *saw* those lewd engravings you sold to Lemore last spring. Those canting crows in cassocks will have us pilloried—or worse!"

Anyone judged guilty of blasphemy could be prosecuted for high treason, locked into wooden stocks, or even executed. A bookseller could be arrested for selling or possessing lewd or infamous reading matter and charged with inciting public disorder.

"I know, I know," her father said despairingly, mortified that his own daughter was now aware of his terrible predicament. "I wouldn't for the world have put us in such jeopardy, but I'm desperate for funds, Sophie! When Lord Lemore first came in the shop and merely desired another Hogarth, it seemed a boon, but then his requests became . . ." His words trailed off. He seemed hard pressed to maintain his composure in the face of such a precarious state of affairs. "After your mother died, I neglected so many things . . . I-I just couldn't seem to . . . and the shop . . ."

As his words became incoherent, his shoulders began to heave. Sophie watched in horror as her father wept for his departed wife and the cruelty of a world in which an obsessed, malicious man like Lemore thought nothing of ruining a gentle, bookish soul like Daniel McGann.

"Oh, Da . . ." Sophie said, heartstruck at his sorrow and mourning her own loss of a calm and competent mother who had kept their family life on an even keel. She put her arms around her father's slight shoulders. "Don't worry yourself so," she soothed, while inwardly groping for a solution to the treacherous problem of Lord Lemore's demands. "We'll sort this out," she comforted him, having no idea how that would be accomplished.

After some minutes, her father's shoulders stopped trembling and he wiped his eyes on his worn sleeve.

"You're a good lass," he smiled wanly. "So like your mum." And then his face crumpled and he began to weep once more.

Chapter 4

Sophie swiftly donned the breeches Daniel wore during the day and poked her head through his linen shirt. She glanced over at her father's sleeping form on the bed tucked under the eaves. Following supper, he had instantly fallen into an exhausted sleep in their shared room above the shop.

Sophie slipped into his coat made of black velvet. It was a bit moth eaten, but serviceable. The garments hung loosely on her small frame, but they were a passable fit when she folded back the coat's sleeves. Then she fastened her auburn hair with cord which she'd used earlier to dry placards in the print shop downstairs. Clamping Daniel's tricornered hat down to her eyes, she slipped quietly downstairs and stealthily headed toward the Royal Infirmary in whose operating theater Thomas Sheridan would impart secrets of her native tongue.

"And let us never forget," thundered the celebrated Irish actor from his podium in the fan-shaped amphitheater, "English is the language of the immortal *Shakespeare*! Whosoever has command of his mother tongue, has command of *much* in this world!"

Sophie glanced around at the rapt assembly and felt her pulse quicken with excitement at being introduced to Sheridan's passionate belief in the power of the spoken word. It was almost as if the concepts he was imparting to his audience were unlocking a secret door in her youthful consciousness.

"Learn everything you can about your language," he exhorted his listeners. "*Read* it . . . respect it . . . cherish its nuances . . . worship its eloquence. English can be the language of guttersnipes or the tool of the noblest in the land. And remember this, the English language is also the form of expression employed by the finest authors, poets, and playwrights the world has ever known!"

Sheridan bowed deeply to the enthralled spectators and informed them he would continue his dissertation on the specifics of proper pronunciation, including the mending of all Scottish accents, in his next lecture scheduled for the following week.

Sophie slipped out of the operating theater unnoticed. It would be safer to collect the money Sheridan owed her for her placards the following day.

Daniel was still sound asleep when she crept upstairs to their living quarters. As she shed the breeches and cuffed coat in the darkened chamber, she mused over Sheridan's thought-provoking concepts. *Could the variety of obscene visual and printed material by which Lord Lemore appeared obsessed merely be* one *expression of language and art?* she wondered. She might revile the prurient nature of those images, but they were, after all, part of the total culture that had descended from Great Britain's Anglo-Saxon heritage. She could—and did—find the pictures summarily distasteful, but perhaps Lemore's relish for such rubbish was nevertheless part of "Culture" in the broader sense.

These thoughts somewhat soothed Sophie's emotions concerning artistic and literary freedom, which were in conflict with her ingrained notion of public decency. Even so, she was disquieted by her certainty that the clerics next door, asleep in their stone cells, would never share such tolerant views.

For Sophie, the remaining weeks in August seemed to fly by. Hunter, perhaps motivated by Sheridan's inspiring lectures, came regularly to McGann's for his reading lessons and was making slow but steady progress. Sophie noticed too that his speech was laced with fewer Scotticisms such as *dinna* and *canna,* which, in some ways, she rather missed hearing. But she knew that his efforts would be rewarded with larger roles when the Canongate Playhouse's season began.

On the night of each lecture, she prepared her father's evening meal earlier than usual and poured him an extra bumper of wine. As soon as he was asleep, she escaped in her borrowed garments and slipped into the back of the operating theater unnoticed. At the lecture's conclusion, she returned home just as silently, jotting down Sheridan's most memorable statements while they were still fresh in her mind.

Around eleven o'clock following the last lecture, she was startled by the sound of the shop's door opening as she was about to put her quill pen away and retire for the night. A tall figure stood in the threshold, his face obscured in the shadows cast by her flickering candle.

"Hunter?" she said, aghast that he should find her dressed in man's clothing.

"I saw the light, my dear," a cool voice said from the darkness. "I thought perhaps 'twould be a good time to call for certain engravings I ordered sometime ago from your father."

Sophie's heart slammed against her chest and she shivered in the night's chill air funneling through the open door.

"I-I-I don't know . . . I don't *believe* they've arrived from London, m'lord," Sophie stammered, desperately trying to remember what her father had done about this unwelcome request. She wasn't certain her father had actually placed the order.

"Since I have taken the trouble to call," Lord Lemore said icily, "I expect you to do me the courtesy of checking your father's records, you little trollop!"

Both stung and enraged at this unexpected insult, Sophie remained behind her father's desk to hide her apparel. She tried to compose her emotions, sensing she was treading on dangerous ground. Lord Lemore stepped into the circle of light cast by the candle on her desk and glared down at her.

Sophie tried not to flinch under his gaze and stared back at him as steadily as she could.

"Only my father would know of your request and its disposition, sir," she said, stalling. "Shall I have him contact you at his first opportunity on the morrow?"

"Oh . . . he's not in the shop?" Lemore asked sharply.

"He's retired for the night," she answered.

"How sensible of him," he chuckled. "And a sound sleeper, is he?" Lemore inquired, drawing nearer. He scrutinized her more closely. "What the devil?" he exclaimed as he extended a bony finger toward her man's shirt and cuffed coat.

Sophie cursed herself for having filled her father's tankard to the brim at supper several hours earlier. Under normal circumstances he would have heard their voices and come downstairs. She could not tear her eyes away from Lemore's narrowing stare. She felt like a helpless field mouse cornered by a stable cat at the Red Lion Inn.

"I was chilled, m'lord," she offered hastily, "and donned my father's jacket while I sat at his desk figuring our accounts."

"Your father must have great confidence in you, leaving you alone so often to run the shop," Lemore said evenly.

"I am merely his assistant," she said as loudly as she dared, hoping her father would stir. "Some of my late mother's duties fall to me."

"Quite a grown up lass, are you now?" he said softly, reaching for her arm. "Despite your mannish garb tonight, you are wise in the ways of womanhood, I expect?"

"Let go of me!" Sophie said, indignantly pulling her arm away from his grasp. Lemore slender white hand began clawing at the opening of her father's shirt.

"Such a little polecat," he chuckled. "I like that."

"No!" Sophie heard herself shout. She pounded her fists against his stomach, the only part of his anatomy she could reach from her sitting position at Daniel's desk.

"Why you little slut—" Lemore growled, slapping her hard across the face with one hand while grabbing her arm once more.

The two wrestled with each other furiously, but

Lemore's superior strength won out as he pulled Sophie to her feet and pinned her buttocks against the edge of her father's desk. Then he began tearing at her shirt again, ripping the fabric nearly to her waist. His kisses on her neck were actually sharp bites, and his teeth dug into her flesh. One hand fumbled at the waist of Daniel's breeches while the other held her fast.

"What in the name of—" he panted. "Why the deuce are you in *breeches*?"

In this instant's hesitation, Sophie lifted her right leg and swung her knee as hard as she could into Lord Lemore's groin. Her attacker bellowed in pain. She pushed against his chest in a frantic attempt to escape.

"Ho! What's this?" she heard her father cry, and then whirled around to see Daniel McGann standing in his nightshirt and cap, holding a candle in his trembling hand. He was peering about the chamber in confusion.

"Oh, Da!" Sophie sobbed, running to his side. "He tried to—"

Sophie looked back at her father's desk. Lord Lemore was leaning against it, bent double, one fist pounding his scrawny right thigh, his thin face grimacing in pain. Her father looked aghast, the explanation dawning on him as to why his sleep had been interrupted by such bloodcurdling screams.

At length, Lord Lemore drew himself up, his face now an impassive mask.

"I was happening by after Sheridan's lectures, McGann, and thought to call for my engravings," he said stiffly. "I'd like them now, if you please."

Daniel stared at his daughter and then back at Lord Lemore. The silence in the book shop lengthened until Sophie heard her father say quietly, "I didn't order them, sir. 'Tis a trade I've given up." He placed a protective arm around his daughter's slender shoulders.

"What do you mean 'given up'?" Lemore repeated, his eyes glittering dangerously.

"I'll not be trafficking in such items in future, m'lord," her father said in a stronger voice, "so perhaps you'd better patronize some other bookseller."

Lemore's face went white with anger.

"I'm warning you, McGann," he said between clenched teeth, "I've means to humble such impudent riffraff as you and this doxy, here! I'll charge theft! Where are the engravings I ordered!"

"You haven't paid for the last set I provided you," Mc-Gann declared, "and you put no siller toward the trash you said you wanted this time. 'Tis no case of theft, m'lord. You'll have to come up with something better than *that*!"

Sophie was astounded by her father's pluck. It was Daniel McGann as she remembered him when her mother was alive —caring and courageous—and she was touched beyond words that he would stand up to this powerful nobleman on her behalf.

"Rest assured, I'll come up with a charge that will make you *both* wish you'd done me the simple courtesy of providing what I asked for!" Lemore said with a meaningful glance in Sophie's direction. And without another word, McGann's best customer whirled on his heel and disappeared into the night.

※

Throughout September, Sophie lived in dread of Lord Lemore's next move. She jumped each time she heard the shop door open or saw the constable stroll past the Luckenbooths. But, as the weeks rolled by and nothing went amiss, she and her father concluded that Lemore's dire threats and fulminations had been sheer bluster.

By early October, her gnawing anxiety that something frightful would befall them had abated. In its place grew a sense of excitement that Hunter would soon debut as a member of the Canongate players. He had been preparing for the supporting role of the servant, Whisper, in Susannah Centlivre's comedy, *The Busybody*.

Hunter's reading lessons had now evolved into sessions in which Sophie tested both his memorization and comprehension of his lines.

"Let's start today with act four," she said late one October afternoon. She was settled comfortably on the low stool in front of the small hearth at the back of the book shop.

Hunter was sitting cross-legged on a small carpet next to her. "Scene one," she said dramatically. " 'Outside Sir Joshua Traffick's house. Enter Whisper.' "

" 'Ha! Mrs. Patch,' " Hunter read slowly from his copy of the play. " 'This is a . . . lucky . . . minute to find you so . . . read-i-ly. My master dies with . . . im-patience!' "

"Very good!" Sophie interjected. "You did that completely on your own, and with nary a Highland burr! Good show!" she added, using one the expressions Sheridan had suggested was commonplace in London's highest social circles.

Just then, the door at the front of the shop opened and in stepped one of the scores of caddies who delivered messages and performed errands around Edinburgh. Sophie rose from her stool and went to greet him, glancing through the square-paned windows. Her breath caught in her throat when she noticed Lord Lemore standing in a knot of elegantly attired gentlemen in front of the Royal Exchange across the road.

"Packet for you, miss," the caddie announced. "From London, by the looks of it. Franked from there, so there's nothing owing."

"Thank you," Sophie murmured numbly as the messenger handed her the thinnish package.

"Books?" Hunter asked, standing up to stretch his long legs.

"P-probably," Sophie stammered, her heart beginning to thud painfully. The only items ordered from London in recent months had been those demanded by Lord Lemore.

She glanced up again, watching the caddie cross the High Street and head down the Royal Mile. Lord Lemore swiftly stepped out of his circle of companions and halted the messenger's progress. Sophie then saw the caddie nod affirmatively at Lemore as he pointed across the road in the direction of the book shop. The nobleman fished into the pocket of his waistcoat, pressed something into the caddie's hand and waved him on his way.

"Aren't you going to open it?" Hunter asked, interrupting Sophie's preoccupation with the tableau she'd just witnessed.

"Oh . . . I'll let Da see to it when he gets back," she replied faintly. She forced herself to walk calmly to her stool and sit down. "S-shall we continue?" she asked.

As soon as Hunter departed for a rendezvous with James Boswell at the Pen and Feather to celebrate the law student's twenty-first birthday, Sophie ripped open the recently delivered packet and stared in horror at its contents. Her hands trembled as she flipped through the lewd caricatures illustrating the amorous adventures of the infamous Fanny Hill. After Lemore's late-night intrusion, Daniel had admitted to Sophie that despite his denials, he had indeed placed an order for the engravings from his agent in London. He had explained ruefully that the Fanny Hill engravings had sold nearly as well as the book itself for more than a decade, even though the government had made countless attempts to suppress both.

When Daniel McGann returned to the shop later that day, Sophie lost no time in confronting him with the engravings and describing Lord Lemore's conference with the messenger.

"Jesu!" Daniel whispered. "What danger I've put you in . . . put us *both* in. When I saw how Lemore put his filthy hands on you, I simply told him that I'd not placed the order. Now he must have guessed that I lied."

"You were so brave that night, Da," Sophie said, flinging her arms around his neck. "I love you so much!"

Furtively, she rewrapped the engravings and buried them under several ledger books in the bottom drawer of his desk.

Hunter's appearances as Whisper in *The Busybody* brought him an excellent notice in the *Edinburgh Courant*. With his Highland burr more firmly under control, he was soon cast by David Beatt as the Duke of Norfolk in *King Henry VIII*—one of Shakespeare's lesser performed history plays—which was presented the first week of the new year. Three days later he appeared as Byam in an adaptation of Aphra Behn's novel *Oroonoko*.

As January wore on, Sophie was pleased when several clients came to McGann's in search of printed copies of the plays that they had recently seen performed at the Canongate, and she was only too happy to sell what few she had in stock. However, the steady stream of customers had apparently caught the attention of the clergy of St. Giles. One afternoon, Sophie found herself exchanging looks with a rotund man in a black cassock, whom she knew to be the Reverend Mr. Meeker. The minister glared through the shop windows at one of his flock who was in the act of pushing several shillings across the counter for a copy of *Oroonoko.*

"So! Once again you are promoting that Jezebel's work!" he thundered from the doorway at Daniel, who simply stared at the clergyman, dumbfounded. "Don't think I haven't seen the comings and goings here!" he announced angrily, refusing to set foot inside the shop. "I've seen that vile Irishman frequenting this place of abomination . . . that *Sheridan* fellow! A *Catholic,* no doubt! And I know you offer wicked, profane texts in *French* for sale!" he said accusingly, as if Lucifer himself might be a clerk at the shop. As the embarrassed customer departed, the minister followed him down the street spewing a righteous torrent of abuse against godless books, plays and playhouses.

The following Sunday, a bitterly cold morning in February, Reverend Meeker's sermon at St. Giles Cathedral was an hour-long diatribe against music, dancing, and all forms of public entertainments.

Two days before Sophie's seventeenth birthday, Constable Munro, normally a friendly fellow, marched through the book shop's door flanked by two red-coated guards from the Tolbooth prison.

"Daniel McGann?" the constable inquired, knowing full well the identity of his long-time neighbor on the High Street, "I have a warrant for your arrest. I charge you by the authority vested in me for the commission of blasphemy and the selling of ungodly texts."

Daniel remained silent but the color drained from his heavily lined face.

"Who has brought this charge?" Sophie demanded angrily.

"'Twas instigated by the clergy and elders of St. Giles, and it charges Daniel to appear before the Justiciary Court," Constable Munro replied. "Since this is a capital offense, Danny, I must take you to the Tolbooth." When Sophie gasped, Munro added with gruff kindness, "Most likely, bail will be set at only sixty pounds or so—"

"*Sixty pounds!*" Sophie wailed. "It might as well be *six hundred*!"

"I'm afraid I must confiscate those Frenchy books mentioned in the Lord Advocate's writ, here," he said, pointing at the document with a detailed list of titles, "and all those printed plays, too, I'm afraid. Need 'em as evidence, it says here."

"How would the Lord Advocate know which books we sell here by *title*?" Sophie asked suspiciously as she surveyed the list. "He and that Mr. Meeker never *shopped* at Mc-Gann's!" she added angrily.

"Now Sophie," Constable Munro cautioned, mindful that the red-coated guards were not above tattling behind his back to the church elders. He wasn't about to tell her that a degenerate peer named Lemore had provided a detailed listing of exactly which blasphemous works might be found at McGann's and had received a blessing from the avenging kirk elders for doing so.

"Shall I search the premises, sir?" one of the two stone-faced guards declared.

Constable Munro nodded before turning to Daniel.

"Don't suppose I need to put irons on you, Danny," he said quietly. "We're close enough to the Tolbooth. I'll take you out the back."

"No!" Sophie cried, but the other guard stepped forward and restrained her as she tried to run toward her father.

Meanwhile, his fellow guard began scooping volume after volume from the shelves. As Sophie sank onto her small stool by the hearth, the other guard systematically searched the rear chamber where the printing press stood. He returned to the book shop with a copy of the broadside she had printed for Sheridan's lectures and a few other examples of her handiwork.

"Check the desk," he grunted to his companion, whose arms were stacked high with books.

"*You* check it, sapskull!" the first guard snapped.

The second guard placed the placards on top of the desk, yanked open the drawers, and rummaged through their contents. Sophie's heart froze. For the first time in her young life, she thought she might faint.

"Holy St. Ninian! Blast me! Sweet Jesu!" the guardsman swore in a string of epithets that were far more blasphemous than anything poor Daniel had ever uttered.

"Let me see those," the other guard demanded, setting his pile of books on the desk beside the placards. "God's bones! Will you look at *that*!" he marveled, gazing over his comrade's shoulders at Lord Lemore's undelivered order of engravings from *Fanny Hill*.

"I'll take those!" Constable Munro intervened, confiscating the pictures. "Bring the rest of the evidence to my chambers," he added brusquely. Then, prodding Daniel McGann into the alleyway located behind the Luckenbooths, Edinburgh's keeper of the peace escorted the haggard bookseller through the granite portals and into the bowels of the forbidding fortress known as Tolbooth Prison.

On the first of April, Sophie, Hunter, and William Creech sat in the Justiciary Court, watching as the prisoner was led to the dock. Despite her effort to steel herself, Sophie was aghast at his condition after two months' incarceration. Her father had not shaved in weeks nor, it seemed, had he bathed. His clothes were in tatters and he was shoeless.

She was further dismayed to see James Boswell's father, Lord Auchinleck, sitting as one of the jurists hearing the case. As she took stock of the courtroom, she noted that among the jury of thirteen men were several friends of Lord Lemore, whom she recognized from the crowd that had attended Thomas Sheridan's lectures at the Royal Infirmary.

The Libel of Indictment for Blasphemy against Daniel

McGann was read in full by the court clerk. Sophie felt her spirits sinking with each damning phrase.

"Said Daniel McGann has most unlawfully, seditiously and maliciously contrived and intended by wicked, artful, and scandalous insinuations to molest and disturb the happy state of this kingdom," intoned the court clerk. "Said Daniel McGann insolently did scandalize and vilify our sovereign lord and king, George III, to incite and stir up the subjects of the realm to insurrection against said king by wickedly and feloniously offering for sale bawdy and ungodly engravings from *Fanny Hill* and other ungodly and blasphemous texts, and did knowingly . . ."

Sophie clamped her eyes shut and tried to blot out the ghastly accusations, but she could not. When Daniel at last stood in the dock, he seemed to have shrunk to half his size, and his voice quavered when he spoke in his own defense.

"I believe, my lords and jurymen," he said softly, "in the rights of men to allow their conscience and sensibilities to choose what they should read, see or hear. I do not, myself, endorse what my accusers consider obscene, but when authorities deem it their right to dictate these matters, there will be no freedom of thought, word, or deed in this land."

Sophie could hear a disgruntled muttering coming from the direction of the bench where the august Lords of Justiciary sat in their wigs and gowns.

"And do you, sir," demanded Lord Auckinleck sternly, "deem it *your* duty to supply society's wastrels and scoundrels with such disgusting fare?"

"No," Daniel replied slowly. "But I believe 'tis their right to seek it if they choose."

"And you make a pretty penny on the stuff, I'll warrant," the judge said sharply.

"If I had, I could have raised the necessary bail," Daniel said mildly.

There were titters from the onlookers, which did not please the panel of judges.

The Lord Advocate rose and requested the judges' permission to call a witness regarding the procurement of the lewd engravings, which had been entered as evidence, but which even the jury had not been allowed to see.

Sophie sank deeper into her courtroom seat as the caddie who had delivered the packet from London approached the witness box.

"And you recall delivering a packet franked from London to McGann's Printers and Booksellers?" the Lord Advocate queried.

"Aye," the caddie said, staring down at his shoes.

"And did the said packet look like this?" he asked, holding up the very wrappings in which the *Fanny Hill* illustrations had been sent.

"Aye. That's the one."

"And is the person to whom you handed this same packet—which the constable's men swear contained the lewd drawings—present in this courtroom?"

"Aye," the caddie replied.

"Will you tell the court who that is?" the Lord Advocate asked patiently.

"Aye . . . 'twas Sophie McGann over there, the bookseller's daughter."

"May it please the court, I call Sophie McGann to the witness box!"

Sophie gasped with horrified surprise.

"You must *go!*" William Creech whispered urgently. "*Go up there, lass!*"

Sophie stood up and made her way to the witness box like a sleepwalker. When she stood to face the spectators, she was even more unnerved to see that Lord Lemore had slipped into the courtroom and taken a seat in the back.

He's come to see himself avenged, she thought bleakly, her legs so shaky that she clung for support to the top of the witness box.

"You are the accused's daughter, are you not?" the Lord Advocate was saying.

"Aye, sir," Sophie mumbled.

"And you were in the shop the day the caddie delivered the packet sent from a London book agent?"

"A-aye," she repeated.

"And did you open this packet?" he asked loudly.

Sophie stared at Lord Lemore, stunned at the obscene cruelty of the man. She wasn't the prettiest wench he could have coveted, or certainly the best tutored in the ways of debauchery. Why? *Why her?* Was it because Lemore was enslaved by simple lust or, rather, that he was a man who invariably got his way?

"Did you *open* the packet?" the Lord Advocate repeated sharply.

"Aye . . . I d-did," Sophie stuttered, suddenly unable to control her words.

"And what was inside?" her inquisitor asked forcefully.

Sophie looked in the direction of her father standing in the dock and her eyes misted over.

"Eng-g-gravings," she stuttered once more, alarmed that she could not seem to master her speech.

"Engravings of *what?*" the Lord Advocate demanded, his patience finally wearing thin.

"Of *F-F-Fanny Hill,*" she choked.

"Will you tell the court the complete title of this obscene work?"

"*F-F-Fanny H-Hill,*" she said, her voice sounding more strangled than ever, "*M-Memoirs of a W-Woman of P-P-Pleasure.*"

Something horrible had happened to her ability to speak out in the hearing chamber. She felt her throat close, and sweat beaded her upper lip.

"And were placards printed in your shop promoting lectures by one Thomas Sheridan, the so-called god of Elocution?" he asked thunderously.

"Y-y-yes," Sophie agreed helplessly.

"My lords and gentlemen of the jury . . . what more can the man stand accused of? We believe there is but *one* God in this land! And McGann's blasphemously crediting such powers to an *actor* is appalling beyond belief!"

Sophie bowed her head in abject misery, tears coursing down her cheeks.

"I think we have heard enough from this chit, m'lords," the prosecutor said disdainfully, ordering her from the witness box. "The crown versus Daniel McGann is ready to proceed to the worthy deliberations of the jury and my Lords of Justiciary."

The verdict was not unexpected. Daniel McGann, printer and bookseller, was found guilty of obscene libel and blasphemy. Sentencing would be pronounced by mid-April, and while Sophie waited for the court's decision, her sleepless nights were filled with anxiety that her father might well be hung.

On April 15, the Justiciary Court pronounced sentence: Daniel McGann would be publicly pilloried for his crimes and remanded to the Tolbooth for six months. The court had, in its mercy, decided to be lenient in failing to demand the death penalty or forfeiture of the convict's whole moveable goods to the crown. "This is done at the intercession of such worthies as Lord Lemore and his friend and fellow nobleman, Lord Creighton, who urged this court to take pity on McGann's daughter, as she has no other means of support than the shop," Lord Auckinleck declared from the bench. Annoyance colored the judge's final proclamation: "This court has shown you its mercy in not punishing you to the full extent of the law for selling books that rot women's minds and tracts that pollute men's. As your confessor would say to you—if you ever had the piety to attend kirk session—'Go, and sin no more!' "

Chapter 5

Flanked by town guardsmen, the prisoner was led bare-headed and barefoot from the Tolbooth prison and into the open square at sun up. Sophie could see her father shivering in the early morning chill and he appeared dreadfully under-nourished. His arms were like pale splinters shed from fresh-cut wood, and it made her wince to watch the guards roughly thrust his emaciated limbs into the stocks' narrow openings. Worse yet was to see them push his head toward the pillory's worn curve where his neck would be clamped until sundown. Daniel seemed listless and glassy-eyed, and there was nary a sign that he had seen Sophie standing in the crowd. Several catcalls and a cabbage were thrown in his direction while the righteous Reverend Meeker, serving the dual role of accuser and prison chaplain, loudly cited examples of his wickedness. But for the most part, both onlookers and passersby stared silently at the bookseller whom the authorities had chosen to make an object of public scorn.

At the end of the long day, the town guardsmen unlocked the pillory and led the prisoner back toward his cell. Sophie crowded close and reached out to give his bruised wrist a squeeze.

"Write your Aunt Harriet," Daniel croaked, "go to her in London . . ."

"No!" Sophie retorted. "I'm staying here with you!"

The redcoat rudely pushed her aside, prodding his charge in the direction of the prison whose menacing walls loomed overhead. Daniel's gait was unsteady, his shoulders stooped, and his head remained thrust forward, as if frozen in the position dictated by ten hours in the wooden stocks.

"'Tis over, lass," Hunter said quietly. "Let me see you home."

Sophie nodded dully and allowed Hunter to take her arm. At least her father's public degradation was at an end. She tried not to dwell on the fact that his prison term still had five months to run.

In late October, four days before Daniel McGann was due to be released from the Tolbooth, Reverend Meeker stood at the book shop entrance wearing an expression of studied calm.

"God has seen fit to summon your father to judgment," Reverend Meeker announced without preliminaries. "He left this life last night."

"W-what?" Sophie stammered, staring at the portly visitor as if he were speaking a language she didn't understand.

"He died of jail fever."

"Why didn't you come for me!" she cried. She picked up a book on her father's desk and slammed it down again. "You only had to walk a dozen paces or so to summon me! Why? *Why!*" she shouted.

The chaplain looked toward the shop door, as if considering an avenue of escape.

"These fevers come on fierce," he explained, a nervous tic tugging at his protuberant left eye. "Four others died besides your da. 'Twas God's will."

"God had nothing to do with it!" she screamed at him. "*You* and all the other sanctimonious little toads have *killed* him. What have you done with his body?" she demanded fiercely.

"The kirk won't have him," the chaplain retorted, stung by her invective. "He was certainly no churchgoer. There'll be no hallowed ground for a blasphemer like him!"

Sophie stared at the chaplain's long black coat and the two white flaps hanging from his linen collar that denoted his calling. Grabbing hold of them, she yanked his bloated face within inches of hers and shrieked, "W-what have they d-done with my *f-father*!" The stutter that had plagued her when she testified at her father's trial now made her words almost incoherent.

Sophie's firm grip on the chaplain's collar mottled his face with pink and white blotches, and his pale eyes began to water.

"T-the Royal Infirmary . . ." he choked out the words. "I heard they took him—"

Sophie shoved her shoulder hard against the chaplain's barrel chest, sending him reeling into a bookcase. Before he could recover his breath, she had stormed out of the shop. She tore down Bell's Wynd past the halls where she'd watched Hunter dance the minuet with assorted beauties of the town, and dashed heedlessly across the Cowgate, a rutted road which paralleled the Royal Mile. The buildings off College Wynd created a confusing labyrinth of stone walls and alleyways. At length, she reached the University of Edinburgh itself and ran pell-mell toward the Royal Infirmary.

The entrance to the stone building was eerily familiar, although in daylight, its walls seemed stark and colorless. Sophie headed impulsively toward the operating theater, recalling how the stairwell during Sheridan's lecture series had been crowded with noisy attendees eagerly anticipating the evening's program. On this day, however, all she could hear was a subdued murmur of voices as she reached the landing.

Without pausing to catch her breath, Sophie flung open the door. Suddenly, her eyes dilated in horror as she stared down on an audience of young medical students, seated in fan-shaped formation. Their attention was focused on a pallet at the center of the chamber. A physician—operating instruments in hand—was lecturing to his student audience. Beside him, a body lay faceup on a table.

It wasn't the vision of her father's frozen profile that wrenched Sophie's guts and made her gasp for breath, but the sight of his pathetic splinter of an arm, now gray in death. And as she stood staring down at the expanse of the operating theater, her gaze was riveted on Daniel McGann's poor, emaciated limb—an extremity that was no longer attached to his body.

Both students and professors bolted to rigid attention when they heard the high-pitched, keening cry rising from the back of the lecture hall. Before anyone could scramble up the stairs to the top row of seats, the young woman, as deathly pale as the cadaver they had been dissecting, had crumpled to the floor.

Daniel McGann had been in his grave barely a day when his daughter chose her method of retaliation.

"No, Sophie! *No!*" Hunter said angrily, frustrated that she would not even look up from the small printing press. "Don't *do* this!" he shouted at her as she continued to fiddle with the handle of the press. "'Twill only make things worse . . . 'twill only put you in terrible danger, like your da!"

"I don't *care!*" Sophie retorted bitterly. She slapped the wooden form containing the metal letters in place, firm in her resolve to seek vengeance. Viciously pulling the handle, she caused a sheet of paper to move beneath the platen. Another fierce tug and the metal type in the wooden form imprinted the sheet with ink.

"Well, *I* care, and so do Will and Bozzy and *all* your friends in the Luckenbooths!" he argued.

"*Bozzy!*" She spat the name. "James Boswell has not come near McGann's since Da was arrested."

"His father sat as judge!" Hunter protested. "'Twould only inflame the old man more to learn his son was your champion. Bozzy's kept his distance to *protect* you. He told me so!"

Sophie merely flattened her lips in a thin, unforgiving line. In truth, the lass's rigid composure since her father's death had Hunter worried. She had maintained an eerie calm during the ten days required to make the unorthodox arrangements to lay his broken body to rest. Hunter and Will had hired livery and a hearse to take them to the burial site. It was located in a back field of a small farm belonging to a distant relative in Penicuik, south of the city. The young men had marveled privately at Sophie's iron resolve to see her father's remains interred in a beautiful spot, as no church in Edinburgh would allow his grave within its precincts.

Then Sophie's pent-up fury had finally burst into the open. Hunter and Will Creech had arrived back in the city at dusk, and the hired carriage had paused in front of the book shop to allow Sophie to disembark. Will then rode with the driver back to Boyd's White Horse Inn while Hunter followed Sophie into the book shop. She walked directly to the composing table and immediately sat down on her stool. With growing apprehension, Hunter watched her methodically select metal letters and slide them into a wooden composing frame. Reading the type backward with some difficulty, Hunter began to understand what form her rage was going to take.

The first broadside to emerge from under the platen confirmed his worst fears. He yanked it from the drying tray and pointed angrily at the screaming headline.

"'The Immorality of Censorship Considered by Sophie McGann, dated fourteen November 1762,'" he read aloud with a facility that would have amazed both himself and his erstwhile teacher, had they both not been so upset. "'. . . wherein she castigates the churchmen of St. Giles, the city magistrates and especially the Lords of Justiciary for their inhuman act of imprisoning her worthy father and letting go free a certain nobleman who possesses engravings of an obscene nature.'" He slapped the broadside on top of the printing press in exasperation. "That's good . . . that's truly bonnie of you, Sophie!" he said sarcastically. "'Twasn't enough that your poor da died of the jail fever. *You* want to libel Lemore so you can hang by your neck on a public platform!"

"You don't want me to tell the truth about what happened to Da because it might have some bearing on *you*," she retorted furiously. "The authorities might exercise their arbitrary powers over *you* and the playhouse—and wouldn't *that* be inconvenient, now that you no longer have to juggle for a living and can prance about the stage with those harlots like Gwen Reardon, who calls herself an actress!"

Hunter colored and remained silent as Sophie lined up a second sheet of paper.

"Well 'tis dangerous, what you're doing, and that's a fact," Hunter said finally, watching her mechanically put the paper under the platen and pull the handle across the press. "And it won't change a *thing*," he added quietly.

"That's the safest way to view it, I suppose," Sophie said acidly, continuing her work in a steady rhythm. "Let someone *else* fight for the freedoms you enjoy."

"Oh, rubbish, Sophie!" Hunter responded with some heat. "You're not printing these placards to preserve my right to 'prance upon the stage with Gwen Reardon,' as you describe it. You're seeking revenge against Lord Lemore . . . you think you can show those churchmen the evil of their ways. You're even cracked enough to think Bozzy's father will somehow see how right you are and how wrong the decisions from the bench. And you're willing to destroy yourself doing it!"

Sophie suspended her frantic activity and looked at him coldly.

"You're on *their* side," she said in a low voice. "Rather than risk a hair on that handsome head of yours, you prattle on about caring for my safety. You're nothing but a pretty, pleasure-seeking coward, Hunter Robertson! Now, why don't you leave?"

Hunter was stunned by the venom in Sophie's voice. It was true, he acknowledged inwardly, that he had always managed to survive by charming and outfoxing his adversaries, rather than by locking horns, as Sophie wanted to do. Did that mean he was a coward? As for the rest, well, the pleasure-seeking part 'twas true enough. Gwen was an appealing bit of fluff, a light o' love that took his mind off . . . the past.

Hunter stared at Sophie's trembling form and the feral, wounded look in her eye. For such a slender wee thing, she was like a wild Highland storm, he thought sadly, driven by her demons and haunted by the hideous memory of her last glimpse of her beloved father. Because she couldn't very well attack her genuine adversaries—except in print—*he* was the safest target for her fury and despair. Hunter understood that, yet he was hurt by her words and confused when his brotherly feelings toward her seemed tainted now by emotions he couldn't quite discover.

"All right . . . I'll leave," he said quietly. "Print these, if you must, but promise me you won't distribute them in the town. *Promise,* Sophie!"

Her ragged breathing had evened out and she seemed calmer, but she remained tight-lipped and refused to answer.

"I'm due to meet Bozzy at the Cap and Feather for a final farewell before he leaves tomorrow for London," Hunter said, eyeing her uncertainly. "Shall I tell him you wish him God speed?"

"I would appreciate, in matters relating to me, that in future you do not allude to *God*!" she snapped. "As far as I have observed, He doesn't exist! As for Bozzy, I bid him adieu."

Hunter, Will Creech and several other of Jamie Boswell's cronies who had lifted glasses all evening in honor of their friend's imminent departure for London decided, at length, to call it a night. It was nearly three in the morning when the raucous group wended their way past the front door of the Cap and Feather, much to the relief of the pubmaster who should have closed his doors an hour earlier. The revelers cursed cheerfully when they felt the frigid winter air sear their skin. Their brandied breath formed clouds of steam in the night sky as they clapped Bozzy on the back, wishing him a safe journey and a grand adventure in the capital.

A loud pounding rent the air, coming from across the High Street. Hunter peered through the gloom, unable to determine the source of the steady thuds reverberating in the chill air.

"Who'd be making repairs *this* time o' night?" one of the lads asked jocularly.

Ignoring his companions, Hunter strained to see a white rectangular-shaped sheet tacked to the door of the butcher shop which stood diagonally across from the Pen and Feather. He crossed the High Street, trailed by Bozzy, who hiccuped occasionally, although he was not quite drunk enough to be insensible.

" 'The Immorality of Censorship Considered,' " Boswell read aloud over Hunter's shoulder, " 'by Sophie McGann.'

Hey, what? Good God, man!" he exclaimed. "What's that minx up to now?"

The steady thud of wood against wood grew louder. It seemed to emanate from behind the row of Luckenbooths.

"You'd better head on home, Bozzy, m'lad," Hunter said quickly, grasping his friend by the shoulders and pointing him bodily in the direction of his lodgings. "Remember, your coach leaves at dawn, and you've got your kit still to pack."

"My man's put most to rights, old chap!" Boswell said, slightly slurring his words. "I say . . . you think they'll approve m'accent in London town?" he asked. "Think I'll manage a posting to the Guards?"

Hunter was aware that the pounding had momentarily ceased. Then the thuds began again, although this time, the sounds had become fainter.

"I'm sure you'll get your commission—but not if you miss the coach. *Home* with you, now," he said, desperate to be rid of Lord Auckinleck's son, regardless of how stalwart a friend Jamie had become during their year's acquaintance.

Fortunately, Will Creech and Andrew Erskine, the fourth member of their party, came to his rescue, offering to escort Boswell to his doorstep. Hunter bid them all a hasty good night and waited until they had disappeared into Parliament Square before tearing down the placard Sophie had nailed to the butcher shop entrance. Walking quickly around the east end of the Luckenbooths, he strode down the alleyway that separated the medieval row of shops from St. Giles Cathedral.

Tacked on the thick wooden door marking the entrance to that ancient seat of Christianity was Sophie's broadside denouncing the ministers, kirk elders, and Lords of Justiciary. Hunter swore under his breath and ripped the printed diatribe to shreds. Groping his way in the darkness down the High Street in the direction of Holyrood Palace, he headed toward the place he wagered would be Sophie's next stop: Tron Church. Hunter had no doubt that his enraged young friend would affix a broadside to the very lodgings of Lord Auckinleck himself, not to mention those of Constable

Munro, Lord Lemore, and even the entrance to the Tolbooth prison!

Approaching the high-steepled church, Hunter heard Sophie before he glimpsed her in the murky light. She had taken off her right brogue and was using its heel as a hammer. Next to her, on the top step of Tron Church, sat at least two dozen broadsides which she clearly intended to plaster throughout the city.

"You insane little *fool!*" Hunter exploded, grabbing her small shoulders while ripping down the placard she had just tacked to the church door. "You may be brain cracked, but *I'm* not—I'll not let you *do* such a thing to yourself!" With that, he pulled her down the stairs into the road.

"Let me *go!*" she screeched, prompting Hunter to clamp his large palm over her mouth to prevent her protestations from raising the dead in the nearby cemetery—not to mention the town guard.

After a brief struggle, he managed to encircle her waist in the crook of his elbow and hoist her onto his right hip like a sack of meal. Bending his knees, he scooped up the pile of broadsides from the church steps with his free hand and headed straight down the High Street in the direction of Sophie's lodgings. He prayed to St. Ninian that the neighbors were sound sleepers and would not wake to her enraged denunciation of him and every man in the town.

Hunter nudged open the front door of the book shop with the toe of his boot and marched over to the hearth at the rear of the chamber. First he threw the offending placards on the low-burning embers. The paper kindled at once, spawning flames that cast a bright glow against the bookshelves nearby. Then, as the blaze waned, Hunter eased Sophie off his hip and set her feet down on the slate floor as gently as he could. He noticed she'd lost a shoe.

"Where else have you posted broadsides?" he asked her quietly. "I'll fetch them back."

Sophie stared at him wordlessly. Then she lifted her hands to cover her face and turned away, her shoulders heaving as she gave way to big, hollow sobs. In the remaining glow from the hearth, her auburn hair turned amber, a brilliant nimbus around her head. An almost unearthly radiance transformed her into a Botticelli portrait like the ones he'd seen in Boswell's book on Italy. Despite the tears sliding down her cheeks, she appeared surprisingly mature . . . a woman weeping, not a sniveling girl exhausted from her fiery burst of temper. She was actually quite lovely, he thought with some surprise, noting her delicate profile and smooth, flushed skin.

This heartsore lass was an entirely new Sophie, and her grief rendered him both uneasy and fiercely protective. He thought of his sister, Megan, and comforted himself that the strange, mildly unsettling sensations coursing through him were distinct from the lecherous impulses prompted by the likes of Gwen Reardon. His sudden, overwhelming desire to enfold this seventeen-year-old in his arms merely sprang, he assured himself, from brotherly concern.

Hunter was relieved to see Sophie wipe her eyes with her sleeve. She turned to face him, swallowing the last of her tears.

"The other broadsides"—she heaved an enormous sigh, as if agreeing, but bitterly, to unconditional surrender—"I posted one at the entrance to Chessel's Court and one—" She bit her lip and shifted her eyes away from his. "I tacked one at Lord Auckinleck's lodgings!" she blurted.

"Oh, no," Hunter groaned, but before he could chastise her further, he heard the tramp of feet outside the shop and a murmur of masculine voices. He raced to the front of the chamber to peer out the square-paned windows, dismayed to see a small detachment of town guardsmen accompanying a disheveled-looking Constable Munro, who held what looked like one of Sophie's broadsides in his hand. From the man's sleepy countenance, Hunter surmised that the man had been roused from his slumbers. "God's wounds, Sophie!" he cursed. "They're coming to *arrest* you! Quick! Out the back chamber!"

"But I've only one *shoe*!" she cried.

But Hunter didn't tarry with such niceties. He pushed her ahead of him past the printing press that bore silent witness to her folly. As soon as they emerged outside, he grabbed her by the hand and hauled her down the familiar alley bordered by the back of the Luckenbooths on his left and the cathedral on his right.

"Stay close to the buildings!" he barked hoarsely, dragging her behind him as he abandoned the protection of the row of shops. The two of them ducked past Bothwick's Close and ran down the Royal Mile toward the only sensible destination under the circumstances: Boyd's White Horse Inn, where the coaches for London departed. Boswell was due to leave for the capital at dawn, only a few hours hence. Hunter's makeshift plan for Sophie's escape would be doomed if Lord Auckinleck chose to rise at cock's crow to bid his wayward son farewell.

The White Horse coaching station was situated a few doors down from Hyndford Close where Sophie's pig-riding friend Jane lived with her two sisters and her imperious mother, Lady Maxwell. Hunter and his charge stumbled into the livery yard and made a dash for the horse stalls.

A sleeping groom was curled up on a pile of straw in a corner. Four bay horses chewed contentedly in their separate stalls, and a small, closed carriage stood sentinel nearby.

"Blast!" Hunter cursed softly.

"What's amiss?" Sophie whispered, her erstwhile bravado having evaporated into the cold night air.

Hunter pointed at the post chaise scheduled to depart at dawn.

"'Tis a closed carriage with only one bench inside to hold two persons. Bozzy mentioned last night that a Mr. Stewart was booked to travel to London, so there's no room for *you*!"

"What about riding beside the driver?" she asked earnestly.

"Not with the town guardsmen looking for you . . ."

Sophie's eyes widened with anxiety. She motioned for him to follow her away from the slumbering groom so as not to awaken him. Suddenly, she gestured toward the post chaise, or "chariot" as some coach makers called the transport Boswell had engaged to take him to London:

"Look!" she exclaimed. "There's a large wicker trunk on board . . . there . . . under the driver's seat!"

Hunter strode over to the carriage and pulled the trunk

toward him. It was heavy and unwieldy. He slid it off its storage platform and opened the lid to peer inside.

"Well," he breathed. "Here's a bit o' good luck. 'Tis Bozzy's gear. If we just rearrange things a bit . . ."

Before Sophie had time to consider whether she wished to ride to London curled up in a wicker trunk, Hunter was prodding her into the woven reed baggage compartment. She coiled herself into a fetal position, nestling her hip just even with the top of the basket. Hunter dropped a smelly horse blanket on top of her. It covered all but her nose.

"For warmth," he whispered. "You'll need it." He dug into his breeches' pocket and pulled out ten shillings, tucking the coins into her hand that, to him, felt as small as a child's.

"I'm sorry 'tis so meager . . . I spent most my siller at Bozzy's farewell fete."

"I've four pounds in a tin box hidden behind the Bibles at the shop," she whispered back. "'Tis all I've got as well. Perhaps you could send a draft to—"

"I'll sneak back and bring the money to you, if I can," he interrupted. Suddenly, a worried frown creased his brow. "I may not be able to inform Bozzy you're on board before you leave, so be sure you reveal your presence only when you're safely beyond the borders. You can ride next to the driver the rest of the way. And ask Bozzy to assist you when you get to London. He's due to see Sheridan and might procure some useful introductions around town. Sheridan will probably remember your help in advertising his lectures . . . go see him with Boz," he told her earnestly.

"Don't worry." She smiled wanly. "Jamie and Mr. Stewart may realize I'm on board rather quickly if I can't breathe in here. 'Tis mighty fierce smelling with this horse blanket you've provided."

She poked her head above the lip of the trunk to glimpse the pink wash that had tinged the night sky.

"Hunter?" she whispered.

"Yes?" he replied, looking down on her small body curled around Boswell's possessions, including the book on Italy and Corsica he had bought from Daniel McGann.

"Thank you. Thank you for saving me . . . from myself." Hunter shrugged and flashed her a rueful smile. "I've an aunt," Sophie continued, "Harriet Ashby is her name, she lives on Half Moon Passage, Covent Garden. If you write me there, I'll critique your hand and grammar," she ventured tentatively.

"Sh!" Hunter said abruptly, cocking his head.

Before they exchanged another word, he slammed down the trunk's top over her head and wedged it back under the driving seat.

Only a tiny fissure of light filtered through the wicker's woof and weave. Sophie couldn't see Hunter depart, but she heard his footsteps fade into silence as he bolted out of the livery yard. Soon she detected the sounds of jangling harnesses and surmised that the groom was preparing to hitch the bays to the carriage.

Less than an hour elapsed before she heard Hunter's voice explaining to the preoccupied groom that he was placing a few more belongings in his friend, Mr. Boswell's trunk. He lifted the wicker top only a few inches, and Sophie felt something heavy drop on her, followed by several coins raining down on the horse blanket.

"Your money and your shoe!" she heard Hunter whisper and smelled the faint aroma of brandy still on his breath from his evening's revels. "God speed!" he added.

And before she could answer, she heard the sound of his steps retreating in the distance. She shifted her weight to gain some comfort among Boswell's thick cloak, linen shirts and breeches, plus several bulky books. Easing the malodorous horse blanket around her shoulders, she reflected on Hunter's final words. Oddly, she found herself comforted by his farewell—even if it did invoke the name of the Almighty.

And then, miraculously, she fell asleep.

Sophie was jerked back to consciousness by the coach driver's "Heigh-ho!" and the lurch of the carriage pulling out of the livery yard. The post chaise swayed through sparse morning traffic down the length of the Royal Mile. In a few moments, the vehicle lurched to a halt and she heard

Boswell's voice extend greetings to his fellow-passenger, Mr. Stewart.

The other passenger climbed aboard and soon the coach surged forward, only to be reined again a few minutes later by the driver. Sophie peered through a broken reed in the trunk and saw Jamie Boswell alight and walk ceremoniously toward the Abbey of Holyrood Palace. She repressed a giggle as she watched her friend make a series of deep, self-conscious bows—once to the mammoth palace itself, once to the crown of Scotland above the iron gates in front, and once to the venerable chapel nearby. Then he marched to the center of the paved court and bowed three *more* times to Arthur's Seat, the lofty mountain that rose behind the ancient home of Scotland's kings and queens. Without a word of explanation for his eccentric farewell or an apology for the delay, he climbed back into the carriage. Sophie felt the vehicle pitch forward once again, rolling past the gates guarding the city of her birth.

Soon the horses picked up speed, their hooves flinging clods of rich loam to the side of the lane. The two-man chaise rumbled on to the old Eastern Road and headed toward Ayton, Berwick, Durham, Doncaster, and Biggleswade.

Not long after crossing the border into England, the chaise threw a wheel, tossing Boswell and Stewart roughly against the sides of their vehicle. Sophie, wedged tightly within the trunk, was shaken but not hurt by the mishap.

"Blast! Several spokes have been splintered," Jamie Boswell moaned when he crawled out of the damaged coach, unharmed.

"I'll have to ride one of the horses to Berwick, sir," the driver noted gloomily. "They have a proper coaching station to repair the wheel."

"I saw a rustic inn a mile or so behind us," Boswell's fellow passenger, Mr. Stewart volunteered. "Shall we wait there?"

"Splendid," Boswell rejoined, sounding more cheerful at the prospect of a glass of port. "Call for us there when all's well."

Meanwhile, the inside of the wicker trunk had become

insufferably hot and stuffy. As soon as Sophie calculated the two passengers were far enough down the road not to hear her cries, she called out to the driver.

"Please, sir! In here! Please open the wicker trunk!"

The coachman was much taken aback at hearing plaintive calls from beneath his seat and took his time freeing Sophie from her small prison.

"Here's three shillings to take me with you on your horse to the next town and not mention my presence to the gentlemen," she pleaded, extending her bribe. She thought it better not to chance Boswell's knowing of her escape from his father's clutches, at least, not until they both had safely reached London.

"'Tis no business o' mine what ye do." The driver shrugged, pocketing the coins.

Within half a day, Sophie boarded the *London Fly* at a cost of three pounds. She was crowded in among five other passengers and their piles of luggage. Fortunately for all concerned, she had none.

After nine arduous days traveling due south, the carriage finally reached Highgate Hill, providing the travelers with their first glimpse of the capital. Anxious to conclude the journey, the exhausted driver urged the horses on. The sweaty steeds strained their harnesses in an effort to pull the mud-splattered vehicle the last few miles toward the city gates—and toward the uncertain fate that lay in store for Miss Sophie McGann, late of Edinburgh, Scotland.

Book 2

62-1498

Book 2

1762–1764

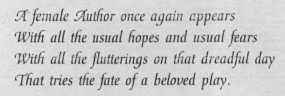

A female Author once again appears
With all the usual hopes and usual fears
With all the flutterings on that dreadful day
That tries the fate of a beloved play.

—JAMES BOSWELL

Chapter 6

Sophie's back ached and her throat felt like straw after nearly a fortnight of bumps and jolts in the enclosed coach dubbed the *London Fly*. However, she had never endured fumes of the type that assaulted her senses the moment she stepped off the coach at the Dean Street terminus in Soho.

As a lifelong resident of Edinburgh, she was accustomed to the noise and bustle of a city and was no stranger to the stench of rotting refuse in back alleyways or the pungency of human offal in the streets. But wafting from the doors of nearly every London shop, inn, cellar, garret, and public house near the coaching station was the biting scent of distilled grain mash, laced with sweetish juniper berries—a brew that resulted in the infamous brand of spirits known as London Gin.

Having secured directions from the coach driver, Sophie began to make her way the half mile down Charing Cross to Bedford Street, which marked the perimeter of Covent Garden where Aunt Harriet and Uncle John Ashby lived. She pulled the horse blanket around her shoulders to ward off the November chill and attempted to ignore the sense of desolation settling on her like a heavy cloak. Coal-laden fog stung her eyes and lungs as she trudged down a road crowded with every type of wheeled and foot traffic imaginable—all crawling through the overcrowded city of seven hundred thousand souls. She longed for Hunter's reassuring presence as she recalled the endless miles separating her from

Edinburgh, and she suddenly felt like weeping from sheer homesickness.

"'Allo, luv . . . a bit of the berry?" leered a bleary-eyed vagabond.

The disheveled creature stepped into her path clutching a half-consumed bottle of gin to his breast. His breath was so rank that Sophie's nose twitched and her eyes watered. Shoving him aside, she hiked up her skirts and crossed to the opposite side of the road.

Continuing on down Charing Cross, Sophie was forced to bat away children who clutched at her skirts and gazed up at her with imbecilic smiles. They too were completely addled by the liquor given them by inebriated adults. A slovenly young soul sat grinning in a doorway, her legs splayed out on the street. A baby was wedged in the crook of her arm, suckling the teat of its mother's exposed breast while the harlot herself guzzled gin from a flagon held in her free hand.

Exhausted and apprehensive, Sophie soon found herself on Bedford Street. She stared at the three- and four-story buildings characteristic of the type that had risen a hundred years earlier, after the Great Fire of 1666, and wondered which residence might house the shop and upstairs lodgings belonging to her father's sister and brother-in-law.

On the corner of the road that had narrowed into a mere alleyway called Half Moon Passage stood a seedy ale house known as Le Beck's Head. Directly across from this establishment was Bob Derry's Cider House, where some half dozen unkempt wretches lounged outside. Nearby, Sophie spied a painted wooden sign displaying a half moon and, aptly enough, peeling gold letters that spelled "Half Moon Tavern." In the middle of this block, squeezed between the two drinking establishments, stood two shops. The left one had a sign declaring it to be "Mrs. Phillips' Green Canister —Salvator," and next to it—much to Sophie's relief— Ashby's Books and Gentlemen's Accessories. A narrow door leading to a dark stairway separated the two emporiums but she noted with dismay that the entrance to the bookstore was shut tight and appeared neglected.

Glancing at the shop on her left, Sophie entered the establishment known by the enigmatic designation Green Canister—Salvator. Inside, she gazed with awe at a long wall whose floor-to-ceiling shelves were stocked with myriad exotic toiletries—washballs, soaps, scented water, powders, oils, essences, pomatums, cold creams, lip salves, sticking plasters, snuff, and even sealing wax. Opposite these stood an enormous glass-fronted cabinet displaying apothecary jars labeled mercury, oil of peppermint, oil of rosemary, spirit of hartshorn, alum, laudanum, nodyneline, sulfate of zinc, and much more. At the rear of the chamber a marble-topped counter ran parallel to the wall and displayed several sizes of mortars and pestles. On a back wall were more shelves on which were arrayed strange, sheathlike objects in a variety of sizes. Some of these mysterious articles appeared to be made of stiff linen, others of sheep gut.

Several gaudily dressed women Sophie took to be trollops were chatting with a lithe young woman they addressed as Lorna. Without meaning to eavesdrop, the visitor quickly learned that slender, fair-headed Lorna was a dancer at the Theater Royal, Drury Lane. She had come to Mrs. Phillips's to purchase foot powder to soothe her aching arches.

A plumpish woman of about thirty-five stood behind the counter pulverizing a substance in one of the mortars. She conversed somberly with a young dandy decked out in skintight breeches and a vivid mustard yellow coat whose velvet sheen was complemented, to startling effect, by yards of frothy lace foaming at collar and cuffs. The young peacock wore heavy white face powder with hand-drawn black brackets accenting his dark brows and black hair and sported a black patch plastered to his cheek.

Why, 'tis a genuine macaroni! Sophie thought, her eyes widening in astonishment at the sight of the flamboyant-looking young man so-named because hordes of young Englishmen had invaded Italy as part of their Grand Tour. Sophie had read humorous accounts of these young coxcombs returning to their native country dressed in garish Italian silks and brocades and affecting a worldliness that seemed ludicrous after so short a sojourn abroad. Some wag had dubbed these outlandish creatures "macaronis" after the national dish of the same name.

"Mix a pinch of this mercury powder with ale to make a tincture and take twice daily for a month," said the woman Sophie took to be the proprietress, Mrs. Phillips. "Let us hope your gentleman's complaint will right itself in time."

"Sink me, madam, at these prices, I most certainly *trust* so!"

"The price of *neglecting* such a dose will be high indeed, sir!" she snapped, tipping the contents of the mortar into a small cloth bag and tying it securely. "I would also recommend that in any future amorous adventures you protect yourself with a French letter." She pointed to the sausage-shaped objects displayed on the shelf behind her.

"Can't stand the feel of 'em!" the dandy said disdainfully. "Sheep's gut gives you blisters and that linen feels like a flannel stocking."

"'Tis at your discretion, of course, sir," Mrs. Phillips replied stiffly, accepting the coins he offered her. "I bid you good day."

As the young man took his leave, the apothecary slipped the coins into her apron, brushed a few specks of powder off the countertop, and wiped the mortar clean with an efficient sweep of a cloth. She then looked up at Sophie. "May I help you, miss?" she asked briskly.

"Aye, I hope so," Sophie said. "You are Mrs. Phillips?"

"Her niece," the woman replied, acknowledging the Scottish lilt in Sophie's voice with a raised eyebrow. "I inherited the Green Canister when Aunt died recently."

"I am sorry," Sophie said sympathetically. "That your aunt died, I mean. You are . . . ?"

"Mrs. Phillips will do." The woman shrugged. "No one seems to want to call me Mrs. Perkins, and I suppose 'tis good for trade to maintain my aunt's name."

"Aye," Sophie agreed. "I, too, have an aunt in trade— Mrs. Ashby, your neighbor. She and Uncle John own the book shop next door, but the door is locked and I—"

"*You're* Harriet Ashby's niece?" interrupted the woman.

"Aye," Sophie replied quickly. "Well . . . actually, I've not seen Aunt Harriet and Uncle John for ages . . . 'tis ten years or so since they were last in Edinburgh. But surely you must know each other? She's my late father's sister. Can you tell me where they are and why the shop is bolted tight?"

"Let me assist these customers and then we shall have a word together," Mrs. Phillips said soberly.

The shopkeeper-apothecary poured musk oil into a small glass vial for one of the two prostitutes and then ground up several unidentifiable substances into a powder for the other.

"Make a paste and put it on the affected area three times a day, and, if you'd heed my advice, Miss Skene," she added acerbically to a woman whose cheap muslin dress was awash with an extraordinary number of flounces and frills, "you'd better stick to ruffle making. Mother Douglas's bagnio isn't a place for amateur bawds, my dear."

Sophie noted with some amusement that Mrs. Phillips "the second" gave a good measure of unsolicited advice, along with each potion, powder and pomatum she dispensed to her customers.

When the shop was finally deserted, Mrs. Phillips withdrew a large key ring hanging on a hook beneath her counter and bid Sophie follow her out of the shop. She locked her premises and hesitated in front of the door frame that led to the wooden stairway separating her establishment from the book shop.

"I'm sorry to be the one to tell you, but your Uncle John died last winter and your aunt's been poorly since before he was taken."

Sophie let out a sigh. She had virtually no memory of her uncle, but it made her sad to think that what little family she did possess had probably been suffering recently as much as she and her father.

"I warned Harriet 'twould all come to a bad end," Mrs. Phillips confided, "but no, she wouldn't touch my infusion of mercury, more's the pity. Perhaps 'twould have eased her a bit."

"Is she ill?" Sophie asked anxiously. "Is that why I found the shop shut up tight?"

"I expect you'd better know the worst," Mrs. Phillips said ominously. But without revealing the nature of her dire news, the shopkeeper gathered up her skirts and led the way to the darkened landing. She fumbled with several heavy keys before she slid one into the lock on the door to the right. "I live just there," she indicated with a nod over her shoulder. "I've taken to keeping her locked up when my shop's open, to prevent the poor dear from coming to harm," she whispered. "If *you* hadn't tipped up, I'd determined to send her to the charity workhouse within the fortnight. I'm too good a Christian, of course, to send her to that dreadful Bedlam where—"

Before Mrs. Phillips could finish her sentence, the door creaked open to provide a sweeping view of the Ashbys' living quarters above their shop. Sophie glanced around the gloomy chamber whose only sources of light were one small window in the ceiling and a casement overlooking Half Moon Passage. Piles of books and stacks of prints, etchings and engravings were strewn everywhere, leaving only space for a bed in one corner, two chairs standing sentry in front of a cold hearth, and an armoire with one of its doors dangling loose on its hinges. A curtain to Sophie's left appeared to lead to a back room.

"In there's the old print shop," Mrs. Phillips revealed, responding to Sophie's inquisitive look, "with a circular stairway that leads down to the book shop. I put planks over it so Harriet couldn't go down there and make mischief like the *last* time!"

Before Sophie could question the woman about the incident, she was startled by a scuffling sound punctuated by low, piteous moans.

"What *is* that?" Sophie asked, alarmed.

"Better light a candle," Mrs. Phillips replied obliquely, reaching high on a bookshelf for flint and a small brass candlestick containing a taper less than two inches high. "I keep these out of harm's way," she said as she managed to strike a light. "Don't want her burning down the place."

Holding the candlestick in front of her ample bosom, Mrs. Phillips motioned Sophie to follow her. She pulled back the curtain and stepped aside, allowing Sophie to pass through to the other room. In the adjoining chamber stood a wooden hand press of a design similar to the one her father had owned, but slightly larger. Dust and cobwebs cast a shimmering net over piles of paper stock stored on the floor.

Sagging ropes, hung in parallel lines, stretched from wall to wall where a few stray placards, broadsides, and other printed works had been pinned up to dry in better days.

Sophie sank to her knees in the corner of the chamber to examine a form curled up and shaking in abject terror. A haggard old woman with Daniel McGann's aquiline nose and with gray hair streaming past her shoulders stared up at Sophie, her eyes black with fright. Scattered in disorganized piles nearby were stacks of engravings so obscene, the kirk elders at St. Giles would surely have demanded the ultimate sacrifice from anyone attempting to sell them.

"*Jesu!*" Sophie said on a long breath. *So this was the source of the lewd prints her da had sought when he was so desperate for money!* She wondered that she had never fathomed the obvious connection. Her father had made no secret of the fact that he did not care for his sister's husband, but the two families had seldom kept in touch once Harriet had married John and moved to London years earlier.

Sophie stared with revulsion at her aunt, who sat huddled on the floor. She knew Harriet Ashby to be about fifty-two, but she looked twenty years older.

"Poor dear," Mrs. Phillips clucked. "She's gone a bit balmy."

"How long has she been this way?" Sophie asked, aghast.

"Only a short time, really," the woman replied. "But quite unable to see to herself, poor thing, and 'tis all *his fault!*"

"Uncle John's?" Sophie asked, glancing at the printing press and some copper plates that leaned against one wall. She wondered if Ashby's Books had made a specialty of actually reproducing and distributing such vulgar work as that which she found staring her in the face.

"Who else?" Mrs. Phillips demanded. "The pox carried the whoring blighter off to his just reward last January—no loss *that* . . . but not before he gave it to his lady wife! Syphilis is *bad*—not like the clap or the drip—'tis *bad* as it gets."

"Aunt Harriet has *syphilis*?" Sophie exclaimed, staring at the disheveled creature who seemed unaware she was the subject of such frank discussion.

Mrs. Phillips nodded.

"No cure for the syph that *I've* ever heard of, and I've heard of 'em all, you can be sure of that!" the loquacious woman said, shaking her head. "I've got nothing but a few poor poultices and some foul brews to offer, but they don't help." Mrs. Phillips leaned forward discreetly, as if she didn't wish Aunt Harriet to hear, although the poor woman seemed far beyond understanding. "It goes to the *brain*, y'know," she whispered hoarsely, tapping her head with a finger discolored from years of potion mixing. "The syph's what's ailing your aunt, the poor dear. The pox is starting to eat her brain like mice nibblin' cheese." She straightened upright, putting her hands on her broad hips. "She has good days and bad . . ."

Judging silently that today was obviously one of the latter, Sophie merely nodded as she stared at her aunt cowering in the corner.

"But now she's got a dear niece to look after 'er, and that's a blessin', isn't it?" Mrs. Phillips declared.

And with that, the proprietress of the Green Canister spun on her heel and disappeared down the stairs.

With sinking heart, Sophie's gaze swept the squalor and disorder surrounding her aunt and wondered what further misfortunes lay in store.

Throughout December and into the first month of 1763, Sophie attempted to bring order out of the chaos at Ashby's Books and Gentlemen's Accessories, and do what she could for her aunt's health and mental state.

Her first task was to bathe the poor woman and dress her in clean clothes. Then Sophie began the overwhelming assignment of straightening out the inventory of books, periodicals and engravings strewn all over the shop and living quarters.

Most days her aunt sat silently in a chair facing the hearth while Sophie worked long hours attempting to set her new home to rights. Every so often, Harriet Ashby would start to sob heartbrokenly, telling Sophie repeatedly what a blessing it was to have her in London.

"If only I'd not been barren," her aunt moaned one dreary winter morning a month after Sophie had arrived. "If only John and I had been blessed with a child as good and kind as you. If I'd had a child, John wouldn't have sought out . . ."

Sophie put her arms around her aunt and allowed her to have another good cry. For a few hours, Harriet Ashby seemed almost to have recovered her spirits and did what she could to help Sophie with the enormous effort of making the shop presentable. Soon, however, the poor thing appeared to slip back into a mental fog that sometimes rendered her mute for hours at a time.

As the self-appointed manager of Ashby's Books, it took Sophie nearly two weeks to sweep layers of dirt and cobwebs from every nook and cranny of both her lodgings and the shop. In a leather trunk, she discovered a sinister collection of short whips and riding crops, velvet bonds and reproductions of male organs whose uses she could only imagine. However, these peculiar finds explained the "Gentlemen's Accessories" in the shop's name. On one dark, moonless night—and without consulting her aunt—Sophie gathered the goods into a sack and deposited it on a pile of other refuse thrown into the alley behind the Le Beck's Head.

She also spent long hours browsing through the shop's books, engravings, and prints. As much as Sophie abhorred many of the images in this collection of erotica, she could not deny the drafting skill of several celebrated artists whose ordinary illustrations were known and appreciated by the general public. Nevertheless, she tossed many drawings into a fire kindled from Aunt Harriet's dwindling supply of coal and stored the rest in the leather trunk.

At first, Aunt Harriet seemed indifferent to the improvements in her creature comforts. Nevertheless, Sophie stubbornly continued to bathe the woman and delouse her hair and saw to it she had a bowl of broth and bread from the tavern at least once a day, paid for by parceling out a few coins from the last of the money she had brought with her when she departed from Edinburgh in the wicker trunk. Before long, however, her efforts were rewarded to the degree that Aunt Harriet would occasionally show flashes of her old self.

"I so regret not having seen Brother before he passed on," she commented one morning in a perfectly normal tone of voice. "But he urged you to come be with your old auntie, and that's a comfort."

"Aye." Sophie smiled tiredly. "He often told me of the lively debates the two of you had in your youth over books in the shop. Now, finish your broth while I just have a go at those filthy windows downstairs in the shop."

An hour later, Sophie pushed a strand of hair off her perspiring forehead as she surveyed the glass panes she'd been polishing with gusto. Recalling the journey to London —part of which she'd endured in Boswell's trunk— prompted her to think of Hunter Robertson. She felt a sharp stab of loneliness, momentarily overwhelmed by the unhappy circumstances that had befallen her in this huge metropolis.

"Have you sold any books since you reopened the shop?" Mrs. Phillips demanded one gloomy morning in early January.

"A few," Sophie replied reluctantly, pausing in her attack on a shelf with her feather duster.

The truth was, she'd only sold one book and a Hogarth drawing. Ashby's clientele was no doubt accustomed to racier fare than the merchandise Sophie had restored to the shelves. In addition, Ashby's suffered the same problem as had McGann's in Edinburgh: a shortage of capital to buy the latest publications.

"This is not the neighborhood for a literary salon, my dear," Mrs. Phillips pronounced dryly. "'Tis the theater district, frequented by rascals and rogues and populated by more harlots per block than any other borough in London! Have you gotten rid of your uncle's entire stock of those nasty drawings and bawdy books?"

"Much of it," she admitted. "I've stored what I didn't chuck out in my aunt's trunk," she added reluctantly.

"Well, my advice is to dust off at least *some* of those

tomes you've packed away, or you'll not be able to pay the rent on this place."

Sophie sighed and nodded her head, discouraged.

"I know, I thought to solicit some print work to add to the till."

Mrs. Phillips considered her words and then nodded sagely.

"But until you do . . . pray, don't dispose of *all* your naughtier merchandise."

Sophie smiled polite acquiescence, but had no intention of selling that filth; she was determined to forge her own path as manager of Ashby's Books.

However, after Mrs. Phillips had left, Sophie's spirits sank nearly as low as when her father had died. A familiar wave of bitter loneliness engulfed her as her eyes swept the deserted book shop. There was no Daniel to consult about inventory and new purchases, only an ill and failing old woman upstairs who seemed to grow more disoriented with each passing day.

Sophie's thoughts drifted to Hunter once again and she felt tears welling in her chest. He had never written to her in care of Ashby's Books and she forced herself to accept the truth that she might well never see him again. His final kindness to her had merely been that of a casual acquaintance and not a symbolic link in a permanent chain of friendship. She stared at several rows of odd-size books awaiting her attention and determined that for all intents and purposes she was now an orphan. Glancing out at the narrow, rain-swept Half Moon Passage, Sophie had never felt more alone in her life.

One mid-afternoon in late January, Sophie peered out Ashby's front window at the steady sleet slanting across the road. She was startled to see a familiar figure heading for the entrance of the Green Canister. Excited, she flung open her door and hailed the pedestrian.

"Bozzy!" she shouted through the biting wind. "Bozzy! Over here! 'Tis I . . . Sophie McGann! Pray, come in and warm yourself!"

With a look of astonishment, James Boswell stared across the ten feet separating them.

"Why Sophie . . . what in the world are *you* doing here?"

"I could ask you what *you* are doing visiting the Green Canister!" she replied with a mischievous chuckle.

Boswell's round face flushed crimson and he ignored her teasing comment as he approached her door.

"The night I left Edinburgh, my father had raised the town guard looking for you!" he exclaimed, staring at her through the icy downpour. "That broadside you wrote put him into a right foul temper. I truly think he might have had you hanged. But you escaped his clutches! How the deuce did you *do* it?" he asked admiringly.

"I'm glad you inquired," she replied saucily, "as you were an accomplice! I was hidden in *your* wicker traveling trunk!"

"Lud, Sophie, you're an amazing wench!"

"When your wheel splintered, I rode postilion with your coachman and eventually caught the *Fly* to London." Her amusement at the episode had blossomed as time and distance lengthened. "Come in, come in, get out of this wretched weather."

Jamie tramped into the shop, divested himself of his coat, and stood in front of her hearth at the back of the chamber, warming his fingers against the glowing coals.

"I dare say I'll never tell Lord Auckinleck the conclusion of this amazing tale . . . the renegade escapes justice in his son's trunk, only to be taken on by yet another scurrilous book emporium!" Jamie laughed, glancing around Ashby's.

Sophie, sotto voce, then explained her dilemma regarding her aunt's frail condition and her own struggle to make ends meet.

"I think, eventually, I can make a success here, selling printed plays and novels and such, but, in the meantime . . ." Her words drifted off uncertainly.

James Boswell was scrutinizing her in a way that suddenly made her feel uncomfortable.

"I must say, Sophie, you've . . . not grown, exactly," said Boswell, "you're still a wee one, as Robertson always called you . . . but, you . . . ah . . ." He had the decency to flush slightly as his eyes strayed to Sophie's bosom which had finally, mercifully, begun to fill out. Suddenly, he reached for her hand and kissed it. "So soft . . ." he murmured against her flesh. His eyes lifted to hers and his lids drooped seductively. "Surely, under the circumstances you face, you'd allow me to offer my protection."

Sophie felt no tremor of excitement at his suggestive words and gently removed her hand from his.

"Bozzy," she said with a smile and a shake of her head. "Don't be ridiculous, especially when I presume you're on your way to the Green Canister for a remedy for your latest dalliance." Boswell looked aghast at hearing such blunt honesty. "I am most flattered that you now perceive me a comely enough wench," she added pleasantly, "but I'd much rather have you as my friend. I've so few in this city." He looked abashed and then grinned, the expression on his broad face almost one of relief. "Tell me," she asked, "have you got your commission in the Guards?"

Boswell frowned and shook his head sadly.

"'Tis devilish hard to arrange, it seems," he said. "I have interviews and appointments and try to make my way, but no, I have not got into the Guards." He looked downcast, but then his face brightened. "But I met the famous Mr. David Garrick of Drury Lane—*and* his most amiable wife. She made breakfast for us, can you imagine that!" Boswell's features were aglow with pleasure. "And here's something you'd fancy, Sophie. Garrick showed me his library, with a large collection of good books and some busts and pictures. At noon he was obliged to attend rehearsal and so I left to come here."

"And have you seen Thomas Sheridan?" she asked eagerly.

"Aye, I called on him almost as soon as I'd arrived. He lives on Henrietta Street . . . number Twenty-four. I'm surprised you haven't seen him yourself."

"I must pay a call," Sophie murmured, excited to have encountered someone from home and heartened to discover that the world she loved and the people who fascinated her most were literally just around the corner. "By the way," she said casually, "has Hunter Robertson written how he's getting on as a bona fide actor?"

"Not a line," Boswell replied cheerfully. "That rogue's probably too busy charming the wenches at the playhouse to put quill to paper."

"Speaking of wenches and the mischief they can cause," Sophie responded pointedly, hiding her disappointment as best she could, "have *you* yet met the famous Mrs. Phillips, dispenser of potions and unsolicited advice?"

"No," he said, embarrassed.

"How did you learn of her shop?" Sophie persisted.

"From my physician," Boswell said stiffly. "He sent me to get a-ah—"

"To get a draught for a gentleman's ailment, am I right?" she asked. Since becoming a resident of Covent Garden she had learned to speak frankly of such commonplace ailments.

"Aye," he admitted, apparently relieved not to have to dissemble further. "A lass who acts at Covent Garden Theater showed me perfidy by not advising me she was . . . unwell. For some days I've observed the symptoms of a strong infection—"

"A gentlemen's disease, indeed! Sounds like the clap, I'm afraid, Bozzy," Sophie commented matter-of-factly. "Poor you!"

"Aye, Señor Gonorrhea has paid an unwelcome call," he confessed glumly. "Doctor Douglas says I must take a draught for some days."

"Well, come along with me. I'll make the introductions to Mrs. Phillips," Sophie said sympathetically, for she knew that Jamie Boswell, as charming as he sometimes could be, would be no sweetheart of hers.

Chapter 7

Sophie clasped Jamie Boswell's hand and dashed fifteen paces through the driving sleet to the Green Canister. Inside the shop, Mrs. Phillips was leading a customer toward the shelves that held a variety of cosmetics.

"I've a lovely selection of rouge pots, dearie. A little color is what you need," the proprietress cooed to the young dancer whom Sophie had encountered her first day in London—the one with the sore feet. "'Twill make those cheek bones of yours so exquisite, you'll catch the eye of a duke!"

The dancer nodded absently and began to sample various colors from Mrs. Phillips's stock, dabbing a bit of vermilion paste from each pot on the back of her hand. Meanwhile, Bozzy surveyed the variety of medicines stored in the large glass cabinet on the opposite side of the apothecary shop.

"Mrs. Phillips," Sophie interjected, "may I present a great friend of mine from Edinburgh, James Boswell, Esquire, a barrister, and mayhap soon a member of the King's Guards."

Pulling his gaze away from the rows of apothecary jars, Jamie inclined his head in greeting. Mrs. Phillips surveyed Boswell's form from the tip of his silver-buckled shoes, up past his ample waistline and soft hands to his moon-shaped face.

"More sensible to stick to your briefs and your books, if you ask me," she declared, bobbing a perfunctory curtsy.

Sophie ignored the look of pique spreading across Jamie's face in response to such unwelcome advice.

"Mr. Boswell needs your assistance in a medical matter," Sophie said in a low voice.

"Does he, now?" Mrs. Phillips responded. "Come with me, Mr. Boswell. Alum, is it you want? Or tincture of mercury?"

She led the discomfited young man to the back of the shop where she proceeded to pulverize various substances that, when combined, were supposed to counteract venereal disease. Meanwhile, Sophie glanced in the direction of the dancer who lingered over her choice of rouge.

"So you've come from Edinburgh, have you?" the young woman asked pleasantly, gazing at Sophie.

"Aye . . . I manage my aunt's book shop, next door," Sophie responded. "My name's Sophie McGann."

"I'm Lorna Blount." She grinned at Sophie. "I gather your establishment has changed its character somewhat."

"Aye, and I hope to get new customers because of it," Sophie ventured. "I plan to stock plays and novels and the latest publications. You know, things that theater people like yourself might enjoy," she added, hoping Lorna Blount might begin to spread the word that Ashby's Books was a place to frequent.

"'Tis a capital idea," Lorna replied enthusiastically, "as long as your prices aren't too dear. Actors are always short of funds, as you probably know. Have you attended the theater yourself since your arrival?"

"No, I'm sorry to say I haven't had a chance."

She briefly recited the formidable tasks that had confronted her as a result of reopening the book shop and alluded to her own lack of funds.

"Well, I'm more than pleased to know you," Lorna responded eagerly. "I dance the hornpipe and do a bit of tumbling in the entre-acts at Drury Lane, but I love to read, so I'm happy to hear of your efforts at the book shop. My father was assistant music master at Covent Garden until he died. He's the one who made sure I learned my letters."

"You can read *and* tumble?" Sophie said, admiringly.

"That . . . and I dance in taverns when Garrick can't employ me."

Sophie turned to indicate the companion with whom she'd entered the shop.

"My friend James Boswell, there, knows Mr. Garrick. He sounds like a wonderful fellow."

"He is," Lorna replied eagerly. "Not like so many of those actor-managers who only offer you a role for a *roll* in the feathers!" Both girls laughed at her joke.

"Garrick's a man who prizes his wife, is he?" Sophie wondered aloud, remembering the loving relationship between her own mother and father.

"Oh, yes, and Mrs. Garrick loves *him*. She gave up her dancing when they married, and quite wonderful she was, too," Lorna replied. She tilted her head to one side, looking thoughtful. "I'm not performing on Wednesday . . . I could gain us free entrance to *The Two Gentlemen of Verona*, if you'd like. 'Tis by Benjamin Victor who shuffled some of the Bard's words to appeal to modern audiences."

"Shakespeare? Oh, that would be *wonderful*!" Sophie said excitedly. "That's really kind of you, Miss Blount."

"Lorna, please," she insisted. "'Tis no bother. The boxkeeper's a friend. He'll find us seats as soon as the play commences."

"I'd quite like that," Sophie said eagerly.

"A few minutes before six o'clock, then," Lorna replied, "in front of Drury Lane."

"Six o'clock," Sophie confirmed, "and thanks, awfully."

Lorna was silent for a moment, fingering the pot of rouge she had finally selected for purchase.

"I don't suppose you'd let me borrow a novel to read once in a while, Sophie?" she asked shyly, slightly embarrassed by her request. "I do so love them, and I have lots of time to read when I'm backstage, waiting to perform."

"Of course," Sophie responded, warmed by the notion that Lorna Blount and she could become fast friends. "When you've purchased your rouge, pop into the shop. I've got one or two really good ones to show you."

Boswell had concluded his transaction with Mrs. Phillips

and approached Sophie's side, his eyes fastening appreciatively on the pretty blond woman standing next to her.

"May I make the acquaintance of your ravishing *amiee*," he requested with an ingratiating smile.

In Sophie's view, James Boswell became a different creature when interested in a woman. His round, intelligent countenance grew animated, his eyes intense. He began to exude a palpable magnetism that invariably drew females to him and made them forget he was certainly not the handsomest of men. Bozzy's alert, intelligent gaze mesmerized his prey and turned them into willing lambs submitting to his wolflike charm.

"Lorna Blount, may I present James Boswell, Esquire, late of Edinburgh," Sophie said, observing Lorna's responsive glance. "Well, Bozzy," she inquired sweetly, "was Mrs. Phillips able to give you something satisfactory for your ailment *d'amour*?"

"Uh . . . why yes," Bozzy replied, visibly ruffled by Sophie's candor.

"How fortunate," Lorna murmured, averting her eyes demurely.

Jamie cast Sophie an annoyed look and begged to take their leave. Impulsively, Sophie put her arms around him and gave him a sisterly hug.

"Forgive me," she whispered into his ear. "I have every confidence you'll soon recover, but Lorna's a friend as well . . ."

He patted her on the back in a gruff gesture of amnesty.

"Until next time, then," James Boswell saluted them with reasonable good grace and bid them both a hasty farewell.

Sophie remained preoccupied with improving the atmosphere at the book shop, but did not forget her rendezvous with Lorna scheduled for a little before six on Wednesday. However, on the morning of the appointed day, Sophie had barely unbolted the shop's door before Lorna arrived, breathless with the news that there would be no performance at Drury Lane that night.

"There was a full-fledged *riot* last night!" she announced, whipping off her cloak with a dramatic flourish and tossing it on a chair nearby. "That rabble-rouser, Thaddeus Fitzpatrick, was spoiling for a fight. You know that Garrick's decreed they'll no longer give half-price reductions in tickets to people who come into the theater after the third act." Lorna scowled. "You can imagine what it's like for the actors, when those rowdy young bucks arrive late . . . but they *like* disrupting things, and they want their amusements cheap!"

"Fitzpatrick . . . is he a theater critic?" Sophie asked, handing her new friend a mug of freshly made hot chocolate from a pot kept warm near the hearth.

"A self-appointed one," Lorna declared with disgust. "Yesterday, he all but called for a riot, and then persuaded some fifty young rogues to wreak havoc on the poor theater, soon as the curtain parted. His confederates even produced axes from beneath their coats and began to chop up the benches!"

"No!" Sophie responded, horrified.

"One ruffian actually climbed on stage and nearly set fire to the velvet drapes that frame the proscenium arch!"

"You can't be serious!" Sophie exclaimed. "Where was David Garrick?"

Lorna took a long sip of chocolate and shook her head. As she spoke, the fear she had felt the previous evening played across her features.

"At the height of the din, Garrick suddenly appeared from the wings and raised his hands for quiet, attempting to speak—but the blackguards howled him down!"

"Not allow *Garrick* to speak?" Sophie cried.

Lorna nodded.

"Fitzpatrick had the temerity to demand that Garrick go down on his knees and *apologize* to the rabble for the new ticket policy, but he utterly refused and declared 'twas folly to share company with such scum."

"So, what's to happen?" Sophie asked urgently.

"Garrick walked off stage, rang down the curtain, and declared the theater closed till further notice and the damages repaired." Sophie shook her head at such a tale and let out a long breath. "Welcome to the world of London theater," Lorna added ruefully, handing back to her friend a borrowed novel she had finished reading. "I owe you a night's entertainment."

A few days following the riot at Drury Lane, Sophie was pleased to receive a note from Jamie Boswell that proved he bore her no ill will.

> *29 January 1763*
> Though I fear I am still somewhat indisposed, I have informed Mr. and Mrs. Thomas Sheridan of your presence in London and they bid you to call at Number Twenty-four, Henrietta Street on Sunday next at noon when they will be at home.
> Your most obedient servant,
> Jas. Boswell

"Bless you, Bozzy!" Sophie said aloud, startling poor Aunt Harriet who sat in front of the small hearth, staring somberly into the flames. "I've been invited to the Sheridans' tomorrow, Aunt—you know, the actor and his novelist wife? 'Tis just around the corner."

"That's lovely, dear," Aunt Harriet replied faintly. This was not one of her good days, and indeed, the feverishness and the throbbing in her joints were assaulting her with increasing frequency.

"Will you be all right here on your own?" Sophie asked anxiously.

Harriet merely nodded, retreating, as she did often these days, into a kind of dreamlike state in which she remained silent for hours at a time.

On Sunday, the bells of nearby St. Paul's were calling actors and others to worship. The columned house of worship down the block was not the domed cathedral of the same name, but a smaller edifice called "the Actors Church" because so many thespians attended it or were buried there. Its ringing bells, however, merely suggested to Sophie it was time to depart for the Sheridan's. Aunt Harriet remained in her odd, lethargic state, but dutifully spooned down a bowl of broth. Sophie settled her into her chair with a rug wrapped around her knees. Then she smoothed her own faded skirt and searched for a shawl that had the fewest moth holes. Securing the door, Sophie practically danced down the steep narrow stairs into the street, anxious to escape the gloom permeating her upstairs lodgings.

"Come in, come in," Thomas Sheridan greeted her warmly, ushering Sophie into a small, rather shabby sitting room crowded with guests.

"Frances, my dear," he said to his wife, a plain-featured woman with warm gray eyes. "Here is the Scottish lass I told you about . . . the young miss is Boswell's friend. 'Twas she who printed that excellent poster touting my elocution lectures in Edinburgh."

Frances Sheridan rose from a chair, begging pardon of none other than the famous David Garrick himself. The actor-manager was flanked by a pretty woman Sophie took to be Mrs. Garrick, who had cooked breakfast for Jamie on his previous visit. Frances Sheridan's expressive eyes registered surprise at Sophie's youthful appearance but she immediately flashed her a warm smile of welcome. The novelist was at least a head taller than Sophie and appeared to be about forty years old.

"So kind of you to come," she said, extending her hand. "Thomas showed me that placard you printed for him. 'Twas excellently done and certainly drew in patrons, I'm told."

"His lectures were magnificent, Mrs. Sheridan . . . *inspiring!*" Sophie replied earnestly, and then promptly blushed.

"Tell me true, Miss Sophie," Thomas Sheridan queried teasingly. "I never saw your father use that ticket I gave you. I wagered to Frances that you somehow managed to attend those lectures yourself. *Incognito*, was it?"

"I-I borrowed my father's breeches," Sophie admitted.

"I thought so!" Sheridan laughed.

"I so love to read," she explained eagerly. "I adore books and language and—" She ceased her torrent of words and stared at them both for a moment. "It just seemed so *unfair* that I should not be allowed to attend, merely because I am female!"

The Sheridans exchanged glances and laughed heartily.

"Sounds a bit like *you*, Frances, when you were young."

"It does, indeed," Mrs. Sheridan acknowledged, smiling. "Come, my dear, you must meet Mr. and Mrs. Garrick . . . we've been consulting with them about my forthcoming play. 'Tis just been granted a license by Edward Capell, that knave in the Lord Chamberlain's office, and we're celebrating."

"Now, Frances," Sheridan reproved teasingly. "'Tis not politic to let people hear of your disdain for the king's servant."

"King's servant!" Frances Sheridan scoffed. "'Twas a miracle Davy got that wretched man to grant a license for any play by a 'petticoat author,' as he calls us."

"You're having *your own play* presented at Drury Lane?" Sophie asked, awed. "I thought your novel wonderful."

"Thank you." Mrs. Sheridan beamed. "'Tis my first play, but then, Mr. Garrick has taken several women scribes under his wing, haven't you, sir?" she added before quickly making introductions.

"Some excellent ones, I'm proud to say," David Garrick answered genially. "Kitty Clive . . . Mavis Piggott . . . and now you, my dear Frances. We've many nights of repertory to fill in a season. We always need a good new play, and *I* don't care who writes it."

Sophie surveyed the Garricks admiringly, although she was quite surprised to see how diminutive a man he was—barely four inches above five feet, she wagered. Both husband and wife were elegantly dressed—he in a midnight blue velvet coat and cream knee breeches and she in a gown of pale peach moiré with an underskirt a shade darker. Garrick looked to be about forty-five, his wife perhaps five years younger.

"I'm pleased to hear Drury Lane will be ready for your play, Mrs. Sheridan," Sophie commented to her hostess. "It suffered less damage than Covent Garden, I gather." Thaddeus Fitzpatrick had led a second disturbance that same week, this time leaving Garrick's rival theater in shambles.

"The riot at old Drury was expensive enough, I assure you," Garrick volunteered, eyeing Sophie curiously. "My partner, Mr. Lacy, has plenty to say to me on *that* score, and frankly, one can hardly blame him. 'Tis outrageous that Fitzpatrick and his mob aren't cast into prison for such wanton behavior!"

Garrick's rich, resonant voice, laced with indignation, utterly dominated his surroundings.

"My friend Lorna Blount told me of the fracas," Sophie disclosed. "Those wastrels were disgraceful! I understand that you, Mr. Garrick, sir, were magnificent putting that scoundrel Fitzpatrick in his place!"

"Thank you, my dear, but I fear my temper got the better of me that night. Those ruffians could have burned us to the ground," he said disgustedly. "Fortunately, I know when 'tis time to make an exit!"

"Who would believe acting could be such a dangerous profession?" Mrs. Garrick said, and Sophie heard the accent of Vienna in her English. "I fear for poor David's life at times," she added, clutching her husband's arm.

Lorna had told Sophie that the Garricks had married more than a decade earlier, at a time when they were two of the most popular performers on the London stage, he, a rising young actor at Drury Lane, and she the principal dancer at the opera house.

"And now," Garrick said to Mrs. Sheridan, abruptly changing the subject, "we must finally decide what to do about the role Mr. Love was to have taken in this play of yours."

"Sadly, the man is quite indisposed," Mrs. Sheridan confided to Sophie. "He believes he won't recover by the time *The Discovery* has its debut next week."

Garrick turned to Thomas Sheridan with a determined look.

"Sherry, my friend . . . please consider what I've proposed. 'Tis my belief that your charming wife had you in mind when she wrote the role of Lord Medway. Say you'll rescue us and play the scamp."

Sophie noticed that Sheridan's features were slightly flushed, as if he were upset but was attempting to disguise his pique.

"Second choice in a pinch, am I?" he said with a thin smile.

Sophie was beginning to see that theater folk were a sensitive breed and prone to petty jealousies, even among friends.

"Oh, darling," Frances said in a rush. "'Tis just that Davy has the Loves under contract. He must use them or be accused by his partner of being profligate with their earnings. You'd otherwise be everyone's first choice, don't you see?"

Appearing somewhat mollified, Thomas Sheridan paused for effect and then nodded his acquiescence.

"Splendid!" declared Garrick. "Absolutely splendid! The part couldn't be in better hands. Now, my next problem is to persuade that miserable printer I employ to run up some new playbills to post around the city announcing the change of cast. He threatened to quit after all the adjustments in scheduling I demanded of him following the riot. Quite a maddening, moody fellow, he is."

Sophie felt her heart begin to race. She noticed Thomas Sheridan looking in her direction with amusement.

"I-I'm a printer, sir," Sophie stammered. "I'm managing Ashby's Books at present and we have a press. I'd be most happy to print your playbills for you. I often did that for the Canongate Playhouse in Edinburgh."

Garrick looked at her with surprise that soon turned to skepticism.

"You'd better take her up on it, Davy," Sheridan urged. "My elocution lectures in Edinburgh were sold out, thanks to Sophie."

This news apparently did not sway the manager of Drury Lane, who remained silent.

"Frances . . ." Sheridan persisted, "do we still have that playbill this young miss concocted? Remember, I brought it back with me to show you the pleasing configuration of lettering."

"Why yes, right here in this drawer, I believe," she said,

glancing sideways at Sophie conspiratorially while rustling through a nearby desk.

"*You* did this . . . completely on your own?" Garrick asked intently, studying the creased placard held up for his inspection.

"Yes, sir," she answered softly. "My father was a printer and bookseller in Edinburgh. He taught me the trade after my mother died."

"And he's with you here in London?"

"No . . . he . . . he passed away too, sir. Just last autumn. That's why I'm living with my aunt, managing Ashby's because she's ill."

Garrick looked at her with sudden sympathy.

"And you say you could have playbills made and distributed in a day's time, before *this* Thursday?"

"Aye, sir!" Sophie said swiftly, although it suddenly occurred to her that she had never printed a single sheet on the Ashby press, nor did she know if it was even in working order.

Garrick studied her a long moment, apparently considering his various options. Then he nodded.

"Right then. Let us work out together exactly what we want." He glanced over at Mrs. Sheridan just as she was winking at Sophie. "Frances, my dear, pray lend us your quill. Have you a scrap of paper we can use to rough this out?"

Smiling encouragement at Sophie, Mrs. Sheridan replied, "Of course." She opened a desk drawer and took out a pot of ink and a sharp-pointed swan's feather. "Why not use the back of Sophie's playbill for Sherry's lectures? 'Tis just the right size."

Sophie's hands and arms were stained with ink when the first placard came off the Ashby press. She sighed with relief. After an hour's search, she had found the necessary letters stored in a tray of unsorted Caslon type jumbled together in a small timber box. Painstakingly, she slipped the type into the wooden frame to spell out:

The Discovery
a comedy by Frances Sheridan

and the rest of the copy that Garrick had dictated to her the previous day. Fortunately, there was paper in stock to complete the job. Within a few hours she had printed both the large playbills that would be posted in front of the theater and the smaller ones for the coffeehouses and taverns around the town. By late Monday afternoon, the fruits of her hard labor had dried sufficiently to allow her to bundle the posters together. She saw to Aunt Harriet's comfort and headed across Covent Garden's Great Piazza toward Drury Lane, passing the steps of St. Paul's.

She walked briskly to Russell Street and turned right on Brydges Street, which fronted the theater. Making her way down a narrow alley, she pushed open the stage door and nodded a greeting to a rotund man perched on a stool just inside the door.

"Good afternoon," she greeted Drury Lane's stage doorkeeper. "I'm Sophie McGann and have been asked to deliver these new playbills to Mr. Garrick."

"Right you are," the man replied pleasantly. "Name's Collins, by the way. Mr. Garrick says you're to bring them to him directly. Shall I show you the way?" he asked kindly.

"I'd be most obliged," she murmured, a sense of awe at the sight of her celebrated surroundings prompting her to speak in a mere whisper.

The doorkeeper hopped from his stool and led the way down a corridor that led into the lamp-lighting room. Stage workers were trimming wicks and replacing candles in several lighting devices that would be used during the next performance. The pungent smell of tallow that permeated the air reminded Sophie of the interior of the Canongate Playhouse in Edinburgh, calling forth the day she'd introduced Hunter Robertson to David Beatt. Unbidden, a pang of homesickness swept over her—for McGann's book shop, the bustling High Street, and her Scottish friends. A sharp image of Hunter's handsome features and rakish grin blocked out her murky surroundings and provoked in Sophie a physical longing for the sight of his familiar face.

With resignation, she continued to follow Mr. Collins's circuitous path through the labyrinth of scene pieces and stage furniture littering the backstage area. An instant later, Sophie had her first full view of the vast stage area and the even grander auditorium. She gasped as Collins and she halted in the wings and stared at the forestage, a platform that extended twenty-five feet in front of the proscenium arch.

"Jesu!" Sophie said in a breath, her eyes widening at the sight of the cavernous performance hall. "'Tis like a temple for some great god!" she whispered.

David Garrick was seated in a chair, downstage right, watching the performers—including Thomas Sheridan—rehearsing the second act of Frances Sheridan's comedy.

Benches that could accommodate some fourteen hundred patrons stretched out before her. Rows of empty seats in an area dubbed "the pit" were situated adjacent to a cluster of straight-back chairs where orchestra members sat with their instruments. Gazing around the hall, Sophie counted three large galleries rimmed by balconies at the rear of the auditorium. Two tiers of elegant box seats to the right and left of the stage were subdivided by low partitions with narrow pilasters supporting them. Soaring some eighty feet overhead was an elaborate, gilded plaster ceiling.

"'Tis at least thrice again as large as the Canongate, back home," Sophie sighed, overwhelmed by the sheer enormity of the place.

"Just wait here," advised the doorkeeper, amused that the familiar sight prompted such wide-eyed admiration. "Mr. Garrick will eventually summon you."

Sophie turned and offered a grateful nod as Collins disappeared behind the flies.

A tall, imposing young woman who looked to be about twenty-five years old strolled out from the Greenroom and stood in the wings, peering down her nose at Sophie with undisguised hauteur. Her almond-shaped eyes fastened on the younger girl's faded blue and white muslin skirt and shabby wool shawl. Sophie concluded that this striking creature was one of the actresses. She stole an envious glance at the lady's magnificent bosom, which was high and fulsome and spilled over her striped silk bodice. Sophie held up one of the playbills.

"I expect your name is on this," she said quietly, in a manner inviting a friendly exchange.

The arrogant young woman squinted at the placard, inadvertently revealing her nearsightedness.

"Ah . . . yes, but, once again, I see my name follows both Mrs. Clive's and Mrs. Pritchard's!" she said petulantly, pointing to the notation "Mrs. Piggott appearing as Lady Flutter."

"The order of players was determined by Mr. Garrick himself," Sophie replied cautiously, regretting now that she had shown this stranger her handiwork. She recalled that Mavis Piggott, along with Kitty Clive, had been mentioned by Garrick as one of the actresses whose play-writing efforts he had nurtured at Drury Lane.

"He does have his favorites," Mavis Piggott commented sourly.

"*Stop! Please!*" Garrick's authoritative voice boomed out suddenly. "Mrs. Pritchard and Mrs. Clive, if you'd be so kind," he said to two of Drury Lane's most celebrated names, "I think 'twill be more amusing if you make your entrance as if you had already been conversing off stage. Can we take that section again, please?"

Sophie continued to watch from the sidelines as the two women dutifully backed off stage and reentered, chattering like magpies. Mavis Piggott wandered away and soon Sophie saw her standing on the far side of the stage, awaiting her entrance.

After ten minutes, Garrick noticed Sophie standing in the muted pool of light cast by a candelabra that was positioned to provide the actors illumination during rehearsal. He signaled her to approach as soon as the scene had concluded.

"Well, well," he chuckled softly, his eyes scanning the copy of the playbill she handed him. She held her breath, praying he would not find some error that had escaped her critical eye. "Excellent work," he said, "and completed so quickly. I'm most obliged to you, Miss McGann."

"Why, thank you, sir," she said with a bright smile, inwardly heaving a sigh of relief.

Garrick called out to a man of equally short stature standing to one side, in conference with a person holding a manuscript.

"George . . . George, come here a moment, will you please?"

The man turned and Sophie knew instantly by his features that he must be David Garrick's brother. Lorna had explained that George Garrick was the actor-manager's right hand in nearly every aspect of operating the playhouse—and, she said, "Old George doesn't let you forget it!"

George Garrick dutifully walked toward them. Behind him, another man followed in his wake clutching a copy of Mrs. Sheridan's manuscript.

"Yes, Davy?" George said, eyeing Sophie with some suspicion.

"This is Sophie McGann, Brother, and I want you to see what a fine job she's done with these new playbills. I've decided to allow her to print up smaller ones, like these," he said, indicating the miniature placards. "I propose she sell them to our patrons for a penny. Should we try out the scheme?"

"Hmm," George said noncommittally.

"She will turn in her profits to you each night, which you will then divide—half to the house, half to her. And if that Featherstone gives us any more problems about making last-minute changes of cast and so forth on the larger posters, Miss McGann, here, is prepared to leap into the breach, am I right, Miss McGann?"

"Oh, *yes*, sir!" she replied eagerly. "Most happy to oblige."

"I'm sure she is," George said dourly.

Despite George Garrick's lack of enthusiasm, Sophie was thrilled. She would be able to run the book shop by day, complete printing assignments between customers, and sell playbills to audiences at Drury Lane during the evenings. With these profits, she hoped to seek some proper doctoring for Aunt Harriet who, of late, seemed more agitated than ever. Eventually, Sophie could begin purchasing plays and novels and turn Ashby's into the kind of establishment of which she could be proud.

Her eyes were shining with gratitude when she shifted her gaze from George Garrick to his brother, and back to George again.

"Well," George allowed, "I suppose 'tis worth giving the lass a trial period. I think Featherstone was just overtaxed by all the changes we demanded, Davy, and will restore his temper soon."

"He'll come around much faster, once he realizes we have Sophie up our sleeves, eh what?" He winked at her mischievously. "And I think my notion of selling small programs during the interval is a capital idea!"

"As I said, I think 'tis worth a trial period over the run of *The Discovery*," George said with measured emphasis. "And speaking of such," he added, tilting his head in the direction of the man next to him holding the manuscript, "Hopkins, here, says he's having a devil of a time prompting the players and noting your changes at the same time. Normally, I would play scribe, Davy, but I still have much left to do to see that the repairs to the playhouse are finished by six o'clock when we reopen on Thursday."

"Could I help, sir?" Sophie said, before she had even considered who would run her shop in her absence. "I have a fair hand."

All three men looked at her and then exchanged glances.

"'Twill just be a day's work . . . mayhap two," George said, eyeing her skeptically.

"Can you spare us the time from your book shop?" David Garrick asked.

Sophie nodded eagerly. 'Twas a chance to learn about *stagecraft*, she thought excitedly, to learn how mere words on a page became the stuff of living, breathing human beings! As her gaze swept around the stage area, Mavis Piggott gave her a measuring glance. Kitty Clive and Frances Sheridan were chatting amiably to one another, bathed in the soft light cast by the overhead chandeliers. Mrs. Sheridan, Mrs. Clive, and Mrs. Piggott—all three women had seen the words they'd written come to life on this very stage! In that instant, it seemed to Sophie that the world of the theater was grand, indeed, and full of infinite possibilities. As for the book shop, she would ask Lorna Blount if she'd like to earn a shilling or two minding Ashby's from time to time!

"There should be no problem about Ashby's, sir!" Sophie said earnestly. "I've a friend who'll look after the shop whenever I might be needed here." She smiled brightly at William Hopkins, the prompter, and added, "Has someone an extra quill?"

Chapter 8

February 1763

"Playbills for a penny! Playbills for a penny, sir!" Sophie cried as spectators streamed into the foyer of Drury Lane, jostling her as they passed. "Thank you, sirs," she said to a pair of effete young men dressed in flamboyant shades of pomegranate and puce. "Get your playbill for only one penny!"

"Odds fish, if 'tisn't little Sophie McGann!" said a voice diverting her from counting the coins in her apron pocket.

"Bozzy!" Sophie exclaimed as she recognized her friend, bundled up in several layers of clothing and accompanied by two young men about his age. "'Tis lovely to see you!"

"What the deuce are you doing hawking playbills?" Boswell demanded.

"'Tis thanks to *you*, Bozzy," she replied, and brought him up to date on the results of her visit to the Sheridans.

"Good heavens!" Boswell replied. "You are the most extraordinary creature . . . a pen-pushing little wonder!"

"We must support such an enterprising wench," Erskine cried, digging into the small pocket of his waistcoat. He handed Sophie a coin and accepted a playbill in return.

"I hope you enjoy the performance tonight," Sophie volunteered.

"'Tis authored by a petticoat scribe," Boswell replied disdainfully, as if that fact alone were enough to damn the entire production. "I'll wager it won't be a memorable evening, but 'tis pleasing sport to mingle with the crowds, eh what?''

And with that, the trio melted into the first-night throng that was streaming into the performance hall. Sophie realized that Boswell and his comrades were there not merely to render judgment on Frances Sheridan's maiden effort, but to see and be seen.

Despite James Boswell's dire prediction, *The Discovery* was a solid success. Eventually, Mr. Love, the actor, recovered and replaced Thomas Sheridan in the role of Lord Medway, prompting Garrick to employ Sophie to reprint the playbills with the new cast. Within a half day of his request, the revised notices were soon posted all over the city.

"You've done a splendid job with this," David Garrick said when Sophie brought in the smaller playbills to solicit his brother George's approval and deliver the week's profits from selling playbills to the patrons.

The two theater men were sitting opposite each other at the desk in the manager's office located above the stairs that led from the stage door entrance. It was a small, windowless chamber that adjoined the Treasure Room, a closet with a metal door in which each night's receipts were locked. Sophie had been excited at being able to turn over nearly one pound fifty to George Garrick, and a similar amount in playbill profits for herself. After expenses, she was clearing nearly fifteen shillings a night—enough to buy a meal each day from the Half Moon Tavern for Aunt Harriet and herself, pay the rent for their leased lodgings, and make a few select purchases for the book shop.

"George and I were just debating the notion of placing daily notices of Drury Lane's offerings in *The Public Advertiser*," Garrick told her. "I think 'twould attract more business. What do you think, Sophie? Would you take charge of seeing to the notices?"

She bit her lip and glanced at both brothers.

"We'd pay for your services, of course," Garrick hastened to add, misinterpreting Sophie's blank stare. "Would a shilling a day be sufficient?"

Sophie silently calculated her new found riches . . . at least six shillings a week, plus what she could earn printing playbills. As she began to give Garrick her answer, he interrupted her.

"Of course, we would continue having you sell playbills at night, as that seems to be turning a tidy profit, according to George," he said, glancing at his brother. George Garrick gave a reluctant nod.

"I'd be most happy to oblige," Sophie said gratefully.

"Well, that's settled," Garrick said. "And now I must see about convincing a certain maturing actress to accept a part suitable to her age." He hurried out, leaving Sophie to calculate how soon she'd have enough funds to take poor Aunt Harriet to a proper physician. Just the previous day, she'd come home from Drury Lane to find the woman sitting stark naked in her chair in front of the fireplace and chewing on the corner of one of the ribald etchings she had somehow retrieved from the trunk. Aunt Harriet's condition was more severe every day, and no amount of kindness or care from Sophie could change that.

By the middle of March, Sophie had fallen into the pleasant routine of calling at Drury Lane each morning to confirm the next evening's play repertory and casting with George Garrick. Any last-minute changes were duly noted, both for Sophie's playbills and for the notices she personally delivered to the editors of *The Public Advertiser*.

Sketch of a Fine Lady's Return from a Rout by actress Kitty Clive began rehearsal in late March. Following the first runthrough on the dimly lit stage at Drury Lane in which Kitty herself was to perform, Sophie, the prompter William Hopkins, and Mrs. Clive repaired to the Greenroom to review the most recent changes in dialogue. The chamber in which actors received their admirers after performances was actually rather dingy and uninviting during the day. A few tapers burning in several wall sconces provided their only source of light.

"Mrs. Clive, could you perhaps insert a line here that would explain *why* Mr. Moody has appeared on stage at this particular moment?" Sophie said tactfully.

Kitty Clive sat on a straight-backed chair next to Sophie and peered at the younger woman's notations over her shoulder. Like Sophie, the actress was rather small of stature, with a heart-shaped face and a prominent nose, down which she gazed with great comic effect on stage. "Do you agree Moody's presence in this scene is unclear, Mr. Hopkins?" Kitty demanded.

"Some explanation would indeed help . . . something simple," he said with equal tact.

"All right," Kitty sighed. "This scribbling's more taxing than one might think," she complained good-naturedly. "Why am I not content simply to speak someone else's words?"

"'Tis wonderful that you write," Sophie volunteered enthusiastically, "but I've noted that precious little time is spent on readying new works for the stage."

"The repertory changes so often, the management has other troubles to attend to. New plays must sink or swim in the rehearsal time allotted them," Kitty replied resignedly. "But I thank you for your concern. You seem to have an ear for this work," she offered thoughtfully. "I like your suggestion . . . now, what could Moody say that would make everything clear?"

Sophie was aware someone had wandered into the Greenroom and was listening at the door.

"I warn you, Kitty, my dear," Mavis Piggott said archly as she sauntered into the chamber, "the little scribe, here, has already bewitched our manager. Beware she doesn't bewitch *you* too. So much has the Great Garrick come to depend on her, his poor brother waxes wroth at the mere mention of the name *McGann*."

"Mavis, we're working here, if you don't mind," Kitty said sharply, returning to her manuscript.

"I'd take care, if I were you," Mavis continued, poking a nail into the melted wax from a taper nearby. "Perhaps the sudden appearance of Miss McGann heralds a *spy* from our rival down the street," she added spitefully, referring to the not uncommon practice of Covent Garden allies attempting to infiltrate Drury Lane for advance notice of the repertory.

Sophie felt her own sharp intake of breath at such an unsolicited insult. Why in the world had this Mavis Piggott taken such a dislike to her? Kitty Clive gazed appraisingly at Sophie for a moment. Then she merely smiled.

"As Sophie has just said . . . there is not enough time at either Drury Lane or Covent Garden to concern ourselves with anything other than getting the piece on the boards," Kitty replied. "So, I'd appreciate it, Mavis, if you'd just trundle on your way. Now, let us see," she mused, "Moody's speech must explain why he has come upon Lady Asquith at such an unexpected moment . . ."

As hard as Sophie attempted to steer clear of Mavis Piggott, she could not avoid the woman entirely. One morning toward the end of April, David Garrick's partner, James Lacy, was just leaving the manager's chambers to attend to some crisis relating to wardrobe for the evening's performance. He barely nodded in greeting as Sophie arrived for her regularly scheduled conference with George Garrick.

"That damnable jade!" Lacy muttered to no one in particular as he headed past Sophie. "She says the ermine on her royal robe looks like a 'fox with the pox! 'Tisn't *good* enough for a queen of England,'" he quoted in a high-pitched voice that Sophie took to be Lacy's mimicry of female speech. "'Twas good enough for all the *other* grand dames who've played the role this season—but not Her Royal Highness!"

And with that, Garrick's partner stormed out of his office. Sophie suppressed a smile, wondering what actress was going to receive an earful of his abuse. She gazed around the office and noticed that the shelves on one wall were piled high with manuscripts—staples in Drury Lane's revolving repertory. Selecting a chair facing David Garrick's desk, she glanced at another stack of plays resting on its leather-tooled surface. Someone was apparently in the process of reading and evaluating them for future presentation. Next to that pile lay open a handwritten manuscript titled *A Lady's Maid; or Danger in the Dressing Room.*

Beside the two-act farce was a half-composed letter in David Garrick's distinctive hand to none other than Mavis Piggott. Unable to stem her curiosity, Sophie scanned the opening lines of the missive. After the usual compliments to the author for having the kindness to submit the work to him, Garrick then wrote:

> However, I beg your indulgence to put forth a basic principle I've found to be of great import, even in my own attempts at play writing . . . that, to wit, 'tis of no merit to have clever dialogue and amiable characters, if there be no fable . . .

Sophie smiled to herself ruefully. The problem of having no "fable," or story line, was precisely the dilemma that had plagued Kitty Clive's latest effort. Apparently David Garrick was informing Mrs. Piggott in the gentlest manner possible that she was not, perhaps, the best of storytellers—at least in this particular case. "'Tis *plot* that counts for an audience's interest," Garrick had emphasized during their conferences with Kitty. "If the audience doesn't care what happens next, then all a playwright's clever words are for naught." Sophie found herself nodding at the truth contained in Garrick's soft reproach.

"And pray, what skulking little pilferer lurks here?" demanded a shrill, angry voice from across the chamber, shattering Sophie's absorption in Garrick's play prescriptives. "'Tis not enough that I am asked to perform in tattered capes and moth-eaten gowns, but now the plays I submit to you in good faith are subjected to the snooping eyes of *this* chit!" Sophie looked up guiltily and was horrified to see Mavis Piggott marching into the office with James Lacy trailing behind. David Garrick himself appeared at the threshold. "'Tis likely you'll see an offering that mirrors *my play* at Covent Garden before the month is out!" Mavis concluded darkly.

Sophie stared at her, aghast. She had been a fool to examine the material on Garrick's desk, but to be accused of out-and-out thievery or spying for the Covent Garden management was beyond the pale.

Before Sophie could get a word out, Mavis marched across the chamber and snatched her play off Garrick's desk. She scanned the manager's half-finished missive, her almond eyes narrowing grimly. Then she glared at Sophie.

"I shall bring an *action* the next time I catch you snooping like this, you little slut!" she declared savagely.

"Mrs. Piggott! You will cease this display at once!" David Garrick said in a voice so chilling, it made the blond hairs on Sophie's arm prickle. "If 'tis anger you wish to express concerning my opinion of this . . . this *submission*," he said coldly, pointing an accusing finger at the manuscript the actress clutched in her hand, "pray vent your spleen at me, my dear. I would wager Miss McGann has no plans to pilfer the mishmash sentiment contained therein."

Speechless with fury, Mavis glowered at Sophie and flounced out of the chamber.

"Please . . . I-I'm s-so s-sorry," Sophie stammered, shaken to the core by the woman's venomous attack and her own regret at having read what lay open on Garrick's desk. "I did glance at what was p-private . . ." she faltered.

"I assume you are no plagiarist or a spy, but surely you will allow that my correspondence *is* confidential," he warned sharply. Mortified by this deserved reprimand, Sophie flushed scarlet. "Lacy!" Garrick said to his partner who had remained rooted to the spot even after Mavis Piggott's dramatic departure. "A bit of brandy might suit at this point, don't you think?"

"Hear, hear," he murmured. "I'm still quaking from that shrew's flap about the ermine cape."

As Sophie rose, chagrined, to make her departure, Garrick bade her retake her seat with a wave of his hand.

"Ah, the wicked stage!" Garrick said with a mocking sweep of his arm. "There's always someone's temper in a stew!" He narrowed his glance in Sophie's direction. "I trust today's theatrics have taught you an important lesson." He walked over to a small cabinet on the wall opposite the bookshelves and pulled out a bottle of spirits along with several crystal glasses. "The theater thrives on competition among players and among writers, and yet the worm of envy can render the entire enterprise rotten to the core. The Mavis Piggotts of this world have always been with us and always will, don't you agree, Lacy?" His partner nodded, sinking into the nearest chair. "'Tis merely the Green-Eyed Monster that's got her in his paw."

"But why would she be envious of *me*?" Sophie asked earnestly. "She's an actress *and* a playwright, and besides, she's the toast of half the beaux in London—"

"You have youth . . . and untapped *potential*," David Garrick said matter-of-factly, handing her a small quantity of brandy. "Mavis is quick to note such things. Although the woman has met with some success, I fear she is beginning to recognize her limitations in both departments. And she doesn't appreciate competition." He gestured to the pile of manuscripts on his desk. "The latest crop, mostly from amateurs," he said with a wry smile. Then Garrick tilted his head and surveyed Sophie soberly. "The prompter, Mr. Hopkins, tells me your suggestions to Kitty Clive were on the mark."

"He did?" Sophie responded, amazed that her contributions had won her any notice.

"If you are willing, I'd like you to read these farces," he announced, indicating the pile of unsolicited manuscripts. "Tell me whether you think they're worthy or egregiously bad or somewhere in between. They don't have to be brilliant—just *passable*. I've worked with many a playwright who had just one good piece in 'im!"

"This playhouse is another kind of monster," Lacy agreed. "'Tis a monster that devours material like a horse eats oats."

"Any whittling away some of this pile would be a kindness to me," Garrick conceded. "'Twill offer you an education of sorts."

"Aye," Sophie said in a breath, relieved that Garrick had apparently forgiven her transgression. "I'd quite like that." She stared for a long moment at the rim of her glass. "Sir . . . I am so dreadfully sorry to have read your letter to Mavis Piggott . . . 'twas unconscionable."

"It was," Garrick acknowledged calmly. "And I'm sure

you won't commit such a faux pas again. Now, let us see
what you can do with this mountain of words . . ."

A liveried footman clad in cream satin and wearing a
prim, white wig answered the door at Number Twenty-
seven Southampton Street, a mere four blocks from Drury
Lane. He bade Sophie enter Mr. and Mrs. Garrick's town
house. Her back still felt warm from the spring sunshine
flooding Covent Garden's vast, stone-paved Great Piazza.

Sophie held several manuscripts in the crook of one arm.
Her other hand fingered a letter posted from Edinburgh that
she kept tucked into the pocket of the simple lawn gown she
had cut down from one belonging to her aunt. Though she
had heard little of Hunter Robertson, of late, what she did
know was disheartening: according to James Boswell,
Hunter had continued his liaison with the actress, Gwen
Reardon. So Sophie had been astounded to receive a letter
this very morning in which Hunter revealed that his pen-
manship had improved markedly and that his grandfather
had died of the ague in February. The missive was short, but
offered her assurances that his season as an actor and singer
at the Canongate was going well.

As the footman led her into the Garricks' drawing room,
Sophie wondered if she dared petition her employer on
Hunter's behalf. Would a strolling player with limited experience as a legitimate actor be a potential recruit at such an
august institution as Drury Lane?

Before Sophie could ponder the question further, the
footman led her into a well-appointed sitting room where
Mrs. Garrick welcomed her with open arms to their traditional Sunday "At Home."

"Sophie, *liebchen*," she said in her lilting Viennese dialect,
kissing the visitor lightly on both cheeks. "My Davy will be
pleased to see you, as am I . . . please come in. We are
examining a new Folio of Mr. Shakespeare which Davy has
just acquired. Come! Come!" she urged, leading the way to
the book room.

The shelves in the Garrick library extended from floor to
ceiling and were enclosed by panels of brass-handled doors

fronted with wire mesh. A handsome mahogany desk stood near a window festooned with rich red silk drapery. Several leather wing-backed chairs and a leather sofa seemed an invitation to a book lover like Sophie to curl up for hours.

Garrick was standing next to a book stand on which sat the edition Sophie took to be the new Shakespeare. On the actor's left stood a man of middle height who had the carriage and demeanor of a gentleman, but whose skin was marred by numerous bright red patches and angry-looking pustules that covered his cheeks, forehead and chin.

"Sophie! So kind of you to come," David Garrick said warmly. "Just put those manuscripts on the desk, and have a look at my new prize!"

Garrick led her across the room to perform the introductions. She tried to keep her eyes fastened on the neck cloth of Garrick's other guest in deference to his dreadful complexion.

"This is Edward Capell, an expert on divining the authenticity of Shakespeare texts—and," he said with meaningful emphasis, "a deputy examiner of plays in the Lord Chamberlain's office."

So *this* was the king's play censor whom Frances Sheridan had called a "little wretch," Sophie mused. Garrick was shrewd enough to ingratiate himself with the very man who would be called on to grant a government license for any new production proposed for Drury Lane. "So delighted to make your acquaintance," she murmured, extending her hand in greeting—a gesture which Mr. Capell unaccountably ignored.

She noticed the man's own hands were blotched with the same, scorbutic patches that covered the remainder of his exposed flesh. She shuddered to think what the *rest* of his body must look like under his elegant clothes.

"Edward did an absolutely *brilliant* job of cataloging my book collection six or seven years ago," Garrick said briskly, his warm approbation a gracious attempt to cover the awkwardness of Capell's refusal to take Sophie's hand. "In addition to his duties for the Lord Chamberlain, my friend, here, has currently embarked on a worthy project—restoring Shakespeare's texts in a completely new edition of the plays.

I've invited him to peruse my latest acquisition, in hopes it may further his work."

"You are too kind," Capell murmured, appearing relieved to be allowed to return to his inspection of the volume.

Sophie watched, bemused. She knew this was important work indeed, if done well—the painstaking process of sorting out which editions were most faithful to the Bard's original writings.

Just then, several other guests arrived, including Frances and Thomas Sheridan. Sophie quickly gravitated to them.

"Alas, Garrick invites me to dine at his table, but not to act at his theater," Thomas said moodily. "We shall be forced to return to Ireland if we can't pry a bit of employment out of him. Some say he dares not allow my tragic muse upon his stage, fearing 'twould outshine—"

"Now, my dear," Frances interrupted in hushed tones, "Davy has a difficult juggling act as manager. He was more than kind to mount my play."

"Yes, he got it past that mincing little sod over yonder, I'll grant him that," Thomas said darkly, shifting his eyes in the direction of Edward Capell.

"Davy does what he can, given the normal obstacles and James Lacy's pinch-fisted ways," she responded soothingly.

"I wonder," Thomas commented, glancing over at Garrick, who was pointing out some facet of the Folio to the peculiar Capell. "He certainly plays the flatterer to *that* piece of—"

"*Thomas!*" Frances interjected sharply. "I agree with you on the subject of Capell, but we are Davy's *guests*! Let us cease this unpleasantness and discover what Sophie has been conjuring up for herself these days. Are your playbills selling briskly, my dear? Such a lovely one you did for my play."

Sophie brought the Sheridans up to date, including the fact that she was reading plays that came to Drury Lane from all manner of odd sources.

"Every tobacconist and wigmaker thinks he can write a play these days," Thomas said irritably. "'Tis enough to make a professional retire to herd sheep or grow vegetables."

"And most of what I read is dreadful. It evokes neither a smile nor a tear," Sophie said. "Tell me, Mrs. Sheridan . . . are you busy with a new work?"

Thomas patted her hand encouragingly.

"Tell her, Fanny . . . tell her what *you* have been conjuring in that clever brain of yours!"

Sophie was struck by Sheridan's contradictory character. On the one hand, envy dripped from his every pore when it came to his unspoken competition with David Garrick. Yet Thomas was wonderfully generous-spirited about his wife's efforts as a writer.

Frances blushed but seemed eager to tell Sophie her news. "I'm working on a new play! 'Tis about a sort of engaging featherhead . . . you know, one of those garrulous females given to aimless, brainless talk."

"It sounds most promising." Sophie smiled encouragingly. "How much I admire you, Mrs. Sheridan!" she blurted impulsively.

"Why, thank you, my dear," Frances replied, genuinely touched. "Perhaps one day you will try your hand at something for the stage?" She smiled affectionately, and Sophie was struck suddenly by the great contrast between this woman's warmhearted generosity and Mavis Piggott's mean-spirited prickliness.

Mrs. Garrick chose that moment to announce that tea and a buffet were being served in the dining room and the group repaired to the front of the town house where a resplendent repast was set before them. The refreshments consisted of a piping hot brew from China, plus a veritable groaning board of colorful cheeses, sweet puddings, maids-of-honor cakes, orange-flavored jumbles, and Shrewsbury biscuits featuring brandy and rose water and served with red raspberry jam.

Sophie watched with fascination as the eccentric Edward Capell studied the buffet carefully. Then slowly, and with great deliberation, the king's play censor began to assemble some decidedly odd choices on the fine bone china plate provided him by Mrs. Garrick's footman.

"Mr. Capell, sir?" Sophie said by way of satisfying her curiosity. "May I help you to a bit of this marvelous jam?" she asked, smiling as she extended a spoon dripping with the rich, ruby jelly. "I'm told it comes from the Garricks' Hampton House estate."

Capell backed away from her in horror. The blotches on his skin had deepened to vermillion.

"God's blood, but I do not *care* for such stuff!" he choked. "My digestion . . . 'tis ghastly to consume such dreadful—I-I only consume edibles that are *white*! All else causes me to—"

Suddenly, he cast her a poisonous glare, as if she had pried an abhorrent secret from him. The plate he held began to shake from side to side, jiggling his sliced breast of turkey, white goat cheese, and creamy pudding into a bland, unappetizing jumble. Sophie observed that, true to his words, there was no item of food on his plate that was not white.

Sophie had once read about the causes of scurvy in sailors. She thought it no wonder that the man had become such an unappealing-looking creature, if his nutritional choices were so narrow. And from what little she'd observed of the man, he *despised* females. She pitied any woman playwright who dared submit her work for his consideration.

It appeared to Sophie that Edward Capell appreciated only two things in life: pale food and the original works of William Shakespeare.

Chapter 9

As spring ripened into early summer and London grew hot and dusty, Sophie sensed a palpable shift of focus among the Drury Lane players. *The Miser,* an old chestnut by Henry Fielding, was slated to be the final presentation of the season. Many of the actors who could sing and dance had signed on for the summer months at the various London pleasure gardens like Vauxhall. Those who could not find employment in London made the passage across the tortuous Irish Sea to perform at Smock Alley in Dublin.

Sophie heaved a sigh of relief when she learned Mavis Piggott would soon depart for Ireland. 'Twould be the best of Irish luck, Sophie brooded, if Mavis were engaged there indefinitely.

One quiet Saturday morning prior to the official three-month closing of the theater, she broached the subject of Hunter Robertson and his talents to the manager of Drury Lane.

"Well, my dear . . . I may not be the one with whom to raise this question of new players," Garrick said. "Mrs. Garrick and I are considering a respite from all this," he added wearily, gesturing to the overwhelming pile of manuscripts heaped high on his desk.

"*Leaving* Drury Lane?" Sophie asked, alarmed.

"Perhaps for a while," he said pensively. "Those half-price riots last January were most disturbing to both of us." His eyes glittered with indignation. "The rabble can destroy in a twinkling everything one builds over a lifetime," he said bitterly. "I've been treading the boards for twenty-two years. Let them do without me for a while."

Sophie was amazed to hear the harshness and resentment that tinged Garrick's words and to see the angry flush in a face that invariably presented a calm demeanor to the world. She stared at him, suddenly at a loss for words. Garrick not play Drury Lane? 'Twas *unthinkable*!

"Your Hunter Robertson sounds a likely candidate," Garrick continued, his kindly manner restored, "but I'd have to see him perform."

"He could sing for you and recite some speeches he's played . . . would that be sufficient?" Sophie asked anxiously.

"I usually prefer to see applicants perform before an audience," the manager explained gently, "or have someone whose judgment I trust report to me of players in the provinces . . . but should he come to London . . . yes, Sophie, my dear . . . I'll be pleased to have a look, if it means so much to you. A sweetheart from home?" he inquired teasingly.

"N-no," she stammered, wishing with all her heart she could claim a higher place in Hunter's affections. "He's merely a friend. But a very *gifted* friend."

Within the hour she had posted a letter to Hunter reporting the exact words of her conversation with the august manager of Drury Lane. She wondered if Hunter would chance leaving a secure position in Edinburgh—and the voluptuous arms of Gwen Reardon—for the Great Unknown of the London theater world.

The closing of Drury Lane for the summer months of 1763 meant that Sophie would soon lose the steady income from printing and selling playbills that had rescued her and her aunt from abject poverty. Ashby's Books would also soon be minus the services of Lorna Blount, who had taken a position for the summer season as dancer at Sadler's Wells, a theater off the Islington Road on the outskirts of London.

Sophie glanced around the shop, her eyes scanning the shelves.

"Well," she said to Lorna, who had come to bid farewell this rain-spattered May day, "I've resolved to raise some funds to tide me over until autumn. I'm selling off volumes that aren't appropriate for my new vision of the shop." She pulled down a heavy tome titled *Sermons of the Established Clergy,* published in 1751 and, next to it, a book by Colonel David Dundas on *Principles of Military Movements Relating to the War of 1757 in the American Colonies.*

"Those must have been purchased by your uncle *before* Ashby's earned its notoriety," Lorna joked, eyeing the weighty volumes.

"Aye," Sophie agreed. "Mrs. Sheridan advised me to try Tom Davies's book shop on Russell Street. He was a player himself, once, she said, and likes doing business with theater folk."

Just then a loud thump reverberated overhead in Sophie's lodgings upstairs.

"God's bones! What was *that*?" Lorna cried with alarm.

Without answering, Sophie flew up the circular stairway at the rear of the book shop, hurtled past the printing press, and froze at the threshold to her living quarters. Aunt Harriet had pulled away the heavy fire screen, tossed it on the floor, and was now sitting among the cold ashes, munching on bits of coal. Black spittle dribbled down her chin as her eyes darted wildly from side to side.

"*Jesu!*" Sophie cursed under her breath. "Lorna!" she shouted, but her friend had just arrived in the chamber. "Get some water, will you please? Come, Aunt Harriet," she said in a calmer voice, "there's a good lass . . . come, let's get you tidied up. 'Tis not very savory what you've been eating, is it now?" she crooned, removing the last bit of coal from her aunt's mouth and tossing it on the cold hearth. Her aunt stared back at her, a flicker of comprehension glinting in her eyes. "No need to eat coal," Sophie chided gently, dipping a rag into the basin of water brought by Lorna.

Harriet Ashby blinked slowly several times and then looked from Sophie to Lorna and back again to her niece. She let Sophie clean her face and brush back her wild gray mane. Sophie's heart contracted at the deteriorating condition of her only living relative. She knew Harriet McGann had at one time been a vibrant, intelligent woman. Gazing at her aunt's miserable state, Sophie wondered silently what in heaven's name she could do to make the woman's life somehow more bearable.

A few days later, when the weather had turned even cooler and rainy in spite of the month, Sophie was cheered by the sight of James Boswell appearing unexpectedly at Ashby's door. However, his gloomy countenance was instantly sobering.

"I have given up my dreams of glory," he announced dramatically, swiftly accepting her invitation to join in a cup of chocolate she'd brewed on the open hearth at the back of the shop. "I shall travel to the Continent in August, and once again attempt to please my father by studying civil law at the University of Utrecht in Holland."

"Are you are not pleased, I take it, about your decision?" Sophie countered quietly, handing him his chocolate when he had settled in a chair. She perched on the corner of her desk.

Boswell sighed and flipped idly through the pages of a book lying on the counter.

"I don't rightly know, Sophie," he said bleakly. "I shall miss my friends and the excitement of the town . . ." His voice trailed off disconsolately.

"You've become a bosom companion of the great Dr. Johnson, I hear," she said, smiling. "I assume he's forgiven you your Scottish origins?" she teased. Dr. Johnson, the incisive pundit and writer of dictionaries, had a well-known antipathy to Scots.

"Aye." Boswell nodded earnestly. "I met him in Davies's book shop last month and we conversed for hours! He's wise in marvelous ways and thinks this trip will settle me in the right path."

"Then why so low-spirited and melancholy?" she asked. Boswell sighed a second time and shrugged despondently but remained silent. "Perhaps 'tis the gloomy weather," she suggested.

"I'd rather be in London among the *literati* and not in some dull college surrounded by bores and law books!" he blurted suddenly. His eyes sought out Sophie's beseechingly. "You can't imagine how terrible 'tis to be a judge's heir . . . to be dependent on his will and kindness . . . for funds . . . for *everything*!"

Sophie thought of her own orphaned state and bit back a tart retort. Boswell continued to sip his chocolate to the dregs and soon bade her a melancholy farewell.

By midafternoon, the sun emerged from scudding clouds, but Sophie found that Boswell's Blue Devils had become contagious. Lorna had long since departed for Sadler's Wells. Meanwhile, Sophie had received no response to her written enticement to Hunter. There was no denying it, she mused moodily. Hunter Robertson was a dreadful correspondent and Sophie could not spare money to frank another missive when there was apparently no realistic hope of gaining an answer.

Upstairs, she could hear Aunt Harriet moving restlessly about their living quarters.

"'Tis cooped up, I've been," Sophie said aloud, "and 'tis making me as balmy as my aunt!" With an air of decisiveness, she locked the front door to Ashby's Books and dashed up the circular stairs. "I'm just going out for a breath of fresh air," she announced to Harriet, who was sitting on the bedstead, staring at nothing in particular. "I won't be long," Sophie added with forced cheerfulness, but received no reply. She settled a shawl on her shoulders to ward off the chilly wind that had blown the rain clouds south of the Thames, and descended the stairs leading from her lodgings into Half Moon Passage, now washed clean by the earlier storm.

Sophie inhaled the scent of summer as her eyes scanned the Piazza. The rain had turned the pavings to silver. Her spirits lifted somewhat merely at being outdoors after such a long time shut away in Ashby's Books. She strolled down Bedford Street and turned through the tall iron gates into the verdant churchyard of St. Paul's. Ancient, moss-encrusted

gravestones tilted at odd angles in the velvet grass that surrounded the simple lines of the Actors' Church. Sophie noticed a plump brown bird busily pulling a worm out of the
moist ground.

"What a lucky fellow." Sophie chuckled softly. "You
have your supper right where you want it, don't you?"

She stared at the bird, absorbed by the sight of its darting
beak and the manner in which the creature cocked his head
and stared back at her. Then she drifted several yards from
the resourceful bird to inspect one of the granite headstones
adorned by an exquisitely carved angel clothed in soft green
lichen. She ran her fingertips over the gravestone's indented
letters, then pulled back with a sharp intake of breath when
she discovered that the marker commemorated the death of
a child who had perished in the Great Plague of 1665. That
was only two years short of a century ago, she mused. From
the dates etched in the stone she determined that the poor
mite buried beneath her feet had only been three years old—
about the same age Megan Robertson, Hunter's sister, was
when she died. Sophie's palm cupped the small stone head of
the angel.

How hard life can be, she thought, *and with what random cruelty life's blows sometimes befall us.*

Her thoughts drifted back, recalling the look of utter desolation that invaded Hunter Robertson's eyes whenever he
made mention of the wee sister who had perished during the
Starving. As a direct consequence of the failure of Bonnie
Prince Charlie to recover his throne, his loyal Highlanders
suffered swift and severe punishment meted out by government troops whose scorched earth policy resulted in the
burning of dwellings and torching of crops throughout
northern Scotland during Hunter's childhood.

Sophie's fingers brushed against the stone angel's wings.
She thought of her father, in his grave less than a year. *Pun-
ished* because religious and governmental authority dictated
he could not read or sell certain books. *Random cruelty,* she
mused, gazing up at the plain, straight lines of Inigo Jones's
St. Paul's Covent Garden rising from the churchyard in
which she sat. *How could there be a God when such things
were allowed to happen?*

Shaking off her melancholic thoughts, Sophie glanced at the sun slanting behind St. Paul's Church and shivered in the shadows swiftly enveloping the graveyard. The drop in temperature reminded her that she'd been away from Aunt Harriet longer than she intended. Bolting past the cemetery gates, she ran down the road to Half Moon Passage toward the shop.

A crowd clustered in front of Bob Derry's Cider House where an excited chimney sweep was pointing a soot-covered finger in the direction of the Great Piazza.

"Shed her clothes in the road and stark neckit, she be," he announced wide-eyed to Bob and the assembly that had gathered in the lane to hear his wild tale. "'Air as gray as Father Time and lookin' as old as 'im, she was," he declared, his gaze acknowledging the arrival of Sophie, Mrs. Phillips and the sometimes-strumpet, Mary Ann Skene, a frequent customer at the Green Canister. They had dashed across the road to listen to this horrifying intelligence. "The Shakespeare Head's in a fair state, and *that's* a tavern what's seen a lot of life, I ken tell ye that! But never seen no neckit creature like Mistress Ashby runnin' through the place, screechin' and hollerin'! The constable's been called!"

"Oh, dear God!" Sophie cried, setting off at a dead run down Henrietta Street, across the wide expanse of Covent Garden's Great Piazza.

The scene inside the public house was worse than Sophie could have imagined. A dozen or so patrons of the notorious drinking establishment had leapt to the tabletops for safety while a platoon of town guardsmen moved toward a corner. There crouched a wild-eyed Harriet Ashby, stark naked. In one scrawny hand, the pathetic soul wielded a cooking pot, and in the other, a sharp carving knife, apparently snatched from the cook.

"I'll play the harlot!" the normally retiring Aunt Harriet was screeching at the prostitutes and dandies who frequented the dark den. Her skin was flushed and her eyes glittered with fever. "Sons-of-whores, all of you! God strike you *dead* for what you've done! Seducing m'husband to your wicked ways! *God strike you dead!*" she shrieked, her hysterical voice renting the air in an ear-splitting crescendo.

One hard-faced Bow Street Runner, as the local keepers of the peace were known, moved toward her, brandishing an iron fire-poker snatched from the hearth. He drew closer, but before he made a move to fell her, Harriet grabbed his forearm and sank what teeth she possessed into her attacker's flesh.

"Ooowww!" he snarled, pushing her roughly against the wall where she collapsed from the force of his shove and slid down to the floor. Dazed, the old woman began to cry in high, keening sobs that racked her bony shoulders.

"She's cracked, Toby!" growled one of the men bent on capture. "Everyone 'round here knows Ashby's wife's got syph in the head."

"Aye!" grunted the man with the lacerated arm. "Bedlam's the place for her," he said, referring to the nickname given to fearsome repository for the insane officially called Bethlehem Hospital in Moorgate. "C'mon . . . let's take her!"

"Can't you blockheads see?" screamed Sophie, running toward Harriet. "She's terrified!"

Sophie leapt between the men and the poor, bewildered soul whose body was trembling uncontrollably. Standing with her back to the sobbing old woman, she stretched out her arms to prevent the two men from charging such a defenseless creature. The man with a crescent of teeth marks on his arm grabbed Sophie's shoulders roughly and gave her a hard shove. Instinctively, Sophie shoved back and slapped the man's face in the bargain.

"Why you little vixen," he cursed, grabbing her by the arm and twisting it behind her back, "you're as brainsick as *she* is!"

"Aye, they're *both* daft!" someone called from atop a table at the side of the tavern. "Bedlam! Bedlam! Take 'em to Bedlam!"

The cry to banish the intruders to London's warehouse for the insane became a rhythmic chant.

"Bedlam! Bedlam! Bedlam!" shouted the patrons who were clearly unnerved by the sight of a wild-eyed, wrinkled old woman, naked as a prune, and her ferocious niece, disturbing their afternoon tipple.

Sophie was defenseless against the mob who roughly seized both her and her aunt and dragged them out into the wide Piazza amid the stares of curious pedestrians. Under the horrified gaze of Mrs. Phillips and Mary Ann Skene, standing helpless on the sidelines, Sophie and Harriet's extremities were trussed with lengths of cord and the two women were dumped unceremoniously into a hackney coach. The Bow Street Runner named Toby rubbed his sore arm where Harriet's teeth marks had branded him and climbed aboard with the driver.

"Fleet Street to Moorgate," he barked.

Sophie felt the coach lurch, dumping both her and Aunt Harriet from their precarious position on the seats into a heap on the carriage floor. Her aunt began emitting high, frightened cries that sent shivers up Sophie's spine.

After several minutes of trying to catch her breath, Sophie twisted in her bonds and was finally able to sit up, her head bouncing against the stained velvet padding of the coach door. Silent tears streamed down her face as she stared through the window and saw the roof of Drury Lane pass by. Everyone she knew who had influence enough to attempt to extricate her from this wretched nightmare had departed London for the summer. She was alone with a madwoman and soon she would be surrounded by hundreds more.

The two guardsmen who had taken them from the tavern hauled Sophie and her aunt from the coach and carried them like sacks of meal into a small, barren room where they were put in shackles and abandoned for several hours. At length, a burly orderly appeared. He unfastened their leg restraints and commanded that they walk ahead of him down a long passageway which funneled into a row of small cubicles barricaded by iron bars.

"In with ye, now!" the orderly growled, shoving them both into a cell eight feet square, crammed with eleven other women suffering various forms of insanity. Sophie staggered and fought to regain her balance on the straw-strewn floor.

She stared, appalled, at the moaning, chattering, thoroughly demented souls surrounding her.

"Please, *please*!" she cried, "I'm not insane! My aunt—"

"'Tis what all the moon-mad say," he interrupted, unmoved. With a practiced twist of his wrist he secured the lock.

Amid the cacophony of human misery rising around her, Sophie clutched the bars in desperation.

"No! Please!" she screamed. "I am *not* mad! 'Tis a mistake by the guards who captured my poor aunt! I'm *not* mad!"

The orderly ignored her loud protests and walked resolutely to his post with nary a backward glance.

The first days in Bethlehem Hospital were so harrowing that Sophie found herself observing her terrifying surroundings almost as if she were watching a tragedy acted on the stage. She soon discovered that the ordinary melancholiacs, with their sobs and silences, were the least threatening. However, the other frenzied, delirious souls who jabbered and raved around the clock often became like snarling animals, ready to attack. She had more than one bruise on her body to bear witness to this fact.

Oddly, there was an intermingling of the mad with the mere down and out: idlers, tramps, and petty criminals. They were quick to steal a comb or grab an extra morsel of food, and Sophie grew to be as wary of their behavior as of the raving fools.

Equally as ghastly as the mood of Bedlam was the sheer, desperate *idleness* of the detainees. The lunatics had virtually nothing to occupy them throughout the endless hours of their incarceration. Sophie's quarters were filthy, and she and the others were shackled to the bed. Such barbarity in the name of medical science would be incomprehensible to anyone who had not witnessed it, she was certain. The physicians who ran Bedlam—and allowed ogling sightseers to peer at the inmates, manacled, naked, and sleeping in foul straw—also prescribed regular blood letting, vomiting, and purges.

"We must drive out the devil!" one physician's aide mumbled grimly as he forced a feeding tube down Sophie's throat after she refused to take a purgative.

The prevalent notion that these medicinals cleansed the body of ill humors prompted all manner of experiments on the patients. Behind the walls of the incongruously majestic building whose front portals were flanked by the famous statues depicting Mania and Melancholy, Sophie found herself strapped into a swing and rocked for five hours until she was so nauseated, she wished only to die. This, she learned through a conversation overheard between the institution's director, Dr. John Monro, and an asylum worker, was part of a new trend in experimentation.

"Therapeutic science, old chap!" the doctor had pronounced gravely. "Mechanical chairs and those swings over there get the blood circulating . . . syphon off the poisonous humors, don't you know. 'Tis the latest thing!"

As June melded into July and the heat and close confines of her cell brewed unimaginably foul odors, Sophie thought of suicide for the first time in her eighteen years. After six weeks in Bedlam, she could no longer conjure Hunter's handsome face or David Garrick's kindly features to soothe her terror. She gazed enviously at her aunt, who seemed oblivious to her surroundings. Harriet Ashby had retreated into a world disturbed only by the rhythmic banging of her gray head against the cell's stone walls. Sophie, in contrast, was only too aware of the horrendous catastrophe that had befallen them both.

One Sunday in early August, Sophie gazed past the clutch of writhing, sobbing women in her cell to stare at a group of visitors who were being conducted, for their apparent amusement, through the asylum by none other than Dr. Monro himself. The callers were kept at a distance for safety's sake, but Sophie could only stare at an extraordinarily tall gentleman, accompanied by a round-faced companion.

"Hunter! Bozzy?" she screamed, and then burrowed her head under the foul straw at the bottom of the filthy chamber, concluding that she had seen an apparition and was, at last, going mad.

Toward the end of August, as the hot days continued to make Bedlam a living hell, the squat, burly man who was so expert at forcing feeding tubes down patients' throats inserted a large key in the lock of Sophie's cell and poked his head in. His eyes surveyed the human wreckage scattered about the abominable chamber.

"You," he bawled, pointing at Sophie. "Sit up, miss . . . and don't you be tryin' any tricks on old Gus, will you now? Put on this smock."

Sophie stared dumbfounded as he unlocked her shackles. Her ankles felt light as swans feathers as she followed him out of the cell and down the hallway. Eventually they entered a well-appointed chamber so flooded with sunlight, she had to squint. Brushing her matted hair out of her eyes, she stared with astonishment at the sight of several people taking tea with the infamous Dr. Monro.

"Ah . . . here's the lass," Dr. Monro said graciously, as if he were introducing an honored guest. "Your friends have come for you, Sophie, my dear," he said, gesturing toward a plump woman whose gloved hands Sophie knew to be stained with various tinctures she compounded for her clients at the Green Canister.

"*Mrs. Phillips!*" Sophie cried joyfully, but before she could truly assimilate the reality of her neighbor's presence in this comfortable sitting room, Hunter Robertson rose to his full height, setting down his tea cup on the rosewood table provided for their convenience.

She stared at him, openmouthed, convinced as she had never been of anything in her life, that he was a cruel specter come to haunt her nightmares in this ghastly hall of horrors.

"Sophie? *Sophie?*" Hunter gasped, visibly shaken by the sight of her matted hair, her painfully thin body, and the dark bruises that formed smudged crescents under her hollow eyes.

She moved toward him in a trance, her bare feet padding softly on the Turkey carpet. Sophie glanced at its rich ruby colors and recalled its near twin in the equally well-appointed sitting room of the lecherous Lord Lemore. She stood stock-still. This *had* to be part of her nightmare. She would waken to the bitter reality that there was no one to save her. No one to breach the high thick walls that had closed off her world for more than two months.

"Sophie, pet . . . 'tis me," Hunter said softly, taking note of the wild, tormented look that had flickered in her haunted eyes. He reached out and grasped her hand gently. "Yes, dear heart . . . 'tis truly me . . . Hunter . . . come to take you away from here."

Mrs. Phillips extended a packet to Dr. Monro.

"Here 'tis . . . as we agreed," she said shortly. She stood up abruptly. "We'd best get Sophie home and scrubbed up. I don't know what you've been dosing her with, but I suggest fewer purgatives for your patients and more hearty beef broth. The lass is as thin as a pike!"

"Wouldn't want this . . . uh . . . unfortunate mistake to be bandied about, now would we?" Dr. Monro said quietly, refusing to accept the packet Mrs. Phillips had proffered to him. "I'll need your promise on that before I release her."

"This *mistake*, as you deem it, doctor, has done great harm, as you can plainly see," Hunter said in a low, angry voice.

"But the tale will remain among *us*," Mrs. Phillips pronounced with a warning glance in Hunter's direction. She pushed the packet into Monro's hands. "We bid you good day."

"Aunt Harriet . . ." Sophie insisted weakly, pulling against Hunter's supporting arm. "We c-can't leave Aunt Harriet."

"Now, any attempt to defend *her* sanity is quite fruitless, you know," Dr. Monro said crisply. "She ran naked through Covent Garden in front of dozens of witnesses!"

"Your aunt must stay," Hunter said gently, once again taking Sophie's arm firmly in his.

"I've seen with my own eyes the last stages of the syph," Mrs. Phillips added bluntly. "Your uncle John was a danger to the entire neighborhood. Mice nibblin' cheese, remember," she said, pointing to her skull, "and when there's no cheese *left* . . ."

"No!" wailed Sophie, "no . . . no . . . NO! We c-can't leave her in this . . . g-ghastly . . . *pit*!"

Dr. Monro's chin jutted forward with an injured air.

"How *dare* the chit rant on like this!" he fumed. "She's mad, too, I tell you, and shouldn't be allowed on the streets! I wash my hands of her!" he pronounced pompously. "Don't think you can bring her back here! I'm finished with her!"

"You've been highly paid to release her," Hunter said icily. "And you know full well her wits are no more addled than yours!"

In the midst of the argument, tears had begun to course Sophie's cheeks, but she couldn't seem to speak or even make a sound. Hunter stared down at her, concern etched on his handsome features. Abruptly, he scooped her up in his arms and carried her to the hired coach whose driver waited patiently outside the hospital's impressive facade. Sophie gazed listlessly through exhausted eyes at the horses pawing the ground near the large statue depicting a weeping giant. The bronze plaque on the base dubbed it Melancholy. Suddenly, Sophie herself began to weep loud, convulsive sobs.

'Twas just like the Tolbooth—only worse! she thought distractedly, raising her head above Hunter's broad shoulder to stare in horror at the statue's tortured features. Poor, benighted Aunt Harriet. She would die in this horrible place, just as surely as Daniel McGann had died of jail fever. And she, Sophie, would live with her guilt over that for the rest of her life.

Book 3

1763–1764

---

*Players, Sir! I look on them as
no better than creatures set upon
tables . . . to make faces and produce
laughter, like dancing dogs.*

—SAMUEL JOHNSON, QUOTED
IN JAMES BOSWELL,
LIFE OF SAMUEL JOHNSON

Chapter 10

Sophie remembered little of her first few days of freedom. She dimly recalled Hunter carrying her up the stairwell to her lodgings at Half Moon Passage and putting her to bed. Her unsettled sleep those first fitful nights was filled with repetitious nightmares, dreams that pulled her back into the filth and horror of Bedlam. And always in her dreams there was the sound of Aunt Harriet's keening cry—echoing her own feelings of helplessness and terror. Sometimes Sophie would waken to discover the entreaties were her own, at which point, Hunter would rise from the pallet resting on the floor of the printing chamber to soothe and cosset her until she fell back to sleep.

Several days after her liberation from Bedlam she was roused by the sound of a loud thump-thumping up the stairs outside the landing that separated her chambers from those of Mrs. Phillips.

"Blast and bother!" a familiar voice cursed.

Then the door swung open on its hinges, crashing with a thud into the wall. Hunter entered the room walking backward, dragging a large tin tub in his wake. Before Sophie could greet him, he disappeared down the stairs once again, reappearing several minutes later with two steaming buckets of water which he poured into the container. Again, he descended the outside stairs and returned with two more pails of water he'd fetched from the well behind the Green Canister and blended the contents with the others. Sophie propped her head on one hand and drank in the sight of his broad shoulders and luxuriant hair pulled back neatly, periwig style, and secured with a black ribbon.

"I quite like you as my lady's maid," she said softly.

Hunter glanced up from the packet of dried flowers he was spooning into the bath.

"Ah . . . at last . . . Her Nibs awakes . . . and saucy as ever, I'm glad to see," Hunter replied. "'Tis a welcome sign you're on the mend." He pointed to the potpourri he was holding over the steaming tub. "Mrs. Phillips's notion," he laughed. "She swears 'twill soothe your body *and* your mind—for a mere sixpence, of course."

"Mmm . . . smells like heather and roses," she said contentedly.

Hunter gave the packet a sniff.

"I do believe you're on the mark, poppet. Now c'mon . . . in with you. I'll let you have your bath while I pop out on a few errands."

Disappointed that he planned to depart so soon, Sophie shyly wrapped the bed linen around her thin body and padded toward the center of the room.

"I must look like a skeleton . . . an *exhumed* skeleton at that. I've not washed my hair in months," she said.

"Aye, you look poorly, pet, but Mrs. Phillips says she'll fatten you up." Sophie was not particularly pleased with his blunt assessment of her physique or with the notion that he planned to turn over responsibility for her rehabilitation to the apothecary next door. "In you get," he said, matter-of-factly reaching for the bedcover she'd wrapped around herself.

Embarrassed more by his impersonal demeanor than if he had absorbed her nakedness with an appreciative stare, Sophie scrambled into the tub, grateful for the masses of rose petals and herbs that floated in profusion in the water lapping her neck. She'd never felt so flat chested in her life. Her bosom's budding roundness seemed to have all but disappeared after the dietary deprivation she'd suffered at Bedlam.

"That's a good lass . . . now have yourself a fair scrub."

"Where are you going?" she asked, halting his progress toward the door.

Hunter turned around, a mischievous gleam in his eyes.

"Bozzy arranged my introduction to some friends of his who may smooth the way for me at Covent Garden. I've promised to pay a few calls to these fellows, informing them of Jamie's departure and extending his deepest regrets for having left their company, and so forth. Can I be bringing you something upon my return, pet?" he asked solicitously.

"I said I'd introduce you to *Garrick*," she declared mulishly. "And don't call me *pet*! I'm not six years old."

"A mere seventeen." He smiled, attempting to humor her. "And I'm most appreciative of all you can do for me at Drury Lane."

"I'm *eighteen*!" she protested. "I'll be *nineteen* in five months' time!"

"Sink me, madam," he said with a mocking bow. "I most humbly beg your pardon. 'Tis just you play the street urchin to perfection!"

Sophie sank deeper beneath the water, cursing for the hundredth time her small stature and, now, her state of emaciation.

"How did you find me?" she asked, more apprehensive than she was willing to admit about being left on her own. "How did you meet Mrs. Phillips?"

"Now there's a story," Hunter said chuckling. "I'll tell you when we dine."

"No! Now!" Sophie cried, and was ashamed how plaintive her words sounded. "Tell me now, for I will never forget what you've done for me, Hunter. *Never!* I thought surely I would die . . . and at times, I wanted to. 'Twas a miracle to see you standing there in that grand sitting room."

Hunter walked over to one of the chairs facing the hearth and turned it toward the tub.

"Well . . ." he began, warming to his story. "Last spring, I considered what you'd said in your letter about meeting David Garrick, and as my grandfather had passed away, there was really nothing to keep me in Edinburgh." He looked at her sheepishly. "I was always meaning to write you, Soph—but with my lack of talent with the quill and the Canongate season ending—"

"What about your mum, Jean?" Sophie interjected, still dissatisfied with his excuses for not answering her letters. "Had you no regrets taking leave of her?"

"Jean Robertson will always make her way in the world," he said, tight-lipped.

"And what of Gwen Reardon?" Sophie parried. "Surely you must have grieved at parting from such a dear friend."

Hunter glanced at her sharply and then shrugged.

"I doubt either of us were plunged into mourning when I took my leave," he replied evenly.

He settled deeper into the chair and stretched out his long legs and the black leather boots that extended to his knees. "So," he continued in better humor, "over the summer, I sang and strolled my way to London town. I called on you as soon as I arrived, only to find the address you'd provided on your letter locked up tight. Mrs. Phillips filled in the rest of your story."

"But how did you get them to *release* me?" she persisted.

"'Twas Bozzy's idea, really. He knew that people visited Bedlam for a bit of sport . . . so as soon as we could, we sauntered through that hellish place, pretending 'twas a rare rip."

He gazed down at her with a look of genuine distress.

"I thought I saw you that day, but I couldn't be sure," he said softly.

"I saw *you* and I thought I'd gone completely mad," she whispered, feeling tears well in her eyes.

"Remember, now . . . our Boswell is familiar with the way certain matters are handled among the authorities with whom his august father deals as judge," Hunter continued briskly, as if he dreaded her tears. "Bozzy suggested we simply *bribe* the director! Dr. Monro, wasn't it? Old Boz hadn't the siller to spare, and neither had I, or not near enough to do the trick, so we asked Mrs. Phillips if we could open up your book shop and try to sell enough merchandise to ransom you."

Sophie was so touched she couldn't speak.

"Mrs. Phillips scoffed at that idea. 'The lass sells two

books a week, if she's lucky,' she said. But then she told us of your uncle's . . . collection of bawdry."

Sophie sat upright in the tub, inadvertently exposing her small breasts. Quickly she slid back down in the water, flushing to the roots of her auburn hair.

"I locked that rubbish away!" she declared angrily to cover her embarrassment. "'Tis not for sale—at any price."

"I'm afraid 'tis *already* sold," Hunter explained, looking apologetic. "I broke the trunk's lock and Mrs. Phillips sold the goods off to a fellow named Jacob Renner . . . some dealer in titillation near here. Got a fair price, she said. "Enough to purchase your release, at any rate." He shrugged. "Mrs. Phillips handled that part of the affair."

Sophie wondered if the canny Mrs. Phillips hadn't turned a modest profit for herself on the transaction. As Hunter stood looking at her sympathetically, Sophie suddenly felt overwhelmed with exhaustion. She leaned the back of her head against the rim of the tub and closed her eyes. Hunter slid off the seat of his chair and knelt beside the tub, enfolding her moist hand in his.

"You've had much to tax you, my poor poppet. 'Tis your penchant for defending the defenseless, I fear."

Sophie's eyes flew open and she glared at him.

"'Twas my *family* I was defending," she said heatedly. "My father and my poor aunt."

"Aye . . . but you battle *more* than that, pet . . . you fight the world sometimes."

"And *you* don't care that such foul places as Bedlam and the Tolbooth exist?" she demanded, tears once again clouding her eyes.

"I care that you don't call down *worse* misery on your head," he retorted with exasperation. "Remember those broadsides you tacked up all over Edinburgh? Well, my dear Sophie, Bozzy's father would have had you jailed—or worse," he added sternly.

"I know enough now not to put my *name* on such placards," she replied defensively, "but in *London*, you should know, carping clergymen don't hold such sway, thank heavens! Folks print all manner of chapbooks and broadsides with strong opinions!"

"And some of them are arrested by the King's Men and sent to the Tower for libel or sedition, aren't they now?" Hunter demanded. "Clergy or King Geordie's toadies . . . 'tis all the same, and 'tis folly of you to think the likes of you or I can put them in their place by printing a few pamphlets!"

"'Tis not the same in London, I tell you," Sophie said stubbornly.

Hunter looked at her narrowly.

"You're not about to treat us to a repeat performance—plastering broadsides condemning Bedlam all over London, are you now?" he demanded. "Because, if you are, I may not always be there to rescue you."

"Not a broadside," Sophie replied, despising the petulant tone that had crept into her voice. The idea of placing an anonymous article about the evils of the asylum in *The Public Advertiser* had sprung to mind as she lay in her bed these last days. She had several acquaintances at the publication who might assist her.

"What then, if not a broadside?" he asked suspiciously. When she refused to answer, he said severely, "Sophie, I know you've had a shock—a series of terrible shocks, actually—but you must cease plotting revenge against forces that you can not overcome." He chucked her playfully under the chin. "Besides, you're altogether too earnest for my tastes these days. Where's the scamp rumored to have dressed in men's clothing and sneaked into Sheridan's lectures?"

"If I am too earnest," she replied hotly, ignoring the thrust of his remark, "you, laddie, are too . . . too . . . *frivolous!*" Splashing water out of the tub, she crossed her arms over her naked chest, looking at him indignantly. "Life isn't just a masquerade ball, Hunter, where you can cavort like some imbecilic court jester with nary a thought for the suffering of the less fortunate! Life is *hard* . . . life is—"

"Life is *short!*" Hunter interrupted testily. "And since neither of us have much faith in a Divine Being or a promised Afterlife . . . I say we'd better enjoy as much of it as we can." He forced her eyes to meet his. "I beg of you, as your friend and rescuer . . . *don't* even *consider* writing any diatribes about Bedlam. That Dr. Monro has much in-

fluence, I'm told, and he particularly demanded no recrimi-
nations when he allowed you to go free. Do you promise?"
he persisted.

Sophie glowered across the metal tub, her anger with
Hunter boiling in the pit of her stomach for reasons she
didn't actually comprehend. Here he was, her *rescuer,* and
yet she wished to slap him across his handsome features for
not understanding why she had no *choice* but to try to help
her father and aunt . . . why she had to try to help *others*
who suffered such unfair and inhumane incarceration.
Hunter had experienced tragedy in his life. *Why* didn't he
understand?

She broke away from his riveting glance and stared down
at the water in an attempt to calm her raging emotions.
Streaks of Bedlam's grime still clung to her skin.

"Now, scrub up," Hunter said more gently, accepting
her silence as assent to his plea. He pulled himself to his feet.
His voice had assumed a more cheerful tone. "And, pray,
delouse yourself, pet, so I may find you fit company for
supper, come evening."

He saluted jauntily and was gone.

Hunter's relentless brotherly treatment during the next
days began to grate on Sophie's nerves. He seemed to be
deliberately ignoring the care she took to bring her hair back
to its auburn glory, and her attempts to gain back the weight
she had lost. Each night he saw that she was safely tucked in
her bedstead before departing to sample the sights and pleasures London had to offer a handsome refugee from Edinburgh. Boswell, before departing for France, Italy, and
Holland, had apparently introduced Hunter to his wide circle of Scottish friends and acquaintances residing in the capital.

"How have you the blunt for all this merriment?" she
asked one evening while they broke bread at the Half Moon
Tavern.

"Blunt?" he asked, puzzled.

"Blunt, siller, *money*!" she repeated impatiently.

"Ah . . . *blunt* . . . what a Londoner you've become," he mocked her.

"How can you afford to play the dandy?" she persisted.

"I can't really," he grinned, talking with his mouth full. "But with such inexpensive lodgings as I've enjoyed with *you*, and the generosity of Bozzy's friends here, I've enough for another few weeks until I find employment."

"We *must* introduce you to Garrick this week," Sophie offered, pursing her lips thoughtfully. Lorna Blount had returned from her summer engagement at Sadler's Wells and was already rehearsing the musical entertainments scheduled for the opening week. "'Tis a bit late for the new fall season," Sophie admitted, "but Garrick often hires on extras when some actors don't return to Drury Lane as planned."

"Are you well enough for such an outing?" Hunter questioned.

"I am perfectly *fine*," she snapped, "not that *you've* noticed!"

"My, my . . . in a bit of a temper, are we?" he teased. "You *must* be much improved. How dull of me not to realize it." He took another sip of ale and smiled at her across the tavern table. "Well, poppet . . . let us get you tucked in your bed so you'll be fit to take me to your Great God Garrick on the morrow."

"And where will you be off to?" she demanded.

"'Tis not fit for your tender ears what plans my mates and I have devised to keep us entertained," he jested.

"Blast you, Hunter," she sighed resignedly. "Why do I bother with you?"

"Because I am your guardian angel and you are mine," he replied lightly. "Now, to bed with you."

❦

At ten o'clock the following morning, Hunter and Sophie strolled across the wide expanse of Covent Garden's Great Piazza, heading toward their important rendezvous.

"Isn't it *grand*?" she exclaimed, gesturing to the Theater Royal's colonnaded facade looming over the narrow path that ran between Brydges Street and Drury Lane itself. "Oh, Hunter," she sighed happily, "'tis so *good* to be back!"

He smiled in return and took her arm as they walked through the stage door. When she introduced him to the doorkeeper, they discovered that David Garrick; his partner, James Lacy; his brother, George Garrick; and the dramatist George Colman were all conferring in the Greenroom.

"Mr. Garrick received your note and is expecting you," Mr. Collins, the doorkeeper said amiably, casting a speculative look in Hunter's direction. "Just poke in your head to see if 'tis politic for you to interrupt the gentlemen," he advised. "There's great goings-on here these days," he added cryptically.

Sophie and Hunter made their way across the murky stage dotted with scenery that Sophie realized was slated for *The Beggar's Opera*, the production scheduled to open the new season.

Her heart sank at the sight of Mavis Piggott's tall, willowy form just outside the door to the Greenroom. From Mavis's determined look, she appeared intent on gaining an audience inside the chamber. At the sound of their approaching steps, she turned and, recognizing Sophie, shot her a sour look. Then, as she caught sight of Hunter, her brow smoothed and a charming smile spread across her voluptuous lips. The sight of Sophie's exceedingly attractive companion made her suddenly loquacious.

"Escaped from the lunatic asylum, have you?" she commented coolly. "I wasn't back from Dublin a day before I heard from Lorna Blount that some handsome gallant had appeared from nowhere to rescue you." She cast a flirtatious look in Hunter's direction. "Pray, don't vex me by avowing you have *two* handsome gallants in thrall?"

"No," Sophie replied curtly, as she realized there was no way to avoid making introductions. "This is Hunter Robertson, late of the Canongate Theater in Edinburgh. Hunter, this is *Mrs.* Mavis Piggott."

"How'd you do?" Mavis murmured coquettishly.

She extended a graceful hand to be kissed and exchanged provocative looks with Hunter, who smiled at her as if they were indulging in some private joke. He brushed his lips against her white flesh and replied, "Charmed, I'm sure, madam."

"Will you be at Drury Lane this season?" Sophie asked Mavis, hoping against hope this would not be the case.

"'Tis not settled," Mavis replied, pouting her puffy lower lip. "As I explained to our dear manager at the end of last season, either I am given larger roles more suited to my talent, and see my plays produced here, or I will have to take an engagement in Bath. The manager there, Mr. Arthur, is quite anxious that I do." She leaned toward Hunter conspiratorially. "But the Drury Lane pinch-pennies would not commit to such a plan before I departed for the summer . . . they have their favorites, don't you know? However, now that Colman's taking on the running of the theater while the Garricks are abroad, perhaps I'll play Juliet after all!"

"Mr. Garrick's *leaving* Drury Lane?" Sophie blurted, aghast.

"On the fifteenth of September, 'tis said, for Paris," Mavis replied smugly. "His doctors are insistent. A breath of fresh air, I'd call it." Her eyes appraised Hunter's blue velvet coat and snug breeches and she smiled merrily as if Sophie were invisible. "But you must tell me of *your* plans, sir . . . theatrical and otherwise," she added seductively.

Hunter smiled faintly at the obvious double meaning of her invitation.

"I've come to town, thanks to my wee friend Sophie, to meet Mr. Garrick . . . and perhaps Mr. Colman as well, if he's to be the manager of Drury Lane this season."

Before this nauseating tête-à-tête could proceed further, Sophie was, for once, gratified to see George Garrick, who suddenly appeared in the Greenroom doorway.

"Mr. Garrick, Mr. Lacy and Mr. Colman will see you now, Mrs. Piggott," George said gravely, raising an eyebrow at the sight of Sophie and Hunter. "We received your note this morning, Sophie, but you'll have to be patient. We've a number of pressing matters to dispense with before we can wait upon you."

"I see," murmured Sophie, attempting to maintain her composure as best she could in the face of so many unsettling developments.

"If your interview with messieurs Garrick and Colman

doesn't produce employment," Mavis said to Hunter in a throaty whisper, "I'd be delighted to forward a recommendation to my good friend, Mr. Arthur, at the Orchard Street Theater in Bath. A note left at my lodgings at Number Seven King Street will suffice," she added with a smile full of unspoken promise. And with that, she swept into the Greenroom with George Garrick in her wake.

"What a *cow*!" Sophie muttered under her breath.

"'Scuse me?" Hunter asked, amusement infecting his voice.

"I just wonder *how* a middling actress like Mavis Piggott can claim such a patron as the manager at Bath. Lacy and Garrick do not hold her in high regard, I can assure you. No doubt this Arthur fellow takes her in his keeping!"

"You allege, I take it, that her acting skills are not sufficient to earn her such devoted admirers," he teased. "But her face and figure cannot displease the audience. 'Tis better reason than some wenches have for parading on the stage. By the way," he wondered aloud, "is there a *Mr.* Piggott?"

"Cuckolded and deceased, I presume," Sophie snapped. "I imagine she'll be prancing on these boards for yet another season," she added gloomily, pointing with a sweeping gesture to the vast performing area and the yawning auditorium behind them, "as long as there are certain gentlemen who appreciate such strumpets with the wrong part of their anatomy!"

"Owww . . . the two of you are like scratching cats!" Hunter joshed. "Tell me, has Mrs. Piggott stolen away some young beau of yours?"

"I hope not," Sophie muttered.

Ten minutes later, Sophie found to her dismay that the meeting with David Garrick and his comanager James Lacy did not run as smoothly as she had hoped.

"I'm not sure how long we'll be abroad," Garrick announced to the small assembly seated in the Greenroom as George ushered Hunter and Sophie into the chamber. "My doctors say I need a long rest to ease this confounded gout. And to tell the truth, I feel the need of a respite after the tumult of last season."

Garrick's interview with Mavis Piggott had apparently

just concluded. As he spoke, Sophie searched the woman's face for some clue to her fate, but Mavis was at least a good enough actress to disguise her sentiments as she approached Sophie and Hunter standing at the threshold. She paused to bestow an enticing smile on Hunter before departing with a swish of her taffeta skirts.

"And as for engaging additional players to round out our company, 'twill be in the hands of my friend and fellow-dramatist, George Colman, here," David Garrick was saying.

Garrick's surrogate appeared to be in his early thirties. He was known by virtually everyone in the London theater as a successful writer of farces and comedy sketches. His biggest triumph had been a full-length comedy, *The Jealous Wife,* based in part on Fielding's novel, *Tom Jones,* performed to great acclaim with Garrick and Kitty Clive in the leads.

"While I am gone," Garrick explained to all assembled, "Mr. Lacy will continue in his normal role looking after wardrobe, scenery, and receipts. Mr. Colman will handle the principal direction of plays. All decisions as to casting I leave in his hands." Garrick noticed Sophie, who'd edged farther into the room. He smiled his welcome to Sophie and abruptly changed the subject.

"Sophie, my dear, how relieved I am to see you looking so much improved," he said by way of greeting. "Mrs. Garrick and I were appalled to hear of your ghastly experience while we were away this summer. You are near recovered, I hope?"

"A bit behind in the rent for Ashby's," she replied candidly, "but otherwise . . . reasonably recovered, sir . . . thank you."

"Colman, old chap," he addressed the man taking on his duties as director of Drury Lane's productions, "I do hope you will consider allowing Miss McGann to continue printing and selling playbills during performances. We made quite a tidy profit from her efforts last season."

"I'll leave those sorts of decisions up to your brother," Colman said absently. "He's promised he will relieve me of such tedious burdens so that I may concentrate on filling your shoes, my friend . . . a task that won't be easy."

"Ah . . . well, 'tis your decision. My doctors say I must remove myself entirely from the cares of this society and thus he recommends I travel to France." He smiled at Sophie apologetically. "I presume this is your friend from Edinburgh?" he added with a curious nod in Hunter's direction.

"Yes, may I present Hunter Robertson, sir," she replied, still shaken by the news that Garrick would soon be departing for the Continent. "He's played Shakespeare and is known as Edinburgh's premier singer and dancer!"

"Well, Colman, perhaps you should speak to this young giant," Garrick offered, giving Hunter's extraordinary height an appreciative stare. "He might be useful in battle scenes and such."

"I hope I may be permitted to lay before you the range of my abilities," Hunter said quickly, addressing the temporary manager.

"Perhaps," Colman said noncommittally. "We have nearly a full complement of players, I fear. You are primarily a singer?"

"Yes, but I have played supporting parts as well . . . at the Canongate Theater," Hunter reiterated eagerly.

"I have more than enough warblers," Colman said flatly. He was of unusually short stature, and gazed up at Hunter's impressive six feet with an air of resentment. "I thought I detected a slight Scottish burr. Pity."

"Well," Garrick said smoothly, filling the awkward silence that had settled between Hunter and Colman, "I fear I must be off. God bless, everyone . . . and good luck."

And so, Hunter and Sophie left Drury Lane knowing little more than when they arrived. After a gloomy supper taken together at the Three Tuns on the corner of Chandois Street, Hunter escorted Sophie to her lodgings and departed with a vague explanation that he would be visiting friends.

The next morning, Sophie marched upstairs to the manager's office and virtually shamed George Garrick into allowing her to continue selling playbills to the patrons each night.

"And I'll be happy to take notes during rehearsals and deliver your notices to *The Public Advertiser* as your brother had me do last season," she said, smiling with false bravado.

"You won't be charming me quite as easily as you did Davy," George Garrick replied evenly, "but for the nonce, 'twill be one less matter for me to worry about. Mind that you report *all* your profits from the playbills, missy," he added. Biting back an angry retort, Sophie simply nodded her head in a sham display of meek acquiescence. "Be on your way now," George Garrick said, dismissing her with a wave of his hand. "The information on the playbills posted out front is correct. And see that you don't lounge around here all day," he said self-importantly. "I want the copy delivered to *The Public Advertiser* in time for the paper tomorrow."

"Yes, sir," Sophie said, her jaw tightening. It took all her willpower to avoid reminding him that she had never once missed a deadline for his brother. Already, Sophie was mourning David Garrick's loss.

With flagging spirits, she completed her round of errands and returned home by early afternoon to set the type for the first batch of playbills heralding the new season. She then spent the rest of the day giving the book shop a thorough dusting and arranging what she hoped would be an enticing display of editions of *The Beggar's Opera*, along with a newly printed playbill announcing the opening night.

Finding she was not tall enough to shake her feather duster along the top shelves, she pulled over a chair and clambered onto it, stretching on tiptoe to reach a line of books covered with grime. At that point, her eye caught two thin volumes standing side by side that bore the arresting titles: *Treatise on Madness* by William Battie, M.D., and *Remarks on Dr. Battie's Treatise on Madness* by John Monro, M.D.

Sophie slipped the books from the shelf. Both had been published five years earlier and detailed what appeared to be a heated debate between the two celebrated physicians on the proper treatment of madness. She leafed quickly through Dr. Battie's treatise, her pulse quickening as she read his castigation of Dr. Monro's practice of restricting patients at Bethlehem Hospital to a spartan diet in the belief that "depleting the system" would aid in restoring their wits. Battie, a well-respected Fellow of the Royal College of Physicians, vehemently disagreed with this course of treatment and with Monro's use of dangerous purgatives. In his essay, Battie issued an urgent call for a fresh approach and pressed those in his profession to create a new standard of care and treatment for the insane.

Still standing on the chair, Sophie turned from Battie's work to the bound remarks of Dr. Monro, written in response to his challenger. Monro did everything but label his adversary a madman himself! Then, her quiet absorption in the controversy was suddenly interrupted.

"What in the world are you doing up there in such a precarious position!"

Hunter's voice startled Sophie so much, she had to grasp the edge of the shelf to keep from falling off her perch.

"Lud, but you gave me a turn!" she gasped.

Hunter advanced across the shop, offering to help her down. His large hands clasped her waist and he lifted her to the ground as if she were a feather. Encircled in his grasp, Sophie found herself staring up at him, her lips inches from his. A palpable current of emotion passed between them and for several moments, neither spoke.

"Any customers?" he inquired at length, finally taking a step backward and releasing her from his grip.

"N-no," Sophie admitted shakily, "but I embarrassed old Georgie Garrick into allowing me to sell programs again. Any luck at Covent Garden?" she asked anxiously.

Hunter shook his head. The highly charged moment had passed.

"'Twas the same story as at Drury Lane. I am late in petitioning them for principal roles and they have 'too many warblers'!" He sounded uncharacteristically discouraged. "I suppose I could go back to strolling and street singing—"

"No!" Sophie injected vehemently. "You're far beyond

such everyday performing . . . there *must* be a way to find you work!"

"I thank you for your loyalty, pet," Hunter said gravely, "but I must sort all this out soon. It may even be too late to go back to the Canongate . . ."

"Oh, you *can't* leave London!" Sophie wailed, and then looked away, embarrassed to reveal so plainly how important his presence was to her. "Let's close the shop and repair to the Three Tuns. We'll think of something."

Hunter looked uncomfortable and shook his head.

"I'm sorry, poppet, but I've made plans to dine with some friends later. Let me run and get you something tasty though. You can eat it in front of the fire while I dress."

Sophie tried to hide her disappointment, but accepted his compromise with good grace.

Before long, she was putting knife and fork to her mutton chop while listening to the sounds of Hunter dressing in the next room. He appeared in front of her hearth looking resplendent in a pair of buff breeches and a burgundy-colored coat that she hadn't seen before.

"When did you acquire those handsome lace collars and cuffs?" Sophie asked admiringly.

"Oh . . . a lass named Mary Ann sold 'em to me not long after I arrived in London," he said with a grin. "Got quite a good price!"

"So I would imagine," Sophie replied grimly. "Mary Ann Skene, was it?"

"Aye," Hunter shrugged, avoiding her glance. "I think 'twas her name." He strode over to inspect his friend's dinner platter. "Good lass!" he commented on her hearty appetite. "You're actually getting a little meat on your bones." He pinched her chin affectionately. "And you've roses in your cheeks again, I'm happy to see." He bent down to the coal box and tossed several black chunks on the low burning fire. "There! That should keep you cozy." He winked at her. "Sleep well."

When Sophie awoke, the fire had gone out and she shivered in her night dress. She was curled up in a chair where she had fallen asleep after rereading the two essays by the physicians whose views on treating the insane were so contradictory. She padded over to the door to the printing room, expecting to see Hunter asleep on his pallet. It was empty. She glanced up at the window in the ceiling, but the sky was pitch black. The church bell in the tower of St. Paul's tolled the hour: four o'clock.

Where was Hunter? her heart cried out, but her whirling thoughts already provided the answer. He was with a woman. Perhaps that jade, Mary Ann Skene, who so cleverly combined the profession of ruffle maker with that of harlot. Sophie was suddenly gripped by a blackness of spirit she had only experienced during her most despairing moments at Bedlam. Mechanically, she pulled back the cold covers of her bed and climbed in, staring at the ceiling with unseeing eyes until the darkness bled into dull gray and the day of Drury Lane's autumn opening finally dawned.

Sophie unlocked the doors to the book shop early and spent the entire morning glancing through the window hoping to catch sight of Hunter walking down Half Moon Passage. At the same time, she feared she would behave appallingly if he *did* come sauntering back after staying out all night. The fact was, she longed to see him under any circumstances.

Get a grip, Sophie, lass! she chided herself sternly. *Whatever happens with that rogue Hunter Robertson, you've got to devise a way to make this book shop profitable to keep body and soul alive!*

At around eleven, Lorna Blount arrived, allowing Sophie to call at the theater to confirm the following day's cast and deliver her copy to *The Public Advertiser*. She returned to the shop around one o'clock, and when she walked through the front door, Lorna gave her a look of concern that signaled trouble.

"Hunter said to tell you he'll write from Bath," Lorna said carefully, tidying the counter, which was already immaculate. "He dashed in here just after you left, packed his belongings and raced for Soho to catch *The Fly.*"

"W-what?" Sophie said, stunned.

"Seems he received word that there's a place for him at the Orchard Street Theater there."

"But he only met Mavis Piggott *four days ago*!" she exclaimed, feeling the blood pound in her temples. Sophie began to pace up and down the shop like a tigress. "I'll wager that strumpet's left with him!" she seethed. "Nary a thought for Old Drury if she can snare a strapping stallion. 'Tis *disgusting*!"

"Mavis remains in London," Lorna replied gingerly, "at least that's what Hunter said. Apparently the chit sent that Mr. Arthur a note the same day you all met, so sure was she that he had need of a player of Hunter's type. As it turns out, someone in Arthur's company had drowned in an accident on the Avon and the manager sent a runner to London, delighted with Mavis's suggestion. The poor lad was in a terrible hurry to avoid missing his coach. It was the only departure available for two days and he was due to play a small role in *Much Ado About Nothing* tomorrow night. He had no choice but to dash for the station by noon."

Sophie stood stock-still, trying not to give in to useless tears of disappointment. Just as unexpectedly as he had arrived in her life, Hunter Robertson had departed. And that was that.

"He left you a note," Lorna said softly, knowing her friend was fighting for composure.

"He *did*?" Sophie said, brightening.

Lorna handed her an old playbill. She turned it over and scanned the uneven lines written in Hunter's untutored hand.

I regret not seeing you before this hasty departure. Since I cannot serve as your Guardian Angel while in Bath, pray, dearest Sophie, refrain from any untoward or foolish actions. I am sore tempted to dismantle your printing press, but have not the time and will trust you to be sensible in all things. Keep well and wish me luck. H. R.

"Blast his bones!" Sophie exclaimed as an unbidden vision of Hunter's empty pallet the previous night rose before her eyes. No doubt he'd slept with that harpy Mavis Piggott to demonstrate his gratitude! He certainly is beyond bold, giving *me* advice on proper behavior, she thought angrily. She took a deep breath in an attempt to control her churning emotions. "Lorna?" she said in a tight voice. "Can you watch things here for a bit longer? I've something I must compose and print before *The Public Advertiser* closes this afternoon."

Chapter 11

October 1763

All of literate London was talking about the controversial article detailing the horrors of the asylum known as Bedlam published in *The Public Advertiser*. The author of the piece had taken the pseudonym "Melancholia," and speculation was rife as to whether it was actually written by William Battie, M.D., to advance his cause, or by someone else— perhaps the same Mr. Wood who had brought an action recently against Dr. Monro for falsely detaining him as a lunatic.

It pleased Sophie enormously that her article had caused such a sensation, even prompting numerous letters to public journals demanding reform. She took great satisfaction from the news that there was to be a Parliamentary inquiry on the issue—with Dr. Monro called to testify.

Inspired by this success, Sophie printed the same article in pamphlet form. She then employed neighborhood waifs to hawk the unsigned leaflet on street corners for sixpence a copy, garnering a tidy profit of three pounds. She derived no small enjoyment from the controversy she had stirred up. Even so, she tried not to think about Hunter's reaction, if he were to learn of her latest attempt to goad the authorities. And at night, when she was alone in her upstairs lodgings, she was often overcome with a foreboding that Dr. Monro would somehow find her out. Fortunately, when the sun rose each morning, her apprehension receded with the night's shadows.

Her routine at Drury Lane remained similar to what it had been when David Garrick was running the playhouse. In the evening, after she sold her complement of programs, the doorkeeper, Mr. Collins, allowed her backstage and the prompter, Mr. Hopkins, permitted her to sit quietly behind the flies, observing each night's performances.

During October and November, Sophie witnessed sparkling productions of two hilarious comedies written by the late Susannah Centlivre, *The Wonder* and *The Busy Body*, as well as Shakespeare's *Richard III*, *Twelfth Night*, *The Tempest*, and *Romeo and Juliet*.

"'Tis something to be proud of, Mr. Hopkins," Sophie declared when the curtain had closed on a particularly well-received performance of *The Busy Body*.

"What is, my dear?" Hopkins asked absently, jotting down his customary notes in his diary of the night's events at Drury Lane.

"The fact that Susannah Centlivre, dead these fifty years, *continues* to have many of her comedies presented on these boards. Think of it!" she said in an awestruck voice. "Twenty-one plays!"

"What about Will Shakespeare?" Hopkins said with mild reproof. "He's been dead some *two hundred* years and he's still the most popular playwright in history."

"Aye . . . the power of the pen," Sophie said softly. "It grants an immortality more sublime than anything promised by those fulminating clergymen."

"What did you say?" Hopkins asked, startled that such irreverent words could be uttered by his polite young assistant.

"Nothing, sir," Sophie said quickly. She smiled at him warmly. "And thank you for all your kindness . . . especially for allowing me to eavesdrop on all this," she added, gesturing in the direction of the backstage servants who were now moving props and scenery in preparation for the next day's fare.

"'Tis a magical process, to be sure, this transformation of lines on a page into living theater," Hopkins agreed, tucking his pen into its holder. "The scenery painters . . . the lighting masters . . . the wardrobe keepers—they all play their part, don't they? That's why so many dilettantes who know nothing of the backstage arts discover to their sorrow and embarrassment that 'tis easier to call oneself a playwright than to conjure something memorable."

"Aye," Sophie said, her eyes shining with pleasure. "I see that now." She impulsively gave the prompter's hand an affectionate squeeze. "I look forward to assisting you any way I can with Mrs. Sheridan's new work. Rehearsals start tomorrow, do they not?"

"That they do, my dear," Hopkins smiled back. "Better sharpen your quill."

The following morning, Sophie trudged through a light December snow, arriving back at the theater a little before ten o'clock. She made for the Greenroom to inform Mr. Hopkins of her arrival, hearing through the partly opened door the sound of loud voices arguing within the chamber.

"And you have the impudence to choose this piece of . . . of . . . *rubbish* over *my* work!" a feminine voice exclaimed.

"How *dare* you call *The Dupe* rubbish, you insolent jade!" retorted a voice Sophie recognized as Frances Sheridan's. "Garrick rejected your play before he left for Paris, so there's no point in crying foul to Colman or me!"

"Why you—" Sophie heard Mavis Piggott shout, and she feared the two female playwrights would soon come to blows.

"You will cease this *at once!*" George Colman thundered.

"Stop . . . stop . . . ladies, I beg of you!" echoed William Hopkins, whose pleas were all but lost in the furor emanating from the Greenroom.

"Mavis Piggott, you have breached all propriety, not to mention your contract—" Colman declared.

"I shall not set foot upon this stage as an actress until I have your word as a gentleman that you will also mount *my* play!" Mavis said mutinously.

"Well, then, my dear," Colman replied in frigid tones, "as I have already selected the new works I intend to present this season, we will have no further need of your services."

"No doubt, you will continue to 'present' more of your *own* drivel," Mavis charged.

"I would have you know that my last play received endless bravos and ran ten nights," retorted Colman icily. "'Tis scheduled by popular demand throughout the rest of the season—which is far more success that *you've* ever realized. Begone, strumpet! Pack your costume trunk and leave here tonight before the curtains part!"

There was utter silence both in the Greenroom and on stage where various theater personnel were preparing the rehearsal space for the first run-through of Frances Sheridan's play. Sophie quickly stepped behind one of the flies as Mavis Piggott stormed out of the Greenroom, pausing at the threshold to impart her exit lines.

"I've read your play, Frances," she spat. "'Tis full of endless prattle and boring detail. Not even Kitty Clive will save your Mrs. Friendly. Mark my words, 'twill be hissed off the stage!"

"Go burn your bridges somewhere else, woman!" Colman ordered furiously. "We've no need of such baggage at Drury Lane."

"You shall rue such words!" Mavis hurled back at the top of her lungs. "And I've plenty of bridges yet to cross, sir! Smock Alley will be pleased to have me back, I'll warrant . . . and I shall tell them of the infamy that rules the playhouse here!"

And with that, Mavis Piggott turned and charged past Sophie, who simply stood and gaped.

"I shall write to Ireland forthwith," Colman muttered loudly. "We shall see if *my* report of this affair does not *keep* her unemployed! Hopkins!" he ordered gruffly. "Now, let us waste no more time. Frances, my dear, have you survived that hissing shrew? Nothing like womanly envy to stir things to a boil, eh what?"

"Mavis Piggott begrudges any who advance ahead of her," Frances averred as she, Colman and Hopkins filed past the Greenroom door. "'Tis not merely my sex that prompts her so to vent her spleen."

"Ah . . . Sophie!" Hopkins exclaimed upon noticing her standing in the shadows. "So glad you are here."

The trio seemed relieved to be able to shift their focus to the assignment at hand. Sophie offered Frances Sheridan a sympathetic smile, which the older woman returned, ruefully shaking her head.

"All right, everyone," Colman was saying, bustling on stage. "Let's get started. Is Kitty Clive here? Players, are you ready? Lighting master? A reflector in the flies will throw more illumination on the scene, if you please. Attention, everyone! Let us begin."

❊

Unfortunately, several of Mavis Piggott's barbs proved to have substance. Even with Kitty Clive portraying the middle-aged featherhead, and with Mrs. Pritchard and Mrs. Palmer doing their best, *The Dupe* desperately needed Garrick's sharp eye and editing skill. To Sophie—and the audience—the work seemed flabby and verbose.

Although the comedy opened December 10, as scheduled, it played only two additional evenings. On each of those nights, it was roundly hissed in the fourth and fifth acts during sections in which Mavis Piggott was to have played a small role. Colman sadly determined that to curry favor with the disaffected public, he would substitute two old chestnuts, *The Conscious Lovers* and *High Life Below Stairs*, rendering Frances Sheridan's profits for her new play virtually nonexistent.

"I'll wager 'tis a cabal organized by Mavis," Kitty Clive asserted when the curtain closed on *The Dupe* for the last time. "Try not to be too disheartened, Frances, my dear."

"What will you do now, Mrs. Sheridan?" Sophie asked with concern. Thomas Sheridan was playing an engagement in Dublin so the poor woman had faced the entire calamity without his support.

"I shall meet my husband in Bath where he's to lecture on oratory," she sighed wearily, "and will try to decide whether to attempt play writing ever again."

"But *The Discovery* was such an enormous success!" Sophie protested. "You shouldn't think of quitting. *The Dupe* simply needed a bit more time to bring it to perfection!"

"You are sweet," Frances said, smiling at Sophie sadly,

"but the battle with Edward Capell in the Lord Chamberlain's office to secure a license each time, plus the vagaries of the stage . . ." she allowed her words to drift off. "I think, perhaps, I should remain a novelist. 'Tis far less treacherous for the author, I think. Especially if one is a woman."

True to her word, the dramatist repaired to Bath before the week was out. For Sophie, the small flame of desire to try her hand at the play writing trade had been snuffed out by this humbling glimpse of the perils facing even experienced women scribes like Frances Sheridan.

Christmas Day dawned bleak and cold, with steady sleet beating against the book shop's windows. Sophie spent the morning reading a book in bed, determined not to feel sorry for herself. After several hours, she gave the embers on the hearth a stir and noticed that outside, a light snow was dusting the cobblestones of Half Moon Passage, now devoid of all traffic. In the eerie quiet, she began to muse about the tumultuous year since she had arrived in London. In two months she would be turning nineteen, she realized with a start. And this very week Hunter had sent her holiday greetings from Bath with a return address that told her he was living on Pierpont Place, in the neighborhood of John Arthur's Orchard Street Theater. In the dim light of Christmas morn, she donned a simple day dress, trundled downstairs to the shop, and extracted his missive from her desk, relishing its contents on this lonely Christmas morn.

I play the occasional Romeo to some plump, middle-aged Juliet, and have done Benedick quite to my liking, of late. Most of my efforts, however, fall in the realm I'm most comfortable playing: songs, skits, and light entertainment. Bath, it seems, is where one comes when one's been sacked or plagued by London creditors. As neither catastrophe has befallen me, I am quite the curiosity among my fellow players.

So much for the tale of my adventures. I thank you for your missives sent care of the theater and apologize I

am such an inferior correspondent, but you were ever
the scholar and the scribe, and I, your poor, untutored
but affectionate friend, H. R.

Ah, how could I forget? The sentiments that prompted
this poor communication—A Happy Christmas, dear
Sophie, from your Guardian Angel who prays constantly that you are behaving yourself. Relieve my
anxiety on this question by writing me at Number Six,
Pierpont Place, Bath.

"Happy Christmas, Sophie!" Lorna's cheerful voice
called out, interrupting her languorous perusal of Hunter's
letter. Sophie looked up and saw her friend smiling outside
the book shop's front window. Short puffs of frigid vapor
rose in the air with each word. "Let me in . . . 'tis *freezing*
out here!"

Sophie swiftly unlocked the door and ushered Lorna inside.

"Quick, I've a fire in the hearth upstairs. Come up and
I'll brew you some tea."

The two young women shared a companionable cup of
the bracing liquid. Then Sophie donned her aunt's best dress
and combed her hair back into a simple style tied with a
scrap of ribbon at the nape of her neck. They had gladly
agreed to join Mrs. Phillips and several shop assistants in
making short work of a roasted goose cooked to order by
the Half Moon Tavern. Sophie had also bought a pastie,
some cheeses, and a sack posset, a delicious custard made of
milk, nutmeg, eggs and sherry that she intended to take to
her aunt in hopes the turnkey would allow his patient to
enjoy such Christmas savories.

The hired coach deposited the two visitors at Moorgate
and the driver was instructed to wait.

"'Tis difficult for you to return to this place, isn't it?"
Lorna asked quietly.

Sophie nodded somberly. She felt her heart thudding in
her chest at this first sight of Bethlehem Hospital's imposing
facade since her hasty exit four months earlier. She sighed
audibly, thinking of the diatribe she'd written, describing the

scandalous cruelties and abuses that took place within its grand facade. Unless one had actually been inside, Bedlam looked ever so respectable.

"Aye . . . even those statues bring back horrible memories," she shuddered as her gaze fastened on the gigantic renderings of Mania and Melancholy that guarded the hospital's entrance.

The two young women mounted the steps and walked gamely through the entry into the impressive foyer.

"So, ye've sweetmeats for that cracked aunt of yours, have ye, luv?" the turnkey leered, his appreciative gaze surveying the visitors and their basket. A ring filled with keys hung from his gargantuan waist and his breath smelled of gin. "Have you considered offering any Christmas cheer to old Jackson?"

Sophie fished out a small pork pie from one of her pockets and two shillings from another.

"I'd be pleased if you would accept these small tokens, sir," Sophie said sweetly. "And much obliged if you'd deliver this basket to Mrs. Ashby, with Christmas wishes from her niece."

"Small tokens, indeed," groused the man called Jackson, "but as 'tis you two pretty things that's asking—"

"Turnkey!" interrupted an authoritative voice. "What, pray, are you doing! You are quite aware that we do not allow such rich, distempering foods to be given our patients!"

Sophie froze, having identified the speaker as Bedlam's fearsome director, Dr. John Monro. She had risked returning to the lunatic asylum because she'd been certain that the head of the hospital would be at home, gnawing the bones of his own Christmas goose. She grabbed Lorna by the hand and was about to make a dash for the door when Dr. Monro blocked their path.

"Well, well, so you've come to pay a call on that demented creature you call aunt," he said, eyeing her narrowly. "I wagered 'twould be a lifetime 'ere I saw *you* in Bedlam again. You had no use for our methods as I recall."

Sophie swallowed hard and exchanged anxious looks with Lorna—the only person she had taken into her confidence after publishing her broadside about the horrors of the place.

"I see there are others far more knowledgeable than I who take issue with what passes for treatment here," Sophie retorted, and instantly regretted her audacity.

"So there are," Dr. Monro replied evenly, regarding her with a penetrating stare, "and I've often wondered who—other than that upstart William Battie—had enough knowledge of this institution to write so descriptively . . ."

He stared at her with an intensity that raised the hackles on the back of her neck.

"I can't imagine what you speak of, sir," Sophie said with feigned nonchalance. "I hope you will have the decency to deliver my Christmas goods to my aunt. I bid you adieu."

"Not quite so fast, missy," Dr. Monro growled, taking a menacing step closer.

"We've merely come to bring Christmas provisions to Mrs. Ashby," Lorna spoke up bravely.

"This does not concern *you*, chit!" he snapped, causing Lorna to clutch Sophie's hand in a deathlike grip. He turned his malevolent gaze back to Bedlam's former inmate. "I can assure you that I have not enjoyed having such outrageous criticism published about me, especially as I suspect 'tis a mere layperson claiming to understand the subtleties of science," he said in a threatening voice. "Nor did I appreciate being summoned to answer queries before Parliament," he added, glowering.

Sophie bit her lip to keep back an intemperate reply.

"'Tis no affair of ours," she managed to answer. "Now if you will simply let us pass, we will trouble you no further."

"Indeed, you *won't*!" he said angrily, his flashing eyes studying Sophie as if trying to piece together a puzzle. "As I recall, your aunt and her husband had that book and *printing* establishment near Covent Garden known for producing foul abominations and selling prints not fit for decent folk." A satisfied smile began to crease his lips. "I doubt the Crown magistrates would hesitate to accept my bill of libel accusing John Ashby's niece—a former *inmate*—of printing lies about me in the paper and distributing scandal sheets around the town."

"That's absurd . . ." Sophie replied faintly.

Dr. Monro began pacing circles around them, his voice rising with each step as he pointed an accusing finger at her.

"Sophie McGann . . . of course!" He laughed harshly, his tone confirming his suspicion that she was, indeed, the author known as "Melancholia." "Who else could write so knowledgeably of our advanced methods here?"

"Don't be ridiculous!" Sophie replied, feeling panic rising in her throat with every word she spoke. "*I* . . . a mere *female* . . . challenging the medical theories of the great Doctor Monro! No one would believe such accusations!"

"You'd be wise never to come here again," he warned. "And just wait and see if I don't bring an action against such outrageous libel!"

Without further hesitation, Sophie tugged at Lorna's sleeve and the two young woman raced for the door. Gingerly they ran down the ice-slicked lane that led to Moorgate and never looked back until they reached the waiting coach.

※

"Here's the k-key to the s-shop," Sophie stammered, her teeth chattering in the chill morning air as she watched the coachman's assistant at the Saracen's Head on Ludgate Hill hoist her trunk to the roof of the conveyance about to pull out of the stable yard. "When you think 'tis s-safe, open the doors for business. I'll share all p-profits with you equally while I'm gone."

"Surely Dr. Monro is all bluff and bluster," Lorna replied reassuringly, taking the key from Sophie's frozen fingers and drawing her own warm woolen cloak tighter under her chin. "He has no real proof against you and has as much to fear as you do, dredging all this up again."

"I can't risk it," Sophie replied, shivering at the memory of her father languishing in the Tolbooth because the influential Lord Lemore had goaded the church authorities into punitive action.

"I'll write you as soon as I think the tumult's died down," Lorna soothed.

"And don't forget to tell George Garrick I've been called

home to Edinburgh on a family emergency and have left you in charge," Sophie added anxiously. "If you simply follow those written instructions I left on my desk, you'll not have any problems producing the playbills. Get Mary Ann Skene or someone to sell them for you the nights you're dancing at the theater."

"I don't know much about operating that printing press," Lorna replied, but the look of dismay spreading across her friend's face caused her to add, "but I'll do my best, Sophie . . . I promise."

"On board with ye, lass!" exclaimed the driver, wrapped to his bushy eyebrows in a knitted muffler. He held out his mitted hand to receive Sophie's pound and five shillings, a sum that depleted the reserves in her purse to under two pounds total. "We've got to reach the inn at Newbury by dusk," he advised.

A gaggle of some five additional passengers trundled toward the *Flying Machine*, a large coach with piles of luggage strapped to its roof.

"Thank you so much, Lorna," Sophie said in a rush, giving her a quick hug. "A true friend, you are."

"And so are you," the slender young dancer replied. "Keep safe and Godspeed."

Sophie settled in beside two beefy middle-aged women, both complaining of gout while discussing the merits of drinking mineral water and floating in hot baths with their fellow sufferers. An arthritic gentleman accompanied by his surly looking son sat facing them, prompting Sophie to turn away and peer out the window. She leaned forward to wave at Lorna with as much cheer as she could muster, comforting herself with the knowledge that Dr. Monro would not have been able to complain to any governmental official until two days after Christmas, which meant later this day.

The coach driver shouted at his team of horses from his perch overhead. The enormous vehicle groaned and then lurched forward, heading toward Kensington and the Hammersmith Road. Despite all the worries besetting her, Sophie felt her spirits lift. If her Guardian Angel couldn't come to her . . . she would go to him.

Less than thirty-six hours and eighty miles later, Sophie had counted the last villages leading to her destination. Overton, Black Dog Hill, Chippenham and Box all whizzed by the coach window, until finally she caught a glimpse of a series of hills dotted with houses made of honey-colored stone. The coach seesawed along the rugged road still sheened with frost, but fortunately no snow had fallen during the journey from London to slow them down.

As they approached the outskirts of the city ahead, Sophie marveled at the amount of building that appeared to be in progress. The coach crossed the river Avon and rumbled down the last stretch of the Bath-to-London Road, passing beside an enormous circle of buildings, elegant even in their half-completed state.

"That's the Bath Circus that John Wood the Elder designed . . . the one his son, John the Younger is constructing," remarked Mrs. Sims, one of the plump matrons who apparently enjoyed serving as tour guide. "'Tis a bit far from the baths, but already the *ton* seem interested in leasing rooms in the section that's now finished."

Sophie stared, awestruck, at a gracefully curved edifice that would eventually form a perfect circle.

"It puts me in mind of engravings I've seen of a Roman amphitheater," she said in a breath.

"Aye." Mrs. Sims nodded. "'Tis said that the elder John Wood found inspiration from that Italian architect . . . Pa-Pa—"

"Palladio?" Sophie asked, recalling the book on Italy her father had sold to James Boswell.

"That's it! That Palladio fellow . . ."

The building was constructed out of the city's characteristic Bath stone, a soft local limestone that conferred a warm beige aura on the small metropolis. Sophie took in a long breath and exhaled. Bath must be one of the most beautiful cities in the *world*, she thought happily. Her excitement at having dared to come to such an unknown place bolstered her spirits.

The coach route led them eventually past the Avon to a pretty square known as the Orange Grove. Then they rolled down Cheap Street where Sophie spotted a startling array of shops—hatters, hosiers, goldsmiths, watchmakers, linen drapers, china-and-glass merchants, circulating libraries, confectioners, silk emporiums, shoemakers, stationers and purveyors of every commodity from cheese to tallow candles. Obviously, Bath was a shoppers paradise, and it impressed her that such a small city could offer holiday makers, inveterate gamblers, and recuperating invalids such an extraordinary array of quality goods.

Soon the coach turned into Stall Street and pitched to a halt in front of a public lodging house called the Bear Inn. It was midmorning and as Sophie stared out of the carriage window, scores of sedan chairs bearing occupants wrapped in blankets were being transported hither and yon.

"They've just come from soaking in the baths and drinking the waters in the Pump Room over there," Mrs. Sims informed her. The building in question was situated across from the Gothic Abbey that rose so dramatically in the middle of a large square nearby. Sophie could hear lively music drifting from the chamber where the medicinal waters were dispensed, and she wondered at such levity being indulged in so early in the day. "Now, they're off to their breakfasts, as indeed, we shall be in a trice," Mrs. Sims stated with satisfaction. "'Tis been a pleasure traveling with you, my dear. Where are your lodgings?"

"On P-Pierpont Place, I believe," Sophie stuttered, the reality of arriving unannounced on Hunter's doorstep permeating her consciousness. "I'll be staying with a family friend," she added bravely.

"Well, I'll be watching for you, my dear," the matron said with a smile. "Everyone knows everyone in Bath."

Sophie made arrangements to store her trunk temporarily at the Bear Inn and wandered across the large square that was dominated by Bath Abbey. She craned her neck, mesmerized by the building's soaring towers and flying buttresses, marveling at its size. Having secured directions to the Orchard Street Theater from a pair of elegantly attired ladies out for a morning stroll, Sophie threaded her way past Sally Lunn's bun shop. She found herself on Pierpont Street next to a columned passageway that led to Pierpont Place and a two-story building with a door painted red marked "Number 6": Hunter's lodgings. Her heart beat faster as she passed it by without hesitating. Instead, she continued down the narrowing road, turning sharp left into Orchard Street. With some relief she saw at the end of the lane a solid-looking structure that could only be the Orchard Street Theater.

It was eleven forty-five, near the hour when morning rehearsals would be concluding and the players pausing for refreshments. She halted her progress in front of the theater, noting its small size in comparison with Drury Lane. Her pulse began to race at the sight of a large playbill announcing productions of *The Jealous Wife* and *The Devil to Pay* due in January. Sure enough, Hunter Robertson's name was listed prominently among the cast members. The next moment, however, her throat constricted and she felt her breath shorten. Playing opposite Hunter in *The Jealous Wife* was the name "Mrs. Piggott." Before Sophie could adjust to the notion that her erstwhile nemesis had fled to Bath instead of Dublin after her battle at Drury Lane, a side door swung open suddenly and a score of chattering players poured into the narrow street.

Immediately, Sophie spotted Hunter, towering head and shoulders above the others. He threw back his dark blond head and laughed at something one of his companions had remarked. Mavis Piggott was strolling just behind him and exchanged glances with Sophie before Hunter was even aware of her presence. Without batting an eye, the tall, striking actress nudged Hunter's arm and possessively slipped her own in its crook.

"Sink me, darling, but isn't that the little London chit Sophie McGann?" she said loudly, garnering the attention of the small crowd surrounding her.

A look of utter amazement washed over Hunter's handsome features and he stood rooted to the spot.

"Sophie! Pray, what in the world are *you* doing in Bath?" he demanded.

"'Tis nearly the New Year," Sophie retorted, flushing

scarlet and feeling utterly foolish. "I felt in need of a change of scene," she added feebly.

The group surrounding the trio of Hunter, Sophie, and Mavis began whispering and a few snickers could be heard.

"Well, well, Robertson," said a young man whose attractive appearance bespoke his profession, "seems you have your hands full. *Two* lovely ladies begging your attention! May I be of any assistance?" he asked mockingly.

"Aye," Hunter replied grimly, "you could escort Mrs. Piggott with the rest of the company to the eating house on Kingsmead, if you would be so kind."

"Delighted to be of service, old boy," the actor replied jocularly, "and in return, I would ask that you introduce me to your newest friend."

That remark prompted suppressed laughter all around and Sophie shrank with mortification. Mavis was glaring openly at her. Sophie was filled with remorse that she had ever thought to seek safety with Hunter. Since she had first met him, she had seen he was a favorite with the ladies, and now he was behaving true to form in his adopted city. She wished for nothing so much as to disappear beneath the cobbled stones on which she stood in the cold light of this wintery day.

"Sophie," Hunter said stiffly, "may I present Geoffrey Bannister, our leading player." He shot a look of annoyance at his fellow actor. "Bannister, this is Sophie McGann, whom I have known since she was a wee bairn in Edinburgh."

"She's no 'bairn' now," Bannister said with an appreciative smile. This reaction bolstered Sophie's spirits somewhat, for she had always felt her looks mousy in comparison to Mavis's dramatic face and figure. "Welcome to Bath, Miss McGann."

"Thank you," Sophie murmured, casting her eyes down to study the tips of her shoes.

Why did I ever think to come here? she mourned silently. She racked her brains for a graceful way to make a speedy exit, but Geoffrey Bannister had already tucked Mavis's arm in his and was nearly dragging the woman down the road and away from the theater. She looked back at Sophie with a murderous glance.

"Shall I see you later?" she demanded of Hunter, almost shouting to be heard.

But Hunter wasn't listening. He grabbed Sophie's hand and strode down Orchard Street in the opposite direction, retracing the route his friend had trod just moments earlier. At the red enameled door marked Number 6, just around the corner from the theater, he hauled a key from his coat pocket, turned it roughly in the lock, and unceremoniously escorted Sophie inside.

Chapter 12

Silently, Sophie watched Hunter strike a flint, igniting the coals in a fireplace that provided his sitting room with its only source of heat. Dim wintery light suffused the small chamber that, from the look of the rumpled bedding on the unmade four-poster standing in the corner, also served as his sleeping quarters. Her eyes rested on the broad expanse of his back as he knelt before the hearth. She dreaded the condemnation he would surely heap on her when he finished his task and rose to his feet.

It was obvious from everything Sophie had observed during the few moments she had seen Hunter and Mavis Piggott together, that the two enjoyed more than just the camaraderie that traditionally exists among players. Sophie could plainly see that Hunter and Mavis had become lovers, and her unexpected arrival in Bath was undoubtedly the last thing either of them wished.

"I've a bit of pottage I'll heat for us," Hunter announced over his shoulder, hooking the kettle's wire handle in the crook of a wrought-iron arm designed for cooking simple dishes over a fire.

"Thank you," Sophie said dully. "I fear I'm a trouble to you."

"That you are," Hunter replied, blowing on the coals. He rose to his full height, turned around and, much to her surprise, flashed her a crooked smile. "But then, you always were . . . 'tis what's kept our friendship interesting."

His tobacco brown coat was new—a sign of his increasing prosperity—and it fit him superbly, as did his matching breeches and fine silk stockings. Despite her shock at having seen the proprietary manner Mavis had displayed toward Hunter, Sophie was desperately happy to lay eyes on him again. However, the fact that the mean-spirited Mrs. Piggott had captured his heart, or at least had appealed to some baser instinct, was a bitter pill.

"I'll just be staying in Bath until . . . 'tis safe to return to London," she blurted, glancing down at her entwined fingers. To her dismay, tears began to sting her eyes.

"Safe?" Hunter echoed her words, taking a step closer. He gently seized her chin between his strong fingers, forcing her to meet his gaze. His blue eyes seemed darker than she remembered and they searched hers intently. Then he shook his head. "You'd better sit down and tell me all about it," he said, indicating a pair of chairs that flanked a table near the fireplace.

Her voice quavered as she described the anonymous article she'd authored about Bedlam in *The Public Advertiser*. Then she pulled from her reticule a copy of the unsigned pamphlet she had distributed—the one that boldly criticized Dr. Monro.

"He guessed that I penned both pieces and he's threatening to bring a bill of libel against me—even though every single word I wrote about him is *true*!" she exclaimed.

Hunter's eyes quickly scanned the pamphlet and his mouth narrowed into a thin line.

"You did *precisely* what I advised against," Hunter said sternly, "and now you come running to me for help. What am I to do with you?" he added with exasperation.

"I can see you've quite enough to cope with as it is," Sophie retorted, her rising temper stemming her tears. "Had I but known you would be so *occupied*, I'd have never disturbed you in your . . . your . . ."—she glanced around the rather untidy chamber—"your *love nest*!"

Hunter had the grace to flush slightly. He cleared his throat and rose to give a stir to the soup in the kettle.

"Actually," he said, his back to her, "I'm rather glad to

see you, although I can't fathom why you've managed to get yourself into yet another scrape."

"Well, you needn't worry," she said tartly, her anger and disappointment stiffening her spine. "I shall get myself *out* of it!" It would never do to allow Hunter to see how close she'd come to flinging herself into his arms at her first glimpse of him emerging from the Orchard Street Theater. "If you will direct me to some cheap lodgings, I shall see if some printer or bookseller would take me on for a while. I shan't be a burden, I promise you. There are ever so many shops here, I see."

"Aye . . . shops to engage all your fancies," he agreed.

Hunter crossed to an armoire and opened its doors to retrieve two plain white porcelain bowls. Crouching again next to the hearth, he ladled out the hot soup.

"Here," he said, rising and handing her a bowl and a spoon, "you must be famished."

"I am," Sophie admitted, watching him take his seat across the table from her. "And sitting here, I can still feel the pitch and sway of the coach on those muddy roads."

Hunter gazed at her reflectively, spooning the steaming soup into his mouth.

"Your health's quite restored, I see."

Sophie felt his eyes appraising her carefully.

"Aye . . . I suppose so," she said, moodily staring into her bowl.

To be sure, her body had convalesced since her release from Bedlam, but her mind and spirit were still in need of healing. For some reason, she found herself thinking back to her childhood in Edinburgh where she had laughed and played pranks with friends. As she faced the new year of 1764, her heart seemed overburdened with all that had happened since those happier days. She wondered if she would ever feel lighthearted and carefree again.

"Well, you're most welcome to stay here," Hunter was saying, interrupting her melancholy reverie.

"W-what did you say?" Sophie replied, confused.

"You can sleep here," Hunter repeated. "'Tis not as if we haven't shared lodgings before, and 'tis the least I can offer after your kindness to me when I came to London last year."

"'Tis not charity that I ask of you, Hunter," she said, irritated, "nor do I expect you to sleep on the floor. I'll find myself somewhere to stay."

"I'll make a pallet for myself, as at Half Moon Passage."

"No need," Sophie responded stiffly. "I doubt that Mavis Piggott would enjoy giving up this bed," she added with a show of pique, nodding in the direction of the four-poster.

"Such subjects are no concern of yours," he replied testily.

"Well, if I lodge with you, *'twill* be concern of mine soon enough . . . and yours as well! Mavis will no doubt try to strangle me while I sleep."

"'Tis of no consequence, I tell you!" he said harshly. "If you wish to stay, you're welcome." Then he added in a gentler tone, "You've proven yet again, we must look out for each other."

Sophie gazed across the table, feeling suddenly exhausted from her journey and the complexities that greeted her at the end of it. Her pride was hurt and her heart was sore and she didn't have the strength left to make any sensible plan beyond surviving this dreadful day.

"Tell me of your life here," she said, determined to change the subject from her gloomy musings. "How goes it on the wicked stage of Bath?"

Hunter smiled faintly.

"Bath is extraordinary, a fantastical place, as you have already seen," he said, warming to his subject. "It attracts the rich, the famous, the royal . . . not to speak of parvenus, gamblers, debtors, fops, dying invalids, match-making matrons—a more bizarre cast of characters you couldn't imagine."

Sophie smiled sleepily at his amusing description. She found the sound of Hunter's rich, warm voice soothing, and soon her eyes began to droop with accumulated fatigue.

"And the theater patrons?" she asked, smothering a yawn. "Are they a similar array of rogues and brigands?"

"To be sure." He grinned. "But fortunately, they seem to warm to my tunes and musical skits." For a brief moment, his engaging smile grew diffident. "As I may have mentioned in my letter, I've found, quite to my surprise, that I enjoy theater management as much as performing. Mr. Arthur is a bit of a blowhard and terribly disorganized, so he's turned to me for some assistance. We open again on January fourteenth and he's allowed me to supervise the entire production of *The Jealous Wife.*"

"Why, Hunter!" Sophie exclaimed, sitting bolt upright. "'Tis wonderful that you've got on so famously in such a short time."

"Aye, in some respects 'tis gone well for me in Bath."

She resumed her posture, propping her head with her hand. Her eyes blinked slowly and her neck felt heavy as a chunk of Bath stone. Hunter scrutinized her closely.

"You're about to fall asleep right in my face, aren't you now, poppet?" he said, the full measure of his old affection resonating in her ears. "Come, now . . . let's get you undressed and into bed." He looked around the chamber. "Where are your belongings? Don't tell me you were forced to flee without even a portmanteau?"

"My trunk's at the Bear Inn," she mumbled, pulling herself to her feet with effort.

"We'll fetch it later. Here," he said, lifting his banyan off a chair and handing her the quilted silk dressing gown. "Put this on . . . behind there," he added, pointing to a four-paneled screen standing in the corner opposite the bed.

Sophie stumbled sleepily toward the makeshift dressing room and fumbled with the buttons on her gown.

"Odds fish!" she muttered in frustration.

"Here," Hunter said, appearing behind her, "let me do those."

She felt his long fingers deftly releasing the fastenings at the back of her gown.

"Once again, my lady's maid," she murmured.

"Aye," he replied, his fingers reaching the buttons below her waist. Her gown gaped open and she could feel his hands resting lightly on her hips. An odd tremor like a trill played on a harp skittered down her spine. Then his fingers began plucking at the laces of her stays.

"You seem well schooled to this task," she asserted over her shoulder. "You've made short work of it."

And as if to provide evidence of her claim, her corset, traveling gown, and quilted petticoat slid down her slender legs, falling into a pool at her feet. She was left clothed only in her shift, a thin garment made of cotton. Slowly, she turned to face Hunter and felt a strange fluttering in her chest. Her eyes traveled up his buttoned linen shirt and halted at the deep cleft that dimpled his chin. She realized she was holding her breath and exhaled with a sigh.

"Feel better?" he asked softly.

Her eyes drifted up to meet his and she nodded. They gazed at each other for a long moment and Sophie swayed slightly with exhaustion mixed with a dizzying sense of suppressed excitement.

"I feel light-headed," she blurted, unable to remove her eyes from his. His glance shifted lower and Sophie wondered if her cotton shift revealed her breasts' new fullness.

"You're fatigued from your journey," he replied, his voice sounding as if he needed to clear his throat. He reached for the banyan she'd draped over the screen. "Here, put this on."

He held the garment while she slipped her bare arms into its sleeves. She knew she looked ridiculously undersize in his dressing gown, but she reveled in its mysterious, masculine scent.

"Mmmm . . . so silky," she murmured. She felt slightly off balance and swayed against his chest.

Hunter put an arm around her shoulders, steadying her.

"Come, soon you'll start to snore standing up," he said gruffly, guiding her to his bed. She watched while he pulled back the untidy covers, smoothing the bed linen as best he could. "In with you," he urged, pushing her gently against the pillows and drawing the counterpane up to her shoulders.

Sophie snuggled into the feather mattress, which was also infused with the faint masculine essence that permeated his dressing gown. She drew the scent deep into her nostrils and sighed contentedly. Within moments she was fast asleep.

Hunter stood next to the four-poster, staring down for

quite some time at the slender figure slumbering peacefully
in his bed. Then he lowered his large frame into the chair
that faced the low burning fire and gazed bemusedly into its
glowing coals until the candle on the small table beside him
sputtered and went out.

Sophie slept all afternoon and straight through the night,
waking the next morning as Hunter was tiptoeing toward
the door with his coat over his arm.

"Hunter, what time is it?" she demanded from beneath
the bed covers, halting his progress.

"Ah . . . the sleeping beauty awakes," he replied, approaching the four-poster. "And none too soon, slugabed!
I'm just off to rehearsal. I'm staging the musical interlude
this week." He pointed to a large object placed near the
screen where she had changed out of her clothes the previous day. "Your trunk, madam. I had two of the stage servants fetch it from the Bear Inn."

Sophie lay back on her pillows and smiled up at him.

"Thank you," she murmured, noting the makeshift pallet
laid in front of the hearth. Its proximity to where she'd slept
symbolized both cozy intimacy and a distinct boundary ex-
isting between them. She and Hunter exchanged a long look
and Sophie was struck by a strange sense that the room had
grown suddenly warmer. "In a curious way, perhaps 'twas a
blessing Colman didn't sign you on for Drury Lane," she
said quickly to fill the silence. She wondered if Hunter had
noticed how flushed her cheeks had become. "It sounds as if
you've been given much more responsibility here than you
might have had in London."

"That's true, Bath is a good place to learn more of my
craft. Still, the London toffs visit here in droves," he
laughed. "Perhaps when they return, they'll urge Colman to
remedy his terrible oversight next season!"

"Let's hope Mr. Garrick returns by then," Sophie replied
fervently. "No one can match him for kindness or fair play."

Hunter set his coat down on top of the bed covers.

"So, my sleepy Sophie," he grinned. "I've been thinking
'twould be easiest to gain you employment as an Orange

Girl rather than chase all over Bath trying to persuade the local booksellers that a lass five feet tall can run a printing press. What say you to meeting me at the theater about one o'clock and I shall try to fix it up with Mr. Arthur?" Noting her look of uncertainty, he hastened to add, "You've sold playbills before, and 'tis nearly the same, except you must be able to pare the fruit into sections. 'Tis sticky work, but a pretty miss can make more than a few pence, I can tell you. And—as you say—'tis only until you can safely return to London."

Sophie gazed at him pensively and then shook her head. "No, I-I don't think that would suit."

"Why not!" Hunter demanded. "'Tis a capital solution to your lack of funds."

"Because I'd be at the theater every night," she said softly.

"What's wrong with *that*!" he protested. "I thought 'twas an excellent part of my plan."

"I'd see you with Mavis!" she blurted, and then banged her head against the feather pillow, mortified that she'd admitted aloud—and to *him*, of all people—her dread of seeing them together.

"God's bones, Sophie, I—"

"*Don't say it!*" she interrupted furiously, sitting bolt upright and pulling the bed linen tightly under her arms. "I know, 'tis silly prattle on my part to protest what's happened between you two . . . you have my apologies," she added more calmly, forcing herself to meet his gaze. Hunter had behaved like a stalwart friend, and she had realized—as she had in the case of Gwen Reardon—that she'd rather have him playing *that* role in her life than none at all. "I *must* secure employment and I won't leave any stone unturned. I'll visit a few book shops this morning and see what possibilities there might be for me—*and* I will meet you at Orchard Street at the time you say." She forced herself to smile at him brightly. "You're very kind to be willing to speak to your manager, and even kinder to have offered me shelter. I won't impose any longer than I must."

His gaze in response to her monologue struck her as uncharacteristically grave, but she supposed he was as disconcerted as she by the awkwardness of their situation.

"Till one, then," he said at length. "Come into the foyer of the theater and I'll meet you there." He fished a key out of his pocket and placed it on the small table near the fire. "Here . . . in case you need it," he added, and turned to depart.

Sophie had barely slipped into her worn blue-and-white striped cotton skirt and white bodice before she heard a key turning in the lock at the front door.

"Hunter?" she said, bending over her open trunk to retrieve a light wool shawl.

"No . . . not Hunter," Mavis Piggott replied. "'Tis I."

Sophie straightened up and turned to stare at the intruder who sauntered into the chamber and pointedly placed the key that had gained her entrance to Hunter's chambers on a nearby table. Then she opened the doors to a small cabinet, withdrawing a bottle of spirits and two glasses.

"A bit of brandy?" Mavis offered calmly. "I find it so soothing when one is out of sorts."

Sophie shook her head, sick at heart to have her worst fears confirmed. Mavis possessed her own key to Hunter's lodgings and was obviously intimately familiar with its furnishings.

"You've just missed Hunter," Sophie said stiffly. "He left for the theater not ten minutes ago."

"I know," Mavis drawled, pouring herself two fingers of brandy. "I saw him leave."

"Then you probably know that I'm seeking employment and will find my own lodgings as soon as I can."

"I should hope so," Mavis replied coolly. "With the babe, I don't think there'd be room for all four of us in here."

Sophie could not hide her shock, nor mask the pain of her reaction. Mavis continued to stare at her boldly, her back to the fireplace.

"You're . . . ?" Sophie asked faintly.

"Yes," Mavis answered abruptly, "so I imagine you'll not be surprised to hear that Hunter and I will soon wed."

"Is there really no 'Mr.' Piggott?" she wondered aloud.

"Dead, I'm afraid," Mavis replied. "So sad—I was barely a bride."

"And Hunter knows of the bairn?" Sophie asked.

"Not yet, but 'twill not change things. In fact, I imagine 'twill hasten them along!" Mavis laughed and took a generous gulp of brandy. "I'm surprised he did not tell you of our . . . ah . . . arrangement." She stared steadily at Sophie, seeming to relish her rival's acute discomfort. "But then, he's a man, and men don't handle these situations very gracefully, do they?"

"He didn't need to tell me," Sophie replied in a strained voice. "I realized how the land lay the moment I saw you together in front of the theater."

"Perceptive little waif, aren't you now?" Mavis snapped. "Well," she added, glancing over at the bed Hunter had devised for himself near the fireplace, "I called on you this morning to spare you further embarrassment. I am glad to hear you seek employment and other lodgings. Under the circumstances, 'tis only fitting."

And without further comment, Mavis Piggott drank the last of her brandy and swept out the door.

Sophie remained rooted to the spot, staring after her. The actress was carrying Hunter's *child,* she mourned silently, sensing that her intricate web of cherished daydreams had just been ripped to shreds.

Sophie spent a discouraging morning calling on various printers and booksellers, including a Mr. Leake at his circulating library in Terrace Walk.

"Have you no references, Miss? No one who'll vouch for your printing skills?" Mr. Leake inquired gruffly. "Not that I've ever heard of a lass your age running a press. A widow lady, mayhap, but not a slip of a girl."

"Hunter Robertson, at the Orchard Street Theater can vouch for me, sir," Sophie said brightly.

"A *player*?" Mr. Leake replied disdainfully. "'Tis like asking a vagabond to swear you won't pick my pocket. Sorry, miss. I've got customers to attend to. I bid you good day."

By one o'clock, Sophie was chilled to the bone by the sharp wind that swept off the river Avon and feeling dreadfully dispirited. She trudged down Orchard Street to the theater and stared dumbly at the various doors marked "Gallery," "Pit," and "Boxes." The door that was unmarked did, indeed, lead into a front foyer. Once inside, she stood in a darkened corner shivering until Hunter appeared, looking harried and out of sorts.

"Ah . . . there you are," he exclaimed, striding quickly to her side. "Come on . . . Mr. Arthur will see you." He paused and draped her shawl more becomingly around her shoulders and smoothed a wayward strand of auburn hair from off her brow. "You'll do. Now smile prettily at the gentleman, Sophie. 'Tis good for business."

And without further instructions, he seized her hand and strode purposefully through the auditorium, up a small flight of stairs, and through the backstage area to an office at the rear of the building.

After introductions were made, the rotund John Arthur, a one-time comedian, surveyed her from head to toe.

"Could be more buxom for my taste," Mr. Arthur commented bluntly as if Sophie were somewhere else, "but she's pretty enough, I suppose. Take her to wardrobe and fit her out in one of those milkmaid gowns." He eyed her chest area critically. "Tell Maude to rig up a corselet . . . *that* might push 'em up a bit." He waved a plump hand distractedly. "You'll be working with Nancy Quinn. Be here five o'clock sharp on the nights we play."

"Yes sir," Sophie said quickly. "Thank you, sir."

Sophie and Hunter moved toward the door.

"Oh, Robertson . . . tell Mrs. Piggott that if she doesn't do us the honor of rehearsing without the book by Wednesday, she'll be replaced by Miss Reed. Tell her I've seen her scribbling that play when she should be studying her role. I'm not paying her to be a bleeding scribe. *Tell her!*"

"Yes, sir," Hunter said and walked quickly out of the manager's office with Sophie in tow.

"For a comedian, he's not very amusing," Sophie said in a low voice as Hunter ushered her down a dark passageway and into a room with a variety of costumes hanging on wall pegs.

An ancient crone sat stitching a swath of moth-eaten ermine onto a velvet cloak in the dim light of the wardrobe chamber.

"Maude," announced Hunter, "this is Sophie McGann, our new Orange Girl. Arthur says, dress her as a milkmaid. Oh, and give her one of those corselet contraptions to push up her breasts so *they'll* look like oranges."

"*Hunter!*" Sophie exclaimed.

Hunter shrugged, grinning.

"'Tis not to *my* taste," he retorted, referring to Mr. Arthur's earlier assessment of Sophie's anatomical shortcomings, "but the man appreciates large mammaries . . . what can we do?"

Sophie giggled in spite of herself and Hunter smiled, seeing that her good humor had returned. She followed the wardrobe mistress to a corner where she was given an orange-and-white striped skirt with several gauze petticoats and a skimpy white blouse with a matching orange laced corset that fitted tightly around her rib cage. The ensemble did, indeed, thrust her breasts to their highest possible elevation. When she stepped from behind the changing screen, Hunter emitted a low whistle.

"Well . . . my, my . . ." he said with a lascivious smirk. "'Tis a miracle of engineering, my dear, but quite effective. You're bound to make those macaronis take notice, so beware!"

"I . . . c-can . . . hardly *breathe!*" she gulped.

"Good," Hunter retorted. "That means 'twill be difficult for you to *talk* and you'll find yourself in less trouble. Would you care to change out of those clothes and take some refreshment with me? I've an hour or two free."

Before Sophie could answer, Mavis Piggott suddenly entered the room. Hastily, the younger woman retreated behind the changing screen.

"Oh, Hunter . . . there you are!" she heard Mavis say.

"You're not due for a fitting as far as I know," Hunter replied tersely.

"No, but you're long over due to take me to the Pump

Room. 'Tis been ages since we went there, darling," she cajoled him. "I'm feeling a bit peckish. We could drink the waters and then have a nice afternoon tea. Besides, I have something *most* important to tell you."

"I'm afraid I—"

"Thank you so much for all your help, Hunter," Sophie interjected brightly, emerging once again from behind the screen. "Oh, hello, Mavis. I'll just be on my way."

And before Hunter could stop her, she bolted for the door, leaving him to arrange to take his midday meal with the mother of his child. In Sophie's haste to escape out of earshot, she nearly collided with a middle-aged gentleman at the end of the passageway that led to the stage door.

"Oh, I beg pardon, sir," Sophie said, clutching his arm to regain her balance.

"'Tis quite all right," the man replied. He squinted at her through a round, metal-rimmed pair of spectacles.

"My name is Sophie McGann . . . I've just been hired as the new Orange Girl."

"Ah . . . yes . . . Robertson's friend from Edinburgh," he said. "My name's Edgar Bryan. I'm the prompter. I've heard a bit about you," he added obliquely.

"I expect you have," Sophie replied.

"First time working in the theater?" he asked.

"No, I printed and sold playbills at Drury Lane last season and helped Mr. Hopkins, the prompter, with his notes."

"You did?" Mr. Bryan said, his eyes brightening. "Well, if our season improves, perhaps I can persuade Mr. Arthur to put you on as my assistant. At the moment, we're doing no new plays . . . just the old tried and true. These people would rather soak in sulfur water with their fellow invalids than imbibe a bit of culture!"

"Too much holiday making," Sophie agreed. "Well, let's hope things improve for both of us." She searched his kindly face and asked him about lodgings. "I can't afford anything fancy . . . just a decent spot that has a fireplace to keep warm."

"I may know just the thing for you!" he said enthusiastically. "'Tis atop my favorite shop in all of Bath. Come. I shall treat you to tea."

Mr. Bryan donned his cloak, guided her past the stage door, and led her up Orchard Street. He motioned her through a small gate on the left that Sophie hadn't noticed in any of her trips up and down the road. It let out into a small paved rectangle fronted on three sides by attractive town houses.

"This is North Parade," he explained. "Your Mr. Garrick stays in this block when he comes to Bath for his gout," he added, pointing at a white door with a handsome brass knocker.

They proceeded down the street, entering a narrow alley Sophie recognized from her trek from the Bear Inn her first day in Bath.

"First we'll have a nice pot of tea," he said, pointing to a sign that said "Sally Lunn's Bath Buns," "and then I'll see if that garret room is still for lease."

"Does Mrs. Lunn own the entire building?" Sophie asked.

"Sally Lunn's been dead for near a century . . . but her sticky buns live on, thanks to Mrs. Hervey."

Sophie craned her neck to scan the four stories soaring above her head. She spied a small, square-paned window under a peaked roof. A delicious aroma of baked breads wafted into the alley. For its odor alone, Sophie thought the garret would be the most heavenly place to live—as long as she had a penny for a bun.

The pink-cheeked proprietress brought them their tea and drew up a chair to join their company.

"Aye, Mr. Bryan," she nodded. "The room's available. Not very large, it is, but cozy and warm."

"Well, this young miss is not very big herself, so perhaps it would suit."

"On your own, are you?" the woman who'd been introduced as Mrs. Hervey asked, eyeing Sophie closely.

"Yes, I'm the new Orange Girl at the Orchard Street Theater."

"Oh, I don't know, Mr. Bryan," Mrs. Hervey said doubtfully. "The Orange lassies tend to be light-o'-loves, you know . . ."

"Oh, please, Mrs. Hervey," Sophie implored, feeling an

unnerving sense of desperation. "I'm a very respectable person, my father was in trade as you are, he owned a book shop in Edinburgh. Please let me have the room! If you find I don't suit, you can chuck me right out into the North Parade."

Mrs. Hervey leaned back her head and laughed loudly. "All right, all right," she said, "the chamber's yours."

In early January, the week before the theater reopened, Sophie offered to help Mrs. Hervey serve in her shop. She had hired two sedan-chair bearers to fetch her trunk from Hunter's lodgings at a time she knew he would be at the theater and she was settled in her new upstairs room before he discovered she was gone. Without informing him where she was, she simply left him a note thanking him for his help and telling him she would see him opening night.

At five o'clock on the evening of Saturday, January 14, sedan chairs and carriages began jamming the narrow lane in front of the Orchard Street Theater as patrons or their servants sought seats on an unreserved basis. The scores of theatergoers were looking forward to an entertaining evening after the Christmas hiatus, and they jostled each other good-naturedly while streaming inside.

Sophie was pleased to have been assigned a position near the entrance marked "Boxes," which meant she'd have a wealthier clientele for her refreshments. One look at Nancy Quinn, assigned to the upper galleries by John Arthur, explained Sophie's own good fortune. Nancy was a young woman with gargantuan breasts that strained alarmingly against the top of her milkmaid costume. Her face, however, was ugly enough to have won her a role as one of the three witches in *Macbeth*.

"Oranges . . . Spanish oranges!" Sophie shouted loudly, just as she had learned to do when hawking playbills at Drury Lane. The throng was in a buying mood and she was kept busy cutting the fruit in sections and exchanging it for six pence.

"Two oranges, if you please, and an extra penny for a kiss," propositioned a dark-haired young buck decked out in frothy linen and an impeccably tailored sapphire brocade coat sporting deep cuffs and matching buttons. His companion's larger frame was handsomely attired in plush black velvet and an ivory satin waistcoat embellished with exquisite yellow and green embroidered flowers. He appeared a few years older than his fellow theatergoer, and made no attempt to engage Sophie in flirtatious banter. Instead he appeared to be surveying her exchange with his friend with detached amusement. Both men, Sophie thought admiringly, had excellent taste in clothes and obviously the money to purchase them.

"Oh, I'm so sorry, sir," Sophie replied saucily, accustomed to such bold advances from her days at Drury Lane, "only oranges are dispensed here tonight! But thank you for the compliment!"

"Well, Peter," remarked the more imposing gentleman to his crestfallen companion, "I'd say you've been rather neatly dismissed. Come, old boy . . . let us take our seats."

Smiling coolly, Sophie turned to aid her next customer as the pair moved on.

At the interval, the younger of the two returned, ostensibly to purchase another orange.

"With this hankering for oranges, you're certain to avoid the scurvy, sir," she laughed, handing him the neatly sectioned fruit.

"Ah . . . 'tis more than oranges that I crave," he smiled. "Would you do me the honor of allowing me to take you for some refreshment after the program?"

"'Tis most kind of you, but we are not acquainted," Sophie replied evenly.

"Well, do let me remedy the situation," riposted the dark-haired young gentleman who appeared to be in his midtwenties. "I am Peter Lindsay-Hoyt, Baronet. My companion is the Honorable Roderick Darnly, the earl of Llewelyn's second son. You've heard of that distinguished peer, I presume?"

Sophie surveyed the young man staring at her with such eagerness. He seemed the classic young aristocrat, full of confidence and bonhomie. She wagered silently that he had recently returned from the obligatory Grand Tour of the

Continent where he had undoubtedly acquired a penchant
for fine silk clothes cut in the latest fashion, as evidenced by
the cascade of lace at his collar and cuffs. His handsome face
was dusted with white rice powder and a tiny black patch
decorated his cheek. His jet black eyebrows arched over
dark brown eyes, giving his features a haughty look, although his manner toward Sophie exuded friendliness and a
fervent desire to become better acquainted.

"I ordinarily reside in London," Sophie replied to his
question concerning the youthful baronet's taller companion, "and I can't say the name of your friend's father is
familiar to me."

"So do *we*!" Sir Peter responded with enthusiasm. "Live
in London, I mean. How coincidental! You *must* agree to
allow me to escort you somewhere so we can share our impressions of that fascinating city."

"Are you a Londoner by birth?" she inquired, efficiently
slicing more oranges while she chatted with the engaging
young fellow.

"No, I come from York," he replied. "My grandfather's
Sir Thomas Hoyt, also a baronet. 'Twill be another title of
mine someday," he added with a sly wink.

"And your honorable companion?" she bantered.

"From Wales," Sir Peter responded hurriedly, as if he
feared she would be more enamored with an earl's son, even
if he wasn't the heir. "Sad to say, Darnly's older brother's in
line to inherit the family's vast coal fields in that wretched
backwater. Roderick prefers the pleasures of city life, as do
I. Now, what of my proposal?" he urged. "It would give me
the utmost enjoyment if you would accompany me to the
Silver Swan this evening."

"You're very kind," Sophie answered smiling, "but 'twill
be dreadfully late before my duties here are finished. Thank
you, no."

Sir Peter had a rather winning way about him, she
thought, watching a look of genuine disappointment flood
his features. She piled the orange sections on to a tray and
prepared to circulate to the far end of the foyer to pick up
any business she had missed. Undoubtedly, this likeable
young man sought a light-o'-love, not merely a dinner com-

panion—a common-enough practice among the swells who regularly attended the theater. Even so, it was pleasant to receive such an invitation, Sophie considered ruefully, especially in light of Mavis and Hunter's liaison. Inside the theater, she could hear the orchestra tuning up for another musical interlude.

"You'll miss that wonderful Hunter Robertson if you don't return to your box, sir," she added with a false note of cheer. "And now I fear I must bid you good night." Before Sir Peter Lindsay-Hoyt could utter another word, Sophie began calling out, "Oranges! Fresh oranges . . . six pence a piece. . . . Oranges!"

During the remaining two weeks of January, Sophie managed to avoid contact with Hunter and Mavis by remaining at the front of the theater tending to her duties, and then skipping out the foyer door each night before the actors had time to remove their paint and change out of their stage attire. Therefore, she had no hint of Hunter's response to the news Mavis would bear his child.

On the other hand, she saw more of Sir Peter and the tall, rather forbidding Roderick Darnly. Both men appeared to be avid playgoers, attending performances of *The Foundling* and *The Deuce Is in Him,* as well as the February debut of *Love Makes a Man* and *The Honest Yorkshireman.*

"You can't expect a northerner like me to miss such a presentation," Sir Peter said to Sophie as he lounged against a pillar in the foyer during the musical interval. "And besides, 'tis my passion, this playacting. I am writing a theatrical piece myself. 'Tis a capital amusement."

"You deem yourself the next Garrick or Colman?" she teased, "nay, another Shakespeare, perhaps?"

Peter looked at her steadily.

"You're not merely an Orange Girl, are you?" he said, his eyes kindling with warmth. "I mean, you've some education. You read and write, do you?"

"My milkmaid's attire didn't fool you, it seems," Sophie murmured with feigned disappointment. "Yes," she added matter-of-factly, "I have a fair hand and I am rather a good speller."

"I really would like to get to know you better," the young baronet said gently, clasping her hand in his. "Please, do allow me to take you to sup," he added earnestly. "Perhaps you would read my play and give me your opinion?"

Sophie met his gaze and thought briefly of Hunter and Mavis playing opposite each other in Act Four of *Love Makes a Man* inside the theater.

"Perhaps we could meet," she said moodily, extracting her hand from his and deftly slicing through another orange.

"Where may I find you?" Peter pressed.

"You may leave a message at Sally Lunn's," she parried.

"*When* may I see you?" he persisted.

A burst of applause from inside the theater hung in the air between them, the result of some amusing exchange between Hunter and Mavis performing together on stage.

"Tuesday next," Sophie replied decisively. "We've no rehearsals or a performance that night. I find that I am perfectly free."

Chapter 13

A driving sleet pierced the darkness cloaking Orchard Street as Sophie trudged the short distance from the theater to her lodgings. By the time she reached her garret room atop Sally Lunn's, the icy rain had turned to a light snow. During the night the wind rattled the square panes, interfering with her slumber. When, finally, she drifted off to sleep, she dreamed of Hunter and Mavis peering into a cradle, staring at a crying infant. In the early hours she rose from her frigid bed to retrieve two of Aunt Harriet's old shawls from her trunk to keep warm.

As dawn broke over the river Avon, the wind finally died down and Sophie dozed off once again. She had no idea what time it was when a loud pounding reverberated at her door, pulling her back to consciousness.

"Sophie! Sophie! 'Tis me . . . open the door!" someone was shouting. The pounding grew more insistent. "Sophie! Are you in there? *Sophie!*"

She stumbled out of bed, pulling a shawl around her shoulders.

"Who is it?" she mumbled sleepily, brushing her tangled hair from her eyes and leaning in a daze against the wall.

"Hunter. Sophie, I need to talk to you."

"'Tis Sunday," she muttered. "Early Sunday morning."

"'Tis one o'clock in the *afternoon*!" he retorted through a crack in the wooden door. "Been keeping late hours, have you?"

"'Tis no affair of yours *what* I've been doing, Hunter Robertson. Go away."

"Sophie, *please!*" he pleaded. "I've come on the authority of Mr. Arthur. Betsy Neep, one of the dancers, tipped up with the ague last night. She made it through the performance, but *tomorrow* night—" He halted midsentence and began pounding on her door again. "*Will you open this door?* Please," he added more civilly.

Sophie turned the key in the lock and cracked open the door.

"How did you discover my lodgings?" she demanded.

"Well, you've had the most extraordinary aroma of Bath buns hovering about you lately," he bantered. When she glared at him indignantly, he added quickly, "'Twas a *jest*, Sophie. I asked everyone in the company where you were hiding, and Mr. Bryan told me he'd found you this abode. May I *see* what kind of closet he secured for you? Or have you a visitor?" he asked suspiciously.

"I asked Mr. Bryan not to tell anyone."

"I had to pry it out of him. As this was an emergency, he finally relented. *Please* let me come in! I'm freezing out here. There's even some snow on the ground."

Sophie reluctantly opened her door. A blast of frosty air from the stairwell swept into the chamber as Hunter immediately walked over to her fireplace and began to ignite the coals with a flint he found on the hearthstone.

"God's teeth, but 'tis cold," he said, blowing on the coals to get them started.

"So a dancer has the ague. Why does that mean you must barge in here and—"

Hunter rose from tending the fire and turned to face her.

"You must dance with me Monday night," he said earnestly. "Time is short, and you're the only one who could do it."

"Go recruit Mavis," Sophie said flatly. "She thinks she can perform miracles on stage."

"Mavis has two left feet when it comes to dancing. Please, Sophie. 'Twould be a great favor to me."

"Hunter, you are granted more than enough favors from

women as it is," she retorted, pulling her shawl closer to her body.

"Sophie . . . I—I don't have *time* to discuss what the complications are between Mavis and me," he said distractedly, beginning to pace before the fire. His worried look was as gloomy as the weather outside her window.

"I suppose you're too preoccupied with this weighty crisis to squander precious moments on such a distasteful subject!" she retorted sarcastically. "See here, Hunter, this is nothing to do with Mavis. The mere *thought* of dancing on a stage terrifies me. I can't do it."

"You danced on the *street* in Edinburgh in front of crowds of people," he said with exasperation. "And you were dying to dance with me at Miss Nicky's Cotillion."

"'Twas different, that," she retorted, chagrined by the memory of remaining a wallflower at the dance.

"Why? Why was it different? These are simple Scottish dances you already know."

"Because—"

She couldn't bring herself to explain how she had been totally captivated by the brash young strolling player the first day they'd met or how much she longed to dance with Hunter that night when all the young women of Edinburgh were making cow eyes at him. But dance *on a stage*? With an audience staring at her, waiting for her to make a slip or a stumble? 'Twas too reminiscent of being called to the witness box to testify at her father's trial.

"I've persuaded John Arthur to pay you a pound a week for as long as you perform," he said, interrupting her disjointed reverie.

Sophie hated to admit that her profits from selling oranges had been quite meager. After paying Mrs. Hervey for her room and board and other incidentals, she hardly had a farthing to spare. She wondered how she would ever earn enough money to pay for her coach trip back to London when the theatrical season concluded in May. A pound a week was no small consideration.

"Do you think this dancer will be ill the entire week?" she asked sharply.

"I'm positive," Hunter replied enthusiastically. "She

sounded dreadful last night. Sneezed through the entire pas de deux!"

Sophie sighed and nodded.

"As long as you *swear* 'tis mostly steps you're sure I already know . . ."

"I'll change everything to make it that way!" he beamed. He looked around her spartan surroundings. "Quick now, get dressed in something simple you can dance in."

Hunter was true to his word. Before the afternoon was out he had simplified the steps of a dance that spoofed the foibles associated with Scottish thrift.

"You certainly toady to the English in this piece," Sophie commented disapprovingly, wiping her damp brow with a corner of her faded blue skirt.

"They buy the majority of tickets," he replied with a shrug. "Let's begin again, I want to go over that section where you pilfer the money out of my pocket . . ."

Hunter hummed the tune the orchestra would be playing and they ran through the steps once again. This time, Sophie thought with satisfaction, she was beginning to feel at ease with the simple musical playlet. Most of it was pantomime, and she felt exhilarated dancing with Hunter in such light-hearted fashion. For the first time in months, her spirits lifted. Suddenly, she found herself grinning as he played the role of a skinflint old swain in love with an avaricious lass determined to separate him from his money. As the routine concluded, Hunter picked her up under her arms and whirled her around in a dizzying circle.

"Brilliant, lass!" he chortled, allowing her body to fall against his as he set her back on her feet.

Sophie stared up at him, acutely aware that he had not removed his arms from around her waist. A strange current of emotion passed between them and as he inclined his head toward hers, she was certain that he intended to kiss her firmly on the lips.

Suddenly, loud clapping erupted from the back of the theater.

They sprang apart, startled and embarrassed.

Mavis Piggott, swathed in a stunning blue velvet cloak, strode through the auditorium toward the stage.

"What a little wonder she is," Mavis said sarcastically. "And I do mean little. She dances those jigs like a regular whirling dervish."

"What are you doing here?" Hunter demanded.

"I paid you a call, darling. When I found you not at your lodgings, there was only one other place you could be."

"Only one?" Hunter replied coolly.

From his distant demeanor, Sophie wondered whether he had yet learned that Mavis was with child. If he had, was he displeased?

"Have we finished?" Sophie asked quietly.

"Well . . . ah . . ." Hunter temporized.

"I didn't sleep well last night," she said quickly, "and this exercise has fatigued me. I'll just be going."

"Be here at ten tomorrow morning for a final rehearsal," Hunter ordered. "No social engagements this evening, mind you," he added sharply. "You'll need every ounce of energy you've got for tomorrow night."

"So will *you*," Sophie retorted sharply, looking pointedly at Mavis. Before Hunter could reply, she quickly departed.

Sophie felt physically ill as she began calling out her wares in the theater foyer. Hunter's "Entertainments" were scheduled after the presentation of the comedy *All in the Wrong,* but already, her skin had begun to feel clammy with stage fright. Even so, she could not afford to pass up an opportunity to earn a bit of extra money and resigned herself to her fate.

"Oranges . . . Spanish oranges . . . six pence for delicious oranges!" she called, feeling her stomach churn alarmingly at the thought of her imminent performance.

"Sophie, my dear, 'tis all the talk in Bath, this debut of yours," Sir Peter Lindsay-Hoyt exclaimed, sauntering to her side with the imposing Roderick Darnly, the Earl of Llewelyn's second son, in his wake. " 'For the first time on any stage! Sophie, the Orange Girl!' " he said, quoting the placard affixed to the theater outside.

"'Tis a tiny part . . . and I'm filling in only until some poor lass recovers from the ague," she explained hastily.

"Well, we shall be your faithful supporters, cheering you on from our box," Roderick Darnly commented with apparent gravity. But his cool appraisal of her face, figure, and ridiculous milkmaid costume did little to bolster her confidence.

"Well, I'd best be getting back stage," she said nervously.

Before she realized what Peter was doing, the baronet had seized her hand and brought it to his lips.

"All good luck, Sophie," he murmured over her fingers. "And I hope you won't forget our plan to meet tomorrow. We can show you all the pleasure spots of Bath and you can read a bit of my play, eh what, Darnly?"

"Miss McGann seems in little need of the medicinal baths, but perhaps tomorrow night's ball might amuse her," Darnly suggested as he raised a scented handkerchief to his aquiline nose.

Sophie stared at the two men, chagrined.

"Oh, I'm terribly sorry," she apologized. "I'm sure I must rehearse. I've a new piece to learn."

"Ah, yes . . . the budding player," Roderick Darnly interrupted. "Another time, perhaps. Come, sir . . . we must take our seats."

Sophie turned over her remaining oranges to Nancy Quinn and dashed out the front door. She bolted down Orchard Street and reentered the theater at the stage door just in time to hear the restless audience hissing something happening on stage that displeased them. Ten minutes later, she was staring, white faced, into the peer glass while the character actress, Mrs. Lee, helped arrange her coiffeur.

"Here, dearie," she said, brandishing a comb. "Let a few of those charming auburn ringlets cascade down your pretty neck."

"Ready?" a masculine voice called urgently from the threshold.

Sophie turned to face her dancing partner who stood waiting at the door, outfitted as an old man with makeup to match.

"I-I'm shaking . . ." Sophie choked. She was amazed by

the transformation of Hunter wrought by stage artifice. He wore a grizzled wig and he'd drawn deep age lines around his eyes. Other charcoal marks extended from the corners of his nose to the corners of his mouth. "You look a hundred and two!"

"And you look absolutely lovely," he said quietly, advancing into the chamber.

"Oh, Hunter," she wailed. "I c-can't do it! I can't face all those people. They've been *hissing*!"

"And well they should. They paid good siller to see *All in the Wrong* and Mavis hasn't bothered to learn her speeches. But no matter, Sophie," he added with mock solemnity. "There's no escape."

"Just smile, dearie," Mrs. Lee said, giving Sophie's hand a squeeze, "and they'll never look at your feet."

With the veteran player's advice ringing in her ears, Sophie allowed Hunter to take her by the hand and lead her to their stage left position to await their entrance. Mavis and her fellow actors were delivering the concluding lines to an audience that seemed more intent on chatting than watching the play. Sophie noticed Hunter's mouth had flattened out into a grim line, but he squeezed her perspiring palm encouragingly.

"Remember, you don't have to utter a word. Take Mrs. Lee's advice: just smile and dance," he said, sotto voce. "Leave everything else to me."

The applause was humiliatingly sparse as the actors took their bows. Mavis stalked off stage and nearly collided with them in the wings.

"Beastly crowd!" she said, looking furious. She scrutinized Sophie's appearance, adding maliciously, "They'll howl a novice like you right off the stage."

Before either Hunter or Sophie could reply, Mavis stormed off and the orchestra began the musical interlude before the second half of the evening's presentations—the much-heralded "Entertainments."

"All right, poppet," Hunter said in a low voice, adjusting his tam on his powdered gray locks, "grin and enjoy yourself."

"As if I *could*!" Sophie muttered, forcing an idiotic smile to her lips as she skipped on stage.

The crowd took its time to settle down, and Sophie could hear whispers buzzing from box to box. Soon, however, she began to concentrate on the simple dance steps and pantomime bits of comedy. An appreciative burst of laughter greeted her the first time she raided Hunter's coat pocket of gold ducats. The music played faster and faster and their droll jig sped to its farcical conclusion. Sophie gazed up at Hunter with a look bordering on amazement. The audience was not only clapping but actually stamping its feet with approval. The contrasting heights of the two dancers and the choreography's blatant buffoonery apparently rendered the portrayal of a Scottish skinflint amusing enough to please the crowd, especially one that had endured the lackluster comedy preceding the act. Finally, the tomfoolery concluded with Hunter chasing Sophie off the stage.

Panting with exertion in the wings, Sophie watched as Hunter hurled himself past the flies. As applause began to rumble across the foot candles, he turned, strode toward her and in an instant, swept her off her feet in a bear hug. Before she could even catch her breath, he set her back on her slippers. Then, slowly, deliberately, he brought his lips down hard against her own. He pressed a palm against each of her ears, blotting out the sound of the raucous cheers and encasing her in a new world of warmth and sensuality. He kissed her long and thoroughly until her legs felt wobbly and she found herself clinging to him fiercely and kissing him back. The audience was still cheering when they finally pulled away from each other, their breathing ragged. They exchanged a look of utter astonishment. Then, as if waking from a dream, Hunter seized her hand and dragged her back on stage where they acknowledged the applause with bows and curtsies.

At length, they exited toward the tiring-rooms, so short of breath they couldn't speak. A beaming Mr. Arthur clapped Hunter on the back and pinched Sophie's cheek approvingly. Hunter barely had time to give her a second hug before dashing to the men's tiring-room to prepare for another musical number. Sophie remained rooted to the spot, trying to still her pounding heart.

Sir Peter Lindsay-Hoyt and Lord Darnly were among the first audience members to greet Sophie in the Greenroom. As she accepted the young men's compliments, she could see Mavis out of the corner of her eye, striding toward Hunter the moment he entered the crowded chamber. The actress had changed into a magnificent gown of burgundy silk, its tight-waisted bodice and low-cut design revealing creamy breasts barely contained by the rich ruby fabric. Resolutely, Sophie turned her back on the pair's animated conversation and gave Peter her complete attention.

"You were a staggering success!" exclaimed the young baronet. "Darnly, wouldn't you call Sophie's debut brilliant?"

"She danced very prettily," his taciturn companion allowed, although Sophie sincerely doubted that he was overly impressed with any portion of the entertainments. She guessed Roderick Darnly was a young man of culture and sophisticated tastes. Bath's local diversions surely could not measure up to his high standard.

Despite her firm resolve to ignore the tête-à-tête taking place between Hunter and Mavis, Sophie couldn't help but stare at the actress as she folded her arm possessively around that of her companion and drew him out of the room.

Hunter Robertson freely dispenses kisses, to be sure, but he never even said a proper thank-you for my taking Betsy's part, Sophie fumed silently. She had a violent desire to fire a cannon through the door where he and Mavis had just disappeared.

"Have you learned whether you can come out with us on the morrow?" Peter asked eagerly, distracting her from brooding further over the couple's abrupt departure. "After all, we claimed you for a friend *before* your fame commenced . . ."

"I think 'fame' is a bit of an exaggeration," Sophie replied, trying to smile. "Actually, though," she informed her backstage admirers, "I've not been notified that I *must* rehearse tomorrow. If your offer still stands, I'd be delighted to join you."

❊

Sir Peter Lindsay-Hoyt and the Honorable Roderick Darnly rendezvoused with Sophie at the early hour of eight o'clock in the morning. Roderick Darnly's coach deposited the trio in front of the arched entrance to the King's and Queen's Bath adjacent to the celebrated Pump Room. Both men had cast an appreciative eye at the green velvet gown Sophie had wheedled out of Maude, the wardrobe mistress, before she'd departed the previous night from the theater.

"'Tis such a pity Beau Nash is no longer Master of Ceremonies," Peter commented on the demise of the legendary social dictator who had died two years earlier in 1762. "I think some of the standards of decorum in Bath have slipped, would you not agree, Darnly?"

Richard Nash had set strict rules of conduct and dress in the baths themselves, the Pump Room where visitors drank the medicinal waters, the card rooms and the assembly rooms. And he had been the only city official successful in forcing the sedan chair men to refrain from tossing their passengers out of their hired vehicles if they balked at paying exorbitant charges.

Inside, they parted company. A uniformed matron led Sophie to the changing room where she was handed an odd garment made of thin yellow canvas.

"'Tis stiff as a board and cut like a parson's gown. 'Twon't cling to the body when it gets wet, I guarantee it, miss," the matron added with a wink and handed her a chip hat made of finely woven straw and a handkerchief "to wipe the sweat from y'face."

Feeling slightly ludicrous in this bizarre costume, Sophie followed the matron down a stone-sided corridor, through an archway and into a hot, humid chamber, open to the air, where a steaming pool fed by natural hot springs stretched at her feet. She could hardly keep from laughing at the sight of Sir Peter and Roderick Darnly padding toward her dressed in drawers and waistcoats constructed of the same sort of thin canvas as was her gown.

"Not the most fetching attire, is it?" Darnly commented dryly.

Sophie had been shocked when first she'd discovered that men and women bathed together in these public spas, but now having seen the getup that was de rigueur, she thought them the least seductive garments imaginable.

"Cross Bath is a delightful temperature, don't you agree?" Peter informed her as an attendant assisted him down the steps and into the water. "At King's, one is all but parboiled!"

Steam was boiling up around Sophie and her costume ballooned out to absurd proportions as she teetered on the last step, nearly submerged in the stone-lined cauldron. Fortunately, she was able to grab on to a ring at pool side where she established her footing on the floor of the basin, floundering in water up to her neck. An opaque mist hovered over the bath itself and she could hear the strains of a string quartet playing Vivaldi. Viewing terraces overhead ringed the mineral pool. When the vapors parted occasionally, she could glimpse elegantly attired ladies and gents promenading in front of the bathers who were taking the waters below.

"Quite the thing, eh Sophie?" Peter laughed, eyeing the spectators. "'Tis nice to be able to socialize while the old pores cleanse themselves, don't you think? Lets out all the poisons, they say . . ."

"Takes some *in*, I'll wager," Darnly asserted. "Too many people with unidentified ailments in one place, if you ask me."

Sophie nodded, growing hotter by the moment. She retrieved her handkerchief from atop her straw hat and wiped her flushed face. Then, she scanned the crowded waters themselves, relieved to see several other women bobbing nearby and she smiled at them tentatively. "I must look frightful," she exclaimed, inspecting her wrinkled fingertips.

"You appear the lovely mermaid," Peter said gallantly, his own face flushed scarlet. "But let us repair to breakfast."

The female attendant took Sophie back to the dressing room where she was wrapped in a flannel blanket while she adjusted to the temperature outside the bath. Feeling somewhat faint, she sank down on a small bench and waited until she felt cooler before dressing. Soon, however, she'd recovered enough to join her escorts in front of the colonnaded bathing area.

"What say you we go to the chocolate house?" Peter proposed as Roderick Darnly. [hailed his coachman.]

Following a hearty repast of Bath buns, eggs and chocolate, the trio advanced to the Pump Room, an enormous chamber large enough to serve as a ballroom. Near one wall stood a tall fountain spilling warm mineral water of a slightly greenish tinge into a round stone basin.

"I drink three pints a day," Peter confided, his eyes briefly scanning the room on the lookout for any luminaries present.

"I never touch the stuff," said Darnly. "I can't help thinking there is some regurgitation from the baths into the cistern of this pump . . . can't abide the thought of quaffing water that's boiled diseased bodies in the preceding hours."

His observation was enough to convince Sophie she would do anything but accept Peter's invitation to sip the warm liquid.

"No thank you." She shuddered but was pleased to see she had earned an approving nod from the imperious Roderick Darnly.

Next, her two escorts led her on a leisurely walk along the Grand Parade, a gravel path that bordered the river Avon. The ice from the previous day's storm had melted and the temperature had become pleasant enough at midday to stroll outdoors. At half past three, Roderick guided them to an eating house on Kingsmead where they dined on mutton, followed by river fish and braised parsnips.

"Darnly and I prefer to arrive at the ball after eight," Peter announced, patting his stomach with a satisfied gesture. "That allows us time to return to our lodgings so you may scan a few pages of my play." Sophie gazed back at him, somewhat unsettled. "Oh, Sophie, for an Orange Girl, you can be such a goose," Peter laughed affectionately. "Darnly's housekeeper will make us tea and 'twill be all prim and proper, we assure you, don't we, Darnly?"

"Speak for yourself, Peter," Roderick Darnly said dryly.

At Sophie's raised eyebrow, he reached over and patted her hand. "I'm sure you shall be safe enough in our company, my dear."

Somehow, Sophie did not feel reassured, but as they had been so generous in entertaining her all day, she concluded the least she could do was skim Sir Peter's play. She was curious to see what he considered an amusing comedy.

Darnly's coach headed up Gay Street, away from the center of town, eventually entering the half-constructed Circus. It soon drew up in front of a handsome door in the solitary row of town houses that had been completed by the celebrated architect, John Wood, the Younger.

"The building will be so beautiful when 'tis finished," Sophie said in a breath, craning her neck to survey the graceful crescent of columns decorating the front facade.

A housekeeper dressed in black bombazine and a white batiste mobcap greeted them at the door and ushered them into a well-appointed sitting room whose fireplace crackled with glowing logs. Darnly and Sir Peter removed their coats and settled in front of the hearth with the day's journals, while Sophie was directed to a desk near the window.

"'*The Footmen's Conspiracy*,'" she said aloud, surveying the sheaf of papers in front of her. She swiveled in her straight-backed chair. "Well, I like the title . . ." She smiled encouragingly.

"Excellent!" Peter beamed, looking up from his reading. "Let's hope you find the rest of the tale amusing. 'Twas capital fun composing the thing. There's pen and a quill there," he added. "If you find gross errors—just change 'em!"

Sophie returned to the manuscript and began to read. Tea was brought in and she nodded her thanks to the housekeeper as the serving woman set a cup beside her on the desktop. Except for logs falling in the hearth as they burned to cinders, the only sound in the room was Sophie's pen scratching against the paper. She had to suppress a smile at Peter's atrocious spelling and some of the stiff, unnatural dialogue—not to mention the severe lack of plot—but she found the setting and characters reasonably engaging. It was, as Garrick would have called it, a noble effort by an amateur.

"Well?" Peter demanded as the shadows lengthened across the sitting room floor. "Your verdict, madam."

Sophie remained silent, gathering her thoughts in an effort to say something sensible.

"The lass is trying to be diplomatic," Darnly interjected. "Allow her time to think of something charitable."

Peter's dark brows knit together in consternation and Sophie hastened to say, "Really, that's quite unfair of you, Mr. Darnly. *The Footmen's Conspiracy* has some very appealing qualities. It wants a bit of story line, and I must admit, your spelling's fairly erratic, Sir Peter, but—"

"My dear, Sophie," the young baronet urged earnestly, "let's dispense with titles . . . 'Peter' will do nicely." He appeared pleased and excited by her gentle verdict. He glanced at his friend triumphantly. "See, Darnly, and you thought I was just an idle scribbler. Sophie, here, is *in* the theater! And she says the work has merit!" He rose from his chair and walked over to the desk. "I see you've made some changes," he noted, peering over her shoulder. "What a fine hand you have. Perhaps you'd be willing to check *all* the spelling . . . and recopy it. I'd pay you, of course. I wish to send it to George Colman before the month is out. Darnly, here, is thinking of purchasing a mortgage on some of Lacy's shares in Drury Lane. The man's always short of cash, is he not, Darnly?" he added, looking over at his companion, who merely gazed back at them expressionlessly. "If Darnly's an investor, that'll add a bit of push, won't it?" He smiled broadly. "With your help—and Roderick's—I just might become a proper playwright!"

"Sophie's corrected your spelling," Darnly said sardonically, "but she hasn't amended your plot."

"He could easily improve it," Sophie said suddenly, irritated by Roderick Darnly's veiled condescension, "if he wrote a scene where all the footmen gather to plan their revenge against the old skinflint character. It should be here," she said, pointing at a sheet of paper with many crossed out sections and additions, "at the beginning of the second act."

"Of course!" Peter agreed, nodding enthusiastically. "That's precisely what's needed. Perhaps you could jot down a few appropriate lines when you do the recopying?"

Sophie looked at her host narrowly.

"Are you engaging a copier or a collaborator?" she asked pointedly.

Peter Lindsay-Hoyt flushed and glanced over at Darnly.

"A collaborator, to be sure," Roderick laughed. "I've enjoyed dabbling in a bit of play writing myself," he avowed, "for little entertainments put on at my club. I've found that two heads are always much better than one . . . and that's especially true in your case, Peter. I suggest you sign her on immediately as your coauthor."

"If you think so," Peter said tentatively. Then he glanced down at all the additions and deletions he had made in his struggle to put his work on paper. He sighed. "Right, then. 'Tis agreed." Suddenly he smiled at both of them with renewed enthusiasm. "Together, Sophie and I shall rewrite this play!"

Chapter 14

Over a glass of champagne provided by Roderick Darnly, Sophie and Sir Peter toasted their agreement to work together to improve *The Footmen's Conspiracy*. Then, as dusk deepened into evening, the three departed for Harrison's Assembly Rooms situated on the east side of Terrace Walk overlooking a formal garden that bordered the river Avon.

Sophie was astonished at the sheer size of the ballroom. It appeared to be nearly a hundred feet in length and its stucco ceilings more than thirty feet high. Huge, ornate crystal chandeliers hung over the wooden dance floor at intervals of twenty feet.

"We shall take tea later," Peter advised, his heightened color betraying his excitement at being part of the lively scene whirling around them. "But first, let's stroll around the ballroom to determine if there is anyone here worthy of notice," he joked.

Ladies adorned in a rainbow of silks and brocades chatted behind fans or sat on straight-backed chairs carved in Queen Anne style and traded the latest gossip and scandal. Scores of gents in white wigs conversed with their companions or clustered around the faro and piquet tables in the enormous card room that featured a coved ceiling. Both chambers were graced with portraits of the late Beau Nash.

"Tell me true, Sophie," Peter enthused, "have you seen anything like this in Edinburgh? 'Tis grand, is it not?" A string orchestra began to play a minuet, a tedious exercise performed by a solitary couple in the middle of the ballroom under the scrutiny of countless critical eyes. Flanked by Sir Peter and Roderick Darnly, Sophie admired the dancers' straight backs and precise footwork, though the performers certainly didn't appear to be deriving much enjoyment from the exercise. "The country dances will start soon," Peter assured her. "Ah . . . there's the tune for 'Drops of Brandy.' Come."

After several lively dances partnered first by Peter then by Darnly, Sophie had become quite flushed and the perspiration had dampened her green velvet gown. Suddenly, she spotted Hunter and Mavis standing among the onlookers. Hunter was scowling, and before Sophie could compose her thoughts, he murmured something in Mavis's ear and advanced to where they were standing.

"May I have the honor of this dance?" he addressed Sophie stiffly, without deigning to look at her two escorts.

"At your service," Roderick Darnly murmured, and melted into the crowd with a disgruntled Peter in tow.

"That was a rather rude performance," Sophie commented icily. "You've not even been introduced and you—"

"I can just imagine their unsavory reputations," Hunter said dourly nodding at their retreating backs, "even if you can't."

"The friendships I enjoy are certainly no business of yours," Sophie retorted. Out of the corner of her eye she could see Mavis staring at them with a look of murderous indignation. "I believe your own companion finds her abandonment quite intolerable," Sophie added pointedly, vexed at Hunter's presumption that she was some rustic—helpless prey to these gentlemen of means.

Hunter narrowed his blue eyes and, instead of joining the crowd on the dance floor, he led Sophie out of the ballroom and into an alcove guarded by a potted plant.

"I came to fetch you to rehearsal this morning and Mrs. Hervey said two overdressed dandies had called for you earlier to take you to the baths," he declared angrily. "It took me less than two minutes and a few shillings to determine which coachman at the Cross Baths was liveried to the Earl of Llewelyn's son."

"How very clever of you," Sophie replied sarcastically. "And how unnecessary. As you apparently know, I have been treated to the entertainments of Bath by these two delightful gentlemen and have no need of a *third* escort. Especially one who is already engaged," she added.

"Those 'delightful gentlemen,' as you call them, are probably a couple of bounders whose creditors will be arriving on the next coach!"

"Roderick Darnly has his own town house in the Circus!" Sophie retorted scornfully. "His credit must be good enough for that!"

"Ah . . . so you've gone to his lodgings, have you?" Hunter countered. "I never expected you to be that idiotic."

"The housekeeper was there the entire time," Sophie replied defensively. "I was merely correcting Peter's spelling on a play he's composed."

" 'Peter' is it now?" Hunter mimicked. "Honestly, Sophie, do I have to draw a sketch for you about the danger to your reputation—nay, the danger to your very *person*—that you risk consorting with such scoundrels?"

"How *dare* you call Sir Peter and Roderick Darnly scoundrels!" Sophie replied heatedly. "When it comes to exploiting women, I'd say *you're* the rapscallion of record! Now, if you'll excuse me—"

"I'm warning you, Sophie . . . I know a few things about the type of company you keep," Hunter said, grabbing her arm.

"And I know something about the company *you* keep," she retorted, yanking free of his grasp. "Now, will you please escort me back to my friends and pray, cease your carping."

"I wish to rehearse the companion dance to *High Life Below the Stairs* tomorrow, ten o'clock sharp," Hunter said, his jaw clenched. "And afterward, I think we should have a serious talk."

"I shall be at Orchard Street at the appointed hour," Sophie replied, straining for composure, "but frankly, Hunter, we've nothing to discuss."

In response, he tucked her arm roughly in his and strode toward a table where a fruit punch was being dispensed.

Mavis apparently could not contain her impatience another moment as she now was stalking toward them across the wide dance floor.

"Betsy Neep is still quite ill. I will also need you at the theater for the entre-act to *Catherine and Petruchio*, which we're performing February twentieth," Hunter declared.

They had arrived at the punch table amid the milling crowd where they encountered Roderick Darnly conversing with several elegantly dressed young bucks of a similar stripe.

"February twentieth's my birthday!" Sophie protested, and then calculated that she would need every shilling to survive until she returned to London. "Oh, never mind . . . I'll be there."

Mavis strode up to Hunter and took his other arm.

"Have you given Sophie the news?" she asked archly.

Sophie stared at Hunter, dreading an announcement of their impending nuptials.

"Mr. Arthur regrets to inform us," he said slowly, "that the theater will be closed most of March and half of April for what he's indicated is a need for urgent repairs."

"*What?*" Sophie said, startled.

"Actually, our manager has spent as much time in these card rooms," Hunter said bitterly, "as he has at the Orchard Street Theater. He is embarrassed by debts and cannot pay us beyond February twentieth."

"The wretch goes to Bristol to play in two comedies to cover his losses," Mavis said disdainfully, "and the rest of us must fare as best we can!"

Just then, Peter Lindsay-Hoyt sauntered out of the very card room that figured in their discussion and joined his friend Darnly, who was standing just a few feet from where Hunter, Mavis, and Sophie had been exchanging words.

"Ah, Sophie," Peter said, eyeing her companions suspiciously. "I feared some common vagabond had snatched you away."

Hunter drew himself up to his full height and glared down at the youthful baronet. It was common knowledge that actors were the legal equivalent of what the government was wont to term, "rogues, vagabonds, and vagrants," and

Peter's comment came perilously close to an out-and-out insult.

"Actually, I feared some coxcomb had exhausted her patience and thus I came to inquire of Miss McGann if all were well," Hunter retorted, as his affront found its mark. He turned to Sophie and added, "I trust I shall see you at the theater at ten o'clock on the morrow?"

"Ten o'clock," Sophie murmured, wondering how in the world she would be able to pay what she owed Mrs. Hervey during the weeks the Orchard Street Theater would be dark. Her eyes somberly followed Hunter and Mavis's retreat.

"'Tis plain to see that actor and his lady have upset you," Darnly observed. "Did I hear that rogue expects you to perform on your birthday? Poor you."

"'Tis of no consequence," Sophie murmured. "What *is* disturbing is that the Orchard Street Theater is closing for six weeks," she sighed. "'Tis bad news for players and house servants alike."

"Not to worry, Sophie!" Peter countered enthusiastically. "In fact, it couldn't have come at a better time! Now you can devote yourself entirely to *The Footmen's Conspiracy*!"

※

Oddly, the next few times Sophie and Hunter were forced to rehearse the musical pieces scheduled for the final performances in February, it was Hunter who avoided discussion of any serious topics. Sophie had been girding herself for an unpleasant dissection of Hunter's entanglement with Mavis, but strangely, he gave no indication now that he wished to take up the delicate subject. Instead, he kept relations strictly professional and she reluctantly decided 'twas all for the best.

On Monday, February 20, a simple nosegay of hothouse violets was left without a card at her door. She was touched to have her birthday remembered and thanked Peter for his thoughtfulness when he called to escort her for a celebratory breakfast.

Sir Peter smiled when she inquired if he had been her benefactor. "Players frequently receive flowers from their admirers. I'm delighted you like them. And as tonight is your last performance for a while," he added eagerly, "I presume I will be employing your copying services as of tomorrow?"

"My *collaborative* services, don't you mean?" Sophie chided gently. It was their first meeting out of the presence of his constant companion, Roderick Darnly. "I think 'twould be best if we are perfectly frank with each other, Sir Peter," she said formally, looking directly into his dark brown eyes that were fringed with short, stubby black lashes.

"Just 'Peter' will suffice," he reminded her softly, sipping his cup of chocolate.

"For your part," she continued, unsettled by the intimate tone of his voice, "you bring the basic idea and some amusing characters to this effort. I contribute my experience of stagecraft, and some literary and copying skills. 'Tis an *equal* partnership," she pronounced, ". . . or *must* be, that is, if we are to proceed."

Peter's gaze turned away from her face and focused on his cup of steaming chocolate.

"Well, Sophie, your suggestions for the piece do seem awfully clever, but, after all, 'twas *my* idea at bottom."

"Yes, and I can assure you, sir," she replied briskly, "that if you take this play as you originally wrote it and submit it to a Colman or a Garrick, you will receive an ever-so-polite note of rejection!" She leaned forward over the small table separating them. "You must decide if you merely wish to dabble so you can tell your friends you've composed a play, or bear down and do the *real* work of play writing—which is *re*writing. I've seen it often enough with writers such as Mrs. Sheridan and Mrs. Clive . . . this business of creating frothy diversions for the stage requires real *effort.* 'Tis not merely some amusement that just anyone can bring off. 'Tis hard, brain-cracking *work!*" She looked at him kindly. "Why not think about it further and let me know what you decide?"

For the first time in their acquaintance, Peter looked discomforted. He toyed with his knife, carving marks in the snowy table linen. Then, he set the knife down purposefully and glanced up at her, a lazy smile spreading across his face.

"You are a hard taskmistress, Sophie, but how can I resist?" he said softly. "'Tis time I did something useful with myself. Starting tomorrow, we are collaborators."

"And we will share in the credit and profits equally?" she persisted. "I will waive my fee for copying, since you've so kindly had me as your guest these several times."

He bit his lip, as if deep in thought. Then he reached over and took her hands in his, intimately lacing their fingers together.

"You're a clever lass," he said finally. "I admire that."

The dance divertissements following the performance of *Catherine and Petruchio* were well received by the audience that evening, but there was no repeat of the passionate kiss between Hunter and Sophie at the conclusion. Sophie bade farewell to her friends in the Orchard Street Company, realizing several of them could not afford to wait out the hiatus until the theater reopened in six weeks' time—and would move on. Hunter was still in the tiring-room when Sophie ducked out the stage door on her birthday eve and walked home alone in the chill February night air.

During the next few weeks, a daily routine began to emerge. Roderick Darnly sent his coach each morning around ten to fetch Sophie to his lodgings while he and Peter took the baths, had their breakfast, and then enjoyed a morning constitutional. Sophie sat at the lovely desk in Darnly's sitting room, recopying sections of the manuscript. She was perfectly aware that most of the changes and suggestions were hers. However, the basic idea, as Peter had pointed out, remained his, and Sophie felt that with their understanding of an equal partnership, the arrangement would be mutually satisfactory.

At around three o'clock each afternoon, Darnly's coach returned to the Circus to collect Sophie and deposit her at whatever eating house or tea shop the men had selected that particular day. After a delicious meal that her two companions insisted on providing, Sophie briefly informed them of the progress of her work. Peter would then respond to the changes she'd made on the manuscript the previous day and offer his opinion on the additions she planned to write during the next scheduled working session. For his part, Roderick Darnly appeared to have carefully scanned every revision she'd left on the desk in his sitting room.

"'Tis immensely improved," Roderick commented one day when they were having tea in the Pump Room itself. Tables dotted one end of the large chamber and a stringed quartet played on a balcony overhead in counterpoint to the splashing mineral water cascading from the famous Bath cistern. While they chatted and sipped their tea, a progression of invalids arrived on crutches or in wheeled chairs to imbibe the murky green liquid. "Who knows, Peter?" he said mockingly, "you may find yourself with a genuine profession. You're lucky to have found an author willing to put herself at your disposal."

"I'm not a proven scribe," Sophie said modestly, but she was nevertheless pleased by Darnly's good opinion. The man was highly educated, despite his apparent preference for a life of idleness, and she valued his judgment on matters of literature and culture. "I think 'tis coming along remarkably well," she opined. She toyed with her fork, poking a tine into the rich crust of her treacle tart. "We still must solve the problem of revealing the truth about Sir Bottomley's deceased wife in the last act," she mused, even as her thoughts drifted from the idle chatter.

"You'll devise something," Peter replied, focusing his attention on a group of fashionables who had arrived for tea at the next table. "The sooner we post this play to Drury Lane, the better for our purse, eh what?"

The need for funds was certainly Sophie's motivation for completing the assignment, and she toiled long and hard over the last act of *The Footmen's Conspiracy.* Peter and his wealthy friend had saved her the expense of her meals, but the money she had earned as an Orange Girl and as Hunter's dancing partner went directly to pay for the other necessities of life, including Mrs. Hervey's lodgings. Sophie worried that she would have nothing left by the time she intended to leave for London, at the end of May. Lorna had written that

she was just managing to cover expenses from sales at
Ashby's Books.

> I fear I've virtually no gossip, nor have I even heard
> mention in recent months of anything concerning
> your pamphlet. Dr. Monro is silent, so I hope this
> means 'twill be safe for you to return soon.
> As for your Aunt Harriet, I do apologize for having
> no news to convey, but I fear to stir up trouble where
> none exists by visiting Bedlam.
> Ashby's muddles along, as do I as your printer's mate
> . . . G. Garrick is as sour as ever, but Mary Ann
> Skene and I continue to ply your playbills.

Sophie dispatched a letter of grateful thanks, and subsequently doubled her efforts to craft the comedy into a work
she hoped would appeal to the managers at Drury Lane.

By mid-April, less than a week before John Arthur
planned to reopen Orchard Street for a month of performances before the summer, Sophie had finished rewriting,
editing, and copying *The Footmen's Conspiracy*.

"If it satisfies you, Peter," she said at last, handing him
the neatly penned sheaves, "I think we should immediately
send it to Colman for his consideration for next season's
repertory."

After a good night's sleep, Sophie awoke refreshed and
buoyed by a tremendous sense of accomplishment. She and
Peter had actually written a *play*! She arrived at Darnly's flat
to find him penning a letter at his desk and Peter bundling
up the precious manuscript into a packet wrapped with thin
cord.

"I have written a note to Lacy to include in the packet
you're sending to Drury Lane," Roderick announced, dusting his missive with sand to dry the ink, folding it, and sealing it with his waxed crest. He slipped the letter inside the
open end of the parcel and Peter tied the knot, patting the
bundle with satisfaction.

"Let us hope your kind words will encourage Colman to
view the play with some favor," Peter said jovially to
Darnly.

"You are truly kind, sir, to smooth the way for us," Sophie said to Darnly. She remembered all too well the pile of unsolicited plays forever cluttering the managers' desk. "Peter and I will need every bit of support to call attention to our fledgling offspring." She smiled. "Perhaps David Garrick himself will return from abroad soon and find the piece has some promise."

Peter and Roderick nodded in unison.

"We've each done everything we can to promote its success, my dear," Roderick Darnly assured her. "Shall I ring for the coach so we may dispatch this precious cargo ourselves, posthaste?"

"Hear! Hear!" Peter said, giving Sophie's hand a happy squeeze.

Within a few minutes the threesome was bumping along Milsom Street in Darnly's carriage, heading toward the Bear Inn, the point of departure for the *London Fly*. Arriving in Stall Street, they climbed out of their vehicle to ensure that the ruddy-faced coachman stored the manuscript in a trunk under his seat. Just as Darnly was handing the man a generous tip to ensure the play's safe delivery to Colman at Drury Lane, Sophie glanced across the street and was startled to see Hunter Robertson marching toward them with a news journal rolled under his arm and a scowl on his face.

"And where are *you* going, may I ask?" he demanded heatedly of Sophie, with a glance at the enormous coach that would soon pull away from the inn, heading for the London Road.

"I am not going anywhere," Sophie replied, surprised and unsettled by his unexpected appearance.

"Excuse me, sir," Peter interjected coldly, "but you have no cause to accost Miss McGann in such a surly fashion."

"I have every cause in the world to protect her from gentlemen of your stripe," Hunter replied as he stared down at Peter with a look of murderous intent.

Peter reacted with shock at his insolence, but, surprisingly, Roderick Darnly intervened with deliberate tact.

"Now, now . . . let us not be bumptious with each other on such a glorious day," he said, eyeing Hunter's superior height and well-developed physique. "Aren't you

Hunter Robertson . . . that fine performer I've seen at the theater here?" Hunter remained silent and bestowed a look of contempt on both men. "I do believe, Peter, that we should allow Mr. Robertson the opportunity to converse with Miss McGann. You must admit we've been monopolizing her of late."

Peter's mouth fell open in protest, but Darnly took his friend's arm firmly in his own. Sophie had heard enough about deadly duels fought on the outskirts of Bath to realize that Darnly was anxious to avoid a needless—and possibly dangerous—confrontation between his agitated friend and the hot-tempered actor.

"Do, please, make use of my coach," Darnly added quickly, indicating the fine equipage that stood nearby. "Why not take the young lady home, and then ask Charles to convey you to wherever is convenient for you, sir? Lindsay-Hoyt and I will enjoy this fine spring day with a walk on the Grand Parade. Please be so kind as to direct my driver to meet us at the bridge in an hour's time. Good day to you both."

And before any of them could challenge Darnly's directives, he had Peter in tow and was headed down the road in the direction of the river Avon.

"Well, at least one of your dandified friends has some sense!" Hunter exclaimed, holding the coach door open and indicating Sophie should step inside.

"Of all the absolute *gall*—" Sophie sputtered, refusing to budge.

"Get in," Hunter commanded.

"I will not, you overbearing oaf!"

Without replying, Hunter unceremoniously lifted her by the waist, thrust her bodily in the coach and climbed in behind her, slamming the door. Shouting through the window, he instructed the coachman to drive to North Parade.

"I thought you were boarding the *London Fly*," Hunter explained in a calmer tone as the coach and horses responded to the driver's whip. "I was angry and worried and, frankly, dismayed to see you play the harlot with those two rogues."

"Harlot! Rogues?" Sophie responded furiously. "How *dare* you accuse me thus. What is your proof?"

"Peter Lindsay-Hoyt is no doubt a blackguard with debts from here to Trafalgar Square, and Roderick Darnly, I've heard rumored, is a mysterious string puller who as far as I can tell hasn't a decent chap he can call a friend."

"You've been *spying* on me!" Sophie exclaimed.

"Of course I have, you little ninny!"

"And *you're* the greatest blockhead I ever—"

"So, you claim you were *not* about to leave Bath without saying farewell?" he interrupted.

"Not *today*, I wasn't!"

"I haven't seen you these last weeks," he said, staring at her gravely across the swaying coach.

"No, you haven't," Sophie confirmed irritably.

"I brought you flowers for your birthday and received no acknowledgment."

She stared at him blankly, and then remembered the violets delivered to her door that Peter allowed her to assume he'd sent.

"There was no card, so I could hardly extend my thanks."

"You've been avoiding me," Hunter insisted.

"I have," she agreed, daring to meet his steady gaze.

"Why?"

"I think you know why," she said quietly, lowering her eyes to her lap.

"I want you to *tell* me," he demanded.

"God's wounds, Hunter!" she retorted, looking up at him and feeling her temper rise. "You've got Mavis Piggott with child! All three of us know it, and that should be enough answer for you!"

Hunter scowled at her.

"That is the situation she claims is the case," he said darkly.

"You deny that you were lovers?" Sophie cried, astonished that he would disavow his own offspring.

"No, I do not deny *that*," he retorted, "but I *do* deny that she is enceinte with *my* child."

"So . . . the jade carries another man's child," said Sophie in a low, angry tone. "Your masculine pride has been dealt a blow, and thus—in exchange for a few kisses—you think that *I* should be your willing strumpet whenever you feel randy and Mavis is in another man's bed! Good God, Hunter, you take me for a fool!"

"Surely I do *not*! That is *not* the bond that exists between us," he responded, his eyes flashing, "and well you know it!"

Sophie was too shocked by the vehemence in his voice to reply. Instead, she merely stared at him, horrified at what, to her, seemed a callous response to the inevitable outcome of the intimacy Hunter and Mavis had shared these last months. The carriage turned into York Street near Sally Lunn's. She extended her hand and knocked smartly on the roof overhead to signal to the coachman to halt his vehicle.

"I'll just get out here," she mumbled, leaning toward the door.

As her fingers reached for the handle, Hunter grasped them in his own and propelled himself onto the same bench seat where she was perched, poised for a hasty exit. Without warning, he crushed her against his chest and began kissing her hair, her forehead, and finally her lips, as if to tell her something his words were powerless to convey.

"Stop!" Sophie gasped, pushing against his chest. "You can't blot out all that's happened like that—"

But that was exactly what he seemed to be attempting to accomplish, obliterating whatever sanity either of them possessed with bruising lips that bespoke some desperate longing.

"Until you came to Bath, I tried to convince myself you were merely a child," he murmured.

"Well, I'm *not*!" she gasped between kisses. "I'm not some little sister you can pat on the head, or kiss and then ignore."

"How well I know!" he whispered hoarsely, at last releasing her. "I've wanted you since the day I threw those placards into the fire at your father's shop and bundled you into that wicker trunk to make your escape. I just refused to see it."

"And now, 'tis too late," she said dully, smoothing her hair off her forehead and inhaling deeply to gain control of her emotions.

"No!" he replied angrily. "Come home with me. Right now!"

The coach had rolled to a halt in front of Sally Lunn's and horses and driver waited patiently for the carriage door to open.

"I cannot do that," she insisted quietly. "And if you refuse to confront the consequences of your liaison with Mavis Piggott, to my way of thinking, you're the same breed of men you call blackguards."

And with that, Sophie jumped from the steps to the ground. Her eyes were filled with a sadness beyond tears as she left Hunter sitting alone in Roderick Darnly's elegant coach.

The dancer, Betsy Neep, once recovered from the ague, had drifted off to Bristol with a promise of better parts at the playhouse there. Sophie and Hunter were required to rehearse the musical divertissements to prepare for the theater's reopening at the end of April. Rehearsals became awkward exercises, with each of them speaking only when absolutely necessary. Once the Orchard Street Theater was back in business, Mavis Piggott's ill-temper added to the miserable atmosphere around the place.

"Those rustics!" she spat, storming into the women's tiring-room after being roundly hissed in *Romeo and Juliet*. "All they want is for a simpering dolt-of-a-Juliet to kill herself and be done with it!"

"I was told that two earls and a marquess were in the audience tonight," Mrs. Lee announced cuttingly. "They are hardly peasants, my dear. Perhaps your strident interpretation of the role is not to everyone's taste?"

"Oh, do be *still*!" Mavis said loudly. She shed her diaphanous Juliet costume and suddenly Sophie was struck by how slender she was for a woman four or five months gone with child. "Well," she announced importantly, "at least I have received *some* good news . . . a celebrated manager has just written that he will mount my play in the autumn." She cast a triumphant glance in Sophie's direction. "So, Hunter and I won't be forced to tread these boards next season, saints be praised."

Sophie was shaken by pure, unadulterated envy, then ashamed to admit to herself how much she begrudged her rival's success. When she and Hunter had performed their duo, she retired to the dressing room without a word, feeling utterly friendless.

Within minutes, a stage servant informed her of a visitor waiting for her in the Greenroom. Hastily, she made her way past clusters of stage furniture in the wings and poked her head into the actors' reception chamber.

"Mrs. Sheridan!" she exclaimed, her spirits brightening for the first time in days. "How lovely to see you!"

"And you, dear child," Frances Sheridan greeted her warmly. "I've come to congratulate you on your dancing tonight and to ask you to come to tea soon, if you have time. We've taken lodgings on King Street."

"Of course," Sophie replied eagerly. "I'd so love to spend some time with you. Would tomorrow afternoon around three suit?"

"Excellent!" Mrs. Sheridan replied. "Till tomorrow then."

※

Sophie arrived promptly at the Sheridans' rather humble lodgings at Number 9 King Street. The two women had hardly begun to sip their tea before Sophie confided in Frances about the rift with Hunter and the play she had rewritten with Peter Lindsay-Hoyt.

"I suppose Mavis's success on so many fronts has made me wish violently for my own," she acknowledged with a rueful smile. "Yet I felt so ashamed of that rush of jealousy when I heard someone was to mount her play."

"Who knows better than *I* what a harridan Mavis Piggott can be?" Mrs. Sheridan said. "But remember, Sophie, whatever you write, 'tis *your* unique vision. No one sees the world through your eyes, nor you through theirs," she smiled encouragingly. "So, you needn't fear that Mavis's success precludes your own. And speaking of that," she added, pulling some sheaves of papers from a nearby desk drawer. "I've finished the first three acts of a new comedy I call *Journey to Bath*."

"You've not given up on play writing then!" Sophie said, beaming. "Oh, I'm *so* pleased!"

"I'd like your opinion if you think the work is of any merit," she replied. "Sometimes I think I cannot judge its caliber any longer."

"You would like *me* to read it?" Sophie asked, her eyes shining with pleasure.

"I certainly would," Frances replied emphatically. "I've created an eccentric named 'Mrs. Tyfort' who, in her desire to sound erudite, mispeaks herself constantly . . . she says words like *progeny* where she means *prodigy* and such."

"I love her already," Sophie laughed.

"Ah, but I'm having difficulty working out the plotting, so many mismatched couples and calculating mamas . . ." Frances sighed.

At that moment, a boy who looked twelve or thirteen burst into the room. His complexion was ruddy from his outdoor exertions and he hardly looked at either woman in the room, heading directly for the tea table to sample the sweets.

"Richard!" his mother said sharply. "Please excuse your rude entrance and pray, pay your compliments to Miss Sophie McGann."

The young scamp nodded perfunctorily, smiled charmingly at his mother, and exited as quickly as he had entered, carrying a sticky bun in each hand.

"Home from Harrow for the Easter holidays," Mrs. Sheridan said tiredly. "He's such an active lad . . ."

April melted into May and the weeping willows along the Avon drooped full-leaved fronds into the river swollen from spring rains. Sophie spent as much time in the Sheridans' company as she could spare, both as a means of enjoying her friendship with the older woman and of keeping her distance from Hunter and Mavis.

The final performance of the 1763–1764 season, a comedy titled *The Old Maid*, was scheduled for late May. Hunter had designed a new musical sketch to accompany the piece. Many in the company had already abandoned the Orchard Street Theater for summer pastures elsewhere. Mavis was forced to learn a new role to cover for a departed actress and was not the least bit cheerful about her task. Hunter, too, appeared to be in an equally foul temper when Sophie arrived to rehearse the new steps.

"No, no, no, Sophie!" he fumed. "'Tis balance, balance, *coupé*, balance."

"That's a change from the last time," she said flatly.

"No, 'tis *not!*" he retorted.

"Yes it is," Sophie insisted. "You said 'balance, balance, balance . . . *then* coupé.'"

"Sink me, if you aren't a slow-witted dolt today," he replied cuttingly. "That's not at all the way I taught it to you."

Sophie put her hands on her hips and glared at him.

"If you cannot keep a civil tongue in your head, Hunter Robertson, sink *me* if you won't just have to find another dancing partner!"

And with that, she stormed off the stage.

Before she reached the exit, Hunter grabbed her wrist and continued her forward progress, dragging her into the alley behind the theater. Instead of berating her, as she expected, he pulled her roughly to his chest and held her fast.

"I'm sorry," he whispered into her hair. "I can't bear this another instant. Please, *please*, Sophie . . . hear me out."

She pulled away from his grasp and stared up at him, moved—despite her anger at his recent behavior—by the look of misery that had invaded his eyes.

"'Tis a lovely spring day," she said quietly, clasping his hand. "Shall we take a stroll by the river?"

Chapter 15

"'Tis a relief to escape the smell of tallow and breathe the scent of sun and sky and grass again," Hunter said, inhaling a deep breath. "Come," he urged her, shedding his coat and spreading it on the grassy bank a few feet from the Avon. "Sit on this while we hold our solemn conference."

Sophie did as she was bidden. Hunter stretched his long legs toward the river and leaned back on one elbow, plucking a fat blade of grass with his fingers.

"Where to start?" he sighed. "Well, here is what I most wish you to know—I have not shared the bed of the female in question since before you came to Bath." He glanced at Sophie, who was staring at the river, expressionless. "Mavis was, indeed, enceinte, but not by *this* swain, although I wasn't able to confirm that until recently," he continued, twisting the blade of grass between his fingers.

"I know this may surprise you," Sophie said quietly, "but the fact Mavis is not with child by you really doesn't alter the situation to my mind. You were lovers in London and here in Bath . . . she *might* have been carrying your child . . ."

"And is it your belief," Hunter finally interrupted, "that when that possible inconvenience reared its ugly head, I simply selected you to be the next object of my affections?"

"Well," Sophie flared, "it certainly appeared that even *after* you had ceased to enjoy a physical . . . liaison with Mavis as you claim, you dined and danced and promenaded with her through Bath continuously. If I were she, I'd have been certain you'd mend the breach and become lovers once again—especially as she'd written a large part for you in her new play!"

"That's *not* the way of it," Hunter replied heatedly. "I have been trying to disentangle myself from Mavis Piggott since *before* you turned up on my doorstep." Sophie bowed her head and cast unseeing eyes on the river flowing at their feet. "I played the typical, randy fool with Mavis," he confessed. "I was lonely and bored when she tipped up from London last Autumn in such a huff. She was eager to renew our . . . uh . . . previous connection. She was charming . . . she was *willing*. I suppose I lacked the moral fortitude to turn down her invitation in the dead of winter to warm her bed."

"And, as the winter wore on, what prompted you to desert such cozy accommodations?" Sophie demanded, sounding unconvinced.

"The lass herself," he said flatly. "Mavis, I must admit, is a fascinating creature, not uncomely, and not a dullard. But she is totally, absolutely, *completely* absorbed in one subject only—herself."

"That must have been uncomfortable for you," Sophie shot back.

"And you think I am like her in that regard?" Hunter demanded.

"Well, let us merely say, you have a healthy estimation of your good looks and your abilities," she replied.

"You are certainly direct," Hunter winced. His level gaze unsettled her somewhat. "Haven't you yet realized one thing about me?" he queried gently. "My good looks, as you describe them, have often been a curse. I rarely know *why* my company is desired, other than for some peculiar fascination with this cleft in my chin, or these blue eyes, or this straight nose," he said, touching each of his classic features with the blade of grass he held in his hand. "But you . . . you were always my friend, my good companion. From that very first day on the High Street, you seemed to wish me well."

"I did . . ." Sophie replied slowly, "but I *was* dazzled

by your . . . your . . . handsomeness and your large stature . . . and the way you have of appearing so sure of yourself. It made me feel safe."

"And when you suddenly sought me out in Bath," Hunter said, smiling at his recollection of that chilly December day, "it finally penetrated my thick skull that what I felt for you was far from mere brotherly affection. All this time I had deliberately cast you as 'little Sophie,' the Edinburgh waif . . . my tutor and my friend."

"But *why*? Why did you fend me off with this pose?" she asked, swallowing painfully.

"You so put me in mind of Megan," he replied slowly. "It rather felt like—"

"Well, 'twas *not*!" Sophie interrupted hotly. "I am Sophie McGann, not your deceased sister, Megan Robertson, and I am thoroughly *sick* of being treated as if 'twas some unnatural thing, this . . . attachment . . . that's grown between us."

"*Exactly!*" Hunter agreed with a teasing smile. "Why did you not call my attention to this fact a bit sooner?"

"Your attention, sir, was riveted elsewhere!" she reminded him bluntly. "We were speaking of Mavis . . . and of your belief her child was not sired by you," she added, forcing the conversation around to matters at hand.

"Ah . . . yes," Hunter said, frowning. "I know this may sound harsh to your innocent ears, but I soon grew tired of Mavis's demands—both intimate and otherwise. It all seemed so . . . so calculated on her part. Long before Christmas, we had ceased being lovers. Within the week of our estrangement, she flaunted Geoffrey Bannister as her latest conquest, so I was fairly certain that her story of my fathering her bairn was false."

"But she told me the day after my arrival here at the end of December that she was carrying your child!" Sophie interjected accusingly. "She had only to inform you of it, she said, and you would be wed."

"But she didn't tell *me* she was breeding . . . not for quite some time," Hunter protested. "She merely hinted at it . . . demanding to see me . . . demanding that I sup with her or walk with her, but never coming out with it until after that evening I encountered you at the Assembly Room ball with Darnly and Lindsay-Hoyt."

"Well, given the news of Mavis's condition," she asked quietly, "what was your reaction?"

"Of course, I was disturbed to hear her claims, especially as my feelings for you were becoming—" Hunter cut himself short. He shifted his weight to his other elbow and stared off, across the river. "You see, your arrival in Bath had prompted Mavis into action. Geoffrey Bannister is *already* married, and she realized she had to move swiftly if she wished to avoid the embarrassment of bastardy, and she liked me well enough, then, I suppose . . . so she used such deception in an attempt to persuade me to marry her." His eyes were now fixed on the blade of grass clasped between his fingers. "When she told me she was with child, I felt I had no right to . . . to make my feelings known to you until I knew the truth of her claim."

"But, how are you now so sure the bairn's not yours?" Sophie said in a low voice.

He flushed with embarrassment.

"Because when last I lay with her in November, her courses came and I had not lain with her since." He looked away, his thoughts as distant as his gaze across the river Avon. "'Tis of no consequence now . . . there is to be no bairn."

"She got rid of it?" Sophie whispered.

"I don't know exactly what happened, but there is no child," he said, sounding strangely bereft.

"Then tell me this, Hunter," Sophie asked tersely. "Why does that fact make you so melancholy, if 'twas not yours?"

Hunter turned to look at her squarely. The strange, haunted expression she'd first seen play across his features when he spoke so long ago of his sister's death invaded his eyes once again.

"Because 'twas a life and 'tis been snuffed out," he reflected, "and, as you have so astutely pointed out, it *could* have been my child."

The pair sat at the river's edge for several minutes, mesmerized by the water's relentless flow. Suddenly Hunter broke their silence, leaning toward her, gently tracing the line of her cheekbone with the back of his fingers.

"I canna believe how much I wish to make love to the lass I once took for near a sister," he said quietly, his former Highland burr creeping back into his speech. At length he stood up, pulling her to her feet by his side. "But I shall not stalk you, Sophie, nor attempt to charm you, nor use those male tricks I know so well," he said somberly, gazing into her upturned face. "I shall simply wait for you to come to me—if you so desire."

Sophie could only stare at him wordlessly, a thousand thoughts whirling in her brain. Hunter seized his coat off the ground, dusting the grass from its nap, and offered her his arm. Their backs were warmed by the spring sunshine slanting across the river as they slowly retraced their steps to the Orchard Street Theater.

The day of the final performance of the season, the entire company was called for a last rehearsal at ten o'clock in the morning. On her way to the playhouse Sophie paused at King Street to bid adieu to the Sheridans who were off to Edinburgh, where Thomas had secured several leading parts at the Canongate for a week or two.

"After that . . . I'm not quite sure where we'll be," Frances Sheridan admitted wearily, adjusting the cloak of her traveling costume as she waited for the rest of her family to appear outside their lodgings. She leaned forward, lowering her voice. "Our son, Richard, will be returning to Harrow," she said, "but our debts are so pressing, Thomas proposes he and I repair to France at summer's end."

"Oh, Mrs. Sheridan, I am so sorry," Sophie commiserated, knowing from her own experience how distressing it was to be counting farthings. "But you're bound to complete *Journey to Bath* soon. Perhaps Garrick will have returned to Drury Lane by then and your fortunes will deservedly rebound."

"You are such a dear," Frances said, gazing at Sophie reflectively. "And I hope your effort at play writing succeeds as well. Remember, Sophie, *no one* sees through your eyes or can write the same play you're capable of creating."

Impulsively, Sophie threw her arms around the woman she so admired.

"Thank you," she whispered, as her breath caught in her throat. "Thank you for all your kindness and confidence in me."

She bid the Sheridans farewell and dashed through Kingsmead Square, barely arriving at the appointed hour. There was much good-natured grumbling, owing to the early hour, among the remaining crew presenting *The Old Maid.* Fortunately, rehearsing the comedy and the musical interludes revealed the program was in a sufficient state of readiness to put most members of the Orchard Street Theater in a good mood.

"Your thoughts seem on the moon today, Sophie." Hunter smiled down at her, wiping the perspiration from his face with a cloth hung round his neck. By this time, John Arthur had dismissed the entire company, and the players were milling about. Some drifted out the stage door into Orchard Street. At that very moment, Sir Peter Lindsay-Hoyt strode through the flies and rushed on stage, excitedly waving a sheet of paper.

"At last!" he exclaimed, breathing hard. "I've been looking for you everywhere. Come, Sophie! I must speak with you."

"What is it?" she demanded, trying not to put too much stock in Peter's beaming countenance.

"It just arrived in this morning's post," he panted. "'Tis from George Colman. *He likes our play!*"

"Sink me, you can't be serious?" Sophie gasped, her eyes glowing. "He really, truly *liked* it?" Peter nodded emphatically. "Give it to me," she demanded, reaching for the missive, "let me *read* it!"

"No!" he teased, holding Colman's letter above her head. "You must come with me, so we can read it together and celebrate our good fortune!"

Sophie turned to look at Hunter, who was staring at her collaborator suspiciously.

"'Tis *wonderful* news!" she babbled at him. "*George Colman likes our play!*"

"My congratulations," Hunter replied stiffly.

"Pray, Sophie, you must come with me," Peter insisted. "We have much to discuss." And without waiting for her acquiescence, he clasped her hand and headed for the rear stage door.

Peter refused to let Sophie read Colman's letter until they rendezvoused with Roderick Darnly at a nearby eating house.

"You can see from that first paragraph that he will require some reworking of the earlier scenes," Peter explained, sipping his second whiskey at the rather early hour of one o'clock in the afternoon. Sophie was holding Colman's letter in one hand. Peter gave her other hand a soft squeeze. "It shouldn't take us too long to make those changes, should it?" he inquired eagerly, his cheeks suffused with color from both the spirits and the excitement. Sophie did not reply as she was reading the letter for a second time. "He says he hopes to mount it in the '64, '65 season, isn't that a rip?"

She raised her head to look her coauthor squarely in the eye.

"This letter is addressed to you alone," she said quietly.

"Does not signify . . ." he shrugged, sipping his whiskey.

"Nowhere is my name mentioned," she added in a low voice. "Peter . . . you *did* submit this work with *both* our names attached to it as authors, did you not?"

Peter looked uncomfortable and glanced over at Darnly.

"I-I thought it more politic to send it with my name as author only—just for the present—as there is so much prejudice against petticoat authors."

"But I shared in the writing of the piece," she insisted. She was trying to keep her temper in check. "I copied it at no fee to you, so it could be *read. I* solved the problems of plot! How in conscience could you have submitted this to Drury Lane without mentioning my name?"

"Now, now, Sophie," Roderick interjected soothingly. "'Twas a small error in judgment on Peter's part, I agree . . . but 'tis not irreparable. I doubt that if the play has merit—and Colman apparently believes it has—the manager would have been dissuaded by the sight of a woman as joint author . . . but Peter wants to give the piece its best chance at acceptance." He smiled coaxingly at Sophie. "You can't blame him for *that,* can you?"

"And you've heard what a menace that Edward Capell has been," Peter added, "despising female wits and refusing them licenses for production of their works. I didn't want to chance it . . ."

Sophie's breath was ragged and she knew her face had flushed scarlet. She looked from Peter to Roderick and back to her collaborator again. Everything they said had some truth to it, and yet she knew Peter had deceived her. She swallowed hard and tried to gather her thoughts.

"Well, now that Colman *has* indicated his interest in our work," she said with measured emphasis, "I wish him to know that I was your coauthor, is that agreed?"

"As soon as he accepts our final version, I promise you, Sophie," Peter vowed earnestly, "he shall know the names of *both* the brilliant playwrights he has in his employ. In fact, we should repair immediately to London, don't you think, Darnly?"

Sophie was also anxious to return to the capital. She had not heard recently from Lorna Blount regarding Aunt Harriet, and had nagging worries about the poor woman and about affairs at Ashby's Books. Hunter, too, should leave for the city before the end of May to confirm his year's employment and to discover if he was, indeed, to be cast in Mavis's play at whichever theater was to take it on.

"I shall be departing Bath for London in a day or two and would be most delighted if both of you would keep me company in my coach," Darnly volunteered.

Sophie thought of Hunter and wondered how soon he had planned to return to the capital. It was probably not sensible to beg a ride for him in Darnly's coach, recalling the men's mutual antipathy. She must speak to Hunter first, she decided.

"I thank you for your kind offer of transportation, sir," Sophie said finally, "and will inform you of my decision on the morrow, after the closing of the playhouse tonight, if that would suit?"

"As you wish," he replied.

Sophie focused her attention on her writing partner.

"So we are agreed we will return to London forthwith to complete the work Colman has suggested," she said in a businesslike manner, "and that we will inform the manager that Sir Peter and I *both* assume credit or blame for *The Footmen's Conspiracy*?" Sophie gazed expectantly at her writing partner, who was toying with his empty whiskey glass. After a long pause, he shrugged, a gesture Sophie took to be agreement with her plan. Formality seemed to be replacing their previous camaraderie, which was just as well, she thought ruefully. She stood up to depart.

"May I direct my coachman now to convey you to your lodgings?" Roderick offered.

Sophie regarded both men for a moment and then shook her head. By the timepiece on the wall behind their table, it was just after two o'clock. Hunter would most likely be resting at his flat prior to leaving to prepare for the season's final performance.

"No, thank you," she said firmly. "'Tis a lovely day . . . near summerlike, I'd say. I shall walk."

Sophie paused in front of the entrance to Number 6 Pierpont Place, her hand resting on the door's heavy brass knocker. Now that she was standing in front of Hunter's lodgings, she hesitated to announce her presence. At length, she rapped twice, feeling suddenly foolish and shy. After a lengthy interval, the door opened only a crack.

"Sophie?" Hunter said, a look of surprise playing across his features. He was coatless and standing in his stocking feet.

"Aye," she answered uncertainly. "If you're resting, we can speak later . . ."

"No . . . no . . ." he said swiftly, flinging open his door. "Come in, 'twas just I was having a wee sleep when I heard your knock . . . I'm a bit fuzzy headed, 'tis all."

"So am I," Sophie replied wryly, following him into his chambers. "I'm very confused about a number of things."

He gave her a quizzical look and bid her select one of the two chairs that sat facing the cold hearth.

"Well, then, do sit down," he urged. "May I offer some spirits? I have brandy, I think . . ." he added, striding toward the armoire standing on the opposite side of the room. He retrieved the bottle and set it and two glasses on the small table in front of them. "Well, Sophie," he said, focusing his attention on the brandy he was pouring, "shall we toast our final performance together at the theater this evening?"

"'Tis finished tonight, isn't it?" she assented softly. "Back in London, I'll simply be 'Sophie McGann, playbill seller.' I don't think my performing compares to dancers such as my friend Lorna Blount."

"Let us not forget you are now a dramatist," he reminded her quietly, sipping his brandy. "Did Colman's letter confirm your hopes?"

"He very much liked the play—with a few reservations and suggestions for changes in the early acts," she parried, too embarrassed to reveal the controversy about her status as Peter's partner. Hunter was staring contemplatively into his glass and Sophie leaned across the table to force him to heed her next words. "Hunter . . ." she said earnestly, 'you don't seem truly pleased about my play—"

"It pleases me not at all that you are in partnership with that fop," he interrupted testily.

Sophie found herself repressing a smile. She reached for his free hand, allowing her fingers to brush his lightly.

"'Tis a *business* association, Hunter . . . I promise ～u."

He raised his eyes from his brandy glass and searched her face for a long moment. She stared back steadily and felt a familiar current of emotion surge between them.

"And you came to tell me that?" he said at length.

"A-aye . . ." she replied uncertainly.

"And you came for no other reason?" he asked, gazing at her intently. He took her hand and turned her palm toward him as if to study it.

"I-I also wished to ask you—as my friend—to be *pleased* for me that this small success has come my way . . ."

"I *am* pleased . . . for *you*," he replied with studied emphasis. He had begun to stroke the soft, sensitive cushion of her palm with his thumb, sending odd sensations coursing up her arm. "And those are the sole reasons you have knocked at my door this quiet afternoon? You are merely paying me a friendly call?" he persisted.

She laughed hesitantly, staring down at her hand to watch the restless circles he was sketching on her skin. Her entire arm had begun to tingle, and she felt the oddest feelings rippling through her extremities.

"This isn't one of those 'male tricks' you told me by the river you wouldn't employ?" she demanded with a weak smile.

"I fear that it is," he admitted, the ghost of a grin pulling at the corners of his mouth. "But I also said then that I would wait for you to come to me, if you so desire—and it appears you have. And you do. Desire, I mean. I can *feel* it, Sophie."

Her heart was beginning to thud so strongly, she wondered if Hunter could hear it. He raised her hand off the table and slowly, deliberately inserted her forefinger an inch into his mouth, his lips tugging on it sensuously.

"A-another trick?" she whispered, feeling as if she were about to fling herself off a cliff.

"Just one of many I have up my sleeve—*if* you so desire," he divulged quietly, his dark blue eyes riveted on hers.

"Oh, Hunter," she said in a breath. "'Tis so unfair . . . you know so much of . . . these . . . matters . . . and I'm a—"

"Novice?"

"Virgin," she corrected him faintly. "I am completely untutored in this subject, I assure you . . ."

Her words drifted off as he pressed the back of one hand to his lips, insinuating his tongue lightly between two of her fingers. Then he gently seized her other hand, and repeated his caress. She swallowed hard as he encased his large palms around her small ones, trapping them on the table between them. Sophie breathed deeply to steady her nerves. Then, he rose to his feet and pulled her to stand next to him beside the small table where their brandy glasses had been abandoned.

"Well, darling Sophie," he murmured, his hands sliding up her arms, past her shoulders and resting lightly at the base of her throat. "You taught me how to read by slow degrees. So . . . turnabout is fair play, wouldn't you say?"

She merely stared up at him, marveling at his startlingly blue eyes. All sensible questions concerning their return to London had flown out of her head.

"You do recall," he continued, carefully releasing the few front fastenings on the plain blouse she had donned for their rehearsal earlier in the day, "how you began my earliest reading lessons with something very simple? *You* said the letter *A* . . . then *I* said the letter *A*? Remember?"

"Aye," she said, biting her lip to keep from sighing aloud as his fingers pushed past the fabric of her bodice and casually grazed the sensitive flesh between her breasts.

"'Tis the same thing with learning to make love," he smiled down at her. "I remove a piece of your clothing; then you remove an article of mine." Sophie's legs had turned to jelly. She found herself leaning against Hunter for support as her trembling fingers did his bidding, unbuttoning his linen shirt.

"Excellent," he chuckled, confirming his approval of her latest actions by kissing her on each eyelid. In response, her eyes flew open to stare at the mat of dark blond hair on his chest.

He continued talking to her quietly, coaxing her gently to mirror his movements. Next he unbuttoned the fastening on her skirt and allowed it to fall to the ground. He made short work of her petticoat and turned her around to unlace her stays.

"Do you remember when I assisted you like this your first night in Bath?" he whispered, nuzzling her ear. "You had nearly fallen asleep, standing upright—over there, behind that screen. I noticed then how beautiful your breasts had become."

"They're small . . ." she murmured over her shoulder, "compared with Mavis's."

He turned her around to face him.

"But oh, so beautiful," he said, stooping to brush his lips against the thin cotton shift covering her bosom. She thought she would faint as his kisses grazed her nipples and then gradually traveled upward toward her throat. "Now, my breeches," he commanded softly, and Sophie blushed. Even so, she felt helpless to refuse his requests since they reflected her own desires in the most frightening fashion. "That's a good lass," he said, assisting her trembling fingers. "I knew you'd be an apt pupil." He kicked off his trousers, but Sophie kept her eyes glued to his face, a sudden feeling of panic enveloping her.

"Hunter, I-I . . ." she whispered, tears unexpectedly filling the corners of her eyes.

"I know, pet," he said soothingly, drawing her close, her nearly naked body pressing against the alarming contours of his muscular frame.

With infinite care, he slipped her shift off her shoulders and pushed it gently down the length of her body as if he were removing a thin layer of skin. Then he scooped her up in his arms, deposited her in the middle of his bed and sat beside her, his large fingers gently strafing her collar bone. He massaged both sides of her neck just below her ears and she felt herself relax, despite her trepidation about what would undoubtedly happen next.

Sophie had received an extensive education on the mechanics of human coupling when she inventoried John Ashby's lurid engravings before locking them away in Aunt Harriet's trunk. Suddenly, she dreaded to consider how such ungainly gymnastics would manifest themselves between Hunter and herself.

"You're afraid now, aren't you?" he said, delicately squeezing her earlobe. She nodded bleakly. "Of getting with child?" he asked quietly.

"No," she whispered. "I've just had my courses," and then flushed crimson once again.

"Then *what*?" he pressed. "What do you fear? The pain?"

She nodded miserably, having no real answer for all the mysterious aspects of lovemaking that frightened her.

"'Twill sting one time only, swift as a pinprick," he murmured, stretching his long body beside hers on the feather mattress. "And then 'tis over for a lifetime." When his hands reached for her, gently drawing her into the circle of his arms, her apprehension began to subside. She suddenly felt small and safe and utterly protected. "And, I promise you, this loving tutor will then proceed to demonstrate wondrous things." He tweaked her nose and leaned forward to whisper in her ear. "I have no doubt, once properly instructed, you shall teach me wondrous things as well."

"And you said you would make no attempt to charm me," she scoffed gently, suddenly smiling up at him.

"Ah . . . you've caught me out. 'Twas a terrible falsehood I told you by the river," he murmured against her hair. "I mean to charm you this day, Sophie McGann . . . charm you to a fare-thee-well."

"But Hunter?" she whispered in a small voice.

"What, pet?" he replied, pulling away and leaning one elbow on the mattress.

Sophie averted her eyes and plucked absently at the counterpane.

"You're such a braw lad . . . and I'm so . . . small . . ." Her words drifted off, leaving her tentative question hanging in the air.

"And your concern is?" he said, smiling faintly.

Sophie swallowed hard and felt her face flush crimson for the third time. The silence ticked away. Finally she blurted, "We won't fit!"

Hunter's blue eyes kindled with understanding as he slowly shook his head from side to side.

"You've forgotten two very important facts, Sophie my love," he said in a low voice. His forefinger traced a slow, languid line from the base of her throat, between her breasts, down her abdomen and finally stopped at the crease where her torso met her slender legs. "You are my own wee witch, you see . . . and, as you well know, I'm a conjurer with many tricks," he continued, as his fingers began gently to probe her tender flesh. Sophie reacted with a sharp intake of breath and stared up at him with eyes that both questioned and implored. "Ah . . . there . . . you see?" He smiled, relentlessly stroking her, coaxing a flood of warmth and moisture to take possession of her. "In this first lesson, I shall demonstrate a most magical feat the two of us can master . . . a genuine marvel!"

Sophie could do nothing but stare at Hunter with astonishment as her body began to respond to his expert ministrations. After several delicious minutes during which his hands and lips roved wantonly over every inch of her flesh, he suddenly rolled flat on his back, settling her body on top of him. He began kissing her eyelids and both cheeks, grazing his lips against her earlobes, everywhere—but her mouth—until she couldn't stand the deprivation another second. She slipped her hands behind the nape of his neck, pushed her forearms against his chest and lifted her head so that she could stare at his lips which had curled in a sensuous grin.

"So Miss Sophie would like to be kissed properly, would she?" he teased, shunting his hips against hers to emphasize his growing ardor. Then slowly, deliberately, his fingers threaded through her hair and he seized her mouth, provocatively tracing his tongue along its velvet lining until she forgot all else except wanting . . . wanting . . . What was it she desired? she thought disjointedly. Hunter's large hands clasped her waist, raising her in one fluid motion so her legs straddled his hips.

"This is the secret of it," he whispered softly, staring boldly at the juncture where their two bodies met. He lifted her above him, and as his rigid flesh began to insinuate itself against her soft interior, Sophie felt as if every pore in her body was opening to the heavens. "'Tis for you to decide . . . when . . ."

Sophie's lips parted slightly and her breath became short and uneven. She steadied herself, bracing her palms against his shoulders and slowly allowing her weight to sink against him.

"*Jesu* . . ." she murmured, feeling her soul being pierced as well as her body. She hung suspended above him, allowing the miracle Hunter had promised to take possession of her. Every few seconds she paused, permitting their bodies to adapt to each other, and then advanced inch by heartstopping inch. A puzzled look suddenly crossed her features; she could descend no further.

"You've done your part, my darling girl," he whispered hoarsely. "Now, I must do mine."

Before Sophie quite knew what Hunter was about, he swiftly rolled her on her back and, with one relentless thrust, pushed past the virginal barrier that separated her from a lifetime of girlish innocence. She stiffened and cried out, breathless from the swift, intense pain radiating between her legs. Hunter tightly clasped her against the length of his body and remained motionless, granting her time to adjust to the shock.

"Shh . . . I'm so sorry, darling," he soothed, "'tis over forever. Only pleasure from now on, I swear. Shh . . ."

He held her quietly for several long moments before he began whispering a litany of endearments and sensual promises so erotic that she felt herself swept up by a torrent of longing. Then the talking stopped and they spoke in other ways, with their hands, their eyes, their mouths. She wondered at the glorious compatibility of their sweat-sleeked bodies and felt herself being initiated in the mysteries of love and sensuality in a manner that bore no relation to the exploitive desires of Lord Lemore or the shocking images of lust and perversion she had viewed at so tender an age. Hunter wished to give, not to take, some lucid portion of her brain cried out . . . to soothe and cosset and pleasure her beyond her wildest imaginings. She reveled in the power and elation of it all as a trembling that began in her midsection rippled through her body with the force of a Highland storm.

Suddenly, it was Hunter's turn to cry out, bathing Sophie in the explosive release that her virgin's body had enticed from him. And now she assumed the role of comforter, whispering her love and gratitude and contentment until they both fell fast asleep.

When Sophie finally awoke, the shadows had lengthened across the chamber. She stared down at Hunter, awestruck by the avalanche of passionate feelings and emotional sensations they had shared.

I'm the same Sophie, she mused, gently brushing a stray

dark blond lock off his forehead, *and yet everything's changed . . .*

The clock on the mantelpiece struck the hour of five and Sophie sat bolt upright in bed.

"Hunter!" she whispered urgently. "Hunter, wake up!"

"Ummmm?" Hunter moaned sleepily. "Shhh . . ." he mumbled. "Come here."

He lifted his head off his pillow and deposited his tousled mane in her lap, brushing his lips against her thigh through the bed linen.

"Hunter!" she protested laughingly. "'Tis *five* o'clock! We should be at Orchard Street! The performance begins in an hour's time. Mr. Arthur will be frantic!"

"Oh . . . God!" he groaned, pulling himself to a sitting position and rubbing the sleep from his eyes. He turned and stared at her, a lecherous grin spreading across his face.

"Well . . . well. My saucy little pupil is wide awake," he teased, leaning over to nibble playfully at her earlobe. "I will expect you to prepare yourself for Lesson Two, commencing immediately after the performance tonight . . . what say you?"

"Hunter!" she remonstrated with mock severity. "I fear you take your role as tutor too seriously."

"Oh, I take it *very* seriously indeed," he answered, cupping her face in his hands and kissing her with a ferocity that sent the blood singing through her veins. "God's bones, but you could make me miss a performance for the first time in my life," he murmured, kissing her again with growing ardor.

"No . . . we cannot," she cried weakly against his lips. "I promise you, professor . . ." she said urgently, "we shall return to my lessons just as soon as the curtain closes tonight."

"Then you wish it as much as I?" he demanded, suddenly serious, his eyes searching her intently.

"Aye, Hunter." She smiled timorously. She swung her legs to the edge of the mattress and looked at him over her shoulder. "'Tis like a dream . . . having you for my own," she admitted shyly.

He lifted her tangled hair from off her shoulders, swiftly kissed the nape of her neck, and gave her a gentle shove.

"Out of my bed, wench," he laughed, "or the dancing we do tonight will never be performed on stage."

Sophie emerged from the women's tiring-room and sauntered dreamily past the flies to stand at her starting position off stage left. Hunter was already standing in costume in the shadows and he gave her hand a welcoming squeeze.

"I shall miss dancing with you in London," she whispered wistfully, standing on tiptoe to reach his ear.

"Not to worry, love," Hunter whispered back. "You'll be dancing with me at Smock Alley. I know I can persuade them to give you employment."

"*Dublin?*" she said, staring at him aghast. Someone nearby hissed "*Shhh!*" and Sophie lowered her voice to a croak. "You're planning to play in *Ireland* next season?"

"Aye, and the summer season, too," he replied, flashing her his most engaging smile. "And so must you. I've already signed my contract . . . last winter, when Henry Mossop came to Bath recruiting for his theater."

The orchestra had begun to play the musical cue heralding their entrance.

"No!" she whispered. "Dear God, Hunter . . . I can't go with you . . . not to *Ireland*! It's to *London* we must go! What about Aunt Harriet? And there's my book shop . . . and my play—"

Sophie's anguished response was cut short by the first strains of the music to which they were to dance. Hunter grabbed her roughly by the hand and pulled her out in front of an admiring audience that seemed determined to enjoy the last presentation of the 1763–1764 theatrical season. Sophie wondered if the onlookers had any notion that despite her bright, hard smile, she was on the edge of dissolving into a fit of loud weeping.

The hours that followed had been agonizing as Sophie endured the closing night festivities, followed by a silent walk back to Hunter's lodgings while many conflicting thoughts whirled through her head. Once they were inside the door at Pierpont Place, however, Sophie could no longer contain her dismay.

"It *was* a trick!" she exclaimed in a low voice as she and Hunter entered his chambers.

"What was?" he demanded, shutting the door quickly.

"You've known all this time you were leaving for Dublin, and this afternoon, you heard me talk about Colman's wanting changes in our comedy. You *knew* that would require my being in London. Yet you said *nothing* about playing next season in Ireland! Not *here*!" she declared, pointing at the rumpled bed standing in the corner, "not as we walked to the theater tonight . . . not *anywhere*! Instead, you plied that dangerous charm of yours to get what *you* so desired—even if it meant asking me to give up my one chance to become a produced playwright! But, no! *You* had decided what was best for me, hadn't you? Because what is most important here is what is best for *you*! Do you deny this?" she demanded.

Hunter refused to reply, his body tense and unyielding.

"Hunter," she persisted, tears edging her voice, "when we made perfect, beautiful love this afternoon, I thought it was safe to show you how much I . . . I care about you . . . have cared for so long . . . because I thought you would want a life that was good for me too."

"Why is it not good for you to come with me to Dublin?" he asked stubbornly.

"Because I left a life behind me in London!" she exclaimed in frustration. "My aunt is in an insane asylum! I must see how she is faring . . . I must *try* to do something to help her." Hunter remained silent as he tugged angrily at his neck linen. "I left poor Lorna responsible for my bookstore and I must see to that," she continued insistently, sensing he was already discounting her reasons for wanting to return to London. "And my *play*, Hunter! I'm no actress . . . my tongue goes all wobbly the minute I speak on stage and my dancing is only adequate. You know perfectly well that I haven't a scintilla of the performing talent you have. But I want to write plays. I know that now. Don't you see how much this chance to have my work mounted at Drury Lane means to me?"

"And can't you see how important this engagement in Dublin is to *me*?" he demanded, shedding his coat and flinging it on a chair.

"You can gain employment as a player in London," she countered, "but I can't secure the same opportunity as a playwright in Ireland—not a chance like the one Peter and I have now at Drury Lane."

"Well, Smock Alley means more to me than merely prancing on a stage," Hunter replied hotly. "I'm to be assistant manager and supervise nearly half of the repertoire this summer and next season as well. 'Tis *my* chance to move beyond being a mere player. I want to *own* a theater someday . . . like your sainted David Garrick."

"I understand that," she whispered, blinking at the tears that had begun to fill her eyes, "and I wish you every chance to realize that dream, but what about *my* dream? Why in God's name didn't you tell me you had signed a contract to go to Ireland before we—"

"Because, Sophie, I was sure that once we made wonderful love together as I *knew* we would . . . as we *have*," he replied hoarsely, "there would be no doubt in your mind that your place was with me. I see I was wrong. Your ambition overrules your heart, it seems."

"But you gave me no choice in the matter!" Sophie replied, stung by his jibe. "You dazzled and beguiled me with hot looks and sweet words and that beautiful body of yours and now you tell me what *you* think is best for me because it fits so conveniently with your plans. Your ambitions are just as strong as mine. *What about what is best for both of us?* Have you *ever* considered that when it comes to a woman?" she demanded. Hunter merely glowered at her. "I thought not," she added, feeling drained and worn out. She turned to face the door.

"The other reason I didn't tell you about Dublin," he interjected in a low voice, addressing his words to her stiffened back, "was that I feared you'd say what you're saying to me right now—and I wanted you so much, Sophie," he continued, barely above a whisper. "I've wanted you for so long." When she didn't turn around or reply, he added bleakly, "And I feared that you wouldn't go to Ireland if . . . if you knew Mavis Piggott's play was to be done at Smock Alley. 'Twas she who introduced me to Henry Mossop when he came here last winter to see whom he might lure to Dublin. 'Tis *nothing* to me that Mavis is going there, but—"

"Mavis Piggott's going to Dublin next season, too?" Sophie demanded indignantly, whirling around to face him. "Ah, so *now* I understand!" she added bitterly, heading for his front door. "Why would you choose to be with me if it means giving up such a choice part in that strumpet's play?"

"Where are you going?" he shouted after her.

"To London," she cried. And she didn't look back.

Book 4
1764–1766

*[I am] . . . forced to write for Bread
and not ashamed to own it.*

—APHRA BEHN
preface to *SIR PATIENT FANCY*

Chapter 16

"Dare you risk it, Sophie?" whispered Lorna Blount anxiously, as she watched her friend don a pair of knee trousers and a small-size coat. The garments were the same ones worn by the actress Kitty Clive in numerous "breeches" parts in which the heroine dressed as a man.

Drury Lane's wardrobe chamber was located at the rear of the stage and one floor below the level of the street outside. Even at midday, the room was full of shadows, with motes of dust suspended in the murky light. Mounds of costumes hung on pegs and spilled out of dozens of wicker trunks. Upstairs, the theater was quiet. Most of the players had departed for their customary summer engagements, and only the scene painters and a skeleton crew remained to prepare for the September opening of the new season.

"Dr. Monro will never recognize me in this garb," Sophie declared with more bluster than confidence. She pulled back her auburn hair and tied it tightly with a ribbon stored in a box nearby. "Have you seen any tricornered hats?" she asked, casting her eyes about the musty chamber.

Lorna burrowed under a mound of cavalier chapeaus festooned with ostrich plumes and handed her friend a sedate black model shaped like a felt triangle. Although Sophie was nervous about appropriating a costume from the hundreds in storage, she soothed her conscience by vowing to donate a larger portion of her opening night playbill profits to George Colman's coffers.

Upon returning from Bath, she had tried to put her unhappy parting from Hunter out of her mind by calling at the
Garricks' chambers on Southampton Street, only to discover
that they remained abroad. Their butler revealed that the
celebrated couple had been constantly on the move, visiting
various countries on the Continent and being feted wherever
they went. Thanks to Lorna Blount's faithful printing and
selling of playbills at Drury Lane, George Colman welcomed Sophie's offer to continue this service and to supervise the cast announcements that would run daily in *The
Public Advertiser* during the coming season.

In a remote corner of her mind, there was never a day
when she didn't mourn Hunter's absence, or long for the
absolute peace—not to mention the passion—she had experienced in his arms. Weeks passed, however, and no letter
arrived, seeking a reconciliation or even informing her of his
safe arrival in Dublin. To dull the pain of regret she determined to keep frantically busy, and this she did.

Her first days back in London had been devoted to revising *The Footmen's Conspiracy* with Peter, as well as running
Ashby's Books and Printing, and dashing back and forth to
Drury Lane on various assignments. Sophie had not been
able to muster the time—or the courage—to call on her aunt
at Bedlam to see how she fared. But now, after a month back
in London, she could postpone her duty no longer.

"What if that sawbones, Monro, should lay eyes on you
again?" Lorna asked worriedly.

"I *have* to see my aunt . . . or at least make the attempt," Sophie responded fervently, clamping the tricorner
on her head. "I shall be all care and caution, I promise you."

"But if Monro should find you out, there'll be no Hunter
to come to the rescue!" Lorna exclaimed, and then appeared
chagrined, as a look of distress flickered over Sophie's features.

"I know," she replied softly, "but I *must try.*"

There had been no secrets between the two friends and
Sophie had shared the sorry tale of her acrimonious parting
from Hunter and her less-than-satisfactory working arrangement with Sir Peter Lindsay-Hoyt. Adding to her distress, Peter had become increasingly adamant that Sophie

not reveal their joint authorship for fear of antipathy toward petticoat scribes.

"Colman had his fill of that Piggott woman . . . he banished her and her play clear out of London! Regardless of the merit of our comedy," he continued forcefully, "Colman or Capell could damn our first effort out of hand, and then *neither* of us would profit. Let us establish ourselves before the public. We'll win their approbation, and *then* surprise the powers that be with the truth about your contribution to this effort."

Sophie had reluctantly agreed because of her fierce desire to see their play mounted professionally. However, the secrecy was far from pleasant.

"When the time is right, all shall be revealed," Peter assured her. "Trust me, Sophie. I know whereof I speak."

With a sigh, she forced her thoughts back to the task at hand and followed Lorna quietly up the stairs that led to the stage doorkeeper's box. She slipped past without Mr. Collins even looking up from his news journal and headed toward Moorgate on an unseasonably chilly afternoon.

A half hour later, her heart quickened when she caught sight of the statues of Madness and Melancholy flanking the entrance to Bedlam. No sooner had she passed through the familiar portals of the asylum when, to her dismay, she spied Dr. Monro greeting dignitaries who were indulging in an afternoon's amusement by observing the antics of the inmates. Fortunately, he failed to give Sophie, in her male attire, a second glance. Within minutes, she had conveyed a basket of food to her aunt by pressing two hard-earned shillings into the palm of the guard, Jackson, who would ensure its safe delivery.

To remain inconspicuous, Sophie joined the Sunday visitors who stared from their assigned vantage points at the cackling, moaning, chattering patients milling about a large room with high windows and virtually no furniture. Aunt Harriet was, indeed, among those herded into the chamber by the orderlies. The old woman had grown more wraithlike and haggard and appeared bewildered by the bustle and noise surrounding her. Soon, she retreated to a corner and curled up on the floor in her customary fetal position.

Tears filled Sophie's eyes as she quickly exited the hospital and walked the long road back to Half Moon Passage in a light rain. As she trudged up the gloomy staircase to her lodgings above Ashby's Books, she wondered, suddenly, if writing plays for a fickle public and hostile authorities was worth the misery and isolation apparently required to accomplish such a feat.

"You're back!" Lorna exclaimed as Sophie lifted the latch to her chambers. "I decided to wait. Come . . . I've started a nice fire in the hearth . . . and here's a cup of tea to warm you. You had no trouble with that wretched Monro?"

"No," Sophie said wearily, hanging her cloak on a peg near the door. "The good doctor never even noticed me." She took the cup of tea Lorna proffered her and sank into a chair near the fire.

"Your aunt's worse?" Lorna asked, observing her friend's gloomy countenance.

"A bit thinner . . . but the same, really."

"Then, why so melancholy?" Lorna asked kindly, drawing up another chair as she balanced her teacup on her knee.

Sophie gazed into the fire and shook her head morosely.

"As I was walking home I was struck by the notion that most women bind themselves to a man to have a center for their lives. Aunt Harriet certainly did that when she married Uncle John. She left an entire life in Edinburgh and followed her husband to London to work in an establishment that ultimately turned out to specialize in bawdry, which I am certain my aunt abhorred."

"Perhaps she loved her husband?" Lorna ventured.

"Perhaps she had no idea what she was bargaining for," Sophie replied, taking another sip of her tea. "And then there's David Garrick's wife . . ."

"Eva-Maria? She was a supremely talented dancer, I'm told."

"And she hasn't danced a step in years," Sophie retorted.

"Well, I suppose her life is awfully pleasant," Lorna considered, "a celebrated husband . . . ample income . . travel . . . two lovely abodes—"

Sophie set her tea cup down on the floor with a clatter.

"But don't you wonder if there are days when Eva-Maria

Veigel, the former toast of Vienna, doesn't long to *dance*? To fly across the stage? To hear the applause . . . to use that God-given talent?" Sophie demanded. "To live *her* life, not David Garrick's?"

"Perhaps on days when Garrick himself is in a foul temper, yes," Lorna jested.

"No . . . truly?" Sophie protested. "Why must Mrs. Garrick be the one to give all that up?"

"Perhaps she wanted to," Lorna said gently. "There are nights my feet ache so much, I would love to have a husband who'd entreat me to remain in my country house and dance him attendance."

"Well, of course," Sophie agreed reluctantly. "I've had days lately when I'm tired and discouraged, but why must a woman *always* put a man's wishes and desires *first*? Why must she invariably honor his dreams and ambitions above all else? Do you really think that's the *only* path to happiness for men and women?"

"Certainly it is for the *men*!" Lorna laughed, and then grew somber at the look of utter dejection that had come over her friend.

Sophie sighed and rose to stir the coals with the fire poker.

"But consider Thomas and Frances Sheridan. They appear to honor each other's abilities in a respectful manner."

"Aye . . ." Lorna replied, contemplating Sophie's words. "But they're often separated by their professional pursuits, and their children are left in Ireland with relatives for years at a time."

"But they seem *devoted* to one another," Sophie noted wistfully.

"That's true, they do," Lorna agreed. She stared at her friend closely. "Are we actually discussing the Sheridans, or is it you and Hunter . . . and the fact that you left him to write your play?"

Sophie sighed once again and nodded despondently.

"I refused to go to Ireland with Hunter because I wanted to see to our play at Drury Lane," she said woefully. "My best opportunity to accomplish that was in London with Peter." She cast Lorna a plaintive look. "I wish Hunter to succeed with his dream . . . why can't he wish the same for *me*?" she cried.

"Because I doubt he's considered that your dream is as important as his," Lorna said quietly.

"That's what I said to him!" Sophie retorted, and then shrugged sadly. "Yet I feel so wretched without him."

"It must be true love then," Lorna said with a smile.

"But I know that I would be equally miserable if I were in Dublin right now, selling programs in the lobby and never lifting a quill!"

"'Tis certainly a coil," Lorna nodded.

"If I persist in wrestling with this subject overmuch," Sophie laughed ruefully, "I'll end up back in Bedlam!"

"You may wait in here, mum," Sir Peter's housekeeper announced with undisguised ill-humor as she showed Sophie into the front sitting room of the baronet's flat on Cleveland Row. As she entered Peter's chambers, Sophie found herself pondering the irony that both his abode and that of his friend, Darnly—a magnificent establishment around the corner at Number 10 St. James Street—were within sight of the entrance to the Lord Chamberlain's office housed in St. James's Palace. Through Peter's front window she could see the black enamel door behind which the scaly faced Edward Capell controlled the fate of would-be playwrights.

Mrs. Hood crossed the carpet in the direction of a floor-to-ceiling window at the far end of the chamber.

"The baronet returned from Wiltshire only yesterday, mum, and was out quite late last night, I understand," the housekeeper announced reproachfully over her shoulder as she pulled open the drapes, allowing hot August sunshine to stream into the room. "I doubt he will rise before two."

"I made today's appointment with Sir Peter before his departure," Sophie replied tartly, unpacking the manuscript she had toiled over during the fortnight Peter had decamped for the country estate of one of his aristocratic friends. Placing *The Footmen's Conspiracy* on a nearby desk, she added sharply, "Please inform the baronet when you wake him that in one hour's time I will proceed to Drury Lane to submit our work to George Colman. That should encourage his *levee*."

"Yes mum," the housekeeper replied resignedly.

As Mrs. Hood departed to convey the message, Sophie took a seat at Peter's desk, withdrawing a long, white quill from its inkstand. She snapped the feathers smartly against her palm as she scanned the final scene of the play with an acutely critical eye. Suddenly, she dipped the pen into the inkwell and began scribbling furiously. More than thirty minutes elapsed before she heard the poshly accented voice of Roderick Darnly in the foyer outside the sitting room.

"Why Sophie, what a pleasant surprise," Roderick declared as he strode into the room. He glanced at the clock on the mantel, which registered ten minutes past eleven. "No Peter yet? What a slugabed! I was up by nine this morning, in spite of our evening's festivities."

"Good morning, sir," Sophie said politely.

Darnly was handsomely turned out in a cream-colored silk moiré suit and white silk stockings. His hand, with its gold-crested signet ring, rested on her desk as the young nobleman leaned over her shoulder and peered at the sheaf of manuscript pages. "*Finis!* it says. Well, well, you two *have* made progress. Congratulations!"

"'Tis *I* who've made the progress," Sophie replied with asperity. "As you must know, your friend has been away from London. Needless to say, this can make collaboration difficult."

"But Sophie!" a voice said teasingly from the doorway, "while I was in the country, I always knew our play was in capable hands. Lovely to see you, my dear," Peter greeted her warmly. "Morning, Darnly. Has Mrs. Hood brought the coffee?"

"Here you are, sir," the housekeeper announced, bustling through the door and depositing a tray on a table standing near a sofa brocaded in mustard silk.

Peter was wearing his dressing gown over his breeches and his shirt was open at the neck, revealing a mat of jet-black hair. He eagerly grabbed the cup extended to him by Mrs. Hood and saw to it that his guests were served coffee as well. As Sophie sipped the chicory brew, Peter perused the pages she had just completed. He actually laughed aloud at some of the passages.

He smiled expansively. "Really, Sophie, these last bits you've conjured up are capital fun."

She found herself smiling with pleasure at his praise.

"I myself think they're quite good," she agreed blandly. "If you have some fresh paper, I can copy over the new material and we can submit it all to Colman—*at last*!"

"Absolutely!" Peter enthused. "Mrs. Hood, find Miss McGann some fresh sheets. Darnly, old boy," he added, "what say you we clear out of here for a bit . . . let Sophie get on with her work undisturbed. Shall we look in at White's . . . have a brief repast . . . something of that nature?"

"If Sophie is amenable," Roderick said, casting her an inquiring look.

Sophie was tempted to demand that Peter remain, if only so she would feel less like a common clerk. However, she knew she would make much faster progress if she had total peace and quiet.

"'Tis perfectly agreeable to me—as long as you promise to return in two hours' time," she replied. "I want this to be in George Colman's hands *today*, Peter. He may already have assumed at this late date that the authors of *The Footmen's Conspiracy* have abandoned their effort."

"Not to worry," Peter assured her cheerfully. "I dispatched a note from the country saying I expected to be able to submit the revised manuscript before the month was out."

"And how were you so sure—out there in Wiltshire—that we'd be prepared to give him the finished version?" she asked pointedly.

"Because I placed my complete faith in your brilliance, my dear." Peter smiled mischievously. He turned to his companion. "Shall we cease distracting the poor girl?"

And before Sophie had dipped her quill into her host's crystal ink pot, she heard Peter and Roderick pass through the front door.

Sophie spent the rest of the week in an agony of apprehension. What would Colman think of the revisions of their play? Did she actually dare reveal her joint authorship at this juncture?

In the first week of September, she had an excuse to call at Drury Lane to secure a cast list for the perennial season opener, *The Beggar's Opera*, scheduled for the middle of the month.

She smiled a greeting at Mr. Collins, the doorkeeper, and quietly made her way up the stairs in the direction of Garrick's office. The familiar refrain of MacHeath's song drifted up the stairwell from the rehearsal taking place on stage. As she passed near the Treasure Room where the nightly receipts were kept, a deep-throated laugh wafted out from the manager's chambers. Peering through the door standing ajar, Sophie was astounded at the sight of George Colman sitting at David Garrick's large mahogany desk holding a copy of *The Footmen's Conspiracy*. Another burst of merriment erupted and he slapped his thigh with amusement. He only looked up when he sensed Sophie was standing in the doorway.

"Sink me, but I never dreamed the man could write so witty a piece!" he exclaimed, motioning her to enter his office.

"Who, sir?" Sophie asked, glancing down to confirm the manuscript in question was actually the one Peter had delivered to Drury Lane.

"That baronet, Peter . . . what's-his-name? I'm just re-reading a manuscript that coxcomb submitted last week."

"Peter Lindsay-Hoyt?" she said. "You like his work?"

"Aye . . . 'tis most droll . . . all about a rebellion of footmen in a great house—they force their master to make all sorts of comical concessions." He pointed a finger at the manuscript. "I want to put this into rehearsal straightaway . . . it will make a good companion piece to *The Platonic Wife*."

"You're mounting Mrs. Griffith's play at Drury Lane?" Sophie said, unable to mask her surprise. For a reputed misogynist, George Colman was certainly offering an important opportunity to a woman novelist like Elizabeth Griffith with no proven theatrical accomplishments—other than as a minor actress at Covent Garden in the distant past.

"Aye . . . she's adapted a French comedy in fairly good form," Colman replied. "That *may* pose a problem with the Lord Chamberlain's office . . . but, with a little persuasion, I hope to realize it in December or in the New Year. *The Footmen's Conspiracy* is as British as a joint of beef. Perhaps 'twill soothe Capell's Francophobia and the little drone will grant licenses to both."

"Let us hope so," murmured Sophie, determined to insist that Peter inform Colman immediately of their joint authorship, now that the manager had acknowledged their play had merit.

Colman scrutinized her closely.

"You have copied parts here on occasion, have you not?" he asked.

"Aye . . . over the summer, in Mr. Hopkins's absence, I wrote out roles for several actors," she replied.

"Well, I need a copy of *The Footmen's Conspiracy* to submit to the Lord Chamberlain's office posthaste. I'll pay you seven shillings if you can deliver it to his chambers by the Thursday."

Sophie nearly laughed out loud. Here she was being asked to make a duplicate of her own play, and neither Colman nor Edward Capell had any idea it had sprung in large part from her pen.

"I'd be honored to assist you," Sophie replied. "Have you comments or changes to incorporate in this version?"

"No . . . surprisingly, 'tis in excellent form," he replied. "Copy it as quickly as you're able and return the original to me for safekeeping. The Lord Chamberlain's office has a nasty habit of not returning manuscripts."

"Then you're really going to mount *The Footmen's Conspiracy*?" she persisted.

"Aye," Colman replied with a smug grin. "The baronet might even earn a few more quid to add to his ample coffers if the work lasts more than three nights."

Sophie raced past the stage doorkeeper and out into Russell Street. Despite the expense, she hired a hackney coach to speed her to Peter's lodgings on Cleveland Row. At the door, his housekeeper, Mrs. Hood, told her that Peter was entertaining Roderick Darnly and could not be disturbed.

"Well, please inform him I am here," she said firmly, "and that I am aware of the excellent news that Drury Lane plans to present *The Footmen's Conspiracy*. I am sure he'll see me."

Within minutes, Mrs. Hood returned and grudgingly showed Sophie into the front sitting room. There sat Peter, Roderick, and to her surprise, Mary Ann Skene, the erstwhile ruffle maker, playing a game of cards at a table set before the empty fireplace. Sophie stared at the homely but well-endowed young woman, recalling that the last time she had seen her was the day Aunt Harriet ran naked down Half Moon Passage. Today, Mary Ann was decked out in resplendent, if garish finery, for this late afternoon tête-à-tête.

"Ah . . . Sophie, I see our good news has caught up with you!" Peter said warmly, taking her arm and guiding her to a fourth chair facing the card table. "I was just saying to Darnly that I must send a note requesting you join us this evening to celebrate at the Blue Periwig. We'll have some supper, a bit of champagne!"

"I–I'm not sure . . . I—" she stammered, suddenly shy. She had severe doubts that her only evening gown, a lavender garment cut down from Aunt Harriet's limited wardrobe, would be suitable for such an elegant-sounding establishment.

"Of *course* you'll join us," Roderick said briskly. "I'll have my coach call for you by seven."

Sophie hurried home in high spirits to make herself ready. Within the hour, the clatter of hooves on the street below told her Darnly's coach had arrived.

Sophie did her best to maintain a calm demeanor when Darnley's party was led by a liveried servant into an elegantly appointed private dining room of the Blue Periwig. The walls were covered in a rich, sapphire brocade. Heavy matching draperies pulled back by gold ties framed the large-paned windows on one side of the ornate chamber. Opposite stood a wide sofa in matching blue brocade that appeared to Sophie to be as large as a bed.

The revelers settled into their chairs at the small, intimate dining table, which was laden with crystal and fine china and illuminated by a five-branched candelabra. Soon, bumpers of wine and delicate shelled oysters were served by an army of white-gloved waiters. A mock turtle soup, rich with carrots, onions, veal broth, and laced with a touch of Madeira was followed quickly by a terrine of potted beef. Next came roasted pigeons smothered in currant sauce presented on silver scallop shells. As more wine was poured into the crystal goblets, Sophie's eyes widened at the sight of glass dishes heaped with whipped syllabub swirling around bits of savory macaroons and featuring the rare condiment coconut.

After the servants had silently departed to allow the guests to enjoy their pudding in private, Roderick rose somewhat unsteadily to his feet and raised his wineglass.

"To our authors!" he toasted Peter and Sophie with an expansive gesture. "May your quills remain sharp!" He then sat down abruptly and leaned conspiratorially toward Mary Ann Skene and whispered something unintelligible into her ear.

"Hear! Hear!" Peter chorused, glancing over at Sophie a bit bleary eyed. "May our pens never waver!"

"I couldn't have said it better myself," Sophie replied, feeling warm and giggly and wondering at how light-headed she was.

Mary Ann was flushed scarlet and seemed more than a bit stewed herself. Even so, she somehow maintained enough coordination to slide spoonfuls of frothy syllabub into the open mouth of her companion.

"Tell me, my partner," Peter said, fingering the scrap of lace that decorated the sleeve of Sophie's lavender gown, "have you thought about what we can serve up *next* to our esteemed manager, Mr. Colman? He asked me if I had any other ideas as witty as *The Footmen's Conspiracy*."

"I will tell you a notion I had," Sophie said, feeling a silly grin spread over her features, "if *you* promise to inform Colman we both wrote the play and if you will tell me what fees you expect!"

"Fees?" Peter replied, looking puzzled. "Unless it plays extremely well, 'twill hardly cover the cost of this fine supper. Fees?" he repeated waggishly, staring intently into her eyes, "I think I'll pay you what's owing you thusly!"

Fueled by his bottle of champagne, he pulled Sophie to his chest and kissed her with the full force of his open mouth. She was so startled by his abrupt action that she lay in his arms unprotestingly. His lips pressed insistently against hers, his tongue, smelling sweetly of spirits, insinuated itself boldly into her mouth, sending an odd languor throughout her body. His hand slid up the front of her bodice and molded itself around her small breast, kneading it with gentle urgency.

"Sophie . . ." he murmured against her lips.

His kiss was quite unlike her memory of Hunter's passionate embrace, but, whether the wine, the lavish banquet or the pleasant fellowship was responsible for her feeling of goodwill, Sophie yielded herself to the warmth of Peter's embrace, and the gentle, pleasurable sensations they evoked. In light of Hunter's continuing silence, she allowed herself the comfort of leaning into Peter's chest, savoring the luxury of human contact after so lonely a summer. At length, some small, sane portion of her mind remembered the presence of Roderick and Mary Ann. She pulled away breathlessly and stared at the youthful aristocrat with some confusion.

"You have quite confounded me," she whispered. "I was asking you about fees . . . or was it you who were asking me?"

"About our next venture." He smiled, pouring more champagne. She stole a glance at their dinner companions who had at some point removed themselves to the blue brocaded couch on the far side of the room. Roderick Darnly was tipping his champagne glass against Mary Ann's lips while she stroked her hand against his satin-clad thigh. "I've racked my brains for an amusing notion, but can't think of a thing," Peter acknowledged candidly.

Sophie licked her lips and smoothed her hair in an attempt to regain her composure. Peter was smiling and his thumb was gently strafing the side of her cheekbone. He looked at her expectantly.

"Now that we've proven ourselves as dramatists," Sophie said earnestly, focusing her eyes with some difficulty, "you *will* tell Colman we're to share author's credit, won't you?" After all, she realized, Peter—with Darnly's help—*had* been the one to get the play accepted by George Colman. "'Tis so much less forbidding to work with a partner, Peter, but I must have your solemn pledge," she added, "that if we succeed in getting our first play past the censor, you shall disclose I am your joint author on this one *and* the next." Peter merely smiled and raised her hand to his lips. "And no more galloping off to the country when we have work to do?"

"You are such a scold, Mistress McGann . . . but a beautiful one," Peter replied, leaning forward to kiss her on the nose. "Now tell me your notion for a new comedy." He looked over at Roderick whose head was tilted against the back of the coach, his eyes closed. His linen was in disarray and Mary Ann was busily nuzzling her lips against his chest in a most provocative manner. "Darnly . . . sorry to interrupt, but we need your thoughts on this. Sophie has an idea for a new play."

The Earl of Llewelyn's son reluctantly rose to his feet and pulled Mary Ann to hers. With his arm draped casually around her shoulder, he sauntered back to the dining table and the couple again took their seats. Sophie, befuddled by the wine she had consumed, cleared her throat and hesitantly proposed a farce about a tempestuous, aging actress who falsely assumes that she remains the public's darling.

"However, behind her back, the younger players invent backstage ploys that eventually trick her into yielding to a prettier, younger, less pretentious actress who takes over her roles while the grand dame is suitably relegated to playing old crones. I thought to call the piece *The Provoked Player*," she finished, and then hiccuped.

"This couldn't be based on that wretched woman in Bath who was so horrid . . . Mavis Somebody?" Roderick chuckled. "We met her with young Hunter Robertson that night at the ball."

"It could be based on any number of actresses," Sophie protested faintly, resolving not to imbibe another drop of champagne.

"Well, Darnly . . . d'you think you could again use the power of persuasion at Drury Lane if we dash this off?"

Peter asked. He nodded in the direction of their benefactor. "My friend, here, has some influence, now that he's quietly purchased a mortgage on some of Lacy's shares, don't you, old chap?"

"'Tis good only for a few free tickets in a favorable box," Darnly shrugged, sipping more wine, "but I shall put in a good word, if I can." His eyes fastened on Sophie's flushed face and he took her hand in his. "I am most happy to advance the fortunes of those who show genuine talent," he added in a low voice.

He stooped to kiss her fingers and his lips lingered an instant too long for common courtesy. Despite Peter's inebriated state, Sophie sensed he had noticed Roderick's gesture and was displeased.

"Sink me, Darnly, if I shall allow you to charm this little morsel away with promises of fame and fortune! You stick to your ruffle maker, old man . . . I shall jolly well reserve Sophie for m'self, thank you very much! Now, if you would be so kind as to allow me the use of your coach, I shall escort the lady home."

"As you wish," Roderick said with a shrug before rising to his full height.

Peter took Sophie by the arm and bid a curt adieu to Darnly and Mary Ann, who was toying with the stem of her champagne glass, looking bored.

"The Honorable Mr. Darnly has reserved the Blue Periwig's finest suite for himself and Mistress Skene, and I think we shouldn't prevent their making use of it a moment longer!" Peter said pointedly. "We bid you good night. I'll settle the account with you later, if I may."

Roderick Darnly bowed to both of them but remained silent. Sophie allowed her escort to lead her from the chamber and down the stairs to the elaborately decorated reception foyer. Highly rouged young women were leading their male guests up the staircase and disappearing into rooms off the landing. It struck Sophie suddenly that she and Mary Ann had been entertained in nothing so grand as a high-class bawdy house.

"Good evening, Sir Peter," a heavily painted woman said as they awaited two servants who fetched their cloaks.

"We're pleased to have you and Mr. Darnly with us again this evening." The woman cast a speculative eye in Sophie's direction. "You'll grace us with your presence again soon, I hope."

"Ah . . . yes . . . thank you," Peter said brightly, assisting Sophie down the stairs in the direction of the waiting coach. A hint of autumn was in the air and the cool breeze that ruffled her cloak cleared Sophie's head a bit. "Cleveland Row, please, Charles," Peter directed the driver.

"Half Moon Passage first," Sophie called up to the coachman who struggled to keep Darnly's four-in-hand steady.

Before Peter could protest, she climbed in the carriage unaided. He settled himself next to her and they rode in silence for several minutes. Their faces remained in shadow as the vehicle turned down a lane leading from the Blue Periwig, to Covent Garden.

"Sophie—" Peter began, drawing her into his arms.

"F-forgive me," she insisted shakily, pushing her hands against his chest, "but I think it best if we keep our association strictly professional."

"But I kissed you and you—"

"I know . . . 'twas quite pleasant," she replied, regaining her composure, "but I believe 'tis better the way I suggest."

Peter sighed and took her hand, caressing it gently before he kissed it.

"Such a scold," he murmured against her flesh, "but so utterly charming."

Three days after the season's opening at Drury Lane, Sophie stood in front of St. James's Palace staring at the shining black enamel door with the brass plaque that read "Lord Chamberlain." The palace itself was only three stories high with white framed windows. To the right stood the gate to the palace itself flanked by red-coated guards standing at strict attention. With bated breath, Sophie reached for the knob and entered the outer office, just as she had been instructed by George Colman earlier in the day. A harried young man looked up from his desk with an inquiring glance.

"I've been asked to see about a license for a Drury Lane production, *The Footmen's Conspiracy,*" she said, struggling to remain calm.

"The author?" the clerk demanded peremptorily.

"Ah . . . Lindsay-Hoyt . . . Sir P-Peter Lindsay-Hoyt," Sophie replied unsteadily.

"Humm," the beleaguered young man temporized, shuffling several piles of paper around on his desk. "Ah . . . yes . . . here is the copy with deletions noted," he added, pointing to the title page where the words *Licensed for Acting* were scrawled.

"So, Mr. Capell has granted the play a license?" Sophie breathed.

"With *deletions noted,*" the clerk said irritably. "Anything with an *X* may not be spoken on stage. Surely you know that!"

Sophie began to flip through several pages of her manuscript and noted with a sinking heart that entire speeches had been crossed out and many lines of dialogue obliterated by strokes of dark black ink. As she surveyed the rest of her work she nearly choked with outrage.

"May I see Mr. Capell, himself?" she asked in a low voice.

"That would be impossible," the clerk snapped. "He's extremely busy and so am I—"

Suddenly an angry voice shouted from the doorway of the inner chamber.

"Confound it, Grieves, you've neglected to sharpen my quills properly!"

"Mr. Capell!" Sophie exclaimed, whirling to face the deputy examiner of plays.

"Yes?" Capell replied with obvious annoyance.

"I am Sophie McGann . . . we met at David Garrick's some time ago . . . the day you were examining his new Shakespeare Folio."

"Oh, quite," said the fifty-one-year-old civil servant who on that day had demonstrated his obsession with white-colored food. Sure enough, his face was still livid with the red blotches. Sophie was certain he had no memory of her whatsoever.

"I've just come to fetch *The Footmen's Conspiracy* for George Colman at Drury Lane. He'll be ever so pleased to see you've granted it a license, but may I tell him, sir . . . pray, why is this amusing exchange in Act One not acceptable? I, myself, heard Mr. Colman near split his sides, he found it so comical."

Edward Capell, his scaly skin flushing scarlet, stared at her disdainfully.

"Then, Mr. Colman is more a lover of tawdry farce than I thought," he snapped. "But I have no need to speak of such things to a mere chit!" he added with a dismissive wave of his hand. "Tell Colman he performs this, word-for-word, as I have licensed it, or I'll send the King's Men to shut him down. Now leave me!"

With that, the malevolent little man turned toward his cowering clerk.

"Grieves . . . come in here at once and bring a penknife. I want these quills sharp as a scabbard, you fool!"

Sophie could feel her body trembling with fury as she emerged from the Lord Chamberlain's office into Pall Mall. Ignoring the bustling afternoon traffic, she whirled on her heel and strode angrily toward Cleveland Row. Barging past Mrs. Hood at Peter's front door, she stormed into his sitting room where she found her collaborator and Roderick Darnly engaged in a game of cards.

Pointing to Capell's blackened deletions in the manuscript, she denounced the heavy-handed cuts. For his part, Peter appeared more upset about Roderick beating him at cards.

"What care we what exact words are spoken on the stage?" Peter shrugged, squinting at the cards in his hands. "As long as Colman pays for the Author's Third Night Benefit, I am content."

Sophie stared at him, dumbfounded. Roderick rose and placed a sympathetic arm around Sophie's small shoulders.

"Ah . . . my dear Sophie," he chided gently. "To Capell, nothing will compare with the Almighty Bard. 'Tis typical of the minions's sensibilities. But at least the work will see the stage. 'Tis more than most dramatists achieve, I assure you. Take heart, my dear girl."

"But that little nobody has changed the timing and the cadences of speeches that I'd toiled over for ages!" she protested vehemently. "I was striving for a certain effect and now the piece is *ruined*!"

"'Tis not ruined," Peter soothed, tossing down his cards to offer her some reassurance. "He's snipped a few words here and there . . . just as you have!"

"He's made minced meat of the *entire* play!" Sophie shouted, her anger at Capell and the situation itself coming to a boil. "Perhaps 'tis just as well you have thus far relegated me to an anonymous scribe!" she cried, striding furiously toward the sitting room door. "If the audience should damn this piece because of these foul deletions, no one shall know I ever had a hand in it!"

And without a word, she flung herself past the startled housekeeper and yanked open Peter's front door. She stormed past a pair of alarmed pedestrians out for a stroll along Pall Mall. As she stalked down the road, she was assaulted by a disturbing memory of black-cassocked clergymen carelessly slinging her father's precious volumes onto the floor of McGann's Printers and Booksellers.

Chapter 17

January 1765

Sophie leaned against the back stage wall for support, staring anxiously through the wings at the players reciting their lines in front of the restive audience. She barely noticed the pungent odor wafting from the stage candles glowing against their tin reflectors. After a few minutes, Peter drifted toward the Greenroom in search of more amusing company while Sophie continued to watch the debacle unfolding on stage.

From her side vantage point, she could see part of the pit and a slice of the first and second tier of boxes. The theater patrons were chatting, making private jokes and generally ignoring Elizabeth Griffith's *The Platonic Wife*, a play that agitated for better treatment of married women. What, Sophie despaired, would be the fate of *The Footmen's Conspiracy* in the face of such an indifferent crowd? Her play was scheduled to be presented after the main selection.

Downstage, the actors soldiered on despite the swelling boos and catcalls. In the face of the audience's obvious displeasure, they gave their best effort to the overlong speeches.

"The gentlemen out front do not like a woman who converts her husband to her own point of view!" Kitty Clive whispered loudly in Sophie's ear. The actress had emerged from the women's tiring-room dressed as Lady Fanshaw and wore a grim look. "Poor Elizabeth," she said, referring to the dramatist who had retired to the Greenroom to avoid hearing her work vilified.

"Well, at least Colman has given her this chance," Sophie

whispered back. "I thought he had no use for women scribes."

Kitty reacted with a puzzled look. In the next instant, however, the incomparable actress turned her attention to the stage and made an amusing entrance that, mercifully, provoked a delighted response from the fickle audience.

By the third act, the goodwill generated by Mrs. Clive's appearance had worn off. And when the curtains finally closed, the applause was painfully sparse. Soon, the Drury Lane patrons were drifting into the foyer, intent on using the interval either to secure refreshments, repair to the out-door privy, or merely seek a breath of fresh air.

By this time, Sophie's stomach was churning at the thought of how this unpredictable audience might react to Peter's and her work. However, she was diverted by the sight of Elizabeth Griffith, emerging from the Greenroom, wringing her handkerchief and babbling to anyone who would listen.

"Surely, the audience response wasn't against the *play*?" she insisted to Sophie, who stood in the shadows backstage. "The actors did their parts poorly, don't you think? 'Tis certainly no crime of *mine*! Oh, if only David Garrick had been here to advise in rewriting and casting . . . all would have been quite different!"

Sophie silently agreed that Elizabeth Griffith's lackluster piece needed Garrick's sensibility and sharp quill, but she soon found herself unable to keep up with the distracted woman's conversation. As the playwright drifted off to seek solace somewhere else, Peter and Roderick Darnly appeared in the dimly lit wings.

"'Tis certainly ladies' night at Drury Lane," Roderick noted dryly, as soon as Mrs. Griffith was out of earshot. "George Colman can't be criticized for not giving female wits their due . . . then again, he doesn't realize he has *two* presentations tonight by petticoat authors."

Just then, Mrs. Clive brushed past, dressed now as the Head Cook in *The Footmen's Conspiracy*. Within minutes, the curtains parted, triggering a series of speedy exits and entrances in the country kitchen on stage. When the first spontaneous laugh erupted from the auditorium, Sophie clutched Peter's arm to brace herself. Another chortle was heard from the audience, and then another, as the comical events of the plot unfolded. Sophie bit her lip and glanced over at Roderick Darnly, who gazed back at her with an amused smile. Despite Capell's heavy-handed cuts, the ironic humor she had woven into the story was apparently intact and the audience was responding.

"'Pon my word, they *like* it!" Peter whispered, incredulous as another burst of merriment rolled back stage across the smoking foot candles. He delightedly clapped Sophie on the back. Sophie, however, remained rooted to the spot, amazed whenever a line she and Peter had toiled over produced a chuckle or burst of laughter. When the curtain on the two-act farce finally closed, the assembly out front took up the chant "Author! Author! Author!"

At the sound of the cheering, Peter sauntered out from the wings, his chest puffed with pride. Sophie watched as he walked to the fore stage and gravely accepted the accolades from the throng.

"The rabble approves of your first effort, it seems . . . especially compared with Mrs. Griffith's lamentable dirge," Roderick commented over the noisy adulation.

Sophie merely stared, torn between delirium and despair.

Afterward, George Colman thumped Peter on the back as he invited his newfound protégé into the Greenroom.

"My faith in your play was completely justified, old boy," he said with some relief, pouring Sir Peter a glass of port. "In fact, I hope 'twill carry the Griffith piece at least to the Author's Third Night Benefit," he added, lowering his voice so as not to be overheard by the unfortunate writer. "I'm just sorry it took three months to get a version of Griffith's work past that damnable censor," the manager sighed. "We should have put yours on earlier in the season, but that's life upon the wicked stage!" Colman laughed. Leaning in toward the baronet, he added conspiratorially, "I liked your notion about the aging actress. Let me see a draft of it as soon as you can!"

And before Sophie could hector Peter into confessing their joint-authorship and his appropriating her latest plot, the manager rushed toward the Greenroom entrance to greet a group of well-wishers who had their hearts set on meeting Kitty Clive.

To Sophie's surprise, Peter hailed a hackney coach in front of Drury Lane and bid Roderick Darnly a resolute good night as he entered his own vehicle. Assisting Sophie to her seat, the baronet climbed in beside her and closed the carriage door. His face was flushed with excitement, and before she could utter a word, he took her hand and pressed it to his heart.

"Ah . . . Sophie . . . what a night!" Peter exclaimed, "and I owe it all to you!" He inclined his head forward, his dark eyes searching hers for some sign that she acknowledged his gratitude. "For the first time, I can see a way for myself in this world . . . I am sick unto death of drifting along as I have."

Surprised by this unexpected confession, Sophie merely gazed at him silently as the carriage bumped along through the wide expanse of Covent Garden's colonnaded Great Piazza.

"I no longer wish to be a mere 'dabbler,' " he told her earnestly. "I see, for the first time, really, that together we could become as celebrated a play writing team as Garrick and Colman! Remember *Miss in Her Teens*? That play is *still* staged year after year . . . the royalties helped Garrick purchase that lovely country house of his, I'll be bound!"

"Aye . . . penning plays is by far the most lucrative way for a scribe to earn a living," Sophie agreed tersely. "I look forward to receiving my half of the proceeds." She stared at him coolly across the coach and removed her hand from his. "And if we are to collaborate on *my* idea, which you have apparently already discussed with Colman," she added tartly, "I will expect full participation on your part."

"We could make a fortune, you and I," Peter said pensively. "The really successful playwrights with one or two pieces a year can earn six hundred pounds, I understand. And the copyright for printed plays, they say, is another hundred! If you produced our work on your own press, we'd probably profit *twice* that!" He recaptured her hand and raised it to his lips. "I wouldn't need a farthing from my grandfather and we could live like princes!" he continued while gazing into her eyes as if looking for confirmation of his dreams of fame and glory. He took her chin between his fingers and kissed her lightly on the lips. "Witty and pretty, that's what you are," he whispered. "What an extraordinary combination." He shifted his weight to sit next to her on the carriage bench and drew her into his arms. "I promise, Sophie, from now on, I shall heed your strictures to work more diligently. And deuced, if writing more plays won't provide an excellent excuse to see you every single day."

Peter's arms were oddly comforting after an evening of such gut-wrenching tension, and she allowed herself to sink into his embrace. Tilting her head to be kissed, she felt his lips press against hers softly, sweetly, and then with a growing ardor that neither threatened her nor aroused her to a fever pitch. What was taking place between them, she thought vaguely, was not at all like the sense-shattering encounter with Hunter Robertson—but then, *that* had led to nothing but misery, and a painful separation. Peter seemed to be offering some form of personal and professional alliance and Sophie was forced to admit the combination had a certain seductive appeal.

"Will you come to Cleveland Row tonight?" Peter murmured urgently.

His breath was warm and his arms enveloped her protectively. His vow to dedicate his life to something more worthwhile was somehow touching. Considering the deafening silence from Dublin, she was sorely tempted to accept his ardent invitation, but a warning voice urged her to observe the behavior of this would-be playwright a while longer. Their success tonight had prompted Peter to promise to improve his working habits—but would he keep his word?

Reaching up to cup his face between her palms, she said gently, "I'd like to be with you tonight very much, but I shan't." She leaned forward to kiss him firmly on the lips. Pulling away from his startled gaze, she smiled mischievously. "However, I *promise* to be at your lodgings tomorrow by ten in the morning to begin our work on *The Provoked Player* . . . how would that suit?"

"Not nearly as much as if I had you in my bed," he

replied with a crooked grin. "But if 'tis the only way to convince you of my sincere devotion, I will gladly make the sacrifice."

※

Elizabeth Griffith's play enjoyed a moderately successful six-night run thanks only to the amusing afterpiece, *The Footmen's Conspiracy*. At both the Third Night and Sixth Night Author's Benefits, Sophie was pleased to discover Drury Lane filled to overflowing, thanks in part, to Darnly's recruiting legions of his acquaintances to support ticket sales. Even so, Sophie hesitated to announce her joint authorship to George Colman and the world, fearing she would jeopardize the vastly improved atmosphere at Cleveland Row.

During February and March, Sophie was gratified to see how studiously Peter applied himself to the work at hand. Together, they penned a first draft of *The Provoked Player* within six weeks. Peter rarely missed one of their writing appointments and virtually ceased imbibing the goodly amount of port and champagne he had been wont to consume. He also curtailed his forays to the clubs he and Darnly had frequented with regularity, including White's and some mysterious organization that required the pair to don black capes and masks. And to Sophie's amusement, neither he nor Darnly ever suggested they repair to the Blue Periwig.

Instead, Peter plied her with cunning little gifts—a silver-sheathed quill pen and a fan painted to depict the interior of Drury Lane itself. And he plied her with kisses, taking every opportunity to tell her how lovely she looked and that he hoped he was earning her trust and admiration.

For herself, Sophie was content to drift along in this odd sort of courtship, happy that she found herself dwelling less and less on thoughts of Hunter. Occasionally, however, she dreamed of her former lover and woke up mortified by her half-remembered nighttime fantasies.

On a day in late March she left Lorna in charge of Ashby's while she dashed next door to the Green Canister to buy a tonic for Aunt Harriet. Her visits to Bedlam dressed as a young boy had become routine and the guards accepted her gifts for her aunt without hesitation, pocketing the gratuity she placed in their palm to ensure delivery. Aunt Harriet would most likely never make use of anything but the food Sophie brought, but she always included in her packages some small token—a special elixir or a small rose sachet in hopes that the poor soul would sense there was someone who cared for her welfare.

As Sophie was paying Mrs. Phillips for her latest purchase, Mary Ann Skene wandered into the Green Canister, appearing thin and sallow.

"Here you are, dearie," Mrs. Phillips said, handing the young courtesan a cotton pouch. "Boil the water and let the packet steep a good half hour. Strain it and drink like tea. Apply the salve several times a day," she directed.

The woman nodded wanly and departed without another word.

"Let that be a lesson to you," Mrs. Phillips clucked. "Señor Gonorrhea plays no favorites, I can tell you that! I suggest, my dear Sophie, that you take care the company *you* keep as well!"

"You mean Sir Peter Lindsay-Hoyt?" Sophie replied, surprised.

"Aye!" Mrs. Phillips nodded. "Mary Ann mentioned he's kept you quite occupied of late."

"He wishes me to live with him," Sophie shrugged, "but I've declined."

"Humph!" Mrs. Phillips snorted, taking Sophie's money for her purchase of the tonic. "'Tis your own affair, of course, but certain men being what I know them to be—*and* since I'm a friend of your aunt—I will make you a present of *this*!" From the shelves behind the counter she selected a sheepskin condom displayed alongside various antidotes for venereal disease. She placed the cylindrical object in its own cotton pouch.

"Really, Mrs. Phillips!" Sophie exclaimed, "I've not slept with the man, if that's what you're implying."

"I am of the opinion the device is also useful in preventing the getting of brats," the older woman continued, ignoring her protest. "I strongly suggest you keep it in your reticule at all times and insist Sir Peter *employ* it!"

One rainy afternoon in the middle of April, Peter and Sophie toiled a solid six hours in one sitting, the rewards for such sustained effort resulting in a completed second draft of *The Provoked Player.*

"*Finis!*" Sophie exclaimed gaily, drawing a line beneath the final speech with a flourish of her pen. "How I *love* to inscribe that word!"

"Bravo us!" Peter chortled, rubbing his thumbs in soothing circles between her strained shoulder blades as she sat at his desk. "Surely, this calls for champagne!" he declared.

He strode over to a nearby wall and yanked a fat, braided silk cord, summoning Mrs. Hood to secure some sparkling wine.

"We've none in the cellar, Sir Peter," the housekeeper responded in her typically uncooperative manner.

"Then go *fetch* some!" Peter said testily.

"I'll need to pay the tradesman," she responded pointedly, extending her hand.

"Oh, blast it, woman!" Peter exploded. "Tell them to send me an accounting!"

Before Mrs. Hood could protest, Sophie reached into her reticule and withdrew several shillings.

"Here . . . let this be *my* gift," she announced. "You've feted me with many a meal while we've been working," she smiled at Peter. "Here, Mrs. Hood . . . two bottles, please."

"Very good, miss," Mrs. Hood sniffed. "I'll send the footman . . . if I can *find* him!"

For the remainder of the afternoon Sophie and Peter sipped excellent champagne in front of the fire and nibbled on toast points and potted shrimp. As the light faded, Peter lit candles around the room and they read aloud the scenes from their play that they found most amusing. When they concluded Act Five—as well as most of the second bottle of champagne—Peter suddenly took hold of one of her hands.

"You're a partner beyond price, Sophie, my love," he said as his eyes sought hers. "These last two months have been better than anything I've ever known . . . I am so terribly grateful for your guiding hand . . . and the confidence you've shown in me . . ."

"We've done well," Sophie responded, marveling at the change in his attitude toward hard work. "'Tis remarkable how splendidly we've done, pulling on the same oar . . ." she noted solemnly before a loud hiccup erupted from her throat.

They burst out laughing and then Peter took her hand in his, pressing it to his lips, murmuring, "Yes . . . that's what you've proven, to be sure." He peered at her gravely. "And that brings me to another topic of supreme importance," he added, licking his lips nervously. "Please, dear Sophie," he pleaded softly, his dark brown eyes attempting to focus intently on her face, "will you do me the honor . . . of becoming my wife?"

Startled and somewhat sobered by his unexpected declaration, Sophie stared at her writing partner in shock. She struggled to muster a suitable response.

"'Tis far too soon to consider . . . such a dire step as marriage," she managed to say, inadvertently tipping over her empty champagne glass. Setting it to rights, she added hastily, "but I am, indeed, esteemed that you should think to offer—"

"Do you not wish to be a baronet's lady?" he entreated. "'Lady Lindsay-Hoyt.' Oh, Sophie . . . it means everything that you've shown such faith in me. If it weren't for you, I'd have turned into a total wastrel!"

"Oh come, now," she giggled, "pray tell me I'm not such a boringly good influence on you as *that*!"

"Well," he said, catching her mischievous mood, "I have found that the notion of your lovely face and form so near— and yet so far—keeps me restless in my bed and anxious to get on with our project each day. And that keen wit of yours is no small attraction, either. I believe 'twill make us *rich*!"

She smiled indulgently, reaching over to smooth a stray strand of dark hair off his forehead. "I thought you *were* rich, sir!"

Peter stared at her for a moment, then grinned foolishly. "Richer! Your wit will make us *richer*!"

"Speaking of riches," she smiled, "when will we be receiving the fees owing from our Authors' Benefits for *The Footmen's Conspiracy*? I'm sure our royalties by now will add up to far more than the price of a dinner at the Blue Periwig," she added pointedly.

Peter frowned and got up to stand beside the fireplace.

"Really, Sophie!" he chided, some of his playfulness evaporating. "You should take some pains to disguise your Scottish miserliness, my love. We can't go groveling to Colman after a few pounds, can we? *The Provoked Player* is the piece that will put you in silks and satin, but you must show some ladylike patience. Stop mewling and come over here, lass," he commanded, stretching out his hand to her.

Feeling simultaneously guilty for raising the issue of money and unfairly chastised by Peter's cavalier attitude, Sophie rose from her chair and walked rather unsteadily toward him, attempting to regain her equilibrium. He drew her against his chest.

"Such a pretty little pinch-penny," he murmured, whispering into her hair as his hands massaged her back in sensuous circles. "Let *me* worry about our funds, will you? When I make you Lady Lindsay-Hoyt, you won't trouble yourself over such trifles, will you, darling?"

"I haven't said I'd become Lady Anybody," Sophie replied tersely, feeling a headache coming on, both from their conversation and far too much champagne.

He pulled her closer, whispering urgently into her ear. "Lady Lindsay-Hoyt. It suits you . . . absolutely suits you, my angel." He wrapped his arms around her waist and pulled her firmly against the length of his body, evidence of his obvious desire pressing against her thigh.

As his lips began trailing kisses from her ear to the base of her throat, a vision of Hunter rose, unbidden, in her memory. It had been nearly a year since they'd parted, Sophie thought, distressed to realize she felt oddly removed from the ardor of Peter's fervent embrace. She had made her choice to return to London, and she had not heard a word from Hunter since. At least Peter wanted her . . . wanted to be her writing partner . . . wanted her to be his *wife*!

His kisses had become more demanding and she forced her mind to attempt to concentrate on the pleasant sensations he was evoking with his thumb as he stroked her breast through the fabric of her gown. She felt nearly cleaved in two as her senses were heightened by his ardor and, at the same time, diminished by a strange sense of detachment, a mere curiosity to see how the scene between them would play through to its conclusion. After several moments, he broke away and strode to the door, locking it with a decisive click of the key.

"What about Mrs. Hood . . . ?" Sophie giggled as he marched over to the window and yanked closed the velvet drapes that fronted Cleveland Row. Then he turned to face her with a determined gleam in his eye.

"The baggage wouldn't dare attempt to come in here unless I rang," he said gruffly, picking up the champagne bottle in one hand and taking Sophie's hand in the other. Draining the last of the bubbly liquid from the container's narrow throat, he set it carefully on the floor beside the satin-covered chaise.

Without further conversation, they divested each other of their clothing, leaving their garments in piles beside the couch. The firelight danced in amber patterns against Peter's skin as Sophie surveyed his naked body for the first time. She could see the dark stubble that shadowed his face this late afternoon was matched by black hairs covering much of his chest, legs and arms. She thought fleetingly of the fine golden hair dusting Hunter's well-muscled torso. Immediately, she banished all memory of that magical afternoon in Bath by holding out her arms to the young baronet.

"You're so fair . . ." he murmured, drinking in the sight of her auburn hair and pale skin. He inclined his head to kiss her as he asked gruffly, "Have you been with a man 'ere this?"

"Yes . . . yes, I have," she said, swallowing as a frown creased his forehead. "If it pleases you not I have had . . . another lover . . . perhaps we'd better reconsider . . ."

Sophie hesitated, her headache growing more severe by the minute. She was overwhelmed by a sudden desire to be home alone in her own bed.

"Sophie, my love," he whispered urgently, pulling her

roughly against him, "what pleases me is *you* . . . just you."

The chartreuse satin upholstery felt cold against her back as Peter's full weight pressed her body against the daybed in his sitting room. She attempted to ignore the dull ache throbbing in her temples, concentrating, instead, on the sensation of his lips pressing against the hollow of her throat. His knees swiftly parted her thighs and when he entered her, she heard him sigh, almost with relief. Then, he began to throw his torso against hers in short, eager strokes, as if he were competing in some contest in which he intended to vanquish his opponent by sheer, physical endurance. She pushed her palms against his chest, hoping to slow down his frenetic pace, but to no avail. Within seconds, he emitted a groan and collapsed against her, sweat drenching the black mat of hair covering his chest.

As Peter lay beside her, panting with exhaustion, a thought suddenly pierced through Sophie's champagne-induced lethargy. She had forgotten to make use of the sheepskin condom Mrs. Phillips had so emphatically warned her to keep at the ready.

Sophie waited anxiously during the following week for any signs of infection resulting from her carelessness that April afternoon in Peter's sitting room. Even so, she was greatly relieved to discover as the month progressed that there was no evidence of Boswell's old nemesis, Señor Gonorrhea. Despite her relief, she battled severe feelings of remorse for having fallen into Peter's bed and, in a weak moment, even entertaining the notion of becoming his wife. This was a step she realized she had no intention of taking, even in the unlikely event Peter's grandfather would give his blessing to such an alliance.

"'Twas a terrible thing to do," Sophie confessed somberly to Lorna one morning as they opened the book shop for business. "I don't require a Calvinist preacher to tell me that!"

"'Tis *not* such a terrible thing, Sophie," Lorna insisted,

wrapping a sympathetic arm around her friend's shoulder. "Foolish, perhaps, but not terrible."

"Yes, it was," Sophie insisted dejectedly. "I see now, I do not truly return Peter's affections, and I *used* him to ease the loss I feel for—" she faltered, looking away quickly to avoid Lorna seeing the tears that invariably sprang to her eyes whenever she mentioned her unhappy parting with Hunter.

"It appears to me that Peter's used you to gain fame—and some fortune," Lorna responded firmly. "'Tis an even exchange, I'd say." She gave Sophie's arm a soft squeeze. "'Twill all come right in the end with Hunter . . . just you wait and see. The man can't play to the bloody Irish forever! But I must admit," she added pointedly, "I'm relieved you've decided to steer clear of Peter's bed. Mrs. Phillips says—"

"Aye," Sophie replied shortly, halting her friend midsentence. "All that's finished."

In truth, she had foresworn champagne forever and, since that day, had repaired to her lodgings in Half Moon Passage each night at the conclusion of their writing sessions. She refrained from all manner of physical intimacy, pleading fatigue—which was real—and the press of her duties as a shopkeeper and printer.

For his part, Peter seemed strangely satisfied with their current arrangement. He showed her the list of revisions Colman had ordered for the final draft. However, as the summer wore on, the more pages Sophie produced of the new draft of *The Provoked Player*, the fewer Peter tended to contribute. Despite her effort to be forgiving, Sophie grew increasingly impatient at the hours spent reworking several troublesome scenes with virtually no help from her co-author.

One sultry morning in early July, Sophie rang the bell to the baronet's flat, only to be informed by the surly Mrs. Hood that his lordship had failed to return from a night on the town with Roderick Darnly.

"No bother . . . I'll just slip in and get to work," Sophie announced brightly, trying to mask her irritation.

Her stomach already felt mildly queasy from a breakfast of cold cabbage and a bit of meat left over from her supper the previous evening. This latest development only made her feel worse. Assuming her customary seat at Peter's desk, she resolutely attributed her biliousness to the long hours she'd been working and to her anxiety over funds. She had been equally distressed by the deteriorating condition of her aunt whom she had visited in Bedlam the previous Sunday.

Suddenly, Mrs. Hood flung open the velvet drapes in the sitting room with an angry jerk.

"Don't know why I put up with it!" the middle-aged woman muttered under her breath. "Seeing to guests when I haven't been paid my wages in *weeks!*" The woman turned, hands on hips and glared in Sophie's direction. "I suppose you'll be wantin' me to serve you tea, like you was some proper lady!"

"Actually, I'd appreciate a cup very much right now," Sophie replied evenly, thinking tea might be just the prescription to settle her stomach.

During the rest of the day she found it difficult to concentrate on the plot problems Colman had accurately detected in the final act. As the day wore on and Peter did not return, she could feel a knot of fury building inside her, choking off whatever comic muse she usually summoned to portray the back stage antics of the competing actors who peopled this new play. Her stomach continued to churn and she wondered if her anger over Peter's increasingly wayward behavior could actually make her ill.

At about two in the afternoon, she heard a bell ringing outside. Her pen was poised over a sheet of foolscap with a thicket of crossed out sections marring its surface. She listened intently when Mrs. Hood opened the front door.

"Lost your key, have you?" Sophie heard the housekeeper snap. "You've company in the sitting room. That scribbler's been here all day . . . wanting tea, like she was mistress of the house!"

"I'll have some too," Peter replied cheerfully as he opened the door to the front chamber. "No . . . make it coffee . . . hot and strong."

"Before I fetch the coffee, sir, I must speak to you," Mrs. Hood said stubbornly, lingering in the foyer.

"I'm afraid 'twill have to wait," Peter replied in clipped tones. "I have a guest."

"I'll be wanting my wages, sir," Mrs. Hood retorted. "I can't be slaving for a gentleman like yourself if you don't pay m'fees!"

"*Coffee,* woman!" Peter pronounced, ignoring her request as he entered the sitting room. "God's bones!" he said for Sophie's benefit, "that wretch is a housekeeper from Hades!"

"One can hardly blame her," she replied as Peter sauntered into the sun-filled chamber. "I, too, have yet to see proper payment for my labors." She rose from the desk. "However, that is merely *one* of my complaints. You are four hours late for our appointment!"

"'Pon my word, Sophie," Peter replied with feigned amusement, "you, too? How many harpies must I endure in my own house?"

"Harpy!" Sophie exclaimed, refusing to fall in with Peter's attempts at humor. "In the last month I have done virtually all of the work suggested by Colman, while you . . . you've done naught but frequent every drinking and wenching establishment in this city, I hear!"

"Well, have you considered that if you hadn't suddenly become such a cold-hearted lass," Peter noted pointedly, heading for his drinks cabinet, "perhaps there'd be a greater temptation to return to my own bed."

Stung, Sophie watched silently while he blithely poured himself a stiff brandy. She was unnerved by the offhanded way he had loudly voiced the fact of their intimacy within earshot of Mrs. Hood.

Mortified by their exchange, Sophie gathered her papers into a pile.

"See here, Peter," she said, turning to face him, "since you have yet to write a single word of this draft, I am off to Drury Lane to submit these changes in *my* name."

"You wouldn't *dare*!" Peter pronounced with an amused smile.

"I certainly would!" Sophie retorted. "You deny that I'm the genuine author of these pages?"

Suddenly, a wave of exhaustion invaded every fiber of

Sophie's body. She sank into a chair near the cold fireplace, next to an ornamental paper fan that masked the hearth during the summer months.

"Sophie . . . look here, I—" Peter began, his tone suddenly contrite.

"Don't bother to apologize or make excuses," she interrupted in a fatigued voice. "You were at the Blue Periwig or some such brothel all night and it doesn't interest me in the least. I just want the play to be accepted at Drury Lane and be *done* with all this!"

She heard cups rattling in the foyer and soon Mrs. Hood marched in with a tray, which she thumped on the table next to Sophie's chair. The aromatic fumes of the rich, sable brew wafting toward her nostrils were inexplicably nauseating and Sophie nearly gagged at an odor she normally found delightful. Her throat felt constricted, and cold sweat broke out on her forehead.

"Sophie?" Peter said hesitantly, his expression registering his alarm at her wan appearance.

But before he could finish his sentence, Sophie bolted toward the fireplace and was thoroughly sick behind the paper fan.

"Good God!" Peter exclaimed to Mrs. Hood. "Go and fetch a bucket of water and a cloth . . . Sophie, what the deuce . . . ?"

"Ooh . . ." Sophie replied weakly as Mrs. Hood beat a hasty retreat to do the baronet's bidding. She leaned against the mantelpiece to steady herself, humiliated by what had just transpired.

"Probably a bad shrimp," Peter suggested, taking her arm and leading her over to the day bed where he urged her to lie down. "I've had it happen to me . . . nasty business, that."

"No," Sophie whispered, tears flooding her eyes. "'Tis not a shrimp that's caused this." Without warning, an overwhelming sadness engulfed her, and she felt a sob welling in her chest. "You've gotten me with c-child," she wailed, "or I've gotten myself with it . . . oh, *God* . . . how could I have been such a rustic—"

Peter sank to his knees beside the daybed, grasping her hands.

"You're enceinte?" he asked incredulously, an odd look of surprise and unaccountable satisfaction passing over his features.

"Aye," she replied, appalled by his ridiculous posture. "I've ignored the signs for weeks, convinced 'twas merely fatigue . . ."

A broad smile animated his unshaven features.

"That's wonderful news, darling," he pronounced delightedly. "We must marry straightaway!"

"W-what?" Sophie stammered, feeling as if the world was whirling in dizzying circles. "No! Absolutely *not!*"

"I must make an honest woman of you, Sophie!" Peter said, almost crowing. "You can't have your babe called 'bastard,' can you now?"

"But what of that formidable grandfather you're always going on about?" Sophie demanded, alarmed by another wave of distress unsettling her stomach. "He'd never agree to it!"

"I've been thinking on that very subject, of late," Peter replied with a pleased smile. "And I've determined that 'tis time I'm free of the blackguard's disapproving prattle. What do I care how dear *grandpère* reacts to our union now?" He raised her trembling hand to his lips. "Our babe's decided it. 'Tis time I made you my wife."

Chapter 18

Lorna and Sophie stayed up the better part of the night debating Sophie's alternatives.

"I'm not the first lass to make a fatal slip," Sophie said morosely, sipping a tisane that Mrs. Phillips had recommended to calm her digestion. "And I fear I won't be the last. At least the bairn will have a proper name. I couldn't stand to have a child treated wretchedly, like those poor bastard offspring I saw growing up in the back wynds of Edinburgh."

"Aye," Lorna Blount agreed sadly. "And some day the babe may have a title and lands to show for your sacrifice. I'm glad, at least, you refused that purgative Mrs. Phillips offered. Mary Ann Skene nearly died taking that same potion last year," she added earnestly. "I heard she aborted a lass missing fingers and toes!"

Sophie shuddered at the thought.

"At least Garrick has accepted the revisions Colman wanted," she said, clinging to at least one shred of good news. The manager and his wife had recently returned to London, full of new ideas for lighting and scenery inspired by what they'd observed on the Continent. Sophie had been too ill to pay them a call but had dispatched a note of welcome. She sighed and shook her head. "Perhaps Peter and I will eventually . . . find our way together," she said, fighting the emotion that sprang from her half-buried dream of

seeing Hunter Robertson one day and having all made right
between them.

Peter had appeared utterly delighted at the prospect of
becoming a father. He would not hear of Sophie's refusing
to marry him and, the following day, appeared on her doorstep with an armload of flowers.

"But your grandfather . . ." Sophie once again interjected, knowing full well what Peter's answer would be.

"Sir Thomas Hoyt be damned!" he smiled at her confi-
dently. "We shall be like Colman and Garrick—a force to be
reckoned with!"

"What will your friend Darnly say?" she demanded.
"Won't he judge you to have married beneath your station?"

"Darnly's departed for Henley to visit friends. Once our
union is a *fait accompli*, he'll have to be gracious about it,"
Peter shrugged. "And besides, Roderick may be a terrible
snob, but I happen to know he quite admires your pluck."

Having considered the problem from every angle, Sophie
felt she really had no choice. Within ten days' time, the
banns were read and she and Sir Peter Lindsay-Hoyt were
wed quietly at the Actors' Church, St. Paul's, Covent Garden. Only Lorna Blount and Mrs. Phillips knew of Sophie's
reluctant decision to marry and served as the sole witnesses
to the ceremony. In spite of her many reservations, Sophie
McGann had, indeed, become the Lady Lindsay-Hoyt.

A week following their wedding, Sophie was reclining
one evening on the daybed in Peter's sitting room, trying to
think of something besides her wretched nausea, when she
heard a sharp pounding on the front door. Mrs. Hood grumbled under her breath all the way through the foyer. The
next instant, Roderick Darnly strode into the chamber in
high dudgeon.

"Ah . . . Darnly, you've returned!" Peter said genially.
"How was Henley, old man?"

But Roderick ignored the friendly greeting.

"What have you *done* you foolish, foolish girl!" he declared loudly in Sophie's direction and then turned to con-

front his erstwhile companion. "Peter, you really have behaved despicably, though I'm not surprised! You've deflowered this poor young woman to secure a scribbling drone who'll keep you out of Newgate."

"'Twas far too late for any deflowering, I fear, old boy," Peter said nervously, pouring himself a brandy. "Some other worthy gentleman had already had that pleasure . . . but, yes . . . I think Sophie's writing abilities should prove useful. What of it?"

Sophie jumped to her feet in the midst of this appalling discourse and immediately regretted such precipitous action. Feeling dizzy, she clutched at the sofa arm to steady herself.

"How dare you speak of me thus!" she cried to her husband of less than a week.

"Ah . . . playing the lady already," Peter chided. "Well, since Darnly's here, we might as well hazard all our cards on the table, shall we? Yes . . . I have given your babe a name and in return, I expect you to earn your keep—as you have proven you are fully capable of doing. A comedy or two a year should bring in a nice annuity . . . and if the world thinks *I'm* the clever one, so much the better," he chortled.

Dumbfounded, Sophie stared at her new husband. The charming smile had vanished, as had his teasing, affectionate manner. In its place, Sir Peter had adopted a smug, self-satisfied air.

"I would advise your bride not to play the 'lady,' as you put it, for an entirely *different* reason!" Darnly declared, his features flushed with uncharacteristic anger. "I regret to inform you, Sophie, that Peter may have given you a name for your child, but 'tis not the name you think! I have recently discovered that he is no heir or even an aristocrat. In fact, Sir Thomas Hoyt of Yorkshire *has* no son. He has a *daughter*—one he has thoroughly disowned—and she is Peter's mother."

"W-wha—?" Sophie stammered.

"This is absolute drivel!" Peter exclaimed, glaring at the visitor. But Darnly ignored the interruption.

"Peter's *mother*, Agnes Hoyt . . . a foolish woman, I am told . . . ran away with Jarrard Lindsay, a stonemason from the Borders. The man had come to Yorkshire to make some repairs on Sir Thomas Hoyt's country mansion. This common laborer then eloped with Sir Thomas's only child, Agnes, when she was sixteen."

"Preposterous!" Peter cried. "Why, the man is inventing this out of whole cloth!"

"By God, but I am *not!*" Darnly thundered, and Sophie knew with a sinking heart, he spoke the truth. "When I returned from Henley, I learned from Mary Ann Skene about the gossip that you two had said your vows at St. Paul's. Frankly, I was appalled," he snapped, gazing sternly at Sophie. "I thought you intelligent enough not to become entangled with such an obvious bounder—"

"Now see here," Peter interrupted with an injured air, "I thought you were my friend! Why are you—"

"'Tis true, you provided amusing companionship, at times," Darnly interrupted acidly, "and as we are both diverted by an interest in theater and certain other pleasures, we had some basis for keeping company. But that presumed you were one of my set. The fact is, you're not."

"He's been posing as an aristocrat?" Sophie asked faintly.

"I called on His Majesty's Officer of Arms this afternoon and asked him to consult the archives regarding some suspicions I had all along." The Earl of Llewelyn's son strode over to the drinks cabinet, poured two brandies and offered one to Sophie, who numbly declined.

"Officer of Arms?" she echoed.

"The King of Arms has the final word when it comes to establishing the legitimacy of aristocratic titles. It was all in their dusty tomes. Your new husband," Darnly said in a gentler tone as he surveyed her pale features, "whose real name is simply Peter Lindsay, by the way . . . has no baronet's title of his own. He simply tacked on his grandfather's name *Hoyt* to make his masquerade appear more convincing."

"Darnly, is this some sort of unamusing jest?" Peter declared heatedly.

"What I find *unamusing,*" the nobleman declared in a low voice, "is having been played the fool. You drank my brandy, frequented my club, borrowed untold sums of blunt, and posed as a gentleman, yet you are in line neither for your grandfather's title—since it descends only through the direct male line—nor the old man's estate." He glared at the object of his scorn. "Will not the fortune, titles, and land pass to a male cousin through your great uncle? And isn't it true that Sir Thomas Hoyt disowned your mother the instant she married beneath herself?"

Peter remained silent, apparently unable to summon a suitable reply.

"Is this so?" Sophie asked, barely above a whisper, staring at the man to whom she was bound for life. "You've lied about your name, in addition to everything else?"

Peter's black eyebrows knit together in a scowl.

"'Tis unfortunate," Darnly interjected more calmly, "but there are some people in this world who seem virtually unable to tell the truth. I believe Peter to be among that group. I've discovered him to be a man who can look one straight in the eye and fabricate such a convincing tale, he eventually believes it himself!"

Sophie gazed at Peter in a state of shock. His customary, lighthearted demeanor was nowhere in evidence. In the brief space of Darnly's staggering announcement, her husband had assumed a truculent stance and merely scrutinized his shoe tops.

"Peter let it be known, for instance," Darnly continued, glancing at his erstwhile friend with a look of disgust, "that his father, Jarrard Lindsay, the supposed baronet with lands near Lockerbie, died when he was a mere babe. The truth is, the blackguard deserted Peter's mother soon after their son was born, abandoning them to live in disgrace and penury in a cottage on her father's property."

"Oh, Peter . . ." Sophie blurted, "I can understand how ghastly it must have been for your poor mother, but why invent—"

"Oh, do be still!" Peter exploded, grabbing Sophie's untouched glass of brandy and downing it in one gulp. Roderick Darnly surveyed him with disdain.

"You were ignored and despised by the old man, although, I'm told, your grandfather, Sir Thomas, did send you to an inferior boarding school. Gave you three hundred pounds when you came down to London three years ago and ordered you to fend for yourself. Those funds, I'll wager, have been frittered away on fashionable clothing and your unquenchable thirst for gambling and drink. No wonder, as your funds ran low, you saw Sophie as a way out of your financial embarrassment," Darnly finished contemptuously.

This last statement seemed to stir Peter from his state of brooding lethargy.

"You, sir, will regret this!" he shouted suddenly, leaping to his feet. "I shall call you out!"

Roderick laughed harshly and waved a dismissive hand.

"Now, now, Lindsay," he answered coolly, swiftly demoting Peter to his genuine name, "no need for histrionics. I promise, for Sophie's sake, I won't reveal the truth to the town. It matters not to me if you style yourself a baron, duke, or prince of the Realm. Just don't try to deceive your betters. And at least Sophie now knows not to invest time or trouble in you as a husband—or a playwright."

"Why ever not?" Peter snapped. "We've done quite well thus far. And even if the world knows she pens most of the stuff, whatever she earns belongs to me."

Roderick advanced toward Sophie who was too stunned to do anything but stare.

"If only I'd known you were considering this match," he said gruffly, "I would have revealed to you my suspicions and gotten you the proof that I now lay before you. Perhaps some alternative could have been found . . ."

"I 'considered this match,' as you put it, only because I am with child," Sophie reminded him dully. Darnly's eyebrows raised almost imperceptibly. "Yes," she sighed, "'tis definitely Peter's offspring."

"I hope it doesn't inherit its father's penchant for reckless gambling," he replied coldly.

"I warn you, Darnly, you go too far!" Peter exclaimed, fists clenched.

"Come, come, my man," Darnly chided. "No need to dissemble before *us*. You know as well as I do that this compulsive wagering's gotten you into a dreadful state. You even welshed on those small bets we made at the Blue Periwig. I checked at White's and found you had even larger debts outstanding. We share the same tailor . . . wigmaker, and of course, ruffle maker . . . need I elaborate?"

Peter flushed. "A few bad nights at faro, 'tis all."

"Face it, man," Darnly said with a shrug, "you're up to your neck cloth in unpaid bills."

Peter had lapsed once again into sullen silence. Sophie was feeling total revulsion toward her husband of less than one week. As bile suddenly rose to her throat, she dashed from the room, heading for a water closet beneath the stairs in the foyer.

"If you ever need me," Darnly called after her, "and undoubtedly you will—don't hesitate to let me know."

For several days Sophie felt so miserable in body and soul, she could barely lift her head from her pillow. Even after the news that Garrick had scheduled the revised version of *The Provoked Player* for a debut in late September, she remained too ill with morning sickness to attend rehearsals, much less declare to anyone that she had conceived the lion's share of the farce.

Peter's mood, in contrast, veered erratically; one minute he was belligerent, the next he was chagrined. He had taken to sleeping in another room away from Sophie, or simply did not return home at all. By week's end, he announced he'd been invited deer stalking at a friend's country estate near the Wychwood Forest in the Cotswolds and intended to depart the following day.

"And, pray, what funds are available to you for such a lark?" Sophie demanded, pulling herself to a sitting position in Peter's large bed as she watched him throw clothing into a small portmanteau.

"'Tis none of your affair!" her husband retorted, making no attempt to maintain his heretofore charming facade.

Sophie lapsed into silence, watching Peter rummage through his armoire. His abrupt gestures were those of a petulant boy who'd been caught out in a tremendous lie, but refused to own up to it. Peter wasn't evil, he was simply pathetic. She saw with sudden clarity that he was a young man driven by forces set in motion long ago—forces that he didn't understand himself and that rendered him incapable of taking responsibility for what he did, or even noticing how deeply his actions wounded others. Her anger and anguished sense of betrayal gradually drained away, leaving a residue of disappointment and quiet despair.

"The truth is, Peter, we are linked forever," Sophie said quietly, attempting to come to terms with the reality of this nightmare alliance. "Every single thing each of us does from now on will affect the other." She looked at him steadily across the room. "Please . . . you must answer just one question."

"And that is?" Peter said cautiously.

"How do you envision this marriage?"

"Meaning what, exactly?" he asked.

"Meaning, what do you imagine our living together as husband and wife will be like?"

"Oh, we'll rub along all right, I expect," he replied evasively, "that is, if you'll do your part by getting up and earning some blunt."

But, will you do yours? she cried silently, knowing in her heart the probable answer.

"And can we at least agree to treat each other civilly within these walls?" she persisted. "What you do on your own *is* your affair."

"I suppose so," he answered disinterestedly. "Now, where the deuce is my hunting jacket?"

Fortunately, when Peter returned from his holiday in Oxfordshire, he seemed to have put the humiliating scene with Darnly behind him and was surprisingly cheerful and pleasant toward Sophie.

"Glad tidings, my lady wife," he said with something of his former bonhomie. He deposited his portmanteau inside the door of the front sitting room. "I've just been round to Old Drury. *The Provoked Player* has survived Edward Capell's ax reasonably intact and has been granted a license from the Lord Chamberlain's office! Garrick plans to launch it in September."

"'Tis wonderful news," Sophie responded, looking up

from the desk and attempting to match his mood. "Let us pray it shall do as well as *The Footmen's Conspiracy*," she added fervently, noting that Peter nonchalantly tossed several scraps of paper into his top drawer.

To Sophie's great relief, the waves of nausea that had tormented her disappeared as suddenly as they had started, now that she was in her fourth month of pregnancy. For the first time in months, she felt well enough to leave Cleveland Row and attend the play's opening night.

She and Peter took their seats in a box in the second tier on stage right. Kitty Clive was perfectly suited in the role of the aging actress and evoked an avalanche of laughter with her ludicrous posturing and comic vanity. Sophie's spirits soared as she observed the audience's amusement.

At the conclusion of Act Five, the assembly rose as one and applauded thunderously, prompting the cast to take repeated bows. Cries of "Author! Author!" filled the hall and Sophie swallowed hard when Peter rose from his box seat to acknowledge the cheers of the assembled multitude. Roderick Darnly was seated in a box with Mrs. Garrick and inclined his head to Sophie in an ironic greeting.

Later, in the Greenroom, Peter was surrounded by well-wishers when David Garrick strode across the chamber, arms extended.

"Sophie!" Garrick exclaimed heartily. "How lovely to see you at last! I understand congratulations are in order," he offered, giving her hands a gentle squeeze. "Darnly informs me you are now Lady Lindsay-Hoyt. I suppose this means you will not be available to sell playbills in our foyer any longer," he teased.

"Well . . . n-no," she replied, "but I still employ staff to run Ashby's and the printing press," she added earnestly, relieved that Darnly had been as good as his word and not revealed to anyone that her new husband was a charlatan. Such intelligence would only intensify his creditors' demands for full payment of his debts—and *that* could land them both in Newgate Prison. "I remain ready to print your smaller playbills, and can also handle the announcements to *The Public Advertiser*," she said. They would certainly need the funds and Lorna, who had injured her ankle dancing in a performance of *The Beggar's Opera*, could help Sophie keep her commitments to Drury Lane, as the dancer was only too happy to have an alternative source of income, however meager.

"I think I can arrange that, if 'tis your wish," Garrick replied, eyeing her speculatively. Sophie glanced down at her abdomen, suddenly aware that her normally trim waist had begun noticeably to expand, now that she was beginning her fifth month of pregnancy.

"You're very kind," she murmured.

"Well, we must keep the lady wife of our new playwright in good spirits."

Before Sophie could reply, Garrick was accosted by one of his admirers and borne away. Suddenly drooping from fatigue, she crossed to Peter's side and suggested they return home.

"To bed?" Peter replied, aghast, "on this night? God's bones, but I intend to *celebrate*, my girl!"

"Then find me a hackney . . . I'm about to develop full-blown vapors," she replied.

"Allow me," Roderick Darnly said, appearing out of nowhere. "My coach waits outside. Charles will happily conduct you to your door. Peter, old boy," he added, as if the pair had never quarreled, "you must allow me to fete you at White's. All of London talks of your brilliance and wit." He offered a mocking wink in Sophie's direction.

"Well . . . I wouldn't say no to a spot of brandy," Peter replied uncertainly, confused by Darnly's renewed cordiality. "Everyone did seem to enjoy themselves tonight, didn't they?" he added with more confidence. "I wouldn't mind having the chaps hoist a few in my honor. Thank you, Roderick. 'Tis damned decent of you."

"Have another port, old man, while I just see Sophie to my coach," Roderick said, taking her arm and steering her toward the stage door.

"Thank you for rescuing me," she murmured.

"You're feeling better, I take it?" he said, guiding her through the diminishing crowd clustered in front of the theater. He stopped midstream and looked down at her pensively. "I'm afraid my anger at Peter for playing me for a fool quite overcame my concern for your . . . condition. I can imagine how upset you were to hear my news. I apologize for the abrupt way I informed you of such unfortunate truths."

"I doubt there was any way to soften the blow." Sophie sighed. "I too was taken for a fool—and rather behaved like one, I regret to say. Now I must pay the price."

Roderick Darnly refrained from commenting further, having spotted his driver amongst the confusion of carriages.

"Ah . . . there's Charles." He helped her aboard and gave instructions for the coachman to wait upon him at White's after depositing Sophie at Cleveland Row. Before he shut the door he said to Sophie, "Congratulations on the play this evening. It shows your fine hand."

"And Colman and Garrick's," she reminded him. "But thank you."

"Will you write another?"

"I must," Sophie smiled wanly.

"With Peter?"

"I hope so. 'Tis a great trial to do it all on my own."

"But you are capable of writing on your own and that's the important thing, isn't it?" he said firmly. "Well, my dear . . . off to bed with you. Good night."

As the coach pulled away from Drury Lane, Sophie turned Roderick Darnly's last words over in her mind. Perhaps she *was* capable of writing a play completely on her own. Then she heaved a tired sigh and prayed that wouldn't come to pass, given her exhausted condition.

She sank against the elegant upholstery and stared forlornly out the window at the luminous September moon. She found herself musing that the same silvery light was also shining over Dublin this night. She wondered how Hunter had fared during his year at Smock Alley and felt nothing but regret. She'd not seen him these sixteen months. It felt like a lifetime.

The next morning, Sophie awoke and, peering into the bedchamber Peter now claimed as his own, realized instantly that her husband had never returned home. Sighing with resignation, Sophie dressed and wandered down to the basement kitchen to brew a pot of tea, as Mrs. Hood had turned in her resignation. Cup in hand, she entered the sitting room and forced herself to take stock of her situation and conceive some plan of action.

A notion for a new comedy about the antics of hypocritical churchmen had been simmering in her mind for some days, although she had kept mum about it with Peter. Sitting at his desk, she opened several drawers in search of some blank paper to jot down a few ideas she'd been turning over in her mind, only to confront the latest pile of unpaid tradesmen's bills. In another compartment, she discovered a series of IOUs contracted in the days following their marriage. The markers, it appeared, were owed to Peter's gambling compatriots at the faro tables at White's.

"Blast his bones!" she declared aloud, horrified by the large amounts she calculated were owing. Whatever profits had accrued from their play to date would obviously go to pay these debts.

Angrily, she stomped into the foyer, grasped her cloak from a peg, and hailed a hackney she could ill afford, instructing the driver to head in the direction of Drury Lane. When she entered the murky stage entrance, she paused a moment to allow her eyes to adjust to the shadowy confines back stage. Heading for the stairs that led to Garrick's office, she heard voices emanating from the Greenroom.

Turning toward the sound, Sophie nearly gasped at the sight of Mavis Piggott, evidently returned from her previous engagement at the Smock Alley Theater in Dublin. Sophie quickly ducked behind a curtained wing to avoid being seen. Ashamed to be such a blatant eavesdropper, she observed Garrick rise to his feet, courtly as ever, and thank Mavis for her reading of Juliet.

"As you well recognize," he said, "it is the end of September and we have nearly a full complement of players. However, if you will be satisfied with second parts, I think, perhaps, we could find you a place in the company this late in the season."

"'Twould suit perfectly," Mavis murmured agreeably. Her acquiescent tone had none of the bluster and bravado

Sophie so associated with the woman. She appeared grateful, in fact, for whatever theatrical crumbs happened to fall on her plate.

"And now, if you'll excuse me, Mrs. Piggott," Garrick said, concluding the interview. ". . . gentlemen . . . ?"

Sophie watched from the shadows as the manager strode across the rear of the stage and up the stairs leading to his office. Before the rest of the group could disperse, she quickly followed in his footsteps, and knocked timidly on Garrick's door. Fortunately, he appeared glad to see her and bade her enter. After an exchange of greetings, and taking courage in hand, she began to describe recent events as objectively as possible, omitting to reveal, however, that she had recently discovered her new husband was posing as a baronet. If Peter Lindsay wished to pretend he was the Prince of Wales—that was up to him, she thought bitterly.

"I am dreadfully ashamed of my conduct and deserve my fate as far as my forced marriage is concerned, but I cannot continue to work in this fashion . . . toiling on plays for which I receive neither credit as a playwright nor even a penny in my pocket!" She flushed, but soldiered on. "I don't wish to sound boastful, sir, but I truly did compose the lion's share of both *The Footmen's Conspiracy* and *The Provoked Player.*"

"I must confess, I'm not much surprised to hear this sorry tale," Garrick said, shaking his head. "I thought it strange such an undisciplined sort could have crafted such skillful work."

"I tell you of my involvement in hopes you'll entertain more favorably a new idea for a play I wish to write *on my own.*"

"You are saying you do not wish to continue this collaboration with your new husband?"

"No, sir," Sophie replied stiffly. "I wish to try my hand alone and thereby profit by remaining anonymous."

"A wife's possessions are usually managed and controlled by her mate," Garrick said gravely.

"But that would mean Peter and I will find ourselves thrown in debtors' prison before the year is out!" she groaned.

"Well, tell me of this new notion of yours," Garrick replied.

As briefly as possible, Sophie outlined her idea, which concerned a miserly parson who, in spite of his sermonizing, was forever promoting luxuries for himself at the expense of his parishioners.

"You'll have to make him a Scots Presbyterian," Garrick warned. "'Tis the only way to get it past the Lord Chamberlain's office. Capell, especially, might otherwise deny a license to a play that spoofs England's religion."

"I could *easily* make him Scottish!" Sophie responded, and Garrick reacted to her vehemence by raising one eyebrow. "But I must have your assurance, sir, that my authorship will be held strictly confidential," she pleaded.

"Of course, my dear," Garrick assured her. "And my response to your work will be as candid as you know it always has been, even though I had no idea you'd turned author . . ."

"I desire that," Sophie answered fervently. "And will you remit all payments, if there are any, to me *personally* while telling no one? I very much need the funds to pay debts, and if Peter—I mean, if anyone should know . . ." she faltered.

"I understand the situation perfectly, my dear," David Garrick assured her. "Your secret is safe with me."

"Thank you so much," she said, preparing to depart.

"Not at all . . . I look forward to seeing the fruits of your efforts. Good day, my dear," he said, smiling.

As Sophie opened the door to the passageway that led to the stairs, she heard a swish of petticoats and caught a glimpse of Mavis Piggott's gown disappearing around the corner. Horrified, she wondered if the chit had turned the tables and had listened at the door. If so, what had she heard?

When Sophie arrived downstairs, her former rival for Hunter's affections was standing next to a backstage wall chatting with Kitty Clive. A rehearsal was in progress on stage. Sophie nearly bit her tongue with the effort required not to demand to know if Mavis had placed her ear to the key hole of Garrick's office and learned of Sophie's plans to write a play on her own.

"I see you've returned from Smock Alley for the new season," Sophie ventured stiffly. Mavis's frosty stare surveyed Sophie's figure from hair to toes.

"And I see you've got an Irish Toothache—as they say in Dublin," she retorted, her eyes narrowing. "When's the babe due?"

"In December or January," Sophie replied, inwardly cursing the woman's keen eye.

"Well, my congratulations," she sneered. "Kitty, here, informs me 'tis *Lady* Lindsay-Hoyt now. Quite a rake you've chosen as your life's mate. But a clever playwright, I must admit," Mavis added grudgingly. "I'm sure your friends across the Irish Sea will be astonished to hear the remarkable news of your marriage to the admirable baronet."

It was clear to Sophie that Mavis Piggott could hardly wait to dispatch the latest gossip to her colleagues at Smock Alley. And she knew it was only a matter of time before Hunter Robertson learned of her pregnancy and marriage—in that order.

※

"Ye'll be wantin' the letter that came for you today, Mr. Robertson," the doorkeeper called out in his distinctive Irish lilt as Hunter entered the back stage area of Smock Alley Theater. "The prompter's stowed it in his box. From London, by the looks of it."

"Thanks, Reilly," Hunter said, wondering if, at long last, Sophie had written him saying she was as ready as he was to declare a truce. The year spent in Ireland had certainly been instructive in one respect. He couldn't get the lass out of his mind, awake or asleep, no matter how hard he had tried—and despite a parade of willing young actresses eager to assist him in this regard.

"Here 'tis, laddie," Mr. Kelly, the prompter, said genially, handing him the missive. He watched a curious play of emotions flicker across Hunter's features as the handsome young actor broke the wax seal and quickly scanned the letter's contents in the dim light cast by a single candle in a wall sconce overhead.

"Well, well . . ." Hunter breathed. "I'm afraid I'll be

leaving midway through this season, Mr. Kelly. 'Tis fortunate I haven't yet signed my articles . . ."

"But sure, the management's wantin' ye to stay, Mr. Robertson?" Kelly responded.

"Aye . . . but by December, 'tis to London I shall go!" he grinned.

Chapter 19

October 1765

Sophie's fingers were cramped painfully around her quill pen, and her eyes felt like the coals burning on the fireplace grate in the sitting room. A draft of frigid air seeped through the crack at the bottom of a window near her desk, causing the taper's flame to flicker erratically. The discarded paper on the floor provided mute evidence that she had toiled far into the night.

As had been her practice for the past two months, Sophie left a few pages of *Double Devils* scattered on the desktop— a work that Peter and she were supposed to be writing together. Meanwhile, she labored on her own original comedy, *The Parsimonious Parson*. It was a deception she'd adopted in case her husband came upon her unexpectedly and wanted to know how she was employing her time. More often than not, he simply ignored her and assumed she was busy on a play that would ultimately earn them urgently needed funds.

"The additional fees from *The Provoked Player* should see us through for some time," Sophie had protested after the second Author's Benefit Night. "Pay some of the tradesmen with those!"

"There's nothing left," Peter announced flatly. "These London merchants are all brigands!"

"'Tis the debts owing your gambling cronies, isn't it?" Sophie pulled several new IOUs from Peter's desk drawer and shook them in front of his nose.

But her husband had stomped out of the sitting room, offering no defense. From the moment Roderick Darnly had revealed him to be a fraud, Peter had abandoned all pretense of functioning as her writing partner and indulged himself in whatever vice or amusement appealed to him most at that moment. It seemed to Sophie as if the charming facade he had employed so convincingly during their year-long acquaintance had simply cracked, exposing all of Peter's character flaws and leaving nothing but rubble at her feet.

Meanwhile, she had been secretly lavishing most of her flagging energy on the new work she had proposed to Garrick in September. For several days, now, she had been struggling with the second act and had been reworking the same passage far into the wee hours of the chilly October morn.

Suddenly, she heard a commotion at the front door.

"I'm fine . . . jus' fine!" she heard Peter saying, his slurred speech bearing witness to an evening imbibing wine and spirits.

He and Roderick staggered together through the sitting room door. The Earl of Llewelyn's son had looped her husband's arm around his neck to prevent his inebriated companion from pitching forward.

"I do believe he's about to faint," Roderick announced sharply, red faced from the exertion.

"Over here," Sophie commanded, pointing at the daybed. "Let him sleep it off till morn."

She watched with disgust as he half-dragged her husband across the carpet and lowered him on the very chaise where she and Peter had first made love. She rubbed her aching back involuntarily and glanced down at her rounded belly, which by now restricted her view of her own feet.

"There!" Roderick gasped, straightening to his full height. "My good deed for the night."

"I thought you two were no longer on friendly terms," she commented dryly. "Why such concern for the drunken sot?"

"I can't let the father of your child be run over in the gutter by a hackney coach, now can I?" Roderick replied.

"Would you be so kind as to offer me a port or brandy? I find nursemaid duties quite enervating."

"Of course," Sophie answered perfunctorily.

Their supply of port was exhausted, but she poured what was left of the brandy into a snifter and handed it to him. As he sipped the amber liquid, his eyes drifted to her desk.

"Working, I see," he said, an eyebrow cocked. "Your muse visits you rather late in the evening, does it not?"

"I write when 'tis quiet," she replied with a glance in the direction of her husband, who was snoring noisily.

"And you're making progress?"

"Not really," Sophie replied evasively. "'Tis slow going when one's writing partner is either absent or unconscious."

Roderick studied her for several moments and then stepped closer, taking her hand in his.

"I do hope you haven't forgotten my offer of help, should you find yourself in need of funds," he said softly, raising her fingers to his lips.

She could smell by his breath that he had kept pace with Peter's drinking. Yet tonight, as was often the case, Roderick Darnly appeared calm and controlled.

"I appreciate your concern, sir," Sophie replied evenly, gently withdrawing her hand from his, "but with Ashby's and my printing work, I expect I'll manage."

"Perhaps you shall," he said with a glint in his eye. "But I can't quite believe you wouldn't enjoy being looked after."

"Ah . . . but there is always a price to be paid for such benevolence, isn't there?" she countered lightly, moving toward the desk in a show of tidying her papers.

For a moment, he merely gazed at her, as if reflecting on her words.

"Give and take, Sophie, my dear," he said at length. "'Tis what makes the world go 'round."

"The weak *give* and the strong *take*," Sophie responded wearily. "That's about the size of it, wouldn't you say?"

"I would say only that 'tis damnably late, and I must be off," he replied, setting down his brandy snifter. "I wish you and Peter success with your new play—and, of course, the best of luck obtaining the endorsement of the censor."

For the rest of October, Sophie felt as if she were growing plumper around her waist with every manuscript page of *The Parsimonious Parson* she produced. Once or twice she feared Peter might discover she was working on something other than *Double Devils*, but in truth she had made slow progress on that play too. It was a light farce depicting the machinations of twins who confound the people to whom they owe money by posing at different times as the Good Twin or the Bad Twin, as the situation warranted.

"I told Garrick I'd have a first draft of *Devils* by mid-November!" Peter groused as he stared at the words *Act Two* which she had just penned. "You've never worked at such a snail's pace before!"

"And *you've* never worked on *Devils* at all!" she snapped.

"Why should I?" he shrugged. "You're clever enough with a quill for the two of us. And, besides, I expect you to earn your keep!"

Before she could stop herself, the two of them were once again bickering like fishwives.

※

The first week of November, Sophie arrived at Garrick's office with dark smudges under her eyes, and feeling utterly exhausted. Still, she had been pleased to deliver a manuscript the previous day that she thought sparkled with some wit. 'Twas strange, she thought, watching Garrick retrieve the five-act farce from the top of a pile of proposed works. Writing comedy had been a welcome escape from the miserable reality of her current predicament.

"*The Parsimonious Parson,*" Garrick pronounced, surveying the first page. "Even the title makes me smile . . ."

"I hope the rest of the work did as well," Sophie replied, awaiting his verdict.

"'Tis an excellent job . . . my notes are few," he granted.

Sophie broke into a broad smile, and felt almost like hugging herself with pleasure. Then her face fell.

"You've not told anyone I'm writing anonymously, have you?"

"I took my dear wife into my confidence, but no others," he replied with a look of sympathy.

"Not even Mr. Lacy?"

"Eventually, I may have to inform him. We're partners. But I thought to wait until I know when we'll present the play. Most likely 'twill be after the Christmas pantomime."

"And Lacy's . . . friend—Roderick Darnly? You haven't told him either?"

Garrick frowned and shook his head.

"I will confess, Sophie my dear, I am not happy that James Lacy has diluted his holdings in Drury Lane by mortgaging even a few shares to that man. I fear the Earl of Llewelyn's son has ambitions beyond those he's willing to disclose."

"Ambitions?" Sophie asked, alarmed.

"As a holder of the King's Patent, Lacy must *sell* his shares outright—and I must approve the buyer," Garrick confided. "He ought not obtain loans using Drury shares as collateral, but I fear that's precisely what he has done. My partner could find his shares wrested away from him by his supposed benefactor." The manager shook his head. "Ever since I returned from abroad, I find myself confronted by this noble interloper who fancies himself an arbiter of theatrical taste. The Honorable Roderick Darnly thinks that by right of his investment, he holds some power here. I've seen his type before," he added somberly.

"But Mr. Darnly seems to have a genuine interest in the drama," Sophie ventured, disturbed that Garrick, whom she so admired, should speak so harshly of a man who had been nothing but kind to her of late.

"These dilettantes aspire to live the lives of artists, but haven't the innate talent or discipline for it," Garrick averred. "Just between us, Lacy's given me his word he'll not mortgage anything further to underwrite his search for coal on his country estate."

"I should not trust the word of men who are short of funds, sir," Sophie observed, thinking of Peter's penchant for breaking promises to himself—and others.

"Nor I," Garrick was quick to agree. "That is why I shall remain mum about the origins of *The Parsimonious Parson.*

Once we begin rehearsals, we shall discuss whether you wish to make your authorship known."

In early December, Garrick announced to Sophie he had scheduled her comedy to begin rehearsal the week following Christmas. Less than an hour later, Sophie burst through the front door of Ashby's Books just as Lorna was closing shop.

"Come with me," Sophie said gaily, "I'm treating you to the finest chop London has to offer. We're celebrating!"

"Celebrating what?" Lorna laughed, putting down her feather duster.

"I can't even tell *you*," Sophie replied mysteriously. "Not for a while, anyway . . ." She retrieved several shillings from the cash box inside the desk drawer. "Come. Let's go to Half Moon Tavern next door and have a fine supper before I return to Cleveland Row."

"What of Sir Peter?" Lorna asked.

"He's rarely home to sup these days," Sophie declared curtly, "so why should I be?"

It was only three o'clock, but the tavern was full of theater people eating their principal meal of the day. Few respectable women would be seen in a public eating house like the Half Moon, but this was Covent Garden, where actresses and whores (and some who plied *both* trades) had no such qualms.

Sophie and Lorna threaded their way through the crowded chamber toward an empty table protected by high wooden partitions. In one booth sat Mavis Piggott, Kitty Clive, and a gloomy-looking Elizabeth Griffith. The three women, who had all enjoyed the success of having plays produced professionally in London, appeared deep in conversation. Mavis looked up at the precise moment Sophie passed their table and curled her sensuous lips into a malevolent smile.

"Well . . . if it isn't *Lady* Lindsay-Hoyt," Mavis said mockingly.

"Why, Sophie, dear, how are you?" Kitty Clive chimed in with genuine warmth. "Growing ever larger, I see. Hello, Lorna," she added, "having a nice meal tonight, are you?

Avoid the parsnip stew at all costs," she warned, rising to make her departure.

"Sophie can't be as interested in tonight's menu, Kitty," Mavis said slyly, "as in news that a certain gentleman we both know *intimately* has just arrived from Dublin."

Sophie felt her heart pound so fiercely she was certain the others could hear it. Kitty's inquisitive gaze shifted from Mavis to Sophie, but Elizabeth Griffith spoke first.

"I was just telling Mavis and Kitty, here . . . 'twas that handsome new assistant manager at Covent Garden—Mr. Robertson—who informed me just now that John Beard preferred some bit of nonsense about a parson to *my* play," Mrs. Griffith complained, referring to the current manager at Covent Garden. "'Tis to be presented before Christmas instead of my *Double Mistake!*"

Hunter was *here*? In *London*? He had obviously made no attempt to find her, Sophie thought morosely. She glanced down at her swelling waistline and then gazed distractedly at Mavis. Had the jade seen him yet? Had she told him Sophie was married—and carrying Peter's child?

Among the confused thoughts swirling in her brain, Elizabeth's complaint regarding the play that had been substituted at Covent Garden finally penetrated her consciousness. *A farce about a parson,* Mrs. Griffith had said.

"A play about a . . . *clergyman* . . . is forcing cancellation of your work, Mrs. Griffith?" Sophie asked haltingly.

"Not canceled," Elizabeth pouted. "But my piece has been postponed till January, and one wonders if that Robertson fellow was sincere about the new date. Do you think he'd be truthful, Mavis?" she said anxiously.

But Mavis was looking at Sophie triumphantly.

"You didn't know our old friend had returned to London either, did you?" she said with a smug smile.

"No . . . why should I be privy to events at Covent Garden?" retorted Sophie. "As you well know, Mavis, my loyalty's to Drury Lane."

Kitty Clive nodded in agreement.

"Elizabeth's just been telling us how the new lad—this Hunter Robertson—is creating dances for a musical confection that Covent Garden is throwing hastily on stage," Kitty prattled, ". . . *The Parsimonious Parson*, was it, Beth?"

"Yes," Elizabeth Griffith sniffed. "According to Robertson, 'tis a thin tale that aims to spoof the doleful Scottish clergy."

Sophie stared dumbfounded at Lorna and the other three women. Everyone in the London theater world knew that the pilfering of plots—as well as out-and-out thievery—between competing dramatists was a common enough occurrence, but this was too much! Kitty Clive reached for her cloak, heedless of the tension whirling around her.

"Well, ladies, I must be off," Kitty sighed. "Mavis, are you coming?"

"No . . . I've nothing till the second act—"

But before anyone else said a word, Sophie whirled on her heel and bolted out the tavern door with Lorna Blount following her, wearing a look of bewilderment.

"A pox on 'em!" Sophie cursed, pointing a shaking finger at a playbill announcing a coming attraction that was posted on the front of Covent Garden Theater. "'Tis actually set to *music*!"

"What is?" panted Lorna, having finally caught up with her friend.

"*The Parsimonious Parson*, that's what!" Sophie exploded. "That's what we were going to celebrate, you and I! Garrick had just scheduled a play I wrote anonymously for Drury Lane. Someone—and I'll wager a hundred pounds 'twas Mavis Piggott—has pilfered my manuscript from his office and given it to that bastard! Look!" she said, jabbing her forefinger at Hunter's name printed on the playbill announcing his authorship of the piece scheduled for Covent Garden in three days' time. "He's even taken *credit* for writing the play and then had the cheek to set it to *music*—may his bones be damned!"

"But how could Mavis or anyone else steal it from Drury Lane without Garrick knowing of the piracy?"

"Someone with access to the manager's chambers could have copied it at night," Sophie replied grimly.

Lorna leaned forward in the gathering gloom to read the print at the bottom of the playbill.

" 'Hunter Robertson,' " she read aloud. She stared at Sophie, dismayed. "You're saying that *you* wrote this and Hunter is falsely claiming to be its author?" Sophie nodded grimly. "Sink me, but this is dreadful!"

" 'Tis more than *that*!" Sophie retorted, seething. " 'Tis *thievery*! And if he and Mavis think I'm going to sit still for this . . ."

Lorna watched, openmouthed, as Sophie stalked down an alleyway toward Covent Garden's stage door and disappeared inside.

"Mr. Beard is not available, Lady Lindsay-Hoyt," announced Mr. Besford. The stage doorkeeper cast a skeptical glance at his visitor's rounded girth. "I'm afraid the manager simply cannot see you now. Performances begin in two hours' time." Privately, the servant was shocked to see a woman, let alone an aristocrat, appear in public in such an advanced stage of pregnancy. Certainly not one with fire in her eye, rudely demanding to see his employer. "I will find the assistant manager for you, if you'll just wait here."

Sophie paced restlessly just inside the entrance until a tall, familiar figure suddenly materialized out of the gloom.

"Sophie?" Hunter said, a look of astonishment flooding the handsome features she remembered so well. "Besford said it was a Lady Lindsay-Hoyt and—" He paused, mid-sentence, the impact of the words he'd just uttered apparently dawning on him. "You mean to say you *married* that sod!" he exclaimed in a horrified voice. "Oh *God*, Sophie . . . you *didn't*!"

"Don't you *dare* pretend my marriage is news to you or that you aren't aware that I am the author of *The Parsimonious Parson*, you lying villain!" she shouted.

"For God's sake, Sophie, what are you talking about?" Hunter demanded, his eyes reflecting his shock as he stared at her bulging abdomen. Besford gazed from one to the other in amazement. Hunter hastily grabbed Sophie's arm and hauled her fifty paces into a deserted scene-painting

room that smelled pungently of turpentine and oils. Once
inside, he let go of her arm but cupped his large hand fleetingly on the side of her hard belly.

"When is the bairn due?" he asked, his features expressionless.

Sophie poked a finger roughly into his chest.

"My babe's due in January, if 'tis any of your business,
which it certainly is not!" she stormed. "But I am here to
discuss my *play*, you swine! *The Parsimonious Parson!* A
'Musical Afterpiece by Hunter Robertson' that I just saw
trumpeted on that placard outside!"

"You are saying that *you* wrote that play?" Hunter asked
with an astonished look.

"Of course I'm saying I wrote it!" she screeched. "By
God, you certainly know that *you* didn't write it!"

"Of course I didn't write it!" snapped Hunter. Now it
was Sophie's turn to look confounded. "It was already in
rehearsal when I arrived from Dublin," explained Hunter.
"Just give me one reason why I should believe *you* wrote
it?"

In sheer frustration, Sophie began to pound on his broad
chest with her fists.

"Because the manuscript titled *The Parsimonious Parson*
—penned in *my* hand—is sitting in David Garrick's office at
this very second, *that's* why!" she shouted. "Someone made
a copy from *that* copy, and I would bet my life 'tis your
former paramour, Mavis Piggott. Or have you two reunited?" she added with withering sarcasm.

"I haven't laid eyes on Mavis Piggott," he retorted. "I
haven't had a minute to myself since I was summoned back
to London by post and this *Parson* claptrap was thrown in
my lap three days ago. I'm expected to invent dances out of
thin air!"

"*Claptrap!* Why you—" Sophie retorted, flailing her fists
against his chest with renewed fury.

Hunter caught her by the wrists and glared down at her.

"Will you stop it?" he shouted. "I know my name is on
the placard outside, but I swear to you, Sophie, I *didn't steal*
the play—*your* play, if you like!"

"It *is* my play, you lout," she shouted between ragged

breaths, "and I would like to know exactly how it comes to have your name attached to it, if you please?"

"The manager, John Beard, bought it through an intermediary who asked, as a condition of sale, that someone *else* put their name on the piece," Hunter exclaimed. "Since I was newly arrived, Beard dubbed me the lucky author and had the placards put up this morning. We assumed the genuine dramatist was some timid woman scribe or a member of the *ton* who desired anonymity," he declared, describing a common practice among authors from the upper classes.

"Or a person or persons wanting to *hide* their identity as a way of committing this shameless robbery!" Sophie retorted bitterly. "Who *was* this intermediary?" she demanded.

"Beard dealt with the person, not I," Hunter replied.

"And why should I believe you?" Sophie snapped. "Why should I not think Mavis Piggott didn't spend a long evening in Garrick's office copying the work and bringing it to you as soon as she heard you'd returned to London? What a lovely gift to the new assistant manager, anxious to make his mark—and she, so desirous of currying your favor once again!"

"Sophie," Hunter said more calmly and with a look of concern for her agitated state, "my only involvement is that Beard has ordered the work turned into a comic opera and asked me to put my name to it to disguise its true authorship. That is all I can tell you."

"That is all you are *willing* to tell me," Sophie maintained stubbornly. "You men of the theater stick together, don't you?" she added acidly.

"I find it surprising you have had time to take up the quill," he said pointedly. "It seems you have been otherwise occupied while I was in Ireland."

"And I suppose *you* played the celibate priest in Dublin all year?" she shot back.

Hunter immediately shifted his gaze and said nothing. As misery flooded her every fiber, Sophie turned away from him blindly, fleeing past a row of painted flats depicting moonlit terraces and castle keeps. The startled doorkeeper gawked as she bolted out the stage entrance.

Behind her, she heard the sound of Hunter giving chase into the narrow passageway. Walking as fast as her cumbersome girth would allow, she had almost reached the end of the lane when he grabbed her by her arm and whirled her toward him. The breathless pair gazed wordlessly at each other for a long moment. A palpable tremor passed between them before Hunter leaned down, seized Sophie's head between his large hands and drew her roughly toward him, kissing her fiercely. Having initiated the passionate embrace, he pulled away angrily.

"I seem always to be kissing you in theater alleys," he announced hoarsely. "You wouldn't go to Dublin with me, yet you married that rake. *Why*, Sophie?" he asked in a strangled voice.

She sighed and smiled wanly.

"I wanted to be a writer of plays," she explained softly. "I wanted to say . . . so many things with my pen. You didn't seem to think that was important . . . it appeared that what was important to me meant little to you . . . only that you wanted me wherever *your* ambitions took you."

Hunter looked down at her and shook his head sorrowfully.

"I see that . . . may have been the way of it—then," he acknowledged quietly. "I understand how my actions must have seemed to you." He forced her to meet his gaze. "And is Sir Peter Lindsay-Hoyt such a paragon of masculine understanding?" he asked more sharply.

Sophie laughed bitterly.

"Peter . . . ah . . . Peter. The gentleman *seemed* to understand that I wanted so much to learn the playwright's craft—and said he did as well."

"And did he?" Hunter asked.

"No," Sophie whispered, near tears. "I allowed him to use me . . . use whatever talent I possessed to help pay his monstrous debts. Peter gave little thought to my dreams or welfare," she finished. "I have totally played the fool."

"I'm sorry for that," Hunter said. "You deserved better." Then he smiled grimly. "Well, at least you've got a title out of all this—*Lady* Lindsay-Hoyt, isn't it?"

The memory of Mavis Piggott taunting her with precisely

the same words not an hour before at the Half Moon Tavern made Sophie's blood boil.

"That's odd," she said caustically, her temper rising once again. "'Tis *exactly* the way Mavis Piggott described my marriage. Yes . . . I am now the *Lady* Lindsay-Hoyt," she declared, referring to her bogus title with as much bravado as her shattered nerves could muster. "And, if you do not reveal who brought you my play—and I am certain you do, indeed, know the identity at least of the intermediary—I shall use the influence at my disposal to initiate legal action!"

"I'm sorry, Sophie, truly I am, for everything that has happened to you in my absence," he said gravely, "but I do not know who appropriated your play and I cannot tell you the name of the intermediary. On that, I gave my new employer my word of honor."

"*Honor!*" Sophie exploded furiously. "Here's *this* for your supposed honor, you thieving blackguard!" She slapped him a stinging blow across his chiseled features, a blow that carried with it all the anguish and despair she had endured since they had parted in Bath.

�֍

David Garrick was more disturbed than shocked to hear the latest developments at Covent Garden.

"I am *certain* Mavis Piggott has done this," Sophie complained. "Why cannot we simply confront her with the facts of this affair?"

"You have no proof, no witnesses, and to pronounce such accusations publicly—that would be slander."

Sophie averted her face from the manager to hide her angry tears. Garrick leaned across his desk and patted her hand.

"As one who has lost sleep toiling over a piece, I know too well what you are feeling," he soothed. "I once wrote a Christmas pantomime that had an unauthorized debut at another theater. My only copy had been pinched right from under my nose, and there was absolutely nothing to be done about it." He smiled sympathetically. "I know 'tis difficult, but I think it best if you simply put this unpleasantness behind you and start work on something new. Have you any other comic notions in that fertile mind of yours?" he gently teased.

Sophie sighed, and then brightened.

"Peter said he'd discussed an idea about twins with you . . . two rakes whose actions confound visitors at a stylish country estate. That was my idea."

"I *do* remember that one!" he said approvingly, "but the young rogue never came forth with it. Can you work on it?"

"Aye, but I don't know what to do about an author's credit . . ."

"We shall wrestle with that issue when there's a play to argue over," he said. "If your husband joins you in this effort—so be it. If 'tis *you* who does the work . . . then credit shall be as you wish and we shall find a new title. And I promise you," Garrick added soberly, "I shall purchase a strongbox to preserve new compositions as they are submitted, to which only I have the key!" Sophie could barely summon a weary smile of thanks for his support. "Now, I want you to get busy, my dear," he urged her. "How are you for funds? Will you have enough to cope with the expenses of your new . . . arrival?"

The actor who could subdue an unruly audience of fifteen hundred souls appeared flustered at the mention of the impending birth of Sophie's child.

"We're as short as ever," Sophie admitted glumly, "but with Lorna keeping Ashby's going, and with the orders I get from you for printing the playbills, I hope to get by."

Nodding, Garrick reached behind his desk and selected a tattered manuscript.

"I plan a Christmas pantomime based on *The Milk Maids*," he said. "It has a part for an extraordinarily short, very rotund old man who does not say a single line the entire performance. Would you consent to play the role *incognito* for the salary of a pound a week?"

Sophie knew his gesture was one of pure charity, but she accepted it with gratitude.

"Now off with you," Garrick said cheerfully. "And I'd like a draft of *Double Devils* as soon as you can manage it."

〰

Harriet Ashby sat on the dirty straw, propped up in the corner of her cell, looking like nothing so much as a living skeleton. Her sunken eyes and prominent cheekbones spoke eloquently of the near starvation she had suffered during the three years she had resided in Bedlam. The sight of her swollen joints and emaciated form made Sophie feel helpless with rage.

"'Tis nasty in here, sir," the turnkey warned Sophie. On this visit to the hospital she was disguised as the fat old man she would soon be playing in Drury Lane's Christmas pantomime. The guard unlocked the door, shepherded his visitor into the cell, and returned to his post.

The stench was overwhelming, and for the first time since the early months of her pregnancy, Sophie was assaulted by a wave of nausea. In her borrowed knee breeches and man's bagwig, she knelt beside her aunt.

"Harriet . . . Aunt Harriet!" she whispered urgently. "'Tis me . . . Sophie . . . dressed as an old man." Her aunt glanced at her with darting, frightened eyes. "'Tis all right, Aunt . . . I'm here," she said soothingly, brushing strands of gray hair off the old woman's haggard face. "I've brought you some food . . . would you like a pastie? 'Tis full of lovely beef bits . . . let me feed you some."

As Sophie dug into her knapsack, her aunt's eyes seemed suddenly to glow with recognition. Without warning, tears began running silently down her cheeks.

"No . . . no . . ." the woman croaked, "'tis no use . . ." Sophie stared, stunned at the spark of sanity that burned in her aunt's gaze. "I wish only to die . . . only to die," Aunt Harriet whispered. "Give me something . . . anything, to make me die . . ."

"Oh, Aunt . . ." Sophie said helplessly.

"Die . . . die . . . *please* let me die . . ." she moaned.

Her aunt continued to sob the phrase in a horrifying litany until Sophie could stand it no longer and fled the cell the instant the turnkey could be hailed to set her free.

Within a week of Sophie's back stage confrontation with Hunter, *The Parsimonious Parson* opened at Covent Garden after a minimum of rehearsal as a companion piece to *The Summer's Tale*.

"Have you seen *The Public Advertiser* today?" Lorna asked tentatively when Sophie arrived at Ashby's Books to set type for a series of Drury Lane playbills.

"Yes . . . yes, I have," Sophie replied tersely as she placed a packet containing two acts of *Double Devils* on the desk where she hoped to work later that afternoon. "As I recall, it said something about the 'clever characterization of the pinch-penny parson' and that 'the lively music and dancing created by author Hunter Robertson gives audiences and critics alike much to praise,' " she added sarcastically, reciting from memory.

"Does Sir Peter know about this theft?" Lorna asked apprehensively.

"No, and since he doesn't know I *wrote* the piece, I don't intend to tell him," Sophie replied firmly, recalling her husband's panicked demands that she spend less time at her book shop and more hours with her quill. Even Roderick Darnly's solicitor had sent word that the due bill from a certain wager must be met by the first of February in the new year.

Perched on a stool in the printing chamber, Sophie slid pieces of metal type into the wooden form. When she pulled the lever on the hand press, the baby inside her delivered a swift kick. She wouldn't be able to function as a printer much longer, she reflected glumly, as she pondered her bloated form. And since her confinement was due in about a month, she wondered anxiously whether Lorna would be willing once again to add the duties of printer to the many others she had already assumed.

By three o'clock, Sophie realized she was far too exhausted to work on her comedy. Gathering the freshly printed placards under her arm, she bid Lorna farewell and trudged through the chill December air to deliver her goods to Garrick's office, thanking the fates that her services were not required in *The Milk Maids* this night.

"Have you seen this *Parson* play of yours?" Garrick asked her casually.

"No . . ."

"Do you wish to?" he queried.

Sophie squared her shoulders. Despite her fatigue, she was burning with curiosity as to how Hunter had adapted her comedy to music.

"Yes, I rather think I might!" she replied thoughtfully.

"Then let us use my courtesy coin," Garrick chuckled, holding up a metal entrance token granted all managers by their rival playhouses. "I'm not playing tonight either. Therefore, might I have the honor of your company in Box Five?"

The celebrated David Garrick and his pregnant companion attracted stares as they took their seats in Covent Garden Theater's vast auditorium. Soon, however, the curtains parted, and Sophie had her first glimpse of Hunter in black clerical garb, prancing comically around the stage. The audience begin to titter, and then to laugh enthusiastically.

"Clever lad . . ." Garrick whispered in her ear, "if he doesn't prove to be in league with our thief, I might try to engage him m'self."

Sophie smiled weakly. How different her life would have been if only Garrick had urged his temporary replacement, George Colman, to hire Hunter on the spot before Garrick left for the Continent.

Two acts later, the comic opera arrived at its amusing conclusion and the chattering spectators made their way out of the theater.

"May I see you to a conveyance, my dear?" Garrick said solicitously, having bid adieu to a gaggle of visitors paying their respects.

"Please allow *me* that honor, sir," a deep voice said from the low doorway to the box.

Hunter, still clad in black clerical clothes, advanced into the low-ceilinged chamber.

"Congratulations on your performance, lad," Garrick offered calmly. "Your friend Sophie and I came to see what you would make with . . . ah . . . this *particular* piece," he commented dryly.

"I saw you from the stage, and I can understand your curiosity, sir," Hunter replied, "as I have already explained to Lady Lindsay-Hoyt, I do not know from whom Mr. Beard bought this play . . ."

"But you *do* know who the intermediary was," Sophie said tiredly, "so your hands are far from clean."

"That is true," he replied evenly, "but I am sworn to secrecy by my employer."

"The man shows loyalty," Garrick commented lightly, "and as a manager myself, I must say, 'tis refreshing to hear you say that." He smiled wearily. "I will leave you young people to discuss this further, if you wish, as long as you promise to see Sophie safely home." He bowed to both and exited the box.

Hunter sat down beside her.

"Well?" he asked somberly. "What did you think?"

"Good writing begets good theater," she replied.

"I saw you smile," he ventured. "Several times."

Sophie shifted uncomfortably in her gilt chair as the baby gave her another of its sharp kicks.

"Yes . . . I admit I smiled," she answered. "And now, I beg to take my leave. I am very tired," she added, struggling to pull herself to a standing position.

Hunter supported her under her arm until she steadied herself.

"You're a very clever lass," he said suddenly. "I enjoyed working with your creation. Perhaps . . . perhaps we could collaborate on another . . . piece sometime . . ."

"If you feel guilty, Hunter, there are other ways to make amends," Sophie responded pointedly.

"That's *not* what I'm doing," he protested. "I *meant* what I just said. I do wish we could work together some day."

Sophie pressed her hand to the small of her back, staring at him coolly.

"No apology? No hint of conscience for collecting fees from someone else's work?"

"Jesu, Sophie!" he exclaimed. "I didn't *know* it was your play! That's why I wished to see you tonight. To give you this," he added, pressing a leather pouch filled with coins into her hand. "'Tis your share of *my* share."

Chastened, she answered at length, "I will accept what's

due me, but Hunter . . . even if you didn't have a hand in obtaining my play, you went forward with it after you knew it to be stolen."

"I told Beard what happened and the man just shrugged," Hunter said defensively. "This purloining goes on more than any of us would like, so there was little I could do, except share what I've made from it. There may be additional monies if it plays three more nights."

Sophie sighed and nodded, turning toward the door. Hunter accompanied her to the front of the theater where he hailed a sedan chair. He helped her aboard and handed the front bearer some coins.

"Lindsay-Hoyt's address?" he asked brusquely.

"Cleveland Row," she said, a lump rising in her throat.

He repeated the address to the bearer and bid her adieu, walking swiftly toward the theater entrance to Covent Garden without a backward glance.

Chapter 20

Peter wandered into the chilly sitting room and stared for a long moment at Sophie sitting at his desk, bent in concentration over a pile of manuscript pages. Another stack of papers were scattered next to her.

"Well . . . making progress at last," he declared, searching among several half-filled bottles on the sideboard for something to renew his dismal mood.

Sophie looked up, startled.

"I thought not to see you till evening," she replied tersely.

He ignored her reference to his current habit of staying out all night and sleeping most of the day. Empty tumbler in hand, he sauntered over to her side and picked a page of *Double Devils*.

"What do you mean, 'by a lady'?" he demanded, pointing to the title page.

"This is *my* work," Sophie said matter-of-factly, easing her swollen body from her chair with supreme effort. "I have told you, I shall never again write another word with you credited as sole author, and *Double Devils* is a perfect case in point. You've contributed nothing but the title, and you half-stole *that* from Elizabeth Griffith's new play."

Peter glanced at her sideways, pursing his lips in thought.

"Well then, my witty wife," he replied, returning to the sideboard to pour a finger of whiskey from a near-empty bottle, "we shall have to strike a bargain, wouldn't you agree?" Sophie shrugged and remained silent. "What matter whose name goes on the deuced thing?" he continued. "If Garrick likes the piece, your author's fees will be mine by right as your husband. I offer you this compromise: put *both* our names on it and be done with it!"

And that solution to the authorship dilemma was exactly what David Garrick suggested when he accepted the farce and scheduled it for presentation in the new year of 1766. Both he and Sophie realized that the woman-hating, Shakespeare-loving deputy examiner of plays, Edward Capell, might be appeased by the joint authorship. Only recently he had made Elizabeth Griffith rewrite her play, *A Double Mistake*, four times before he deemed the work acceptable.

"Do you think it risky to open the same night as Griffith's play at Covent Garden with such a similar title?" Sophie asked.

"They pinch our play . . . we mock their title," the actor-manager said with a determined look. He quickly seized a quill and wrote a cover note to Edward Capell, requesting the manuscript be granted a license for debut Thursday, January 9.

"Shall I spare the prompter a journey to St. James's Palace and submit this myself to the clerk at the Lord Chamberlain's office?" Sophie asked. "'Tis mere blocks from Cleveland Row."

"Only if you'll allow me to treat you to a hackney coach," Garrick said, appraising her enormous girth. Pressing a shilling into her hand, he added, "Sophie, shouldn't you be home resting?"

"As soon as the playbills are finished for this week's fare, home to bed I go." She smiled with forced cheer.

As Sophie laboriously reached the bottom of the stairway that led from Garrick's office, Roderick Darnly emerged from the Greenroom. She saw him coming and going from the theater often, of late. Perhaps he had loaned additional funds to Garrick's partner, James Lacy, and now considered Drury Lane part of his fiefdom.

"Ah . . . just whom I was hoping to see—" He halted midsentence and stared at her. "Good heavens!" he exclaimed. "You risk life and limb gadding about in your condition."

"I'm fine . . . just—"

A sharp pain in her abdomen suddenly cut off her words and Sophie gasped aloud.

"You are not at all well . . . come in here and rest for a moment," he insisted, taking the manuscript from her hand and guiding her into the dimly lit Greenroom. "That's better . . . take a deep breath," he urged, settling her into a chair.

The pain disappeared as quickly as it had come, and Sophie guessed that Mrs. Phillips's warnings about the likelihood of false labor had just materialized.

"Thank you," she said, inhaling deeply. "I'm all right now, I think."

Darnly studied the title page of the play script he held in his hand.

"Submitting *Double Devils* to the censor, I see," he noted. "So . . . it bears both yours and Peter's names. Did he write a word of it?"

"Two words: *Double* and *Devils* . . ." Sophie retorted, and then heaved a sigh of resignation. "'Tis probably for the best. The man has pressing debts, as you certainly know. This promise of future fortune may stave off his most obstinate creditors."

"Do *you* have need of money?" he asked gravely.

"Of course I do," she snapped, and was immediately apologetic for her shortness of temper. "You're kind to voice concern, but I have every reason to believe I can earn my keep by my pen—given time and freedom from the profligacy of my noble husband."

"I have absolutely no doubt that you can," Darnly replied mildly, "but given the debts I personally am owed, I thought perhaps you might be critically short of funds at a time you'll be needing to do things like hire a midwife."

Sophie gazed thoughtfully at Peter's erstwhile friend. "Why are you being so solicitous, Roderick?" she inquired bluntly.

"Among other things, I admire your writing talent," he replied evenly. "'Tis wicked how your husband appropriates your work and your hard-earned funds for his own pleasures."

Sophie gazed at him skeptically. Her husband owed the man who stood before her a large sum of money. Yet, he was offering her assistance. Why?

"Sir," she said quietly, "is there something you wish of me?"

Roderick Darnly allowed the semblance of a smile to linger on his face. He was a large man, appearing even more imposing dressed in a suit of garnet-hued brocade decorated with black braid and a double row of lace on each cuff. When he smiled, he was quite attractive, Sophie allowed, although she knew instinctively that beneath his pleasant demeanor was a thirty-five-year-old nobleman with an iron will who was accustomed to achieving his goals through influence and persuasion.

"Well," he acknowledged, "I was intending to ask you to do me a service that would benefit *both* of us."

"And pray, what is that?" Sophie asked warily.

"As you may remember, I have had a casual association with a young woman named Mary Ann Skene."

"Yes . . . the ruffle maker from the Blue Periwig," Sophie replied, vividly recalling the woman with the voluptuous body and horse-faced countenance.

"I have decided to end this liaison," Darnly said imperturbably, "but I do not wish to abandon the girl."

"How kind . . ." Sophie murmured dryly.

"So, I would like to lease your lodgings above Ashby's Books for Mary Ann, since you are now living at Cleveland Row."

"I often go there to write," Sophie objected, torn between the idea of pocketing a much-needed regular monthly fee for space she rarely used, and the realization she hardly admitted to herself—that she might soon decide to move back to Half Moon Passage, washing her hands of Peter and his increasingly dissolute habits. Thus far, she had avoided making a decision until determining the legal implications of such an action.

"I have warned Mary Ann that you return to the flat often to do your printing work and that you would still have free use of the premises. However, those terms were agreeable to her."

"Oh," Sophie said, at a loss for any additional objections.

"So . . ." Darnly countered, pulling a bank draft for twenty-five pounds, "let me give you this for six months' rent."

"But 'tis the exact amount!" she exclaimed, staring at the elegant handwriting denoting funds for a half year's lease.

"My noble friend, the Duke of Bedford, who owns the freehold on that street, informed me of the rents you pay when I saw him at White's," he replied calmly. "So . . . 'tis agreed?"

Sophie tucked the bank draft into her reticule. Ironically, this meant that in effect, Darnly's own money would settle Peter's IOU, but *she* would be without her privacy above Ashby's Books. Ah well, she thought. There was nothing to be done about it. At least Peter and she would not be thrown into debtor's prison, come February, when the note was due.

"Mary Ann can bring over her belongings whenever 'tis convenient," Sophie replied quietly.

"Excellent," Darnly smiled. "Now . . . let me order Charles to deliver you home in my coach."

"Thank you, but Mr. Garrick has thoughtfully seen to that," she demurred, and bade him farewell.

Climbing into the hackney, Sophie directed the driver to take her to St. James's Palace and ordered him to wait while she delivered *Double Devils* to the clerk in the Lord Chamberlain's office. No sooner had she handed the manuscript to the reedy assistant, than a door to the inner office burst open and Edward Capell stalked out of his chambers.

"Grieves!" he said sharply, clutching a pile of plays in his arms, "I distinctly recall ordering you to remove this pile of manuscripts cluttering my bottom shelves!"

"I have some of them here, sir, and was just about to—" began the clerk, pointing to several works on his cluttered desk. Sophie assumed the hapless fellow had a habit of allowing orphaned manuscripts to molder in some cupboard in the warrenlike chambers.

"These works are all vile, disgusting attempts at humor,"

Capell declared, dumping the stack he carried onto the clerk's desk. "The sooner you return them to their misguided authors, the better!"

The Deputy Examiner of Plays interrupted his tirade to stare at Sophie who, in her advanced stage of pregnancy, was apparently unrecognizable. As a result of his outburst, his mottled skin had grown even more blotchy and scarlet than usual.

"Kindly tell me, Grieves," he said, eyeing Sophie disdainfully, "why you have allowed a female in this revolting condition to lounge willy-nilly in these chambers?" He addressed Sophie directly. "Madam, you belong with a midwife. I cannot *bear* such fecundity to be flaunted in this place of business. Pray, absent yourself from my sight *at once!*"

"I am Sophie McGann . . . I-I mean, Lady Lindsay-Hoyt," she stammered. "I have just delivered a manuscript from Mr. Garrick for your amiable consideration sir." She envisioned her months of hard work evaporating in the hostile atmosphere prevailing in the Lord Chamberlain's office. "Mr. Garrick sends his kindest regards . . . and please excuse me, if my appearance causes you offense." Backing out of the chamber, she bumped into a chair and nearly lost her balance. "I-I beg your leave," she mumbled and exited as quickly as she could, disgusted at her own obsequiousness.

Sophie was able to work off some of her righteous anger during the hour required for her to print a new batch of playbills due at Drury Lane.

"Sophie . . . here, let me do that," Lorna said from the top of the circular stairway that spiraled into the back of the book shop on the floor below. "You shouldn't be pulling on that lever that way . . . 'twill bring on your labor prematurely."

Sophie wiped her brow on the sleeve of her dress and arched her aching back.

"I think I *will* rest for a while," she agreed wearily. "Shall I brew us a cup of tea?"

"No, I shall," Lorna said firmly.

But Sophie had no sooner eased her tired frame onto her bed than she heard the sound of footsteps on the stairs that separated her lodgings from those of Mrs. Phillips across the landing. Her door swung open and there at the threshold stood Mary Ann Skene, her gown resplendent with frothy ruffles. Behind her, a burly young man carried a large trunk. The harlot eyed Sophie with irritation.

"Roderick said I'd be able to sleep here during the *day*," she whined. "If you wish to sleep here at night, 'tis your affair, but m'lord *guaranteed* I'd have a place to sleep during the *day* and—"

"And so you shall," Sophie interrupted tiredly.

She heaved her heavy body upright, and swung her legs over the side of the mattress. "The bed shall be yours . . . no doubt your labors at the Blue Periwig leave you quite exhausted."

Mary Ann gazed at her suspiciously while the porter carrying her trunk dumped it noisily on the floor and departed.

"Peculiar chap, that baronet of yours," Mary Ann proclaimed spitefully, opening the trunk and pushing Sophie's few belongings to one side of the battered armoire standing against one wall. "There's some that drinks and gambles . . . and there's some that wenches themselves skittle brained. Then there's rogues like him who do it *all* to a farethee-well!" She paused midway from trunk to armoire, cradling a pile of lacy shifts in her arms. "But isn't that the way of it when the wife's breeding?" She boldly stared at the enormous bulge protruding under Sophie's gown.

Sophie merely nodded and retreated to the printing chamber, silently vowing not to lose her temper. Lorna shook her head with sympathetic disgust as she stacked the last of the week's order of playbills into a pile.

"I'll brew the tea downstairs and bring you up a cup," she whispered.

Sophie created a thick, soft pallet on the floor near the printing press out of piles of Harriet Ashby's abandoned clothes. A few minutes later, Lorna reappeared and handed Sophie her tea.

"That doxy should be lying here, and you on the bed!" she whispered indignantly.

But Sophie smiled faintly. In a strange way, she felt rather comforted to be sleeping in the precise spot Hunter had chosen when he shared her lodgings during his first trip to London. After a few minutes, she set her tea cup quietly on the floor, and in a trice, she was napping peacefully.

The front facade of Drury Lane was aglow from the light of flambeaux carried by servants escorting their masters up the colonnaded entrance to the theater. Sophie inhaled the smell of snow in the air as she trudged down Russell Street and made her way to the stage entrance, relishing the palpable excitement and anticipation backstage that invariably gripped the players just before the performance was to start.

"Evening, Sophie," an actress named Mrs. Love called as she hurried in the direction of the women's tiring-room. "I believe we may have a bit of a blow later tonight."

But before Sophie could summon a cheerful response, the woman had been swallowed up by the velvet wing curtains backstage.

"Allow me, Lady Lindsay-Hoyt," insisted Collins, the Drury Lane stage doorkeeper, as he relieved her of the stack of playbills she was carrying. "I'll see that they get these right away."

Thanking the man for his assistance, she retraced her steps, and hailed a sedan chair that was just then unloading a theater patron. When the single-passenger vehicle arrived at Cleveland Row, the house was shrouded in darkness. There had been no funds to hire a replacement since Peter's disagreeable housekeeper had departed. Sophie groped her way through the front door, found a flint, and lit the stub of a candle she located in a sconce hanging on the paneled wall in the foyer. With considerable difficulty, she started a small blaze in the fireplace. Too weary to climb the stairs to her bedchamber, she sank, fully dressed, onto the daybed in the corner of the sitting room.

She hadn't been dozing more than a few hours when she awoke with a start. Groggily, she stared around the shadowy chamber and heard voices in the front foyer. The fire in the sitting room had burned to embers, and she was momentarily confused by her darkened surroundings. Male laughter suddenly rent the air.

"But my Turkey carpet is *ever* so soft, my lovelies," she heard Peter say in the slurred voice she knew so well. "You haven't experienced love's transports until you've put your exquisite backsides on my hearth rug while I play walrus with your tusks—"

Peals of high-pitched hilarity greeted this sally as the door to the sitting room swung open and a shaft of light from Peter's unsteady candle beamed across the carpet.

Sophie's husband, his shirt gaping open to his waist, stood in the threshold with his arms around two women. He was busy fondling the pendulous breasts of each.

"All right, my little pigeons . . ." he chortled, pushing them along, "which of you would like the honor . . . nay, the *duty* . . . of removing my vestments?"

He nearly lost his footing as the two harlots left his side and sought to warm their hands in front of the low-burning fire. By this time, Sophie had struggled to her feet.

"By God, you shall not behave so monstrously in our own *home*!" Sophie exclaimed and stalked into the small circle of light provided by the fireplace and Peter's candlestick.

The two trollops stared at her, their painted mouths agape. Peter appeared startled at first, and then drew himself up.

"'Tis *my* house, you damnable bitch!" he shouted drunkenly, "and I shall do as I please!"

Sophie snatched the iron fire poker from its stand and brandished it over her head.

"Remove these bawds from my sight or you're a dead man!"

Peter glanced at her weapon and took a step backward.

"Upstairs!" he ordered. Instantly, his two companions exited the chamber and could be heard stumbling up the center stairway, two stairs at a time. Peter gazed at her unsteadily. "Your wish is my command, m'lady," he said mockingly.

A jumble of mad thoughts collided in Sophie's brain. How could she have been so blind to the true character of this man? How much worse than *this* could it have been, to have borne her bairn on her own?

Suddenly, a sharp pain cleaved through her abdomen. Sophie gasped and lowered the fire iron from over her head. She clutched the mantelpiece to steady herself and wished she were dead. Peter appeared both sobered by her agonized expression and relieved to see she was no longer in a mood to strike him.

"I did not appreciate hearing from Darnly tonight that you have been hoarding funds from me!" he growled.

The brief stab of pain now diminished, Sophie's eyes widened in dismayed surprise.

"Wha—?"

"The blighter said he'd housed his doxy above your book shop," he said contemptuously. "Paid you plenty, I understand."

"Just enough to settle the gambling debt *you* owe him and save us both from Newgate!" Sophie snapped.

Peter laughed mirthlessly.

"The man's rolling in wealth," he sneered. "He can wait for his blunt." He stared at her sharply. "I suppose you view him as your savior . . . well, he's arranged it so his good deed doesn't cost him a farthing!"

"At least 'tis better than having nothing to placate his solicitor!"

"I doubt he'd take it to court," Peter said moodily.

"Peter . . . please . . ." she begged, wishing to conclude this ugly scene quickly. "Darnly's given us a second chance of sorts. We should be grateful. I'll pay him the money he's owed and we can clean the slate. If you'd merely drink less and work with me as you did on *The Provoked Player* we could make our way splendidly. You're not an untalented man and—"

"I need not be lectured by *you* on the subject!" He picked up an empty wine bottle and flung it across the room. Sophie flinched as it shattered against the opposite wall. He stepped toward her menacingly. "You'll be very sorry before this is through if you think Roderick Darnly is your knight in shining armor . . . or that he does anything that is not in his own interest."

"Just like *you*," she retorted, her temper rising once more.

"I could tell you a few choice morsels about—"

"No doubt you could," Sophie interrupted wearily, "but all that is beside the point." She shook her head sadly. "Let us face facts, Peter. Our marriage is as empty as your bogus title. I have no wish to harm you. . . . I want only to be left in peace."

"You want to be left with all the fees earned by our plays!" he retorted.

"*Our* plays?" she retorted, her voice rising. "I ask only for *half* . . . the half I *more* than earned!"

"As your husband, I have the legal right to give you *nothing*!" he declared. "I want that money Darnly gave you . . . I *demand* the money! *All* of it!"

"You do, and I'll call down the King's Officer of Arms on you and you'll find yourself in the Tower of London for posing as an aristocrat!" she shouted.

Another cramping sensation gripped her vitals, although this time the pain appeared milder. Slowly she made her way back to the daybed, feeling as if she were walking underwater. She sank, exhausted, onto the couch. Peter stared at her uncertainly. She closed her eyes, her breathing ragged. Silence filled the room.

"Just leave me," she murmured, and after a moment, she heard him stumble out of the room and tread unsteadily upstairs. She realized she didn't care in the slightest what he was doing—or with whom.

Sophie tiptoed past the open door of Peter's bedchamber, determined to collect her few belongings in the room next door. Her husband of six months was sprawled naked between the two snoring strumpets he had enticed to his bed. In the gloomy light of the overcast December day, Peter's face was shadowed by his customary black stubble, giving him the dissolute appearance of a man far older than his twenty-eight years.

She threw open the door to the armoire and angrily snatched several items of clothing off the pegs. Stuffing them into her portmanteau, she glanced up to find her husband, clothed in a rumpled dressing gown, swaying against the door frame.

"What are you doing?" he croaked, his eyes shifting nervously between the armoire and her baggage.

"Leaving this place," she answered quietly, looking across the room to meet his gaze. "Leaving you."

"Oh, Sophie," he groaned, sounding contrite, "that was the spirits talking last night. Please . . . those strumpets mean nothing to me. 'Twas wretched of me to bring them here . . . but you've been so—so *disapproving,* of late. And with the babe and all, I grew . . ." His disconnected sentence drifted off. He smiled tentatively, a naughty little boy pleading forgiveness. "Henceforth, I promise you, Sophie, I will—"

"'Tis no good making promises," Sophie interrupted. She gazed at him with something close to sympathy. "You seem —for some reason I don't understand—to be unable to keep your promises. And I can see from what transpired between us last night that we might one day do each other physical harm." She sighed wearily and seized her portmanteau. "I'm sorry, too, for my part in this debacle. I was not truly in love with you either, and I should never have succumbed to—" Halting midsentence, she glanced down at her swollen abdomen. "'Tis best we separate. I must have some peace 'til the baby comes."

Confounded by her quiet determination to leave, Peter stepped aside to let her pass. He seemed so preoccupied with his own thoughts that he never offered to assist his pregnant wife with her luggage as she swiftly departed his lodgings for good.

"Sophie, you're *mad* to go to Drury Lane tonight!" Lorna protested, watching her friend lift her cloak from a peg beside Ashby's front door. "Someone else can play your part in *The Milk Maids*! 'Tis bitter cold outside, for one thing, and you're in very great danger of having this babe in the *wings*!"

"I feel perfectly well," Sophie responded firmly. "'Tis

remarkable what a simple change of scene will do for one's morale."

"Well, *please* take care," Lorna urged her friend, shivering in the frigid blast of air that swept through the shop's open door. "And good luck with the play," she called after her friend, aware that Sophie had been anxious to hear whether Edward Capell would grant *Double Devils* a license.

An anemic ray of late December sunshine shone weakly through the clouds as Sophie trod gingerly along the paved roads crusted with several inches of snow. Mary Ann Skene would soon be rising from the bed over the shop to make her toilette and ready herself for another evening of trade at the Blue Periwig. In the four days since Sophie had quietly departed her husband's abode, the strumpet had reported Peter's new offenses with unfeigned enthusiasm.

"He looks bad . . . very bad," Mary Ann pronounced.

When, at length, Sophie arrived at Drury Lane, she discovered that the largest breeches from the wardrobe chamber would barely accommodate her swollen waist. An hour later, *The Milk Maids* slowly creaked toward its conclusion. Sophie had done her level best to look cantankerous, as her part required, but her heart wasn't in it. Suddenly, near the end of the final act, a searing pain, much worse than she had experienced before, gripped her abdomen.

"*Jesu!*" she gasped, clutching the arm of Mrs. Love who was playing Sophie's wife.

"Will you manage till the end?" whispered the alarmed actress.

Sophie nodded gamely, momentarily relieved that her discomfort had abated. Within a few minutes, however, another contraction wrenched every fiber of her small frame. She put a hand on her abdomen as the reality of what was happening came over her with frightening intensity. Her bairn was fighting to escape the prison of her womb, she thought frantically. Would the baby live or die? Would *she* live or die?

Cold, stark terror gripped her as fiercely as the pain itself. Blindly, she stumbled off stage and sank onto King Lear's throne, which the stage servants had removed temporarily to the wings.

She tried to catch her breath, and did everything in her power to keep from screaming. However, she couldn't stifle the low moan that escaped from her lips, causing the prompter, Mr. Hopkins, to cast a horrified stare in her direction. Just as the players recited their closing lines and the audience began applauding, David Garrick appeared by her side.

"Good heavens, dear girl!" he exclaimed. "Hopkins . . . flag a hackney and send a runner to Mrs. Phillips. Tell her Sophie will be needing her attention immediately!"

At length, the contraction subsided and Sophie found herself surrounded by the entire cast of *Milk Maids.*

"Clear the way!" shouted George Garrick pompously. "Give the lass some air!"

"Here . . . George! William!" David Garrick barked at the bystanders with the authority of a stage director. "Help me get her to the coach!"

Sophie barely remembered being bundled into the hired carriage for the short drive to Half Moon Street. The Garrick brothers eased her gently up the stairs to her chambers, trailed by Lorna Blount. Sophie's friend had just been leaving Half Moon Tavern following a late supper and spotted the commotion taking place at the entrance to Ashby's Books. Mrs. Phillips was already inside Sophie's flat, readying the bed that Mary Ann Skene had not long since vacated.

"Excellent, gentlemen . . . right in here," Mrs. Phillips called brusquely, "onto the bed with her . . . that's right . . . there you are, my dear . . . here, drink this," she ordered, handing her a cup of something hot.

"What is it?" Sophie asked weakly.

"A bit of camomile tea with a drop of laudanum to soothe your nerves . . . that's a good girl," Mrs. Phillips said.

David and George Garrick prepared to depart.

"Send word immediately when she is delivered . . . please God, we hope safely," David Garrick said to Mrs. Phillips in a low voice. And much to Sophie's surprise, she

felt George Garrick give her hand a gentle, encouraging
squeeze.

Within two hours, Sophie was delivered of a tiny but
robust daughter.

"You're a mite narrow to bring forth so quickly, but you
labored well," Mrs. Phillips declared with a nod of satisfaction, laying the bundled child in the crook of Sophie's arm.
Then she added with immodest pride, "May I say this was
due in no small measure to my own midwifery skills which I
learned from the original Mrs. Phillips, God bless her admirable soul!"

"Indeed," Sophie agreed in a weak voice, grateful to have
come through the ordeal alive and with little Danielle, warm
and pink as a peach, nestled in her arms. Mrs. Phillips was
overbearing, to be sure, but she had known a good deal
about midwifery, and for that Sophie would be eternally
grateful.

"The name you've chosen for her is hardly Scottish,"
Lorna teased, peering down at the softly mewling babe.

"Oh yes 'tis . . ." Sophie murmured groggily. "She's
named for my father . . . Daniel McGann."

During the first week of the new year of 1766, Sophie
found herself showered with gifts from the Garricks, as well
as presents from a number of friends at Drury Lane. Even
crusty George Garrick sent over a soft woven blanket from a
shop in Covent Garden.

For her part, saucy Mary Ann Skene delivered a silver
and bone rattle, courtesy of Roderick Darnly, enclosed with
five pounds. While Sophie put Danielle to the breast, the
young courtesan sat at the desk holding a hand glass, meticulously applying a small black patch near the corner of one
eye. Despite having been relegated to the makeshift pallet in
the printing chamber, Mary Ann departed for her nightly
chores in reasonably cheerful spirits.

Meanwhile, Lorna saw to Sophie's comfort and then retreated down the spiral stairs into the book shop. Little

Danielle slept peacefully in the roomy confines of Aunt Harriet's open trunk placed next to Sophie's bed. The fire burned brightly in the grate and Sophie snuggled sleepily beneath the fresh bed linen.

She was roused from this pleasant state by a light tap on the door leading to the landing. Fearing it could be Peter, come to see his progeny, she felt her heart thump uncomfortably.

"Who is it?" she called out warily.

"A former pupil . . ." responded a deep voice, ". . . come to congratulate an old man who nearly gave birth on Drury Lane's stage!"

"Hunter?" Sophie said in amazement.

In an instant, the door swung open and Hunter Robertson's tall frame filled the threshold.

"Your final performance is the talk of Covent Garden," he announced, advancing into the chamber. His eyes searched her face as if to assure himself she were, indeed, alive and well. "I can only stay a moment . . . must get to the theater soon but I—" His attention was drawn to the open trunk at the bottom of the bed. "Ah . . . so here's the babe . . . and a fine wee mite it is. Lad or lassie?" he inquired, his handsome features softening as he stared down at the baby whose eyes were serenely closed.

"Her name's Danielle . . ." Sophie answered in a low voice, ". . . for my da."

"Yes, she's lovely," he said in a breath. He looked at her across the bedstead. "And you? You're truly well?" She nodded as a strange silence fell between them. "I was surprised to learn you'd shunned the comforts of Cleveland Row to have the bairn here," he commented, glancing around the chamber.

"I . . . ah . . . do not wish to live with Peter any longer," she replied, feeling abashed by the rush of happiness at his interest. Obviously Hunter cared enough about her welfare to pay her this visit.

"I had heard something to that effect," he acknowledged.

"So my return to Half Moon Passage is the subject of tittle-tattle?"

"Yes, m'lady," he answered dryly, "but no one knows the grounds for it. Why have you left?"

"There is no need to call me lady, even in jest," Sophie announced with an ironic smile. "My husband, it seems, is no baronet."

Hunter lifted his brows slightly and then he shrugged.

"Actually, I'm not particularly surprised to learn of this," he responded at length. "Yet, I doubt that losing a title would be the sole reason you would depart his lodgings so abruptly."

"'Tis not," she said shortly, and then added, "I cannot live with a man wedded to strong spirits and endless wagering."

"Then come live with *me*," Hunter suggested calmly. "I wish to be your lover *and* your friend."

Sophie stared at him across the bed linen, stunned by his bold proposal. It was amazing that he seemingly didn't care a farthing that she was another man's wife or that Danielle was living proof of her intimacy with a man he reviled.

"Would a friend not tell me who pilfered my play?" she asked quietly.

"If that's all that stands in the way," he countered seriously, "Beard agrees I can at least tell you this much—*The Parsimonious Parson* was delivered to Covent Garden's manager by a man none of us recognized. We were directed by him to leave the author's share of the profits at a sedan chair stand in the Great Piazza." Hunter sank down on the edge of her mattress and seized her hand. "Sophie, please," he said urgently, "believe me . . . I had no hand in stealing your work."

Sophie's heart turned over at the sight of him sitting so near her on the bed. Her hand in his felt safe and secure. He seemed utterly sincere, yet, she reminded herself, he was an *actor*. She recalled how earnestly Peter had sworn all sorts of rubbish during their short acquaintance. Men could say the most astonishing falsehoods if they wanted something from a woman. She found herself silently considering the remarkable coincidence that Mavis Piggott and Hunter had both returned from Dublin this season and that she had spied Mavis disappearing down the hall the very day she proposed to Garrick in his office that she write *The Parsimonious Parson*. As much as she longed to believe Hunter, given everything she'd endured, she simply couldn't risk trusting him . . . or trusting *anyone,* for that matter. She gazed at him sadly and gently withdrew her hand.

"'Tis quite an astonishing proposal you offer a woman not yet risen from childbed," she said soberly.

"I meant it to be," Hunter replied, scanning her face for an answer. "'Tis what we should have done in Bath," he insisted. "We were both fools and now we should make the best of our mistakes. At least *live* with me . . . and marry me one day, if you can."

She gazed at him bleakly.

"Your proposal presents rather a large problem," she said, recalling her recent journey to the law chambers to pay Peter's debt to Darnly's man of business. "I had an occasion to inquire of a solicitor, a Mr. Beezle, about the possibility of a woman divorcing herself from an adulterous spouse who is forever in his cups. Shall I tell you what this man of the law revealed to me?"

"What?"

"He explained that no woman in England has ever successfully petitioned the House of Lords for a divorce. However, it seems that thirty-three men—commoners and peers alike—have severed themselves legally from their wives."

"But, if *they* obtained relief from adulterous wives, why not wives from adulterous husbands?" he wondered.

"The worthy Mr. Beezle explained that even if a husband committs adultery, beats his wife, or squanders her dowry, it can only mean she hasn't been a good enough companion to the man! He may be a rake, a gambler, a philanderer—*even give his wife the clap*! But English law says the husband is the victim!"

"But what about Scotland?" Hunter asked. "'Tis a different legal system, you know. Courts there have granted wives divorces in extreme situations. . . . I'm sure of it! One could say that a man posing as a baronet had committed fraud, if nothing else."

"You seem to have forgotten how you managed my escape from Edinburgh just a cat's whisker before the constable would have arrested me," she reminded him glumly. "I doubt I could obtain much justice in Scottish courts."

Hunter reluctantly nodded his agreement. The two of them exchanged somber glances.

"My life's a terrible coil, Hunter," she stated finally. "I must sort it out before I can do much of anything . . . write, live with someone—"

"Or love?" he asked, gazing at her steadily.

Sophie felt a sharp intake of breath. How did he read her thoughts so exactly she wondered? She smiled sadly.

"Or love," she echoed.

Hunter stood up wearily.

"You *will* permit an old friend to visit from time to time, won't you?" he asked, bending over the trunk to peer down again at Danielle. He brushed the back of one of his fingers lightly against the baby's cheek. It was a gesture of such gentleness that Sophie thought her heart wouldn't stand it.

She nodded to avoid having to speak past the lump that had risen in her throat. Danielle could have been *their* child, she thought sorrowfully. If only she had not fled from Bath to London to collaborate with Peter. Her eyes drifted involuntarily to the table where she did her writing. Her quill pen rested jauntily in its stand, awaiting the time when she would sit down to work on a new idea for a play that had come to her as she lay in bed recovering from her ordeal. She needed to write as much as she needed to breathe. Could Hunter ever really understand that? Could he understand how her love for him and her love for her work often pulled her in opposite directions? And then there was Danielle. How in the world could she manage it all, she wondered, as Hunter rose to his full height and prepared to depart.

"When you've worked out this puzzle . . . I'll be waiting," he said quietly and leaned down to kiss her lightly on her forehead. Then, he strode out of the room.

Chapter 21

"Good day, m'lady," said Mr. Collins, addressing Sophie from his perch at the entrance to Drury Lane. The look on his face bespoke his surprise at seeing her only ten days after childbirth.

Sophie offered a hurried greeting to the stage doorkeeper as she moved silently toward the wings to watch the final rehearsal for *Double Devils* unobserved. Despite her determination to see how well the actors recited the speeches she had labored over with such intensity, Sophie worried that Lorna would find minding both the book shop and the infant Danielle too much for one person to handle.

She heaved a sigh and tried to concentrate on the actors' characterizations, the flesh-and-blood creations that had sprung from her imagination. Mavis Piggott, playing the hapless fiancée engaged to one of the rakish twins, was sobbing into a series of handkerchiefs provided her by Kitty Clive, her match-making mother.

Garrick had taken for himself the role of one of the twins and West Digges, dressed in matching wig, makeup, and costume, played the other. Even the supporting players seemed to know their lines, and Sophie's spirits rose at the prospect of a delighted audience at the opening performance the following evening.

"Excuse me, sir!" Collins's voice cut through the dialogue being exchanged on stage. "You cannot go in there!"

Sophie shrank back into the shadows at the sight of her

husband, Peter, weaving his way past the stage doorkeeper
and into the first set of wings.

"Ah . . . Garrick, my good man . . . so sorry to disturb you," Peter said, the familiar slurring of his words indicating he had been on one of his now-frequent binges.

The action on stage had halted midsentence, and the cast
turned their attention to David Garrick, whose policy on
interruptions during rehearsals was inviolate.

"We are at work, sir," Garrick said frostily. "I'll thank
you to remove yourself to my office. Collins!" he commanded. "Show Sir Peter the way."

"This can't wait, I'm afraid." Peter grinned inanely, leaning against a painted column that was part of the garden
terrace set. At that point, the piece of scenery gave way beneath his weight. He stumbled forward and was only saved
from falling on his face when West Digges swiftly grabbed
his arm to steady him. "I lost a bit of blunt at White's last
night, don't y'know," he said conspiratorially to his rescuer,
". . . thought I'd collect my author's fees in advance from
the Great Garrick, here." He peered unsteadily in the direction of the actor-manager, "Great God, Garrick!" he announced loudly, executing an exaggerated bow, "can you
spare me a few quid?"

There was a collective gasp of horror from the assembly,
and Sophie suddenly wished she could disappear through
one of the trap doors carved in the Drury Lane stage. Garrick's stentorian answer rang to the rafters.

"Sir! Kindly hold your tongue until this rehearsal is concluded!"

"Perhaps I could be of assistance," declared Roderick
Darnly, materializing suddenly from the Greenroom opposite Sophie's vantage point.

"Ah . . . Darnly . . . my old friend . . . the Patron,"
Peter said mockingly, turning to his former companion.
"Pulled a few wires, did you, to get that peevish censor to
approve this magnificent work of art . . . for which I'd like
to be recompensed . . . now!"

"Come, Peter," Darnly said firmly, taking the inebriated
man by the arm. "Let me help you, old chap."

"You helped, all right," he growled. "You helped my

wife desert me, that infernal bitch! The polecat didn't wish to share credit for this piece when she knows *I* wrote all the good speeches m'self!" Sophie could hear an undercurrent of reaction to this blatant falsehood ripple through the players lounging on stage. "The wretched vixen!" Peter added spitefully. "Don't even know if her babe is *mine*! Could it be *yours*, old chap?" he asked drunkenly.

Sophie felt her pulse begin to pound and her cheeks turn red with anger and humiliation.

"Come, Peter," Darnly repeated as he half-led, half-dragged Sophie's husband toward the stage door. "Collins!" he barked, "take his other arm!"

The entire cast watched in stunned silence as Peter was hustled off stage.

"Take my advice," the unwelcome visitor said loudly over his shoulder, "and never marry a female wit. God's wounds, they destroy a man! Only thing to do now is divorce the slut. Takes an act of Parliament, but you'll testify in my behalf, won't you, Roddy old man?" he inquired as his knees suddenly buckled. "Where are you taking me?" he appealed to his escorts. "The Bedford? . . . or the good ol' Blue Periwig? Must warn the chaps about jades like my lady wife . . ."

Sophie shrank deeper into the shadows, mortified that anyone should know she had witnessed this appalling display.

Garrick scowled at the retreating backs of the three men exiting the theater and announced, "Ladies and gentlemen! I would advise you to disregard the reckless statements of a man besotted with drink. Let us continue, please. Mrs. Piggott? Mrs. Clive? We will commence with your entrance."

There wasn't a spare seat in Drury Lane the night *Double Devils* was presented on stage for the first time. Elizabeth Griffith's *The Double Mistake* was also making its debut at Covent Garden that January night, and the London theatergoing crowd was abuzz that Drury Lane had thrown down the proverbial gauntlet to its nearby competitor. This, coupled with Sir Peter Lindsay-Hoyt's public declaration that he intended to drag his collaborator through the mud in a threatened Parliamentary divorce trial had been excellent for ticket sales.

"It appears the scandal of our warring playwright-spouses has been a boon for business," Mavis Piggott pronounced loudly as the cast gathered backstage for the start of the performance. "I hope their strategy of airing their private quarrels so publicly succeeds beyond first night."

"If you think I'd wish this tittle-tattle on myself, Mavis, you've quite gone 'round the twist!" Sophie snapped.

Kitty Clive listened from nearby.

"My, my, Mavis . . . pull in your claws, my dear," she said sweetly. "Just try to do your very best with this choice part Sophie's written. Take it from an older woman. Your days playing young misses are sadly numbered!"

As the first act curtain parted, the two actresses were all smiles, conversing with the identically dressed Garrick and Digges. Kitty was promptly rewarded with a burst of laughter from the audience as soon as she leaned toward her "daughter" and said as an aside, "What matter which man strikes your fancy, m'dear? If we can catch one of 'em, we'll *both* be the richer for it!"

By the middle of February, Garrick summoned Sophie to his upstairs chambers at Drury Lane and handed her half the proceeds from the Third, Sixth and Ninth Author's Night Benefits.

"Your husband threatened legal action when I paid him his share only," Garrick sighed, counting out Sophie's fees, "but I think 'tis only bluster. All in all, I'd call *Double Devils* a resounding success," the manager smiled encouragingly. "Did you see the excellent notice in the *St. James's Chronicle* this week?"

"Giving all the credit to Peter," Sophie replied morosely. "Thank you," she added, tucking away the money.

"Is that why you appear so glum, my dear?" Garrick asked with a look of concern.

"Peter's creditors have taken to hounding *me* now," Sophie replied. "His threat to petition Parliament for a divorce may also just be bluster, but I have no idea, really. Meanwhile, he's suggested his creditors attach my earnings, which they have a clear and legal right to do."

"The blackguard!" Garrick muttered, shaking his head.

"In spite of the scandal, I rather wish he *would* divorce me," Sophie acknowledged grimly. "My only hope to keep us out of Newgate is to continue writing. 'Tis challenging indeed to craft a comedy under such circumstances."

"One of these days you'll reap your due, dear," he assured her. "How's *The Bogus Baronet* progressing?"

Sophie shook her head and laughed.

"Quite nicely, despite what I just said. Fortunately, 'tis a plot that almost writes itself!"

Ice and sleet howled outside Ashby's Books for several days following Sophie's interview with Garrick, and virtually no customers came to call. Sophie had made a daybed for little Danielle in one of the roomy bottom drawers in her desk at the shop. She was able to keep an eye on her sleeping baby while she worked on the new play, luxuriating in the peace and quiet of her surroundings.

"Morning," Mary Ann mumbled, arriving at the shop with a blast of cold air after her night's labors at the Blue Periwig. Within minutes the exhausted prostitute had mounted the stairs to the second-floor living quarters and crawled into the bed Sophie had vacated less than an hour earlier.

Overhead Sophie heard the sound of Lorna methodically pulling the lever on the printing press. Thanks to their mutual efforts, Sophie and Lorna had managed to stay solvent since the baby was born, though just barely. Nevertheless, to Sophie 'twas a far more pleasant existence than the life she'd shared with Peter Lindsay.

Danielle stirred in her makeshift crib. Puckering her tiny features, the infant began to cry. Swiftly, Sophie lifted her daughter from the bedding, uncovered her breast, which was hard and full of milk, and allowed the baby to find its source of greatest contentment.

Suddenly another gust of frigid air swirled into the book

shop, scattering the pages of *The Bogus Baronet*. She looked up in annoyance and then stared, openmouthed, at the two figures standing in the doorway.

"*Bozzy!*" she exclaimed, jumping up from her chair with the baby still nursing in her arms. "Oh, Hunter, you've brought Bozzy to my door, just as you did in Edinburgh!"

James Boswell, round and pink and hearty as ever, strode into the book shop after an absence of nearly two and a half years abroad.

"You had no suckling babe when last we met, that's certain," he exclaimed, staring at her with curiosity. "Greetings, Sophie," he added with a flourish. "The wanderer has returned!"

Startled by the noise and sudden movement, little Danielle pulled her head away from Sophie's bosom with a jerk and began to wail at the interruption. Boswell flushed scarlet at the sight of Sophie's swollen breast, and Hunter appeared no more at ease than his companion.

She smiled at them apologetically, soothed the baby, and urged her tiny daughter to resume nursing, pulling her shawl discreetly over Danielle's tiny head. She beckoned the two men to take seats by the fire at the rear of the shop and called quietly up to Lorna to come downstairs and greet their guests.

"So, you're back!" Sophie said, settling herself gingerly into a chair beside her visitors. "You must tell me everywhere you've been and everything you've done."

"From what I gather, you've done quite a lot yourself, lassie," Boswell said with a meaningful look at the baby.

"Oh, Bozzy," she sighed, "so much has happened since we last saw each other."

"Aye," he replied, with a hint of melancholy.

"Jamie's mother died in Edinburgh on the eleventh of January," Hunter explained, casting a sympathetic look at his friend.

"Oh, I am so very sorry to hear of it," Sophie replied softly.

"A letter from my father caught up with me in Paris as I was about to depart for home . . ."

Boswell's slightly protuberant eyes begin to fill with

tears. He reached into his pocket and withdrew a crumpled handkerchief.

"But you *must* tell Sophie about your adventures in Corsica," Hunter interjected hastily. "He's been consorting with desperadoes and revolutionaries and all manner of renegades. 'Tis sure to plague his father, if he should ever hear of our lad's exploits!"

Boswell warmed to the subject of his romantic adventures all over Europe. His descriptions painted such vivid pictures that Sophie could almost imagine herself traveling beside him. After a quarter of an hour, she put the sleeping Danielle back into the padded drawer near the desk and then accepted a cup of tea brewed by Lorna. For an hour or more, Jamie regaled them with tales of meeting General Pasquale Paoli, a leader bent on freeing Corsica from the sway of Genoa.

"We could speak of everything, he and I," Boswell said of the General, "politics, philosophy, history, marriage, even the intelligence of beasts. I dressed as a Corsican during my stay and they called me their English ambassador. I played the flute in public . . . Scot tunes, and they loved 'em!"

"And don't forget Rousseau," Hunter said admiringly. "Our Bozzy's become an intimate of the great philosopher."

The mention of Rousseau instantly transported Sophie back to the day when the clerics from St. Giles invaded her father's book shop and she hid Rousseau's *La Nouvelle Heloise* beneath chunks of peat in a box near the hearth. That was the day she first met Hunter.

"I have also become a devoted admirer of Rousseau's mistress, Thérèse le Vasseur," Boswell revealed impishly.

"To what degree are you 'devoted,' you scamp?" Sophie smiled.

"*Quite* devoted," he replied.

"Oh, *no!*" Sophie teased. "You don't mean you—"

"Only twelve times," Boswell said nonchalantly, and Hunter, Sophie and Lorna collapsed with laughter.

"No wonder you've come to call . . ." Sophie chuckled, wiping her eyes, ". . . you were actually intending to visit the Green Canister, next door . . . now admit it!"

"Odds fish, I pray *not!*" Boswell retorted.

Just then, a stranger bundled in a cloak to combat the

bitter cold entered the shop, and the resulting draft stirred the embers on the fire. The man of middle stature quickly shut the door behind him and unravelled a yard-long wool muffler he'd wrapped around his throat.

"I've word for Sophie McGann," the man announced in a gruff voice. "A very rotund friend of hers what used to visit her aunt at Bedlam paid me to fetch her if the old lady should take a turn for the worse."

"I am Sophie McGann," she said, rising to her feet, a chilly feeling of dread clutching at her. "What is it?"

She recognized the visitor as the turnkey from Bedlam—Jackson—whom she'd paid handsomely the day she disguised herself as the fat old man in *The Milk Maids*. He was to bring her word of any trouble.

"I'm sorry to have to tell ye, m'lady . . . yer aunt's dead. Slit her wrists this morning, she did, with the edge of one of them feeding tubes."

"Oh, God," Sophie whispered, feeling Hunter wrap his arm around her shoulder to steady her.

"Where is she now?" Hunter demanded.

"College of Surgeons, I expect," the man said dourly.

Sophie felt her legs turn to jelly. Even so, she pulled away from Hunter and stepped closer to the woeful messenger.

"Does Bedlam make a profit delivering bodies to the medical school?" she asked in a low voice, her eyes glittering ominously.

"Old Dr. Monro collects a pound or two, I expect. There's no one to stop him, don't you know." Jackson glanced nervously at this small-statured woman staring at him with furious intensity. "I'm sorry to bring you such ill tidings, surely I am, but the gentleman what's called to see the old lady was quite insistent I find you the instant anything hap—"

"You've done exactly right," Sophie interrupted. She strode over to her desk drawer where she located a shilling to give to the man. When he had departed, she quickly donned her cloak.

"Lorna, would you—"

"Of course," her friend said, looking at her with concern. "Sophie . . . *please* . . . I beg of you . . . don't—"

"I'm only going to see her," she interrupted dully.

"I'll go with you," Hunter announced, gathering up his cloak. "Boz, I shall see you anon."

"Right-o," Boswell responded, appearing relieved to remain in such cozy and inviting surroundings. "I'll just keep Lorna, here, company for a bit."

Hunter took Sophie's arm, guiding her toward the door. "Quickly now . . . before darkness falls."

The hired coach picked its way slowly through the driving snow and pulled up in front of the somber edifice which housed the College of Physicians and Surgeons.

Once inside, it didn't take long to locate the morgue.

"'Tis common practice for bodies to be sent here when there's no known family," the orderly said meekly as he ushered them to the back of the building where the cadavers were stored. He pulled a sheaf of papers from his pocket, pointing to a document sent to him earlier in the day by Dr. Monro. On it were the words, "body unclaimed."

"May I see her?" Sophie asked quietly.

"You understand the body is now officially the property of the College of Surgeons?" the orderly inquired carefully.

"It hasn't been disturbed?" Hunter intervened.

"No," replied the orderly. "Dissection studies are Tuesdays and Thursdays."

"I understand all that . . . may I see her?" Sophie insisted.

"Very well." He shrugged, gesturing for them to follow him down a passageway where they entered a shadowy chamber at the rear of the large building. Inside, several corpses lay on long wooden tables. Sophie stared hollow-eyed for several minutes, searing the memory of her aunt's rigid form into her brain. She recalled the vision of her father's severed body lying in the operating theater at Edinburgh's Royal Infirmary. In the dim light surrounding the gray remains of Harriet Ashby, the purplish marks on the poor woman's wrists looked like slender jeweled bracelets fashioned of amethyst.

"Thank you," Sophie said faintly, turning to exit the chamber of death.

Hunter was relieved to find the hired carriage still waiting for them in the swirling snow.

"Bow Street," he called up to the driver as he assisted Sophie into the coach.

Inside, Hunter pulled her rigid body against his chest, encircling her shivering shoulders with his own cloak. Sophie couldn't seem to stop shaking, her body racked with waves of involuntary trembling.

"Ah . . . poppet," Hunter said sympathetically, tightening his arms and kissing the top of her head repeatedly. "You've had so much to bear, haven't you? I'm so sorry about your aunt . . ."

Sophie could feel the first sob welling up in her chest, and the second one behind it, threatening to burst forth like a swollen river in a rain-soaked glen. Scene after anguished scene during the years she had tried to care for the benighted woman assaulted her memory afresh. Those visions, compounded by the hurt and degradation she, herself, had endured at the hands of Peter elicited wrenching cries from her breast, and she wept for her family that was no more. The storm of tears lasted several minutes as Hunter continued to hold her close, brushing his lips gently against her forehead as if she were a child.

"Will you come home with me?" he whispered. "Will you let me care for you a while?"

The coach rocked along and a silence fell between the passengers inside. Sophie felt drained and exhausted and unable to think logically. The wheels crunched to a stop and Hunter helped her down to the narrow, snow-choked street that passed by Covent Garden Theater itself.

"You live *next* to the theater?" Sophie said, watching Hunter hand the driver some coins.

"No . . . I live *in* it," he replied with a smile. "There's a small lodging at the top of the house. They offered it to me as an inducement to come over from Dublin. See . . . I've my own private entrance, but many stairs to get there, I'm afraid." He put his arm around her shoulders, drawing her close. "Come . . . let me heat up a bit of soup . . . as I did for you in Bath."

Sophie's heart contracted at the memory of her first meal with Hunter in his lodgings on Pierpont Place. As they trudged up the stairs, she tried not to think of the events that had complicated her life so bitterly since that fateful day.

His tiny flat consisted of one room with a fireplace and a sleeping alcove curtained off from the principal chamber. He urged her to keep her cloak on until he could get a cheerful fire going.

"'Tis a stew, really," he said, poised on his haunches in front of the fire while he stirred a thick, flavorful ragout in an iron pot. "The cook at the Nag's Head on the corner always saves me a bit of whatever she's brewing up for tavern fare."

"Neither of us are very domestic, are we?" Sophie laughed mirthlessly. "Most of what I eat I make sure someone else prepares."

"We're artists!" Hunter joked. "We have to make allowances for our lack of culinary skills. Come, now . . . sit in my one decent chair and sup from my one decent bowl. I'll eat from the pot."

Hunter handed her the food and sat cross-legged on the floor at her feet. The two of them ate in companionable silence. The room grew warm and Sophie felt the knot in her stomach begin to dissolve.

"Some ale?" Hunter asked, extending his tankard.

"Mmm," Sophie replied, accepting a draught and handing it back to him. She watched him finish his meal and sighed.

Hunter took the bowl from her and pulled her to her feet as he rose to his full height beside her.

"Better?" he asked, gazing at her intently as his thumb stroked the inside of her wrist in gentle little circles.

"A bit," she nodded, as their gaze met. "I-I should be getting back to Danielle . . . she'll soon be hungry and poor Lorna's not equipped to cope," she joked weakly, involuntarily glancing down at her swollen breasts. "You've been so kind—"

"You're a lovely mum," Hunter interrupted in a low

voice, "and you've a lovely child . . . but right now, I can't let you go back to Half Moon Passage."

"No?" Sophie said, her gaze drowning in his.

"No," he repeated firmly, pulling her body gently against him. "I don't think you've quite thawed out from our coach ride." His arms tightened around her shoulders and he rested his chin on the top of her head, making her feel small and protected.

"'Twas bitter cold," Sophie mumbled into his chest.

"Aye. Warmer now?" he inquired, deliberately pressing his thighs against her skirts. Sophie could only nod. "See what sharing a simple bowl of stew has done to me?" he whispered, nuzzling her ear. "I know I said I'd wait until you'd sorted out the coil you're in . . . but I can't."

"You can't?" she whispered back.

"Aye, wench, I cannot," he said. "I confess it in front of God and this empty pot of stew . . . I want to keep you safe from harm and I want . . . *you*. Things can't have changed so much between us . . . you can't have forgotten that afternoon in Bath," he murmured.

He plunged his hands into her hair, causing the pins securing her auburn mane to scatter to the floor. His lips sought hers with a fervor that demanded she answer his caress in the same abandoned fashion she had that first heart-shattering time they had made love nearly two years earlier.

"Remember how I taught you to do this?" he whispered, extending the tip of his tongue into the shell of her ear. "And you can't have forgotten the pleasures of *this*," he added, trailing hot kisses from her ear lobe to the base of her throat.

Sophie moaned involuntarily and leaned into his tall frame, unable to resist the avalanche of longing that held her in its grip. Without a word, they repeated their former ritual of taking turns to remove articles of each other's clothing. Then, Hunter gently pulled the curtain masking his sleeping alcove and drew her down on his bed. As he gazed at her, his brows knit together and his eyes were suddenly filled with apprehension.

"Could I injure you, so soon after the babe?" he questioned softly, his body hovering above hers, his desire rampantly obvious.

"'Tis nearly a month," she whispered, touched by his concern.

"Then we shall be gentle . . ." he murmured against her hair. "Let us be gentle and kind with one another."

With infinite care, he cradled her in his arms and began to whisper a litany of endearments. With murmured tributes to her eyes, her hair, her slender form, his lips drifted lower, brushing feathery kisses across her sensitive breasts, plump and voluptuous from nursing her baby.

"So beautiful," he whispered wistfully, but instead of taking possession of her still-tender flesh, he slowly strafed his hand across her rounded abdomen, stroking and tantalizing every inch of her heated body until she begged for deliverance, which ultimately manifested itself in wild bursts of sensation radiating in response to the strong, rhythmic pressure his hands had exerted between her thighs. Humbled by his selflessness, she could only murmur her incoherent gratitude, bewildered and chagrined by turns.

"Hunter . . . what about . . . ?" she whispered.

"'Twould be dangerous to risk making a new baby so soon," he soothed, resting his chin on the top of her tousled hair as he waited for her ragged breathing to even out. "'Tis enough just to touch you . . . at least, that's what I'm trying to tell myself," he laughed ruefully, as they felt the evidence of his unquenched ardor pressing against them both.

"In Bath, I had but one lesson from my dear professor," Sophie ventured, staring into his blue eyes, still smoky with desire. "I'm sure you neglected some of the finer points of . . . ah . . ." she swallowed hard.

"Ah yes," Hunter chortled. "What an eager pupil you are, my love. Lesson Two . . . 'tis quite simple, actually." He seized her hand and with no hint of embarrassment, instructed her in the art of pleasuring him.

"Yes?" she asked, her eyes seeking his.

"Oh, yes," Hunter confirmed hoarsely, all his senses ablaze as he stared into her triumphant gaze.

Then he could only close his eyes and allow incredible sensations to sweep over him until, at last, he gave up all pretense of control. For her part, Sophie exalted in the heady feeling of power he had granted her. At length, she kissed him beneath his ear and snuggled close.

"Oh, God, Sophie," he groaned, pulling her even more tightly against him so she could feel his heart still pounding wildly in his chest. "I am filled with pity you can never experience what you just called forth from me . . ."

"Oh, but I can," she responded softly. "I did." And then, inexplicably, a sob welled in her chest.

"I should never have left you!" she blurted, tears filling her eyes as she raised her head from his chest, gazing at the face that had always been so dear to her. "Somehow we could have found a way . . . but now . . . 'tis all a dreadful muddle!" She buried her head in his shoulder once more to prevent his seeing the moisture running down her cheeks. "Soon, 'twill be summer . . . you'll be going—"

"I'll be going to Sadler's Wells," Hunter interrupted reassuringly, using the bed sheet to wipe the corners of her eyes. "The manager there wants me to produce the musical fare. 'Tis just an hour's coach ride from London."

An hour away from Covent Garden might as well be a week, as far as Sophie's life as a shopkeeper was concerned. She pulled away from his embrace and turned to stare into the fire.

"Come with me for the summer," Hunter said softly, lifting the hair from her shoulders and gently kissing the nape of her neck. "Bring your quill and Danielle and we can take a cottage together. There's lovely country all around. You can write your plays and watch the bairn and I'll support the three of us."

A vision of sweet-smelling grass and clear blue skies like the ones she'd known in Scotland conjured up a welcome contrast to the dirt and grime she remembered from summers past in London.

"Oh, Hunter . . ." she sighed, turning around to face him. She was sorely tempted to accept his proposal then and there.

"Lorna can look after the shop as she did when you were in Bath," he continued eagerly, as if he'd thought about this idea for a considerable time. "Please, Sophie . . . let's not miss this chance the way we did the last time . . ."

"But Peter—" she began.

"Peter Lindsay be *damned!*" he said angrily, pulling himself to a sitting position and leaning his naked torso against the wall. "You can't allow that brandy-breath blackguard to rule your life!"

"He has the entire weight of English law behind him," she protested. "Despite his drinking and gambling and philandering, the law says that *I've* deserted *him!* He's threatened to petition the House of Lords . . ."

"For *what?*" Hunter demanded. "A divorce? Don't be daft. If you were no longer his wife, he could not claim your author's fees, nor your profits from the book shop. Besides, he's pretending to be a baronet! I doubt the House of Lords would look on *that* nonsense with much favor."

"He may be a counterfeit aristocrat, but he's still a *man,*" Sophie pointed out moodily pulling the counterpane around her exposed breasts and tucking it under her arms. "He could take away my child! That Mr. Beezle told me that successful petitioners not only shed themselves of their wives—they gain complete possession of all progeny."

"Has Peter even come to *see* the bairn?" Hunter asked bitterly.

"No . . ." Sophie replied, "but—"

"He's all bluster and brass . . ." Hunter said disgustedly. "He uses these threats to bend you to his will . . . when are you going to call his bluff?"

He stared at her, his handsome features scowling in frustration.

"I don't know . . ." she replied despairingly. "'Tis frightening to be linked to the likes of him . . . he's so unlike the man I first knew in Bath. I suppose 'tis because he drinks constantly now. He was so twisted by his childhood, so despised by his kin . . ."

"You actually sound sorry for the sod!" Hunter exclaimed. "Perhaps you still have some tender feelings him," he added, hurt.

"Dear God, Hunter, you cannot think that . . . not *now?*"

"He's the father of Danielle—"

"Sheer bad luck," Sophie retorted.

"I imagine he can be extremely charming when he chooses," he averred, and Sophie knew instinctively that Hunter was imagining the physical intimacies she and her estranged husband had shared.

"Aye . . . that he can . . . when one doesn't notice the deception."

"Well, my offer remains," Hunter said stiffly. "If you wish to spend the summer with me, I wish it also, assuming you're willing to stand up to Peter's empty threats."

"I *wish* to very much," Sophie replied softly. "'Tis just I must see my way clear to . . . to resolving certain problems . . ." Suddenly she felt her breasts begin to tingle with an onrush of milk. "And now I must get back to Danielle. Thank you for being so kind about . . . everything . . . and especially Aunt Harriet," she said earnestly as they both began to dress.

"I'll walk you to Half Moon Passage," he said quietly.

Despite the emotionally charged atmosphere, there now existed between them a watchful reserve. As they descended the narrow stairwell, Sophie felt an impulse to fling herself in Hunter's arms and retreat back to his cozy chamber. She wanted to leave behind forever the problems that plagued her in Covent Garden. Instead, she silently followed him out the door into Bow Street, now cast in shadow and blanketed with four inches of snow. Their breath became visible puffs of white vapor as they walked across the deserted Great Piazza, down Henrietta Street and up to Sophie's door. Mrs. Phillips's Salvator was locked tight, as was the darkened book shop next to it. A hungry babe's thin, high-pitched wail could be heard at the top of the stairway leading to Sophie's chambers above.

"Good night," she whispered at length, standing on tiptoe to kiss him gently on his cold cheek.

Hunter nodded brusquely and quickly retreated down Half Moon Passage, his steps following the white hollows they'd both trampled in the snow.

In the growing twilight, she wearily trudged up to the landing that separated her chambers from those of Mrs. Phillips. Fumbling for the latch, she stood rooted to the threshold as she gazed past the open door into her own lodgings. There, in her bed, a large body lay huddled, shaking under the counterpane.

"God's wounds . . . what is *he* doing here?" Sophie demanded of Mary Ann Skene, who promptly reached for her cloak on its peg the second she had seen her flat mate open the door.

"'Tis your husband and he's quite ill," Mary Ann said defensively, flinging her wrap around her shoulders. "I couldn't let the blighter freeze to death in front of the shop, could I?"

"You could send him back to his own lodgings!" she retorted.

"He's been evicted for nonpayment, I'm afraid."

"Where's Lorna?" Sophie asked, raising her voice over the wails of her hungry daughter who was crying in the trunk at the foot of the bed.

"She had to deliver the placards due Drury Lane," Mary Ann replied. "We assumed you'd be home hours sooner," she added reproachfully, pointing at Danielle crying in her bed. "I didn't know what to do about *that* one."

Sophie hurried over to the child and scooped her up in her arms, unfastening her bodice while she demanded to know why Peter was installed in her bed.

She shrugged. "He collapsed in the snow. 'Tis a nasty ague, Mrs. Phillips called it."

"Probably just the spirits," Sophie replied bitterly, staring down at her estranged husband who was moaning faintly in his sleep.

"Nay, feel him. He's burning up," Mary Ann countered.

Sophie placed her fingertips lightly on his forehead. His flesh was unnaturally flushed and hot to the touch.

"But he could give this ague to Danielle!" Sophie protested, glancing worriedly at the infant in her arms. "How could you be so thoughtless to allow him in here! Had you no care for the child's safety," she demanded, "not to mention your own?"

"I've already been exposed and am perfectly fit."

Sophie stared at her narrowly. She took a step closer, her eyes flashing.

"Exposed by whom?" she asked accusingly.

"By . . . a . . . well, several patrons have had something of the sort, and I—"

"Peter was not found collapsed on the road, was he?" Sophie said in a low voice, glaring at the woman about to depart for her nightly rendezvous with customers at her bawdy house. "He has been your client at the Blue Periwig for weeks, hasn't he, you trollop!" she demanded. "He became ill there and couldn't pay and they forced you to turn him out . . . told you to take him to his wife and get the money from *her* . . . isn't that so?"

"No! Of course not!" Mary Ann retorted, flicking a piece of imaginary lint off her cloak. "Ask Mrs. Phillips if he wasn't about to breathe his last!"

"I'm sure she thought he was . . . she knows how dangerous these agues can be."

"Well, he *is* your husband," Mary Ann retorted, "and I've done my best with him. Now, I must be gone."

Sophie stared at Peter huddled beneath her counterpane. She had deserted her husband's lodgings on Cleveland Row, only to find him now in Half Moon Passage, unfortunately ensconced in her own.

Chapter 22

Peter's fever raged all that night and into the next day. Sophie got virtually no sleep as she applied moist linen rags to her husband's flushed forehead and tended to the needs of a fretful Danielle.

"Cold compresses are the only thing to bring the fever down," Mrs. Phillips preached across her counter the following morning. "And a bit of watered broth, if he'll keep it down. Either the fever will break, or he'll die."

When Lorna arrived at the shop around noon, Sophie shouted to her that she was not to come upstairs.

"We can't have you ill too," she called down. "Just fetch some broth from the tavern and set it halfway up the stairs."

For several days, Sophie divided her time between nursing Peter—who thrashed in her bed, barely conscious—printing the usual round of playbills that Lorna was kind enough to deliver to Drury Lane, and praying that neither she nor her daughter would be affected by the virulent illness. She routinely sponged Peter's feverish body, spooned soup down his throat and applied a few poultices left by Mrs. Phillips on the landing. She hardly heard her customers coming in and out of the book shop below, so preoccupied was she with her duties as unwilling nursemaid. As for Peter, he seemed oblivious to the fact that he was being looked after by the woman he had publicly called a shrew.

By the fourth night of Peter's forced occupation of her lodgings, his fever broke and his skin became cool and dry to the touch. By morning, he was sitting up in bed, a full half inch of beard shadowing his face.

"I'm very hungry," he announced plaintively. Behind the black stubble, his skin was pale as parchment and his hands shook. "Can you fetch me something to eat from the tavern —and a whiskey?"

Before Sophie could think of a reply, the door opened and in walked Mary Ann Skene. Sophie's lodger had stayed away from Half Moon Passage since the day she claimed she'd rescued Peter in front of the shop.

"Ellen Gardener owes me a quid!" Mary Ann declared, removing her cloak and hanging it on the peg. Her dress was made of cheap muslin but sported an overabundance of frills and flounces that had become the harlot's trademark. "I said to Ellen last night, I said, 'By now he's up and about, or in his grave,' and here you are. Outfoxed the Grim Reaper, did you, squire?"

"No thanks to you," he grumbled. "You didn't even try to persuade that old bawd to look after me."

"Well, you never pay what's owing and Mrs. Douglas wouldn't hear of your remaining with an ague like that! Infect the whole house, you would!"

"If you two don't mind," Sophie snapped, her patience worn to the breaking point, "Peter, you must remove yourself from here immediately! I'll expect you to be gone by the time I return from delivering the week's play listings to *The Public Advertiser*. Lorna should be here within the hour, Mary Ann. Until then, please look after the bairn for a bit. She should go off to sleep soon."

Mary Ann appeared to be about to refuse, but remained silent, probably because of her lodgekeeper's display of ill temper. Sophie picked up Danielle, who was fussing in her makeshift bed. Soothing the fretful babe, she glanced uncertainly at the child's father.

"You were too ill for me to make introductions earlier . . . but this is your daughter," she said, raising Danielle in her arms and taking a step closer to her husband who lounged against pillows propped behind him on the bed.

"*Is* it?" he said coldly, gazing at the fretful baby with obvious disinterest. "Are you sure?"

Sophie gasped at the insult and felt blood pound in her temples.

"Get out!" she shouted as Danielle began to wail. "Get out of my sight, you rotten sot! And if you or your creditors *dare* disturb me again, I'll take more than play listings to *The Public Advertiser*," she fumed, "I'll write for all the world to know the sorry tale of your so-called title! I swear it on my daughter's life, Peter *Lindsay*! Be gone before I return!"

Glaring at both her husband and the startled whore, she handed the baby to Mary Ann, grabbed the newly printed placards, and stalked toward the door, trying her best to close her ears to the infant's anguished cries.

"So you're *not* a bloomin' baronet!" Sophie heard Mary Ann laugh as she flung open the door to the landing. "Darnly hinted that, but I didn't believe him."

Sophie did not catch Peter's sullen reply as she slammed the door shut and ran down the stairs into Half Moon Passage. Crossing into Henrietta Street, she glanced through the iron gates into the little cemetery bordering St. Paul's. She paused briefly to stare at the trees rising starkly between the tilted gravestones. Their leafless branches swaying in the icy wind looked like a skeleton's fingers scratching at the gray sky overhead. Poor Aunt Harriet wasn't even allowed a decent burial. Shivering, she stuck her chin into the folds of her cloak and quickened her pace, striding across the Piazza quickly to escape the cold.

Within ten minutes, Sophie had arrived at Garrick's office at Drury Lane. A conference between him, James Lacy, and Roderick Darnly was apparently just concluding. From the snippets she could pick up while waiting for Garrick outside the door, it appeared that Roderick Darnly was proposing to underwrite several large productions in the form of loans for the following season. In exchange, the partners would grant him the right to receive a mortgage on some additional shares.

"As I believe I've made clear several times before," Garrick said patiently, "I am grateful for your suggestions of new wardrobe and scenes, sir—and certainly your willingness to invest additional funds—but I have no wish to dilute my holdings by granting my shares as collateral. Lacy? What of you?"

Sophie heard James Lacy clear his throat nervously.

"Well . . . the Honorable Mr. Darnly has some capital suggestions for adding spectacle to our presentations, Davy . . . you must own that . . . but if you do not wish to participate in this venture, I'm afraid, my dear sir, I wouldn't wish to mortgage any more of my shares either . . . at least not at the moment."

Sophie stepped back into the hallway as the door opened and a disgruntled-looking Roderick Darnly strode into the passageway.

"Ah . . . Sophie . . . we wondered when you were going to emerge from the sick room," he said frostily. "Is your husband likely to recover?"

Sophie flushed, wondering how word that Peter had been convalescing at her lodgings could have circulated around Covent Garden so fast. Awkwardly, she recounted how Mary Ann had put him to bed above her book shop without her permission.

"In fact," she concluded with heavy emphasis, "he has made such a good recovery, he's vacating my chambers _today._"

"Well, that's a blessing, I'm sure," Garrick interjected from the doorway.

The manager handed her the cast list for the week's fare and, without further discussion, Sophie quickly departed for the newspaper offices. Worried that she had been away from Danielle nearly an hour, she virtually ran back to Half Moon Passage, arriving just before noon.

Rounding the corner at Henrietta Street once again, she was surprised to see Hunter stalking toward her from the direction of Ashby's Books. She began to call out a greeting when she saw from his expression that he was in a towering rage. He halted several paces from her and pointed a finger up at the second story window above the book shop.

"I came to call on you . . . like a foolish, love-sick Romeo," he fumed.

"And you're angry because Peter is upstairs," she said sympathetically. "He's only—"

"Naked! In your bloomin' *bed*!" he shouted.

"Hunter, please, I can—"

"Please don't misunderstand me," he said, lowering his voice menacingly. "I'm not merely angry at you for choosing to lie with that sod . . . I'm *disgusted*! Disgusted by your judgment . . . disgusted by your character, and most of all, Sophie McGann . . . disgusted to have actually thought I was in *love* with someone who could behave as you have!"

Sophie stared at him, stunned by the vitriol that laced his words.

"Dear God, Hunter . . . what is the *matter* with you—" she began, but Hunter brushed past her, stomping down the road. Sophie gave chase, grabbing at his arm. "Please! Let me explain," she pleaded.

Hunter whirled around to face her, his features contorted with fury.

"There *is* no explanation, so, pray, don't bother to lie to me! You've made it up with Peter . . . that's plain to see. All right. Perhaps I can accept that. Women are famous for such treachery. But apparently you think nothing of abandoning that poor child . . . frightened and ill and whimpering pitifully in the printing room while you cavort—"

"Danielle . . . she's ill?" she cried, turning toward her lodgings. "Oh, God . . . NO!"

Sophie began to run, her heart pounding furiously. When she reached the shop, she hardly noticed that the public door to Ashby's was still closed, awaiting Lorna's imminent arrival. She raced up the flight of stairs that separated the two shops and burst into the flat.

Halting at the threshold, she stared at two figures sitting up in bed, each holding a mug which she assumed contained spirits of some sort. Mary Ann wore a transparent batiste dressing gown edged with an ostentatious cascade of lace she had undoubtedly filched from her previous employer. Peter, with the counterpane wrapped around his waist like a toga, was convulsed with mirth. "Where's Danielle!" Sophie screamed. "What's wrong with Danielle?"

But the pair were doubled up in a paroxysm of laughter. Sophie whirled and made for the printing chamber where she found her daughter, listless and feverish, abandoned in her little bed. Her skin was flushed scarlet and her breathing was labored. A burst of Mary Ann's giggles rent the air.

"At least, Peter, I had the decency to *hide!*" Mary Ann chortled, trying unsuccessfully to control her merriment. "But there you sat, like some pasha, bold as brass, conducting a bloody *conversation* with the gentleman!"

"Well," Peter declared between guffaws, "I had to say *something!* After all, we were in bed when the knave nearly knocked the door down!"

"I jumped in the trunk quick enough, but as you two were blathering on, I began to feel a tickle in m'nose inside that dusty bin. I was sure I'd *sneeze* and be found out!"

The pair exploded in another fit of hilarity. Sophie lifted her daughter into her arms and ran to the doorway connecting the two chambers.

"What did you say to Hunter?" Sophie demanded furiously. "What damnable lie did you tell this time, husband?"

"I informed the blighter," Peter said, slurring his words, "that Lady Lindsay-Hoyt would be returning momentarily to minister in proper wifely fashion to her adored husband. However, it appears that the honorable Mr. Hunter Robertson didn't wish to wait."

During Peter's rambling description of his unexpected encounter with the visitor, Sophie backed toward the fireplace and reached for the poker.

"This time I swear by St. Ninian I will *kill* you if you are not gone from these premises in five minutes!" she said in a low, menacing voice, pointing the fire iron at Peter as if it were a pole-axe. It was clear now what scene had greeted Hunter when he opened the door at Peter's bidding—her supposedly estranged husband, naked, lying in her bed; Danielle in the adjacent printing chamber, whimpering with fever and apparently ignored by her parents.

I should never have left her with them! she cried in silent anguish and bitter remorse, staring down at her daughter's listless countenance. *I should have sent Mary Ann to Drury Lane and* The Public Advertiser . . . *or simply shirked my duty, for once . . . I should never have left my child with such—*

"Fetch Mrs. Phillips from downstairs, and be *quick* about it!" Sophie ordered harshly.

The strumpet did as she was bidden. Sophie held Danielle in one arm and the fire poker in the other, while Peter clumsily reached for his breeches and rumpled jacket.

"I never want to see you in Half Moon Passage or anywhere near me again, do you hear?" she cried, as he hastily donned his shoes with their tarnished silver buckles. "And if you try to take any more of my money, I'll have Roderick Darnly see you're thrown into Newgate." She took a step closer, poking him with the tip of the cold fire iron. "And there'll be no more public threats about petitioning the House of Lords to take my child or charge me with desertion, do you understand me?" Peter hiccuped involuntarily and nodded nervously, anxious to be gone. "And may you rot in *hell*, Peter Lindsay, for how you've treated me and our daughter! *Now get out!*"

Her husband of less than a year retreated out the door without a word. Sophie glanced down at her infant, aware for the first time that Danielle was trembling in her arms.

"Oh, no!" Sophie whispered as the baby's face began to contort while a seizure took hold.

She tossed the fire poker aside. Her child had begun to writhe convulsively, her entire little body taking on the hue of cooked beets.

"Mrs. Phillips! *Mrs. Phillips!*" Sophie screamed, running to the landing and shouting down the stairs at the top of her lungs.

"What's a do? What's a do?" she heard her neighbor say as she rounded the corner, and mounted the stairs. "I've a shop full of people . . . I can't be—"

The apothecary arrived out of breath at the threshold, with Mary Ann scampering up the stairwell behind her. The older woman's bosom heaved and her face grew somber as she placed her hand on Danielle's forehead. The baby's eyes were rolling backward, and the infant's little body was racked with violent tremors.

"'Tis the fever's grip . . . we must break it. Water!" she ordered. "You must plunge her in cool water. Quick! There's a tub at the back of my shop."

The trio hurried downstairs and into the Green Canister past a gaggle of customers who watched the frantic procession with mild curiosity. In a room at the back of the shop, Sophie stood cradling her trembling daughter in her arms while Mary Ann filled the wooden tub from buckets of water fetched from the neighborhood well. Within minutes, Sophie plunged Danielle into the bath, but the child continued to shake as if seized by a frenzy. Each pathetic cry protesting the chilly water sluicing Danielle's parched skin tore at the fabric of Sophie's soul.

Finally, the baby stopped shaking and lay still, her breathing shallow. Sophie lifted her from the tub and wrapped her in a blanket, but the child's eyes remained closed. She silently carried the small bundle past Mrs. Phillips' customers, and slowly ascended the stairs to her own lodgings.

The infant's fever persisted for another day while Sophie held her gently in her arms, sitting waxlike in front of the low burning hearth. She spoke and sang to Danielle constantly, despite the babe's apparent unconsciousness. At length, as dawn broke on the second day, Sophie suddenly realized that her daughter had simply stopped breathing.

Later that morning, Mary Ann, who had disappeared soon after the infant had died, returned with an undertaker carrying a small coffin into the chamber.

"'Tis arranged by Darnly," Mary Ann said, pointing at the casket. "I told him what happened and he's seen to the little one's burial . . ."

Sophie stared at the diminutive wooden box and nodded vacantly.

"Thank you," she whispered, silently forgiving Mary Ann her role in the tragedy, while castigating herself more severely than ever for having left her child in the care of a prostitute and a drunkard. "That was kind of you to seek him out—"

"I was happy to be of service," a voice said from the threshold as Roderick Darnly strode into the chamber, his coachman, Charles, following in his wake.

Sophie stared, dumbfounded at the Earl of Llewelyn's son who had never come nearer her lodgings than the elegant confines of his coach waiting downstairs at her door. He strode over to the bed where Danielle lay swaddled in a blanket, her tiny face now tinged gray in the stillness of death. In a low voice he gave instructions to the undertaker, who placed the infant in the coffin that would hold her tiny remains for eternity. Sophie quickly looked away as the lid closed shut. The sound of the wood being nailed was a stark reminder of the finality of her daughter's passing. Then, Darnly's minions bore the casket downstairs.

"I will see to the internment," Roderick told her calmly, referring to the common practice of the day which dictated that mothers did not attend their children's funerals for fear of disgracing the assembled mourners with an unseemly emotional display.

Sophie's skin was pale from lack of sleep and her grief did not allow for tears.

"I cannot be spared, whether I attend services for Danielle or not," she replied, dry-eyed. "I shall bury my child."

When the mourners arrived at St. Paul's, a small plot had been excavated in the hard earth in the corner of the churchyard. Patches of pale blue sky shone through the slate gray clouds overhead. The snow from the March storm a week earlier had disappeared entirely, leaving the earth soft and muddy—a boon only for the grave-diggers, Sophie thought forlornly.

She felt Lorna seize her hand and squeeze it as the rector intoned a brief service. Roderick Darnly, Mary Ann, and Mrs. Phillips stood silently by during the few minutes it took the churchman to lay to rest a child barely two months old.

Soon the weather turned cold again and for the remainder of March, London was buffeted by a return of rain and sleet. Sophie lay in bed late into each day, refusing to rise even when Mary Ann returned at dawn from the Blue Periwig. Most days the harlot was laden with food and provisions supplied at the behest of Roderick Darnly, although Sophie barely noticed and ate very little.

Lorna shouldered most of the responsibilities for running

Ashby's Books and fulfilling the printing orders Garrick continued to commission. Boswell had departed for Scotland, writing her a brief condolence note that she did not have the curiosity to read until mid-April.

From Hunter, she heard nothing.

For two months, Sophie could not bear to take up her quill or even peruse the first act of *The Bogus Baronet*. Books and plays and even writing itself had come to symbolize the series of tragedies that had befallen her.

I am alone, her heart cried into the night. *I am utterly alone.* In the absolute stillness of dawn in Half Moon Passage, nothing contradicted that assertion, nor soothed the injury to her soul.

One day in early May, Lorna brought an ultimatum along with Sophie's morning tea.

"You must do something to rouse yourself from this blackness of spirit," her friend announced decisively. "Ashby's is foundering without your attention and Mary Ann announced yesterday she has found herself a new protector. Her subsidy from Darnly is due to terminate in a month when she moves in with some wool merchant." She marched over to Sophie's writing table and pointed at the thin pile of sheets gathering dust. "I suggest you tackle your play and finish it. 'Tis a capital time to submit it to Garrick for next season."

"What I've written thus far is rubbish," Sophie retorted peevishly, staring vacantly out the window.

"Rubbish or not, you've *got* to work on it!" Lorna said firmly. When Sophie didn't respond, the dancer pursed her lips. "If you choose to continue in this manner, I shall be forced to seek an engagement at one of the pleasure gardens for the summer to earn my keep, and you'll have to cope with Ashby's on your own. You won't have *time* to write or wallow in this misery."

Her tone was sharp, edged with the frustration of a friend who has offered abundant kindness and compassion—to no avail.

"As you wish . . ." Sophie replied dully, pulling the counterpane more tightly under her chin.

Lorna stood in the center of the chamber, staring down at

the woman who had become such a dear and treasured friend.

"Good God, Sophie!" she exclaimed. "I won't allow you to go on this way. Come! Get dressed. At least, let us escape these four walls. We can close the shop for an hour and take a walk around the Great Piazza. 'Tis a glorious spring day."

Reluctantly, Sophie allowed herself to be persuaded to rise from bed, don a simple blue cotton dress, and descend the stairs into Half Moon Passage for the first time in more than a month.

"May I visit her grave?" she said in a small voice as they approached the tall, gated entrance to St. Paul's churchyard.

"Of course," Lorna replied, putting her arm around her friend's shoulders. "Look at all the lovely crocuses and paperwhites," she exclaimed, pointing at the clusters of spring flowers dotting the graveyard.

The friends stood side by side in front of the small mound of earth whose miniature headstone gave witness to the short life of Danielle McGann Lindsay. Several bouquets of dead flowers lay strewn on the grave itself. Sophie stooped to pick up an array of dried roses with a small card noting they been sent by David Garrick and his wife.

"Here's one from Mr. Lacy!" Lorna exclaimed, fingering a batch of dead daffodils. "And one from Darnly, of course."

But Sophie was staring down at a small bouquet of violets, petals stiffened, now, into a shade of dark magenta. She noticed a scrap of parchment attached to the short stalks with a piece of wool. Her hands began to shake as she squinted in the bright May sunshine reading the words inscribed.

Long mayst thou live to wail thy children's death . . .

Lorna peered over Sophie's shoulders to get a better look. The card was signed *H.R.*

"From the third act of *Richard III*," she said in a breath.

"'Tis about the murder of the little princes," Sophie said, her voice shaking with hurt and shock. "Hunter thinks that

what happened was the same as if I murdered my
child . . ."

"Oh, Sophie, no!" Lorna replied swiftly.

"Yes, he *does!*" she responded, tears edging her words.
"And he is right, of course. I did leave her . . . I was worried about her, but I was more worried about getting Peter
out of the flat and fulfilling my obligation to Drury Lane.
. . . *I left my sick child!*" she cried, her voice filled with
anguish.

Sophie turned away from Danielle's grave and covered
her face with her hands. Sobs racked her body. Lorna
quickly put her arms around her friend, cradling her head
against her shoulder.

"You had so much troubling your mind . . ." she
soothed, stroking Sophie's hair. "You were seeing to things
as best you could, Sophie . . . no one blames you for
that—"

"*He* d-does!" she gulped. "His own sister d-died when a
wee thing, and I t-think he always blamed his m-mother for
it."

A new wave of grief seemed to sweep through her and
her shoulders continued to shake with inconsolable crying.
The edge of the parchment engraved with Hunter's reproach
cut against her hand, and its words burned into her memory
forever.

Long mayst thou live to wail thy children's death.

How prophetic those words were, Sophie thought, as
fresh tears coursed down her cheeks. She doubted that in the
years to come she would ever feel free from the remorse she
carried in her heart.

"Oh, Sophie . . . 'twas not like that at all!" Lorna insisted fiercely. "This ague can vanquish children of noble
houses with seven nannies in attendance! You were worried
about having money to be able to look after Danielle and
you did what you thought best. You mustn't torture yourself like this! Hunter has no idea what problems confronted
you. You did the best you *could!*"

Sophie raised her head from Lorna's shoulder and wiped her eyes on her sleeve.

"But he thinks I willingly let Peter stay with me . . . that I allowed him to bed me and ignored my sick child." She shuddered, holding out the crumpled parchment in her hand as living proof.

A pensive look crossed Lorna's features.

"Men can be such fools . . . so ready to think themselves cuckolded and their honor besmirched. 'Tis an abominable trait." Her face brightened and she smiled at her friend. "But you're a *writer*, Sophie! You must compose a careful missive explaining exactly what transpired. 'Twill convince him that what he *thought* he saw was not the truth. You must write him."

Sophie stared at Lorna, a ray of hope shining in her eyes.

"No," she said firmly, straightening her shoulders. "I shall go right now to speak to him. 'Tis nearly three months hence . . . certainly we're both calmer now . . . perhaps I *can* make him understand. 'Tis not that I am blameless . . . who knows that better than I? But surely, he can't truly think me a murderess!"

"Good lass," Lorna said approvingly. She brushed a strand of auburn hair back from her friend's forehead and settled her light wool shawl tidily on her shoulders. "Get on with you."

Ten minutes later, Sophie greeted the stage doorkeeper at Covent Garden with a forced smile and asked to see Hunter Robertson.

"Sorry miss, but Mr. Robertson appeared in *Blind Man's Bluff* on the nineteenth and departed for Comely Gardens the next day."

"He's gone to *Edinburgh*?" she said as bitter dismay infected her manner and voice. "I thought—to lure him from Dublin—the management here had bid him stay for at least two *years*!"

"Oh they did, right enough," the doorkeeper confirmed, "but he left in a rush, soon as the season concluded—or at least, his part of it."

"But surely he'll return next autumn?"

"Well, Mr. Beard and the other managers want the lad's

services, to be sure," the doorkeeper volunteered, "but I heard he's signed on in Bristol next season. Seems foolhardy to me to play the provinces when one can be the toast of London town . . . but there's no accounting for these actors. Children, all of 'em. Willful, spoiled children, I calls 'em!"

Sophie mumbled her thanks and retreated past the stage entrance before she allowed fresh tears to stream down her face.

"He's left London . . . because of me," she cried as Lorna rushed up Hart Street to her side. "He's gone to Edinburgh and then signed for next season with the theater in Bristol!"

"Well, then . . ." Lorna said, trying to find some shred of hope, "you'll write to him *there*! Only the emotion of the moment could have persuaded him to take such a rash step."

A feeling of irreparable loss gripped Sophie, nearly cutting off her breath. The crumpled parchment was a reminder of the depth of Hunter's abhorrence at the circumstances of Danielle's death. 'Twas no rash step, Sophie thought disconsolately. 'Twas only after several months' consideration that he'd given up a coveted position at one of the finest theaters in the world to escape from her presence.

Sophie closed her eyes and attempted to breathe evenly. The line from Shakespeare's *Richard III* ran through her mind in a kind of anguished litany. He had posted the hex on Danielle's grave before he fled from London. 'Twas not a missive from a cuckolded lover, she thought, an ache tightening her chest. Hunter wished her to suffer as much as he imagined little Danielle—or his own sister—had suffered from neglect at the hands of the very people charged with protecting them. The note left in St. Paul's churchyard was intended as a curse . . . and accursed by him she was.

"'Tis over," she said, her belief in her words settling on her like a mourning cloak. "He will never think well of me again."

"Sophie—" Lorna began, staring at her friend worriedly.

"I love Hunter with my life," she said with hollow resignation, ". . . but 'tis finally finished between us. If I think anything else, I shall drive myself mad."

Book 5

1768–1769

At Stratford-on-Avon what doings! Oh rare—
What poetry, music, and dancing was there!

—THE CAMBRIDGE MAGAZINE

Chapter 23

April, 1768

Sophie watched numbly as two burly men, obeying the instructions of bookseller Thomas Davies, carted the last of Ashby's inventory out the door of her shop.

"Did I purchase these?" Davies asked, pointing to a pile of tomes resting on the windowsill.

Sophie glanced at the volumes of Shakespeare, along with a few other of her favorites that she'd culled from the shelves, and shook her head. Then, suddenly, she snatched a copy of *Richard III* from her private reserve and handed it to Davies.

"Here," she said abruptly. "Take this. I don't want it."

She couldn't bear to have the stinging condemnation contained in the play's pages among her few possessions upstairs.

Long mayst thou live to wail thy children's death, she pondered involuntarily, watching the bookseller toss the leather-bound play into a nearby bin.

Rather than wailing, she had been silent—practically mute—these last two years, unable to write, unable to carry on a coherent conversation, accomplishing little aside from the odd printing job that occasionally came her way.

She had found it impossible even to run the book shop and was glad to find a buyer in Tom Davies, whose establishment at Number 8 Russell Street was a couple of blocks from Drury Lane. The proceeds would sustain her for a year or two while she decided what to do . . . or where to go.

The Duke of Bedford, who owned the freehold on the shops along Half Moon Passage, had let out the lower chambers to a staymaker who hoped to attract the same prostitutes who patronized Mrs. Phillips' Green Canister next door.

She stared gloomily at the motes of dust floating in the shaft of April sunshine pouring through the shop's front window and wondered how Lorna Blount was faring. That first summer following Danielle's death, Lorna had sought work at Sadler's Wells where she had taken up the art of tightrope walking. It was a dangerous occupation. Thus far, Lorna had not been injured; at least Sophie had not heard that she had, and for that she was grateful.

Smoothing her hand over the leather surface of one of her few remaining books, Sophie knew she should make the effort to locate her friend and bid her farewell before another summer season at Sadler's began. However, the mere thought of venturing beyond Half Moon Passage prompted familiar feelings of suffocating despondency. The only blessings she could contemplate were that Mary Ann Skene had long since departed her lodgings to enjoy the patronage of her wool merchant, and Peter Lindsay had kept a safe distance from his estranged wife.

For months, Sophie had been avoiding David Garrick and everyone else at Drury Lane. She'd been grieved to hear that Frances Sheridan had died in September, eighteen months past, of a sudden fever while living in France with her ever-impecunious husband Thomas, the Great God of Elocution. As for Roderick Darnly, he had departed for an extended tour of the Continent and she'd heard nothing from him either.

"Good God, Davies!" boomed a voice, shattering Sophie's reverie. "I assumed you were joking! She really *is* giving up Ashby's! Sophie McGann, I can't imagine you without a book shop, but I'm deuced glad to see you, nonetheless!" said James Boswell. He strode through the door and bussed her heartily on both cheeks.

"Jamie," she replied, using every ounce of willpower to summon a welcoming smile. "What are you doing in London?"

He pulled out a book from a wide pocket sewn on the inside of his brocaded cuffed coat and waved it at her.

"I'm here to promote my *Account of Corsica*. I see you haven't heard I've become a full-fledged book author," he chided her. "'Tis been a great boon since I've been raising money to fund arms for the independence campaign."

"You're raising money to buy arms for Corsica?" she said incredulously.

"You don't see me as a soldier of fortune, wagering my life for a good cause?" he asked with an injured air.

"No, I do not!" she replied, trying not to smile at such an absurd notion.

"Well, you're right. I just send money to General Paoli when I can."

"Well, that's a relief. How has your sainted father taken to your career as a published author?"

"Even *he* admits I've taken a toot on a new horn!" he exclaimed proudly. His eyes were shining. "Ah, Sophie . . . I am no longer a carriage dog, running after the wheels of the great. I've written a book and people are *reading* it! Davies tells me he think 'twill go to another printing!"

"I'm happy for you, Bozzy," she said quietly.

"And what of our old friend Hunter? Have you heard from him?" Boswell asked carefully.

"I— No," she replied, the familiar suffocating feeling tugging at her throat. "Have you?" she asked, and then cursed herself for probing an old wound.

"Aye, when he was playing Comely Gardens outside Edinburgh. I had to pry it out of him, but he told me something of what transpired between you." Boswell looked at her unhappily and blurted. "I *tried* to tell him you would never deliberately endanger your child, but—"

"Please, Bozzy," Sophie interrupted, feeling her rigid control beginning to slip, "please don't speak of him again."

At that moment, outside, a coach with a gold crest on its polished black door drew up in front of the shop. A footman wearing red livery stepped through the door and handed Sophie a note sealed with wax. The servant waited patiently for an answer to his master's missive.

Would you do me the honor of celebrating my return to London by dining with me this evening at seven? My coach will return to call for you at the proper hour.
The Honorable Roderick Darnly

"Dining with an earl's sprig?" Boswell said, unabashedly reading the note over her shoulder. "Don't tell me you've taken up the harlot's trade! Not *you*!"

"Don't be absurd!" Sophie snapped. "Roderick Darnly has been abroad for more than a year. And for your information, he's been kinder to me than *anyone*. He arranged for my daughter's burial and even paid for her coffin." She turned to the lavishly attired footman. "Please tell Mr. Darnly I would be delighted to accept his thoughtful invitation."

Everything in Roderick Darnly's dining room seemed to glisten. The highly polished table was set with cut-crystal glasses filled with sparkling champagne. Tall tapers flickered like evening stars in the five-branched candelabra and the diamond-paned windows overlooking St. James's Street glimmered with pinpoints of light as Sophie sipped her wine and considered her host's startling proposal.

"I've already seen to preparing the gardener's cottage for you," Roderick said calmly. "'Tis hidden behind a grove of trees in the parkland behind Evansmor House. You can have peace and tranquility and a place to ply your quill—if you're ever of a mind."

Sophie gazed at him down the length of the long dining table. She was still recovering from her surprise that she was his only guest.

"I'm both touched and flattered you should think of arranging something so kind for me," she said. "But why ever should you wish me to accompany you to Wales?"

Roderick Darnly's unruffled demeanor seemed suddenly strained, as if he wished to divulge a secret and then thought better of it. He signaled his scarlet-clad footmen to grant them some privacy.

"Let us just say that whenever I am summoned home by my coal-obsessed father, I find I am very soon in need of good companionship."

"I am certain there are many other women in Covent Garden far more suited to such a mission," Sophie said primly.

Roderick chuckled and leaned back in his chair.

"Now *I'm* the one who is flattered, my dear Sophie," he replied. "I would not presume to think you would consider sleeping in my bed," he continued smoothly. "When I say *companionship,* I mean exactly that. Wales, as I hope you will soon discover, is a beautiful, untamed land, and the Glamorgan region, where my father has his estates and coal fields, is wilder yet. There are few entertainments of the type one might expect to find in London, and I merely thought we might both profit from a joint expedition to that back-of-the-beyond place. I can't avoid this visit, after so long a sojourn abroad, and now that you've given up Ashby's Books and have severed all personal entanglements, I assumed a much-needed change of scene would do you good. If you assent to come with me to Glamorgan, we shall be rendering each other a service, I assure you."

Sophie was momentarily nonplussed. Obviously, Roderick Darnly had lavished considerable thought on her particular circumstances and was extending a tempting invitation. At that same time, he made it clear she would actually be doing him a favor. But was that all there was to this proposal?

"You've been very kind on several fronts, but—" she began.

"Well, here's your chance to show your appreciation," he interrupted deftly. "I could face my godforsaken homeland far more cheerfully, knowing I had someone there to converse with about theater and writing and all the artistic pursuits we both enjoy."

"And what would the Earl of Llewelyn think of such an . . . arrangement? Mightn't the sight of a female scrivener living at the bottom of your garden unsettle your father?"

"I am the second son," Roderick explained with an ironic smile. "As long as I attend the requisite number of dinners at

Glynmorgan Castle and pay appropriate respects to my brother, Vaughn, and my mother, the countess, his lordship couldn't care less what I do."

"I fear it could still prove awkward for both of us," Sophie mused, taking another sip of champagne.

"But why? Evansmor, where I live, is my mother's former family seat—it's a good mile from the castle gates. You could pass the entire summer and autumn without ever laying eyes on the earl."

"Well, I—" Sophie hesitated. She was running out of excuses, especially because the notion of escaping from London and its painful memories had great appeal.

"As I've said before," Roderick intervened, "I do believe you would enjoy being looked after. In my case, I have an army of servants in Wales, so you needn't worry 'tis a burden on my part, and I truly would enjoy your company. 'Tis as simple as that."

For an instant, Sophie reflected on her darkest days these last two years when she truly thought she would go mad with the double loss of Danielle and Hunter. Darnly's offer was a chance, at last, to put the tragedy of her daughter's death and its aftermath behind her, and to bury forever all thoughts and feelings and memories concerning a certain brash Scotsman.

"Wales in the summer . . ." Sophie responded softly. At length she met Roderick's gaze. "It sounds delightful."

※

Sophie allowed Roderick to support her arm as she sank onto her trunk which had been unloaded at dockside. A stiff breeze blew off Swansea Bay, the same wind that had made the trip by boat from Bristol to this small port city in Wales a nightmare of tossing waves and seasickness.

"Feeling better?" he asked cheerfully.

"Yes, much, thank you." Sophie smiled wanly.

Actually, now that her feet were back on land, both her stomach and her spirits were improving by the minute. She scanned the long, low warehouses near the docks where bales of wool and bins of coal were stored before being shipped to myriad ports in England and Ireland, thus creat-

ing enormous wealth for the likes of Roderick's father. As
with so many powerful Anglo-Welsh aristocrats in South
Wales, Basil Darnly, the Earl of Llewelyn, had the good
fortune to possess vast tracts in the Glamorgan region.
Among his holdings were forty thousand acres of coal-rich
land that stretched from the treeless mountains called
Brecon Beacons to the Vale of Neath whose river emptied
into Swansea Bay.

The luggage was loaded into Darnly's waiting coach, and
an hour later they had crossed the river Tawe and begun a
slow, gradual climb up the hilly road that ultimately wound
through dramatic crags, gorges, and wooded glens.

"Are you sure your coachman is on the proper route?"
Sophie gasped after five miles of being tossed about in the
wildly rocking vehicle.

"Welcome to Wales and its appalling roads," Roderick
replied, bracing himself for the next pothole by placing a
palm on each wall of the coach. "If you can manage, look
out the window," he directed. "There are the gates of
Glynmorgan Castle."

Sophie's mouth literally went slack at the sight of the
forbidding gray stone structure. She was astounded by its six
gargantuan round towers and its walls-within-walls design.

"Whoever built it must have had powerful enemies," she
breathed.

"It was started a short time after the Norman conquest,"
Roderick explained, "and added to by my father's ancestors
in the reign of King Edward the First."

"There should be a jousting tournament in progress in
front of the moat," she jested. "Is the drawbridge actually
pulled up at night?"

"Not anymore," Darnly assured her with a smile.

"How many chambers are there?" she asked.

"Hundreds," he replied. "I've never seen them all."

"And the coal mines? Where are they?"

"Out of sight . . . up yonder, behind that ridge. I'll take
you there, if you like, to see the colliery and ironworks."

The coach continued past the castle keep without stopping and soon the land evened out, although the rutted path
they were traveling did not. A parkland with a high, gray

stone wall ran parallel to the road, broken by a pair of imposing wrought-iron gates. As the coach turned into the drive, Sophie gazed down the graveled entrance. In the distance, she could see a vine-covered manor house three stories high with neat rows of square-paned, arched windows flanking its columned front entrance.

"The former abode of my mother, the Countess of Evansmor," Roderick explained casually. "Mother had the misfortune of having been born an heiress without any brothers to protect her from the avaricious Darnlys who resided next door. Before she turned eighteen, she found herself married to Basil Darnly and her father's lands absorbed into the Glynmorgan estate."

"Who was your English ancestor?" Sophie asked, referring to Darnly's surname.

"My father's mother was also an orphaned heiress, forced to make a match with an Anglo aristocrat during the last century. In fact, of the fourteen prominent Welsh families in this part of the world, twelve tipped up with no male heirs in the last fifty years. It makes it so much easier to be an absentee landlord if one has English blood, don't you know?" he added with grim humor. "Send the local buggers down into the mines and have the bank drafts for their labors forwarded to London."

"So you have no interest in your father's coal business?"

"Not really," Roderick replied. "And thank God, he has no interest in my affairs. Ah . . . here we are!"

Sophie felt awkward as Darnly helped her out of the carriage and turned to greet the large staff that stood rigidly at attention on the mansion's front steps.

"Welcome, sir," greeted a slender man of about Darnly's age who peered past his master's shoulder to have a look at Sophie. "'Tis good to have you with us again."

"Thank you, Trevor," Roderick replied, and Sophie guessed this was the factor who supervised his master's property. "I would like you to take Miss McGann to her cottage so she can rest before dinner. I assume everything is in readiness, as I instructed?" he asked sharply.

"Yes, sir. I've chosen Evelyn as her lady's maid, if you think it best."

"Excellent," Roderick agreed, every inch the grand seigneur. "Well, then, Sophie . . . 'til dinner. Have a good rest. Trevor, have Evelyn ride with Miss McGann down to the cottage and see that she has a pony at her disposal in the paddock nearby."

"'Tis already seen to, sir."

A plump, sandy-haired lass stepped out of the line of servants, smiled shyly, and climbed into the coach after her.

"Good afternoon, mum," she volunteered, eyeing Sophie with curiosity. "The master's never had his guests stay in the gardener's cottage before, but don't worry," she added hastily, "'tis been done up good and proper!"

"I've been ill," Sophie fibbed, salving her conscience by telling herself she had been suffering a malaise of spirit. "Mr. Darnly was kind enough to invite me here to have a complete rest. I won't be the usual visitor," she said, smiling. "I'm a playwright, and if I begin to feel better, I may spend most of my time at my desk—if there is one."

"Oh there is, to be sure!" Evelyn said, clearly awed to meet a writer who was female. "He had his own from the library carted down, he did. It very nearly didn't fit through the door!"

In short order, the coach pulled up to an ivy-covered one-room dry-stone cottage that embodied everything Sophie allowed herself to dream of in terms of comfort and privacy. Its gray slate roof and gaily painted green door were shaded by a grove of towering beech trees artfully planted to hide the structure from view of the manor house.

"Oh, what a sweet, wee kitten!" Sophie exclaimed delightedly as she spotted a ginger-colored animal daintily licking its paws on the threshold.

"Strayed from the new litter in the barn, I expect," Evelyn said. "I'll have the coachman take it back."

"Must you?" Sophie said, reaching down to stroke the cat. "'Twould be a bit of company for me."

"As you wish, mum," Evelyn smiled. "What shall you call him?"

Sophie picked up the purring feline and cuddled it under her chin.

"Marmalade!" she pronounced and carried it into her new abode.

Inside was a fireplace one could walk into, a mahogany four-poster festooned with sheer batiste hangings overhead and matching white curtains on the windows. A pale silk coverlet sheathed the goose-down mattress.

Except for the stone walls, there was nothing rustic about this abode. The large room was warmed by a thick, Turkish carpet, silver candlesticks on a rosewood sideboard, and two leather-covered wing-backed chairs flanking the fireplace.

"Will the desk suit, mum?" asked Evelyn anxiously.

Sophie stared at the exquisitely carved piece pushed beneath the leaded window overlooking the grove of beech trees outside.

"Oh, yes . . ." she said in a breath, stroking Marmalade's soft fur. "'Tis perfect."

※

Nearly a month passed, filled with poetry readings by local bards, concerts held in Darnly's well-appointed music room where Welsh fiddlers played both plaintive and jaunty melodies to entertain just the two of them, and with outings both on foot and in Roderick's coach to explore the eighty-foot Clyn-Gwyn waterfalls and other natural wonders in the Vale of Neath.

By July, Sophie had grown accustomed to the luxury of clean linen and a tidy house. She often curled up alone in Roderick's library with a selection from his well-stocked shelves, reading undisturbed for hours at a time until she succumbed to napping.

One afternoon, she was awakened by Roderick's fingers lightly brushing against her cheek.

"Ready for your tea?" he asked softly, looking down at her. "I've asked Mrs. Williams to serve us in here, if that suits you."

"W-why, yes," Sophie stammered, pulling herself upright on the leather sofa and tidying her hair. His touch on her cheek was the first intimate gesture her host had ever extended toward her and she was forced to admit, it felt rather lovely. "Forgive me for—"

"No apologies warranted," he smiled faintly, gazing at her steadily. "I quite like seeing you feel so at home here."

Sophie remained silent, rescued from her own confusion by the arrival of afternoon tea, which Evelyn served her everyday at four.

As they didn't dine together every night, she assumed Roderick was making the required appearances at Glynmorgan Castle. Evansmor, which she learned from Evelyn was not owned by Roderick outright, but still part of the family estates, was run by his efficient staff, and Sophie had never enjoyed herself more in her life. She had the freedom to spend her days as she wished, pampered by all the creature comforts a person could wish, including the use of a sweet-tempered pony named Powis.

The only problem was, Sophie had no desire to take up her quill.

"You will in time," Roderick told her reassuringly.

"Perhaps I don't wish to find out that my muse has abandoned me," she said somberly as their coach headed up a particularly rutted road that lead to the Darnly Colliery. At Sophie's request, her host had agreed to give her a tour of the coal fields before partaking in the annual celebration at the conclusion of the haying season scheduled to be held later in the day on the grounds of Glynmorgan Castle.

"Why not try your hand at an amusing playlet for the house party I'm giving at Evansmor during grouse season?" he suggested. "In keeping with tradition, it can mock anything its author likes . . . the grouse, the hunters, the host —whatever strikes your fancy."

"I-I don't know if I could conjure anything suitable," Sophie said hesitantly, feeling like an ingrate. Writing an entertainment 'twas the least she could do to show her appreciation for everything Roderick had done for her. "But I shall think on it."

"Splendid," he said. He glanced down at her kid boots, which he had provided—in the correct size—earlier in the day. "You'll be glad you're wearing those if we slog around the mines."

"Is the earl likely to be here?" she asked nervously, gazing at the dark heaps of slag that obliterated the green hills on both sides of the narrow valley they were now entering.

"No worry there," he assured her. "I'm told he's gone to Bristol this week."

Darnly assisted Sophie out of the coach and led her on a promenade around the colliery that included a huge wooden building where ribbons of molten metal spewed out of huge iron kettles fired in white-hot furnaces.

"'Tis like some monster from Hades," Sophie said in a breath, staring at the roaring fire pits and the blackened-faced workers toiling in the heat. "What do they make with the iron they produce?"

"Engines of war," Roderick replied. "In another building on the estate they cast cannonballs. The cannons themselves are made near the port of Swansea, so they can easily be shipped wherever the British government needs them. The latest batch produced by the Darnly Colliery was dispatched to Saratoga, New York, to keep the American Colonists in line." He glanced at Sophie's face to gauge her reaction to his pronouncements. "Surely you realize, Sophie, my dear, that every great fortune is built on something as necessary as bloodshed?" Sophie studied his expression to determine if he were teasing her, but he abruptly changed the subject. "Are you game to go down into a mine shaft?"

"I don't know," she answered truthfully. "May I look at it first?"

Roderick lead her across the rubble-strewn landscape that looked rather like what she imagined the surface of the moon would be—treeless, rough terrain, with pock-marked depressions dotting the landscape. They soon came to a cave framed by thick timbers and burrowed in the hillside. Colliers, their hands and faces completely covered with soot, were emerging from its maw carrying lanterns they soon extinguished. They looked, to a man, utterly exhausted.

"For five hours they've been digging lumps of coal by candlelight, waist-deep in water at close to three hundred feet beneath the ground," Roderick informed her.

Before Sophie could respond to this disturbing information, one of the men stopped in his tracks and then began to wave. Though his face was a bit soot-covered, the cut of his clothes distinguished him from the gaggle of miners who trooped on down the lane.

"Roddy! What a shock to see you here!" the man exclaimed. "I bet 'tis been five years since you've graced us with your presence at the mines."

"I've brought a friend who asked to see the operation," Roderick replied stiffly. He was suddenly no longer the cool, urbane aristocrat Sophie had always known. He seemed ill-at-ease and reluctantly made introductions. "Sophie, this is my brother Vaughn, Viscount Glyn. Vaughn, this is Miss Sophie McGann. She's a playwright."

"So *this* is the reason Father has complained all summer that your visits to the castle have been so infrequent." Vaughn laughed, surveying Sophie appreciatively. "You've been hiding this fair scrivener from your own twin brother, naughty boy!"

"T-twin brother?" Sophie couldn't help but stammer, for Vaughn Darnly was a head shorter than his sibling and sported a mane of bright red hair above his soot-flecked countenance.

"Obviously, we're fraternal twins. I was the lucky one, though—born two minutes before poor old Roddy, here," Vaughn said cheerfully. "I get the land and the mines, but then, I have to deal with Father every day. There is nothing for free in this life, is there?" He grinned.

Sophie liked him at once. Not nearly as handsome as his "younger" brother, the stocky viscount had an open friendliness that seemed utterly at odds with Roderick's cool guardedness. She sensed the heir to the Darnly Mines and forty-thousand Welsh acres was observing her intently, as if it surprised him his brother would have a person of her sort as his guest at Evansmor.

"Can we offer you a ride to the castle?" Roderick said. "From the look on Sophie's face, I doubt she wants to descend very far into that mine shaft, and I'm sure Mother and your new bride hope you'll clean yourself up before the evening's festivities."

"You're coming to the haying fete?" Vaughn asked incredulously. "My, my, Miss McGann, you certainly seem to be having a remarkably good influence on the lad. Old Basil won't believe his eyes!"

"Father will be there?" Roderick asked sharply.

"He returned from Bristol this morning," Vaughn answered, as Sophie felt Roderick grow tense by her side. "He's brought parts for my mechanical pump with him, I hope. I've had the lads fabricate most of this contraption I'm building in the foundry, but there are one or two items—"

"You're *not* still tinkering with that fool pump!"

"I was just down in the shaft trying out a new notion I had before you came," Vaughn said in an animated voice. "If we can syphon out more of the water that collects in the bottom of the shaft, 'twill be far easier for the lads. Less water, more coal. More coal, more money. 'Tis as simple as that. My mechanical pump is bound to make the miners more productive."

"So they can die at an even earlier age, is that it?" Roderick said snidely, glancing down the road at the men who had begun disappearing into a bleak row of stone houses built into the hill.

"If you care so much about the miners," Vaughn snapped, "why do you spend most of your time poncing around London, instead of working with me to try to improve their lot?"

Suddenly, the friendly atmosphere had completely evaporated, replaced by a contentious rivalry Sophie wagered had existed in the Darnly family ever since the brothers were small boys.

"Forgive us our internecine squabbles," Roderick said, scowling at his brother. "I think it best to let Vaughn fend for himself. I promised the countess we'd be on time, for once."

✖

Sophie and Roderick entered the wide, grassy, square-sided area of the inner castle keep. It was now filled by hordes of guests eager to partake of the free cider, cockle soup and rich Welsh cheese served in generous chunks on slices of coarse bread. Although the haying fete had been blessed with warm July sunshine, Sophie shivered in the shade of the gray stone round towers that loomed overhead. In her imagination, she could almost hear the screams of attacking soldiers in King Edward's time, their chests pierced by flaming arrows or scalded by hot oil poured on them from the parapets soaring overhead.

"Can I serve you a whiskey, sir?" asked a voice behind them. "With the earl in attendance today, I imagine you'll need it."

Sophie turned to find Darnly's factor, Trevor Bedloe, clutching a bottle of homemade spirits and two glasses.

"Sophie, would you like to try this witch's brew?" Roderick asked, accepting Trevor's offer. "'Tis a Welsh tradition to get as drunk as possible when one emerges from the mines, and this is the means to do it."

"No thank you," Sophie replied, watching Trevor pour his master a drink and then one for himself.

The trio sauntered over to one of the hulking round towers where a fiddler was flailing away. A hundred guests danced themselves into a frenzy on the broad expanse of green grass. Sophie's breath caught in her throat as she spied an old man leaning against an ancient harp, gazing at the boisterous crowd with a weary air.

"T-the harper?" Sophie stammered, her thoughts thrust back instantly to the first day she met Hunter juggling to the accompaniment of the festive tune plucked by his late grandfather.

"Old Taf . . . he was harper to my mother's father, and she forced Basil to grant him grace-and-favor status here before she agreed to marry. He can't abide the old man . . . thinks he's gone quite scatty, which I suppose he has, but Mother won't hear of him being turned out. Though he forgets the simplest things, like whether he's had supper or not, the man can still sing long ballads praising the valiant deeds of the ancient House of Evans. We Welsh put our bards only one rung below our kings."

"Ah . . . so you consider yourself more Welsh than English?" She smiled, accepting his proffered piece of cheese.

"I expect I have more poet in me than coal baron, wouldn't you agree, Trevor?" he asked his retainer as his eyes scanned the huge crowd.

"Fortunately for you," Trevor responded, his watchful gaze shifting from Sophie to his employer whom he'd known since they were children. "A second son is not expected to be serious about much of anything, is he? Allows one more time for pleasure, wouldn't you say, sir?" he added with a wink that Sophie wasn't sure was intended for her or Darnly himself.

"Or if he *is* serious, there's always the heir to garner the accolades," Roderick added dryly.

He sounded bitter, despite his ironic smile. But before she could press him further on the subject of his divided loyalties, a handsome women in peasant attire, her gray hair flowing freely to her shoulders without combs or artifice, strode toward them with a determined look.

"Prepare yourself, Sophie," Roderick warned under his breath. "You're about to meet my mother, the incomparable Rowena."

"Vaughn wagered me a new Welsh pony you'd never come, but I assured him you would," Rowena pronounced before introductions could be made. "Have you tasted the cheese? Terribly good this year. I churned much of the milk myself." She surveyed Sophie closely. "So you're the playwright, are you?" she said. "'Tis about time my son brought someone to Wales besides those raucous London rakes who invade the hills every August to massacre grouse. Delighted you could join our midsummer fete, my dear." She leaned forward and lowered her voice conspiratorially. "I had it put in my marriage contract, the brigand *had* to keep at least ten thousand acres in crops and not rape every inch of my father's landscape. It pleases me enormously how very cross this haying celebration makes my husband each July, not to mention my wearing the clothes of a common laborer. Have you met him yet?"

Sophie attempted to collect her wits after this barrage of words and merely shook her head no.

"Well, keep her away from the man as long as you can," the countess advised her son. Then she paused and her glance narrowed as she surveyed Roderick's factor.

"Plying my son with whiskey, are you, Trevor?"

"He requested a glass, Countess," Trevor replied, lowering his eyes to the bottle he still held in his hand. And Roderick, as if to deliberately provoke his mother, held out his empty glass for a refill.

"Well, see that you two behave yourselves for once!" she snapped as if she were talking to naughty eight-year-olds. She rested her glance on Sophie again and her eyes softened. "So happy you are staying at Evansmor. 'Tis lovely, isn't it? I'd exchange this pile for that cottage in the grove like *that,* if I could," she exclaimed, snapping her fingers for emphasis. "Roderick," she said sternly. "Have you provided Miss Mc-Gann every comfort so she'll stay through the autumn?"

"Yes, Mother," Darnly said with a thin smile grazing his lips. "There's absolutely no possibility she can escape back to London."

As dusk stole across the keep, the pitch-soaked torches positioned in wrought-iron holders mounted on every wall and staircase cast a golden glow that softened the hard, sinister stones of Glynmorgan Castle. The music grew louder and more frenzied as additional fiddlers and harpers joined the fray in a kind of peasant orchestra, urging the tireless dancers, tanned and muscled from their summer of haying, to cavort under the full moon now rising above the pair of round towers to the east.

Trevor and Roderick had nearly finished the bottle of Welsh whiskey and were quite the worse for it. Vaughn sauntered over to where they sat on a stone staircase that spiraled to a rampart somewhere, silently observing the festivities taking place on the grass. His face was scrubbed of the coal dust that had coated it earlier, and Sophie was happy to welcome him to their strange little group.

"Father wishes to meet your guest," Vaughn said pleasantly. "Says he can't endure the music another moment. You'll find him in his study."

Sophie's heart began to thud and she looked at Roderick nervously, having absolutely no interest whatsoever in meeting his forbidding-sounding sire.

"Tell him," Roderick said with an effort not to slur his words, "that I have no wish for her to meet him."

"Oh, for God's sake, Roddy," Vaughn responded. "Pray, stop performing your little dance. Basil's pleased you have a presentable woman as your guest for a change, and one who's clearly not a whore!" He shot an apologetic glance at Sophie. "Sorry, but that's precisely what he said when I told him about you."

"'Twas not your place to go tattling to him about my private affairs," Roderick said, glowering at his brother.

"Well, your entire family will be pleased to learn it's advanced to that stage," Vaughn riposted.

"Bastard!" Roderick exploded, jumping to his feet and glaring at his twin.

"If only I *was*, eh, Roddy old boy?" Vaughn shot back. "*Your* being the first born might have smothered this poisonous envy of yours. 'Twas no fault of mine Mother produced an heir and a spare."

Trevor Bedloe stepped between the brothers and put a restraining hand on Roderick's arm.

"Come on, sir," he urged, his voice thick from the effects of the alcohol, "a bit of food might be in order."

"That's right, Trevor," Vaughn said with disgust. "Take care of his every need. That's what you've always done, isn't it, man?"

Sophie watched, astounded, as Roderick allowed himself to be lead away by his factor, leaving Vaughn and her standing amid the swirling dancers.

"How long will the fete last?" Sophie asked uncomfortably.

"Into the wee hours, I'm afraid," Vaughn sighed, watching his brother's retreating back. "Shall I see you to Evansmor?"

"I'll ask Roderick's coachman to drive me back. Good night."

※

Sophie swam to consciousness, aware someone was flinging pebbles at the cottage window above her desk. She peered through the gloom illumined only by the embers burning on the hearth. She was startled to see Roderick beckoning to her through the glass. Reluctantly, she removed Marmalade, asleep on the bed in a furry ball next to her feet. She padded across the floor, alarmed that both her inebriated host and Trevor Bedloe had apparently decided to end their night of debauchery on her doorstep.

But Roderick was alone.

"Please . . . Sophie . . . please . . . I must talk to you," he pleaded through the window cracked open a few inches. His voice was that of a child, full of self-pity. After everything Sophie had ever known of the man, his tone, not his words, shocked her profoundly.

"Roderick, I think you're very drunk, and since I remain married to Peter Lindsay, I know whereof I speak. Go back to the house. You'll feel better in the morning. We can talk then if you like."

"I'll feel worse . . . much worse, after what happened tonight," he mumbled. His hands reached out to grasp the windowsill, but the next moment, he slid to his knees. Sophie ran to the door, unlocked it and raced around the corner of the cottage to find her host still in a praying position.

"Come on, then," she said, slipping her hand under his right arm. Miraculously, Roderick was able to rise to his full height and stumble into the cottage, collapsing into one of the two leather chairs facing the high-mantled fireplace. "Would you like me to fix you some tea?" she asked sympathetically.

"No . . . but I would like you to tell me if you find me at all attractive?" he asked solemnly, and Sophie's heart began to beat faster as she silently berated herself for inviting him to come inside the cottage. He pulled out a flask from beneath his coat and took a long swig. Wiping his mouth in a surprisingly uncouth gesture, he peered at her perched on the other chair. "I ask you this because my dear mother believes you were too intelligent to consider linking your life with mine, even before your marriage. For once, my father agrees . . . says you'll soon guess that I—" He stopped midsentence and suddenly covered his eyes with the hand not holding the flask of whiskey. To Sophie's abject horror, his shoulders began to heave, and deep, anguished sobs tore from his chest. She flew out of her chair and knelt beside him.

"Roderick, what's the matter?" she asked compassionately. "What has made you feel so wretched?" But he merely continued to weep and shake his head disconsolately. "Let's get you to bed," she urged firmly. "I'll make a pallet for myself in front of the fire. Come, now, let me help you with your jacket."

He allowed her to divest him of his coat and boots and staggered toward her rumpled four-poster. Just as she was about to pull up the counterpane to cover him, he caught her hand and hauled her roughly against his chest.

"I would have considered marrying you, my pretty little scribe . . . if you hadn't been so foolish as to wed that bounder. From the first, I liked your small, boyish frame," he said, clumsily running his hand down the front of her night dress. Sophie recoiled and tried to pull away from his grasp. "And I liked your intelligence and your cleverness with words . . . we could have made a go of it . . . at least enough to satisfy my bloody fam—"

"Roderick, please!" Sophie cried. "You'll regret every word in the morning."

"That's why I'm so drunk, my dear. So I won't remember . . . I can't *bear* to remember what they said—"

"Just let go of my hand and—"

"How could I be anything other than what I've become?" he asked plaintively, pulling her toward him again with such strength that she was half-lying on the bed. "What would *you* be if your mother cosseted you till you were seven and then banished you to school? And all the while, pampering you and petting you and teaching you to hate your da," he rambled garrulously, "telling you that you were *hers* and your brother, your father's property?"

"Roderick, stop!" Sophie pleaded.

"And your father," he continued, ignoring her entreaties, "what if your father found you too similar to the wife he despised? Would you be drawn to men or women now? Tell me!" he demanded, his eyes blazing with sudden anger. "Which would it be?"

"Roderick, I can't help you with any of this!" Sophie cried, desperate to silence this tortured discourse.

"Yes, you can," he mumbled fiercely, holding her in a

viselike grip with his left hand and unbuttoning his buff breeches with his right. His breath, reeking from the enormous amount of whiskey he'd been drinking for hours, made her eyes water. "You can help me, Sophie . . . truly you can," he half-sobbed, reaching into the mysterious region between his legs. "See if you can merely—"

"No!" Sophie cried, appalled. She wrenched her arm with all her might, but to no avail.

"Please, Sophie . . . I won't think you a whore if you . . ." he pleaded incoherently. "Just help me prove him *wrong*! I've managed it with jades like Mary Ann, but I must find out if—" He yanked down the flap of his breeches and stared at his flaccid flesh, shaking his head helplessly. "Oh Christ! I hate the man! I hate them both! I hate their bleeding guts!"

A paroxysm of sobs overcame him, and he rolled over on his stomach, releasing her from his grip. His entire body continued to shudder, until, at length, his cries subsided, replaced by ragged breathing, and finally, a drugged sleep.

Chapter 24

Sophie trod the short distance through the damp grass from the privy to the gardener's cottage. She inhaled the moist morning air, and wondered how in heaven's name Roderick would face her—or she him, for that matter—when he woke up. She could only imagine the tumultuous family scene that had prompted him to flee to her door in the wee hours. What had happened to Trevor Bedloe? And, what part had Vaughn Darnly played in the domestic debacle?

It was barely first light. Shivering because of the chill, she reluctantly approached the corner of the vine-covered bungalow and peered cautiously through the leaded windows.

Her bed was empty.

She scanned the linen draped untidily on the floor and noticed Roderick's empty flask tipped over on the carpet near the wing-backed chair. She jerked her head back, afraid she would see him fumbling to dress himself or be forced to meet his gaze after the dreadful events of the previous night.

Tense as a bow string, she leaned against the stone wall, frozen in place for what seemed like an eternity, feeling at a loss as to what to do next. Finally, she concluded that the long silence from within could only mean Roderick had departed for the manor house as soon as he had heard her rise.

At eight o'clock Evelyn arrived as usual with Sophie's breakfast tray.

"Good morning, mum," the maid servant said cheerfully. "And did you enjoy the haying fete last night? I wager I danced till the cock crowed, but feel no worse for it," she added pertly.

"Did you?" Sophie murmured, busying herself with the pouring of her tea. "No worse for wear, then?"

"No!" laughed Evelyn. "As long as I don't touch a drop of that deadly Welsh brew so many were drinking last night, I'm perfectly fit the following day. Not like some people we could name," she added slyly. Sophie glanced intently at the housemaid, but did not respond. "Trevor Bedloe's half-dead this morning," Evelyn disclosed blithely. "And the master looked none too well, if the truth be told. Oh!" she exclaimed, turning around at the cottage door. "I'm to tell you that he's off to Bath."

"Mr. Darnly's gone to Bath?" Sophie echoed faintly.

"'Twas ever so sudden. He just this minute left. He called the coachman not more than a half hour ago and bid him take Trevor and himself immediately to Swansea. He's sending the poor driver all the way back to Evansmor to fetch his trunk. That wretched Glynnis is upstairs right now, packing like a dervish. Master said he and Trevor had urgent business to attend to at the warehouses before the ketch sailed for Bristol this afternoon. What business could be so pressing the day after the haying fete, can you tell me?" she chattered on. "He instructed us to look after you good and proper, mum," Evelyn added hastily, "so you're not to have a care."

"I see . . ." Sophie sighed, realizing with a shock that without the funds derived from the sale of her books to Thomas Davies—the majority of which she had left in Mrs. Phillips' safe-keeping—Roderick Darnly's abrupt departure had rendered her a virtual prisoner in Wales.

The warm days of July continued without a word from her host or any firm indication of when he would return to Evansmor. Thanks to Darnly's efficient staff, Sophie wanted for nothing, but she was restless. She considered dispatching a request that Mrs. Phillips forward a bank draft to her, but she was at a loss how she would discreetly convert it to shillings and pounds so she could pay her fare on the boat to Bristol and then catch a coach back to London.

Trevor Bedloe returned from Swansea after a few days and behaved pleasantly enough when they encountered one another around the estate. Even so, Sophie was reluctant to reveal to the man her burning desire to declare her holiday over and return to London forthwith.

Instead, she spent hours devouring the books in Evansmor's library, and justifying her inaction by telling herself that she might as well enjoy having her whims attended to for a while longer. But after a fortnight of this, with still no word from Roderick Darnly, Sophie took quill in hand and began a spoof about a feeble-minded local laird invited to shoot grouse merely because his fellow hunters coveted his well-trained dog. The playlet would be a thank-you present to soften the news that she was departing.

"This is for you, mum," Evelyn announced, plunging her hand into her apron pocket and handing Sophie a note. "The master has returned. The coachman went to fetch him at the dock early this morning. Seems ever so pleased you've been writing again," the housemaid blushed. "I hope you don't mind my tellin' him when he asked after you?" She picked up the silver breakfast tray, bobbed a curtsey, and was gone.

Although Sophie was relieved to learn her host had finally reappeared, she also felt a flush of irritation as she scanned the lines of his short missive.

I have returned from Bath delighted to learn you have taken up your quill in my absence. Please do me the honor of dining with me tonight in order to discuss my plans for the approaching grouse season.
Yr. most obedient servant R. D.

The man had disappeared for nearly a *month* without a word of apology to his stranded visitor. But if Sophie thought Roderick Darnly would voluntarily take note of their disturbing exchange inside the gardener's cottage, she seriously misjudged her host.

He sat across the table from her, sipping his wine and behaving for all the world as if nothing unusual had occurred at their last meeting. When she raised the subject of her forthcoming departure, he deflected her request as quickly as she'd voiced it.

"Well, of course, if you insist," he replied coolly, "but I do wish you'd stay long enough to see to your playlet mounted. You're the only one who can supervise it properly, especially with the amateur actors whom you shall, perforce, recruit from among the guests."

"Roderick," Sophie said quietly. "You absented yourself from Evansmor for nearly a month. Your staff has been wonderfully kind, but 'tis necessary for me to return to London. And besides, I've never even held a shotgun, let alone taken aim at a moving target. I fear that my being in residence with a houseful of your friends will only prove awkward," she insisted.

Roderick took a long draught of his wine, set the glass carefully near his dinner plate, and gazed at her steadily across the long dining table.

"I fear I . . . owe you an apology for the night of the haying fete," he avowed reluctantly. "I'd had far too much to drink of that lethal Welsh concoction and I'm sure I behaved appallingly. Did you get home all right on your own that evening?" he asked.

Sophie suddenly wondered how much of that dreadful night he remembered.

"Oh yes," she replied, watching his expression carefully. "I commandeered your coachman and then sent him back to Glynmorgan to fetch you later. Did he follow my instructions?"

Roderick actually appeared sheepish, a quality Sophie had never before seen in him.

"To be honest, I have no idea. I don't remember much of anything until I woke up in the gardener's cottage and you were nowhere to be seen. I deduced from the counterpane on the floor that after *I* commandeered your bed, you made a place for yourself in front of the fire. The entire business was most unfortunate. I hope I wasn't too much trouble to you," he finished with a questioning smile.

"You were quite inebriated," she said gently.

"No doubt," he nodded. "I must have stumbled out of

the stables when I returned to Evansmor late that night and walked through the first door in my path."

"A-aye," Sophie agreed uncertainly. "Well, then, no harm done."

"I must admit I was rather daunted by the prospect of facing you when I woke up, given the condition I was in," he acknowledged. "So I took myself off to Bath for a bit . . . an attempt to restore my abused body, don't you know? I hope you'll accept my apologies?"

"Of course," she replied perfunctorily. "But, even so, I really must get back to Lon—"

"The shooting season commences in three days' time and lasts three weeks," he interrupted. Sophie's heart sank at this intelligence. "I'll be traveling to London directly afterward. 'Twould be a help to the staff if we all departed at the same time. And besides," he said gravely, "I'd consider it a keen personal favor if you'll stay and supervise your little entertainment."

Inwardly, Sophie sighed, surrendering to her innate sense of good manners and the inevitability of the task ahead. If he *did* remember anything of that dreadful night, Roderick Darnly was clearly determined to ignore what had actually transpired between them.

Gazing past the tall candles illuminating their dining chamber, she nodded her acquiescence, accepting the fact that she really had no choice but to sing for her supper.

The next day, Sophie reclined comfortably on the leather sofa in Darnly's library while key members of his staff stood nearby, absorbing the litany of orders issued by their employer.

"Mrs. Williams, I've arranged for several girls from Swansea to come up to help you in the kitchen for the remainder of the summer. Glynnis," he said, addressing his remarks to the amply endowed housemaid who had packed her master's trunk in such a hurry, "see that they have pallets in the attic. And Trevor, have you lined up enough beaters?" he inquired, referring to the teams of men who were responsible for tramping through the heath to rouse the birds so his guests could shoot at them.

"'Tis attended to," Trevor assured him.

"Excellent," Roderick replied. "The performance of Miss McGann's play shall commence the last Saturday in the month. Have your men construct a platform at the end of the great hall, and on the day of the performance round up enough chairs to seat the audience. What backdrop will you require?" he said, addressing Sophie.

"Something simple," she replied promptly. "A green background of some sort will suit admirably. Merely a suggestion of a forest scene will do."

"The green velvet draperies in the countess's sitting room might serve," he mused. "I'll dispatch a note to her today," he added, scratching on a sheet of paper. "Perhaps she would order her gardener to supply us with some yew branches from the grove behind the castle to add to the set decorations. She'd doubtless enjoy playing a role in the only bit of culture during what she considers an otherwise barbaric exercise."

Darnly dismissed his staff but beckoned Sophie to remain.

"Is there anything else you'll need? Anything at all? I like the playlet quite a lot," he averred, gesturing to the manuscript nearby. "'Tis clear, you've not been abandoned by your muse."

"Why, thank you," Sophie responded, feeling the barrier of studied politeness lower a notch. "I very much wanted to demonstrate my appreciation for your hospitality these last months, so I am delighted it pleases you. Let's hope your guests will also find it amusing."

"They're sure to . . . and Mother will adore it. She used to organize Vaughn and me to perform little skits when we were boys, complete with costumes and scenery. Old Taf provided the musical accompaniment on his harp and the entire staff and company at Glynmorgan Castle were required to attend. Except for the earl, of course, who despises such frivolity. Now that we're grown, she often pitches in on our trivial diversions here just to twit him, I think."

"Your father has no taste for the theater?" Sophie wondered aloud.

"Can't abide it. Which is one reason, I'm sure, why my mother enjoys mounting such spectacles. She has a true Welsh strain in her . . . insisted on teaching us to speak the language. She reveres poets above all men, especially over her supposed Lord and Master—my father."

"You are able to speak Welsh?" Sophie exclaimed admiringly.

"When I was a lad, she'd have me recite druid incantations after tutoring from Old Taf." He laughed harshly. "I think she did it just to annoy the earl."

"And does your father not enjoy poetry at all?" she wondered.

"A bit of Shakespeare, I suppose. There were always rows between my parents over my mother's patronage of various odd local characters and aspiring artists." He looked at her closely to gauge her reaction. "Just a cozy Welsh family, to be sure."

"Does Vaughn enjoy theatricals as much as you seem to?" she inquired cautiously, marveling at Darnly's sudden openness, which seemed so out of character. She guessed he was employing every bit of charm to convince her of the correctness of her decision to remain at Evansmor.

"As soon as we were sent away to school when we were eight, it became clear that Vaughn's bent was of a much more scientific nature," Roderick disclosed with a wry smile. "His tinkering with that mechanical pump is a perfect example. I seriously doubt he can make it work, but it amuses him to try. I, however, continued to dabble in the dramatic societies when I was at Oxford, so Mother won out where one of us is concerned."

"And thus, your interest in Drury Lane?" she ventured.

He shrugged. "Better *that* than wagering a fortune at faro —as certain 'gentlemen' of our acquaintance prefer."

Sophie managed a polite smile at his allusion to her estranged husband and reached for her manuscript.

"Well, I hope the play will suit," she said. "I should let you get on to complete all the arrangements . . ."

"Oh, and Sophie," Roderick said, interrupting her exit.

"I fear I must warn you that there is likely to be a fair amount of . . . imbibing among my guests in the evenings during the shoot," he informed her casually. "Please feel free to join us for dinner or have your meals sent down to the cottage—whatever you'd prefer. Just have a word with Evelyn."

"Thank you for offering me the choice," she murmured and took her leave, quite sure from these tactful remarks that she was meant to confine herself to her quarters behind the grove of beeches until she was needed to supervise her play.

Each day during the following week, new guests began arriving at Evansmor, and the staff had its hands full every minute. Roderick's coach was on perpetual duty to and from Swansea, and the lasses imported from the town were kept relentlessly busy peeling potatoes and stirring cauldrons of hearty soups overseen by the efficient Mrs. Williams. Many guests brought their own servants and they, too, had to be accommodated.

Sophie found it rather dangerous to venture out into the parkland as the season wore on. Shots rang out for hours at a stretch as the hunters bagged brace after brace of black grouse, the stated object of the annual exercise. Mrs. Williams's dinners began to feature grouse in red currant sauce, grouse *encroute*, grouse fricassee. At any moment, Sophie expected to see grouse served in a sea of frothy syllabub.

One moon-filled night, she was awakened by the faint strains of a harp being played in the distance. The odd, musical intrusion had interrupted a dream in which Hunter flung juggling pins high above the roofs of Edinburgh. Shaken by how tangible his presence had seemed, she pulled on her dressing gown and stumbled toward the desk near the window. She pushed it open several inches and the melancholy music grew louder, shifting suddenly to a fierce, staccato plucking sound that had about it a dire, ominous quality.

Her eyes grew wide at the unlikely sight of a column of hooded figures weaving in and out among the beech trees at the far end of the grove. To her vague alarm, the procession was wending its way in her direction, led by Sir Bartle Por-

ter-Jones, whom Sophie had met the previous day at the
manor house.

Old Taf, the harper, had installed himself behind a tree
not fifty yards from her cottage door. A tall robed figure she
recognized as Roderick broke from the ranks of druidlike
specters and strode up to the musician, bidding him to cease
his playing as he pointed in the direction of the gardener's
cottage.

From her shadowed vantage point, Sophie watched,
transfixed, as the dozen or so robed gentlemen, each one
carrying a lighted taper, formed a circle around a large boulder encrusted with moss and lichen that stood in the center
of the grove. Among the masculine faces draped in monk's
cowls, she identified several of the shooting aficionados who
had been summoned to Evansmor at Darnly's invitation.

Sir Bartle Porter-Jones ceremoniously placed an object of
some sort on the uneven surface of the stone "altar." Intermittently, moonlight streamed in silvery shafts through the
trees as wisps of clouds drifted across the night sky. Sir Bartle leaned toward the waist-high boulder, fumbling with
what appeared to be a small cage. Suddenly an animal attempted to make its escape as Porter-Jones swiftly withdrew
a long knife from beneath his flowing black robe. With a
flash of steel, the baronet pierced the defenseless creature to
the heart.

Sophie gasped, feeling ill, and leaned against the windowsill to steady herself. Could this be one of those rituals associated with the Hell Fire Clubs she'd heard whispered
about? Articles in *The Public Advertiser* had boldly hinted
at certain associations of men—mostly among the nobility—
who dressed in medieval garb and cavorted in strange ceremonies before a statue of Venus—or worse, who practiced
the black arts in obeisance to Satan himself. Despite her re-
pugnance, she found herself incapable of pulling her eyes
away from the strange and horrifying spectacle unfolding in
front of her.

Next, Sir Bartle dipped his fingers in the animal's blood
and in turn, solemnly anointed the forehead of each robed
figure. As he made his way around the circle, he appeared to

be mumbling some incantations whose words Sophie could not quite catch.

The harper, Taf, suddenly abandoned his instrument and made his way unsteadily toward the group, muttering in a strange tongue Sophie took to be Welsh. As he approached the circle, the assembly made a deep bow, as if to a druid priest, and Taf held up his trembling, arthritic hands to the shrouded moon, murmuring a slow, rhythmic chant that grew gradually more intense as Darnly and a few others joined in, speaking in the tongue only they understood. The chorus of dissonant sounds sent shudders down Sophie's spine.

At length, another cloaked figure stumbled toward Old Taf, prodded forward by none other than Trevor Bedloe, swathed, like the others, in black. The prisoner was forced to kneel on the brown leaves that carpeted the grove while the elderly Welshman dipped his fingers into the carcass of the slaughtered animal and painted an obscure symbol on the forehead of the hostage.

Suddenly Sophie gasped and her hands flew to her face. The moon had emerged from behind a small curtain of mist and, for the first time, she had a distinct view of the pathetic animal sacrificed senselessly in this hideous rite.

"Oh no!" she whispered, stricken by the sight of a cat, its fur stained dark red. She raced across her chamber and snatched its litter mate Marmalade off the bottom of her bed. Sophie held the ball of fur tightly under her chin as tears streamed down her face.

Then, drawn inexorably back to the window, she gazed into the grove as Taf's bloodied hands fumbled with the tie securing the kneeling captive's cloak. With a dramatic gesture, he flung the garment aside, revealing the naked, trembling form of the housemaid, Glynnis. The woman slowly raised her head to the heavens, allowing her long hair to cascade down her glistening white shoulders and bare back. Her full, pendulous breasts heaved with fear—or excitement —as each man in turn stepped forward to caress some portion of her body.

Shaking uncontrollably, and fearing for the poor young woman's safety as well as her own, Sophie stumbled to the sideboard, poured a brandy and gulped it down. She splashed a second into her glass and ran over to her door, checking to be sure the bolt was shut tight. Then, with nary a glance outside, she secured every window, feeling light-headed from the spirits she had consumed so compulsively. Crawling into her four-poster, she pulled both the covers and the pillow over her head, clutched her cat to her bosom, and fervently prayed to be swiftly delivered from this foul Welsh den of iniquity.

"Sophie, dear, you must erase that worried frown from your lovely face," Rowena Darnly insisted, rearranging a clump of yew branches installed to the right of the small stage that now stood in Evansmor's great hall. "A bad dress rehearsal means a stunning first performance! You, of all people, must know that!"

But Sophie was hardly listening. Instead, her gaze was drawn to Glynnis, the housemaid, who was silently clearing away the tea things. Her long hair was tucked neatly beneath her housemaid's cap and her uniform was immaculate. Observing the young woman's composure, Sophie concluded that Darnly's servant must have derived some dark form of pleasure from having been the center of attention during the bizarre rite that had taken place earlier that week.

Roderick was about to excuse himself to consult with Mrs. Williams and her minions who were in the last stages of preparing for the final banquet.

"I beg your leave as well," his brother, Vaughn, said politely. "I plan to spend the rest of the day at the foundry, readying my mechanical pump for its first full-blown test tomorrow morning."

"I doubt, after this evening's festivities, you will garner much of an audience at the mine for such a feat at so early an hour," Roderick commented wryly.

"No matter," Vaughn shrugged. "Father is curious enough to see if it will function properly to have agreed to accompany me down the shaft to give it a go, and that's all that matters."

"Always anxious to please the guv'ner, aren't you,

brother?" Roderick drawled. "Well, if any of us can, 'twill be you, I have no doubt."

"With all your preoccupations this week," Sophie intervened hastily, "at least you and Vaughn have both learned your lines."

"Which is more than I can say for Sir Bartle," Vaughn said sympathetically.

Sophie stiffened at the mention of his name. A vision of the baronet plunging his knife into the gray cat's body flashed before Sophie's eyes. She silently berated herself for lacking the nerve at rehearsal to administer the dressing-down the man deserved for not having memorized one speech in its entirety, let alone for his barbarism toward that poor, defenseless creature.

"Now, not to worry, Sophie," Rowena hastened to assure her son's guest, whose frown had deepened. "I've chastised that reprobate so severely, Porter-Jones dare not show his face at dinner if he hasn't mastered his speeches by tonight. All will go swimmingly, I'm sure! And besides, tradition dictates that the playlets presented at these fetes contain a surprise or two."

"Surprise?" Sophie said, alarmed. "What do you mean *surprise*?"

"Oh, the cook tips up, dressed like a duchess," Vaughn explained, "or if someone among the company is truly in his cups, a pony may be led into the drawing room."

"Oh, dear," Sophie responded faintly.

"'Twill go swimmingly, I tell you," Rowena soothed. "'Tis all in good fun."

"Let us hope so." Sophie smiled wanly, her nerves still raw from the scene she had witnessed among the beeches near her cottage. All she wished for now was that this wretched house party would come to its expected conclusion and she would find herself on her way back to Half Moon Passage two days hence, as planned.

"Even the earl has deigned to join our company tonight," Rowena volunteered. "Something amusing is bound to take place."

"Can't you direct that confounded harper to stop twanging out those Welsh dirges?" demanded Basil, the Earl of Llewelyn.

The head of the Darnly household, whose height, though somewhat stooped, matched that of his second son, cast a disgusted glance in Old Taf's direction. The earl's scowl served only to emphasize his prominent eyebrows, the narrow furrow between them creating a single slash of grizzled hair. The soiled silk waistcoat covering his paunch forecast what Roderick himself might one day look like if he continued, as he had this night, to match his father in the consumption of claret and grouse.

"The bard sings of ancient battles, the great victories that secured the very castle you call home," Rowena added bitingly. "Surely, m'lord, you would not deny our sons their heritage?"

"But why deny *me* a respite from this infernal din?" Basil demanded. "When will they begin the play?" he asked of no one in particular. "Tell your cook, Roderick, that the cockle soup was off. I've got the beginnings of an ache in my gut, and now a headache to boot, from that infernal musician from hell." He cast a disgruntled look around the room as more guests filed in and selected their seats. "I've got to be up early, you know! I promised Vaughn I'd watch him make a fool of himself, didn't I son?" he declared, giving his heir a skeptical look from beneath his bushy gray eyebrows. When no one commented, he loudly thumped his gold-headed cane on the floor. "Roddy, for God's sake, man . . . tell that female scribe of yours to get your mincing friends on the boards and let's be done with it!"

The earl's booming voice blared over the assembled crowd and their low chattering ceased at once. In its place bloomed a sudden, embarrassed silence. Sophie, dying a thousand deaths, stood near a door adjacent to the stage in the great hall as Roderick, Vaughn, and Vaughn's bride of four months, Dilys, hastily entered the changing room to prepare for the play.

Dreading every second of the next half hour, Sophie nervously glanced down at her attire. She was dressed as a scullery maid whose task was to retrieve the downed birds from the mouth of a hunting dog, played by Vaughn, who was just donning a canine mask the same color as his bark brown suit. His bride, Dilys, looking as miserable as Sophie felt, had put on the apron of a cook into whose pot Sophie would soon be throwing an abundant number of dead grouse.

"All right, everyone!" Sophie hissed to the assembled players, "all I expect is that you do your best and help each other if one of you should forget your speeches," she added with a pointed look in the direction of Sir Bartle Porter-Jones, cast as the kennel master, and Trevor Bedloe, who appeared petrified—now that the time had come—of playing the role of the dog-owning laird in front of the irascible Earl of Llewelyn.

Roderick strode out and recited the prologue without missing a word, much to Sophie's relief. She smiled at him with heartfelt gratitude as the first players made their entrances and the one-act piece got underway.

The play had reached its halfway point when, out of the corner of Sophie's eye, she noticed Sir Bartle and Trevor Bedloe making unscheduled appearances. In lieu of his assigned kennel master's costume, the baronet had donned an elegant suit and sported a walking stick that could only belong to the earl himself. He had managed to attach bits of moss to his own eyebrows, giving him the unmistakable appearance of Roderick's sire. Walking arm-in-arm with Trevor Bedloe, who ad-libbed some nonsense about the prowess of his celebrated hound, Sir Bartle made his way toward Vaughn and executed a swift kick to the scion's backside. The supposed bird dog tumbled painfully to his chest, momentarily stunned by this unexpected bit of business.

Sophie shot a horrified glance at Roderick and Rowena as Sir Bartle began to swagger around the stage, insulting each player in turn. Finally, he approached Sophie and boldly reached out, pawing the front of her dress.

"Come here, my sweet scullery," he pronounced heartily, swiftly plunging his hands down the front of her bodice while from behind, Trevor pinned her arms against her sides. "Let me have a glimpse at those fair paps," Sir Bartle leered.

"Not quite a handful, are they, dear?" he declared bumptiously, cocking an exaggerated eyebrow in the direction of Sophie's chest. "Better yet!" he exclaimed effusively to his cohort, Trevor Bedloe, "where's the housemaid, Glynnis? 'Tis in *her* arms I always find I can forget that cursed wife of mine!"

There were nervous titters from some of Roderick's guests in the audience, but most of the assembly were staring at the earl to gauge his response.

"You *dare* to do this!" Roderick's father roared, leaping to his feet and shaking his cane at his second son, who stood frozen next to the panelled wall. "You *dare* insult me and your guest in my own *house!*"

"But, Father—" Roderick countered.

"Evansmor is Roddy's abode," Rowena spoke up boldly, overriding her son's attempt to defend himself.

"By God, it's *not!*" he shouted, glaring at his wife. "Not till I die, by that foul marriage contract I wish to Christ I'd never signed!" His eyes glittered with fury as he shouted at his son. "'Tis *you* who are behind this! Your mother is merely a maker of mischief, but you . . . you have always been a plague on my house! If you were not my own flesh and blood, I would call you out, you worthless puppy!"

"'Twas *my* little joke," Rowena insisted, her voice rising shrilly. She stared uneasily at her husband of nearly forty years. "'Tis traditional, as you well know, Basil," she said in a calmer tone intended to soothe the situation, "to be a bit larky at these events. I see you've not the stomach for it, and I'm sorry."

The earl utterly ignored his wife's mollifying words and turned, instead, to face the group gathered motionless on stage. Trevor's uncertain grin had faded and even the brazen Sir Bartle looked discomforted.

"You, Bedloe, are discharged forthwith! And without references!"

"But sir—" he began, looking from Rowena to Roderick, "I only—"

"Discharged, I say! Now get out, or I will have you shot for trespassing." He turned to the baronet from Henley. "Porter-Jones," he ordered, "you are to leave this house at

once! And you, Roderick," he added, addressing his second
son coldly, "will vacate these premises within the month.
You and your perverted friends can go back to the London
stews, where you belong. You'll have your two thousand a
year, but you'll not spend it under *this* roof!"

The Earl of Llewelyn drew himself up with more dignity
than Sophie would ever have imagined the cantankerous
man possessed. Turning to face the audience in Evansmor's
great hall, he scanned the collection of two dozen house-
guests whose mouths were all agape.

"Need I say, this evening is at an end!"

Loud pounding and insistent shouts roused Sophie from
a drugged sleep brought about by the brandy she'd deliberately consumed to blot out the calamitous evening.

"Sophie! Wake up! Sophie, 'tis *me* . . . Rowena
Darnly!" a voice cried at her door. Sophie lifted her head—
which felt stuffed with cotton wool—from the pillow and
pushed herself upright in bed. "Sophie! Is Roderick with
you?" Rowena pleaded, now shouting through the closed
window and rattling its frame. "There's been a dreadful accident at the mines! I must find Roderick!"

Sophie leapt up and fumbled for her dressing gown as she
raced for the door, flinging it open.

"He's not here, Countess," Sophie protested, "nor has he
been," she added, noticing Rowena's pony tied to a nearby
tree.

"He's not in his chambers!" Rowena cried distractedly.
"There's been a cave in! Basil and Vaughn . . ." her words
drifted off.

"Come in," Sophie said swiftly. "I'll just dress quickly
and help you search." She grabbed a simple wool gown from
a peg, forgetting her stays, and began to fasten the row of
buttons at the back of her bodice.

"Here, let me do that," the countess said grimly. "I was
hoping against hope he'd be with you, although I suppose
that was too much to wish for."

Sophie barely heard her remark as she mentally reviewed

places where Roderick might logically have ended such a dreadful evening.

"Shall you try the stables and I'll check the hay byre?" Sophie asked, donning the kid boots Roderick had provided her.

"Right!" the countess agreed, looking haggard and distraught. "I've got the entire household looking for him. If you don't find him, meet me back here in ten minutes' time," she commanded.

Sophie snatched a wool shawl off a chair and dashed into the chilly September morning. Several of Roderick's hunting dogs ran through the trees and barked at her heels, having escaped, she surmised, when Rowena checked the kennels for signs of her son. Yapping ecstatically, the hounds ran joyful circles around Sophie as she trotted in the direction of the hay byre fifty yards away.

When she reached it, she was panting from exertion. Attempting to catch her breath, she went round to a side door and cracked it open six inches. One of the hounds slipped through in a flash, its nose glued to the ground, sniffing intently. Sophie was about to open the door wider and enter the musty interior herself when her eyes widened in shock.

There, not twenty feet in front of her, lying on a mound of fresh hay, were three sleeping figures. Articles of clothing were strewn everywhere. Roderick and Trevor Bedloe slumbered side-by-side, naked and entwined in each other's arms. Snoring softly, with one thigh cast across her employer's flank, lay Glynnis, the housemaid.

I've managed it with jades like Mary Ann, but I must find out if— Roderick had cried in his drunken stupor the night of the haying fete.

Sophie stared at his nude form, an incipient paunch marring his otherwise well-proportioned build. He was twice the size of Trevor Bedloe in every way, and Sophie shuddered at the thought of what acts the three had committed during the hours she was asleep in her cottage bed.

The man must be utterly twisted, Sophie thought, recoiling from the sight that met her eyes this misty morn. Was he a lover of women or a lover of men . . . or perhaps merely a seducer of *both*, if licentious circumstances presented themselves, as they obviously had the previous night.

And yet she felt a strange sympathy for a man whose brutally disdainful father ignored him out of contempt for his artistic leanings. What did it do to a son, to see his brother so favored while he was despised?

She stared helplessly at the three naked forms that recalled to mind the foul engravings for *Fanny Hill*. As long as Roderick Darnly wasn't insensibly drunk, he had always been thoughtful and utterly correct in his manner toward her. And he had been so kind when little Danielle had died . . .

Unable to wrestle with the dark complexities of the Darnly clan, Sophie stumbled backward, her trembling hands quickly shutting the barn door. The hound trapped inside began barking frantically. The noise was certain to arouse his master, however dulled with spirits Roderick's brain might be. Instinctively, Sophie ran as fast as she could into the grove, hiding behind a fat hedge that bordered the beech trees.

Within five minutes, Roderick burst through the door Sophie had surreptitiously shut, hastily tucking his shirt into his wrinkled breeches. He was heading in the direction of the gardener's cottage just as Rowena rounded its vine-shrouded corner.

"Oh, God, Roddy!" she screamed. "Come quickly!" She was mounted on the pony she had ridden to Evansmor. "Basil and Vaughn are trapped in Number One shaft! Some timbers overhead apparently loosened when the pumping began, and a portion of the mine fell in. Hurry! Everyone's massing to try to dig them out."

Roderick's already pale face had turned ashen. He glanced around anxiously as his mother rode off, her pony's hooves throwing divots of grass in all directions. Meanwhile, Sophie ran pell-mell through the grove, emerging at the far end and then circling back toward the cottage.

"The countess told me what has happened," she panted, running to his side where he stood motionless near her door. "We've been looking for you everywhere. I thought you might be at the kennels. I've just come from there," she lied, anxious he should not know she was now privy to the morbid secrets of his private life.

"I was just—" he began, appearing unmistakably relieved.

"Come!" Sophie interrupted, firmly taking his arm. "I'm sure your mother's ordered the stable lads to saddle your mount."

Within minutes, she was riding behind him on his horse, her arms wrapped around Roderick's waist. She held on with all her strength as he thrashed the beast's sides and urged the steed up the rutted road that led to the bleak, windswept coal fields.

Men were already digging frantically by the time they arrived. Darnly threw himself off his horse, grabbed a shovel, and disappeared into the shaft. A clutch of women huddled around the countess, who was barking orders like a steward.

"All you women, take off your petticoats *now*, and we'll tear them for bandages. Mattie, make a big cauldron of tea, will you? And, Dilys, be a love and help her carry it back here, swiftly as you can," she commanded Vaughn's tearful young wife. "John, have your men find something that will serve as stretchers. Quickly, now!" she urged.

Slowly, painstakingly, the men carted away a ten-foot-square section of dirt fifty feet from beneath the surface, shoring up the tunnel with stout timbers as they made progress. Then, several miners with stretchers disappeared into the entrance of the shaft. Ten minutes later, two reappeared, carrying the earl, who seemed barely to be breathing. Sophie's eyes shifted to the sight of Roderick emerging from the mine, blinking slowly in the bright September sunshine that had broken through the clouds. His cheeks were bathed with moisture and in his arms he bore the broken, lifeless body of his twin brother. Vaughn's clothes were soaked through with water and his red hair was now completely covered with mud and black soot. In a kind of daze, Roderick stared straight ahead, as if seeing his future stretch before him.

Sophie battled all sorts of wild musings. Thanks to this tragedy, she thought, Roderick Darnly had suddenly become Viscount Glyn, heir to the estate of the father he so bitterly despised.

Chapter 25

April 1769

Sophie sat quietly on a stone bench, fingering a clutch of yellow daffodils. She gazed at the small granite slab that burrowed into the spring grass in a corner of St. Paul's churchyard. After three years, the sharp edges of her daughter's miniature headstone had been softened by gray-green lichen. Purple irises pushed their heads through the mounded earth near Danielle's resting place. Glancing down at the yellow petals she held in her lap, Sophie wondered if spring had come to Wales, gracing poor Vaughn Darnly's grave near Glynmorgan Castle with flowers like these.

She heaved a sigh, struggling to put out of her mind both the vision of Roderick carrying his brother's battered body out of the Darnly mine, and her memory of the forlorn bouquet of violets strewn on her daughter's burial plot by Hunter on the eve of his angry departure from London in 1766. These dual recollections invariably haunted her whenever she visited this quiet spot sequestered from the normal bustle of the Covent Garden district.

Long mayst thou live to wail thy children's death.

Would she ever be forgiven Hunter's stinging condemnation?

Suddenly, Sophie was startled by the touch of a hand on her shoulder.

"Hello, my dear," a familiar voice said gently. "How good it is to see you this fine spring day."

She turned with a start and found herself looking up into the penetrating gaze of David Garrick.

"H-hello," she stammered, unnerved at meeting Garrick in the churchyard where her daughter was buried. She had been too embarrassed by her long silence these last years to call on him when she returned from Wales. Also, she wondered what the Drury Lane impresario would think of her having traveled to Swansea with Roderick Darnly? She'd been back in London more than seven months now, yet she'd once again become a recluse, declining, out of some numbing inertia, to renew old ties.

"I'm just on my way to the theater," Garrick informed her with a smile, "and I saw you through the iron fence. Kitty Clive is bidding adieu to the theatrical profession in her farewell performance tonight—making her exit before the cheering stops, she says. Intelligent of her, don't you think?"

Sophie merely nodded, unable to speak. A further assault of memories had rendered her tongue-tied.

"'Tis been too long, Sophie," Garrick volunteered quietly as he took a seat beside her on the churchyard bench. "We've all missed you."

"I've missed you too . . ." she replied, looking down so Garrick wouldn't see the tears that suddenly filled her eyes.

It was strange. Except for the terrible day she had found Hunter's note, she had hardly shed a tear since Danielle had been laid in the ground not ten feet from where they sat. Yet seeing Garrick again after so long an interval made her feel as if she wanted to weep like a child.

"Have you been writing any plays in that garret of yours?" he asked, nodding in the direction of her lodgings.

Sophie blinked and swallowed hard. Garrick's kindness never failed to touch her. Despite the man's strongly held views regarding proper decorum inside the theater itself, David Garrick had never seemed to judge her harshly—despite her ill-fated marriage and estrangement from Peter. And he always appeared interested in her play-writing efforts.

Suddenly, she felt ashamed of the way in which she had retreated from many such friendly overtures during the last three years. Worst of all, Sophie had simply allowed former confidantes, like Garrick and her friend Lorna Blount, to drift out of her life.

"I've done very little writing . . ." she acknowledged slowly, thinking back to her one-act comedy that had been performed at Evansmor with such disastrous consequences. Roderick Darnly had been so distracted in the aftermath of his twin brother's death and his father's virtual incapacitation, that he had seemed relieved by her request to travel to London on her own. Disclosing he would remain in Wales indefinitely to see to his family estate, he had generously provided the funds for her return trip—and then some. She had been anxious to escape a place so abruptly plunged into mourning, but found, once back in London, that she simply hadn't the heart to pick up her pen and enlarge on the few dusty pages of *The Bogus Baronet* lying in a drawer in her desk upstairs. "Ever since Hunter—since Danielle died," she finally managed to tell Garrick, "I-I've had difficulty . . . especially with comedy . . ." she confessed with a rueful smile. What she didn't tell her old friend was that simply returning to the capital had stirred up too many unhappy memories.

Garrick leaned toward her on the stone bench.

"To any other woman, the death of a child or the loss of a love is dreadfully sad, but . . . to a writer, 'tis also the *stuff* of tragedy. Why not put those feelings . . . that heartbreak I know pains you so deeply into a play you *believe* in?"

Sophie felt a kind of inward tumult.

Dissect Danielle's death and its circumstances in order to present it as a play? Tell the world Hunter considered her a murderess? Dear God, she'd kill herself first!

"I-I couldn't!" she cried.

"Perhaps not yet," he said, "but trust me. These trials that life provides are, in the end, a source of inspiration for the artist. Don't squander them."

Despite her efforts at self-control, Sophie again felt tears begin to fill her eyes.

"Forgive me," she said in a tight voice. "'Tis just . . ."

"I know, Sophie . . . I know," he assured her softly.

"Excuse me, sir," she replied tersely, "but you *cannot* know."

"About that talented young man, Hunter Robertson, and how his abrupt departure wounded you so?" he asked sharply. "Of course I know. Melodramatic gestures such as leaving quotes at grave sites are the grist of gossip in our tightly knit theatrical community. I also know 'twas no one's fault your babe expired, except perhaps that drunkard husband of yours—the so-called baronet. That Phillips woman told the entire neighborhood how that blackguard arrived at your doorstep without an invitation and carrying the ague."

"But Hunter thought I had reconciled with—"

"I'm sure he did, the young peacock!" Garrick snapped. Then he smiled and said in a gentler voice. "I observed long before your marriage to Peter Lindsay that there was a genuine rapport between you and young Robertson. Can't you and he untangle this misunderstanding?"

"I fear 'tis gone on too long to be a mere misunderstanding," Sophie sighed. "'Tis not jealousy on Hunter's part . . . 'tis something to do with Danielle's death, I think. Something that runs deep . . . deep in his own childhood."

"I think someday soon he'll come to see that he's grievously misjudged your conduct," Garrick said reassuringly. "Meanwhile, the lad is cutting quite a swath with audiences in Bath."

"He's in *Bath*?" Sophie blurted. "You've seen him?"

"Yes . . . when I was taking the waters there for the gout this spring. I discovered he'd come there after a year in nearby Bristol. He's taken on some of the managerial duties at the Orchard Street Theater as well as mounting musical afterpieces."

"You saw him . . . you actually saw him perform?" she said faintly, his words triggering vivid recollections of the spa town.

"I delivered him my personal congratulations back stage," Garrick replied. "He'll soon smooth his feathers and return to London. Perhaps next season. At least that's what I *hope* he'll do. I suggested that he come see me before summer's end and he said he would consider it."

Sophie felt her spirits uncharacteristically lighten. Then she frowned. Hunter's returning to London was no guarantee he would ever understand what had happened about Danielle, or truly forgive her for her role in the child's death.

"Now . . . may I tell you a little secret?" Garrick asked with a twinkle in his expressive eyes.

"What?" Sophie replied.

"Soon, I am to be made a Freeman of the City of Stratford-upon-Avon and given a medal! In return, the city fathers wish me to provide—at my own expense, naturally—a statue of William Shakespeare destined for the new town hall, along with a portrait of myself."

"How wonderful!" Sophie enthused, happy to change the subject. "But they should do more than simply hang a medal around your neck, sir, for all you've done to revive interest in Shakespeare's plays. They should name the *building* after you!"

Garrick looked at her mischievously.

"I think so too!" he laughed. "Matter of fact, when they present the actual medal to me on the eighth of May, I have decided to propose a jubilee be held in late summer in Stratford itself. 'Twill honor the two hundredth birthday of the Bard, give or take a few years, plus laud the city from whence he sprang—not to mention"—Garrick put his hand over his heart and bent at the waist in a mock bow—"also pay homage to your faithful servant, who believes that a celebration of Shakespeare's birth is just the thing to launch the '69, '70 theatrical season at Old Drury. What think you, lass?"

Sophie clapped her hands and laughed delightedly.

Garrick looked at her narrowly. "How would you like to be part of the preparations?" he said. "I could use a good scribe, someone with general skills who could tackle everything from getting orders printed up when we needed them, to dealing with the details I won't have time for."

"It sounds wonderful, but I—"

"You must help me coax those balky actors into trekking to Stratford at their own expense. I plan to stage a grand costume parade of Shakespeare's characters," he announced, "right in the streets of Stratford itself! I'll use players from *all* the theaters—Old Drury, Covent Garden, Edinburgh, Bristol . . . *Bath,*" he added with a sly smile. "They'll all want to be part of it, if we can just make them think 'twill be good for their careers. I expect *you* to help me make actors like Hunter Robertson see it that way."

Garrick's eyes were shining and Sophie knew the great showman was already visualizing the details of his festival.

Sophie hesitated, wondering if she could afford to volunteer her time, despite the worthiness of the project.

"I shall make you a paid member of my staff, of course," he assured her. "Since you've given up the book shop, I would hope you could come to Stratford with my brother, George, and me to survey the site of the festivities. Perhaps you two could remain there to oversee things until I am able to rejoin you late in the summer. Do I have your support?"

Sophie was touched both by Garrick's boyish enthusiasm and his generous desire to include her in his fanciful plans.

"Of course I'll help you, sir," she said finally.

"Splendid!" he crowed, "and now I must be off . . . curtain time approaches, you know."

She offered him the bouquet of daffodils she was holding in her hand.

"Perhaps you'd deliver these to Kitty Clive this evening," she asked solemnly. "Please extend my heartiest congratulations for her extraordinary career as an actress—*and* a playwright."

"Why not come with me now and deliver them yourself?" he replied with a smile. "She's often asked after you."

❈

Throughout the tumultuous summer of 1769, Sophie never ceased speculating whether Hunter Robertson would heed Garrick's call for "Actors of Merit" to come to Stratford-upon-Avon and participate in the very first Shakespeare Jubilee.

Nearly five months to the day after her encounter with David Garrick in St. Paul's churchyard, she stared apprehensively out a window of Stratford's White Lion Inn, her home during the period of feverish preparations.

"Oh no! Not more rain!" she groaned, eyeing the dark,

foreboding clouds that blanketed the skies overhead, threatening yet another round of thundershowers. Except for a few pleasant days in July, the festival planners had been confronted with months of appallingly damp weather.

On this Saturday morning, the second of September— four days before the official opening of the Jubilee—Sophie sat sipping black coffee with Mr. Latimore, designer of the Rotunda, an octagon-shaped, fifteen-hundred-seat wooden structure where many of the Jubilee activities would be held. Through the diamond panes in the large window illuminating the inn's coffee room, they watched scores of newly arrived waiters, hairdressers, itinerate tradesmen, and as expected, prostitutes bustling down Stratford's narrow streets. One heavily painted tart had already staked out territory on Henley Street and was busy soliciting customers in front of William Shakespeare's birthplace.

Suddenly, two runaway horses thundered by a few feet from the leaded window where Sophie and Latimore were sitting. Wild-eyed and nostrils flaring, the fugitive steeds frantically sought an escape from the tumult in the streets.

"Someone's bound to be run down!" Sophie worried aloud. "And *where* will all these people find shelter, especially if it rains again?" she demanded of her colleague. For weeks now, the drenching weather had delayed preparations for nearly every aspect of the Jubilee.

"They'll sleep in their coaches, if need be," Latimore sighed.

"If they *have* coaches," Sophie rejoined. "A journalist from London told me last evening that people were paying a fortune for beds in henhouses and alms tenements—in spite of all those bedsteads we've imported from London," she complained.

She looked for some further reassurance from Latimore, but the beleaguered architect merely sipped the last of his Turkish brew. Obviously, the poor man was bracing himself for his return to the Rotunda to supervise the finishing touches on his temporary masterpiece.

Just then, the clamor of bells rang out, officially heralding the arrival of members of the "quality" to the small market town. A raft of dukes and duchesses had already come to

Stratford, along with half a dozen earls and untold numbers of lesser peers and peeresses.

"Let's hope the toffs are reveling in their humble surroundings," Latimore commented finally. "Perhaps they'll consider the entire adventure a lark."

"I only pray they do," Sophie muttered.

Just then, one of Latimore's workmen burst into the coffee room.

"Sir! Sir! Mr. and Mrs. Garrick have arrived!" he exclaimed. "They're lodging in William Hunt's house on Church Street and bid you join them there."

Sophie and the architect leapt to their feet, nearly upsetting the small table where they'd been sitting.

"Thank heavens he's here!" Latimore said fervently.

Sophie felt a surge of excitement in place of the anxiety that had gripped her during these final weeks of preparation. Garrick had arrived! The Shakespeare Jubilee was about to get under way.

"Here's the revised schedule of events," Garrick said briskly as he handed Sophie a piece of foolscap covered with notes. Ever since his arrival he had been directing the final preparations like an army general from both his lodgings at William Hunt's house and from an apartment provided for his use by the owner of the White Lion Inn. Now that the Drury Lane manager was in command, Sophie had hopes that everything would somehow come together before the next day's opening ceremonies. "I want you to run off the program at Fulk Weale's printing shop right away," he directed, "so that the list of tomorrow's opening day events are distributed to every door in Stratford by tonight."

"Yes, sir," Sophie replied, glancing anxiously out the sitting room window at the ominous gray clouds roiling overhead. Rain had been pelting the village of Stratford intermittently since Saturday, but thus far today, there had been no serious downpours. In less than twenty-four hours, the event they'd all worked the entire summer to create would begin.

"And has Mr. Jackson of Tavistock Street arrived with

costumes to let for the masquerade ball?" Garrick inquired sharply.

"One hundred and fifty cases of them—and he's *doubled* his normal fees," Sophie replied tersely.

"Can't be helped," Garrick replied with a wave of his hand. "I've just been informed Charles Dibdin has arrived," he continued, referring to the mercurial composer whose works had been commissioned especially for the Jubilee. "I've instructed him to rehearse this evening with the flutists, guitarists, and singers who, God willing, will coax the visitors out of their beds tomorrow morning in time for the opening ceremonies at eight o'clock. I want you to make sure that Dibdin's 'Dawn Serenade' will actually begin at *dawn*! Speak to him tonight at his rehearsal in Town Hall."

"Yes, sir," Sophie repeated, wondering if the chorus would be loud enough to drown out the sounds of frantic hammering now reverberating throughout the village as last-minute projects raced toward completion.

Unfortunately, Garrick's brother, George, had spent the better part of the summer supping with cronies and drinking port with Mr. French, the artist charged with painting banners and silk transparencies. Various projects had gotten so far behind by late August that David Garrick had dispatched fifty-eight carpenters from London at extraordinarily high wages to meet the deadline.

By late Tuesday afternoon, Sophie was dismayed to see a new layer of heavy clouds gathering in the darkening sky. A chill wind blew against her cloak as she rounded the High Street and the temperature seemed to drop suddenly by several degrees. However, both the townsfolk and visitors appeared oblivious to the elements and remained gathered around crackling bonfires on nearly every street corner. On the Avon, flotillas of river craft had begun tying up at the quays and every available docking spot. The rattle of arriving coaches and the staccato of premature fireworks elicited a kind of excitement that Sophie hadn't felt in ages.

On this evening before the official commencement of festivities, candles glowed in the windows of the newly constructed Town Hall as Sophie mounted the steps leading to the stone edifice. The air was filled with the sound of singers practicing the "Dawn Serenade" to the accompaniment of strumming guitars and softly beating drums.

Let Beauty with the Sun arise,
To Shakespeare Tribute pay,
With heavenly Smiles and sparkling Eyes,
Give Grace and Luster to the Day.

Sophie paused at the door to the large room where the city fathers would eventually be holding their deliberations. In the amber light cast by wall sconces, the musicians played a rich melody, and the singers' voices blended lushly with guitar arpeggios enlivened by the flutes' counterpoint.

Then, a tall young man with dark blond hair that was pulled back and fastened at the nape of the neck stepped forward. Sophie found herself staring directly into Hunter Robertson's piercing blue eyes as he began to sing a solo.

Each Smile she gives protects his Name,
What Face shall dare to frown?
Not Envy's Self can blast the Fame,
Which Beauty deigns to Crown.

Sophie's mouth had gone dry and she clasped her hands together to stop them from trembling. She tried to pull her gaze away from Hunter's face, but she could not, frozen as she was by the shock of seeing him in the flesh. It was one thing to fantasize about his coming to the Shakespeare festivities, quite another to have him standing ten feet away. She sensed a familiar feeling of suffocation begin to descend on her as she recalled his damning words blaming her for Danielle's death. She inhaled deeply, trying to steady her nerves, wishing only to escape from Hunter's presence—and his censure.

He returned to the company of singers as the chorus continued with the song. At its conclusion, Sophie quickly approached Charles Dibdin to confirm he had, indeed, scheduled his minstrels to perform at the crack of dawn.

"The music is absolutely lovely," Sophie hurriedly assured the composer. "Mr. Garrick looks forward to your serenade at dawn's light . . . and so do I. I bid you good night."

She spun on her heel, preparing to leave the building at a dead run, when a steadying hand settled on her shoulder.

"Hello, Sophie," Hunter said, gazing down at her intently. "Do you think our morning concert will roust everyone out of bed, as intended?" He spoke in an even, controlled voice, in total contrast to the angry shouts he'd hurled at her in front of her book shop three years earlier.

"I-I'm sure the music will have its proper effect," she stammered, backing toward the door. "I'm a-afraid I must be off . . . I've a number of chores still to do for Mr. G—" she said inanely and bolted for the exit.

The following morning, there was virtually no sunrise to greet Dibdin and his minstrels' rendition of "Dawn Serenade." Thick, gray clouds all but obscured the horizon. Sophie was roused from the comfort of her feather bed by the thunderous sound of thirty cannons blasting away on the banks of the Avon at six A.M. Volley after volley was fired, followed by church bells that tolled for at least ten minutes. She speculated that only those residents of Stratford who were stone deaf could possibly continue to slumber after such a clamor.

She slipped out from under the covers, pulled the counterpane off the bed and wrapped it around her shoulders to shield against the dank morn. She opened her window and peered into the stable yard, giggling at the sight of carriages that suddenly began to bounce and sway. At one coach window appeared a befuddled gentleman with a tousled wig; at another, an elderly crone, now nearly bald, who had sensibly removed her hairpiece before retiring for the night.

Dibdin and his singers, dressed in tattered clothes, masked and smeared with grime to represent innocent country lads, marched into the innkeeper's yard and began one of a series of short concerts intended to wake the honored guests lodged about the town.

Staring down into the muddy stable yard, Sophie instantly recognized the tall figure towering over the rest of the musical troupe. "Dawn Serenade" began and Sophie found herself exchanging stares with Hunter throughout the song. At the conclusion of the brief performance, cheers resounded from the carriages and from windows thrown open for the early morning recital.

Most of the performers waved gaily to Sophie as they departed, but Hunter stood rooted to the spot. Sophie felt herself begin to tremble once again at the mere sight of him standing there, not twenty paces from her window. Then he bowed slightly and proffered a solemn salute before striding off with his colleagues through the gateway that led to Henley Street. With trilling flutes and strumming guitars the minstrels headed for William Hunt's house to serenade the Garricks on this opening day of the Jubilee.

Shaken by this encounter, Sophie dressed quickly while making a valiant attempt to keep her thoughts on the business at hand. She made her way to the Town Hall as quickly as she could after being jostled by the milling crowds overflowing the streets. She passed Kitty Clive, the Duke of Dorset, the Duke of Manchester, and a gaggle of earls and countesses, all elbowing their way through the throng to secure a decent seat for the opening ceremonies and the breakfast to follow.

Blessed St. Ninian, 'tis as crowded as a Drury Lane first night! Sophie thought excitedly. Garrick's name and prestige had drawn actors and visitors from all over Britain!

She spotted George Colman, Garrick's one-time friend, now his rival as one of the patent holders at Covent Garden Theater. He was busily scribbling notes on a folded piece of foolscap. Sophie had caught a glimpse of him the evening before in the parlor of the White Lion, handing a messenger his daily report on events in Stratford for a London paper. She wondered how charitable he would be.

"Why Sophie McGann!" Colman hailed her. "You're the very person I should talk to." His cool, appraising glance told her that if she wasn't careful, he would use what she might say as a means of insulting her employer. "As you've been here these past months, assisting the Great Garrick in preparing for this grand event . . . you must tell me . . .

is it *true* that the locals charge a shilling if one asks them the time?"

"Well, good morning, Mr. Colman! So nice to see you in Stratford!" Sophie responded sweetly. "No . . . that's not been my experience at all. But, 'tis time for the breakfast, and I fear I must be off. Enjoy the Jubilee, sir!"

"Oh, I shall, indeed," Colman called after her. "I've seen enough tomfoolery at this festival to supply me with plots for a thousand farces!"

As Sophie mounted the steps to the Town Hall, a carnival atmosphere had gripped the crowd. Banners flew on buildings everywhere, and tradesmen were hawking souvenir medals, caged birds and all manner of "memorial" bric-a-brac. Perhaps the Jubilee *was* part flummery and nonsense, calculated to please the crowds and not just lovers of literature. Even so, Sophie told herself, Garrick would have been more than pleased to balance this type of frivolity with more substantive celebrations. Conspicuously missing from this event, however, were the serious Shakespearean scholars Garrick had hoped to attract: Dr. Samuel Johnson and other leading members of his circle, including the detestable Edward Capell. As for Dr. Johnson's greatest admirer, Jamie Boswell, Sophie doubted he would appear, lest he offend his mentor.

In fact, many of Garrick's presumed allies had actually waxed vituperative about his efforts to mount a Shakespeare Jubilee and had shunned the event. A mere actor as Keeper of the Flame of the Immortal Shakespeare? The scholars were appalled. To Sophie, one word explained it all: *envy.*

"Sophie, my dear," David Garrick greeted her as she entered the assembly room, "you've done a marvelous job of distributing the programs. Just *look* at those crowds!" He was dressed in the height of fashion, wearing a suit of amber velvet with a long cream silk waistcoat, which sported gold buttons down the front. His hands were sheathed in white doeskin gloves reputed to have belonged to the Bard himself. "Have you any extra copies? I'm sure there are people to whom you could hand them at the door."

"Yes, I brought extras . . . I'll just go to my post." She smiled encouragingly, for her mentor had a distracted air.

Suddenly, brass trumpets announced the arrival of the mayor. John Meacham was accompanied by his alderman and burgesses, resplendent in their official velvet robes and hats. William Hunt, the town clerk, presented Garrick with his staff of office as the steward of the festivities.

"Huzzah! Huzzah!" rang out the throng, packed cheek by jowl into the assembly room.

Garrick patted the medal, grasped the wand firmly and made a bow to the spectators much as he would opening night at Drury Lane.

"I accept with the greatest pleasure this honor you have done me and shall do all in my power to prove my veneration of Shakespeare and my great regard for all of you."

As he finished speaking, the cannons on the riverbanks boomed once again and the town bells rang clamorously. By half past ten everyone—peer and commoner alike—poured out into the road and paraded down Chapel Street, thence down Old Town Lane and into the gray stone church, the Gothic spire of which jutted toward the glowering clouds swirling above. As she entered the nave, Sophie offered a blasphemous prayer to the rain gods to hold off the downpour that was threatening to drench Shakespeare's devotees.

Inside Trinity Church, adjacent to the playwright's grave, while the oratorio "Judith" was in its final chorus, an extraordinary figure emerged from the gloom near the nave where Sophie stood. The man was covered in mud and dirt, his matted hair straggling about his ears. His suit was of black cloth, damp and horribly stained.

The apparition walked toward Sophie and whispered hoarsely, "Sophie?"

"Yes?" she replied, squinting in the gloom to try to make out who exactly this creature could be. "*Bozzy?*" Sophie exclaimed, and then clamped her hands over her mouth.

"*Shhh!*" he hissed. "I am *incognito*! Where is Garrick?"

"Over there," she replied, suppressing the desire to laugh hysterically. Certainly the Shakespeare scholars would never recognize him.

The oratorio had just concluded to warm applause, and members of the audience were beginning to dribble out the door into the misty churchyard.

"Is Hunter here?" Boswell inquired cautiously.

"He just sang in the oratorio," she replied stiffly, pointing in the direction of a group of singers milling about the nave. Then she stared once more at Boswell's outrageous attire. "Pray, *why* are your clothes in such a state, Jamie?"

"I've been riding all night . . . 'tis raining buckets to the east . . . ah, there's Garrick," and without another word, the Man of Letters strode straight toward the Man of the Hour who, after a startled greeting, gallantly welcomed him.

Sophie soon was swept along with complete strangers in yet another procession—without any sense of rank or precedence—that marched up Old Town Lane to Henley Street where public homage was paid to Shakespeare's birthplace located next to the White Lion Inn.

By four o'clock, hundreds of people were crammed into the Rotunda where dinner was served from the temporary kitchens nearby. Sophie grew alarmed at the undercurrent of grumbling she heard around her when John Payton, the owner of the White Lion tacked on another ten shillings six pence for the meal itself, even for Jubilee ticket holders. Fortunately, the danger passed when the hungry crowd tucked into their meal.

Following supper, a concert of popular songs written in honor of Shakespeare and the Jubilee itself was presented for the crowd's amusement. Sophie found it painful both to watch Hunter bewitch an entire throng with a roundelay about the Bard's mulberry tree and to hear the rich full sound of his baritone rolling over the heads of his rapt audience.

> . . . *Bend to thee,*
> *Blessed Mulberry,*
> *Matchless was he*
> *Who planted Thee,*
> *And thou like him immortal be!*

Hunter's familiar, teasing smile, which he bestowed liberally on his audience, eventually came to rest on Sophie, only serving to make her more miserable. His warm, friendly gaze was part of his performance, she told herself bleakly, a fact that wounded her all the more. Anxious to escape the sound of Hunter's voice resonating in her ears, she swiftly left the Rotunda.

Golden beams of light from the candles glowing inside the amphitheater cast a bright path across the swirling waters of the Avon. Piles of firewood that had been heaped high in the surrounding meadow were being set alight, and soon the entire riverbank was awash in a saffron glow.

By the time she reached Meer Pool Lane, dusk had descended on the village. On each street corner a bonfire blazed, highlighting the bright flags and bunting that hung everywhere. Most thoroughfares sported at least one window draped with an illuminated silk painting depicting a Shakespeare play. Brightly burning lamps positioned behind the thin fabric cast purple, crimson and blue shades into the night.

Inside Fulk Weale's printing shop, Sophie handed the proprietor her list of the following day's events and watched while he set the program in type.

"Please instruct the lads to slip the programs *under* the door sills . . . I think we shall have rain tonight," Sophie predicted.

"Aye, mistress," he nodded obediently as she took her leave.

Sophie returned directly to Henley Street, exhausted from the sheer tension of the opening day's festivities and most especially from Hunter's presence in Stratford. She crawled into bed and eventually drifted off to sleep using a pillow over her ears to blot out the lilting sound of minuets being played in endless succession at the Opening Day Ball held in the Rotunda a few blocks away.

Sophie awoke to the clanging of church bells, the explosion of the ubiquitous cannons, and the steady sound of rain streaming down in torrential sheets.

"Oh, no!" she wailed, leaping out of bed. "The Pageant!"

The program Fulk Weale had printed the previous night foretold a gala, costumed procession of Shakespeare's characters through Stratford's streets, ending at Latimore's Rotunda. There Garrick would recite his *Ode to Shakespeare,* accompanied by a full orchestra.

The timbers under Sophie's bare feet felt dank and clammy, and a dark expanding circle of moisture tinged the walls surrounding the small window that looked out over the stable yard. Rain-swollen clouds slicked the thatch roofs with sheets of water that emptied noisily into the gutters and trenches along the roads, pooling into mammoth puddles everywhere.

"Jesu!" she groaned aloud. "'Tis raining *bloody buckets*!"

She scrambled into her clothes and donned her cloak, draping most of it over her head to prevent her hair from getting drenched on her way to the college, an old monastic building serving as the staging area for the Parade of Shakespeare Characters. By the time she arrived within its great stone walls across from Trinity Church, some two hundred actors, along with local volunteers, huddled in the damp in various stages of undress. Costumes lay about in heaps, and dozens of children ran around the great hall in a frenzy of excitement at being asked to participate in the great parade.

"I can't find my witch's wig!" bleated a hawk-faced Stratford matron to Sophie. "Where are the *wigs*? I must have one, you know!"

"'Scuse me, miss, but George Garrick said you'd know where the swords are kept," demanded a gentleman in a Roman toga. He pointed at his belted paunch. "I'm one of the senators who's supposed to stab Caesar. Without a sword, I can't do the foul deed!"

Sophie's heart sank when she spied George Garrick himself scurrying around the room from one disorganized group to another, hopelessly attempting to reestablish order.

"Quite chaotic, isn't it?" an amused voice remarked behind Sophie. She whirled around and found herself staring up at an elegantly dressed Prospero, Duke of Milan, from Shakespeare's *The Tempest.* "Will I see you at the masquerade ball this evening?" Hunter inquired calmly.

"The ball?" Sophie echoed blankly, her nerves raw from the disaster that seemed ready to befall the Jubilee and its planners.

But before Sophie could respond, David Garrick strode

into the vast hall, accompanied by his wife and his Drury Lane partner, James Lacy.

"I beg your leave," Sophie replied to Hunter hastily, grateful for an interruption that would spare her the embarrassment of trying to make small talk. "I must attend Mr. Garrick."

She rushed to her employer's side, only to be met by a horrifying sight. The celebrated face of Drury Lane's actor-manager was severely nicked in several places and Mrs. Garrick was fluttering around her husband, attempting to staunch the blood with her lace handkerchief.

Acknowledging Sophie's shocked expression, Garrick explained, "that blasted barber was still in his cups from last night's celebration when he shaved me this morning." Sophie could see that he was tired and his voice sounded hoarse.

"Now, now, Davy," Mrs. Garrick consoled him. "I'll just find the kitchen and brew you a cup of tea . . . 'twill sooth your sore throat."

Suddenly James Boswell pushed through the throng, brandishing some verses he had written during the night on the subject of his recent book about the plight of Corsica. He apparently intended to distribute his poem among the patrons of the fancy dress ball.

"Ah . . . David . . . just the man I need to see," Boswell declared. "I'd like to read you these rhymes about the tyranny afflicting my beloved adopted land—*Cor-si-ca*!"

"Oh, Bozzy! Good heavens!" Sophie remonstrated crossly. "The man has a day filled with responsibilities ahead of him, including reciting his *own* verses!"

James Lacy, utterly ignoring Boswell and Sophie, complained loudly, "God's wounds, Davy! These costumes will be *ruined* if you expose 'em to such wretched weather! They're tatty enough as it is!" he added, pointing to a cloak whose threadbare velvet and worn fur would do little to create theatrical magic if exposed in the light of day. "I've said from the very first, this was a moronic idea, planned for the wrong time of the year, set in a ridiculous country town . . . I say we quit! Abandon this folly!"

"*No!*" roared David Garrick in the first show of violent temper Sophie had ever seen from him.

Lacy blinked, startled by his partner's vehement reaction.

"Be reasonable, Davy," he said in a more conciliatory fashion. "Who the devil would hold the procession in this weather? All the ostrich feathers will be spoiled and our property damage will come to easily five thousand pounds! 'Tis folly, I tell you!"

"Ladies and gentlemen!" Garrick boomed over the noisy, milling throng made up of legitimate and would-be thespians. "Your attention please!"

Sophie worried that Garrick's badly strained voice would soon give out completely and admonished people near her to be quiet.

"The Shakespeare Procession will be postponed until tomorrow, for obvious reasons," he bellowed, amid groans from the half-dressed participants. "Please remove your costumes carefully and return to the amphitheater forthwith. Chorus and orchestra members . . . report immediately to the Rotunda. The *Ode to Shakespeare* will commence in a half hour's time!"

Mass confusion descended on the entire proceedings. Sophie lost sight of Hunter as she broke into a run in an effort to catch up to David Garrick. Within the hour he would be risking his entire reputation—as an actor and as the impresario of the Jubilee itself—before an audience of drenched, disgruntled Shakespeare lovers.

Chapter 26

The rain continued to pour down in torrential sheets as Sophie sloshed through the muck behind Garrick. The meadow in which the wooden Rotunda stood had become a muddy quagmire, and the river Avon was now lapping perilously close to the corner of the amphitheater. Sodden crowds were filing gloomily into the auditorium—many cold and hungry.

Inside Sophie immediately spotted Hunter among the hundred members of the chorus and orchestra arrayed around the statue of Shakespeare, the one commissioned and paid for by David Garrick. The conductor, Dr. Arne, took his place, baton raised, preparing to conduct the overture he had composed for the occasion. In the center of the front row of singers was a large gilt armchair with a high back. At this point, it seemed less like a throne for the finest Shakespearean actor the world had ever known, and more like an execution block.

Suddenly, the phalanx of cannons positioned along the river unleashed another tremendous volley. Garrick walked purposefully to the front of the orchestra and sat on the gilded seat.

Sophie found herself clutching the edges of her soggy cloak in anguished apprehension. Could Garrick, nursing a sore throat, still summon his wondrous voice? Could he possibly tame this drenched and angry crowd?

Dr. Arne lowered his baton and the orchestra plunged

into the booming overture. As the last musical notes faded, Garrick rose, bowed, and began to recite his *Ode to Shakespeare* in an atmosphere that was suddenly charged with palpable excitement.

> *To what blest genius of the isle*
> *Shall Gratitude her tribute pay . . . ?*

A swelling chorus of singers blended behind Garrick's words, their voices conjuring up the poignancy and wit—the sheer brilliance—of the greatest writer in the English language. Garrick's ode was a compilation of lines from both the poetry and plays, allowing the actor freedom to interpret a dozen aspects of Shakespeare's art—along with his own.

As the ensemble interwove the spoken word with music and song, Sophie suddenly recalled Thomas Sheridan's exclamation at his final lecture on elocution delivered in the Edinburgh operating theater so many years earlier.

Never forget! English is the language of the immortal Shakespeare! And whoever has command of this man's mother tongue, has command of much in this world!

On this rain-drenched September day, David Garrick had never been more in command of his audience. For Sophie, the sounds caressing her ears were like a healing balm. Something was happening to her, something startling and full of renewal.

Certainly, she could never dare to consider herself a writer in Shakespeare's class, or anything approaching him, but she loved her native language and felt a sudden desire to return to play writing. Her eyes glistened as she absorbed the sounds of Garrick's magical voice, so powerful, so controlled. By the time Garrick delivered his concluding lines, which resonated with his love and reverence for the playwright whose works had made Garrick himself the toast of his age, the entire audience had been beguiled out of its apathy and forgot its soggy feet.

As the last notes of music faded, Garrick rose from his gilded chair. He stood motionless in the hall that was now completely silent except for the steady downpour on the Rotunda's roof. He was alone—without costume, without paint—and his performance had been a triumph. He simply bowed and the spectators went wild.

With tears streaming down her face, Sophie watched as the audience in one body stood on its feet and applauded rapturously. As the tumultuous clapping continued to thunder in her ears, she made her escape. David Garrick had saved the Jubilee, but Sophie McGann still had tomorrow's program to deliver to the printer's shop on a mud-soaked Stratford street. And then there was the question of Hunter Robertson and tonight's masquerade ball.

Sophie procured a candle stub, along with a bowl of hot pottage from the kitchen, and carried both to her little room adjacent to the stable yard. Painstakingly, she made a fire on the hearth and lit the wick of a tall candle on the table next to her bed. As mellow light filled the low-ceilinged chamber, she noticed a large box resting on her mattress. Curious, she pried off the top and stared at its contents.

Lying neatly folded inside the carton was a finely wrought, filmy costume made of shimmering sage green silk with pale satin streamers cascading from the shoulders, cuffs and beneath the bosom. The garment was scandalously skimpy, with no waist and a ragged, handkerchief hemline that she wagered would hardly reach below her knees. When she lifted the airy confection out of its wrappings, she discovered the package contained a pair of fine silk stockings in a matching shade of pale green and two petite sage-colored satin slippers. A tag sewn into the neckline of the sheer raiment revealed the name of the dramatic character it had clothed at Drury Lane.

"Ariel . . ." Sophie murmured aloud.

She stared at the gauzy costume. It appeared to be constructed principally of silken cobwebs, reminding her of a performance she had witnessed of *The Tempest* in which the airy sprite who attends his master, Prospero, flew across the stage in wild abandon. In this untamed sorcerer, Shakespeare had created a being who could magically invoke the wind and rain to do his master's bidding. Both men and women played the much sought-after role, and when a woman was cast as Ariel, the nuances of sexual tension between Prospero and his supernatural servant contributed an added depth and excitement to Shakespeare's romantic drama.

Prospero! Sophie thought, startled. Hunter had been wearing Prospero's costume earlier in the day—a purple velvet doublet and hose and a paste coronet, denoting his rank as Duke of Milan.

With trembling fingers she began to dress for the ball, shivering before the fire. Who but Hunter could have arranged to have these gossamer garments delivered to her door?

※

"God's wounds, but you'll *freeze* in that rig!" James Boswell exclaimed as he caught sight of Sophie entering the public room in the White Lion Inn with her cloak over her arm.

"So will *you!*" she retorted, eyeing Jamie's portly figure costumed in the attire of an armed Corsican chief, complete with feathered miter hat and a tall staff shaped like a snake. He had a rifle slung over his back and a large leather ammunition pouch strapped around his ample belly.

Around them milled assorted Dutchmen, Chinese Mandarins, Pierrots, Highlanders, Nubians, and some rather unoriginal types: foxhunters, dustmen, milkmaids, and charwomen.

"Shall we depart?" Boswell inquired with a mischievous glint in his eye. "A particular friend of ours has asked me to see you safely to the amphitheater. We can watch the fireworks en route."

Unhappily, in the continuing downpour, the event was a disaster. Poor Dominico Angelo, grand master of Drury Lane's special effects, together with his assistants, lit one battery of fuses after another on his marvelous constructions —to no avail. The flints fizzled, the wicks sputtered and died, and every attempt to light the sodden touch papers ended in failure. Pinwheels got stuck and wouldn't rotate. The rockets remained steadfastly earthbound.

When Angelo finally admitted defeat, Sophie and Boswell joined the disappointed crowd wending its way back to the

Rotunda. By now the meadow was submerged in several inches of water, so their legs were caked with mud by the time they arrived at the ball.

"Here," Sophie said, leaning against a wall just inside the amphitheater's door. "We'll use my cloak to wipe our feet."

Together they quickly repaired the damage to their costumes and Sophie donned her mask. Then she put on the green satin slippers she had stowed under her cloak to protect them from the rain. She took several practice steps and found the shoes were a miraculous fit, considering the diminutive size of her foot.

"I'll wager Mr. Jackson has rented four hundred quid's worth of rags tonight," said a deep voice as the orchestra ceased playing minuets and struck up a lovely country dance tune.

Hunter had suddenly materialized by Sophie's side, and from the startled glances the two of them received from nearby spectators, she concluded that their coordinated costumes and their disparate sizes had rendered them a striking couple. Hunter nodded his thanks to James Boswell and immediately led Sophie in the direction of the dance floor. As soon as he touched her hand, she felt a current of excitement shoot up her arm.

"Do you . . . think Mr. Garrick will object to your borrowing these handsome pieces of . . . of wardrobe?" she asked shakily, clutching her costume's filmy fabric between her fingers. Hunter's blue eyes stared down at her from behind his mask.

"To the contrary, he practically commanded that we wear them," Hunter replied, pulling her closer to him. "I wished to seek m'lady's approval several times these two days on the matter of our fancy dress attire, but you kept disappearing."

"'T-tis an occupational hazard for airy sprites," she stammered, feeling her pulse quicken. "You must keep a sharp eye on nymphs, you know, or they vanish at regular intervals."

"Not Ariel," he murmured against her ear. "Don't you know your Shakespeare, lass? Prospero is lord and master."

"But if Ariel's more man than sprite . . . ?" she challenged.

"Not this night, I assure you," Hunter replied, staring down at her steadily. "May I have this dance?"

Sophie rested her hand on his arm to prevent moving on to the dance floor.

"Hunter I . . ." she began, and then swallowed hard. "First, I think we should . . . I . . . well, three years ago when—"

Sophie halted, failing to find a way to express her remorse and hurt and confusion about the events surrounding Danielle's death and Hunter's violent and unfair response to what he had seen in her flat above Ashby's Books.

But he merely smiled and slowly shook his head, leading her, instead, to join the throng of dancers. He surveyed the costumed figures gliding across the floor in time to music played by Dr. Arne's orchestra.

"I command my Ariel"—he ordered softly, as if delivering a speech written by Shakespeare—"to harbor no thoughts of the past. For now there is just the tempest outside, the magic of this night—and thee and me."

For hours, Sophie and Hunter hardly spoke. While the rain pounded relentlessly against the Rotunda's roof, they whirled among the gods and goddesses, Merlins and Guineveres cavorting all around them. Dr. Arne directed his orchestra to play louder to drown out the cloudburst thundering above their heads—and to a great extent, the musicians succeeded. The masquerade ball grew more boisterous by the hour.

"No one can leave this place without drowning, so we might as well dance all night!" Sophie said gaily, gasping for breath as a particularly rollicking gambol came to its rowdy conclusion.

She and Hunter stared down at the dance floor beneath their feet. A full inch of water had seeped through the floorboards and was now lapping at their toes.

"*Jesu!*" Hunter exclaimed, clasping her hand. "'Tis the

Great Flood all over again. Come . . . let's have a look outside."

Removing their masks, they peered out of the amphitheater and were shocked to see that the Rotunda was completely surrounded by a lake. Candlelight from the
building's interior cast paths of gold across the acres of water that stretched on all sides.

"The Avon's breached its banks!" Sophie exclaimed.

"Aye, but look . . . the water's only a few feet deep on
the village side," Hunter said. He took her chin between his
strong fingers and gazed into her eyes. "Well, Ariel . . . 'tis
past four in the morning. Can you fly home, or shall I lend
you some assistance?"

Before Sophie could render her decision, he scooped her
up in his arms and proceeded to wade into the low-lying
meadow that was now a pond. The sky had begun to lighten,
signaling the hour was actually closer to five.

"We've truly danced all night," Sophie murmured against
Hunter's broad expanse of shoulder.

Fifty yards from the Rotunda, a cluster of carriages
waited axle-high in mud near a dirt lane that led back to the
heart of the village. Some costumed gallants were carrying
their ladies on their shoulders, piggyback style.

"Hunter! Have a look over there!" Sophie giggled, pointing toward a portly woman dressed in shepherdess attire.
The benighted soul stood knee-deep in muck and was bellowing for help.

"Not to worry," Hunter laughed. "See . . . there's a
chivalrous devil attempting to rescue her!"

The black-caped Lucifer trod over to the large-framed
figure whose batiste apron was streaked with mud. Her
shepherdess's crook had slipped from her grasp and was
floating downriver. Lucifer heaved the distressed damsel
over his shoulder and staggered toward higher ground.
Then, in the midst of his exertions, he suddenly halted and,
without warning, tossed the poor drenched baggage into a
water-filled ditch.

"I fear the devil discovered *she* is a *he*," Sophie shouted
through the rain, and they both began to howl at the comical
sight.

She laughed so hard, her tears mingled with the rivulets of water cascading down her cheeks. Hunter, too, was nearly doubled up with mirth. Suddenly, he seemed to lose his balance and the pair toppled into the mud.

"Oomph!" Hunter grunted as Sophie fell on top of him.

"Hunter!" she screeched as he rolled her over into the muck. "You did that on purpose!"

"I merely wish to confirm that in your case, *he* is, indeed, a *she* . . ." he laughed, his eyes drifting from Sophie's face to her sodden costume.

Despite the fact they had landed quite close to the road, the two found themselves lying in nearly five inches of water. Sophie's silk garments were plastered against her skin. Her coiffeur had utterly disintegrated as strands of her long hair clung to her face and neck.

"You've transformed yourself from air to water sprite," Hunter chuckled, his large frame looming over her small one. He held her head above the saturated meadow by the nape of her neck. "But just look at the front of you. 'Tis a scandal! Have you no shame?"

Sophie glanced down at her bodice and gasped. Soaked with water, the filmy fabric had become completely transparent. Her breasts and nipples stood at attention, plainly visible through the gossamer cloth. Slowly Hunter lowered his face within an inch of hers, his breath warm against her lips.

"What an absolutely fetching ensemble . . ." he said.

"Hunter, I—"

"'Tis a pity that we must soon strip you of these soggy rags . . . but first—"

His lips brushed lightly against hers, and then he probed her mouth with the tip of his tongue, deepening the kiss until Sophie forgot they were embracing in a muddy quagmire in full view of hundreds of refugees from the ball. Strangely, the mud felt warm against her back as she pulled him closer, reveling in his weight now pressing against her chest. She tasted the rain on their lips, savored the downpour grazing her eyelids. She felt as if she would soon be engulfed by the tide of sensation that rippled through her body.

"God's bones, Robertson!" a familiar voice exclaimed. "You'll *drown* the lass!"

James Boswell, his Corsican chief's outfit streaked with dirt, stood over them. Sophie's forgotten cloak was draped over his arm. Peering up at him, Sophie began to laugh hysterically. Hunter struggled to his feet, extending both hands and assisted her in rising from the mire.

Boswell's gaze drank in the sight of Sophie's disarray, including her near-naked state. She snatched her cloak from Jamie's arm and tossed it around her shoulders, pulling the woolen edges across her chest. She could feel herself flushing scarlet in the gray light of dawn. Overhead, the skies loomed dark and menacing as the extraordinary rain continued to pour from the sky.

"Well . . ." said Boswell with an envious glance in Hunter's direction, "I bid you two good night . . . or rather, good morning."

※

"Shed those clothes while I light the fire," Hunter ordered as they made for Sophie's small chamber through the deluge pelting the stable yard at the White Lion Inn.

"The flint's by the hearth," Sophie replied, hanging her drenched cloak on a peg. She shivered as she attempted to peel off her skimpy garments.

The soaked costume landed in a sodden pile at her feet. She snatched the counterpane off the bed and just as quickly, held the clean white bedspread at arm's length.

"What shall I do?" she wailed. "I'm freezing . . . but I'm filthy!"

The fire was sputtering to life as Hunter rose from his haunches and began to divest himself of his waterlogged garments.

"There's only one thing for it!" he laughed, throwing his velvet doublet on the floor and pushing his silk hose toward his knees. "Outside with the both of us . . . the rain shall wash us clean!"

"But what if people see—"

"'Tis so murky abroad, no one shall spy you but me," he

laughed, taking her hand and heading for the door. "And that's just what I was counting on," he added with a grin.

Giggling at the sight of each other's nakedness, they tiptoed out the door that led to the stable yard, gasping as the chilly air pimpled their skin with gooseflesh. Hunter stretched his arms in the shape of a human cross while torrents of rain cascaded down his six-foot frame.

" 'Now would I give a thousand furlongs of sea for an acre of barren ground!' " Hunter bellowed, quoting from *The Tempest.*

Sophie cast a furtive eye in the direction of several coaches parked in the courtyard. She was certain they contained visitors slumbering the night away. It was almost morning, and she prayed they would stay asleep until she and Hunter finished bathing.

Sophie closed her eyes and lifted her face to the heavens, letting the sheets of water shower down on her. What a wonderful evening it had been, she thought, smiling into the raindrops that grazed her lips. She had giggled and laughed and had felt as carefree as a child. And now, as the relentless storm washed the mud off her body, it almost seemed as if the torrential downpour was cleansing her of years of sorrow . . . her father's death, the horror of her aunt's demise. The one remaining sadness locked inside her heart was the loss of little Danielle.

Sophie closed her eyes more tightly, willing the pangs of guilt to leave her undisturbed for once, praying not to be forced to confront, on this perfect rain-soaked night, the bitterness that Hunter must surely still harbor towards her.

"There's not a speck of dirt left on this lovely body of yours," he said softly, his lips licking moisture off her neck. "I know, because I gave you a thorough inspection while you weren't looking."

Sophie's eyes flew open and she took a step back. Her gaze drifted from Hunter's face, with his blond hair slicked against the handsome shape of his head, down the broad expanse of his chest to his tapering waist, down . . .

"No fair sizing up the condition of your opponent," he chided gently, reaching for her hand and pulling her body close to his.

"Are we adversaries?" she asked softly, staring at the rain drops clinging to his lashes.

"No. We are not," he replied gravely. "Come back to your chamber and I'll prove it to you, my winsome water sprite."

Sophie awoke to the rolling sound of thunder and sleepily attempted to determine whether the noise was from the natural world or the cannons blasting their assigned wake-up call to Stratford's populace. Soon, the town's church bells added to the cacophony, prompting Sophie to burrow more deeply beneath the bed linen.

"Oh, no . . . it can't be time for another of those infernal breakfasts at Town Hall," she groaned.

She felt Hunter shift his weight, pulling her against him.

"Not even ducks would venture out in this weather, Sophie love . . ." he murmured against her ear, insinuating his tongue languidly as he spoke. "Not even the Great God Garrick, himself."

Sophie shivered, excited by his touch. She lay in his arms, allowing his hands to skim over the surface of her naked body, blushing at the memory of her impassioned demands during their tumultuous lovemaking a few short hours earlier. Now his approach was gentler as his lips explored her collarbone and the valley between her breasts. She reached up, pulling him against her, her fingers sinking into his thick blond hair. The length of her body absorbed his weight as if he were another feather mattress.

"You shall have *me* for breakfast," he teased softly. "Does that please you, my Ariel?"

" 'All hail, great master, grave sir, hail I come . . .' " she whispered, quoting her character's first lines in *The Tempest*, " '. . . to answer thy best pleasure, be it to fly, to swim, to dive into the fire—'." She smoothed her hands along the contours of his muscular back, welcoming him like some wanton, suddenly possessed by an insatiable desire to have him within her.

" '—to ride on curled clouds, to thy strong bidding task . . .' " Hunter murmured against her ear. He slipped his palms around her waist, pulling her closer toward the obvious evidence of his desire. "You shall answer my best pleasure . . . and yours as well."

As he entered her swiftly, she cried out, calling his name. Strange, ethereal spirits seem to fill the room, sighing like the wind that was beating against their window. Hunter moved gently at first, as if pushing her playfully on a garden swing. Higher and higher she sailed among gentle breezes, the soft air fragrant with columbine and dwarf carnation, higher and higher until she thought the swing would tear from its moorings, flinging her among the curled clouds where Ariel played havoc with the wind, summoning the tempest at Prospero's bidding. Hunter might still blame her for Danielle's death, she thought with what small coherence was left her, but his body's thirst for hers had not been slaked by the turbulent passions they had shared when they'd sought refuge from last night's gale. And for her, 'twas the same. She wanted him to seep into her pores like the rain, fuse himself to her forever.

Somehow in the vortex swirling around her, Sophie wrestled with the conscious thought she could conceive . . . she *would* conceive a child from such an impassioned coupling . . . if not today, then someday, because she could not find the will to fling herself—now or ever—out of the whirlwind that had taken possession of her.

"'Tis like the storm," she cried, seizing his face between her hands and whispering fiercely. "I must dash myself upon the cliffs, or die . . ."

"Aye," he said harshly, pressing her more deeply into the feather mattress that supported them, "'tis the same for me . . ."

And the tempest caught them up once again and they drowned in their love of it and their fear of it and it finally played itself out—as they regretfully knew it would.

They lay quietly in bed for some minutes, listening to the rain's ceaseless rhythm on their roof.

"How came you to Stratford for the Jubilee?" Sophie asked softly. "I never sent you the invitation that went out to the players."

"Garrick. He bade me come to London," Hunter replied,

absently caressing her shoulder, "to talk about the new season and to hear what part I was to play in this fiasco at Stratford."

"It hasn't *all* been a fiasco," Sophie said defensively, turning to face him.

"No . . . Garrick's delivery of his *Ode to Shakespeare* shall be talked of and written about for a hundred years or more . . . but much of this was flummery, Sophie darling. Amusing, but flummery nevertheless."

"I suppose so . . ." she replied moodily. "If only those stuffy scholars had cooperated."

"Garrick wishes to engage the public, to make Shakespeare come alive for them," Hunter said gently, wrapping a lock of her auburn hair around his finger. "Literary folk who revel in the exclusiveness of what *they* know cannot abide that fact about him. He pleases the masses, which pleases not the scholars!"

"And you?" Sophie asked, catching his hand in hers and kissing it softly.

"I'm like Garrick . . . a mere fool upon the stage, and one day, a full-fledged manager, I hope, though never as brilliant as your Great Garrick," he smiled.

"You like him, then?" Sophie said, brightening. "You see there's more to him than the vain little man many judge him to be?"

"Oh . . . yes, indeed," he replied with a grin. "After all, perhaps his greatest role has been that of Matchmaker."

Sophie shifted away from him slightly. No amount of matchmaking could quell the revulsion she had seen in Hunter's eyes the day he stormed from her chambers after finding her drunken husband in her bed.

Hunter poked a finger lightly under her chin, forcing her to meet his gaze.

"Garrick was quite skillful, you know," he continued, "bringing our conversation quickly around to his hardworking assistant—you."

"And what did he say?" Sophie asked cautiously.

"That he was gravely worried about you."

"Worried?" she said, puzzled.

"Yes . . . that he feared you had never quite recovered

from the death of your daughter because he knew that a great and good friend wrongly believed you had been neglectful of the child."

Sophie felt a familiar despondency settle over her, and she blinked back tears. Hunter looked suddenly serious at the memory of his meeting with her employer.

"Garrick gave me one of his famous *looks*," he disclosed, "and then he told me what every gossip in Covent Garden had told *him*."

"And what was that?" Sophie whispered.

"That Mary Ann Skene was responsible for Peter's being in your flat and that you had only left your child in her care for an hour because you were fulfilling your obligation to Garrick himself . . . that the money you earned from Drury Lane went for food and much-needed medicinals."

Hunter paused, waiting for her to respond.

"Aye. 'Twas Mary Ann who had just risen from Peter's bed," Sophie said in a tight voice. "I found them together after I ran from you in Half Moon Passage. She'd been hiding in the trunk when you came into my chambers. 'Twas she who had banished my ailing bairn to the printing room."

Hunter shook his head morosely.

"I was a great, bloody, conceited, idiotic fool," he acknowledged in a low voice. "Please forgive me, Sophie. I despise myself for having added to your grief over your loss of Danielle."

She stared at him for a long moment. Then, deep, wracking sobs began to escape from her chest as she flung her arms around his broad shoulders, fiercely drawing him to her. She buried her tousled head beneath his chin and cried until she could hardly breathe. She sobbed out her anguish over the death of her daughter and the misery and guilt engendered by Hunter's condemnation.

"Those violets!" she cried brokenly. "Even now, I can't bear the sight of violets . . ."

When her storm of weeping finally abated, she clung to him, attempting to recover her composure. Much to her astonishment, she felt Hunter's shoulders begin to heave against her own.

"Darling?" she asked. "What is it? Shhh . . . 'tis all right now . . ."

"No . . . 'tis *not* all right . . ." he answered, his voice choked with emotion. "'Tis *never* been right with me . . . sometimes I truly think I'm *cracked*!"

Sophie drew away from him, seizing the corner of the counterpane to wipe her eyes. She sat up cross-legged in bed and gently daubed his moist cheeks.

"Look at us," she chided weakly. "We're producing nearly as much water as the storm outside." She stroked his temple tenderly and then pulled his head gently against her breast. "Why, pray, do you think you're cracked, my love? Most times you seem a sensible sort to me."

"When Garrick—and now you—relate to me the facts . . . I'm bloody *ashamed* . . . ashamed how I jumped to conclusions." He raised his head from her chest and shifted his weight to his elbow, staring somberly into her eyes. "Since I was a wee lad, I've *always* concluded the worst . . . especially about women . . . especially about Jean and what she did . . ."

Sophie felt her breath catch. Rarely, in all the years she had known Hunter, had he spoken more than a few curt words about his mother, and never had he elaborated on his unhappy relationship with her.

"And what did you conclude about Jean Hunter Robertson?" she asked quietly.

"That she had as good as murdered my sister, Meg!"

Sophie felt her heart begin to pound. A terrible fear that threatened all the hard-won understanding between them nearly strangled her. Instinctively she realized that whatever had happened in Hunter's family so long ago was part and parcel of their three-year estrangement.

"'Long mayst thy live to wail thy children's death?'" she whispered. "You cursed us both in the same breath, didn't you?"

"Oh, God, Sophie! How dare I accuse you of what I always judged my mother to have done."

"Killed wee Meg?" Sophie said, horrified.

"As good as . . ."

"*How?*" she asked, wondering if she really wished to know.

A faraway look invaded Hunter's eyes and she knew his thoughts had slipped back years to his childhood.

"'Twas the Starving . . . a year or so after the Rebellion of '45 the disastrous Battle of Culloden Moor. My father was dead. The *Bonnie* Prince had fled back to France," he said with bitter emphasis, "all was lost for Clan Robertson . . . or at least for my family. I was about five and Meg, barely two. There was no food. *No food!*" he cried, anguished. "My mother took us far up into the hills above Inverness . . . she found a deserted bothy with most of its thatched roof intact and, miraculously, my grandfather stumbled through the door one day with a bag of barley he'd stolen from a farm. She used a little of the grain to make a broth and fed a bit to her father-in-law—he'd saved us, after all. She took a mite for herself and gave the rest to me." Hunter stared out the window heedless of the muddy stable yard or the arch that led to the Birmingham Road. "She did that each day . . . made a little broth and fed it to the three of us. She gave none to Meg."

"*Jesu* . . ." whispered Sophie. "But could Meg not have still been fed at the breast?"

"Jean's milk had dried up. She had to make a choice, you see . . ." Hunter continued tonelessly. "There were such limited rations to last us through the winter. I was the son and heir and she chose me. She did what she supposed my father would have wanted. She chose me to live . . . and Meg to die." Hunter shut his eyes tight as if to obliterate the memory. "I watched my wee sister perish by *inches* . . . and I hated my mother." His eyes flew open. "I expect I hated her to avoid hating myself for consuming that bit of barley broth each and every day. 'Twas why I believe I treated you so harshly, Sophie. I couldn't bear to think of my mother's deliberate neglect of Meg . . . to remember it all again. 'Twas less onerous to cast blame."

Sophie clasped Hunter's face between her hands, heedless of the tears dampening her face. She kissed him gently on both eyelids.

"Sometimes . . . 'tis as difficult to be the favored child

as the spurned one, Hunter," she said softly, suddenly thinking of Lord Darnly, the Earl of Llewelyn's second son, whose entire life had been tainted by being born a mere two minutes after the heir.

"But Meg *died* . . . surely that was worse!" he answered curtly.

"You *both* were children . . . and what child can dictate to the fates?" Sophie asked gently, ignoring his accusing tone. She recalled Danielle writhing from a fever contracted from her father. "'Twas not my fault my daughter caught the ague from her thoughtless, reckless da . . . and 'twas not you who are to blame for the decision made by Jean Robertson."

"But that's the *coil*!" Hunter said, his eyes filled with remorse. "I blamed my mother for what she could not help . . . for what none of us could help. All these years I've *hated* her, just as I hated you . . . for a time."

Hunter's look of abject suffering mollified the shock Sophie felt at realizing that this man, who was so dear to her, could have heartily despised her.

"Well," she said quietly. "You've asked my forgiveness, and I've granted it. Perhaps one day you'll ask hers."

"Perhaps . . ." he repeated faintly, pulling Sophie hard against his chest. "One day . . . perhaps . . ."

As Hunter had predicted, not even ducks would venture out on the third morning of the Jubilee. The Parade of Shakespeare's Characters was canceled for the second time. But the Shottery Horse Race—held a mile or so outside Stratford—finally got under way at around noon when the weather began to clear.

By evening, they returned to Sophie's room, donned warm, dry clothes, and arrived at the Rotunda for the last communal dinner, only to learn that several inches of water had inundated the entire pavilion and ticket holders were left to seek out what victuals they could at the various inns. Sophie used her influence and secured them a corner in the coffee room at the White Lion where the owner handed out several dishes salvaged from the makeshift kitchens next to the waterlogged amphitheater.

"I shall be off on the morrow," James Boswell remarked as he took a seat at their small table, joining them for a brandy. "Pity, though, it cannot be sooner, for I weary of this soggy burgh." A printer named Richardson had offered to share a chaise with him to London. "I had to borrow five guineas from Garrick for the fare. I'd spent my money having my verses struck."

"God's wounds, Bozzy, you do have cheek," groaned Sophie. "Did you ever give them out?"

"I passed out copies at the ball in the wee hours and after the horse race," Boswell said complacently. "When do you two leave this veil of mud?"

"I must stay a while to help put things to rights here in Stratford," Sophie said.

Hunter glanced at her sharply.

"Must you?"

"Why, yes," she replied, eyeing him curiously. "'Tis what I promised Garrick when I was engaged to work on the Jubilee. What's left of the costumes and props must be packed into their boxes, put on wagons and returned to Drury Lane for the opening of the new season on the eighteenth," she explained. "'Tis only ten days' hence. And you?" she asked, suddenly wary of Hunter's answer.

"George Colman's taken me on at Covent Garden," Hunter replied slowly. "I must return to London immediately. Have you room for another passenger in that chaise of yours, Boswell?" he asked.

"You'll not work for Garrick this year?" she asked, distressed.

She had been so certain, when she'd had time to think of it during their busy day, that Hunter would have been offered full employment by her mentor.

"He tendered me a place before I came to Stratford," Hunter acknowledged, shifting his gaze back to Boswell, "but at Covent Garden I shall drill the chorus and create musical interludes, as well as perform. It appeared the better choice for me."

"You'll be a *London* manager soon, laddie!" Boswell enthused.

"Not with the state of my purse," Hunter replied ruefully, "but perhaps one day I shall purchase some shares. 'Tis a start."

Sophie was forced to admit that there was considerable truth to Hunter's assessment of his fortunes in London. It appeared that Garrick and Lacy had lengthy, successful careers ahead of them, but the situation was far more fluid at Covent Garden. With a bit of good luck, he might one day join Colman as one of the managers. But how, she wondered, would she and Hunter avoid the rivalry and competition that inevitably arose between the two royal theaters?

"I'm pleased for you," she said sighing, "though I wish you were to be at Old Drury . . . I fear we shall be beset with . . ."

Her sentence trailed off, for there was really no answer to the quandary she divined would plague them in the future.

"Mayhap you'll write plays for Colman one of these days," Hunter ventured with a crooked smile. "Surely 'twould make things simpler for us, don't you think?"

Simpler for you! she replied silently, and then instantly chastised herself. 'Twas the same dilemma they had faced in Bath, and they couldn't ride that way again. Hunter was only stating a rudimentary truth, not asking her to be disloyal to David Garrick.

"I've written very little these last years . . ." She shrugged, forcing a smile. "I'm not sure I know how to wield a pen anymore."

But already she'd been mulling over plot twists for *The Bogus Baronet,* the comedy that lay abandoned for three years in her desk at Half Moon Passage. Garrick had liked the notion for the play when she had first proposed it to him in 1766, and she was certain he would be pleased with some new ideas she had thought of. She summoned a laugh and raised her glass.

"We'll all be back in London's hurly-burly soon enough," she said, realizing with a start that legally, she was still a married woman. London, to her, meant Peter Lindsay and Mavis Piggott, and the two of them meant trouble. She tried to rid herself of such gloomy thoughts. "Let us enjoy this last evening together," she added, reaching across to caress Hunter's hand resting on the table. "The stars are out tonight. . . . I believe 'twill be fair tomorrow. Let us drink to having *survived* the Shakespeare Jubilee!"

"To Shakespeare and survival!" the men chorused and the trio clinked glasses in a jaunty toast.

Book 6

1769–1770

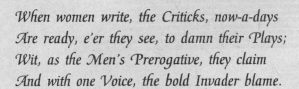

When women write, the Criticks, now-a-days
Are ready, e'er they see, to damn their Plays;
Wit, as the Men's Prerogative, they claim
And with one Voice, the bold Invader blame.

—MARY DAVYS,
"PROLOGUE," *THE SELF RIVAL*

Chapter 27

September 1769

St. Paul's church bells tolled as Sophie approached the stage entrance to Covent Garden. She found herself taking deep breaths to calm her nervous anticipation. She was certain she would find Hunter either just finishing an afternoon rehearsal for the season's opening of *Love in a Village* or down the road at the Nag's Head, having his early evening meal.

"Why, Lady Lindsay-Hoyt," exclaimed Besford, the doorkeeper. "So good to see you. Mr. Colman told me you had quite a time of it among those rustics in Stratford. Have you dried out?" he joked.

She was startled to hear herself addressed as "Lady," but, of course, only a few people—Hunter, Garrick, Darnly, Mary Ann Skene, and her friend Lorna—knew that Peter's ascension to the peerage was fraudulent.

"I have indeed, Mr. Besford. May I inquire if Hunter Robertson is here?" she asked.

She smiled graciously at the doorkeeper, surprised that the gossip-loving Mary Ann had kept the secret this long. Sophie didn't much care one way or the other, since she had been employing her maiden name for three years now. However, she was glad Mary Ann had been discreet, as there was always the danger that Peter's creditors would pursue her for redress—especially when they realized there would be no fortune coming to the supposed heir to the sizable Hoyt estates in Yorkshire.

"I'm terribly sorry, m'lady," Besford said with a nervous smile, "I've just been informed that Mr. Robertson will be in rehearsal for several hours into the evening."

"But 'tis quite late, isn't it?" she asked, ". . . nearly time to sup, I should think."

"I do regret the situation, m'lady," Besford apologized again, "but I have my instructions from Mr. Colman. No one but staff is permitted backstage. Strict orders."

Sophie could hear faint strains of music that sounded vaguely familiar wafting from the front of the house. Suddenly, she recognized the tune: Dibdin's "Dawn Serenade."

"I wouldn't dream of barging in," Sophie replied, weighing the significance of the Covent Garden orchestra playing a piece of music commissioned by the manager of Drury Lane for his Stratford Jubilee—and now, this order to bar outsiders from attending rehearsals for a coming attraction at Drury Lane's rival theater. 'Twas all very curious. "Would you kindly inform Mr. Robertson that I have returned to London and will see him anon?"

"I'm certain he'd want to know of it right away," Mr. Besford replied with a knowing smile. "I'll see he gets your ladyship's message directly."

Sophie strolled the quarter mile down Bow Street to Brydges Street where she exchanged similar pleasantries with Mr. Collins, the stage doorkeeper at Drury Lane.

"Wonderful to have you back," Collins said warmly. "'Tis especially good to see you in such fine fettle, if I may say so, Sophie."

"Thank you," she said, smiling. "Is Mr. Garrick about?"

Collins's face grew somber.

"Yes . . . he and Lacy are upstairs in the Treasure Room," he confided, lowering his voice. "They've been going at it to a fare-thee-well today—unpaid bills, you know, from the Jubilee. Lacy's screaming like a banshee."

"Oh, dear," Sophie sighed. "Perhaps I should—"

"No . . . they've both asked me today if I know whether you've returned from Stratford. Better go up. You don't have more accounts to place before them, do you?" he asked cautiously.

"Aye, a few," Sophie admitted. "And George Garrick's

bringing the final tally with him when he returns in two days' time."

"Oh my," replied Collins, shaking his grizzled head. "'Tis been quite a t'do, this Jubilee affair. The news journals have been having a great squawk about it all."

"Oh . . . but Collins," Sophie said, her eyes shining. "Garrick's *Ode to Shakespeare* was magnificent! I wish you could have seen him!"

"So I've heard," Collins said, appearing more cheerful. "Even the most vicious writers—did you see what Colman wrote!—acknowledged it was Davy's finest hour."

"*Colman!*" Sophie said with disgust. "I can't imagine *he'd* be a fair correspondent."

Sophie mounted the stairs, anxious to report to the managers the good news that the loose ends at Stratford were nearly tied up. As she approached Garrick's office and the Treasure Room, loud voices floated down the passageway.

"John Payton charged us for every sip of porter, regardless of who imbibed it!" Lacy fumed. "Look at these accounts, Davy! They've ruined us! *Ruined us*, I say!"

"Oh, do be quiet about the porter, James!" Garrick replied. "If it upsets you so, *I'll* pay for the bloody drinks."

"Excellent!" Lacy retorted. "Your *brother* drank most of it!"

Hesitantly, Sophie ventured a few soft raps on the door.

"Who is it?" Lacy barked.

"'Tis I . . . Sophie McGann," she said through a six-inch opening, "with the pleasant news the Jubilee is no more . . . the last of the properties and costumes should arrive here tomorrow."

"In tatters, I would wager," Lacy groused. "Come in, come in, might as well give us the bad news all at once and get it over with."

"We'll turn this around, I tell you!" Garrick insisted. "Hello, my dear . . . forgive us partners arguing like fishwives. We both returned home weary and out of sorts—"

"And out of blunt!" Lacy snapped. "And each day it has only grown worse as Davy surprises me with new accountings—like eighteen pounds for *porter*!"

"James," Garrick said sharply.

"Well, let me assure you," Sophie hastened to interject, "the costumes are in reasonably good condition, except, unfortunately, for the one *I* wore to the ball . . . Ariel must be made anew, I'm afraid, and I fully intend to cover the cost."

"Nonsense!" Garrick replied. "For all your hard work, 'twas the least we could provide."

James Lacy looked as if he might protest Garrick's largesse, but instead lapsed into moody silence.

"Well," said Garrick, indicating that Sophie should take a chair near his desk, "tell me of Stratford—not that I ever wish to see that mud hole again."

Sophie smiled sympathetically.

"The Rotunda is just about pulled down and all the materials are to be sold in lots, so perhaps you will recoup funds there."

"Well, that's something," Lacy commented sourly.

"And the silk transparencies sustained no damage and were rolled and packed carefully. You certainly will be able to employ the fabric in some future production—"

"Oh, that *is* good news!" Garrick interrupted. "Lacy, did you hear that? The transparencies are intact! 'Twill make mounting our new project much easier if both the costumes and scenes have survived."

Sophie gazed at her employer closely.

"You are planning something new?" she asked.

"'Tis all very confidential but I intend to stage our Parade of Characters."

"You mean you hope to recreate part of the Shakespeare Jubilee at Drury Lane?" she asked incredulously.

"Yes . . . a comic version of it," Garrick declared, some of his old enthusiasm visible in his expressive eyes. "I have been writing a play about the entire event . . . a kind of spectacular parody . . . the good and the ill, the successful and the ludicrous, *everything* will be incorporated!" He began to pace up and down the chamber. "Most exciting of all," he continued, "I shall *at last* be able to present the Shakespeare pageant we lavished so much time and attention on—only to be thwarted by the deluge. What think you, Sophie, my girl?"

Sophie ventured a quick glance in Lacy's direction, and saw that Garrick's partner was already shaking his head in the negative. Even so, she smiled encouragingly.

"How witty to poke fun at the rain and the other annoyances. I think 'tis a capital idea, sir . . . most of the expenses for such a presentation have already been incurred, and I would wager near everyone in London who was unable to remove themselves to Stratford will come to see the Jubilee at Old Drury—if only out of curiosity to learn what all the flummery was about."

"My sentiments exactly!" Garrick enthused.

"Have you yet begun rehearsals?" she asked suddenly.

"I am still writing . . . but I hope to have it ready by the end of October."

"Sir," Sophie said slowly, recalling Mr. Besford's polite but firm resolve not to allow her beyond his doorkeeper's box at Covent Garden, "have you heard rumors that anyone else has anticipated your plans?"

Both Lacy and Garrick looked at her sharply.

"What mean you?" David said. "Have you heard something?"

"No one has told me anything precisely," she admitted. "As you know, I've just returned to the city . . . but 'twas something Colman said to me when I saw him in Stratford."

"And what was that?" Lacy demanded.

"Well, begging your pardons, sirs," she said apologetically, "he declared that day that he had witnessed enough tomfoolery during the Jubilee to 'create a score of farces,' and today when I called at Covent Garden to inform Hunter of my return, I was barred from proceeding beyond the stage door because a closed rehearsal was taking place—"

"They've got something up their sleeves!" shouted Lacy. "Damnable cheek!"

Sophie hesitated, torn by her loyalty to Drury Lane and her wish to see Hunter succeed at Covent Garden. But what if Colman was mounting a piece aimed both at appropriating the entertaining aspects of the Jubilee and ridiculing Garrick at the same time? What if Hunter's prodigious talents were being used in aid of such a project?

"You were about to tell us something else?" Garrick said quietly as Sophie bit her lip. "You needn't, you know."

"The lass works for us!" Lacy declared. "You must tell us everything you know about those blackguards!"

"I'm fairly certain that I . . ." Sophie began, feeling miserable. ". . . that I heard a few measures of 'Dawn Serenade' being rehearsed on stage while I stood at the doorkeeper's box."

"God's bones!" Lacy groaned.

Garrick slammed his fist against his desk, which was piled high with the customary number of play scripts. "Well, so be it!" he bellowed. "I will match my musical extravaganza with Colman's any day! He may mock me, but I'll wager he could never guess *I* intended to poke fun at *m'self,* and therein lies our secret weapon. Lacy! We must strike first! We must discover exactly what they plan to do upon their stage—and *when!*"

Both men stared silently at Sophie who returned their gaze, feeling deeply distressed.

"I cannot ask Hunter . . . I simply cannot," Sophie declared, anguished. "I would be forcing him to be disloyal in a way I would never be disloyal to you!"

Garrick sighed and stole a look at his partner.

"You shame us, my dear. Of course, you cannot be our spy."

The two men exchanged glances for a moment and then declared simultaneously, "Mavis Piggott!"

"Fortunately, Mrs. Piggott has not your scruples, Sophie," Lacy snorted. "We shall ask her immediately to nose about and see if she can confirm what they're up to—and when they plan to strike!"

"Meanwhile," Garrick mused, "just in case they're quite advanced in their devilish plans, I shall mount my *Ode to Shakespeare* on stage *this* week and bill it as the precursor to a spectacular production to be presented soon at Drury Lane. At least we shall gain the credit for recreating the most successful aspect of the Jubilee ahead of our competitors!"

"How soon can you put it on . . . the ode, I mean?" Sophie asked.

"Well, let's see . . ." Garrick replied, his eyes scanning a schedule of the repertory lying on his desk. "Let us say we present the ode in three . . . four . . . *five* days time! September thirtieth! How is that? Covent Garden's already posted its fare for the week. Old Drury will perform the ode as a surprise afterpiece *this* Saturday and stage it like an oratorio . . . the singers round me in a semicircle . . . the orchestra on a platform behind me . . . and my chair. *Jesu*, Sophie . . . did my chair leave Stratford in one piece?"

"'Tis here, 'tis here," Lacy said soothingly. "I saw the stage servants uncrate it today."

"Splendid!" Garrick declared. "And we shall go ahead full tilt on our major extravaganza. I can begin rehearsals on the first act tomorrow, in *strictest* secrecy, of course." He glanced at Sophie. "Will that be possible for you, Sophie dear?" he asked intently.

She smiled wanly and shook her head.

"Until all this is concluded," she replied, "my personal policy shall be—that I shall repeat to both you and to Hunter *only* what is publicly known about events unfolding at the competing theaters. 'Tis all I can think to do. Will that be satisfactory, gentlemen?"

Lacy scowled but Garrick patted her hand approvingly.

"We shall employ Mavis to do the nasty bits and reward her with a juicy part in *Romeo and Juliet*, shall we not, Lacy?" he chortled. He placed his hands on his desk. "So, 'tis decided. Closed rehearsals, tight security. I shouldn't think we could be ready with the full-length version of our musical spoof until . . . mmmm, I'd say Saturday, October thirteenth. Colman's production may beat us to the stage, but we shall have taken the wind out of his sails with our *Ode to Shakespeare*, eh what?" Garrick jumped up from his seat. Extending his arms to sketch his ideas in the air, he announced, "Then we shall hit them with the Parade of Characters, the ode again . . . the jugglers, the harlots, the runaway horses . . . the hawkers, the hairdressers, the toffs sleeping in their coaches! Drury Lane will present the most stupefying spectacle London has ever seen!"

"Bravo!" Lacy exclaimed, slapping his partner on the back, his ill humor now transformed into a burning desire to hoist George Colman by his own petard. "And you know what I like *best* about this little scheme of yours, Davy my boy?" Lacy said with a baleful gleam in his eye. "We've already paid the bills for the scenery and costumes, and . . . it never *rains* inside Drury Lane!"

Garrick nodded emphatically.

"By God, we shall best 'em," he declared, "and make a fortune *doing* it!"

※

On her way out, Sophie waved as she passed by the stage doorkeeper's box once again.

"Sophie?" a voice called after her. "Sophie, wait! 'Tis me . . . Lorna! Lorna Blount!"

Sophie whirled and walked toward the curtained wings, throwing her arms around her friend.

"Oh, Lorna, how good it is to see you!" she exclaimed. Sophie stepped back to survey her. "So, you've signed with Old Drury, have you?"

"Aye," Lorna beamed, "and Collins, here, says you've been working with Garrick too! I can't tell you how wonderful it is to see you looking yourself again. Will you be printing the playbills?"

Sophie nodded, humbled by her friend's lack of rancor, considering the indifference she had shown toward Lorna in the years that followed Danielle's death.

"Aye, and some play *writing*, I hope," she said quietly. She gazed somberly at her former companion. "I was going to seek you out . . . I've only arrived back in London this afternoon. Can we sup tonight?"

"If you make it early," Lorna answered eagerly. "I'm dancing in the afterpiece following *School for Rakes.*"

"Ah, so Mrs. Griffith still earns her keep by her pen," Sophie noted, encouraged by such news.

"Not without great assistance from Mr. G.," Lorna replied in a low voice. "When *Rakes* was in rehearsal, Garrick nearly went mad with her moaning at every juncture." The dancer cocked an ear toward the stage. "I must go back, but shall we say six tonight? I'm due at Drury by eight or so."

"Half Moon Passage at six, and we shall make our plans from there," Sophie agreed happily. Impulsively, she gave her friend another hug. "You are a prize, Lorna Blount! And I a—"

"A dear friend as well," Lorna interrupted. "At six, then," she called over her shoulder and disappeared backstage.

※

At around the appointed hour, Sophie heard a knock at the door of her second-story chambers.

"You're early," she called gaily, reaching for the latch.

"Sophie McGann?" asked a fresh-faced young man with alarmingly crossed eyes.

"Y-yes," Sophie replied, startled by the lad's peculiar canted gaze.

"This is for you," the boy replied. "Says I was to deliver it to your hands only. Must be off now. Good night."

And before Sophie could reward him for his trouble, the lad disappeared down the gloomy stairway, passing Lorna, who was trudging up in the opposite direction.

"Not bad news, I hope," Lorna said, as they shut the door behind them.

Sophie unfolded the sheet of foolscap, relieved to see the missive was written in a familiar hand.

"'Tis from Hunter. May I?" she asked of her friend.

"Of course," Lorna replied taking a seat before the empty hearth. "I must admit your appearance at the Jubilee masquerade ball with that handsome rogue has been well-reported around Drury Lane," she teased.

"I've no doubt," Sophie replied, glancing down at the letter in her hand.

Darling Ariel . . .
'Tis torture to know you are here across the Piazza, yet I cannot be with you—for a time. Colman keeps me his slave with performances and rehearsals. Tonight I play in *Busy Body* against DL's *School for Rakes*— both pieces by Petticoat Authors. You female Wits have captured both houses, it appears, and tomorrow 'tis Pistol in *Henry Fifth*.
Know that I long to ride the wind with you once again

. . . and will escape from these constant rehearsals for a new piece Covent Garden debuts as soon as I am able. For the nonce, think of me as your duke who dreams of "answering your best pleasure" . . . soon . . . soon . . .
Your Prospero

Sophie gazed at the sheet, disturbed as well as elated. Then she heaved a sigh and slid the letter in the desk drawer.

"Something amiss?" Lorna asked with concern.

"Hunter is apparently working night and day on some new creation to be presented at Covent Garden. Have you heard any whispers as to what it could be?"

"'Tis about the Jubilee," Lorna confided. "Mavis Piggott heard that from someone late this afternoon who had it straight from an inside player. Colman plans to mock the entire affair and Garrick will bear the brunt of it. The blackguard has rewritten some old chestnut and turned it into a *farce* satirizing the recent festivities in Stratford."

Sophie was shocked how few secrets could be kept within the theatrical community. She glanced in the direction of the desk where she had stored Hunter's letter.

"Now, Sophie," Lorna chided gently. "Hunter is merely a contract player at Covent Garden. Did he say in his letter that he's part of the new production?"

"Yes, but he didn't disclose that 'tis intended to revile David Garrick," Sophie replied moodily. "I realize he has little choice in the matter, but Garrick has been nothing but kind to him! It pains me to think he would be part of an attempt to publicly humiliate the man!"

"And has not Garrick, in times past, parodied his rivals?" her friend queried gently. "'Tis the way of things between the two playhouses. 'Tis what gives spark and fire to our profession. As with love and war—all's fair, Sophie dear."

"I suppose you're right," she acknowledged with a sigh, "'tis just—"

"'Tis just the way things *are*," Lorna interrupted. "Now get us to the Half Moon Tavern or your long-lost friend will faint from hunger during tonight's *tours jêtés*!"

※

Sophie spent the remainder of her first week back in London tidying her musty flat and printing the playbills for *Ode to Shakespeare,* which were to be distributed only hours before the Saturday performance. One afternoon she took her courage in hand and read through her partial draft of *The Bogus Baronet.*

Later, over a cup of tea with Lorna, she acknowledged, "'Tis an amusing premise for a farce, but the dialogue lacks any spark."

"If you recall that dreadful time when you wrote those pages," Lorna protested, "'twas a miracle you even penned a word! You had just quit Peter's flat and were hard-pressed to pay the lease on these rooms. You even took in Mary Ann Skene as a paying lodger!"

"Ah, yes, my amiable husband Peter," she said with grim humor. "I haven't laid eyes on the man in donkey's years. What hear you of his health and welfare?"

Lorna shook her head with disdain. "'Tis said he has attached himself to a high-born woman of disrepute. She presides over a nightly faro table at her home on Cheyne Walk."

"And what of Roderick Darnly, our new Viscount Glyn?" she asked carefully. "Has he returned from Wales, do you know? He made no appearance at Stratford."

"I'm told his father has little use of his limbs since the accident and that Darnly shoulders most of the responsibility for the family's estates. Collins says, though, that the viscount has wearied of Wales and has written Lacy of his intention to return soon to consult about our new production," Lorna said, raising a blond eyebrow.

"Ah, yes, Lacy likes it not if these extravaganzas cost too much. I don't wonder that he wrote to Darnly first, to see if the nobleman had blunt to spare," Sophie replied, wondering silently what changes she would find in the demeanor of the enigmatic man who had been her host a year ago.

"Perhaps my lord Darnly will underwrite the new scenery that depicts Stratford's principal street," Lorna speculated with a look of concern, "and thereby garner for himself more shares in Drury Lane?"

Sophie shrugged. "I doubt Lord Darnly would wish—or

have the time, now—to manage such an enterprise, even if he should acquire more influence through mortgages on Lacy's shares. 'Tis my view this pastime merely provides the viscount with amusement.'' She smiled reassuringly. ''Rather like Peter and his passion for faro.''

"I sometimes wonder," Lorna replied dubiously. ''Truly, I do.''

A few days later, the same cross-eyed messenger from Covent Garden appeared on Sophie's landing bearing another missive.

> Finally, the tyrant's set me free! I dance only in *The Maid of the Mill* tonight and rehearsal for *The Recruiting Officer* Saturday concerns me not.
> So, prepare thyself, O Water Sprite.
> H. R.

As dusk approached, Sophie found she was both nervous and excited. Earlier in the day, she had delivered the notice to the local press that *Ode to Shakespeare* with chorus and orchestra would make its surprise debut at Drury Lane the following day, opposite *The Recruiting Officer* at Covent Garden. Saturday morning, the sudden change in program at Old Drury would be all the talk. Once it became generally known that Garrick also planned to present his own expanded staged version of the Stratford Jubilee, rumors about Covent Garden's elaborate satiric broadside were sure to surface, especially because both presentations were being rehearsed at a frantic pace and involved scores of participants who dearly loved to gossip. The battle would soon be joined.

The night watchman called out the hour of twelve. Sophie looked up from the sheet of dialogue she had rewritten several times during the last hour and pulled her dressing gown more tightly around her shoulders against the September chill. In her abode, all was quiet. She dipped her quill once more into the pot of ink nearby and penned a few more lines, which she promptly crossed out, pursing her lips with frustration.

A few minutes later, she heard the sound of a heavy tread upon the stairs. The door to her quarters flew open, and Hunter burst into the chamber. His imposing presence filled the room.

Flinging down her pen, Sophie jumped to her feet and ran toward him, allowing him to fold her into his embrace. She tilted her head, fully expecting to be kissed. Instead, he leaned down and pressed his nose against hers.

"You received my missives?"

Sophie nodded, bumping noses.

"And you understand why I've not slept in your bed till now?" he asked with mock severity.

"You've been rehearsing," she teased in return. "That, or you've been consorting with some other wench."

"One wanton of your caliber is surely all this laddie could handle," he retorted, pulling her close. "And do you know what I've been rehearsing?" he asked, wrapping a fistful of her hair around his hand and inhaling its scent.

"Rumors abound," she whispered, staring into his blue eyes.

"Ah, yes . . . rumors," he said softly, leaning forward to nuzzle his lips below her ear. "I hear all sorts of rumors as well." He reached for the fastenings on her dressing gown and slowly, deliberately began to unhook them, grazing his fingers against her breast. "Let us forget about the playhouse tittle-tattle for tonight," he said on a low breath. His fingers parted the thin fabric as his eyes absorbed the sight of her nakedness. "Bless me, Sophie . . . let us not talk at *all*!"

Chapter 28

The sound of hawkers calling their wares along Half Moon Passage roused Sophie from a deep sleep. She released herself from Hunter's possessive grasp, guessing the time to be just past dawn. She eased gingerly toward the edge of the mattress, motivated by her obligation to distribute the playbills that were stacked in the printing room. But before she could pull herself to a sitting position, she felt Hunter's forearm hook around her waist, pulling her close to him again.

"No . . . no, dinna rise yet," he mumbled, his Scottish accent reasserting itself in his groggy state. "I'll not let you escape our bed . . . not for the entire day, wench!" he growled playfully, nibbling at the nape of her neck while he cupped one of her breasts in his large palm. His fingers gently massaged the sensitive nipple, and he smiled when it stiffened like a thorn.

"Hunter!" she remonstrated, and then began to squirm as his hands and lips relentlessly tickled her tender flesh. "You'd best beware, you rogue!" she parried, darting her hand out to grasp the most sensitive portion of his anatomy.

However, before she could effectively neutralize his assault, Hunter captured both her hands and rolled her on her back. Entrapping her beneath his larger frame, he seized her wrists, pressing them into the pillow above her head.

"Surrender, minx!" he commanded, lowering his head to kiss her while pinning her firmly against the mattress. "Surrender, or I shall extract full punishment!"

They stared into each other's eyes for a long, spine-tingling moment. Then Sophie smiled.

"Please do."

He took her swiftly then, sensing, as she did, that they had no need of preliminaries this time. Their bodies, so in tune, ached with the same insatiable desire. When, at length, they lay quietly in each other's arms, Hunter rested his head on Sophie's shoulder.

"I think I shall sleep for a week and 'tis all your fault," he declared softly, threading his fingers through hers. "You've quite exhausted me."

"Well, sleep if you must, but I have work to do," she teased, kissing the top of his head.

"You insult me," he retorted in mock protest. "How can you think of your ink pot when such a handsome knave is in your bed?"

"'Tis not writing I must do. I have placards to deliver."

"For Drury?" he asked, shifting his weight to his elbow. "What plays there this evening?" he inquired casually, toying with an edge of the counterpane.

"I'll hazard a guess you know full well what's playing tonight," she declared, sitting abruptly upright in bed.

"I have my suspicions," he laughed.

Without warning, Hunter bolted out of bed and sprinted naked into the printing room, with Sophie in hot pursuit. He snatched a playbill from the pile stacked on the wooden printing press.

"Why, the old fox . . ." he said in a breath, staring at the placard. "The rascal restages his ode to beat us to the punch." Hunter turned to Sophie and encircled her throat with one hand in a sham attempt at strangling her. "I should have known that as his printer, you've been privy to these plans." Sophie stared up at him, refusing to answer. He then relaxed his grip and grinned down at her. "I expect you've learned something of *our* scheme as well," he said, leading her back to the bedstead that was pushed against the wall in the other room. "Too many players are involved . . . 'twas bound to get about the town."

Sophie shrugged and pulled the counterpane up to her chin.

"I suppose half of London knows by now that Colman plans to satirize the Jubilee," she admitted.

Hunter climbed in bed next to her, leaning against the mahogany headboard.

"He's taken the easy path . . . adapting *Man and Wife* so as to send the main characters to Stratford for the Jubilee."

"And I suppose he portrays events there as a disaster?" Sophie asked glumly.

"Of course!" Hunter chortled. "I play a character unmistakably like George Garrick. I drink porter night and day, and I'm driven crazy by local rustics who blame the cannons for causing the deluge. 'Tis hilarious." His smile faded, and he cast her a sidelong glance. "In fact," he continued, choosing his words carefully, "you could help me prepare for the role." Sophie remained silent in the face of Hunter's request. "What were some of George's most ludicrous foibles?" he asked. "His little mannerisms or phrases that could help me create the part?"

"Surely you do not expect me to aid you in deriding the people with whom I work?" she chided.

"Well . . ." Hunter replied uncertainly, "I'd hoped you might—" Sophie stiffened and he halted midsentence. "'Tis only a little thing I'm asking," he protested.

"You are asking me to help you mock a man who's been unerringly kind to me," she said in a low voice, "and kind to you. Your play at Covent Garden ridicules a man who gave much of himself—and his pocketbook—to the Shakespeare Jubilee. His brother, George, for all his faults and vanities, is kin to David Garrick . . . and my colleague!"

Sophie sat up in bed, yanking the bed linen under her arms. Her mouth was set in a grim line and she stared straight ahead.

"Sophie . . . really, there's no need—"

"People like your Colman and . . . and Dr. Johnson find it ever so much simpler to snipe from the sidelines," she fumed. "None of those people truly wish Garrick well, and yet they claim to be his friends. Can't you see, they're simply *envious* and they use *you* to spread their venom!"

Hunter tweaked her nose playfully.

"'Tis not venom . . ." he countered lightly. "'Tis for the public's amusement. Surely you must admit, Sophie, Garrick *is* a mite vain. He's been good to you and me, but perhaps our production will shrink his head to the correct size."

Sophie turned to face her lover with clenched fists.

"You simply parrot the backbiting you hear at Covent Garden!" she exclaimed, suddenly furious.

"Now, don't scrape your claws on me, Sophie, my love," Hunter retorted. "Admit it, lass . . . Garrick's a bit of a peacock, like all of us actors."

Sophie jumped from the bed and angrily donned her dressing gown, tying its sash with an angry jerk.

"I don't think you should put yourself on the same cast list as David Garrick—yet!" she glared at him.

"God's eyeballs! What is wrong with you?" Hunter demanded, swinging his long legs over the mattress.

"I *hate* disloyalty!" she cried passionately. "I *hate* uncertainty about who one's friends are!" She began to pace the room. "There must be people one can count on not to snipe and snivel. *Someone* who wishes one well, wants one to succeed! 'Tis how I feel about you!"

"And I about *you*!" Hunter retorted, exasperated.

"Oh, *do* you?" she demanded. "If it advanced your suit at Covent Garden, would you tell Colman what you know of *my* work before it sees the stage at Drury Lane? All this reminds me of *The Parsimonious Parson* . . . you were willing then to play toady to your employer in service to your own ambitions!"

Hunter was now angry himself.

"As I've told you a number of times," he said coldly, "I had no hand in stealing your precious plot. I didn't do it then and I wouldn't do it now—or ever. If you will remember, Sophie, I shared my pay packet with you."

"To ease your conscience, I suppose!" she retorted.

"How unlike you to be so vicious," he said quietly.

"No more vicious than your words about David Garrick," she replied defensively.

"'Tis not the same! David Garrick is certainly a brilliant manager and a sublime player, but anyone would tell you he's a man with a healthy sense of his own importance." He gazed at her quizzically. "Why is my simply stating that fact making you so angry?" he asked. "What are you afraid of, Sophie? This display of pique cannot merely be about whether or not Garrick is a wee bit vain. If the truth be known—all we actors are."

"How true!" Sophie shot back. Then, she heaved a sigh and said sadly, "What I suppose this argument is about, Hunter . . . is that I don't know if I trust you to put my welfare . . . ahead of your desire to succeed at what you do."

Hunter stared at her for a long moment.

"Perhaps 'tis *all* men whom you distrust after marrying a lying wastrel like Peter Lindsay."

"Perhaps you're right," she replied tersely. "Perhaps I've had good reason."

Hunter rose from the bed and quickly donned his breeches. In a trice, he had slipped on a cambric shirt.

"If you do not trust me after all we've shared—and especially after these last weeks," he said, his words clipped, "perhaps you are incapable of trust itself."

Stung, Sophie blinked back tears. A heavy weight seemed to press against her chest. She turned her back to him and tried to control her emotions. Hunter lay a gentle hand on her shoulder.

"Surely you know I love you," he said softly, ". . . that I would do nothing to hurt you."

"You *have* hurt me," she said with more sorrow than anger. She turned to face him. "You do not hesitate to chastise me for what I fear myself—that I shall never feel safe or trust men who believe their welfare and advancement invariably comes first, regardless of how much they convince themselves they love a woman."

Hunter didn't reply and his silence hung heavily between them. At last he said, "We work for rival playhouses. As you mentioned on our last night in Stratford, 'tis a situation fraught with peril. I said then, 'Why not write your comedies for Colman?' " He placed his hands on both her shoulders and added insistently, "Why do you not? 'Twould help untangle this coil."

"I don't think you've been listening very carefully," she

replied tiredly, looking away to stare out her window at the morning traffic in the street below. "Garrick has been my champion—he even brought us back together! I cannot be disloyal to him now, when everyone is out to humiliate him. Including you."

"Well, what about your loyalty to *me*?" Hunter protested. "You've known me far longer than David Garrick—and I've certainly championed you in a few scrapes."

"You've done that to be sure, Hunter," she agreed, seeking common ground. "And I do love you for it . . . just as I love Garrick for the care and kindness he's shown us both."

"*Just* as you love Garrick?" he quoted with feigned dismay. He sat on the bed and grasped her hand, pulling her next to him.

"Well, not *exactly* as I love Garrick," she admitted with a ghost of a smile, impulsively kissing him beneath his ear. Then, her hands flew suddenly to her face. "The placards!" she said urgently. "I must deliver the placards!"

❄

Garrick's *Ode to Shakespeare* was as resounding a success at London's Drury Lane as it had been in the waterlogged Rotunda in Stratford. Then, a week later, Colman's spoof of the Jubilee made its debut. Anyone not performing at Drury Lane that night trooped down Bow Street to join excited audience members crowded into Covent Garden's large hall.

"God's bones, what if it's brilliant?" Sophie whispered in Lorna's ear as the orchestra commenced playing an overture that was clearly reminiscent of *Dawn Serenade*.

It soon became apparent, however, that Colman's effort at Covent Garden was far from stellar. It was not even very original or witty, despite Hunter's hilarious mimicry of the well-known idiosyncrasies of George Garrick. In Colman's grand finale, the parade of Shakespeare characters wore lackluster stock costumes and his players strolled across the boards in no particular order.

"I do believe Colman's best cannot sink our ship." Lorna beamed smugly at Sophie.

Lorna's confident prediction proved resoundingly true.

Hunter learned, as did many of his fellow players at Covent Garden, that, indeed, David Garrick had yet another card to play.

"You knew Garrick was mounting more than just the ode, but you never said a word!" Hunter exclaimed, as he and Sophie took their seats in the gallery at Drury Lane on opening night of Garrick's *Jubilee* satire. Members of the Covent Garden company who were not working on this particular night had flocked to the rival theater.

"I've repeated nothing about what I know of this play, nor has anything you told me about Covent Garden's spoof been repeated to Garrick or his people," she protested. "'Tis all I can think to do in such a situation!"

He nodded an acknowledgment as Drury Lane's curtain parted and comedian Tom King trotted on stage, dressed as a waiter, to recite the prologue. Soon, the audience was convulsed as scene after scene realistically depicting the astounding, ludicrous, and outrageous events of that momentous rainy week in Stratford unfolded brilliantly in front of their eyes.

At one point, the crowd exploded with laughter as an ostensibly empty coach parked on stage began to rock wildly back and forth. Mavis Piggott's former amour, Geoffrey Bannister, playing one of the morning serenaders, stepped forward and made his musical observations:

Blankets without sheeting, Sir,
Dinners without eating, Sir
Naught without much cheating, Sir
Thus 'tis night and day, Sir,
I hope that you will stay, Sir,
To see our Jubilee!

"He's portraying *you*, darling!" Sophie whispered teasingly.

Hunter pursed his lips and did not reply because the stage was now filled with a whirl of activity. Porters juggled baggage, waiters flew back and forth carrying trays piled high with food, a cook chased two men stealing ribs of beef. Even a figure dressed like James Boswell in a Corsican costume ambled across the stage offering his book for sale while the sounds of exploding cannons blasted off stage!

Sophie and everyone around her howled with laughter at the comical sights that cheerfully satirized everything negative that had been said or written about the actual Jubilee—including comments George Colman had himself published as a "correspondent" for the London news journals.

Sophie glanced sideways at Hunter, who appeared glum despite the prevailing hilarity. He slumped deeper into his chair as the pageant of Shakespeare's characters finally made their much-heralded entrances. Garrick had wisely identified each of the bard's plays with a short, instantly recognizable vignette—Shylock pleaded for justice in *The Merchant of Venice;* Titania and Oberon swept across the stage in a gilt carriage drawn by cupids and butterflies as part of *A Midsummer Night's Dream.* If that weren't enough, banners identifying each play guaranteed that everyone would get the message. Sophie's eyes widened at the scores of characters brandishing flaming swords, brass trumpets, and gaudy umbrellas. Garrick had employed everything and anything to achieve a startling visual effect. It was the largest spectacle London theatergoers had ever witnessed.

Afterward, Hunter and Sophie threaded their way through the chattering crowds and walked across the Great Piazza in silence. Once inside Sophie's chambers, he turned to her and said morosely, "Covent Garden has been put to shame."

Several days afterward, Sophie entered The Nag's Head before Hunter's nightly performance at the appointed hour. As she slipped into the bench opposite him, she saw from the scowl on his face that something was very wrong.

"I've been sacked," he announced without preliminaries, taking a deep draught from a tankard of ale. "Colman has accused me of telling Garrick—through you—the precise details of what we were planning so that Drury Lane could counter him with its own version of *The Jubilee.*"

"But that's preposterous!" Sophie declared. "Garrick

came up with the notion of spoofing the event during the return coach trip from Stratford!"

"Preposterous or not," Hunter replied, tight-lipped, "Colman blames me for having to close down his version of the *Jubilee.*"

Sophie reached across the table to clasp his hand.

"Oh, Hunter, I'm so sorry—" she began.

"Well, *did* you inform David Garrick what we'd spoken about?" he demanded. "Did you tell him I was to play George Garrick, for instance?"

"Of course not! I never repeated a word to Garrick of anything you ever said to me regarding Colman's *Jubilee!*" she exclaimed. Sacked! In the middle of the season! 'Twas the worst fate that could befall an actor. Sophie squeezed Hunter's hand sympathetically. "That's a terribly unjust accusation for Colman to make, Hunter," she continued heatedly. "I'm certain, if I went and assured him that neither of us did any such thing—"

"It seems to me, the less you are involved in my professional life, the better!" he retorted angrily.

Sophie felt as if she'd been slapped. She stared at him, her empathy dissolving with his bitter words.

"Hunter," she said in a low voice, "you know as well as I do that there are theatrical spies at both playhouses. But I assure you, I wasn't one of them! You can't blame *me* for what has happened?" Hunter merely cast her a measured glance, but remained silent. "That Colman's a spiteful wretch! He should look to his own deficiencies of talent for the reason his *Jubilee* has failed!" she exclaimed. "Garrick also knows you and I have become lovers, but has he sacked me from my job printing placards? Of course not! Colman is a perfect beast!"

"Why should Garrick care if anything you knew got back to Colman?" Hunter retorted. "His *Jubilee* is the big success."

"Right! 'Tis more amusing and better produced!" Sophie blurted. "The fact is, Hunter, I didn't tell people at Drury Lane that you were playing George Garrick . . . but, what if I had mentioned to *you* something about Drury Lane's production . . . merely in passing," Sophie pressed, her eyes blazing. "Would you have then informed *Colman* of the details?" Hunter's expression wavered, and he toyed with the handle of his pewter tankard.

"Probably not," he answered finally.

" 'Probably not,' " Sophie echoed sarcastically. "Probably not isn't a comforting answer!"

Hunter leaned against the high-sided booth and gazed across the table, his face expressionless.

"Well, my dear Sophie, perhaps your standards of conduct are simply too high for a mere mortal like me."

" 'Tis simply a standard of loyalty and decency," Sophie replied wearily.

Hunter was silenced by the finality in her voice. He breathed deeply and gazed at the tavern's low-beamed ceiling, as if to collect his thoughts.

" 'Tis *you and I* who concern me . . . not Colman or Garrick," he said in a more conciliatory tone. "I wish *us* to succeed, and now I don't have a place at Covent Garden." He banged his fist on the table. "Jesu! To be a mere wandering player again . . ."

Sophie suddenly felt a renewed sense of sympathy. Hunter had ambitions beyond acting, and she understood his frustration and humiliation at losing his job as assistant manager at Covent Garden. She reached for his hand once more.

"Perhaps . . ." she began hesitantly, ". . . perhaps you could speak to Garrick to see if he'd take you on. After all, he selected you especially for the Parade of Characters in Stratford—"

"That was more a favor to you than an endorsement of my performing talents," he responded harshly.

" 'Tisn't so!" Sophie protested. "He did us both a kindness, but he truly admires your work, Hunter. Let me ask him."

"No!" Hunter thundered, and several diners turned from their conversations to stare at them. The muscles in his jaw line grew taut and he took a moment to compose himself. "Thomas Arne will be staging the musical portions at Drury Lane forever. I'd have no future there, and I *won't* have a woman playing the pimp for me."

Sophie felt a flush of anger infuse her cheeks.

"Have you never let a woman procure for you, Hunter?" she asked icily. "What about the employment secured by your dear friend Mavis Piggott at the Orchard Theater in Bath? I don't recall your spurning that offer . . . and didn't she arrange a position for you at Smock Alley that year?"

Sophie's barb hit its mark. Hunter rose to his feet and flung several coins on the table.

"You're a clever, quick-witted woman, Sophie McGann," he said testily. "Clever enough, I'm sure, to see yourself home." And with that, he stalked out of the Nag's Head and marched down the road.

Sophie fully expected Hunter's temper to cool and for him to get in touch with her—but he did not. After a week of silence, she finally summoned the courage to visit his lodgings. There she discovered that Colman had required Hunter to give up his quarters above the theater as a result of having been discharged.

"He's departed without a word!" Sophie wailed to Lorna who shook her head helplessly. "When there are problems, he simply decamps for another bloody playhouse in the kingdom!"

Soon afterward, Sophie noticed in a billboard in *The Public Advertiser* that a certain H. Roberto was dancing the *allemande* in a production of *Il Padre E Il Figlio* at the King's Opera House. She begged Lorna to accompany her to a performance on an evening when her friend was not scheduled to dance at Drury Lane. They soon spotted a tall, distinctly non-Italian player carrying a spear and dancing briefly in the elaborate musical production.

"'Tis a total waste of his talents!" Sophie exclaimed as they hailed a hackney to return to Half Moon Passage. "Why would Hunter prefer this to an honored place at Drury Lane?"

"'Tis his pride," Lorna shrugged. "And your stubbornness. Why don't you seek him out?"

Sophie merely shook her head angrily, silently recalling

the hurt she'd felt when she discovered Hunter had moved lodgings without saying a word.

Roderick Darnly strode into the foyer of his magnificent dwelling on St. James's Street as soon as his butler had opened the door.

"Thank you for responding so promptly to my pleas," he welcomed Sophie, raising her hand to his lips in greeting. He gestured at the scaffolding encasing the grand staircase behind him. "I found the entire house in a shambles when I arrived from Wales last week."

"I expect these refurbishments always take twice as long as one intends." Sophie smiled, allowing her host to guide her into his mahogany-paneled study where a bountiful tea was laid out. The viscount's silent parlor maid poured them cups of the steaming brew and departed discreetly. "How are things with your family?" she asked quietly.

"You mean what's left of it?" he responded grimly. "My mother keeps to her suite, mostly. We secured a wheeled chair for Father, so he can still make everyone miserable when he leaves his sick chamber. But, in truth, his health is frail and his speech is quite impaired."

"He suffers from paralysis?" she asked sympathetically.

"On one side, only. 'Tis most peculiar. But even when he slurs his words, he lets everyone know he is still the Earl of Llewelyn."

"And Evansmor?" Sophie asked tentatively.

"Shut up tight, as he ordered," he said shortly. "I've taken a wing of Glynmorgan Castle so far removed from the family quarters, I might as well be living in Bath," he joked tersely. "But, it makes supervising the estates less taxing."

"So, the earl has allowed you to shoulder the burden of running his affairs?" she asked tactfully.

"He won't admit it, but he hasn't much of a choice," Roderick said with a bleak smile. "No matter how much bad blood exists between us, it *is* thicker than water."

"But, here you are in London, pulling your house apart."

"I must have some reward for all my hard work this year," he said lightly. "Father's factor and the mine and ironworks stewards are perfectly capable of keeping things going, now we've made the adjustment since the . . . accident. This house has needed attending to since I first purchased it."

"And Trevor Bedloe?" Sophie asked cautiously, surmising that a viscount's coffers must be far more ample than those of a mere "Honorable." "What of him?"

"I've employed him to supervise the refurbishments here," Roderick answered levelly. "In fact, would you like to see what we've managed to accomplish thus far? I'd like your advice about some things that need a woman's touch."

As Sophie sipped her tea and nibbled on a morsel of cake, the tumultuous events she had witnessed in Wales almost seemed to have happened in another life. Could she possibly have stumbled upon a slumbering Roderick entwined in the naked arms of Trevor and the parlor maid, Glynnis? And then there was her memory of her host in a monk's cowl, participating in the horrifying rituals at the beech grove, and later, the new viscount emerging from the Darnly Mines carrying the broken body of his twin brother. Sophie's hands trembled slightly as she conjured up such unlikely recollections.

A few minutes later, Roderick commenced a tour of the redecorated ballroom upstairs where workers on tall ladders were installing two impressive crystal chandeliers. The two of them ambled down a long corridor, glancing through open doorways at a series of bedrooms in various stages of renewal. Then, descending several flights of stairs, Roderick halted at a door at the end of a hallway and gazed gravely at Sophie.

"'Tis not the gardener's cottage, but my idea for these rooms was rather on that order."

He opened the door to a suite with its own entrance featuring a beautifully appointed sitting room. Pushed against one wall was the handsome carved desk Roderick had provided for Sophie's use while in Wales. Through an adjoining door she glimpsed Trevor Bedloe conferring with a carpenter who was in the process of attaching ornate moldings to the walls.

Trevor turned at the sound of their entrance and inclined his head in greeting.

"Good afternoon, m'lady," he murmured. "Sir," he added, acknowledging his employer.

"Mr. Bedloe," Sophie replied softly, doing her best to retain her composure.

Roderick casually pointed out the improvements he had ordered for the elegant bedroom, including an indoor water closet. Sophie found herself nervously chirping effusive compliments as they retraced their steps to the foyer.

"'Tis reserved for you, whenever you desire a quiet, secluded place for your writing," he announced, gazing at her steadily. "The selection of curtains, bed hangings, and counterpane has yet to be made. . . . I rather hoped you'd have some notion of what would suit in the way of color." Sophie was speechless and attempted to appear occupied with fastening her cloak. What did this generosity truly signify, she wondered? "You were a marvelous companion in Wales," he continued, as if talking about the weather. "'Tis been a lonely time for me, as you can imagine. I thought, with your own entrance leading out to the mews, you could come and go here as you liked. But we could enjoy each other's company on occasion, as we did at Evansmor."

"Roderick I . . . I—" she stammered.

"'Twill be weeks before the house will be finished," he interjected smoothly. "No need to make up your mind," he added. "Just say you'll think on it."

Before Sophie could summon a sensible reply, Lord Darnly had called for his coach to transport her back to her own lodgings.

Sophie stared distractedly out of the coach window as the vehicle rolled along the perimeter of St. James's Park. When the carriage encountered a knot of traffic near the King's Opera House, she leaned forward suddenly, convinced that the tall figure walking toward an alleyway leading to the stage entrance was Hunter Robertson.

"Driver!" she shouted out the window. "Stop! Please!"

The coach lurched to a halt and Sophie flung open the door.

"Hunter! Hunter!" she cried, waving in his direction.

The object of her frantic appeal halted in his tracks and observed her dashing to his side. "Oh, Hunter," she panted, reaching out to take hold of his arm to steady herself, "why have I not heard from you? 'Tis ridiculous, your carrying spears when I know if I—"

"Used your influence, you could secure me employment?" he said coldly, staring over her head at Roderick Darnly's coach emblazoned with its familiar gold crest. "Thank you, but no thank you," he declared, turning toward the alleyway.

"Hunter! Blast your bones, what is wrong with you!" she cried.

"Absolutely nothing," he replied grimly. "The problem lies with you, I believe, and your penchant for seeking favors from the likes of Peter Lindsay and my lord Roderick Darnly whenever you're short of funds."

"Good God, Hunter!" she exclaimed. "I merely accept a ride to my lodgings in the carriage of a friend and you—"

"Or a trip to Wales, where you had your own cottage in a secluded grove," he snapped, "and where your host could come and go as he pleased?"

Sophie stared up at Hunter, horrified that his accurate recounting of her time spent on the Darnly estates did, indeed, imply that she had played the strumpet with Viscount Glyn.

"Who gave you such a description of my conduct?" she demanded.

"Who hasn't?" he retorted. "If you thought we theater folk are discreet, you greatly miscalculated."

"Mavis Piggott," Sophie said wearily, recalling the languid looks cast by the actress in the direction of Drury Lane's enigmatic patron.

"'Twas the talk of Drury Lane, I'm told."

"I have not behaved like a harlot with anyone—except you," she said in a low voice.

"No?" Hunter said. "Then why did you not tell me of your four-month sojourn in Wales with Darnly?"

Silently, she recollected the frenetic pace of the Stratford Jubilee and the brief snatches of time she and Hunter had spent together since their return to London—time mostly spent savoring each other's charms in bed.

"Shall I tell you why I never mentioned it?" she asked quietly. "I simply forgot. The viscount and I were never lovers, and I am still not even sure we are friends. Once I was with you again, I never gave Roderick Darnly a single thought."

"Well, it appears he's given *you* a great deal of thought," Hunter declared, nodding toward the coach.

Sophie looked at him with something close to pity.

"Hunter," she said slowly, "it appears your old devils have returned to plague you. Think what you will."

And with that, she strode toward Darnly's carriage and bid the coachman to proceed to Half Moon Passage immediately.

March of 1770 proved to be a cold, blustery month conducive to remaining indoors. However, after a week of confinement, Sophie donned her warmest clothes and made the trek to Garrick's country manor, Hampton House, where she was invited to discuss *The Bogus Baronet*, the play which, at long last, she had submitted to Drury Lane's manager.

"Your recommendations will improve it immensely," she agreed, retrieving her manuscript from Garrick's desk in his library.

"Excellent!" the actor-manager smiled, "for I would like to present it before the current season ends."

"Truly?" Sophie said, her spirits lifting for the first time in months.

"Absolutely," replied her employer. "And I believe 'tis safe to submit it in the name of Sophie McGann, if you like. 'Tis a theme that might appeal to Edward Capell, as he despises pretentious fops."

But in April, David Garrick was taken ill with gout and repaired to Bath for ten days to take the waters. In his absence, James Lacy charged his apparent confidante, Viscount Glyn, with the responsibility of personally delivering Sophie's manuscript to Edward Capell and waiting for his decree.

Suddenly, the black enameled door marking the Lord Chamberlain's office at St. James's Palace swung open and Lord Darnly strode toward Sophie, his lips curling in a satisfied smile.

"Well, my dear," he chuckled as he assisted her into his waiting coach, "you are now a scribbler of farces in your own name. Capell has granted your play a license."

Emitting an unladylike squeal that could have startled the horses, Sophie snatched the manuscript from his hands and stared at the precious imprimatur scrawled on the title page in Capell's own hand: "Licensed to Act."

Garrick's infirmities improved enough for him to mount *The Bogus Baronet* as the last original play presented during the 1769–1770 season.

"Sophie," Roderick chided from his front seat in box three, "for pity's sake, move your chair forward a bit or you won't see a whit of your own play." The viscount had not pressed her again on the issue of residing in his home, but had proved remarkably supportive during the nerve-wracking process of mounting her play.

"I can't bear to watch," she groaned, moving her seat deeper into the shadows behind the velvet swag attached to a nearby wall. One of the programs she had printed, touting "a five-act farce by Sophie McGann" lay crumpled at her feet.

But, by hour's end, she was leaning against the railing, drinking in the audience's delighted reaction to the unmasking of a pretentious young scalawag who eventually received his just desserts for attempting to pass as a member of the nobility.

As the actors took their bows, cheers rang in her ears, and eventually, she was prompted by Roderick to rise to her feet and acknowledge the cries of "Author! Author!" Inclining her head graciously, she could only wish that Hunter were there to witness it all.

The Bogus Baronet enjoyed a respectable run of eight evenings, yielding two Author's Night Benefits for Sophie that were worth nearly two hundred pounds. She rather hoped to receive congratulations from Hunter, but no word came, and as the summer began in earnest, she sadly assumed he had taken employment outside of London.

"He'll eventually recover his temper," Lorna reassured her on the eve of the dancer's departure for Sadler's Wells.

Sophie merely gazed at her friend pessimistically. The following day, she bid Lorna farewell at the Soho coaching station and braced herself for a long summer in the city.

On a sun-filled afternoon in early June, Sophie sat across from David Garrick in the Treasure Room and stared in awe at a pile of coins worth some £189—money she had earned in her own name from her own pen!

"Have you any notions for other projects you'd like to discuss?" Garrick asked, expectantly.

"I-I'd like to write about Bedlam," she said softly. "I'd like to show the true insanity of the methods employed there."

Garrick gazed at her thoughtfully.

"A tragicomedy, I should think . . . nothing too heavy-handed, else your audience will consider themselves scolded, not entertained."

"I suppose you're right," laughed Sophie ruefully.

"However, my dear, I think you should refrain from such a weighty subject until you've had a bit more experience in the trenches." He pulled a manuscript bound in a battered leather binding from a nearby shelf. "Perhaps this might interest you . . . and could prepare you for such an effort in the future." He patted the manuscript. "This is a play by Aphra Behn . . . do you know her work?" he asked.

"I know some of it," Sophie replied, her interest piqued. "My father stocked many of her plays, though she died . . . what . . . eighty years ago?"

"Excellent!" he smiled. "Well, she was a brilliant but eccentric woman, some would say 'indelicate.' She was despised by polite society for her audacity in taking up a calling essentially reserved for men in that day. Sad to say,

Aphra was left destitute and abandoned at her death. But she wrote at least thirteen novels and had some seventeen plays mounted in seventeen years—more than any gentleman of that age I could name," Garrick smiled. "At any rate, this play, *Forced Marriage,* has always intrigued me."

Sophie peered at a date scratched on the first page.

" '1671,' " she read in awe. " 'Tis almost exactly a hundred years ago."

"Precisely my thought," Garrick smiled. "Would you like to read it and consider adapting it for us for next season? 'Tis a tragicomedy, like your notion about a play concerning Bedlam. 'Tis well structured, but I think it could be made more appropriate to our age. Will you have at it?"

Sophie was touched by Garrick's offer to learn this form of play writing from such a mistress of it as Aphra Behn. Swiftly agreeing to his proposal, she made her exit from Drury Lane's Treasure Room with a pouch of heavy coins in one hand and the ninety-nine-year-old manuscript by Aphra Behn in the other. As she paused in the passageway to tuck the money into her bodice, she was unable to repress a smile of pleasure.

Downstairs, Sophie groped her way through the murky candlelight that barely illuminated the back stage area.

"Ready to take up the quill again so soon?" a gruff voice said from the shadows.

"Wha—?" gasped Sophie, unnerved by a tall figure emerging from the darkness. Her heart began to beat erratically, followed immediately by a crushing sense of disappointment. "G-good afternoon, Roderick." She faltered as Viscount Glyn strode toward her in the gloom. "You startled me. . . . I thought the place deserted."

Sophie was amazed at how Roderick Darnly always seemed to know the smallest details of what transpired at Drury Lane. Then again, he was a partner of sorts, a mortgage-holder of some of Lacy's Drury Lane shares, and thus privy to much playhouse business.

"As you may know," she replied, observing him closely, "Mr. Garrick has asked me to adapt a play by Aphra Behn—a tragicomedy."

"Really?" he said laconically. "Isn't that a bit of a stretch for a mistress of frothy tales about counterfeit aristocrats?" Sophie grasped the worn leather cover of the manuscript Garrick had entrusted to her.

"Fortunately," she replied gamely, "Mr. Garrick believes I am eminently suited to the task of adapting this particular work."

"Forgive me, Sophie, but I believe your high aspirations have wrongly prompted you to abandon what you do best— amusing farce," he opined. "For myself, I am disappointed by this news. I had hoped to try to place your next comedy with someone eager to revitalize a certain playhouse this summer."

As she had always suspected, it now appeared that Roderick Darnly had higher theatrical ambitions than merely controlling a few shares at Drury Lane. He would not wish to accept crumbs from Garrick's table. Extending his sway at some summer pleasure garden was undoubtedly his next goal.

"Perhaps, if I can find the time, I can write both," she suggested brightly.

Much to her consternation, he nodded.

"I would like that very much indeed," he said calmly. "It needn't be Shakespeare, my dear," he continued dryly, "it need merely be amusing—and quickly conceived, I might add. I would need a manuscript by the end of July, at the latest."

"I-I shall do my best," Sophie said faintly.

"And if you seek a quiet place to work, the chambers I showed you are at your disposal," he added.

"You're very kind," she murmured, "but for the nonce—"

"As you wish," he interrupted.

Begging his leave, she quickly left through the back stage door, wondering how in the world she could ever live up to the demands being made of her. For the second time in an hour, she was startled practically witless by another figure accosting her from the shadows as she entered the stairwell to her lodgings.

"Ah . . . at last!" exclaimed an emaciated man suddenly blocking her path.

"Peter!" Sophie gasped as the husband she hadn't seen in years grabbed her wrist.

His coat and knee breeches were wrinkled and frayed, and his linen was in a scandalously filthy state. His nose was laced with a web of fine purple lines that plainly told the story of the damage done by his penchant for strong spirits.

"Ah . . . my fine, *successful* lady wife," he said, lurching forward in a mocking attempt to kiss her hand. "I heard the playhouse was full for both Author's Benefit Nights. You must have earned a fortune from your spoof of old Peter, here."

"Be gone, you drunken fool!"

" 'Bogus baronet' I may be, but I remain your beloved husband," he said sarcastically, tightening his grip. "By rights, whatever money you garner from your pen is mine anyway, and I've come to collect my due," he said menacingly.

Sophie glanced desperately up and down the road. A few men lounging in front of the Cider House across from the Green Canister seemed unlikely to come to her aid.

"I owe you *nothing*!" she hissed. "You lied and cheated and stole from me since the day I met you. And you *killed* our daughter with your reckless behavior!"

With all her might she jerked her hand from Peter's grasp, propelling him against the building. Then, she swung the leather-bound manuscript by Aphra Behn at her estranged husband's midsection with all the force at her command.

Peter folded like a paper fan. His limp body slid down the side of the Green Canister until he landed in a sitting position in the road. She had succeeded in knocking the wind out of him. Lest he should try to retaliate, she spun on her heel and fled up the stairwell to her lodgings, sliding the rusty bolt securely across the door for added protection.

Chapter 29

The latch protecting Sophie's lodgings remained firmly bolted during the summer, as much to shut out any distractions as to guard against unwelcome intruders like Peter Lindsay.

On warm days when she arose, Sophie donned a light cotton shift and remained at her desk for hours at a time in a marathon attempt to complete her commissioned adaptation of Aphra Behn's *Forced Marriage* as speedily as possible. She found the long hours of concentrated effort helped numb the painful truth that Hunter continued to believe the worst of her.

Outside her small window, the darkened city was utterly quiet. Sophie pulled open her desk drawer and withdrew the letter she had received that day from Lorna.

> Our owner, Tho. Rosoman, has seen fit to engage as music and dance master at Sadler's Wells, the very one spurned by Colman. I thought, at first, to spare you knowledge H. had fled the town without a word to you, but 'tis my belief you'd want to know he is not far off.
>
> I volunteered that you are well and toiling over yet another playscript. He feigned indifference in a most unconvincing manner. 'Tis my hope, my dear friend, that the two of you will show some gesture of good-will and soon remedy this senseless discord.

Sophie heaved a tired sigh as she replaced Lorna's letter in a drawer. She straightened the growing pile of papers that constituted the new manuscript and crawled into her bed, too exhausted to debate what she should or should not have said to Hunter during their last encounter in front of the King's Opera.

By the end of the month, Sophie sent word to Garrick, who was vacationing at Hampton House, that she had completed her version of Behn's play and had retitled it *A Maid Most Modestly Made*. The reply from his Thames estate upriver from London urged her to bring the work to his country house the following Sunday. He also informed her that Roderick Darnly would be among the invited guests and that he had offered to transport her and several other friends to their destination aboard his private barge.

Reasoning that Garrick was making every effort to maintain a show of cordial relations with Lacy's lender, Sophie arrived dockside at the appointed hour and boarded Roderick's boat for the leisurely trip on the tide.

"Ah . . . Sophie . . . welcome," Lord Darnly greeted her as she stepped on deck. "I see at last you've emerged from your warren. Let's find you a comfortable seat."

The finely appointed barge sat low in the water on this sunny July day and provided bench seating for the guests gathering on deck for the short trip. Roderick cast a glance at the leather-bound manuscript by Aphra Behn that Sophie was returning to Garrick's library, along with her own version of the play tied with a thin silk ribbon.

"May I give these to my footman?" he inquired, extending his lace-cuffed arm.

"Please, no, no thank you," she replied, clasping both scripts more tightly in her hands. Just then, she caught sight of a stooped-shoulder gentleman stepping aboard the barge.

"Ah . . . Capell, my good man," Lord Darnly exclaimed, extending his hand to assist the deputy examiner of plays. "Delighted you could join us." He graciously conducted another round of introductions among the guests on board. "And, of course, by now, you are acquainted with our young scribe, Sophie McGann."

"I am," Capell said sourly.

"Ah . . . well . . . yes," Lord Darnly said with wry amusement. "May I provide you with some small libation?"

"Have you milk?" Capell demanded, confirming Sophie's suspicion that the man clung to his aversion toward any food or drink that wasn't white colored.

"Milk?" Lord Darnly repeated, his lips twitching slightly. "I fear not, sir, would champagne suffice? 'Tis of an ivory hue?"

Capell nodded, but Sophie noticed he touched nary a drop as the liveried servants began poling their way to Hampton House.

"So, you have completed your commission for our august manager, I see," Roderick commented quietly, taking a cushioned seat next to Sophie. "But what of my request? Have you commenced work on the comedy of which we spoke?"

Sophie glanced at him uncomfortably. Squinting into the bright sunlight, she gazed at the rolling downs sloping toward the river, charting the course of a man on horseback leaping handily over a five-barred gate, his hounds braying loudly as they scrambled to keep pace.

"T-to be quite honest with you, Roderick, I've only just finished this piece. I . . . plan to begin the play we spoke of immediately."

"Why that is indeed good news," he replied pleasantly. "Pray divulge, at least, the subject you intend to take up."

Sophie swallowed and shifted her glance once again to the sloping fields on the opposite side of the river. The horseman she had glimpsed was now nearing a copse of larches. He and his steed plunged into the wood, trailed by his pack of excited barking dogs. Absently, she wondered if the foxes were likewise preparing themselves for the approaching hunting season.

"Ah . . . my idea for this farce . . ." she temporized. Then she smiled, her eyes full of mischief at her sudden inspiration. "The exotic South American settings sometimes employed by Aphra Behn put me to mind of the Amazon. I've read her novel *Oroonoko*—"

"Do you not think the subject of slavery offers little in the way of mirth?" he asked blandly.

"*My* notion is to create a magical jungle kingdom where the beasts gain the upper hand over the hunters," she laughed.

If Roderick didn't appreciate her sense of humor, she thought, he could simply cancel his request that she write something for him.

"Hmmm . . . perhaps 'tis an interesting notion," he said. He rested his manicured hands on his brocaded breeches and looked at her intently. "Since it will be rather taxing for you to produce the piece in such short order, perhaps you would like to avail yourself of the suite of rooms I've prepared for your use. I'll have my staff look after your daily needs so you'll have nothing to concern yourself with—except your writing."

As always, Roderick's manner was cool and correct, yet Sophie felt a disconcerting intensity lurking beneath the surface of his ostensibly generous invitation. Having unwittingly been privy, while in Wales, to Darnly's disturbing personal secrets—in addition to having witnessed the sinister ritual performed in the beech grove on his property—she wondered if there weren't even darker disclosures about which she preferred to remain innocent. And besides, even if the viscount's motives toward her were merely prompted by the altruism of a genuine patron of the arts, such a move on her part would only confirm Hunter's worst suspicions. She couldn't for the life of her think of a graceful way to decline his request to write the play, but she was certain about one thing: she had absolutely no intention of taking up residence on St. James's Street.

"You're terribly kind," she replied with as much aplomb as she could muster, "but since my work on the Behn play went so well, I fear I'd feel more comfortable continuing to write in my own flat. Need I say I very much appreciate your thoughtfulness," she added, summoning a smile to her lips.

Roderick's gaze narrowed slightly, but the viscount made no further attempt at persuasion.

"Whatever you deem best, Sophie, my dear," he replied calmly. "Shall we say you'll show me something in a fortnight?"

Sophie suppressed a weary sigh and nodded her agreement.

"I'll do my very best," she said with forced cheerfulness.

"You always do," he replied. "Ah . . . here's the landing to Hampton House. We have arrived."

Sophie was amazed when David Garrick, after warmly greeting his guests, immediately relieved her of both manuscripts and retired to his library while the rest of the company toured the grounds.

"Sophie, you must see our orangery," Eva-Maria Garrick declared in her endearing Viennese accent. "And we have just created a grotto . . . 'tis lovely and cool."

Following their hostess, Sophie, Lord Darnly, Edward Capell, and company trooped back outdoors and were treated to a bracing constitutional, touring points of interest on the riverside estate, including a visit to the Garricks' Temple of Shakespeare, a lovely Greek-style cupola with its own statue of the bard.

"Come, everyone . . . a buffet has been prepared," Eva-Maria called to them gaily, and even the scaly faced Edward Capell appeared cheered by the prospect of refreshments.

Sophie tried not to stare as the government censor loaded his plate with white bread and butter, a slice of pale brie served in honor of some guests visiting from France, plus a dollop of chicken breast. She waited shyly at the edge of the ravenous group until nearly everyone else had served themselves.

"Sophie, may I steal you away before you have your lunch?" David Garrick said, appearing suddenly at the threshold.

Sophie followed her host down a paneled passageway into his library, which was lined to the rafters with books.

"Now, my dear, please do have a seat," he offered, taking a chair behind the desk opposite. He indicated her manuscript which lay open to its final page. "I couldn't be more pleased," he smiled, watching with some amusement as a look of utter astonishment flickered across Sophie's features. "It needs very little work. I think 'tis good you kept the

setting in the French court and retained the dissension between the prince and the king's favorite warrior over the
heroine's affections." He nodded with a satisfied expression.
"But I was glad to see the speeches more naturally phrased
and fewer sword fights. . . . I shall talk to Lacy about finding a place for it in this season's schedule."

"'Tis acceptable?" she said, delighted and amazed.

"'Tis more than acceptable . . . 'tis a marvelous reworking of old Aphra's tale." Garrick frowned suddenly. "Of
course, we shall have to persuade our friend Capell to grant
it license . . . but I'll do my best to see it mounted this
season."

Feeling elated, Sophie followed her host out of the library
and along a corridor that led to the dining salon where she
obtained a plate of food. Then, unobtrusively, she made her
way to a sun-filled terrace, perching happily near an open
window where she was soon able to overhear Garrick chatting inside with the ill-tempered censor, Capell.

"Edward, my good man," Garrick said genially. "I
thought to save my sending a messenger to your chambers
regarding this new work we hope to mount early in the
autumn. May I present it to you myself for your swift perusal?" he added, all charm and good cheer.

Sophie thought she heard the rustle of pages being
turned.

"An adaptation of a work by that Behn creature . . .
mmm . . . I see," Capell said obliquely. "*A Maid Most
Modestly Made,* is it? Don't much like the title, I can tell you
that."

"That certainly presents no problem," Garrick hastened
to assure him. "'Tis a trifle to change a title."

"'Tis admirable of you," Lord Darnly commented, apparently privy to the exchange, "to show such confidence,
assigning a complex subject like marriage contracts to a
young and relatively inexperienced playwright. A new view
of the topic, perhaps?"

Sophie grimaced at hearing Darnly's back-handed com-
pliment, which she feared would only serve to arouse
Capell's antipathy. Was Roderick fanning the flames of
Capell's prejudice against women writers in hopes that her

play for Garrick might be refused a government license? That would certainly serve to free up her time to pursue the comedy he wished her to write. Or was this merely his form of retribution for her having recently spurned his offer of hospitality? Was this supposed patron of the arts becoming increasingly possessive of her play-writing skills—or her person—she wondered?

"Miss McGann's talent and sensibility make her eminently suited to this task, I believe," Garrick replied mildly.

"She may well know how to hold a pen and make scratches with it," Capell remarked rancorously, "but she has failed to learn the proper decorum for a member of her sex. I have heard the woman shamelessly deserted her husband."

"Her husband is a notorious drunkard and a rake," Garrick noted sharply. "Surely, you know that?"

"I fear I am, like Jonathan Swift, of the opinion that these female scribblers do naught but expose the faults and misfortunes of both sexes," Capell retorted, "at the expense of public morale. But, of course, sir," he added, making an effort to appear fair-minded, "I shall read it from first act to last and consult with you directly."

"I'd greatly appreciate that, Edward," Garrick said in his most amenable manner. "Have you tried a bit of white asparagus? Mrs. Garrick thought you might prefer it. She ordered our gardeners to plant some in your honor last season."

The following Tuesday in London, Mrs. Phillips called up to Sophie that a messenger from Drury Lane had just delivered a letter for her. Sophie dashed down the stairwell to fetch it, breaking Garrick's seal with trembling fingers.

I most regretfully inform you that the Lord Chamberlain's office—for reasons left unarticulated—has refused licence for *A Maid Most Modestly Made*. I hope you will call on me at the theater at your earliest convenience.

Yrs., D. Garrick

She stared at the missive with anger and dismay. All those hours toiling past midnight! Her cramped shoulders and bloodshot eyes! All that effort obliterated with the stroke of a pen, thanks to the capricious judgments of one spiteful, woman-hating little bureaucrat!

"What is it, my dear?" Mrs. Phillips exclaimed, observing Sophie's angry scowl.

But Sophie hadn't heard the query. She was already marching down Half Moon Passage to The Strand where she hailed a hackney and directed the driver to speed to St. James's Palace.

Storming through the black door with its discreet brass plaque denoting the Lord Chamberlain's office, Sophie pulled up short at the sight of a tall figure lounging in the antechamber, his long legs stretched out halfway across the room. In Hunter Robertson's lap lay a manuscript Sophie deduced he was delivering personally to the deputy examiner of plays on behalf of the owner of Sadler's Wells. Before either of them could speak, Edward Capell himself emerged from his inner sanctum and peered at them myopically.

"Ah . . . Mr. Robertson," Capell said genially, staring admiringly at Hunter's muscular thighs as he rose to his full height. "My clerk said you'd be calling here with Mr. Rosoman's manuscript. I did so enjoy you in *La Costanza* at the opera in April. Such diction . . . such a *voice!*"

Capell was virtually fawning over the man! Sophie fumed. Hunter, who seemed as shocked to see her as she was to see him, thanked the censor distractedly for his kind words.

"I'm in no hurry to commence that hot ride back to Sadler's, sir," he ventured. "Why not confer with Miss McGann, here? I shall be happy to wait."

"I believe I know why she has called—*without* an appointment," Capell replied peevishly, "and I can tell you, mistress, there is really nothing to discuss. I've explained my reasons for refusing your play in a letter to Mr. Garrick."

Sophie summoned every ounce of will to control her raging emotions.

"But that is just the problem, sir," she replied, her jaw

clenched. "Mr. Garrick's note to me said the reasons for refusal were not made clear. Could you please elaborate?"

"Here?" he asked, looking pointedly at Hunter.

"In your chambers, if you please."

"Very well," he replied churlishly, "if Mr. Robertson, who *has* an appointment, has no objection."

"None," Hunter assured him, apparently enjoying her discomfort.

Capell led the way into a room cluttered with manuscripts. Neglecting to offer her a chair, he sat behind his desk and formed his forefingers into a pyramid supporting his pointed chin. The blotches on his skin were more alarming than ever.

"Not to put too fine a point on it, Miss McGann," he announced with relish, "I find the work offensive. The mutinous daughter disobeying the sensible directives of her father . . . the warrior who challenges his king. The piece has a shrill, strident tone that society would not deem acceptable."

Sophie swallowed hard in a herculean effort to keep her temper.

"I'm rather surprised at such a finding," she said slowly, "for, as perhaps you know, *Forced Marriage*, from which my play is adapted, is a work that has been presented on and off in Britain for some ninety-nine years."

"My point precisely!" he snapped. "If Aphra Behn were writing today, I doubt if *any* of her plays would be granted license. Her type of bawdry is the reason Parliament saw fit to *establish* the Licensing Act in 1737!" He looked at her narrowly and stood up in a gesture of dismissal. "When will you female scribblers realize you have no business blathering on about serious subjects that are unsuitable . . . or, as they say in your native Scotland, beyond your *ken*!" he added scathingly. "Now, if you will be so kind . . ."

Fearing she might strike this repulsive little government functionary, Sophie whirled on her heel and stormed out to the antechamber.

"So sorry to have kept you, Mr. Robertson," Capell said unctuously. "Now what have we here? Something that will

suit your stellar skills, I should hope. What's this I hear
about your becoming dance master at—"

Hunter had better guard his privates! Sophie thought
darkly, stalking past the two men into St. James's Street and
heading down Pall Mall. No hackney or even a sedan chair
was in sight, so she walked all the way home. As soon as she
slammed the door to her upstairs lodgings, she flung herself
in exhaustion and despair onto the bed she had once shared
with Hunter. She pounded the mattress with both fists, feeling capable of murder. All those hours of fine tuning the
dialogue to give it a contemporary ring . . . all the brain-
cracking labor attempting to strike just the right tone to
highlight the ludicrous implications of arranged marriages!
She knew instinctively that before many more years passed,
young women—even in aristocratic circles—would be demanding freedom from the tradition of being sold to the
highest bidders like mere cattle.

She sat up on her bed with fists clenched so tightly, her
knuckles had bleached themselves the color of chalk.

"*Blast them all!*" she cried aloud. "*Blast every bloody one
of them to hell!*"

※

Sophie awoke the following morning with the same fury
and outrage boiling inside that had gripped her vitals the day
before. She had barely gulped a mug of tea before she
grabbed her swan's feather quill and dispatched a note to
David Garrick, thanking him for his faith in her skills as a
dramatist, but acquiescing without protest to the verdict of
the Lord Chamberlain's office. Then she began to compose
the piece requested by Lord Darnly.

Two weeks of white-hot activity eventually produced a
two-act diversion she titled *The Vanquishers Vanquished*.
Rather than portraying animals enslaving local hunters, she
had devised a plot with a comical gender reversal in which a
group of Spanish soldiers invading the Amazon jungles were
conquered by the formidable women of the region and
forced to do their bidding.

"'Tis just far-fetched enough to be amusing," Roderick
Darnly pronounced the day Sophie called at his chambers at

Number 10, St. James's Street to receive his verdict on the commissioned work.

"I desire that this piece be submitted to the Lord Chamberlain's office anonymously," Sophie responded tersely. "And unless you are prepared to agree to such an arrangement, I will throw these pages on the hearth!" she added, gesturing toward the crackling fire warding off the unseasonable chill.

"No need for such theatrics," Darnly replied, raising an eyebrow at her outburst. "We shall call it 'A Musical Confection' and intersperse some ballads and rope dancing at the interval. That way, the piece will be considered a 'concert' and we avoid having to submit it to the examiner altogether. I shall let you know immediately if I can place the piece before summer's end."

"Excellent," Sophie agreed, mollified. Preparing to make her departure, she inquired, "Are financial arrangements for authors at such pleasure gardens similar to the author's Third Night Benefit?"

"Just leave the fiscal matters to me," he assured her.

"Forgive me, Roderick," Sophie insisted, gazing at him steadily, "but I wish to know *before* I submit my work precisely how playwrights at these houses are recompensed."

"We will fashion a sort of partnership in this venture. You will receive a portion of the profits, after expenses."

"In effect, a Third Night Benefit?" Sophie repeated stubbornly.

"'Tis possible it could be even more advantageous than that," he replied. "You will receive your share based on the entire run of the work—after expenses—however long it plays."

"However long it plays?" Sophie mused, relieved to hear this intelligence. "Lud, but those rope dancers must attract a crowd!"

"They've taken *The Vanquishers Vanquished* at Sadler's Wells," Lord Darnly announced with a satisfied air the morning of August first as soon as Sophie had boarded his well-appointed carriage. "Thomas Rosoman has already put it into rehearsal. We are expected there by noon to confer about certain production details."

"Sadler's Wells?" Sophie repeated, dismayed. "But I thought surely you would have submitted it to Ranelagh Gardens or Vauxhall here in the city as a first choice. "I never dreamed you'd—"

"Sadler's suffers from its distant location and is in need of spectacle to draw the crowds away from the popular pleasure gardens in town . . . hence, Thomas Rosoman's willingness to take on silent partners in some new ventures. Surely, Sophie, you can't object to my having sold it to him?"

"No . . . only . . ." Her words drifted off as she stared across the swaying coach.

Hunter was at Sadler's Wells! However, she could not bring herself to disclose her personal problems to the viscount, especially because Hunter believed Roderick meant more to her than a mere patron.

"The plan is to lace the tale with melodies and lively dancing," Darnly continued. "Rosoman wishes to confer with you about the most likely places such songs could be inserted."

"I see," Sophie murmured, glancing down at the manuscript laying in her lap. "Then, if you don't mind, I'll just spend the hour's ride thinking about where that might be possible," she suggested, relieved not to have to maintain a conversation with her fellow passenger when her mind was in such a whirl.

Darnly's coach grew hot and stuffy by the time they approached Rosebery Avenue, a dusty road that led to the entrance to Sadler's Wells. Gravel crunched beneath their wheels as Sophie leaned forward to glimpse the elegant iron-gated entrance to the theater itself.

"Word is, Rosoman spent the moon enlarging the brick building you see over there," Darnly observed as the carriage rolled deeper into the grounds of the pleasure garden. "He calls it his music house. And over there at the edge of the green? That's an English grotto garden that he hopes will attract a larger summer crowd."

Sophie gazed out the window to gain a better view of her surroundings. There was a river in the distance and a revolving mill and fountain whose splashing waters were very pleasant, indeed. Several acrobats and tumblers were practicing their routine on a wide expanse of lawn, while, above her head, a stout rope stretching between two large trees supported a man and a woman dancing on the slender cord with astounding agility. Sophie was relieved to discover that Lorna Blount was not among these daredevils. Fortunately, she'd been cast as a dancer.

Sophie heard the sound of music floating through the theater's open windows. Down by the river, a round-shouldered worker was fastening what looked to be fireworks on a wheel that would, when lighted later that evening, spin spirals of flame in a spectacular display of pyrotechnics.

A harried-looking man of middle years emerged from the brick building and walked briskly toward their coach as they rolled to a stop in front of the theater's entrance. Sophie stifled a groan at the sight of Hunter walking a few paces behind him.

"Welcome . . . welcome," Thomas Rosoman hailed Darnly and his companion descending from the coach. He shook the viscount's hand as if they had somehow come to his rescue. "We are delighted to see you. You both know Mr. Robertson, I gather."

Lord Darnly surveyed Hunter coolly. Sophie wondered if the nobleman recalled their unfriendly exchange six years earlier in Bath. For her part, she nodded brusquely and kept her eyes glued on Rosoman.

"Robertson," Darnly murmured, inclining his head in a curt greeting. "So this is where you tipped up after Colman sacked you." He ignored Hunter's cold stare as he addressed the owner of Sadler's Wells. "Rosoman, I suggest we discuss our matters of business privately. I take it you intend these two to sort out the practicalities of adding music to Miss McGann's comedy?"

"Certainly, certainly," Rosoman agreed, beckoning the viscount to follow him into the building. "Robertson, explain, if you will, the type of songs and dances you envision for the piece."

Sophie gazed fixedly at the departing pair, too ill at ease to look in Hunter's direction.

"Have you your copy of the manuscript?" he asked, tight-jawed.

"Yes," she replied, forcing herself to meet his gaze. "I left it in the coach."

"That's as good a place as any to have done with this," he answered, yanking open the door and climbing inside without extending a hand to assist her.

During the following fifteen minutes, Hunter proceeded to detail every single fault he found with Sophie's script. Attempting to keep her temper in check, she merely nodded as he made his points.

"In fact," he concluded, "there are so many changes required to make this piece work with music and dance, I suggest you ask Rosoman if you can remain here a few days to revise the play completely . . . that is, if m'lord Darnly will grant his lady permission to leave his side to pursue her profession."

Sophie stared at him bitterly.

"Lord Darnly in no way dictates to me where I reside or what I do!"

"Oh, really?" Hunter retorted sarcastically. "From what Rosoman told me, he has recently assumed the role of fawning patron as well as personal protector."

"Viscount Glyn is not fawning over me, I can assure you!" Sophie fumed. "Why is it, if a woman makes her way in the world, that men imagine she could have accomplished such a feat only by becoming someone's mistress!"

"Because that is often how it happens," Hunter retorted.

Sophie glared at him, her face flushed with irritation.

"Roderick Darnly has merely submitted my work to Rosoman and will invest in the production, I expect. However, may I inform you that he and I are not . . . and have not *ever* been what you so rudely imply! Believe me, I long ago learned my lesson about the futility of combining business with pleasure! The viscount merely submitted the piece to your manager, and Mr. Rosoman liked it well enough to take it on."

"'Twas *I* who recommended that he take it on," Hunter snapped.

"*You?*" Sophie scoffed. "You hate every other sentence! Why in the world would you recommend it?"

"I don't hate it," Hunter said in a calmer tone of voice. "I rather like it . . . 'tis so like you . . . the women triumphing over the men and all of that. With music and dancing to soften its sting, I conceive it as a harmless piece of fluff that will amuse and delight an audience on a summer's night."

"How kind of you," Sophie retorted caustically, trying to sort his insults from his compliments.

"It needs a lot of reworking," Hunter continued, "and the music and dance will certainly bolster the fable itself." He peered across the coach at her. "How quickly did you compose this piece? Your little debacle with our beloved censor occurred hardly three weeks ago, did it not?"

"If the plot seems a bit thin, it is," she admitted glumly. "I wrote the blasted thing in two weeks' time."

"Well, how soon can you start revising? If this is to be mounted before September, we'd best get cracking."

"If Rosoman will provide lodgings at his expense, I can begin work immediately," she answered snappishly. "I shall return to the city with Lord Darnly, gather up some belongings, and arrive back here tomorrow."

"Alone?" Hunter asked bluntly.

"I fear you haven't been listening!" she retorted. "Of course, alone!"

"Good," Hunter shot back. "Rosoman will guarantee you lodgings—or *I* will."

Sophie didn't know whether to feel indignant or dismayed. She grasped the coach handle, pausing to stare at him across the vehicle's shadowy interior.

"I presume you know," she said in a low voice, "that you behaved like a complete crackbrain when Colman sacked you from Covent Garden."

"'Twas humiliating to be discharged like that in the middle of a season . . . surely, after your encounter with Edward Capell the other day, you can understand my ill-humor."

"Certainly I can," Sophie replied acidly, "but the difference is, Hunter, that I didn't blame *you* for the censor's idiocy."

"Ah, but there is another difference . . . Edward Capell feels little jealousy when it comes to women—and I do."

"Jealousy?" Sophie echoed in a puzzled tone. "I *told* you, Roderick and I—"

"Not Darnly!" he interrupted defensively. "Garrick! You were so bloody loyal to your darling mentor and his version of the *Jubilee.* Heaped upon Colman's dismissal, it stuck in my craw."

"My allegiance to David Garrick in no way diminished my concern for what had happened to you," she replied angrily. "Surely you should have realized by now that my feelings for you fall—fell—into quite a different category than my admiration for Garrick. And besides, I made it no secret that night at the Nag's Head that I thought Colman's behavior toward you disgraceful!"

"And mine toward *you*—disgraceful as well, I imagine?"

Sophie shrugged, saying, "I assumed that you would at some point acknowledge that I was not the enemy and didn't deserve to be treated like some . . . some tale-telling harridan . . . but you never—"

"I acknowledge it *now,*" Hunter interrupted. "You were not the enemy with Colman. But when Mavis gleefully volunteered—and others confirmed it—that you'd spent four months in Wales under the protection of Darnly and never even mentioned it me—and that you *continued* to associate with him, I think I went a bit mad."

"I will say this only once more," Sophie declared between clenched teeth. "Yes, I went to Wales to lick my wounds after Danielle's death. Yes, I lived for four months in a cottage on the Darnly estates. And, yes, Roderick's offer of safe haven at a time you'd cast me as a murderess had certain appeal," she declared brutally. "But I have not had, nor do I intend to have an intimate association with him. *I am not Darnly's mistress, you great oaf!*" she finished, nearly shouting to show her frustration.

"Of course you aren't," Hunter replied thoughtfully. "And I just this minute see *why*! I was utterly mistaken in thinking you were." He grinned rather sheepishly at Sophie's look of astonishment. "Apparently, Edward Capell is so taken with the beauty of my person that he inquired the other day if I would consent to join a small group of people interested in the arts who . . . ah . . . meet in the exclusive company of men. He cited Roderick Darnly as one of the sterling members of this elite society who greatly admire the ancients—especially the Celts and the Greeks—even to the extent of practicing some of their rituals. Need I elaborate?"

"No," Sophie replied, "you need not. In fact, I venture to say I could add a dimension or two on that subject that even *you* could not imagine. However," she continued, ignoring his questioning glance, "that's neither here nor there. Even *before* Mavis poisoned your mind regarding Roderick Darnly and me, you blamed me for Colman's sacking you. Why did you persist with such nonsense?"

"You were enjoying so much success with *The Bogus Baronet*," Hunter admitted, "I feared you'd spurn apologetic overtures from a lowly spear carrier at the King's Opera—"

"If you'll recall," she cut in, her voice raw, "'twas not in my character to tattle to anyone—including David Garrick —about something that could do you harm. And after what we shared during the *Jubilee*, how could you think I'd ever play the harlot with the likes of Roderick Darnly? Yet, *once again*, you thought the worst of me! It seems, despite our long, intimate acquaintance, you know me very little, Hunter."

She flung open the coach door, poised for flight.

"Sophie," he said gravely, halting her progress, "there are many aspects of your character—and my own—that I am slowly, painfully, beginning to learn . . . even after all these years."

"And what is *that* supposed to mean?" she demanded, one foot on the coach's running board.

"'Tis a compliment as far as you are concerned, I assure you," he replied with a mischievous glint in his eye. "Now, then," he continued, "let us see about securing you your lodgings. We have much work to do."

Chapter 30

"That last speech in act one is a bit shrill," Hunter declared
sotto voce as he and Sophie watched a final rehearsal of their
joint effort. "Can you amend it with something more amusing?"

"What?" she demanded, feeling irritated. "Amend it with
what? I've changed the bloody thing five times!"

"Well, of course! You're the *bloody* playwright!" he shot
back. "I'm sure with that clever little brain of yours, you'll
come up with something witty before tonight . . ."

And she did. Much to Sophie's relief, *The Vanquishers
Vanquished* proved a great success with Sadler's Wells summer patrons. By the third night, swarms of Londoners were
making their way from the city to the famed pleasure garden
to enjoy the fine summer weather and the "delightful diversion"—as one London critic had dubbed the two-act fable—
served up with rope dancing and fireworks.

"Will you look at all the toffs!" Lorna Blount crowed as
she and Sophie peered through the peephole at the milling
audience. It appeared to be a lively crowd, elegantly dressed
and decidedly in the mood for enjoyment. Sophie and Lorna
hugged each other like excited five-year-olds.

Following another series of performances in early September that were packed to the rafters with enthusiastic
ticket holders, Sophie stood at the door of Thomas

Rosoman's Treasure Room late in the evening, her hand poised to announce her presence with a knock.

"Sophie!" whispered a voice, interrupting her attempt to summon Rosoman from his counting chamber. "I called at your lodgings after the performance and you weren't there." Hunter walked swiftly toward her along the gloomy corridor. "I was afraid you had returned to London without so much as a fare-thee-well."

"Not yet," she replied quietly, worried her employer might hear their exchange. "Not before I discover how close to an heiress I've become," she added with an ironic smile. She was determined to keep matters between Hunter and her pleasant—but distant. During rehearsals, they had fought battles over content and form, but in the end, Sophie congratulated herself for having kept their association strictly professional during the ten days she had lodged at the nearby Myddleton's Head Inn.

"Old Rosoman'll be counting his shillings for hours," Hunter declared, reaching for her hand. "Come. I wish to speak with you. Your silver will still be in the strongbox tomorrow."

Reluctantly, Sophie allowed herself to be led outside into the warm summer night. Several coaches belonging to theater patrons were departing through the iron gates, while an army of snuffers fanned throughout the grounds extinguishing the glowing lanterns hanging in the willow trees and along the paths leading to the grotto.

Hunter bid Sophie follow him down the sloping lawn in the direction of the river, now awash in moonlight. Moist air drifted off the water, along with a hint of some sweet-smelling flowering vine. The resident swans clustered together in the reeds near the bank, settling in for the night.

For a few minutes, Sophie and Hunter spoke casually of both the high points and near disasters that affected the string of performances of *The Vanquishers Vanquished*. Their meandering stroll led them beside the "Magic Waterfall." Its artificial cascades—generated by a lad hidden behind a rock, turning a water wheel—were silent now that the crowds had gone home. Sophie turned to glance up at

Hunter. Illuminated by the moon's silvery beams, his tall frame cast a gigantic shadow across the lawn.

"Hunter, I—"

Her voice caught and she was suddenly unable to complete her thought. The space between them seemed filled with an emotional charge as potent as the sputtering fireworks ignited earlier that evening. Hunter reached across the short distance separating them and pulled her roughly against his chest. He leaned down and kissed her hard.

"Ah . . . Sophie," he murmured. "I've wanted to kiss those lips since the day we sat in Darnly's coach arguing over your play," Hunter confessed, as he traced the outline of her mouth with his forefinger.

"And I've wanted to clear up once and for all this business about Colman's dismissal and—"

Hunter pulled her close again, his chin resting on the top of her hair.

"Colman's hired me back," he announced.

Sophie took a step backward and stared up at him.

"He *has*?" she said, her voice betraying her utter amazement. "But why? When? Did he apologize?"

"Apologize?" Hunter laughed shortly. "Not bloody likely."

"I suppose not," Sophie responded tartly. "I have learned to my sorrow 'tis difficult for your sex to admit you're ever wrong."

"You may be correct in your assessment," he said dryly, "but Colman *did* offer me managerial responsibilities, in addition to my performing roles."

"And you've accepted his offer?" she asked.

He smiled down at her ruefully.

"I don't think I could have endured another season as 'H. Roberto,' mucking about with all those mad Italian opera singers."

"Well, I think 'tis wonderful," Sophie said slowly, "only I—"

"Sophie?" Hunter said, grazing her cheekbone with the back of one finger. "Did you ask Garrick to hire me this season as well?" She refused to meet his glance, recalling how angry he had become at the Nag's Head when she had offered to do just that. "Because if you did," he added quietly, ". . . thank you. That was very generous-spirited of you." She glanced off across the river to hide her disappointment that Hunter had apparently turned down the offer Garrick kindly agreed to extend—at her urging. "The rumors of Drury Lane's interest in me may have inspired Colman to let bygones be bygones and offer me a superior post at Covent Garden."

"Garrick told me he wrote Colman a letter attesting that you had not betrayed your theater," Sophie responded slowly, "and he offered you a place at Drury Lane because he greatly admires your talent. Knowing you were . . . ah . . . my friend . . . played only a small part," she added, staring vacantly across the water.

"*Were* friends?" he asked with emphasis. Sophie remained silent, her eyes irresistibly drawn back to his. "And are you still adamant about not mixing business with pleasure?" he queried.

"To do so has been disastrous thus far," Sophie replied in a voice tight with emotion.

"You are the most difficult woman of my acquaintance," he blurted. "And you probably consider me as vain as David Garrick and as disagreeable as George Colman."

"'Tis a fair assessment," she murmured as his thumb began to massage the soft skin beneath her ear.

"And once again, I find myself apologizing for . . . not only jumping to conclusions about you and Darnly—"

"Which was too *stupid* a notion for words," she exclaimed crossly.

"Sophie!" he cut in. "Now *you're* the one not listening! I am apologizing for . . . blaming you for my troubles and for being too proud to ask for your help. Instead, I hurt us both. Forgive my conceit," Hunter concluded quietly.

Sophie gazed up at him for a long moment, then impulsively seized his hand and held it against her cheek.

"Thank you for . . . saying that," she replied simply.

Hunter leaned forward and kissed the top of her head.

"As your friend Lorna Blount has repeated to me often enough this summer," he added with quiet firmness, "with some goodwill on both sides, perhaps we can untangle the coil that has complicated our lives and held us in its grip."

"How?" Sophie asked earnestly. "Until now, the answer has always seemed that one of us must compromise too dearly in either our life or our work."

Hunter laced his hands through hers.

"I think 'tis something you said long ago . . . we should be guided by our *common* good."

"And who decides what that is?" she asked warily.

"We both do . . . we can consult, like Garrick and Lacy," he grinned. "As partners, they do not always agree, but they wish to see their theater succeed, and thus always seem to come to an accommodation that pleases them enough to continue their joint venture." He gently grasped her chin between his fingers. "I wish, my darling Sophie, for us *both* to succeed in the venture I see stretching before us—in our lives together . . . and in our work." He shook his head with resignation. "I know 'tis taken me overlong to understand that what we both do in the world has import and value . . . but, truly dearheart, if I didn't see it before we slaved together over this captivating story of Amazons and soldiers, I see it now." As her throat tightened with emotion, Sophie could only nod agreement. "So . . ." Hunter said, coaxingly, "as a first order of business, I would like to propose—for your consideration, I hasten to add—that you permit me to spend this night with you atop that tavern, there." He pointed across the lawn in the direction of the Myddleton's Head whose candlelit windows glowed like a friendly beacon in the velvety night air.

"'Tis very noisy in my garret," Sophie whispered, feeling herself begin to tremble as his thumb strayed along her jaw line. "My chambers are directly over the pubroom, I fear."

"Dinna ye worry, Sophie, m'lass. We winna hear a thing . . ."

He clasped her by the hand and set off toward the inn at a determined trot. Sophie grew breathless keeping pace with his longer stride, and was quite flushed by the time they reached the side entrance to the noisy inn and tiptoed up the back stairs like guilty children.

He slid the bolt shut with a resounding thud. The chatter

from the patrons downstairs faded into oblivion. Then he turned and leaned his long frame against the door, his head nearly touching the ceiling of the miniature chamber. Moonlight streamed through the window over the bedstead, filling the room with silvery radiance.

Staring at her lazily, Hunter shrugged off his coat and began pulling at the buttons of his cambric shirt, tossing both to one side. Sophie's breathing became shallow and her mouth went dry as he reached down and swiftly removed his buckled shoes, padding in his stocking feet to her side. She leaned against her writing table to steady herself, while Hunter made quick work of stripping her down to her shift.

With his thumbs he eased her last garment past her waist until it fell to the floor of its own accord. Then, as his eyes bored into hers, he took her quill pen off the desk and grazed its feathered tip back and forth around the base of her neck, sending delicious shivers of excitement from her scalp to her toes.

She felt gooseflesh rise on her skin as he skimmed his instrument of exquisite torture between the valley of her breasts, hesitating at her navel and then continued its teasing path to the tops of her legs. There, he began to strafe her thighs with the stiff plume in side-to-side strokes calculated to drive her insane.

"I can't believe my cursed temper kept me from this," he whispered hoarsely, kissing her lips. "Or this," he added, nuzzling her ear, "or this . . . or this . . ." His lips sought the tip of each breast, tugging gently. Then, sinking to his knees, he threw the quill aside and pulled her roughly to him, pressing his cheek against her abdomen and then grazing his lips across her flesh like a parched traveler at a desert well.

Sophie threaded her fingers through his hair and held him tightly. She tried to keep her knees from buckling while his lips sought silent answers to his unspoken demands.

"You are a witch," he murmured, at length rising to his full height again and playfully shoving her toward the bedstead. "Nay, a sorceress who has powers to exorcise from me those evils of my sex . . . my arrogance . . . my awful—"

"No, no, wizard mine," she cried softly, settling against the pillows while she watched him swiftly divest himself of his breeches. She held out her arms to him. "We conjure this magic together, don't you see?"

"Aye," he replied gruffly, looming above her momentarily before slowly and with infinite deliberation taking possession of her by inches. Then, he began the instinctive dance, its pulsing, whirling rhythms beguiling her, as they always had, into playing her part. Her arms, her legs mirrored Hunter's every move until his whispered demands evoked in her a kind of desperate incantation.

"Yes! Yes! Oh please . . . yes!" she moaned as her love and sorrow and regret and new resolve blended in a potent brew. She arched against him and raked her nails down his back, unashamedly demanding the release they both craved. The next moment it came, blinding them to the moonlight, the restless chatter below their garret hideaway, to everything but the enchantment of this night.

"I missed you so much!" she heard herself cry out.

"Oh, God, Sophie . . ." he whispered hoarsely, "so did I."

Thomas Rosoman, his wig resting jauntily on a peg near the doorway, greeted Sophie cheerfully enough the next morning, but his smile faded as soon as she explained the purpose of her Sunday visit to his Treasure Room.

"We managers of pleasure gardens do not employ the same system of payment as the Patent Theaters, I'm afraid," he explained. "Hasn't Lord Darnly made that clear?"

"He has said you pay a percentage . . ." she replied tentatively.

"Exactly," Rosoman agreed, looking relieved. "We pay author's fees based on a percentage of the profits at our season's end—*after* expenses. We shall declare profits and losses at the end of . . . ah . . . let me see now," he hesitated, ". . . the end of October."

Sophie's glance drifted to the enormous pile of coins that Rosoman had begun to stack like castle turrets across his desk.

"As *The Vanquishers Vanquished* has been such an obvious success, are you able to disclose what the house receipts for the piece have been, after ten performances?" she asked with a forced smile. "I would imagine you could, at least, *estimate* what share I am likely to receive. I must plan for the future, you know, sir."

Rosoman's glance fell on the pile of money he had been counting and he shifted uncomfortably in his chair.

"Ah . . . I was led to understand that Lord Darnly is looking after your interests," he said stiffly.

Indignant at the suggestion, Sophie took a deep breath to steady her nerves.

"I am sure you've mistaken his meaning, sir," she said as calmly as she could. "Lord Darnly was kind enough to serve as agent for my play, but monies for my share are to be paid to me directly. That was always my understanding."

Thomas Rosoman appeared nonplussed and glanced down at a ledger into which he had been entering figures.

"Well, I am afraid you shall have to take up this matter with Lord Darnly himself," he said gruffly. "He is a participant in this particular venture, along with Mr. Robertson and myself. You'll have to speak with him and settle this between you."

"But, I pray you—" Sophie began to protest.

"I beg your leave," Rosoman said sharply. "I fear I must ask you to allow me to continue with my work. Lord Darnly is due here soon, and I have a visitor from America waiting for me at Myddleton's Head to sup midday. So, if you'll excuse me . . ."

Sophie knew she could go no further with the matter and exited the Treasure Room as gracefully as she could. She seethed with frustration over Rosoman's assumption that she was to be treated as Darnly's scribbler.

A short, stocky man in his midthirties lounged in a corner of the principal chamber of Myddleton's Head Inn. His rough, homespun linen and outdated clothing revealed him to be the "visitor from America" with whom Rosoman was scheduled to dine.

"Do you know who he is?" Sophie asked, postponing her discussion with Hunter about author's fees to avoid spoiling their pleasant Sunday meal.

"His name is John Henry," Hunter said, sipping his tankard of ale. "Rosoman tells me he has come to England to recruit actors for a new theater being erected in Annapolis, in the Colonies. 'Tis opening in the autumn season of 1771."

"You would not consider embarking on such an adventure, would you?" Sophie asked with sudden alarm.

"Of course not," Hunter smiled across the wooden table. "When I have such prospects in London and you are with me here. The New World holds no enticements, I assure you."

Sophie felt relieved as the tavern owner's wife set a steaming pot of ragout on their table and handed them wooden bowls and spoons. They soon fell to eating their supper, but when they had nearly finished, Sophie knew she could postpone her questions about her author's fees no longer.

"I did not realize you were actually partners with Thomas Rosoman and Lord Darnly in the mounting of my play," Sophie said casually, scooping up a last spoonful of spicy stew.

"I doubt that 'partners' quite describes the arrangement among the three of us," Hunter replied, reaching for his tankard of ale. "From the first, I liked the basic notion of your play, but I knew we would have to adapt the work for music and dance. Therefore, I insisted that I be paid a percentage fee beyond my wage as a performer. Rosoman agreed. His arrangements with Lord Darnly were made separately—on the day you first arrived at Sadler's, I believe."

"I see . . ." Sophie said thoughtfully. "I have just been told I am not to be paid my author's fees until the season ends. Rosoman refuses even to estimate the house profits—though, clearly, they are considerable. I saw with my own eyes an amazing amount of blunt in Rosoman's Treasure Room this very morning."

Hunter grinned at her across the table.

"So *that*'s where you got to at the crack of dawn . . . sneaking off to count the treasury and abandoning me in your bed! To be honest, I've been so bloody busy all summer, I figure if I can garner enough wages to buy myself an ale and a chop when I remember to eat, 'tis sufficient! I haven't even asked Rosoman for an accounting yet." He looked at her intently. "Do you need funds?"

"No . . . not yet," she answered, "but I want my author's fees . . . or at least I'd like to know what I can expect. There's something afoot here, Hunter, and I don't like it."

"At least, this time, you don't suspect me of trying to cheat you of your wages, do you, my love?" he asked lightly.

Sophie knew instinctively that his question was in dead earnest. She gazed at him for a long moment and then reached across the table to lay her hand gently on his.

"I believe that the boy I taught to read and the man who rescued me from the clutches of Lord Auckinleck's ire—not to mention the bowels of Bedlam—would never dream of doing me harm."

"At last!" Hunter gently chided, clasping her hand. "I wondered when you'd realize I, too, am your champion."

"You, my father, and Garrick," Sophie grinned.

Hunter raised his eyebrow in mock resignation at the inclusion of Garrick in her pantheon of heroes.

"Well . . ." he ventured, smiling crookedly, "unlike David Garrick, I owe my entire professional life to *you*, not to mention my future happiness. Could that be the reason we've never become utterly disgusted with one another?" His smile faded and he looked at her solemnly. "I cannot honestly imagine another woman sleeping in my bed—or complicating my life."

His voice had lost its bantering tone and the depth of his emotions was reflected in his eyes.

"Even if I cannot be your legal wife?" she replied sadly.

"Even if you cannot . . ." he repeated.

"And children . . . ?"

Her questioning words hung in the air between them.

"Why not have a bairn or two?" he answered, his blue eyes gleaming with mischief. "After a night like ours in the garret room, here, I cannot imagine how we can avoid . . ."
Sophie flushed crimson with embarrassment, but Hunter

merely reached for his tankard and took a healthy swig.
"So?" he continued expectantly, setting his drink to one
side. "What shall we do about getting you your author's
fees?"

"I wish there was some way to have a look at Rosoman's
ledger books," she said, sighing with discouragement.

Hunter seized her hand again and raised it to his lips.
"You're not to worry on that score," he said softly, intimately grazing her flesh. "We shall find out the truth—"

His words were suddenly interrupted by the tavern door
banging open and Lord Roderick Darnly appearing at the
threshold, commanding in an elegant black cape. He glanced
swiftly around the room, surveying every patron in the
chamber. His eyes narrowed as Hunter lowered Sophie's
hand to the table, keeping it tightly in his grasp.

Behind Darnly stood Thomas Rosoman, appearing harried and out of sorts, despite its being Sunday when no performances were scheduled. The manager of Sadler's Wells
nodded a brief farewell to Viscount Glyn, then spotted the
visitor from America, John Henry, and quickly headed for
his table. Darnly marched over to Sophie and Hunter's table
and bowed curtly.

"May I join you for a moment?" he asked, taking a seat
before either of them could extend even a perfunctory welcome. "I understand you were pressing poor Rosoman for
your author's fees this morning," the viscount said coolly,
after hailing the barmaid for a brandy. "I was under the
impression we had agreed that I would take charge of such
financial arrangements."

Both Hunter and Sophie bristled at the nobleman's con-
descending tone, but Sophie quickly intervened before her
companion could speak.

"I merely wished to know what fees I could expect,
Roderick," she replied evenly. "Since you are so well informed on these matters, I would like you to estimate for
me, then, what percentage you will pay me when accounts
are closed."

"As you have been told, Rosoman will not close accounts
until the end of October . . . therefore, as much as I would
like to be of service, I cannot forecast the amount."

"And are you saying, m'lord," Hunter injected, despite Sophie's tempering hand pressed urgently on his forearm, "that *you* have not received any monies owed your original investment, despite the play's great success?"

Lord Darnly turned to gaze imperiously at Hunter, his icy glance signaling his disdain.

"I am not in the habit of divulging my business affairs to common players, sir!" he snapped.

"But *The Vanquishers Vanquished* has been enormously popular!" Sophie protested. "I saw stacks of coins in Rosoman's office this morning . . . surely, you—"

"God's bones, woman!" Darnly barked in a rare display of temper. He pulled a tooled leather pouch from his embroidered waistcoat and slapped down several gold coins on the table. "Here's ten pounds, if you are so presumptuous as to *beg*!"

The silence crackled between them and Sophie sensed several patrons, including Thomas Rosoman and John Henry, watching their little drama intently. Sophie extended the fingers of her right hand across the table and slid the coins to her left, balling her fist around them.

"I shall accept what is due me," she said stiffly, "and hope that soon I shall receive the rest of what is owing."

"And a goodly sum it should be!" Hunter growled.

Lord Darnly took a long sip from his brandy snifter and seemed to regain his composure.

"One can be permitted to hope," he said mildly. "The play has certainly been an outstanding success, but, sadly, Rosoman warned me this morning that the scenery and costumes were costly beyond compare. Really, Sophie, if your fees don't rise to what I fear are your unrealistic expectations, at least your reputation as a female wit is assured."

"Reputations don't pay the butcher, my lord Darnly," Sophie replied pointedly. She took pleasure from the fact that Roderick was offended by her use of his formal title and she no longer cared if the sight of her sharing an intimate moment with Hunter only added insult to injury. "Will you excuse me?" she added, rising abruptly. "I find I'm really rather tired. Hunter . . . shall we go?" she asked, gratified when her companion rose to his feet. "We bid you farewell, sir."

❊

Outside Myddleton's Head, the late afternoon sun had given way to dusk. Billowing clouds scudded across the sky, plunging the Sadler's Wells grounds into deep shadows.

"They're all still downstairs, drinking," Hunter said as he reentered her chamber atop the pub. "'Tis a good bet they'll be there till they close the place."

Sophie, relieved he had returned from his reconnaissance, wrapped her arms around his waist and rested her cheek against his chest, taking comfort from the steady beat of his heart.

"Roderick Darnly is beginning to frighten me," she said in a low voice. "'Tis evident he already surmises that you and I are . . ."

"Lovers?" Hunter teased. "From what *I* surmise from my odd conversation with Edward Capell concerning their little 'club' honoring certain Greek traditions . . . the love between a man and a woman shouldn't be of much interest to men like Darnly and him."

"I don't know," Sophie said, biting her lip. Haltingly, she related the sinister scene she had witnessed in the beech grove, where Darnly and his confederates performed the strange druid rite that involved stripping naked and fondling his female servant.

"Was that the 'other dimension' to Darnly you so cryptically mentioned a few weeks back?" Hunter wondered aloud.

"That . . . and something more," she acknowledged reluctantly. Shuddering at the memory, she described Darnly's troubled family relationships, his anguished ramblings in her cottage the night of the haying fete, ending with her account of coming upon her host, entwined in the arms of his factor and the parlor maid.

"Jesu!" Hunter breathed. "The man seems not to know *what* he is. And then, for his brother to be killed and his father maimed the very next day after your play ended so disastrously . . ."

"Aye," Sophie said somberly. "I think he's quite tortured by it all. Even before Vaughn died, it seems this terrible duality in Roderick's character affected every aspect of his life. Does he wish to be a lover of women, or men? Is he a poet or mere patron of the arts? He appeared genuinely distraught when his twin brother was killed, yet up to the moment he emerged from the mine shaft after the accident, he acted as if he wished the man had never been born!"

"I doubt we can ever fathom Darnly's true intentions," Hunter said quietly, "but whatever his private devils may be, he doesn't have the right to deprive us of what we've rightfully earned. Are you up to a little sleuthing, my love?" he asked.

She glanced out her window at the broad expanse of lawn below.

"But what if they come upon us while we're in the Treasure Room?" Sophie ventured. "There's no telling what they'd accuse us of."

"I am assistant manager!" Hunter declared. "And a partner in this particular venture, as Rosoman told you. I have a perfect right to examine the books. You needn't come with me, you know," Hunter added. "In fact, 'tis probably better that you don't."

Sophie fell silent for a moment.

"No," she said at length. "We are both owed the fees and should equally assume the risk of being discovered."

"All right, my lovely," Hunter agreed, shaking his head resignedly, "don your cloak against the foggy night and let us be done with this snooping among the ledger books."

Stealthily, the pair crept downstairs, peering through a crack in the door to satisfy themselves that Rosoman, his guest, John Henry from Maryland, and Lord Darnly remained preoccupied with their bottle of port.

"Excellent . . ." Hunter said in a breath. "Quickly, now . . ."

When they had made their way to Rosoman's chambers inside the theater, Hunter pulled out a candle and a flint from his pocket and soon illuminated the way into the Treasure Room itself.

"I fear they may notice our light from the tavern," Sophie said anxiously.

"I doubt they'll look up from their snifters," Hunter replied.

"Oh, no!" she moaned, noting that the manager's ledger she had seen earlier in the day was nowhere in sight. "Do you suppose 'tis locked in the safe?"

However, Hunter strode over to the large cupboard leaning against one wall and flung open its wooden doors. In the flickering candlelight Sophie breathed a sigh of relief as he shoved several items of clothing to one side and pulled the heavy account book from the bottom shelf.

Hunter sat in Rosoman's chair and lay the book flat on the desk. Quickly, he flipped through several pages before stopping at one inscribed with flowing script—*The Vanquishers Vanquished—August, September 1770.* Indicated in the tidy columns were numbers charting ten days of full attendance.

"My play has brought in more than two thousand pounds!" Sophie whispered excitedly. *"Two thousand pounds,* Hunter!"

"And all from that clever little head of yours," he teased affectionately. "Let us see," he murmured, ". . . disbursements . . ."

There were amounts listed for candles, costumes, scenery, house servants, players fees, and the normal expenses associated with running an establishment like Sadler's Wells.

"Look!" Sophie said in an awestruck voice. "Under today's date—September fifth. Rosoman notes—"

" 'Roderick Darnly, Viscount Glyn . . . one thousand pounds!' " Hunter read. "The blackguard had *just* received his percentage of the profits, yet he had the temerity to tell us at the tavern that you wouldn't be paid until October—"

"And he had the *gall* to hint expenses were such that I shouldn't hold 'high expectations,' " she mimicked scathingly.

"The brigand!" Hunter cursed. "I'd like to—"

"Shh!" Sophie hushed him suddenly, her eyes wide with fright. "Sink me . . . but I hear something! Someone's *coming!*"

They both froze and strained their ears. The sound of running footsteps pounding down a nearby passageway filled the air.

"Quick! Hide in the cupboard! Behind the cloaks! *Hurry,* Sophie!" Hunter whispered hoarsely.

Before she could protest, he shoved her inside the large cupboard where Rosoman had stored the ledger and shut the door tight. Sophie found herself nearly smothered by several cloaks hanging from pegs above her head. Her hiding place was black as ink, except for a pale sliver of light that seeped through a crack at the bottom of the door.

"What did I tell you, Rosoman!" a voice shouted angrily. "It *was* him stealing across the lawn!"

Sophie identified Roderick Darnly from his accusatory tone.

"The man's my assistant manager, m'lord," Rosoman replied timidly. "He has the run of the place . . ."

"Is it his habit to invade your Treasure Room on a deserted Sunday night?" the viscount demanded. "He intends to rob you, I tell you, and you're too much of a simpleton to notice!"

"*Rob!*" Hunter exclaimed angrily. "'Tis you, m'lord, who could be accused of committing *that* crime!"

"Robertson!" gasped Rosoman in a horrified voice. "Lord Darnly is our patron . . ."

"Your savior, is more like it," Darnly snapped. "This man is in your Treasure Room, snooping about and readying himself to invade your safe. If you are not willing to guard the assets of Sadler's Wells . . . *I* certainly will not hesitate to do so. I have my investment to protect. As a Peer of the Realm," Darnly thundered in stentorian tones, "I accuse you, Robertson, of attempted robbery. You will come along with me to London and—"

"What is your proof?" Hunter interrupted angrily. "I would be careful whom you accuse of thievery, m'lord. I have seen Rosoman's ledgers!"

"You presume to invade the privacy of those accounts?" Darnly shouted.

"You have received your percentage—fair enough," Hunter countered, "but you have lied about the profits of this venture and no doubt intend to withhold from Miss McGann—"

Sophie heard the sudden, loud report of flesh against flesh.

"You dare to slap me—" Hunter growled.

She could hear the sound of a scuffle taking place a few feet from where she crouched huddled in the cupboard.

"God's bones, Robertson . . . let go of him . . . don't squeeze his throat like that . . . don't—" Rosoman was shouting.

Grunts and curses filled the air. Suddenly Sophie heard a thud of knuckles, followed by a groan.

"You've done it now, lad!" Rosoman screamed.

"I've . . . knocked the villain . . . senseless, but he'll . . . live," Hunter said, gasping for breath.

"But when he wakes up, he'll call you out or have you hanged!"

"For what?" Hunter retorted. "For trying to determine if he's cheated a poor defenseless woman of her author's fees?"

Without warning, Sophie slammed open the cupboard door with a bang and startled Rosoman nearly out of his wits.

"I am *not* a poor defenseless woman, Hunter Robertson!" she cried. "But I *am* the writer of *Vanquishers Vanquished*, Mr. Rosoman, and Roderick Darnly never did intend to pay me my fair percentage, did he?" she demanded. "You knew full well this was so, and did nothing about it!"

"I-I—" began Rosoman, flustered.

A groan from beneath the desk startled the trio.

"Our manager will pay you something from *his* share, won't you, Thomas my man?" Hunter announced, his jaw set. "Just as you will pay me my share right now! Quickly!"

Thomas Rosoman fumbled with a clutch of keys fastened to a ring he had withdrawn from his inside pocket. With trembling fingers, he began to unlock the safe.

"What are you going to do?" Sophie whispered anxiously to Hunter.

"Hurry, Rosoman!" he ordered, ignoring her question.

"Two hundred pounds is about what you owe me for my summer's labors, don't you agree?"

"'Pon my word, Robertson! You've made a fine mess of things . . ." the manager exclaimed, hurriedly counting gold coins into Hunter's broad palm. "Darnly's a very powerful man, you know . . . he has friends in high places . . . you'll be hanging from a gibbet at Tyburne, if he decides that's where he wants you."

"A hundred pounds on account for Sophie . . . *Now!*" he growled. "And I advise you to pay promptly whatever is legitimately due her when the season concludes. Otherwise," he added threateningly, "I assure you that word will go out to all players that you're as big a double-dealer as your silent partner—and you'll never again lure decent performers to this burgh!"

Rosoman shoved the correct number of coins in Sophie's hand as if it were his last farthing.

"'Twas never my intention to cheat you, Robertson," Rosoman replied sulkily, "but you've gone too far. . . . Darnly will see you in Fleet prison, or worse!"

"From what I know of the man," Hunter declared, stuffing his wages into his waistcoat pocket, "I rather think you're correct. As I have no desire to play the role of condemned prisoner, I shall bid you adieu for the season," he said, his good humor returning. "My thanks for your confidence in me to date, sir."

Another groan emanated from under the desk.

"Odds fish, Robertson! He's coming to . . ." Rosoman said, wringing his hands.

"I believe a fast exit is called for! My regards to the rope-dancers!" he said almost jauntily.

Hunter seized Sophie by the wrist and pulled her down the darkened passageway and then through the backstage area, releasing her hand only after they had exited the theater. They dashed through the swirling fog across the broad expanse of lawn, arriving breathless at the front of the Myddleton's Head Inn.

A coach and driver were just pulling up to the front entrance with harnesses jangling, awaiting the last of the tavern's guests scheduled to make the trip back to London. Out of the corner of her eye, Sophie saw the stocky visitor from the Colonies, Mr. Henry, head toward the carriage on unsteady legs, the result, she surmised, of consuming a quantity of port.

"Darnly neither saw nor heard you," Hunter panted, leaning against the tavern's wall. "You shall be able to remain here tonight in all innocence while I make myself scarce for a while."

"But Hunter!" Sophie protested, "he'll look for you at Covent Garden! He'll charge you with—"

"You're a mere twenty-five years old now, are you not?" interrupted Hunter.

"This is no time to call me an old crone!" she snapped.

". . . and I, not yet thirty," Hunter grinned at her lopsidedly. "If you have to wait another year or two to be my love . . . you will, won't you?"

"Of course, but—"

He leaned down and kissed her fiercely on the lips. Then he pushed her from him roughly and stared into her eyes. "Now, listen carefully," he said urgently. "'Twill probably all blow over . . . but from what you've told me and what I've heard here and about, Darnly has a cruel and curious nature. I think I should make a graceful exit while I still can."

"*Where?*" Sophie demanded. "For how long?"

"If I must leave London for a time, I shall inform you of it as soon as I can . . . can you trust me on that?"

"Yes . . . but—"

"Heigh-ho!" the coachman shouted for the benefit of any laggards. The horses pawed the dirt road, their nostrils bellowing steam in the chill night air.

"Whatever happens, you must continue your writing, Sophie," Hunter said earnestly. "Take a man's name, or write anonymously if you must, but don't let what's happened here stifle your muse. Just keep your distance from Darnly . . . for your own safety."

"Yes, but . . . you sound as if you're—"

"You've talent enough to overcome whomever tries to thwart you," he said intently. "Garrick saw that long ago. *I* see it now as well, and I hope—"

Full of fear, Sophie glanced around her shoulder and gasped. A pinpoint of light was dancing near the theater's stage-door entrance across the green. She could barely detect the murky outlines of Rosoman carrying a lantern in one hand while supporting Lord Darnly with the other.

"God's eyeballs . . . they're coming this way!" Sophie gasped.

"Then, 'tis farewell," Hunter said quietly, bending quickly to kiss her hand.

Sophie threw her arms around his neck.

"God's blood, but I love you!" she cried.

"So many unladylike curses," he teased. "No wonder women scribes are said to be such jades."

"'Tis no time to jest!" she protested as tears filled her eyes.

"I know . . ." he replied, suddenly solemn. "You are truly my heart's own, Sophie. Never forget that . . ."

The coach driver cracked his whip. Hunter bolted for the departing vehicle and leapt onto the running board. Sophie ran after the spinning rear wheels, calling after him.

"Thank you . . . thank you for being my champion," she cried. "Please, *please* Hunter . . . please come back!"

"I will!" he shouted, unlatching the door and flinging himself next to a very startled John Henry of Annapolis, Maryland.

Sophie waved until her arm nearly fell off her shoulder. Then she whirled around, relieved to see the slow progress of Rosoman's lantern across the green. As Hunter's conveyance lumbered down the Rosebery Avenue, Sophie stealthily ducked into the side entrance of the inn to avoid being seen.

❈

Covent Garden was abuzz with the scandal concerning the altercation that had taken place between the Welsh viscount and the handsome Scottish actor, Hunter Robertson, late of Sadler's Wells. The Myddleton's tavern keeper had related the details of the fracas to Darnly's own coachman, who had whispered the tale to Darnly's parlor maid, who had described it all to her sweetheart whose job it was to deliver coal to residences throughout the theater district. Soon *everyone* knew some version of the story.

No charges had yet been filed with the magistrates—either for assault, or thievery, or even embezzlement—but the fact was, Hunter Robertson was not among the cast of Arthur Murphy's *The Way to Keep Him* at Covent Garden on September 24, the first day of the new theatrical season. Nor was Lord Darnly seated in his box for Drury Lane's seasonal opening that same week. Tattletales said he was so bruised, he wouldn't show his face.

Meanwhile, Sophie had been frantic with worry over Hunter's whereabouts. Arriving back in London, she found a note slipped under her door at Half Moon Passage. She quickly unfolded the foolscap and stared at the familiar handwriting. Then her eyes widened with dismay:

> *26 September 1770*
>
> I exit this stage to seek my fortune entertaining the savages in America. My spies tell me the viscount nurses his injuries with bad grace and I need make myself scarce to save my neck. Thanks to that Colonial John Henry, I depart from Norfolk aboard the *Jenny,* a brigantine bound for the West Indies and thence to Maryland. Write this player at the American Company, Annapolis. In haste and with all my love. H. R.
>
> *A season will fly by like Ariel on the wind . . . courage, my love.*

Book 7
1771–1779

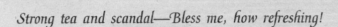

Strong tea and scandal—Bless me, how refreshing!

—DAVID GARRICK,
PROLOGUE TO
THE SCHOOL FOR SCANDAL

Chapter 31

May 1771

The *Jenny*'s bow cut across the glassy surface of Maryland's Chesapeake Bay. Standing in the forecastle next to Captain Marshall, Hunter Robertson could discern the barest outlines of the colonial metropolis—with its neat brick row houses lining the south bank of the Severn River—that was their destination.

The seasoned crew took their stations, their bodies glistening with sweat from the oppressive heat beating down on the New World harbor like a layer of cotton flannel. The men nimbly darted up rope ladders to reef the sails, lashing the canvas to the cross spars, keeping the brigantine under control as it approached its anchorage.

"Glad to see there's no trouble brewing with the natives today," Hunter grinned, referring to reports of sporadic rebellion inspired by the taxes imposed on the Colonies by Parliament.

"Don't be so sure," the ship's master replied grimly. "Last year, at the end of February, the *Good Intent* wasn't allowed to land in Annapolis . . . the merchants and planters didn't fancy paying King Georgie his duties on the imports she was carrying. So, despite the governor's squawks, the ship sailed right back to London . . . with all her cargo!"

"She didn't!" Hunter responded.

"Aye. Fortunately for us, Parliament rescinded the bloody Townsend Acts 'bout the time we sailed from Norfolk—but they left the levy on tea, just to show the Colonials that England hasn't yielded its right to tax 'em," Captain Marshall explained. "The merchants and the customs collectors are an explosive combination, lad. My guess is the natives will fight this tea business too."

Hunter stared across the water at Annapolis, shimmering beneath the hot sun this sultry spring day. So far, he observed, the town had been left undisturbed, despite its defiance of the king and his counselors.

Several other passengers ventured up on deck, including a number of Hunter's fellow players. Their recruiter, John Henry, had remained in England to sign up additional actors from the nation's provincial theaters. Suddenly, the men on deck were treated to the festive sound of pipes and drums, punctuated by the high-pitched whistle of piccolos, wafting over the gentle ripples in the bay.

Captain Marshall shook his head. "Damnation, if I know what they're celebrating with such a bang. What day is this, Robertson?"

"May fifteenth, I believe," replied Hunter, adopting Marshall's bantering tone. "Perhaps 'tis some special holiday alien to us foreigners," he jested.

Privately, Hunter had been keeping track of the passage of time during the months it had taken the *Jenny* to reach the West Indies and then—after waiting out a spate of hurricanes in St. Thomas—sail north to the Colonies. Their trip had been delayed further by port calls at Savannah and Charleston along the east seacoast, but the eight-month journey had provided Hunter with a fascinating glimpse of the land he would call home for a year.

As so often happened, he was struck suddenly by an intense desire to be with Sophie. Inevitably, his reaction to the new sights, smells, and tastes he had experienced since his mad dash overseas to escape Lord Darnly's revenge for a righteous punch in the eye was to wonder what *she* would make of it all.

As soon as the ship was made fast, Captain Marshall gave the signal for the gangplank to be lowered, allowing Hunter and the rest of his fellow passengers to venture on shore. The sun beat down on his back and he could feel sweat seeping under the arms of his linen shirt. He made his way through knots of people who had come down to the quay to greet the ship and inquire about its enticing cargo. The piccolo brigade, it appeared, had been recruited to attract a crowd for just that purpose. The colorful sights, the smell of the fresh oysters and crabs piled high in baskets, even the steamy air filled Hunter with a happiness he had not felt in months—not since he had gathered Sophie in his arms in the small garret room above the inn near Sadler's Wells.

Pushing such provocative memories from his mind, he focused on a sign board plastered on one of the brick buildings standing on the far side of the street. The announcement trumpeted a production of *The Beggars Opera* currently playing at the Annapolis Assembly Rooms, "temporary quarters of the American Company while the new theater is completed." Nearby, a young boy called out headlines from *The Maryland Gazette,* founded, according to the masthead, in 1745 by one Jonas Green and maintained under the current editorship of his widow, Anne.

Sophie would certainly be pleased to know that! he thought, smiling to himself as he tucked a copy of the journal under his arm. Hunter again found himself wishing Sophie were here to share this unexpected adventure. If only their situation had not been so risky, he would have sprinted back to Half Moon Passage and insisted she come with him!

Suddenly, a wave of unadulterated lust came over him, and for the first time in his life, he realized there was only one woman on earth who would satisfy the ache he felt— and she was two thousand miles away.

※

London, on the fifteenth of May, was not nearly as sultry as the Maryland Tidewater, but Sophie thought she would surely suffocate if she didn't get some air.

"Please!" she pleaded weakly with Mrs. Phillips, who looked down at her with concern, "the bed linen . . . 'tis too hot . . ."

"You must keep warm . . . rest . . . 'tis too soon by at least a month for the bairn to be born," the older woman replied firmly. "If you remain quiet and drink that watered brandy there," she said, pointing to a glass filled with amber liquid, "you might not lose—You might wait till your time. Lorna will call on you before she's due at the theater late this afternoon. I've customers to attend to."

And without further comment, the apothecary returned to her shop downstairs.

Sophie stared at the enormous bulge that was her own distended abdomen. A wave of fear washed over her. What if she died? What if the baby died? What if Hunter were *already* dead? She had not heard a word since she received the letter slipped under her door nearly eight months ago telling of his escape to the Colonies. Viscount Glyn, true to his threats, had filed charges of assault and embezzlement last October and departed for Wales, where he had remained all winter and spring, much to Sophie's relief.

She pushed her hands under the counterpane and pressed her palms on the mound below her swollen breasts.

I couldn't bear for you not to know your da, she said silently, the familiar longing for Hunter invading her thoughts. *Please, please keep safe . . .*

She didn't know whether she was praying for Hunter or the baby. In fact, she was astounded to find herself praying at all, having despised the clergy and all it represented for a lifetime. Tears welled in her eyes and rolled down her cheeks. *If you are there and are capable of any goodness or kindness at all . . . please keep my baby and his father out of harm's way, even if you decide I must—*

She pulled herself up short. She knew from past experience there was no bargaining with the fearsome deity the Presbyterian clerics insisted inhabited places like St. Giles in Edinburgh. She was angry with God, and He—it *certainly* was a He, she thought moodily—was angry with her. How else could one explain her becoming pregnant and Hunter departing far across the sea in one fell swoop?

Sophie's eyes drifted toward her desk. She had buried the silver-tipped quill Peter had given her in the bottom of one drawer, preferring to use a swan's feather pen she had purchased at Davies Book Shop. Despite her anxiety and loneliness and her concern about the blood spots and cramping that plagued her of late, a satisfied little smile tugged at her features. She had two additional plays to her credit since Hunter's departure! Well, not precisely to *her* credit, but just after Roderick had vanished to Wales last autumn, Garrick had asked for her help on an adaptation of a play called *Almida* by Dorothea Celesia, a dramatist Garrick had met on his European travels.

"She married a Genoese," Garrick had explained one day in his dressing chambers. His foot was elevated on a stool, the result of an attack of gout brought on by too many fulsome dinners and abundant rounds of port. "She's written an adaptation of Voltaire's *Tancrede*. I'd like you to read my notes on the piece and see what you can do."

"But what of Capell?" she had queried. "After the way he refused to license my *Maid* . . ."

"We'll devise a way to outfox that scrofulous little bureaucrat!" Garrick exclaimed. "He oversteps himself, even if he *is* an expert on Shakespeare." Sophie had wondered whether Edward Capell's complicity with Dr. Johnson and several other Shakespeare scholars in withholding support of Garrick's Stratford Jubilee had finally soured the actor-manager toward the Deputy Examiner of Plays. "I swear Capell's getting more peculiar every day," he added.

When Dorothea Celesia's play was finally rewritten to Garrick's satisfaction, Sophie resolved not to risk Capell's wrath and kept her involvement in *Almida* a secret.

"This was an adaptation to begin with," she reasoned in a final meeting before the play's debut held with Garrick atop Drury Lane, "and you, sir, solved the plot problems yourself."

"But even if you remain anonymous, you have no objection to a nice fee for the speeches you penned, if it plays well?" he had said chuckling.

Fortunately for all concerned, the tragedy had done quite nicely when it opened in the new year of January 1771. It had featured the compelling Mrs. Barry and played ten nights in repertory, alternating with the usual Drury Lane fare.

Even before the work had gone into rehearsal, Sophie had been certain she was pregnant. After her initial shock and her concern about what her estranged husband would do if he found out, she began to revel in her new state.

"You've not been sick, or you've hidden it well!" Lorna had marveled, giving her friend a hug when Sophie told her the news.

"I'd *best* hide the fact I'm not pregnant by my legal husband," Sophie had replied, wondering how long her ample cloak, which she wore constantly, would keep her condition a secret. "Peter might be tempted to sue for damages claiming loss of honor!"

"You've not lived together for *years*!" Lorna exclaimed. "And he has taken shelter with any woman who would buy his victuals!"

"Ah . . . but he's a man!" Sophie rested her hands gently on her belly. "Despite the dangers, 'tis a wonderful thing, this bairn," she added softly, patting her belly. "'Tis as if Hunter's left part of himself . . ."

And now his babe would soon be born—and born too soon, by the looks of it. Sophie shifted her weight on the mattress in an attempt to find a comfortable position—not an easy task, given her enormous girth. Despite her discomfort, she took pleasure in the memory of how, soon after *Almida*'s debut, she and Garrick had concluded an agreement for her to alter the character names and many of the scenes of her censored *A Maid Most Modestly Made* as a way of finally getting it on a stage.

"Shall I employ a male pseudonym?" she had asked her mentor.

"A capital idea!" Garrick crowed. "'Twill be a true test for that carping Edward Capell!" Garrick struck a dramatic pose, his forefinger pointing skyward. "Can that mincing little pen pusher sniff out a petticoat author under any and all circumstances? Let us see! What name will you take and when can I see the new pages?"

"I thought *Sydney Ganwick* might be nice," Sophie said with a wicked gleam in her eye. "The name's English as ale . . . but with a tip of the tricorner to McGann. I hope to have a completed draft by March, if that will suit?"

Garrick considered the pseudonym for a moment. Then he asked another question.

"And have you thought of a new title for the work?"

"*Strife for a Wife*," she answered promptly.

Garrick threw his head back and laughed.

"If we outfox Capell, I'll schedule it for . . . ah . . . let's see." He consulted his list of plays planned for the remainder of the 1770–1771 season. "April Fool's Day seems a fitting date, *Sydney*!" He reached for a glass of port, despite his doctor's orders, and saluted her. "Here's to our mutually successful *Almida* . . . but I'm putting my faith in Mr. Ganwick. I hear he's a brilliant young fellow."

In a twinkling, McGann's *A Maid Most Modestly Made* had been transformed to Ganwick's *Strife for a Wife* and was speedily approved by the Lord Chamberlain's office. Sophie's share of the profits came to more than a hundred pounds. Not a paltry sum, she thought, for a play she had assumed would never see a stage. And with a man's name on the title page, it had sailed past Edward Capell's censorious quill! Who knew what future successes dear Sydney might pen?

At that point, Sophie was roused from her reverie by the sound of a sharp rap at her door.

"Lorna?" she called. "I'm so glad you're here. Mrs. Phillips told me—"

"Sophie, my dear," Roderick Darnly exclaimed, striding into her chambers, "I've just returned to London and was terribly upset to learn from the apothecary downstairs that you were ill—"

He halted halfway across the room, his eyes glued to the enormous mound protruding from under the coverlet.

"No . . . I am not ill," Sophie cut in, dismayed to see Viscount Glyn, of all people, entering her lodgings, "merely enceinte."

"And the father?" Roderick asked in a stunned voice. He seemed to be attempting to master his emotions as he took a step closer.

She glared up at him as he approached her bedside. "Surely you can hazard a guess," she snapped. "The man you've falsely accused of embezzlement." She gazed at him narrowly. "And, pray, what brings you to my humble abode? I see your celebrated injuries left no lasting damage."

"So you know of that blackguard's attack? Well . . . of course, you do," he amended himself, eyeing her belly. "Actually, my time in Wales did me a world of good," he continued, regaining some of his composure. "My temper eventually cooled, despite Robertson's unprovoked assault. You've no call to cast such baleful glances, my dear," he added. "'Tis Thomas Rosoman, not I, who persists in demanding that the full extent of the law be brought to bear on that cheat."

Sophie opened her mouth to protest this blatant falsehood, but Darnly gave her no chance to speak.

"Really, my dear, you do have the most atrocious taste in men. I am sorry to learn you have again been played false by yet another rake, but then, what else can one expect from such scoundrels? All the more reason for you to come live with me . . . after your confinement, you can give the baby over to a wet nurse—which I shall be happy to provide—that is, if the whelp survives. Then you shall be free to write in peace."

She stared at him, dumbfounded by his gall, and tempted to confront his bold-faced lies. Instead she eyed him coldly, saying, "As I am in great danger of having this baby very soon—perhaps even *today*—I would appreciate it very much, Roderick, if you would take your leave."

"Whatever you wish," he replied, grim-faced. "But do give my proposals serious consideration. I stand ready and willing to serve as your protector."

"And why, in the name of St. Ninian, would you wish to do that?" she demanded.

Roderick cocked an eyebrow and smiled faintly.

"It never fails to astound me how much you undervalue your appeal to a man of my artistic sensibilities," he replied, ignoring the look of disbelief flickering across her face. "Have you heard from the miscreant?" he asked mockingly. Sophie maintained a stony silence. "No? I thought not. I'm certain that eventually, dear Sophie, you'll come to see that what I offer you is in our mutual interest. But . . . perhaps you merely need more time to think on it."

He turned toward the door as if to depart.

"Oh, before I go . . ." he added, facing the bedstead

once again. He pulled out a leather pouch, reached for her hand and placed the purse in her palm. "I nearly forgot the primary reason for my visit. Here's the rest of your share of *Vanquishers Vanquished*. Rosoman has, at last, done up his final accounts at Sadler's and wished me to give you this," he said, to Sophie's astonishment.

"May I inquire how much *more* I am due?" she asked curtly, fingering the contents of the pouch.

"As I feared," the viscount said shrugging, "the play's expenses were astronomical. That man Rosoman's a squanderer . . . but there should be a respectable forty-seven pounds in there, my dear."

Sophie remained silent, forcing herself to quell her temper. There was no point in stirring up trouble, she reckoned, because, fortunately, Roderick Darnly was still unaware of her presence in Rosoman's cupboard that night.

"Have you been well enough to work on any plays during these months of your confinement?" Roderick inquired blandly.

"Hasn't anyone told you?" she retorted, in no mood for a chat. "I've given up the muse." She was fed up with the man's dishonesty and constant interference. "I've discovered to my discouragement, there's not enough blunt in play writing, what with managers' expenses and so forth," she added pointedly. "I've found I do far better with my little printing business, thanks to Garrick's kind patronage."

"Surrendered your quill, have you?" he murmured, appearing disconcerted by her announcement. "I'm sorry to hear of this."

"Aye," Sophie replied, feigning indifference. "'Tis of no consequence. I shall be more than occupied caring for the bairn."

She began idly drumming the bed linen with her fingers, longing for Roderick to depart, when, suddenly, she was gripped by a stabbing pain that started in her groin and ripped through her abdomen like a scimitar. Just then, the door to her upstairs lodgings swung open and Lorna Blount stood in the threshold with an armload of daffodils.

"Sophie?" Lorna exclaimed, alarmed by the look of agony distorting her friend's features. "What's wrong?"

"Oh, God," Sophie groaned. "Oh, God! *No!*"

Just then, Sophie's birth water gushed out between her legs, soaking the linen as another pain relentlessly bore down on her.

"Fetch Mrs. Phillips!" she gasped to Lorna. "*Quickly!*" she cried, her voice rising to a shrill scream.

Frantically, she grabbed the bedpost behind her head, riding out the contraction as best she could while Lorna tossed the daffodils on a table and dashed back downstairs to alert the apothecary-midwife. Struggling for breath, Sophie opened her eyes to find Lord Darnly, standing stock-still in the middle of the chamber wearing a horrified expression.

"For God's sake, Roderick! Don't go all glassy eyed! I'm having a *baby!*" she cried angrily.

The viscount had taken a step backward, bumping awkwardly into a corner of the armoire that stood against the wall near the door. His face had drained of color.

Sophie watched her unwelcome visitor stumble toward the exit. She wished, suddenly, to inflict on him the same kind of physical suffering that now held her entire body in its grip. She was furious that the man who drove her bairn's father from her side should be a witness to her distraught state.

"Did you know that Hunter and I have *long* been lovers?" she inquired brutally, as the first contraction finally ran its course. At these words, Lord Darnly halted midstep and turned to stare at her. "Eight months ago *exactly,* on the afternoon you were drinking your port downstairs at the Myddleton's Head Inn, we were upstairs in my chambers directly overhead, making wonderful, *passionate* love!" she exclaimed, gratified to see a look of misery invade his gray eyes. "I can't imagine why you filed those patently false charges," she added with a withering glare. "He was only trying to ascertain what was owing the two of us."

"And what did the villain claim to have seen in those ledgers?" Darnly asked in a low voice.

"I have no idea," Sophie lied boldly, bracing for another contraction that appeared about to seize her. "As you are well aware, he was obliged to make a hasty exit and I never—"

"The man embezzled three hundred pounds, I tell you!"

"Whatever you claim, 'tis *his* flesh fighting to escape this womb of mine!" Sophie retorted scathingly, as another excruciating pain began to tear through her abdomen. *"Damn you, Viscount Glyn! You forced my bairn's father to flee . . . I want . . . Hunter!"* She half-sobbed, reaching behind her head to clutch desperately at the bedpost.

" 'Earl,' " Roderick corrected her dully, closing his ears to her agonized shrieks as he passed Mrs. Phillips bustling through the door. "I really came here to tell you I am now the Earl of Llewelyn. My father has died, you see, and—at long last—I can do whatever I please."

Afterward, Sophie only dimly recalled Darnly's hasty departure. However, she remembered the pain of childbirth, and was grateful how short her labor had been. The babe was fragile looking—very long but extremely thin.

"Tall . . . like his da," Sophie whispered tearfully.

"More like a spider than a babe," Mrs. Phillips had pronounced as she severed the umbilical cord on the bloody sheets. "When they're eight-month bairns—they come out faster. I doubt if he'll live," she added flatly.

"He *will* live!" Sophie replied fiercely, seeing how Lorna and Mrs. Phillips exchanged worried looks. "Here . . . please clean him and put him to the breast!"

As if sheer will could keep an infant alive, Sophie accomplished what Mrs. Phillips privately predicted was impossible. Within a few weeks, little Rory McGann Robertson had gained weight and filled out a bit, "although he still doesn't look quite human . . . a monkey now, instead of a spider," Mrs. Phillips declared as Lorna made her way upstairs to bring her friend a warm caudle she'd had the tavern keeper concoct out of eggs, milk, and nutmeg.

In the middle of June, the apothecary pronounced the month-old infant almost out of danger, barring some unexpected fever.

"Have you written Hunter yet that he's a father?" Lorna asked, holding the baby while Sophie sipped the caudle.

"I thought to wait till midsummer, when we're more certain the bairn will . . ." She left her sentence dangling. She thought of little Danielle, so pink and robust at birth, carried off by ague when three months old. Sophie reached out to take Rory from Lorna's arms. She stroked his cheek and kissed him on each eyelid the way Hunter had so often kissed her. The baby's tiny hand wrapped itself tightly around her forefinger. "That's a good lad," she crooned. "You must grow stronger every day."

The London theaters closed once again for the summer season and most of the players and fellow theater people deserted Covent Garden in their customary fashion. Sophie had revealed her pregnancy to David Garrick during rehearsals for *Strife for a Wife* and had sworn him to secrecy. Now, on the eve of the Garricks' annual departure for Hampton House, she informed them personally of little Rory's premature birth.

"I wondered how you'd bear to keep your cloak on when the weather grew warm." Garrick smiled as he hobbled across the sitting room in Southampton Street to offer her a chair. Despite his latest trip to Bath, he was still suffering intermittent attacks of gout and biliousness.

"And the babe is well?" Mrs. Garrick asked hesitantly. "Only eight months term, David said."

"Aye, he surprised us with his early debut, but he's blooming. In fact, I'll wager he's gained half a stone!" She laughed at her own exaggeration. "I can only stay a short while. Lorna Blount was kind enough to mind him during this visit, but there is no substitute for mama on occasion . . ."

David cleared his throat.

"And what of the babe's father . . . ?"

"I've received my first missive from Hunter just this week," she confided. "He doesn't know of the bairn, of course. I would have distressed him needlessly if something had happened before my confinement . . . and then, when Rory was born so prematurely, I wished to wait and see if—"

"We understand," Eva-Maria interjected kindly. "And what of Mr. Robertson's journey to Annapolis?"

"The ship sailed to the West Indies in record time, thanks to a hurricane!" she related, warming to the tale of Hunter's unusual crossing of the Atlantic Ocean. "In fact, the months of inclement weather in the Caribbean forced the *Jenny* to remain in St. Thomas all winter. That's where he wrote the letter. I haven't heard yet of his impressions of Annapolis, but the new theater is scheduled to open in September and— depending on the situation here in London at the end of the season next spring—I imagine he hopes to return . . ."

Both Garricks peered sympathetically across their teacups at their guest. Now that her baby had been born healthy, Sophie's situation was even more precarious. Wretch though he might be, her legal husband was still alive and full of ploys to wheedle money from his estranged wife. To make matters worse, the father of wee Rory had resorted to fisticuffs with one of the premier peers of the realm. Garrick had not been surprised to learn of Darnly's larcenous treatment of Sophie at Sadler's Wells, but, in all, 'twas a circumstance that did not bode well for the return of young Robertson, even though the new Earl of Llewelyn seemed to spend little time, now, in London.

Drury Lane's ailing manager listened to the young woman he almost considered a daughter chatting with his wife. Her petite figure was enhanced by her newly rounded bosom, full of mother's milk, and for a brief, painful moment, he considered his and Eva-Maria's own childlessness.

Sophie was such a vibrant, intense young thing, he reflected, wry and witty one moment, eyes flashing and full of righteous indignation over the world's folly at another. Absently, he glanced at the ornate harpsichord standing in the corner of his parlor. In many ways, she was like a pianist's tuning fork, he mused, sensitive to every sound, every nuance in the atmosphere. The joys as well as the chaos and personal catastrophes that had beset her had made her more sympathetic to life around her, giving her the ability to reflect in her writing all that she had seen and experienced.

"Well, then," Garrick said to his wife who busied herself pouring another round of tea, "a bit of business, if you don't object, my dear. In the autumn, Sophie, will you wish to continue printing our playbills and such?" he asked.

"Certainly," she responded eagerly, relieved to have some promise of income to tide her over until she fully regained her strength and had confirmation that Rory remained healthy.

"And over the summer, will you be up to any pen scratching?"

"Well . . ." Sophie said slowly. "Hunter's recent letter describing some of the dandies traveling to the Colonies on board his ship put me to mind of those outrageous young men who return from the Continent. I find their garish costumes quite comical, to say nothing of their display of what they consider the latest in fashionable manners and *bon mots*. I thought to spoof the English fops on tour . . . and contrast with them plain and prudent British folk."

"A satire of the macaronis?"

"I think you've found a title for your new comedy," Mrs. Garrick smiled encouragingly.

"Should I write it as Sydney Ganwick?" Sophie asked doubtfully. "Lorna told me recently that someone is spreading rumors that the name disguises a female pen."

"We shall decide that question in autumn," Garrick shrugged. "It will help if *The Macaronis*'s theme conveys the notion that staid English ways are best," he suggested. "And come September, I shall ensure that certain anonymous articles find their way into the gossip journals speculating just who—of several worthy gentlemen named—this Ganwick could be. I think 'twill hide your identity well enough."

"And this remains our secret?" Sophie asked earnestly. "You'll not tell Peter or Roderick Darnly or even Mr. Lacy that I am writing again?"

"All shall be as before," he reassured her.

Sophie smiled at the couple who had been so kind to her, despite the chaotic state of her personal life. "Have a good respite at Hampton House," she urged. "I worry that this year's wrangling among your players has exhausted you both."

"You mean Mrs. Abington, and the Barrys, and that viper Mavis Piggott?" Mrs. Garrick exclaimed. "They dare to refuse the parts Davy assigns them! 'Tis disgraceful!" Eva-Maria added indignantly, nodding at her husband. "They drive my poor Davy to distraction! His foot swells and his belly aches!"

"Now, now, dearest," Garrick soothed his wife. "For a few glorious weeks we shall forget our woes and eat strawberries and punt along the river. Replenish the well, we shall, so we can return to London, refreshed and ready to see what we can do with *The Macaronis*! The more I hear the title, the better I like it."

Sophie noted the drawn, exhausted look pinching Garrick's celebrated features and realized that despite his cordiality he was in considerable pain. She quickly thanked her hosts and made a hasty departure. As she strode through the Great Piazza past St. Paul's, she turned over in her mind the notion of adding a colonial dandy or two to her cast of characters. Hunter's letter had described well-dressed travelers returning to America who, he said, prided themselves on their sartorial splendor.

A familiar feeling of longing swept over her. If only Hunter could magically be waiting for her at the top of the stairs above the Green Canister. If only—

Sophie pulled up short in front of the staymaker's shop. Directly in her path stood Mavis Piggott. The actress had apparently been shopping for undergarments at the former site of Ashby's Books, for she was carrying neatly wrapped purchases under her arm. The lusty wail of a hungry, indignant infant wafted down the stairwell adjacent to the shop. As one, the two women stared up at a window that was slightly ajar.

"I wondered if you still made your abode here," Mavis said with a self-satisfied air. "We've seen little of you at Drury Lane this spring. Is it true you've produced another brat? Was it by your dear, departed Hunter Robertson? Or perhaps Old Drury's patron," she said cynically, "our new Earl of Llewelyn? You can't have reconciled with that addle-pated *husband* of yours?"

Ignoring her unsubtle jibes, Sophie parried the actress's rude questions as best she could.

"Is it true what Lorna Blount tells *me*," Sophie retorted,

"that you've not signed articles for Drury Lane next season? Pray, what playhouse in the kingdom will be graced with your presence?"

"I sail on tomorrow's tide for Maryland, to join the American Company in Annapolis," Mavis answered with a malicious gleam in her eye. "'Tis a delightful establishment that engages only the finest actors Britain has to offer—as *you* must surely know." The tall, imposing woman nodded curtly. "So, I fear I must bid you and your new babe farewell. And you can be sure I'll convey the latest tidings to all who know you across the sea. Adieu!"

Chapter 32

October 1771

A chattering group of Covent Garden and Drury Lane veterans sought the cooler chambers of Reynolds Tavern on West Street across from Annapolis's new theater. Their morning rehearsal had been conducted on a typically muggy Indian summer day and what they desired was a bit of refreshment and a breath of the breeze off the bay. The resident acting company was still basking in the success of its gala opening nearly a month earlier, on September 9.

"Gadzooks!" Mavis exclaimed, mopping her damp brow with the lace attached to her sleeve, "is it always so hot in October?"

"Aye," replied Hunter, studying the fine lines that now creased the corners of Mavis's almond-shaped eyes. "But by December, the weather will be bracing, I'm told."

To Hunter, Mavis Piggott was still a handsome woman, but there was something disturbingly feline about the secretive smile and faraway looks she had been casting at him all morning. Ever since her unexpected arrival in Maryland the previous week, he had kept his manner friendly, but he had deliberately steered clear of any personal exchanges. However, now that they had both been cast in *Cymbeline*, he had the uncomfortable sensation that she was extremely eager to speak with him alone. She had been assigned the role of queen, and he, Lord Cloten, her loutish son, so they had several scenes together.

"Hunter," she said, lowering her eyes to her tankard of

ale, "I feel so in arrears in the mastery of my part . . . would you do me the kindness of working on my speeches with me this afternoon? Perhaps we could find a quiet spot down near the river under a tree where 'tis a bit cooler . . ."

Why not? he thought to himself. Perhaps she would have some current intelligence about Roderick Darnly's state of mind. Hunter didn't put much stock in whatever she might have to say of Sophie, but 'twould be good to hear news of London.

"If you wish," he nodded. "We're not due at the theater until four o'clock or so. Shall we?"

They walked slowly down Franklin Street where the poplar trees offered some shade from the oppressive heat. Mavis had taken a fan from her reticule and was trying to cool the damp hair clinging to her forehead. They found a shady space near the flowing river and began to recite their lines.

After a half hour or so, Mavis suddenly glanced over at Hunter from beneath her eyelashes and announced, "This queen certainly hatches plots for the benefit of her son, does she not?"

"Aye, she wants *him* to steal the throne from her own husband—the devious wench!" He laughed.

"And have I not plotted, in the past, for *your* advancement?" she asked with an innocent air.

"And for your own as well, I'll wager," he replied warily, startled by her abrupt forwardness.

"It seems you're succeeding in this land of transplanted Englishmen," she said pleasantly. "You've been given excellent roles and a hand in managing, I see."

"I've done well enough—for a Scot," he reminded her.

"And do you plan to return to Covent Garden next year?"

"I hope to . . ."

"And do you not worry that Lord Darnly—now that he is Earl of Llewelyn—can do you harm?"

Hunter gazed at her steadily.

"So . . . he has advanced a rung in power and importance."

"Yes . . . and, no doubt, will try to wrest more mortgaged shares from Lacy, if he can. This cannot be good for *your* advancement at either theater . . ."

"Ah, you heard about our little *contretemps*?"

"Who has *not*?" she laughed. "And who hasn't heard of your rekindled passion for Sophie McGann, thanks to the Shakespeare Jubilee?" she added, that mysterious smile once again playing at her lips. "I thought it odd, at first, that you spirited yourself across the sea following your row with Darnly. Dublin's Smock Alley would have been distance enough, it seemed to me. But now that I am acquainted with the . . . ah . . . *situation* facing you at Half Moon Passage, I quite understand."

Hunter's eyes narrowed, but he continued to stare at her coolly.

"What *situation* do you understand, Mavis?" he asked quietly.

"About the babe," she shrugged. She smiled at him in a show of sympathy. "'Twas born in the middle of May, I'm told. I suppose a brat on your hands was the last thing you desired, with her being married to that shiftless sot, Lindsay-Hoyt. He's just the type to threaten a suit for adultery as a way of extorting your blunt. It must have been a shock to learn she was enceinte just when *you* were wrestling with such troubles of your own with London's newly minted earl. But then, I thought, no, perhaps her patron, Lord Darnly was the father . . . or she'd reconciled with her husband and you—"

Hunter grabbed the fan out of Mavis's hands and was tempted to slap her across the cheek with it.

"I didn't know about any bairn before I left," he said in a low, menacing voice. "Was she well when you last saw her? Is the babe lusty? Don't play parts with *me*, Mavis!" he said snarling. "I know your tricks too damnably well!"

Mavis glanced at his angry features and then looked away, her eyes full of uncertainty. She wondered now if she had interpreted events correctly. The baby could be his . . . or could be anybody's, she supposed. Word of Hunter's precipitous flight to the New World had left her assuming he had been only too pleased to escape everything: Darnly's wrath, Peter Lindsay-Hoyt's demands for money, and Sophie's entreaties that the baby was his, despite her valid marriage to that counterfeit baronet. There had even been rumors that Sophie's play *The Bogus Baronet* was based on the vagaries of her own life.

Mavis felt the heat of Hunter's glare. Perhaps she had miscalculated his true feelings for the chit. Ah . . . no matter . . . If the truth be told, she and Hunter never had got on very well. Should she desire someone to warm her bed in the New World, there was always that attractive young man playing Belarius in *Cymbeline* who had been throwing her bold looks during rehearsals.

"See here, Hunter," she said, pulling herself to a standing position and meticulously brushing the blades of grass from her skirts. "All I know is I saw Sophie briefly on the street the day before I sailed last July. She looked well enough, as it was six weeks or so after she'd risen from childbed. I heard a lusty baby's cry coming from her lodgings. That is all I know. I thank you for your help with my speeches, and I bid you adieu."

Hunter watched her stride up the slope and head back toward town along Franklin Street.

Sophie has had a child! Is it a lad or lass?

His head was swimming with the import of Mavis's news. Thank God Sophie had survived childbirth and was apparently well. Then the notion of fatherhood began to penetrate his consciousness. The poor lass had faced her ordeal alone, just as she had the birth of her daughter. Mid-May the bairn was born, Mavis had said. He mentally subtracted the months. They'd been together in their garret at Sadler's Wells in September. Those two days had been the only time they'd been lovers in over a year.

October, November, December . . . He counted on his fingers. The middle of May added up to just over eight months. He swallowed hard. Bachelor though he might be, even *he* knew bairns were born nine months after . . .

Slowly, Hunter rose to his feet and stared vacantly across the river, leaning against a huge poplar that shaded its bank. Mid-May . . . the arithmetic ate at him like a canker.

❦

The autumn storm that native Marylanders predicted would bring cooler temperatures blew against Hunter's window in the low-ceilinged chambers he had leased on Bloomsbury Square. He stared into the burning embers on the hearth, unable to fight his old devils of doubt and distrust.

If not he . . . who could be the father?

Surely not Peter Lindsay. No, the man was too pathetic. Hunter rejected the notion as soon as it entered his head. But what if—

Darnly! Lord Darnly—now, the Earl of Llewelyn!

Several times, Hunter had accused Sophie of having a liaison with him, and it had driven him mad to discover she had spent four months as a guest on Darnly's estate in Wales. Sophie had indignantly denied his charge, revealing, in fact, the earl's all-night rendezvous with his factor and housemaid in the hay byre at Evansmor.

Did she play the wanton with you, Robertson, to find a father for the babe she might have already known she was carrying?

A black fog of melancholy invaded Hunter's soul. Lord Darnly! The man whose wrath and power had driven him across an ocean. The man he had punched in the face for the way he had treated the woman he adored . . .

Sophie, Darnly's sometime mistress?

Then he chastised himself. He was jumping to conclusions again. And each time he had, he had brought them both pain. But then, why had she not *written* him of the babe? He thought of the sly look on Mavis's face when she had so cheerfully dispensed her news. Mavis Piggott had always caused him nothing but trouble, yet . . .

He slammed his fist against the nearest wall. One day he would judge for himself whether the babe looked anything like him. But how could he endure the uncertainty? What if, in the end, the babe's visage reminded him of no one so much as that nobly born scoundrel, the Earl of Llewelyn!

In early November, as if in answer to his prayer, Mrs. Reynolds, the tavern keeper's wife, handed him a watermarked letter posted from London the previous July. Ignoring his fellow players' urgings to join them for a tankard of ale, he carried the missive back to his chambers, breaking its seal with a trembling finger. His eyes misted over as he read her familiar hand.

. . . I watch wee Rory slumber in this dawn's light, but my heart is sore. Oh, Hunter, I was so frightened to face his early birth without you here! I know now Mrs. Phillips and Lorna surely thought he'd die. . . . I even prayed to God to keep us safe for you! Me, Sophie, the cleric-hating harridan! I feared to tell you of his puny spider's body and weak squall in case he should perish and you would have the added sadness of having lost a son.
But a miracle happened! The babe began to thrive and now is so dear, my heart stops when he looks at me with that mischievous smile so like his da's. The pain of birth . . . the fear for my own life as well as for the babe's, are nothing compared with what I endured during those months of not knowing if you were dead or alive.
I beg you, Hunter, write often as you can, for I fear half your letters may go astray if the rumors of conflict in the Colonies are true. Each day I long for word of you across the sea that separates us.
I must confess, ancient fears I harbor that Mavis could bewitch a lad far from home come over me sometimes, but I cannot but believe there is forged between us now a bond of enduring love that will link us forever. My greatest anxiety, however, is that you might meet some terrible fate in that strange land.
I find I cannot work, or sleep with any peace, until I know you have received this letter and rejoice in the birth of your son.
Peter has learned of the bairn, it seems, but appears more intent on soliciting a few shillings than protesting his honor. He tried to flush a bit of blunt from me when he accosted me near St. Paul's a fortnight ago. The poor blighter has never looked more parched

for spirits or disheveled . . . but he allowed me to pass for a shilling and sixpence, once satisfied that I'd given up writing plays to tend to my bairn.

The same excuse for the absence of plays by Sophie McGann has been given to that wretch R. D. Now that he has inherited the earldom, he will no doubt attempt to use his influence to thwart our advancement where he can. Thus far, he tarries in Wales, though his false charges against you remain at King's Bench.

As much as it pains me to urge you to endure where you are, you daren't risk returning until I deem it safe enough. Please, please, Hunter, heed this warning! I grow increasingly wary of this Patron of the Arts and fear some darkness in his soul could do us both great harm.

What has sustained me these long months is the dear face of our bairn, who, with the tiny cleft in his chin and his laughing blue eyes—not to mention his remarkable size for a lad of his age—are the only remnants I possess of my dear childhood friend, loved so devotedly tonight by

Your Sophie

As Hunter scanned the lines once again, his breath began to feel hollow in his chest. Besides the harrowing description of their son's premature birth, he was humbled by the words that contained Sophie's outpouring of love and concern for his welfare.

A tiny cleft in Rory's chin . . . the baby's blue eyes. His large size. His mischievous nature.

Of course he is my child! Hunter thought, more ashamed than he had ever felt in his life. *I have pride and conceit and an inclination to distrust women as surely as Sophie once distrusted men!* Yet, she was willing to voice her fears regarding Mavis's wiles and have faith in his constancy, nonetheless.

Gratitude and remorse swept over him for the thousand foolish doubts that had plagued him since his conversation by the river's edge with that devious wench!

Distractedly, he stared out of the window of his rented quarters on Bloomsbury Street, gazing past the tops of the poplar trees toward the harbor at the bottom of the hill, seeing nothing. He would do as she had pleaded and remain in this outpost of British civilization, but oh, how he longed to jump aboard one of the brigantines anchored in Chesapeake Bay!

"That wretch Capell may have granted Sydney Ganwick's work a license, but he's *gutted* my play!" Sophie said morosely, tossing the Lord Chamberlain's copy of *The London Heiress* back on Garrick's desk. In the two and a half years since Hunter fled London, Sophie was grateful to have earned her and Rory's keep by her pen. Even so, Deputy Examiner of Plays Edward Capell, was growing increasingly difficult to please, regardless of which author submitted plays for his approval. Sophie's latest effort under her male pseudonym was defaced with *X*'s, and the word *Out!* had been scratched by Capell on nearly every page.

"Our worthy royal servant enjoyed the theme in *The Macaronis*, but grows testy, it appears, when it comes to ladies outwitting gentlemen of means," Garrick replied wearily. The actor-manager had his swollen foot elevated on a stool, and his face appeared drawn and pasty. The poor man had recently suffered a painful sore throat and yet another attack of gallstones. "I shall cast your farce with our best players, Sophie, and trust your remaining witticisms will carry the day," he sighed. "And now, my dear, I must face those warring queens of Thespis over their designated roles in *The West Indian* . . . One day, these harpies will inspire me to retire from this wretchedness, and I shall live the life of a country squire!"

And what would happen to Sydney Ganwick without Garrick's protection? Sophie wondered silently, alarmed by his prediction. She watched sadly as her mentor hobbled down the stairs to soothe the contentious actresses who awaited him in the Greenroom.

I am one man away from literary destitution, she thought somberly. *'Tis like being a gentleman's mistress!*

The run of Sophie's *The London Heiress* in early March did not leave its author exactly destitute, but she blamed Capell's neutering of her play's biting humor for the production's lackluster three-night run. It had garnered a mere fifty-seven pounds for her solitary Author's Benefit.

"Twill have to see me through until I can somehow conjure up another idea and try to get it mounted six months from now," she groused a month later to Lorna, who had her aching feet plunged into a pail of water. Sophie's friend was feeling all of her twenty-eight years after a season in the *corps de ballet* at the King's Opera.

"You'll think of something to put that pen of yours to work," Lorna said encouragingly. "You always do. But how do I procure a new pair of arches, will you tell me *that*, Rory Robertson!"

"Feet! Feet! Feet!" crooned Sophie's little boy.

Rory thrust his short arms into the pail and playfully splashed as much water as he could all over Sophie's floor.

"Will you *rub* my feet, wee Rory, instead of sloshing water everywhere?" Lorna laughed.

"No, no, no, you little minx!" Sophie cried, retrieving her twenty-one-month-old son and diverting him with an old feather pen. She tickled him under his chubby chin and in the crease of his elbow until he was squealing with mirth.

Suddenly, a loud knock at the door startled all of them into abrupt silence.

"If you'll stop cackling in there, I've a letter—and a visitor—for Miss Sophie McGann!" a voice boomed.

Sophie dashed across the chamber and flung open the latch.

"Bozzy! Oh Bozzy!" she cried, staring at the rotund form whom she had not seen in London in donkey years—not since James Boswell's marriage to his first cousin, Margaret Montgomerie in the autumn of 1769 following the tumultuous Shakespeare Jubilee. "Your entrances are always so *dramatic*!" she said, throwing her arms around his bulky neck. "Oh Lorna . . . 'tis Bozzy!"

"Bozzy! Bozzy! Bozzy!" Rory cried delightedly, casting his plump arms around James Boswell's knees.

"Well, well, well . . . and who might *you* be?" he said, crouching to examine the child eye to eye. "Jesu, Sophie," Boswell said with mock severity. "Each time I leave you alone in London, you produce a bairn . . . and never by *me*! Let me have a look at you, my young lad. Those eyes . . . that chin . . ." James gazed up at Sophie. "There can only be one sire of this fine laddie. Where's Hunter?"

Sophie bit her lip and struggled to squelch a wave of self-pity.

"America . . . acting in the Colonies . . . in Maryland. You haven't heard about the celebrated altercation between Hunter and Roderick Darnly? The villain's pressed bogus charges, but Hunter dares not fight the word of an earl in court!"

"Aye, the man has vast influence, I'm told, now that he holds sway over his father's coal-rich lands in Wales." Boswell eyed her with a sympathetic glance and then, rising to his full height, he looked over at Lorna. "But how very good it is to see you both," he said, easing the three of them past the uncomfortable moment.

"And lovely to see *you*, Bozzy," Lorna said, glancing self-consciously at her bare feet, as she busily dried them with a piece of linen. "But I'm sure you two have much catching up to do. Rory, how would you like to go visit the man with the musical monkey in the Great Piazza? Would you like that?"

"Monkey! Monkey! Monkey!" Rory beamed.

"Yes . . . you may go and visit the monkey," Sophie said, adding in a low voice, "Thank you, my friend."

Lorna and Rory soon departed while James sank into a chair. Sophie stirred the dying embers on the hearth and put the kettle on its iron peg over the fire for tea.

"Sink me . . . I've brought a letter!" James Boswell exclaimed, pulling a missive out of his pocket. He pointed to the return address. "From Annapolis, it says. It must be from our friend. 'Twas just being delivered to Mrs. Phillips at the Green Canister when I called earlier. I said I'd convey it to you and here I've gone and nearly forgot it!"

"James! You haven't contracted Señor Gona—?" Sophie said, taking the letter from her friend.

"Just precautionary, just precautionary," Boswell mumbled, avoiding any mention of his wife of three and a half years. "I've come down to London to persuade my friend Sam Johnson to make the trip to Scotland that he has been promising for years. Our tentative plan is to depart in August."

"Ah, the Scot-baiting Johnson. I pray a visit to our homeland may change his opinion of it. May I . . . ?" Sophie asked, holding the letter postmarked *Annapolis* as her heart began to pound.

"Of course," Boswell assured her. "I think I can manage to brew us some tea while you read it."

Sophie sank into the chair next to his and broke the plain seal. Boswell watched curiously as a succession of emotions played across his friend's lovely face while she scanned the lines of Hunter's latest missive.

"Is all well with the lad?" he asked gently after a few minutes.

"Well enough," she sighed, allowing the pages to fall to her lap. "He tries to keep my spirits up with tales of his life on the colonial stage." She smiled wanly, pointing to the letter in question. "He and his fellow players have been touring with the American Company in Philadelphia and New York. Do you remember that jade, Mavis Piggott? She's had a falling out with yet another manager. Apparently, he refused to mount her latest play."

"Why are you so glum, then, after receiving such a packet full of news?" he asked in a kindly voice.

"Because he doesn't remain in one place long enough for me to post a reply from England," she complained morosely. "I send my missives off to Annapolis, knowing he won't hear news of Rory and me for nearly a year."

"He'll soon come back," James Boswell reassured her.

"And if he can't?" she whispered, her eyes growing misty.

"You'll go to him."

"But that dreadful voyage . . ." she replied fearfully. "Rory's such a wee lad . . ."

"'Twill all come right in the end," Boswell reassured her. "I never saw such a pair as the two of you that rainy night in Stratford. Of course you shall be reunited, Sophie. 'Tis your destiny."

Brushing the moisture from her eyes with her sleeve, Sophie impulsively kissed her guest on the top of his broad forehead.

"Except for Hunter and Mr. G., my darling Bozzy, you're the dearest man in Christendom!"

Her composure once again restored, she calmly proposed they celebrate Boswell's return to London by attending a performance of Oliver Goldsmith's wildly popular *She Stoops to Conquer.*

"I've heard there's not a ticket to be had in the kingdom," Boswell warned her.

Sophie reached in her pocket and withdrew Garrick's metal manager's token.

"Ah . . . but I've friends in high places," she teased. "We'll use Mr. G.'s courtesy coin and sit in the best box in Covent Garden tonight!"

By the end of 1773, Sophie had written a five-act farce she titled *The Rattecatchers,* about a group of reckless London bucks who form a drinking, dining, and wenching society and are subsequently conspired against by a coterie of *femmes,* one of whom infiltrates their club dressed as a man.

"'Tis brilliant! Your best work to date!" Garrick enthused, "although you'll have to rework that bit where the rakes sup at their private club. Tone down the raspberry tart–slinging scene . . . you know how Capell despises colorful food."

As he handed her the manuscript across his desk, Sophie nearly gasped. Gout had almost crippled the poor man's fingers, twisting them nearly into claws. Throughout the year, his health had been deteriorating alarmingly. Clearly, he had aged far beyond his fifty-six years.

"Well then, shall we aim to see your play mounted before season's end?" Garrick said, grimacing as he shifted in his chair.

It was a miracle that the ailing actor was still able to perform on stage, Sophie thought sadly. However, when he appeared before an audience, she marveled at how his infirmities seemed to disappear, and his voice and presence were as compelling as ever. But gazing at him now, Sophie realized suddenly that Garrick couldn't continue much longer with the double burdens of managing the playhouse and playing the taxing roles of Lear, Richard III, and Hamlet during a typical month.

"And are you coping with the playbills and such?" Garrick asked gently, shaking her from her reverie. "Making enough, are you, to keep little Rory in chops and biscuits?"

Sophie's gaze shifted to the manuscript she held in her hand. She would, indeed, *just* make ends meet if Sydney Ganwick's *The Rattecatchers* survived Edward Capell's censorious pen and *if* the comedy reached the stage before the end of the 1773–1774 season.

"I believe I will, sir," she replied. "I do so appreciate the print work you've given me."

"I know, my dear," he said wearily. "Friendships like ours prosper because they've been good for both of us."

"Like your partnership with Mr. Lacy," Sophie ventured.

Garrick looked at her strangely.

"Not quite like that, but I take your meaning," was all he would say on the subject.

When Sophie later reflected on that brief conversation, she concluded that Garrick may have known something of his cantankerous partner's final illness. On January 21 of the new year, 1774, James Lacy died in his sleep, bequeathing his share in Drury Lane's Royal Patent to his feckless son, Willoughby.

By February, everyone around the Covent Garden district had heard that the fabulously wealthy nobleman with an abiding interest in London's theatrical life, the Right Honorable Lord Roderick Darnly, Earl of Llewelyn, had decamped from his sizable estates in Wales and taken up residence again at his elegant town house at Number 10, St. James's Street.

What these changes would portend for the theater folk at

Drury Lane—and for the dramatist Sydney Ganwick—was
anybody's wager.

Sophie was not particularly surprised to see a crush of
visitors milling about the stage door a quarter of an hour
before *King Lear* was scheduled to unfold this fine May
evening. In the months since James Lacy's death, theatergoers and players alike seemed to sense that an era in theatrical
history was slipping away each time the ailing David Garrick appeared in one of Shakespeare's titanic roles.

Throughout the spring of 1774, David Garrick soldiered
on, despite a lingering cold, a bilious stomach, and the trials
of having a new partner, the slow-witted Willoughby Lacy.
Even the unexpected death in April of his friend, the brilliant playwright Oliver Goldsmith, from a sudden fever,
didn't keep Garrick from meeting his obligations to his
players and his public—although Sophie could see that
Goldsmith's loss had been a shocking blow.

"What a tragic waste," Garrick said to Sophie sorrowfully during one of their private conferences in his Drury
Lane chambers, "that he should die at a mere forty-six years
old." In the next breath he had given her the unwelcome
news on her play. *The Rattecatchers* could not be mounted
until the 1774–1775 season, commencing the following September.

"Unfortunately, Lacy left debts from trying unsuccessfully to mine coal on his property in Isleworth."

"What does that mean for his half of the Patent?" Sophie
asked, alarmed.

"He has mortgaged more of his shares than I would
like," replied Garrick. "Young Willoughby struggles with
many . . . ah . . . impediments, and I worry he may not
be quite up to fending off predators. Meanwhile, our playhouse must trim its expenses. As far as new plays are concerned, we shall be forced to stick with the old chestnuts for
a time, to keep costs down. I am sorry to have to disappoint
you, my dear. Eventually, we shall prevail."

Recalling this rather ominous conversation, Sophie stood
quietly in the wings as the stage servants put the final

touches on the set for *King Lear*. Garrick emerged from his tiring-room costumed in a furred robe and flowing white wig. He wore severe makeup that aged his features to a degree almost too alarming to behold. The prompter, Mr. Hopkins, called for places.

"Hello, my dear Sophie," a melodious voice said into her ear.

Startled, she turned to find the actress, Kitty Clive, who was now retired, standing by her side.

"Mrs. Clive!" Sophie exclaimed with pleasure. "How lovely to see you! You've come to London to see the *Lear*?"

"But of course," she nodded and then lowered her voice. "It may be his last season, you know . . ."

"Do you really think so?" Sophie asked, unsettled to hear so knowledgeable an insider echo the tittle-tattle repeated everywhere these days.

Kitty did not reply, but inclined her head in the direction of Garrick, who was accepting the subdued greetings of the three women who played his stage daughters, Regan, Gonevil, and Cordelia. As was their habit, the actresses knelt ceremoniously to receive Garrick's blessing. Sophie felt a lump rise to her throat as she noticed the painful swelling that disfigured the hand Garrick laid on their heads in benediction.

"The daughters he never had," Kitty murmured in a low voice and then cocked her head to study Sophie closely. "You rather fit that role too," she added softly. "He's always been terribly fond of you, you know. Tell me, did you truly abandon writing?"

"I, ah . . ." Sophie temporized.

"That was a dreadfully rude question," the actress blurted. "Disregard it entirely. Shall we take our seats?"

Sophie had been invited by the Garricks to share their box. Eva-Maria sat regally in her customary chair, dressed in the height of fashion in a gown of gold tissue silk. Much to Sophie's surprise, a dowdy woman in her late twenties occupied the seat next to her. Two other women of a similar age and description had tucked themselves into seats at the back of the box.

"May I present Miss Hannah More?" Eva-Maria said

graciously, "and her two sisters—Sally and Patricia. This is
Sophie McGann, a dear friend of ours." The three guests
nodded at Sophie. "The Miss Mores are from Bristol," Eva-
Maria said by way of introduction. "They've come to Lon-
don for several months, and have taken a flat in Henrietta
Street around the corner from our new house on Adelphi
Terrace," she added. "Hannah has written the most wonder-
ful, complimentary letter about Davy's performance in *Zara*.
When it was forwarded to him by her friend Mr. Stone-
house, he insisted they should meet."

"I was so embarrassed to learn Mr. Stonehouse had
shown it to Mr. Garrick," Hannah said breathlessly. "I, a
fledgling dramatist, having my feeble words perused by a
master of the quill!"

"You have written a play?" Sophie asked skeptically.

"A poor piece, surely. . . . I call it *Inflexible Captive*,"
Hannah More said coyly. "Mr. Garrick has agreed to read it.
. . . I have some faint hopes for it to be mounted in Bath."

"I see . . ." Sophie murmured as the curtain in front of
them opened and the tragedy of Lear and his daughters began to unfold.

King Lear had been the fifth major tragic role Garrick
had played in his first season as a professional actor thirty-
four years earlier. He had become phenomenally successful
as the cantankerous king who was spoiled by power, turned
mad by exhaustion, and pierced to the heart by the ingrati-
tude of his daughters. Sophie stared down at the proud,
hard-bitten monarch storming around the stage. Gone was
any trace of stiffness and pain. Garrick was full of fire and
fury, then by turns, pathetic and weak.

> *How sharper than a serpent's tooth*
> *To have a thankless child . . .*

Sophie's thoughts drifted to Eva-Maria, sitting beside her,
her eyes shining with pride. In truth, the Garricks had no
thankless daughters, or sons, either. Their family had become the 130 people who comprised the company at Drury
Lane. Their circle was ever enlarged by the inclusion of even
such sycophantic hangers-on as this Hannah More, who had

inveigled an introduction to the celebrated actor-manager through artful flattery and had immediately and generously been welcomed into his domain.

Sophie stole a sideways glance at Miss More and was struck by a quality of calculation barely disguised by her prim demeanor.

She has a plan . . . and she is determined to execute it, Sophie mused.

After the performance, close friends and acquaintances crowded into the Greenroom backstage. Hannah More rushed to Garrick's side, full of praise and girlish delight at having sat in the manager's box. Her sisters were likewise effusive with their accolades, and Sophie could see how it lifted the exhausted actor's spirits to hear such fervent tributes paid to his art.

"Pray, what is the meaning of so many Miss Mores purring about Garrick with their plays and their pretty compliments?" Kitty Clive hissed within Sophie's hearing. "He should send them back to Bristol with a flea in their ears!"

"You know the More sisters?" Sophie smiled to hear Kitty echo her own sentiments.

"I hear this Hannah creature had some small plays produced in private houses and now thinks her work ready for a grander stage. Clever of her to flatter a sick old man, don't you think?"

"Oh, pray, don't call Garrick old!" Sophie said ardently.

Kitty arched one eyebrow.

"You truly do love him, don't you?"

"Love?" Sophie replied, startled by Kitty's use of the word.

"Love," she repeated matter-of-factly. "I'll wager you are as close to a true and loving daughter as that jackanapes is ever likely to have . . . but I fear he *is* a bit vain and subject to flattery, especially from ladies such as the mincing Miss Mores. Ah, well,"—added the actress, who had had her share of friendly spats with her former employer over the years—"all these intrigues do not concern me a whit any longer . . . and that's a blessing, to be sure. Adieu, Miss McGann . . . and God bless."

And with that, the indomitable Kitty Clive departed for

the peace and tranquillity of Strawberry Hill, her place of retirement on Horace Walpole's estate outside of London.

Mulling over the woman's rather curious pronouncements, Sophie was oblivious to the crowds jostling her in the Greenroom. She was startled, therefore, when she felt a hand placed on her shoulder.

"I do believe you've been avoiding me," Roderick Darnly said benignly. "Avoiding me for an age, in fact." Sophie whirled around and stared at the Earl of Llewelyn, feeling suddenly at a loss for words. "I understand from young Will Lacy that despite the adoring Miss Mores, you still have Garrick's approbation."

"He has been kind enough this year to allow me the playbill printing concession again," she replied stiffly.

"And you remain hardened against your muse?" he asked.

"I have shunned the quill a long while, now," she lied, wondering how to make a graceful but immediate exit. "Also, my young son occupies a great deal of my time," she added pointedly.

"Pity, that," the earl commented. "And do you ever hear from . . . his father?"

"No," she replied, meeting his gaze steadily as her heart thudded in her chest, "I do not. I haven't seen, spoken to, or heard from him in ages. Now, if you will excuse me . . ." she murmured, grateful to make her escape.

Chapter 33

November 1774

Hunter Robertson, David Douglass, and John Henry—all of the American Company—disembarked at Boston Harbor with the captain of the *Rose* following a stomach-churning trip through choppy coastal waters along the eastern seacoast. They had come north hoping they could somehow put together another acting company, despite the political storm brewing between England and the Colonies.

"Do you think the good citizens of this fair city plan to dump more tea into the Back Bay, Captain Ogilvie?" Hunter asked one of his four companions as they trudged up a dusty road in search of food and lodging.

"I've come to think that *any* Colonial is capable of such dastardly behavior!" the captain grumbled. "Shipping has become a dangerous game."

Now that England had added still more import duties to its rolls, the Colonists had taken to calling the new laws passed by the British government The Intolerable Acts. As a result, there was no end of sabotage committed by the rebels these days, and few ships were crossing the Atlantic in either direction.

In view of Roderick Darnly's long-standing threats to have Hunter arrested, and Peter Lindsay's legitimate claim that he had cuckolded him, Hunter had no clear notion about the degree of danger facing him if he returned to London after four years in the Colonies. Up to now, he had reluctantly heeded Sophie's warnings to remain in America, but with political unrest simmering everywhere, the theaters were virtually empty. Most ironic of all, this land of refuge was fast becoming a dangerous place for a transplanted Briton.

The foursome entered a tavern near the dock, only to learn from the pubmaster that the upstart Continental Congress had just passed a resolution suspending all public amusements.

"Well, that's it then," John Henry said sadly to his companions. "All the theaters will be officially closed." He pulled a leather pouch from his coat and began to count out their money. "Well, Robertson," he sighed, "this should just be enough to buy you your passage home—if you can secure one."

But even if he decided to risk it, Hunter thought morosely, as he fingered his slim profits, it was now early November, a treacherous time to hazard a transatlantic journey. And from the looks of the deserted harbor, there might not be a single ship willing to ply an ocean full of marauding American privateers.

"I expect I'll have to wait until spring, when the weather improves, and hope some daring English captain may be willing to hazard a trip. I wonder if the good congressmen include *juggling* in their list of public prohibitions during this time of civil strife?" Hunter speculated dryly. "'Tis about the only way I can imagine to keep myself from starving this winter!"

On a bone-chilling January afternoon, Sophie dashed for the door of *The Public Advertiser*, and once inside, was cheered by the sight of the fire glowing in the grate.

A handsome young man was conversing animatedly with the editor, Mr. Shaw, to whom Sophie regularly submitted the daily calendar of Drury Lane events.

"Yes, Mr. Sheridan," the editor said wearily. "I've said I would publish your piece before your play opens on the seventeenth, and I shall do just that, if you would be so kind as to allow me to get on with my work and assist Miss McGann, here."

The brash young visitor sported wavy brown hair that was powdered in the current mode. He cast his gray-blue eyes in Sophie's direction, watching her attentively as she handed Mr. Shaw the following day's playbill. Sheridan's curved and almost girlish mouth seemed instantly prepared to smile, as if such primed cheerfulness would somehow assist him in achieving his aims. His clothes were of the highest fashion, replete with lacy ruffles at collar and wrist.

"Sink me, if I shall be the cause of delaying this lovely miss even a moment longer!" the young man replied gallantly. He eyed Sophie closely.

"Your name is Sheridan?" Sophie smiled, deflecting his inquisitive glance with a cool but friendly manner. The impudent dandy was at least five years younger than she. "Can you be related to Thomas Sheridan, the great lecturer on elocution?"

"My esteemed father," the young man replied dryly, his ironic tone revealing that he esteemed his sire very little. "I am Richard Brinsley Sheridan . . . a playwright rather than player . . . with a comedy I believe will succeed wildly at Covent Garden!"

Sophie was brought up short by a fleeting memory of the rambunctious young Richard spiriting sweets from his mother's tea table in the Sheridans' sitting room years earlier in Bath.

"I knew your parents," she said. "Your mother was quite a heroine of mine. I was so sorry to hear of her passing. What has it been . . . nearly ten years now?"

"Nearly that."

"And pray, what is the name of your new play?" Sophie pressed, curious to know what this stylish young beau had concocted.

"'Tis called *The Rivals* . . . set in Bath, where I lived for quite some time. 'Twill open soon at Covent Garden. I hope you'll do me the honor of attending it," he added, pointing to the article he was submitting to the editor of *The Public Advertiser.* "This is a bit of puffery about the work . . . written anonymously by *me,* of course!" He laughed.

Despite her intuition that Richard Brinsley Sheridan remained a bit of a scamp, Sophie couldn't hide her smile.

"You may count on my attendance, sir . . . and I wish you the best of Irish luck with it!"

However, when Sophie went to see *The Rivals* at Covent Garden with Lorna Blount, she was more outraged than impressed. The play had opened, as planned, on January 17 —and had failed. Sophie had heard the author quickly withdrew the piece, rewrote it, and on this night, January 28, again laid it before a skeptical public.

This time, from the very first scene, the audience shouted with laughter, although Sophie could only sit in her seat and scowl.

"'Tis a *steal*, that's what it is!" she whispered fiercely to Lorna during the interval.

"Of what?" Lorna asked, wide-eyed.

"Of his blooming *mother*'s play, *A Journey to Bath*, that's what!" Sophie muttered. "I read the manuscript years ago . . . it had its problems, and Garrick ultimately rejected it for Drury Lane. But Frances Sheridan's character, Mrs. Tyfort, is a matched double for this Mrs. Malaprop's idiotic misstatements!"

"You jest!" Lorna gasped. "But still, you must admit, 'tis hilarious fun," she smiled.

"Why shouldn't it be?" Sophie demanded peevishly. "He had a good first draft written by his mum . . . only he conveniently *forgot* to give her credit on the playbill!"

"No one but you will notice," Lorna noted dryly.

One frosty February afternoon a few weeks later, Sophie received another shock. She mounted the steps to Number 5 Adelphi Terrace, the Garricks' new residence near Covent Garden, and was soon shown into the charmingly decorated sitting room.

"Sophie!" Mrs. Garrick exclaimed, "I'm so glad you could join us. Davy and Miss More will be along from the library in just a moment."

"Hannah More is in London again?" Sophie asked, startled.

"Ah . . . yes . . . she has beseeched Davy to help her with her tragedy. She asks so prettily, how can he refuse?"

Mrs. Garrick laughed, offering Sophie a seat by the tea table. "I do think the poor girl finds Bristol—her home, you know —a bit dull," she confided in the sympathetic tone of a protective parent.

Just then, the young woman in question appeared in the sitting room. David Garrick leaned on her arm as he gingerly walked on his gout-afflicted limbs.

"Sophie my dear . . . I'm so happy you could join us for tea with our Miss More, here," he said, smiling in fatherly fashion at Hannah.

"Oh, pray, sir, have a care," Hannah cautioned her host as she helped him into a blue upholstered wing-backed chair and then hastened to slip a footstool under his pain-racked ankles.

Sophie glanced appraisingly at the primly attired young woman whose thick eyebrows and small pursed lips gave her the demeanor, even when smiling, of the self-satisfied schoolmistress she once had been.

"Mrs. Garrick was just telling me of your feverish efforts," Sophie said, attempting to project a graciousness she hardly felt. "*Inflexible Captive* . . . is it?" she asked as nonchalantly as she could. "Will it be mounted at Drury Lane this season?"

Meanwhile, Sophie wondered with rising annoyance if her own neglected *Rattecatchers* would ever see the stage!

"My play?" Hannah simpered. "Oh, dear me, no! Mr. Garrick believes 'tis safe only to hazard a production in the Provinces. He was kind enough to propose persuading the Orchard Street Theater in Bath to present it in April when we all go there to take the waters," she added, beaming in the direction of her benefactors.

"You suffer from gout?" Sophie asked archly.

"No . . . but the Garricks have been kind enough to invite me to join them there." She smiled brightly at Sophie. "As you can imagine, I am filled with gratitude!" She bestowed on her host the full force of her tiny smile. "If you truly write the epilogue, Mr. Garrick, your name on the playbill alone will help attract a crowd."

"We shall see," Garrick said mildly. "In the meantime, I've invited Sophie for tea to inform her that we plan to begin rehearsals for a Sydney Ganwick play titled *The Rat-tecatchers* in early March," he said with a sly wink at Sophie. "Mercifully, we have Edward Capell's approval—with the usual additions and deletions of course. Therefore, I must speak with you later this afternoon, my dear, concerning the playbills and such."

Sophie forced herself to focus her eyes on the teacup clutched in her hand to mask the discomforting combination of pleasure, irritation, and guilt that washed over her.

You are an envious, covetous, ungrateful little snipe! she railed at herself, mortified that she should allow the manipulative Hannah More to cast doubt on the Garricks' long-standing friendship for her. Miss More could, indeed, flatter and beguile. But, when it came to Drury Lane, neither David or Eva-Maria compromised their standards.

"Will you attend your Author's Third Night?" Lorna asked in a low voice, rising from her table at the Half Moon Tavern to prepare to depart for the theater to dance during the interval following *The Rattecatchers*. "I've heard rumors that some of the toffs have found the piece an offensive jibe at their hallowed traditions," she added, nodding at a group of boisterous young blades decked out at the height of fashion.

"The 'traditions' of not paying their bills? Of using women shamelessly?" Sophie scoffed. "'Tis beneficial that someone holds a mirror up to them."

Lorna tied her cloak under her chin.

"Sophie, you're becoming a bit of a bluestocking!" Lorna laughed. "The next thing you know, Hannah More will be pleading with you to become your dearest companion."

"Not bloody likely!" Sophie retorted, taking a draught of her ale. "I'll look in at the interval."

But by the time Mr. Collins waved Sophie through the back stage entrance, she realized that a near riot was in progress at the front of the house.

"'Tis those damnable young aristos again," Collins said, shaking his head disgustedly. "Only this evening, they've really gone wild . . . this Sydney Ganwick fellow, whoever he is, has come in for a lot of abuse this last hour. Garrick may have to—"

The boos and catcalls rose to a deafening pitch, drowning out Collins's words. The claps and hisses and stomping of feet heard from the boxes became so loud, it was impossible for the actors to continue. Sophie slipped into the shadows near the wings just as David Garrick, looking weary and at the end of his tether, ordered the curtain rung closed.

"I'm sorry, my dear," he said quietly, "but 'tis for the safety of the players."

"I understand," Sophie replied glumly.

"Come . . . let us repair to the Greenroom for a brandy."

The reception area for players was awash with chatter about the evening's developments. Hannah More and Mrs. Garrick rushed through the throng that jammed the chamber.

"Oh Davy, I'm so sorry," Mrs. Garrick exclaimed.

"'Tis a pity, is it not," Hannah said soothingly, "that a play with such amusing partisanship prompts such divisiveness. Whoever this Sydney Ganwick is," she said sanctimoniously, "he would be better served if his next topic did not have so prejudicial a tone. 'Tis dreadful for you to have been subjected to such misery, sir . . . you, who have given us playwrights such indispensable advice and support."

Sophie stared at the prim young woman, speechless at the way in which Hannah More could turn everything that transpired around her into a reinforcement of her ostentatious concern for Garrick's health and welfare.

"Well . . . I fear I must be off," Sophie announced tensely, doing her utmost to ignore the self-satisfied Miss More's cheery farewell.

"You must be as exhausted as I," Garrick sympathized. "But perhaps you'll allow me to have a quick word before you go," he added. "Hannah, dear, would you be so kind as to fetch me a brandy from the sideboard?"

While Hannah happily did Garrick's bidding, Garrick patted Sophie's hand reassuringly and said quietly, "Don't be too discouraged. In fact, I think 'tis time you began work

on that play you've talk about over the years . . . the one
about Bedlam. You had such a good title for it, I recall."

"*School for Fools*?" Sophie asked, surprised that he would
remember her mentioning it so long ago.

"Ah, yes . . . *School for Fools*," Garrick mused. He
cocked his head and cast her a piercing glance. "Now *there*'s
a subject worthy of that biting wit you possess—and worthy
of our stage as well. I hope you'll consider my suggestion."

"I shall, sir," Sophie said humbly. And Hannah More be
hanged!

"Captain Marshall! Captain Marshall!"

At the sound of his name, the master of the privateer
Jenny halted his progress up the gangplank leading to his
ship. He turned to stare at the tall, fair-haired man carrying a
knapsack slung over his broad shoulders, who had hailed
him from the dock. The traveler's handsome features were
moist with perspiration, thanks to the hot July sun.

"Robertson?" Captain Marshall exclaimed. "Why, greetings, my man! Had enough of juggling? I saw you perform
in that tavern near Boston Common last week. I wondered
how long you'd remain in this land of rebellious savages."

"The rebels fought bravely enough at Bunker Hill in
June, till they ran out of ammunition." Hunter hiked his
baggage further up onto his shoulder as he mounted the
gangplank and followed the captain aboard. "But yes, I've
had enough. Whatever might face me in London cannot be
more dangerous than the bloodletting on these shores. Have
you a berth for a man who can pay half fare and work off
the remainder?"

Captain Marshall's crew had been depleted by deserters
seeking fame and glory in the British army that was massing
against the upstart Continental forces. All he wished for
now was to outrun any Continental ship that dared to challenge the swift *Jenny*, and return to safer waters around Britain. He gazed at Robertson speculatively, then nodded his
assent.

"Grab a bunk below, laddie," the Captain grinned. "At
least you didn't puke your guts out on that horrendous

crossing in '70 . . . and I fancy you're strong enough to hoist a jib. It may be chancy escaping these waters and avoiding the hurricanes, but we'll call at St. Thomas and then make straight for home."

※

Sophie clutched the first act of *School for Fools* beneath her cloak to protect it from the icy sleet pelting Drury Lane this January morning in the new year of 1776. Ducking her chin beneath her collar, she wondered whether spring would ever warm the British Isles again.

"Is he in?" Sophie asked Mr. Collins, who was presiding, as usual, over the theater's stage entrance.

"Aye . . . in the Greenroom with the players and stage servants," Collins replied gloomily. "'Tis finally come."

"He's *retiring*?" Sophie whispered.

Collins, his eyes brimming with emotion, nodded.

"The contract for the Patent was signed this morning."

Sophie took a step closer to avoid being overheard.

"And who *are* the new owners of the Patent?" she inquired.

"Young Willoughby Lacy decided not to sell, so George Colman's backed out. He didn't want Will as a partner if he had the job of manager. What remains is a strange mishmash of investors. Richard Sheridan, at least, makes some sort of sense," Collins commented dourly. "He's a playwright and the son of theater folk. And I suppose that singing-master father-in-law of his, Thomas Linley, knows something about the theater. But there's a *man*-midwife named Doctor James Ford who's involved, and some say even a brandy merchant! They've pooled their funds to purchase Garrick's half of the Patent!"

"And the Earl of Llewelyn?" Sophie asked sotto voce.

"That's the mystery in all of this," Collins said, shaking his head. "I would have bet a month's wages he'd be involved, but instead, his friend Doctor Ford, the physician to the queen, has stepped up to the mark."

"Perhaps Llewelyn is a *silent* partner," Sophie mused aloud.

"He's a string puller, all right," the doorkeeper commented glumly. "Likes to stay behind the scenes, that one does . . ."

"And he knows Garrick has no great fondness for him," Sophie whispered. "If he were a declared partner, perhaps Garrick wouldn't have sold to this group at all."

"I hear our Davy got thirty-five thousand pounds for his shares," Collins confided, his voice full of awe. "With his health so poorly, he was relieved to get the offer, I imagine."

A brandy merchant and a man-midwife—supervising Drury Lane!

Would the public ever truly know who had purchased the right to manage and profit from one of the finest theaters in the world? Sophie wondered bleakly. And how could Sydney Ganwick continue to sell her wares and keep her true identity hidden among such unpredictable theatrical entrepreneurs?

Quietly, she made her way across the open stage, glancing at the cavernous auditorium's gilt boxes. She tiptoed to the door of the Greenroom and melted in among the crowd listening intently to the actor-manager as he said his goodbyes. Mavis Piggott, who had suddenly reappeared in London the previous autumn, stared curiously at Sophie and, in an unexpected move, nodded in a gesture of welcome.

Mrs. Garrick sat in a chair near her husband. Next to her, Sophie noted with a sinking sensation, sat Hannah More. The former school mistress' play had received a polite reception in Bath the previous spring, but the ambitious young woman had achieved much greater success in the role of surrogate daughter to the Garricks. Indeed, Hannah had recently left her lodgings on Henrietta Street and was now the Garricks' semipermanent guest.

"I decided to wait till after Christmas to make this announcement to you all," Garrick was saying calmly to his attentive listeners. "The contracts were concluded this morning. I shall remain a player until the end of this season, and after that, I shall be available for consultation as the new managers shall require—and as my uncertain health permits."

As murmurs of reaction bubbled around her, Sophie's spirits rose a trifle. Garrick would be "available for consultation." Perhaps, then, he would remain willing to forward Sydney Ganwick's work to them for their consideration, thereby preserving her secret authorship.

Sophie's eyes drifted over to the Garricks' new houseguest and they exchanged glances. The young woman wore a smug, self-satisfied air. In future, thought Sophie glumly, it might prove difficult, indeed, to obtain access to Garrick if it meant getting past the watchful Hannah More.

Once Garrick's announcements were concluded, Sophie was among the first to depart the Greenroom.

"'Tis bloody bad luck for us all, that's what it is," a familiar voice said behind her. "A *midwife* running Drury Lane! What about it, Sophie . . . feel like a nip of ale to drown our sorrows? No point in not letting bygones be bygones, is there?"

Sophie turned and stared dumbfounded at Mavis Piggott. Her attitude of common cause made it appear churlish to refuse such an unexpected invitation.

"A quick one only, for I must get back to the print shop," Sophie said, affecting nonchalance, and wondering silently if Mavis had any news fresher than Hunter's latest missive.

The two women braved the cold January winds sweeping across the Great Piazza as they made their way to Half Moon Passage.

"So," Mavis said abruptly when they had settled into a wooden-sided booth at the back of the tavern, "everyone tells me you've given up the quill." Sophie nodded, guiltily fingering the few pages of *School for Fools* she'd hidden under her cloak when shedding it moments before. "Well, so have I," Mavis announced grimly. "Now that I've been on both sides of the Atlantic, I see I cannot fight them—all those men. The managers, the dilettantes who think that by virtue of their station their words should reach the stage— not to speak of the *other* male playwrights who resent any woman who can write as well as a man."

"I take your meaning, believe me," Sophie murmured, wondering at Mavis's candor.

"At least in America, one doesn't have to contend with swine like Edward Capell, whose distaste for our sex pre-

cludes any impartial judgment of our works. However, I'm
sure, when those Continental soldiers have had their ears
pinned back by the redcoats, the British government will
install some sort of examiner of plays in the Colonies as
well."

"Perhaps they'll send Capell over *there*," Sophie noted
wryly. "That would improve things in Britain immensely!"

"But we would still have to compete with *female* wits
who write a few fawning letters and versify on occasion and
consider play writing a lark. These petticoat authors pout
prettily in order to flatter failing old men—"

"Mavis!" Sophie interjected. "Garrick is ill, not old!"

"Oh, I know . . . I know . . . in your eyes the Great
God Garrick can do no wrong," Mavis protested, "even
when he is soothed and petted by that sanctimonious charlatan, Hannah—"

"Really!" Sophie giggled. "Someone might hear you!"

"I don't care!" Mavis pronounced, taking a last swig
from her tankard and signaling the barmaid for another. She
cast Sophie a speculative look and abruptly changed the subject. "I have it on good authority that my face and parts do
not please our Mr. Sheridan, who, rake that he is, likes his
morsels a bit fresher . . ." Mavis stared soberly at her companion. "I fear I shall be forced to become a common whore
if I cannot get someone like the Earl of Llewelyn to keep
me," she announced bluntly.

"The earl has offered you protection?" Sophie asked, attempting to disguise her astonishment.

"Not yet," Mavis admitted candidly, "but I think he's
going to. And that is why I've asked you to join me in a bit
of refreshment. The earl may pose as a patron of the arts, but
I'll wager he cannot bring himself to dirty his hands with the
real work of the theater. Lately he has shown some interest
in my person and my ability to wield a pen. I think I could
keep him entertained on both accounts . . ." She gazed at
Sophie with a narrowing glance. "Darnly's not still sniffing
at your skirts, is he?" she asked sharply, "because if he is,
and you play the rival with me, I'll poison your next brew!"

"Blessed St. Ninian!" Sophie scoffed. "Whatever would
make you think such a thing!"

"He quite fancied you at one stage," she said matter-of-factly. "When that reprobate, your husband, was courting you in Bath and using the earl's coach to do it, and Hunter and I had broken it off . . . I watched him watch *you* when the three of you were together. And after all, you did spend those four months in Wales . . ." Sophie did not respond, recalling only too well what Hunter's reaction to that intelligence had been. "Since you and I have had the same taste in gentlemen in the past—"

"Well, I can assure you, Mavis," Sophie interrupted at length, "I am not, nor have I *ever* been in the slightest fashion interested in an . . . ah . . . intimate association with the earl."

Silently, she wondered if a voluptuous quasi-courtesan like Mavis Piggott could tip the scales in favor of the fairer sex as far as Darnly's carnal inclinations were concerned. *I can manage it with jades like Mary Ann,* he had confessed when dead drunk on Welsh whiskey. Well, thought Sophie grimly, eyeing her longtime rival across the table—bully for her. Sometime soon, she wagered, the nobleman would certainly need to father an heir. Perhaps, if he took a mistress, or even a wife, he would finally resolve this inner conflict for himself—if that were, indeed, the reason he would consider Mavis as a companion.

"Some say your son is by Darnly," Mavis suggested coolly, her eyes turning watchful and cunning.

"That's pure rubbish!" Sophie laughed harshly. "One look at Rory would put *that* lie to rest!" she added firmly. She leaned over the table, her face inches from her long-time rival. "You may rest assured that your plans to snag the Earl of Llewelyn will receive no interference from me. I wish you success with all my heart!"

"*Your* heart still pines for that rogue Robertson, doesn't it?" Mavis asked cynically. "I wouldn't hold your breath on his account, if I were you. He went off with some third-rate American manager to try to play New York, or maybe Boston, and he's probably been chasing every petticoat in the New World."

"One hopes not . . ." Sophie replied softly, mentally seeking assurance from Hunter's numerous love letters that she had tied with silk ribbons and stored in her desk drawer not fifty yards from where they sat in the Half Moon Tavern.

"I warned the fool that war was coming, and now it has," Mavis said. "My ship was the last to sail freely out of Annapolis. I'll warrant you'll not be seeing Hunter Robertson any time soon."

Sophie attended as many of Garrick's performances that presaged his retirement as she could, often joining Mrs. Garrick and Hannah More in their private box at the behest of Garrick himself.

Then, on May 15, she and Lorna celebrated Rory's fifth birthday by taking him to a puppet show at Ranelagh Gardens. They secured a tub of syllabub and three spoons to eat the white, frothy confection in a quiet section of the park.

"'Tis excellent, Mama!" Rory pronounced. "Are you and Aunt Lorna sure you're quite as hungry as I?"

The two adults erupted into peals of laughter, prompting a crooked grin to spread across the lad's face that was so reminiscent of Hunter's, it made Sophie's heart ache.

"Have as much as you like, darling." She smiled sadly. "Enjoy it."

During the following week, Sophie had to force herself to continue working on *School for Fools.* Her coffers were dangerously depleted, and with each of Garrick's "final" performances, she found that she was becoming increasingly melancholy—both for her mentor and herself. Worried for Hunter's physical safety and disturbed by the lack of correspondence due to the recent upheavals in the Colonies, her heart wasn't in her writing and she made very little progress.

One evening in early June, following Garrick's last performance as Richard III, a voice hailed her in the foyer of Drury Lane.

"Sophie, my dear . . . 'tis charming to have seen you and Hannah More pay the Great Man such devotion of late."

Sophie whirled around to confront Roderick Darnly, resplendent in a pale blue velvet suit decorated with yellow-and-white embroidery.

"You couldn't have seen Miss More tonight," Sophie replied mildly. "She has recently departed for Bristol."

"Actually, I wish to ask of you a slight favor," Darnly said, surveying Sophie's serviceable tobacco-colored silk gown, which was etched with a minimum of ruffled batiste at the neckline and cuffs.

"And what might that be?" Sophie inquired warily.

"I cannot discuss it publicly, I fear," he replied, taking hold of her arm and guiding her down the front steps of the theater where a confusion of carriages and sedan chairs waited to convey patrons into the night. "It concerns a theatrical endeavor. Would you do me the honor of taking a glass of wine with me?" Without waiting for her answer, he hailed his coach driver.

Was Roderick, at last, making an overt bid to gain control of Drury Lane? As much as she longed to flee his company, her future as a playwright might depend on discovering his intentions.

He swiftly opened the coach's door, assisted her inside, and sat on the bench seat opposite. The coach lurched forward as the horses picked their way through the snarl of traffic clogging the road that flanked the theater.

"I saw you sitting in Garrick's box with Mr. Sheridan this evening," the earl began pleasantly, pulling down the window shades inside the coach. A single candle shielded by a glass lamp cast a ghostly light in the narrow confines of the swaying carriage. "Has he agreed to grant you the playbill concession next season?"

"I imagine such concerns have a low priority, considering the other problems he faces in assuming the reins from Garrick," Sophie responded cautiously.

"Well . . . the reason I ask, is that I have a little proposition to offer you that might require some of your time. You would not be adverse to being paid for writing anonymously, would you?" he asked, gazing at her speculatively across the moving coach.

"My quill is blunt and my ink pot dry," she replied, "not to mention my dulled imagination."

"What I have in mind won't require much in the way of work," he said smoothly.

"What won't?"

"A little amusement I've written to entertain the fellows in my club. I'd like you to read it and give me your opinion. There may be one or two scenes you could improve. I'm prepared to pay you ten pounds for your trouble."

She was relieved to hear that the earl apparently had not captured enough shares at Drury Lane to hold sway over the managers and was still confining his artistic efforts to his social circles. Then, she considered her dwindling coffers, funds that couldn't be replenished until—and unless—Sheridan formally granted her the playbill concession for the 1776–1777 season. Perhaps if she helped the earl with his playlet, she could earn enough to tide her over and, in the process, would have an opportunity to soothe his unwarranted ire toward Hunter.

"I would prefer first to read the . . . comedy . . . is it?" Sophie replied carefully. "Then, depending on the amount of work involved, we could further discuss my fee."

"Always the canny businesswoman, eh Sophie?" he said. "Ah . . . here we are at Number Ten."

The coach pulled up to his imposing town house, its columned facade ablaze with candles. Outside, liveried servants lit the path to the imposing front door with flambeaux. A butler greeted them at the threshold, and a maid whisked Sophie's shawl from her shoulders. She wondered if Mrs. Phillips, who had agreed to allow Rory to sleep on her couch until Sophie returned from the theater, would be alarmed by her lateness.

"Come . . . a little refreshment is in order while I fetch the manuscript for you."

Sophie was handed a glass of sweet wine and beckoned to choose a delicacy from several puddings and sweetmeats laid out on a sideboard in Darnly's paneled sitting room. The chamber's windows were decorated with forest green brocade draperies edged with yellow fringe and tied back in deep swags by yellow tassels. Sophie sat expectantly on the edge of a tapestry chair near the marble hearth, nibbling on a bit of treacle tart.

"Thank you, Trevor," Roderick said bruskly to his erstwhile factor through the open door as he reentered the room with a thin manuscript tucked under his arm. "I'll see to the locking up."

Quickly, Sophie set her glass and plate on a table nearby and rose, as if to depart.

"I shall read it at my first opportunity, and shall give you my honest account of it," she said, mimicking the diplomatic tone David Garrick invariably employed with untried authors.

"What I would really like is for you to collaborate on the work with me," Darnly persisted, retrieving Sophie's abandoned wineglass from the table and folding it into her hand.

"I-I have said to you innumerable times, Roderick," Sophie stammered, as she gently attempted to free herself from the nobleman's grasp, "I have retired as a scribe. I have my son to raise and my print work. I can only agree to read your play and . . . and perhaps offer some few suggestions . . ."

"Ah, yes, your son. A handsome lad, I'm told," Darnly replied, withdrawing his hand and reaching for his own wineglass. "It must present some difficulty, managing alone as you do."

"I manage quite well, actually," she replied, sipping her wine to cover her increasing nervousness.

"Do you?" Darnly said. "And a fee as my joint author would not be a boon? Come, now Sophie, no need to prevaricate with me."

"I am perfectly at ease with the life I have created for myself since my muse utterly abandoned me," Sophie insisted, desperate to escape the earl's penetrating stare. "I fear I would only taint your work with my lackluster efforts. However," she added, in a last-ditch effort to appear gracious, "if you would wish me merely to *read* what you have written . . . to offer a reaction as befits a member of an audience . . ."

The Earl of Llewelyn took a draft of his wine and then smiled at her, appearing to have come to some decision.

"Since **you** **h**ave promised me an honest account of my play, shall I give you an honest account of another reason I am so delighted you have joined me in my home this evening?"

A *frisson* of apprehension shot down Sophie's spine.

"After giving the matter considerable thought, I would like, my dearest Sophie, to offer you an important place in my life and work," he said slowly. "I have it on excellent authority that even if Richard Sheridan grants you the play-bill concession for next season, he is famous for not paying his creditors. In such strained circumstances, this could produce a situation quite miserable for you and the boy." He took another sip from his wineglass, observing her closely during his next words. "Sadly, should Hunter Robertson ever attempt to return to London, he would immediately be apprehended by the authorities. However, if you and I could come to some arrangement, perhaps I could have a word with Lord Mansfield to put aside the charges, after all this time."

"Is the judge likely to do such a thing?" Sophie asked carefully.

Roderick smiled at her calmly, despite his blatant attempt at bribery.

"I would imagine so . . . if I asked it of him. Then Robertson could return to his homeland and pursue his considerable talents, without this cloud hanging over him. 'Tis a sensible solution for all concerned, don't you think?" he added pleasantly. "Between our common interests in the theater and our . . . long acquaintance . . . I could offer you shelter, good companionship, and a worry-free environment that might well prompt a return of your muse." He reached for her hand, raising it to his lips as his eyes bore into hers. "And in future, I may possibly be allowed to seek your hand in marriage. At the rate Peter Lindsay is abusing himself, he can't live forever . . ."

Marriage! Putting aside the earl's sexual ambivalence, she thought, as she reeled from his pronouncements—why in the world would a peer of the realm wish to wed a commoner like her who, for all he knew, didn't possess the ability to write plays any longer? In the whirl of thoughts caroming through Sophie's brain, one notion repeatedly struck her conscious mind.

Mavis Piggott will be absolutely livid!

But did this enigmatic, secretive man lust after *her*—or her *pen,* Sophie wondered, her heart thudding as she withdrew her hand from his.

"Thank you, sir, for your concern for my son's welfare," she replied, struggling to maintain her composure. She was certain, now, that Roderick's offer had some baffling, hidden purpose, though what it could be, she had no idea. What was clear, however, was that he was a man who had spent most of his life coveting what others possessed: titles, honors, poetic genius . . . even inner peace. Suddenly, she was frightened by the thought of how far the powerful earl might go to secure what he wanted. He had lied and cheated at Sadler's Wells and, like her husband, Peter, was capable of looking one right in the eye in executing such larceny. She had little confidence he would keep his promise to withdraw his bogus charges against Hunter, calculating that this gambit was simply his latest, diabolical maneuver to persuade her to do his bidding. *But why?*

She sipped slowly on her wine to gain time, acutely aware Darnly was observing her closely. She forced herself to summon a grateful smile to her lips.

"Unfortunately, there is one, immovable impediment to your generous proposal," she noted quietly. "Legally, I am a married woman. This arrangement you propose could put you at considerable risk from extortion by my wily husband."

"I assure you, my dear, I am more than a match for a bogus baronet and am willing to provide for your every need and desire," Roderick replied, suggestively allowing the tip of his tongue to linger at the rim of his wineglass.

"Ah, but could I provide for *your* needs and desires?" she responded, unflinchingly meeting his gaze. "I fear my poor talents would not be sufficient to render the kind of . . . *personal service* . . . I am certain you desire in exchange for such generosity."

The atmosphere between them suddenly crackled with tension. Let the blackguard wonder at the meaning behind

her words, she thought recklessly. She was putting him on
notice that she was well aware his proposal was certainly not
all it appeared to be.

She placed her wineglass decisively on the table.

"And now, I fear, I must bid you adieu," she said firmly.
"Would your driver be so kind as to escort me home?"

Roderick set his glass abruptly beside hers. His offer
spurned, he picked up the manuscript he had fetched from
his library.

"No matter about this," he said curtly. "I have decided to
turn over this small writing chore to your husband. The
rogue still owes me blunt. Let Peter work it off!"

The butler, not the earl, saw her to his coach. As she
rocked along in the soft evening air, she wondered if tonight
she had, indeed, turned a sometime friend into a powerful
enemy?

Chapter 34

All of London spoke of nothing but Garrick's upcoming *final* final performance, scheduled for Monday, June 10. Sophie was touched to have received an invitation from the great man himself to join his wife and several intimates in his box for the occasion. Thankfully, the party would not include Hannah More, who had been forced by family obligations to remain in Bristol.

"And you thought you'd have to watch from the rafters!" Lorna scolded Sophie, fastening the hooks on an exquisite pale green gown her friend had spirited out of Drury Lane's wardrobe after a wink from the costume mistress. "There! Turn around! Look, Rory . . . don't you have a beautiful Mama?"

"I want to go too!" the lad pronounced, his lower lip trembling.

"Oh, Rory, 'twould be dull as sin," Mrs. Phillips chimed in, offering her hand. "Besides, I've a mind to teach you to play whist tonight, if you think you'd like that. Perhaps later, if you're *very* good, we could pop over to the Half Moon for a dish of syllabub . . . how would that suit you, lad? Then, you could have a wee sleep on my sofa here, till Mama returns . . ."

His protests forgotten, Sophie's five-year-old kissed her dutifully on her cheek and trundled toward Mrs. Phillips's outstretched hand.

It was approaching the hour of six when Sophie turned

the corner to Drury Lane. The light slanting across the Great Piazza bathed the square's arched buildings in the amber tones of the setting summer sun. Sophie held another invitation in her reticule, one that had arrived by messenger two days earlier, requesting her presence at a fancy dress ball at Number 10 St. James's Street. The elegantly lettered card announced that the event was to be given in honor of the evening's momentous occasion and hosted by the Right Honorable Roderick Darnly, the Earl of Llewelyn. Mavis Piggott's newly forged liaison with the nobleman was no secret around Covent Garden, a turn of events that filled Sophie with nothing but relief. In Mavis, the earl had found a suitable substitute for Sophie's services in this mistress skilled in the carnal arts and playwright of some note. What's more, his invitation to the ball signaled that he apparently bore her no grudge.

"Aren't we the fine strumpet, my lady wife!" a voice said from the shadows as Sophie trod down the narrow lane that lead to the playhouse's front facade.

"God's bones!" she gasped. "Don't startle me like that!"

She peered at Peter Lindsay, lounging against the shabby entrance to a seedy tavern. His bark brown suit was threadbare, and he appeared rumpled and disheveled, though reasonably sober.

"Turnabout's fair play, wouldn't you say," he said, falling into step beside her. "You certainly startled *me* several years ago . . . producing a brat that everyone says is Robertson's get."

"My son is five years old and his father departed for the Colonies in '70 and never returned," Sophie replied wearily. "You and I have not been together for ten years. Surely, you cannot claim your honor's been besmirched! You had scores of wenches before I abandoned your bed and an equal number since. 'Tis only blunt you're sniveling after, and as I've told you many a time before—I don't have any!"

"From the look of your silks and satins, I'd say you could get some from whoever's keeping you these days?" he sneered.

Sophie halted on the edge of the throng heading for the theater and put her hands on her hips.

"My finery is borrowed, and I'm as penniless as you appear to be," she said with exasperation. "I thought my Lord Darnly was to give you a writing commission?"

"He gave me a commission, all right," Peter groused. "Forced labor's what I call it! I tried to make something of that mishmash he calls a comedy! Says it was for his club, but I think he intends to push it on Sheridan next season so he can boast that he's the cultivated genius who wrote it!"

"Well . . . perhaps you could make a living as his anonymous scribe," Sophie suggested, hoping she could withdraw from Peter's company gracefully and avoid a scene.

"I did my best with it and then he went and applied my fee toward an IOU."

"And do you owe him blunt?" Sophie asked quietly.

"'Twas from years ago. 'Twas so large and impossible for me to pay, I thought he had forgot."

"Oh, Peter," Sophie sighed. "Unlike Roderick Darnly, you have some talent in you! Why not apply yourself? Why not take up your quill in earnest and make your way honestly, instead of falling in with titled thieves and gamblers?"

"I see you're still the little reformer, aren't you?" Peter retorted, and then heaved a despondent sigh. "'Tis my powerful need for spirits, Sophie, that makes me so beholden to the likes of Llewelyn . . . and my fear that, on my own, my words fall short . . ."

"I know a bit what that's like," Sophie replied, feeling a perverse sense of sympathy for her estranged husband, "fearing one's words fall short, I mean. And I'm sorry your craving for drink has brought you such grief. But, perhaps—"

"Perhaps," Peter interrupted eagerly, "you and *I* might—"

"I couldn't do that," she interjected, shaking her head. "I am as fearful as you that my words no longer have the power to please," she added, contemplating her difficulties with the second act of *School for Fools*. "I realize this may sound strange coming from me, but I hope someday, Peter, that you will pen something as good as you are capable of. I promise to offer you a favorable price to print it on the Ashby Press!" The crowds were beginning to surge through the entrance to the playhouse in waves. "And now, I must leave you to take my seat," she said. Impulsively, she reached over and softly squeezed his ragged sleeve. "I wish you every good luck. Truly, I do." Then she turned and quickly entered the theater.

As she made her way down the narrow corridor that led to the Garricks' private box, she found herself wondering how much longer Peter Lindsay could continue to lay waste to his body with his addiction to strong spirits. Beneath the bluster, he had always seemed to Sophie a frightened little boy, spurned by those he most wished to please. 'Twas some sort of blessing that his problems weren't hers any longer, but, even so, she took no satisfaction from his disheveled state.

She knocked discreetly on the door to the box.

"Good evening, Mrs. Garrick," Sophie said quietly, taking a seat at the rear of the familiar box that overlooked a sea of silks and satins occupying the pit. "How is he tonight?"

"Pale . . . but calm," Eva-Maria said of her husband.

Sophie had never seen such a gorgeously attired audience in all her years of attending Drury Lane as she did tonight from her choice vantage point. The Garricks' friends and theatrical colleagues occupied the choice locations, relegating half a dozen duchesses and countesses to seats in the upper boxes. Even baronets and wealthy gentry had fought for lesser seats in the highest galleries in order to witness Garrick's momentous formal retirement.

"Mr. G. must be pleased that a packed house will benefit the Decayed Actors Fund," Sophie volunteered.

"Yes, indeed," Mrs. Garrick responded. "Profits may be more than three hundred pounds tonight. Ah . . . the Sheridans and the Linleys have arrived!" she exclaimed, rising to greet the new theater owners who filed excitedly into the box. Sophie nodded a greeting to each in turn, and soon everyone settled into their seats, spending the remaining moments before the curtain gazing about the theater in an effort to see and be seen.

Sophie noticed that the Earl of Llewelyn had secured a box nearby, sharing it with Dr. Ford and the brandy merchant. Darnly curtly inclined his head in her direction. Mavis was backstage preparing for her small role in the evening's presentation, but the actress would undoubtedly serve as Roderick's hostess at the masquerade ball later that evening.

Garrick had chosen a comedy for his final farewell performance. *The Wonder* was by Susannah Centlivre, a dramatist dead nearly fifty years, but whose works were still extremely popular.

"I prefer they remember me with a smile than with a tear," the retiring actor had confided to Sophie earlier when discussing Garrick's selection of the roguish character Don Felix as the last role his legion of admirers would see him perform.

The orchestra had to play four melodies before the audience eventually settled down, but as the curtains parted and Garrick stepped forward to speak the customary prologue, the only sound that could be heard was the resonate baritone of the master himself. Soon the comedy launched into its rollicking plot and Sophie began to relax and enjoy its humor, willing herself to avoid dwelling on the fact that this was the last time she would ever see Garrick on a stage. Her eyes swept the tiered horseshoe-shaped balconies where the patrons, for once, weren't surveying the scene around them, but seemed, as one, to have glued their eyes on Garrick's every move. Before Sophie was quite ready for the play's inventive conclusion, the actors were bowing amid thunderous applause. Then Garrick raised his hands and addressed his audience.

"It has been customary," he began, "with persons in my circumstances to address you in a farewell epilogue." He smiled ruefully and shrugged. "I had the same intention and turned my thoughts that way, but I found myself as incapable then of writing such a piece as I should be now of speaking it."

Sophie glanced over at Mrs. Garrick, whose lovely gray eyes were glistening with tears.

"The jingle of rhyme and the language of fiction would ill-suit my present feelings." Garrick gazed up at the penny gallery and then allowed his eyes to sweep the ring of box seats and the crowded pit. "This is to me a very awful moment . . . it is no less than parting forever with those from whom I have received the greatest kindness, and upon the spot where that kindness and your favors were enjoyed."

Garrick's voice broke and tears began to run down his cheeks. Sophie felt her own eyes fill and dared not look at Eva-Maria sitting to her right. Then he seemed to gather his strength and raised his chin in a gesture of determination to continue.

"Whatever may be the changes of my future life, the deepest impression of your kindness will always remain here," he said with renewed vigor, placing his palm against his chest, ". . . here in my heart . . . fixed and unalterable."

He stared up at his wife, his penetrating gaze conveying the thirty years of love and triumph and the hardships they had shared. He smiled faintly, and then shifted his glance to Richard Sheridan and his colleagues sitting next to Eva-Maria.

"I will very readily agree to my successors having more skill and ability than I have had . . . but I defy them all," he said, his voice rising with emotion, "to take more uninterrupted pains for your favor, or to be more truly sensible of it than is your grateful humble servant."

The master of drama allowed his last words to hang in the air. He bowed respectfully to each section of the playhouse. Then his shoulders suddenly sagged and he retreated a few paces behind the open curtain and disappeared into the wings, never to walk the boards of Drury Lane again.

Sophie raised her gloved hand to her mouth and bit on her forefinger to keep from sobbing. Others in the audience could not restrain their emotions and a strange wail amid the wild applause rang out on all sides of the auditorium. The scheduled afterpiece was abandoned and the orchestra began sawing away as the audience gathered its collective wit and somberly pushed toward the exits on all sides of the playhouse.

Sophie smiled wanly at Mrs. Garrick who was being led by Richard Sheridan down to the Greenroom to greet her husband. Eva-Maria bent down and brushed her lips against Sophie's cheek.

"I doubt we shall attend the earl's ball . . . so this is farewell . . . for now," she said quietly. "Do come see us when we've recovered from all this, my dear."

The rest of those occupying the box filed out after Mrs. Garrick, but Sophie couldn't seem to move her limbs. She remained in her seat, her body paralyzed with the suffocating sadness that washed over her from the moment Garrick began his farewell address.

"Well, lassie . . ." a voice suddenly said in her left ear, "I'm happy to see you've neither a swain by your side, nor a ring on your finger."

Sophie twisted around in her chair and gave a startled cry. Her eyes scanned the length of a black wool traveling cloak and rested on the visage that was an exact image of her son Rory. She jumped to her feet and backed away, stumbling against the chairs that had been scattered around the box as her fellow theatergoers had departed.

"You!" she choked, taking refuge in the shadows behind a small curtain that hung to one side of the theater box. Staring mutely at the tall figure in front of her, she flattened her back against the red brocade lining of the small chamber in which they stood facing one another.

"Yes . . . 'tis *I*!" the intruder exclaimed, taking a step closer, "that rascal Hunter Robertson . . . the father of your son! The ground beneath my feet still pitches from riding a ship that braved storms and hurricanes and dodged privateers these seven months to bring me to your side . . . and all you can utter by way of greeting is—'You'?"

"You!" she repeated, her eyes widening with shock as the reality of his presence in Garrick's box sunk in. "What are *you* doing here?"

Sophie glanced frantically across the auditorium from her place of refuge. She received another shock when she saw Lord Darnly pause, his opera cloak over his arm, and stare at the drama that was unfolding in the box opposite. Sophie impulsively reached out and grabbed Hunter's sleeve, hauling him into the protective shadow of the brocaded curtain.

"Jesu, Lord Darnly! He mustn't recognize you or he'll have you arrested!"

"Darnly be damned! Come here, beauty."

She quickly untied the curtain's tassel, allowing the fabric's heavy folds to hang down straight, affording them protection from the earl's prying gaze.

"Ah . . . now, that's better," Hunter breathed, framing her face with his large hands and kissing her resolutely. Then, his blue eyes surveyed her from the tip of her head to her green satin toes. "I had almost forgotten how small you are," he murmured. He placed a hand against the wall beside each of her shoulders, preventing her escape. Slowly, he traced a line down her neck with his lips, pausing at the base of her throat where her pulse was beating erratically.

"Hunter!" she whispered, trying to ignore the ripples of pleasure his touch evoked, "Darnly's *spying* on us from his box!"

"No matter," he murmured huskily, his tongue now playfully bathing the shell of her ear. "'Tis been so long . . . I would do this on center stage for all the world to see, my love."

"You must stop, truly . . ." Sophie begged, leaning slightly forward in an attempt to catch sight over Hunter's shoulder of Roderick's whereabouts. She was distressed to see the earl had remained in his box and was staring in her direction, his expression alternating between shock and outrage.

"I will cease nothing," Hunter murmured, moving his lips from her ear to her mouth and boldly pressing his body against hers. "Not until I have you in my bed."

He suddenly pulled his hands away from against the wall where he had entrapped her and once again cupped her face with his palms. Gently at first, his tongue sought the velvet lining beyond her lips. Sophie's conscious will to resist his caresses had nearly vanished, and a familiar sexual tension began to boil between them. The darkened theater box, with its low ceiling grazing the top of Hunter's blond mane, reminded Sophie suddenly of the small garret chamber where last they had made love . . . where Rory had been conceived.

"Rory . . ." she whispered, battling as best she could the tide of longing rising in her. "We must get back to—"

"I've seen him," Hunter mumbled between fervent

kisses. "Asleep at Mrs. Phillips's . . . she told me where you were . . . he's lovely . . . like his mum . . ."

"No . . . he's not like me," she protested weakly, rediscovering the contours of his face with her fingers and lips. "He's exactly like *you*—"

Hunter pressed his frame roughly against her pale satin skirts, forcing her to acknowledge his rising ardor. He smothered her lips once more and kissed her passionately. "If you don't tell me here and now how much you want me too," he whispered hoarsely, "I shall perform an act among the gilt chairs in this box that shall, indeed, garner the audience's attention . . ."

Summoning all her willpower, Sophie pulled away from him.

"Dear God, Hunter, you know I do," she pleaded, "but *please* . . . you must heed what I say! The earl—"

Reluctantly, Hunter turned to gaze across the auditorium. The Earl of Llewelyn's box was empty.

"See," he smiled down at her in the shadowy light, a Scottish lilt having taken possession of his voice. "He's left us in peace. The matter may still rankle a bit, but 'twas *six years ago*," he said soothingly, "and the charges were bogus to begin with. I have it on good authority, Thomas Rosoman never joined Darnly's original complaint and won't stir the pot at this late date, either." His fingers held her chin gently as he again began to brush his lips against her ear. "As you can imagine," he said softly, "I've had months aboard ship to scheme exactly how I propose to seduce you this night . . . and my plan just so happens to involve that invitation to the ball Mrs. Phillips tells me you have in your reticule."

"We daren't attend!" Sophie exclaimed. "I fear you underestimate the grudge Roderick holds against you, especially since I have rebuffed his numerous schemes to—"

"Well, I should hope so!" Hunter scoffed, interrupting her. He gathered up her cloak draped on the back of her chair. "We shall be so heavily disguised and the earl so preoccupied with his many guests . . . he shall not even know we are there! 'Tis my first day home, lass!" Hunter exulted. "And I intend to dance all night . . . but first—"

He leaned forward, kissing her once more, insinuating the

thumb of one hand inside her bodice. A soft moan escaped her lips and Sophie felt she would fall off the edge of the theater box if he didn't cease etching feathery circles on her flesh.

"Oh, Hunter . . . my darling—" she moaned, dazed by the erotic sensations coursing through her and by the shock of Hunter's having materialized virtually out of thin air.

"Come with me," he whispered. He took hold of her hand and led her out of the Garricks' private domain. In full view of the wizened old box keeper who doffed his cap as they passed by, Hunter suddenly turned and kissed her ceremoniously on each eyelid. Smiling broadly, he added, "And now, my love . . . into this magical night!"

❈

"This is not the way to the ball!" Sophie exclaimed as Hunter ignored the shouts of hackney drivers and led her by the hand toward Covent Garden Theater on nearby Bow Street. "'Tis to be held at Lord Darnly's! I wonder, really, if you should be seen—"

"Have faith . . . have faith, lassie!" he said, repeating his earlier admonishment.

Without further explanation, he entered the stage door entrance and waved jauntily at the doorkeeper, Mr. Besford, whom Sophie remembered from the days when Hunter was Covent Garden's dance master.

George Colman, who had sacked Hunter for erroneously believing the actor had been disloyal over the mounting of the rival Jubilees, had broken up his managerial partnership with Thomas Harris in 1774 to take on similar duties at the Haymarket Theater. On this night, Covent Garden Theater was deserted, having closed a few days earlier for the summer months. A single candle glowing in a wall sconce illuminated a corridor, and Sophie found herself being playfully propelled by Hunter down the darkened passageway. Lifting the taper from its holder, he then escorted her through a maze of rooms, past an open door, and into a large cavern filled with bins piled high with costumes.

Like the wardrobe chamber at Drury Lane, this room was also packed chock-a-block with theater props and pieces of stage furniture, including a massive four-poster used in innumerable dramatic death scenes.

"Our London quarters this night," Hunter explained smugly, sweeping his arm expansively around the room, "complete with a royal bed and canopy. Harris said we could lodge here for the nonce." He pulled her close, resting his chin on her head. "My other news is that I ran into Tom King tonight."

"Tom King? The comedian?" Sophie asked, drawing away.

"Aye . . . I saw him before the performance tonight. Fortunately, he remembered me from the Stratford Jubilee. Old Rosoman has retired and Tom now runs Sadler's Wells. He has need of an assistant manager this summer, starting immediately—providing I refrain from fisticuffs with the likes of Darnly! What say you, Sophie, m'lass? You and Rory and I shall, at last, have our cottage in the country," he added, his gaze softening. "I very much want to know the lad as a son . . ."

"He's a lovely little chap," Sophie reflected softly. She gazed at Hunter in the murky light that scarcely illuminated the overflowing bins of hats and swords, wimples and ruffs. "You and he shall have your battles. Rory believes himself king of all he surveys . . . rather like his da!"

"Two voyages across the Atlantic Ocean can humble a man," Hunter responded ruefully, fingering a felt cavalier's hat that sported a crimson plume. "As a wise old soul of thirty-three years, I shall be happy in future with just good work and the two of you forever in my life . . ." he added, brushing his lips on the tip of her nose. "'Tis settled then? We shall take a cottage near Sadler's and you can work on . . . whatever it is you wish to write."

Sophie took a deep breath to steady herself, unsure if she could articulate the happiness flooding over her. She seized Hunter's hand and kissed it, certain that the love she bore this man—had *always* borne him—was mirrored in her eyes. She was a thirty-one-year-old woman . . . married, but not married . . . an author, but not truly an acknowledged author . . . in love with a wandering rogue who was not a rogue at all, but a man of constancy.

"And this is the place you dreamed of . . . while sailing home to me?" she asked quietly, glancing around the wardrobe chamber.

"Aye . . . I kept picturing you in this very bed," he replied with a wolfish grin, gesturing toward the ornately carved four-poster festooned with swags of heavy, wine red velvet. "When I worked for Colman, I often came down here to find a doublet or pair of hose . . . and each time I'd see this massive bed, for some strange reason I'd invariably think of *you*! After a while, I would feel quite randy, just approaching this door!" he laughed, pointing toward the portal they had entered. "And, as I conjured you while lying on my hard bunk aboard the *Jenny*, this royal setting seemed rather an apt spot for . . ."

Drawing closer, she stopped his words with a kiss and then placed her forefinger at the spot marking the cleft in his chin.

"Tell me, sir," she said in a husky voice, "exactly how do you intend to make love to me on this mammoth mattress?"

He placed the single candle in a holder on a table next to the looming bedstead and pronounced solemnly, "Not tell . . . *show*."

He pulled her against his chest and slowly bent down to kiss her, softly, tenderly—almost as if they were still youngsters tasting the sweetness of each other for the first time. His fingers began to explore the fastenings on the back of her bodice, plucking at the buttons that imprisoned her in the borrowed green silk gown. As his kisses grew more ardent, he intensified his efforts to free her from the stiff-boned garment, but to no avail.

"Damnation!" he swore under his breath in frustration.

Sophie pulled away from him with a deep-throated laugh.

"You will have to stop kissing me in this zealous fashion and *concentrate* on your task if you ever hope to succeed!"

"Blast, but you speak the truth, as usual," he grumbled good-naturedly, whirling her around and commencing the difficult assignment of unfastening the buttons marching down her back.

His gentle caresses at the base of her neck during the minutes it required to complete his task sent a delicious warmth coursing through her, stimulating sensations of such primal longing that she felt an impulse to spin around and fling herself against his chest. He soon set to work on the laces of her stays. In no time, cool air grazed her skin. Hunter's lips brushed between her shoulder blades, sending shivers rippling down her spine.

"God . . . you're so lovely . . ." he murmured.

He coaxed her gown off her shoulders and loosened the rest of her stays. Soon he was implanting a trail of kisses along the length of her backbone as he knelt to unfasten the petticoat tied at her waist. Whether she was trembling from the chill or simply wanton with desire, Sophie's last vestiges of control had totally dissolved by the time he pushed a mass of undergarments and yards of green satin into a frothy sea around her ankles.

"Dinna turn around yet," he said softly, rising again to his full height.

She heard a rustle of fabric that she assumed was the sound of his coat and breeches dropping onto the floor.

"Now," she heard him whisper. "May I see you, Sophie darling?"

Slowly, she turned to face him and her mouth went dry as she observed him pull at a length of neck linen attached to his shirt. It was the only item of clothing left on his long, lean frame.

Their eyes riveted on each other, Hunter cast aside his linen garment. Then his gaze drifted from her lips to her throat and glided slowly downward, feasting on her figure that, she reminded herself, would never be a match for Mavis Piggott's. In a fluid gesture, Hunter gathered her up in his arms, bracing one knee against the mattress while he tugged on the burgundy coverlet.

"No . . ." she whispered into his ear, ". . . don't remove it. I want velvet everywhere . . ."

He lay her gently on her back and then retreated momentarily into the shadows.

"Hunter?" she whispered, startled by his disappearance.

In an instant he was again beside the bed, easing his body down next to hers. He cradled his chin in his right hand.

"Velvet?" he said mischievously, revealing that he held in

his other hand a crimson ostrich plume snatched from a cavalier's hat perched on a nearby bin. Smiling faintly, he began
to trail the downy edge between the valley of her breasts,
strafing a gossamer line across her abdomen. "Remember
your quill that night at Sadler's Wells? I shall show you
again how 'tis velvet everywhere," he whispered, gently
stroking the plumage up and down her thighs. After several
minutes of this delicious torment, he transferred the
feather's tip to the secret site of her pleasure.

Sophie closed her eyes, allowing the incredible sensations
to take full possession of her. The plume's light, teasing
strokes were soon replaced, however, by a gentle, rhythmic
motion that she realized was Hunter's own touch.

"Here 'tis pure velvet," he murmured urgently, his fingers gently probing her flesh, "and *here* . . ." His erotic
caresses called to her, insistent and demanding, rousing her
from her sensual torpor to match him, touch for touch.

Her eyes had grown dark and luminous when she
reached for him.

"And so are you," she said in a breath, ". . . velvet and
iron and velvet again . . ."

She searched his face for confirmation that she was be-
stowing on him the same intense pleasure he had granted her
moments before.

"St. Ninian, but you have the power to bewitch a man!"
he exclaimed, allowing her full reign over his most vulnerable self. At length, he captured her wandering hands, pinning
them against the pillow that cradled her head. When she
dared repeat her passionate assault by teasing him with her
hips, he responded by hovering above her, brushing against
her torso with tantalizing deliberation. "So . . . Miss Sophie McGann knows exactly what she wants, does she?" he
noted, his features alight with amusement. "That pleases me
greatly," he murmured, parting her legs with his knees. "Because, if swathed in velvet you wish to be, my darling . . .
'tis velvet you shall have . . ."

His blue eyes blazed with a strange cobalt fire. Then, he
slowly sheathed his body in hers, deliberately prolonging
their pleasure in a heart-stopping demonstration of restrained but superior strength.

She reached up and pulled him close, luxuriating in the feel of his weight bearing down on her as they lay in the wide expanse of their elegant bed. She found herself encased in a plush cocoon . . . an opulent canopy arching overhead and red velvet pressing against her back. Hunter's muscular frame began to surge against hers, advancing, retreating, and advancing anew, fusing them in a sumptuous, undulating universe of warmth and heightened sensation.

He *had* cloaked her in velvet, she thought with dreamy satisfaction. Her senses were becoming drugged by his bold possession of her deepest self, his tongue savoring the soft lining of her lips, his powerful long legs cushioned against her thighs.

He plunged his hands into her hair, kissing her lips, her eyelids, the hollow at the base of her neck, each breast in turn until she had lost all notion of where her boundaries ended and his began. All that existed was a burning, glowing, incandescence that bloomed between them with unbearable intensity. Finally, he cupped his palms beneath her, pressing her body relentlessly against his in concert with the rhythm of their dance. Longing and heartbreak and reclaimed happiness and sheer carnal delight—woven from the disparate threads of their complicated lives these last fifteen years—forged the velvet bonds that linked them forever.

"Sophie, I—"

"Oh, God . . . *yes!*" she cried, startled to hear her voice ring out in the chamber piled high with the silk and satin raiments of fictional characters whose loves and lives seemed as real to her at this moment as her own.

Hunter whispered her name over and over as they clung desperately to one another. Velvet fire roared in their ears, enveloping them in a burst of white light.

Then, the silence in the room was punctuated only by their ragged breathing. Lying in the sanctuary of Hunter's arms, her skin slick with sweat, Sophie felt herself to be, at last, warm and safe—vibrating from an inner core of happiness she'd not thought possible. The other nights they'd been together were merely a prelude to *this* night, she thought humbly. Yet the pleasures they had bestowed on one another seemed a mere preamble to what they could and would mean to each other in the years to come.

She thought of darling Rory and wondered if tonight, beneath the scarlet canopy of King Henry's bed, she had conceived another bairn. She wanted another baby by Hunter Robertson, she thought fiercely, a child he would celebrate in the womb and cherish from the first day of its birth. Suddenly years of unshed tears of anxiety and loneliness poured down her cheeks and her shoulders began to heave with sobs.

"Sophie, what is it?" Hunter whispered.

"I—I am so desperately *grateful* you're here," she choked. "I c-can't seem to *stop* cry—"

"I'm here . . . I'm here, indeed . . ." he comforted her.

"Oh, Hunter . . . thank *God* you came back to me!" she cried, seeking his lips once more with a fervor that nearly consumed her. "Truly, I was so frightened at times—"

"Shh . . ." he soothed. "At times I was frightened as well. You're safe, now, my darling . . . absolutely safe with me."

And for several long minutes, he rocked her in his arms as if she were a child.

Number 10 St. James's Street was aglow with hundreds of candles. Carriage and sedan chairs jammed the street and sedate music wafted through open windows from a ballroom on the second floor.

As Sophie gazed at the manse jammed with merrymakers, she suddenly shook her head.

"Let's not tempt fate," she pleaded. "We can dance the night away another time . . . I—"

"Oh, Sophie . . . Roderick Darnly can't still be provoked by the likes of me," he scoffed. "He's got a bloody earldom! What more does the blackguard want from this life?" he protested. "If, after six years, the bloke can't let bygones by bygones, this country *is* in a sorry state." He grinned down on her, admiring her high-waisted ruby silk gown and steepled hat with its gauzy veil spouting from the crown—courtesy of Covent Garden's production of *Taming of the Shrew.* "Anyway, he'd never guess 'tis you in this garb . . . though, to me, madame, it seems the perfect choice."

Sophie smiled weakly, not wishing to dampen his soaring spirits on this first night of his homecoming.

"You have a rather warped sense of humor, sir," she retorted, eyeing his short, padded tunic and the tight, fitted hose of a Renaissance nobleman. "Pray, don your mask. You'll hear my shrewish tongue, indeed, if you dare take it off while we're here."

For several moments they observed the parade of nuns and cavaliers, harlequins and milkmaids making their way toward the earl's elegant front door. Clearly, it was the social event of the year.

"It reminds me of the Jubilee Ball," Sophie commented as they brushed past the majordomo who had given up all attempts at announcing new arrivals. "Except I'll wager we'll not be caught in a downpour on a night like this."

Upstairs, Darnly's ballroom was aglow with candles and crowded with revelers. Sophie and Hunter secured glasses of punch for themselves and spent several minutes attempting to identify people they knew, despite the entire company being disguised with masks.

Mavis Piggott had decked herself out in a magnificent brocaded court gown which Sophie recognized as having come from the same source as the green satin dress she had worn earlier to the theater. Darnly's mistress wore an elaborate white wig bedecked with several ostrich plumes. The actress's neckline plunged scandalously, displaying her two most celebrated assets to their fullest advantage. The Earl of Llewelyn was dressed in full court attire as well, looking for all the world like France's Sun King in a red velvet coat and matching breeches embroidered with silver.

"Well, well," Hunter said in a breath. "I return after all this time to find my old nemesis as self-satisfied as ever."

Steering well clear of their hosts, Sophie and Hunter wandered into a room where card playing was the principal diversion.

"God's bones . . . is that *Peter*?" Sophie gasped.

They both stared across the chamber at an emaciated figure cloaked in a monk's robe who was sitting at a table where three other faro players wearing a variety of costumes were demanding payment for their winnings. Peter Lindsay appeared white and shaken. Trevor Bedloe, dressed in matching monk's garb that Sophie wagered he had worn in the beech grove at Evansmor, was dispensing gold coins to the winners from a metal strong box. Then Darnly's employee handed Peter paper and quill with which he presumably was signing an IOU to his host who, it appeared, had staked him to tonight's play. Quickly, Sophie and Hunter retreated to the ballroom, anxious to lose themselves in the crowd.

The string orchestra had by this time ceased playing stately minuets, and its leader announced *The White Cockade*, a lively Scottish country dance. Joining the bottom of the set, Hunter and Sophie began to execute the rollicking steps with great enthusiasm. When at length, the tune came to its boisterous conclusion, the couple laughingly collapsed on the nearest straight-backed chairs. Suddenly, a voice snarled from behind them.

"You *dare*, Robertson, to presume upon my hospitality?"

Sophie and Hunter turned to discover Roderick Darnly glaring down at them, his eyes blazing like an enraged Lucifer through the holes in his crimson mask.

"Roderick," Sophie intervened quickly, "you were kind enough to send me an invitation . . . Mr. Robertson has just returned from the Colonies and I assumed after all this time—"

"Well, you assumed incorrectly," Darnly cut in coldly. "I observed your disgusting display in the Garricks' box tonight and the moment he took to the dance floor, I knew the identity of this six-foot rogue. I wish this man to leave my house at *once!*"

"My lord," Hunter said, rising to the full height that had apparently foiled his disguise, "I will respect your request and shall depart immediately, but I would hope, after six years, we can put our differences behind us and—"

"I should call you out, you Scottish cur!" Darnly snapped, "but to save Sophie embarrassment, I shall merely, for the nonce, take pleasure in watching you leave my house and consider what charges Rosoman and I shall renew upon the morrow."

"I doubt you will find a supporter at Sadler's Wells or anywhere else for legal action at this late date," Hunter retorted. He clasped Sophie by the hand. "Come, Sophie . . . we shall not keep the earl from his remaining guests. We bid you good night."

"And I bid you good riddance!" Darnly retorted.

Outside, Hunter hailed a hackney from among the lines of coaches hoping for a fare and quickly assisted Sophie inside.

"Dear God, Hunter . . . I felt it in my bones—we should have never put ourselves in harm's way," Sophie agonized. "He'll seek to injure you . . . I *know* it!"

Hunter shifted his weight to sit beside her in the swaying carriage and put a reassuring arm around her shoulders.

"I spoke to Tom King about the affair only this evening," he replied soothingly, "when we discussed my summer engagement. Rosoman long ago confirmed to him that Darnly was a pirate. He told King the man is mental on the subject of my catching him out cheating . . . but if I *wasn't* stealing from the till, and Darnly *was* stealing from *you* . . . and if Rosoman was a witness to the earl's striking me first— then there's no proof against me. Dinna worry, sweetling," he added softly, stroking her cheek with his thumb. "I didn't come all this way from America to let the likes of Roderick Darnly do us harm."

Chapter 35

On the Wednesday following the Earl of Llewelyn's ball, Sophie paused while packing her portmanteau, alarmed by the sound of boots tramping up the stairs to her lodgings. She glanced apprehensively at Hunter, who sat at her desk with Rory on his knees. With a sense of foreboding, she opened the latch in response to the insistent pounding at her door.

"Are you Hunter Robertson, late of Annapolis?" demanded a guardsmen in the king's livery, addressing Sophie's companion as he strode across the chamber to stand behind her.

The room was cluttered with trunks and valises in anticipation of their departure to Sadler's Wells the following morning.

"Yes," Hunter said, clasping Sophie's hand reassuringly.

"Are you a king's man?" little Rory chirped at the visitor, a look of awe playing across his youthful features.

"Aye lad . . . come to serve summons, I'm afraid."

"Summons?" Sophie gasped. "For what? From *whom*?"

"By the authority vested in me," the guardsman intoned, reading from a writ he'd pulled from his coat pocket, "I charge you, Hunter Robertson, with the civil crime of Criminal Conversation with one Sophie Lindsay-Hoyt, the proof of which is a five-year-old boy named Rory, whom the plaintiff will prove is your issue, the product of your seduction of Sir Peter Lindsay-Hoyt's true wife, depriving him of the physical congress of her person and tainting, by this spurious offspring, the future happiness of his house. The plaintiff further charges damages of ten thousand pounds for the loss of the comfort and society of said wife and the deprivation of her maternal services. On the Monday, you will appear at King's Bench to answer this summons. Failure to appear will result in fines and imprisonment."

Sophie leaned against Hunter to avoid sinking to her knees in despair.

"This lodging will be watched, so I wouldn't contemplate any thoughts of flight," the guardsman intoned, indicating the presence of a comrade who had stepped from the shadows on the landing separating Sophie's abode from that of Mrs. Phillips.

The first guardsman handed Hunter the parchment from which he had just recited and nodded curtly at Sophie. The uniformed pair then retreated down the stairs where one of them took up his post across the road in front of Bob Derry's Cider House.

At this point, the color had drained from Sophie's face. She stumbled toward the chair facing her writing desk and sat down. Rory glanced with alarm from his mother to Hunter.

"Will they send you to p-prison?" he asked tremulously. "What have you done?"

"I have loved your mother, and our love has created you, my little man . . . and that is no crime," Hunter said quietly. "'Twill all come right in the end, so you're not to worry . . . but Mama and I need to speak privately of this matter. Would you be a good lad and pay a call on Mrs. Phillips? Here," he added, digging into a pouch of coins resting on a table nearby. "Perhaps you could persuade her to take you for a syllabub . . . I hear you're the grand champion when it comes to eating this confection."

"A-all right," Rory replied, looking at them both tentatively. "But you won't leave before I get back?"

"No . . . I shall not be leaving at *all*!"

The five-year-old had departed from the room before Sophie allowed her tears to fall freely.

"'Twill be all right, I tell you," Hunter exclaimed, kneeling beside her chair. "Ten thousand pounds is a ridiculous sum! You and Peter have not lived together for more than *ten years*! They'll dismiss the case forthwith!"

"No . . ." Sophie moaned. "Don't you remember *The Way of the World*?" she cried. "Congreve's play says it all. 'Tis not to secure faithful wives that these criminal conversation suits are brought. . . . 'Tis to *ruin* us and enhance the malicious husband's coffers!"

Sophie angrily brushed away her tears on her sleeve. She jumped up from her chair and began to pace in front of the empty fireplace while Hunter took the seat she had vacated. "'Tis an action carried on *exclusively* between two *men*!" she added bitterly, "the legal husband and the wife's alleged lover. Only in our case, Rory is proof positive that our so-called Criminal Conversation was more than a conversation! The wife is not permitted to play any part in these trials. . . . I cannot call witnesses or testify in my own defense. . . . I cannot tell the jury of men that when Peter and I lived together as husband and wife, he drank and whored and gambled and claimed my written words to be his own." She balled her fists to keep from screaming her outrage. "That bastard has seen the possibility of wheedling money and now tries common *blackmail* to get it. He thinks, in his usual cunning fashion, that perhaps you have returned from the Colonies a wealthy man! And to think I spoke so kindly to him the other night, and actually wished him *well*!"

During Sophie's stormy monologue, Hunter stared thoughtfully at the silver-tipped quill sitting on the desk. It was the feather pen that Sophie had reluctantly revealed had been a gift from Peter years before.

"Your husband realizes perfectly well that neither of us has ten thousand pounds," Hunter said slowly, "nor even a *hundred* pounds. He lost heavily at cards that night at Darnly's and he's deeply in debt. And he realizes *we* know he's no baronet and can humiliate him publicly on that score. He had no choice but to bring this suit!" Hunter said, banging his fist on the desk. "No . . . Peter is as much a victim of this scheme as you and I . . . he's been *forced* to bring these charges!"

"Forced? By whom?" Sophie whispered, horrified.

"Darnly . . . I'll wager 'tis the nobleman's string pulling revenge," Hunter replied in a low voice. "He knows perfectly well that his accusations of embezzlement and assault will not hold up in court. Since he's failed in that ploy, he's put Peter's feet to the fire to accomplish the same purpose by manipulating a man who owes him blunt. He probably believes he can manipulate the courts whose judges are his friends—"

"And he wishes to manipulate *me* into serving . . . or servicing him in some perverted fashion," Sophie interrupted, the truth of Darnly's ultimate strategy dawning on her with frightening clarity. "Either with my quill or my person—or both."

"*What?*" Hunter exclaimed.

"Not long before you returned, the earl made me a proposal that quite mystified me at the time. He asked me to be both his anonymous scribe *and* his mistress in exchange for supporting Rory and myself. His ultimate enticement was that he claimed he'd drop his charges against you if I would comply with his wishes."

"The bloody bastard!" Hunter growled, slamming his fist once more on the desk.

"He even offered to wed me—at some future date, he said," Sophie recalled carefully.

"But the man isn't even convinced he *prefers* women!" Hunter exclaimed. "And surely he, of all people, knows of your valid marriage to Lindsay?"

"That was why it all seem so farfetched," she agreed. "Why *me*, for pity's sake?"

"I would marry you in a trice, if you were free!" Hunter grinned crookedly, attempting to lighten the atmosphere. "I think you underestimate your charm, my love . . . even to that twisted sod."

"Roderick once said something similar," Sophie mused. "He said I underestimated my *value* to a man of his artistic sensibilities . . . and he then took up with Mavis Piggott!" She shook her head in despair, her voice edged with tears once more. "Dear God, Hunter . . . what are we to *do*?"

"Attempt to get the damages reduced," Hunter said grimly. "Otherwise Lord Darnly will have succeeded in using this ruse to imprison me for debt for the rest of my natural life."

�

Oddly, neither Peter nor Hunter was allowed to testify personally in court. Hunter's barrister, Mr. Lasley, swiftly proved that Peter Lindsay had falsely styled himself "baronet" by calling the head of the King's College of Arms as a witness. Lasley asserted, on Hunter's behalf, that a man of no rank and such perfidy was not entitled to such astronomical damages as ten thousand pounds.

Sophie sat at the back of the courtroom disguised in a pair of breeches and a man's cuffed coat, a tricornered hat pulled down to shield her face. She watched grim-faced as the court proceedings moved to their astonishingly swift conclusion.

"Foreman, what is your verdict?" demanded the judge, Lord Mansfield.

Darnly's guest, the gentleman to whom Peter had lost at cards the night of the earl's masquerade ball, rose to face the bench.

"We, the jury, find the defendant guilty as charged," he declared, "with costs and damages to be seven hundred pounds. Had not the plaintiff been proven a fraudulent baronet," the foreman continued, "ten thousand pounds would have stood, m'lord."

Lord Mansfield peered down from the bench at Mr. Lasley.

"Seven hundred pounds seems prudent," he nodded, ". . . for a wife's adultery is a grievous crime against society, as we all would agree. As the plaintiff is related legitimately to noble stock and has been cuckolded by the defendant's own admission, seven hundred pounds shall be entered as the court's judgment." Lord Mansfield motioned for Hunter's barrister to approach. "If Robertson cannot pay in full," the judge advised, his wig dangling over the edge of the bench, "he will be arrested forthwith and dispatched to debtor's prison. You have a day's time to secure payment of damages. Court dismissed!"

✲

For Sophie, the summer and autumn of 1776 rivaled the horrifying months she'd spent in Bedlam with Aunt Harriet, although this time, she was the visitor and Hunter the inmate.

At first, he had been assigned a chamber in Newgate prison at the Old Bailey with felons of the most notorious sort. Recalling the fiefdom of turnkeys that had existed at Tolbooth Prison, Sophie bribed the warden with whatever money she could spare to secure a small, private chamber in which Hunter could sleep, write, and even entertain guests. Debtors in Newgate could import food, wine, and even whores, if they had the funds.

"Many here are as unfairly imprisoned as I," Hunter commented bitterly one afternoon when Sophie came to visit. They had repaired to what amounted to a public house inside Newgate, as the sale of beer was recognized as a legitimate source of profit to the jail keeper. "I have learned that the size of potential damages in these criminal conversation suits has tempted all sorts of scoundrels to sue third parties as a means of earning blunt."

"Darnly's not after money," Sophie replied grimly. "He's after blood."

A day later, Sophie's worst fears were confirmed.

"Peter, I must speak with you!" she cried, falling into step beside her estranged husband as he emerged from the Blue Periwig around midday. He looked haggard and frail, weaving unsteadily down the road away from the whorehouse. "I want the truth! Did Darnly put you up to the suit?"

"Don't challenge him on this," Peter warned hoarsely, looking around furtively to see who might overhear them. "None of us is safe."

"What do you mean?" she demanded. "Do you stand to make money off of this, Peter? Because, if you do, I shall—"

"Ha! The paltry hundred pounds he gave me doesn't begin to cover what I owe that Jack Nasty!" Peter exclaimed bitterly.

"So why are you doing this?" Sophie wailed.

"Darnly threatened to have *me* shut up in Newgate for my debts if I didn't agree to the scheme."

"Oh, Peter . . ." she groaned.

His skin was like pale parchment except for the web of broken blood vessels on his nose and cheeks. He paused, a look of utter misery flooding his eyes.

"What a botch I've made of everything," he whispered. ". . . your life . . . mine . . ."

Sophie watched, full of pity as well as repulsed, as he stumbled into a nearby alley and was thoroughly sick behind some rubbish.

When Sophie informed Hunter of this latest development during her next visit to the infamous prison, he actually appeared encouraged by the news.

"Bribing someone to bring suit against a third party and then threatening him if he refuses *is* a form of extortion, you know," Hunter said thoughtfully.

"Believe me, darling," Sophie said heatedly, "we cannot fight this battle in the courts when our opponent has the ways and means to control the powers-that-be. We must simply find a way of raising seven hundred pounds and *buy* your release."

Hunter glanced at the thick walls surrounding them.

"We'd best start penning some clever farces, Sophie my love," he replied. "Else I could have served you better by remaining in the Colonies. I'd have joined the rebels to fight against this wretched king and his diseased government."

"Speaking of that," Sophie said, happy to shift the subject from their predicament. "Has anyone told you? The upstart Colonists officially declared their independence from Britain on the fourth of July in Philadelphia!" Her eyes suddenly widened with excitement and she suddenly clapped her hands. "What a brilliant notion we've just had!" she crowed. "What if we write something that spoofs *both* sides of this tempest? Nothing too terribly rude, so we avoid infuriating that toad, Capell . . . just a witty little farce based on the latest news dispatches—calculated to merely amuse and divert!"

Hunter leapt up and whirled her around his small prison cell.

"A brilliant notion!" he chortled, bussing her on the cheek. "Lud, but you are a little treasure, Sophie!"

During the remainder of 1776 and into the early months of the new year, Sophie and Hunter worked furiously in their separate quarters on a project they ultimately called *Battle Royal*. Each wrote a scene and then traded with each other for a critique. Soon they had created a series of vignettes that chronicled the foibles committed by both sides in the conflict.

"We must take care to make the Colonials appear more obstreperous and inane than the British," Hunter warned one chill day in February after Sophie bribed the warden to remain in his cell for the day. "Else your nemesis, Capell, will never approve it."

"I suppose you're right," Sophie said moodily, staring out Hunter's barred window as she chewed on her quill's feathered tip, "although I'd like to write what I truly think of those British generals—"

"*Sophie* . . ." Hunter exclaimed with exasperation.

"I know . . . I know . . . I'll be good."

"You *are* good," he chuckled, extending his arms. "Come over here, lass . . . have you an extra shilling to buy permission to spend the night? Since I am already incarcerated for having Criminal Conversation with you, my love, I'm ever so anxious to commence conversing," he added, boldly stroking her breast through the bodice of her cotton gown.

"Oh, Hunter . . ." Sophie groaned, peering over his shoulder to see if the turnkey was staring in at them, "you know I cannot concentrate on my work if you persist . . ."

"I shall persist, so you might as well surrender your quill," he whispered, nuzzling her neck.

"We *mustn't*," she said in a breathy voice, feeling a familiar warmth seep into every pore. "I neglected to bring the French letter Mrs. Phillips so kindly provided us . . . as much as I long to— If I were to get with child now, I—"

"I know . . ." he said, suddenly sober. He kissed her gently. "'Tis just the sight of you nibbling that quill makes me randy . . . it makes me think of—"

"Don't *say* it!" she laughed ruefully. "I'm in quite the same state, I assure you, you rake. Let us return to our task!"

❄

Sheridan had, after much delay, granted Sophie the play-bill concession under his new management at Drury Lane. Just as Darnly had predicted, however, he often neglected to pay her in full. When she requested the dramatist-manager settle his accounts, he simply shrugged and protested 'twas a trifling amount and she would have to wait a while longer.

"Sheridan hasn't the skill Garrick had in managing the business of a playhouse," Lorna commented sourly one morning. "He's so preoccupied with mounting his *A Trip to Scarborough* this month and writing some other new farce, he scarce attends to anything else."

"Well . . . I *must* have my funds," Sophie said unhappily. "The lease on my lodgings will soon be owing and I need money to give those brigands at Newgate to purchase Hunter's comforts. The poor man hardly complains, but 'tis galling for him to be caged like an animal and dependent on me for every tankard of ale . . ."

Finally, by March 1777, Sophie and Hunter felt prepared to submit *Battle Royal* to Garrick for his opinion.

"He received your note that you wished to see him, but he's not been at all well," Hannah More said, peering at Sophie over the butler's shoulder when the servant answered the door. "I'm sure you will understand if today he does not—"

"Why, Sophie McGann!" A Viennese-accented voice called down from the second floor of the Garrick residence on Adelphi Terrace. "How *kind* of you to call! Davy, 'tis Sophie come to see you. I'm sure Hannah will make you welcome. I shall be down directly!"

"I only thought to spare him—"

"Of course you did," Sophie cut in sarcastically as the butler ushered them both into the small front sitting room. "And how goes your latest play?"

"Mr. G. and I have conferred for nigh nine months, and without him, I'm certain I should have cast it in the fire long ago . . . but everything he touches turns to gold . . . literary gold, I mean," she corrected herself primly. "He says he will write the prologue and epilogue for *Percy*. Isn't that wonderful?"

Sophie smiled weakly in reply as Mrs. Garrick entered the room and bestowed a friendly kiss on her cheek.

"He's had another bad attack of the stone, you know," Eva-Maria said worriedly. "He bids you visit him upstairs."

Relieved to escape Hannah's unwelcome presence, Sophie was shown to a small study on the second floor where David Garrick was propped in a wing-backed chair looking unwell.

"And have you brought me something to read?" he smiled faintly after Sophie had given him the latest details about Hunter's incarceration for debt.

"Yes, we've both authored it," she replied, withdrawing the manuscript from beneath her cloak. "Although I'd like to submit it as Sydney Ganwick, if you consent," she proposed.

"A wise choice," Garrick agreed, leafing through the manuscript. "And young Rory . . . how is he?"

"Nearly six, sir," Sophie smiled. "And the image of his da."

Within two days Sophie received a note with the welcome news that Garrick considered *Battle Royal* an amusing diversion.

> Considering that all London talks of the rebel general George Washington driving British troops from New Jersey, this comical approach might bring relief . . . I shall send it on to Sheridan in the name of S. G. as we've agreed.
>
> My regards to your joint author and I pray this work shall win him his freedom. If not, you must consider my offer of assistance.
>
> Yrs. D. Garrick

"Perhaps we should accept his offer of a loan," Sophie ventured on her next visit to Newgate.

"I wish to earn my own way out of this trap, if you don't mind," Hunter replied tight-lipped.

Seeing the last remnants of his tattered pride stretched to the breaking point by the thought of her benefactor loaning them the enormous sum of seven hundred pounds, Sophie merely nodded and kissed him lightly on the forehead.

In early April, Sheridan sent word to Garrick who informed Sophie, also by letter, that although he very much liked Sydney Ganwick's latest effort, the Drury Lane managers could not afford to mount it until the 1777–1778 season.

The week before Rory's sixth birthday, Sophie and her son celebrated the occasion by her teaching him how to operate the hand press located at the back of her lodgings.

"That's right, lovey . . . just slip those metal letters in the form. *There!* You've done *The School for* perfectly," she smiled down at his tow head industriously bent over his work. "Now, how do you spell *Scandal*? One more word and the name of Mr. Sheridan's play will be correct. Just think, you've become my printer's apprentice and learned to *read* at the same time!"

"But Mr. Sheridan's taken the title for *your* play," Rory complained, his small fingers deftly sliding an *s* into the form.

"No . . . no he hasn't," Sophie corrected her son, smiling. "I've not finished writing *School for Fools* yet. And playwrights have always been fond of using the word *School* in their titles, for some reason. There's *School for Rakes* . . . *School for Wives* . . ." she laughed. Then her face grew sober. "Rory, dearheart, you must *never* discuss with anyone besides Mrs. Phillips and Lorna that mama writes plays, for it could go badly for us," she added urgently, wondering if Hannah More had pried out of her mentor the true identity of Sydney Ganwick.

"Not even tell Papa?" Rory asked anxiously.

"Of course Papa knows," Sophie acknowledged.

"But he's in prison," Rory said sadly, "so he won't tell."

"Aye . . ." Sophie nodded, her heart constricting. "That's why 'twill be such a help if you can learn to print these single sheets, my lad. Then your da and I can concentrate on writing some plays whose author's fees are bound to bring him home!"

To Sophie's dismay, nearly a year had gone by without their having the funds to secure Hunter's release. Reflecting on this desperate situation, she stood quietly in the wings watching Richard Sheridan supervise a rehearsal for his latest play, *The School for Scandal*. Despite the obvious brilliance of its dramatist-manager, Drury Lane had foundered the previous season without Garrick at the helm.

"No . . . no, that will not *do*, Mrs. Abington," Sheridan declared to the formidable actress who glared back at him. He leapt from his chair on the forestage. "You mustn't *whine* when you say 'How dare you abuse my relations!' You are to turn and sweep down on your nemesis like a *volcano*! Don't you agree, David?" Sheridan asked, turning to the former manager of Drury Lane.

Perhaps in response to the rumored production problems, Garrick had been at the author's side during most rehearsals and had written the prologue to the play in preparation for its debut the following evening.

"Exactly, Richard," Garrick nodded, resting his gout-ridden feet on a footstool.

"There's worse to come!" whispered a voice in Sophie's ear. The prompter, Mr. Hopkins, who had just arrived backstage, pointed to a copy of Sheridan's play tucked under his arm. "Capell's just refused Sheridan's play a license!"

"No!" she replied with disbelief. "That toady can't have turned it down!" Despite her irritation with Sheridan, Sophie was the first to admit that *The School for Scandal* was among the wittiest comedies she'd ever seen performed on a stage. "What will Richard *do*? The play's to debut *tomorrow*! I have already finished the placards . . ."

"Capell's objections involve some foolish political nonsense," Mr. Hopkins explained in a low voice, "that have nothing to do with Sheridan's intentions in writing the play." Hopkins squared his shoulders and marched across the stage, conferring in whispers with Garrick and Sheridan. The playwright's face grew flushed and he suddenly picked up the chair he was sitting on and hurled it across the stage, narrowly missing the surly Mrs. Abington.

"I shall go at once to speak to the Lord Chamberlain myself!" Sheridan declared, practically shouting.

"Now, now, Richard," Garrick urged, "try to compose yourself. Make your protests to his lordship reasonably and calmly, my boy."

Fortunately, Lord Hertford found this tempest in a political teapot as ludicrous as Sheridan, and the Lord Chamberlain himself quickly overrode the verdict of his deputy examiner of plays. *The School for Scandal* was speedily granted a license, and it opened May eighth, as scheduled.

"'Twas absolutely brilliant!" Sophie reported excitedly to Hunter the next morning, having witnessed Sheridan's triumph from the vantage point of the Garricks' private box. "Richard got so drunk following the performance, however, he was nearly arrested by the watch!" Hunter stared gloomily out the window of his prison cell, and offered no response. "Drury Lane's managers have no excuse not to pay their debt to me now," Sophie added cheerfully. "I heard they took in three hundred pounds last night!"

"I shouldn't count on him paying," Hunter said morosely.

Sophie glanced at his scowling countenance with concern. The bright green leaves sprouting on the trees outside the prison reminded them both of the full year that Hunter had been shut up in Newgate. His spirits had been steadily sinking in the face of another long summer during which the major playhouses would be closed. Worse, there was still no guarantee their *Battle Royal* would be mounted in the new season, come September.

"Please, darling," Sophie urged, placing her hands on Hunter's shoulders as he continued to stare moodily out his cell's narrow window, "you can't lose heart now . . . *Battle Royal* is witty and pithy and bound to be popular with audiences—"

"Even if Sheridan fails to gamble away his winnings from Drury Lane's current success," Hunter prophesied darkly, "and even if he chooses to mount our play, it will never survive Capell's razor!"

"Now, you're sounding like *me*!" Sophie teased.

"At this rate, I'll be an old man before 'tis acted on a stage," he replied, failing even to smile at her jest.

During July and August, Hunter's morale grew even worse. And as the summer evenings turned cool and crisp and Drury Lane prepared for the 1777–1778 season, Sophie feared Hunter's dismal forecasts might prove correct, but for a reason even he did not anticipate.

The School for Scandal was such an enormous favorite with theater patrons that London audiences wished to see little else. The play had been presented an unprecedented twenty times at the end of the prior season and was in demand from critics and public alike as the new season got underway.

"*The School for Scandal* seems to be the *only* play the public wants to see!" Sophie complained good-naturedly when she paid a visit to the Garricks in late October at their country house in Hampton, outside London. Rory had been whisked away by a jovial nursemaid, thus allowing Sophie and the Garricks to repair to their sitting room, which was decorated with exotic Chinese furniture. To Sophie's infinite satisfaction, Hannah More remained in Bristol with her family.

"I shall have a word with Sheridan when we return to London," Garrick said reassuringly. "*Battle Royal* is timely and would, I believe, please the public—especially now. I've just heard that Ben Franklin managed to coax money and supplies out of the French foreign minister!"

During the autumn and winter, however, Sheridan and his partners wrangled among themselves about everything from the costs of candles to the casting of plays. Despite their box-office successes, it was February before the managers agreed to mount *Battle Royal* prior to Drury Lane's closing in late May.

"Sheridan hasn't committed to a specific date, mind you," Garrick warned across his desk back at his apartments on Adelphi Terrace in London, "but 'tis a hopeful sign that he wants those provocative scenes about the bumbling British generals excised from the manuscript before the play is forwarded to Capell."

"Do you honestly believe Drury Lane will ever mount our play?" Sophie asked, feeling deeply discouraged. "I *must* earn some blunt to prove to Hunter we're making progress in paying off the blasted judgment! The poor darling grows more morose by the day . . . 'tis not possible to keep a man of his size and sensibilities caged up and sane much longer. He's even searching for some means of escaping the prison walls," she added worriedly.

Garrick shifted painfully in his chair, his swollen limbs wrapped snugly in a checkered rug.

"Sophie, why will you not accept my offer of a loan for the seven hundred pounds?" he urged.

"Hunter won't hear of it," she replied, with a catch in her voice. "Seven hundred pounds is simply too enormous a sum to borrow from anyone—even a dear and generous friend." She smiled wanly. "If *only* our play could see the light of day!"

As the spring of 1778 wore on, Sophie became so desperate for funds, she even agreed to allow the strumpet Mary Ann Skene to pay her two shillings a week to sleep on a pallet next to the printing press at the back of her lodgings.

"My wool merchant's gone bankrupt. Down on my luck, I am," Mary Ann complained with a pleading look when she encountered Sophie in Half Moon Passage and begged for temporary shelter.

"No more than I am," Sophie retorted, recalling the ghastly trouble the whore had caused the day she brought fever-ridden Peter to her door more than a decade earlier. "Why not ask your former benefactor, Lord Darnly, for assistance?"

Mary Ann's pinched, haggard face grew more anxious still.

"That actress . . . Mavis what-ever-her-name . . . she's got him under her thumb these days," she whined.

"I doubt any woman can dictate to an earl," Sophie retorted, offering silent thanks that Roderick Darnly had given her a wide berth since their confrontation the night of Hunter's homecoming.

"I'll pay you proper, see if I won't," Mary Ann promised as she pressed two shillings into Sophie's palm. "That harpy

Mrs. Douglas has played nasty with me at the Blue Periwig, but 'tis certain Mother Griffith will give me a place in a few weeks."

"You're to have nothing to do with my son, do you understand?" Sophie said sharply. In her mind she had already spent the two shillings on some fresh linen for Hunter. "You're simply to be pleasant to the lad, sleep in your bed, and leave it at that. And as soon as you find a new . . . situation . . . you're to be on your way. Agreed?"

At last, in early May, Sophie received word that *Battle Royal* had miraculously passed Capell's critical eye after numerous changes and cuts. As promised, David Garrick kept the true identity of Sydney Ganwick secret, forwarding sealed requests for changes and new dialogue by messenger to Sophie, and then personally conveying Hunter and Sophie's altered manuscript back to Sheridan.

"There's great excitement about the debut of Sydney Ganwick's latest comedy!" Sophie joked, attempting to rouse Hunter from his lethargy. "Even Mavis Piggott told Mrs. Abington at rehearsal today 'tis bound to please our patrons."

Hunter merely shrugged and remained silent.

On the day of *Battle Royal*'s debut, however, Sophie was on edge herself.

"You're like a cat on a griddle," Mrs. Phillips declared, having shared a meal of coffee and smoked kippers that she'd fetched from the Half Moon Tavern. "A bit of camomile tea to calm your nerves, perhaps?"

"I'm sorry," Sophie said contritely to her old friend whom she had taken into her confidence regarding the authorship of *Battle Royal,* "but so much depends on the play's success tonight!"

Her eyes followed her son as he gloomily returned to the printing room to correct a mistake he had made selecting letters to slide into the wooden form. Just then, Mary Ann stumbled through the door looking haggard from a night of plying her trade.

"Mornin'," grunted the strumpet as she padded toward her bed. She began shedding articles of clothing as she progressed toward her ultimate destination. The woman seemed oblivious to the clanking of the printing press Rory operated adjacent to her sleeping chamber.

"God's eyeballs!" Sophie said under her breath. "I play landlady to a whore, and then ask a seven-year-old to pull a lever I can barely manage myself! The season's nearly ended, Mrs. Phillips," she said in a low voice. "If the play fails tonight, I don't know if Hunter will be able to stand—"

"'Twill go splendidly!" the apothecary reassured her. "Lorna says the new scene is highly amusing."

"What new scene?" Sophie said, surprised that any changes would be instituted at this late stage.

"I don't know," Mrs. Phillips replied vaguely. "She was in earlier for those soothing foot salts I sell . . . mentioned some bit of business that was taken out and then restored. You'll see soon enough yourself."

But Sophie added this information to her catalog of worries: *What have they done to my play?*

A few hours later, backstage, she began to pace up and down near the wings as the orchestra played the customary melodies intended to quiet the restive audience.

"Why so nervous, Sophie?" Roderick Darnly said, appearing suddenly from the shadows.

"Oh!" Sophie gasped. "You're forever startling me . . . rising like a ghost out of the gloom. I . . . ah . . . I am only concerned for my friend Lorna Blount . . . she has quite a substantial part in tonight's performance."

The earl advanced into a circle of light cast by the candle glowing in the wall sconce overhead.

"Ah, yes . . . she dances a jig as that Martha Washington creature, I gather," he replied, observing her steadily.

"Um . . ." Sophie merely nodded, wondering how she could gracefully escape Darnly's odious presence.

"But let us not talk of such frivolous matters as *Battle Royal*," the earl said pleasantly. "You must tell me how *you* are faring . . . your son is well, I hope? We haven't spoken for an age."

Not since Hunter's trial for Criminal Conversation initiated at your behest, she thought bitterly.

The earl's tone had become conciliatory. Suddenly, he

reached for her hand and began to gently caress her wrist with his thumb.

"Hunter's son is well," she replied coolly, wishing he would release her hand. "The lad just celebrated his seventh birthday. The three of us get along as best we can, under the circumstances."

"Seven hundred pounds . . ." Darnly said softly. "A man in Robertson's plight could go forever without securing such a sum . . ." He raised Sophie's hand and grazed her flesh with his lips. "If I can be of any assistance whatsoever . . ." he murmured.

Sophie snatched her hand away, her eyes flashing.

"Let us not play parts, m'lord!" she snapped, barely holding her temper. "And let us not mince words, either. 'Twas *you* who brought Hunter to such indignity, not Peter Lindsay!" she exclaimed. "I cannot fathom why you wish to cause us so much grief, but clearly you do."

"Robertson's conduct toward your husband is the cause of his misfortunes, not mine toward him," Darnly replied stiffly.

"That's absolute *twaddle*!" Sophie replied angrily. "We know you forced Peter to sue Hunter for astronomical damages, blackmailing him with threats to have *him* cast in Newgate for past debts owed you if he did not do as you insisted."

"A gentleman must make good on his IOUs," Darnly replied.

"Gentleman!" Sophie spat. "I feel nothing but pity for Peter and compassion that his addiction to gambling and drink has drawn him into the web of a man like you," she added scathingly. She narrowed her eyes, unable to restrain herself further. "*Your* conduct lately seems to include the rather nasty habit of employing *extortion*, m'lord, to attempt to accomplish whatever twisted purposes you devise. I don't pretend to understand *why* this should be . . . all I know is that we all suffer for it . . . and if Peter should ever have the courage to tell the court he no longer demands these unwarranted damages from Hunter . . . the matter would be moot."

"Peter Lindsay cannot afford to abandon hope of collecting money from the man who cuckolded him," Darnly responded cuttingly, "for he owes *me* too much."

"But, what if the judge, Lord Mansfield, learned 'twas you who forced Peter to file suit merely to seek revenge against Hunter for proving you a cheat?"

Darnly appeared momentarily startled by her words, but replied calmly, "'Tis my word against a bogus baronet, and against Robertson—a player of little note."

"But if Peter himself should reveal to the judge what threats you used against him to bring this case to court," she persisted, "or if Rosoman bore witness to the fact that you struck Hunter first and have a motive for revenge . . . what then?"

Darnly stared sharply at Sophie and then shrugged. A mocking smile began to play across his lips.

"Lord Mansfield surely knows that many things in this world are not what they appear. Take the mysterious author of tonight's diversion, as one example," he continued. "No one knows, really, who this Sydney Ganwick might be. Edward Capell is in the audience tonight, I understand," he added. "It seems our government censor is annoyed by rumors certain cuts have been restored."

"Really?" Sophie said tensely, feeling the color drain from her face. Had Roderick somehow discerned the identity of Sydney Ganwick? "'Pon my word, but I can't imagine such frothy fare as *Battle Royal* would merit his august attention."

"From what I've seen of the piece, it doesn't," Darnly retorted, inclining his head in an abrupt farewell before striding off toward a door that led to his box.

Shaken by this exchange, Sophie raced for the peephole. Her spirits sank even lower at the sight of the mottled-faced examiner perched in the second gallery, a manuscript cradled in his lap. Just then, Mr. Hopkins, the prompter, called for places. Sophie then made her way in the semidarkness to the Greenroom where she found Richard Sheridan pouring himself a glass of spirits from a decanter on a table near the door.

"Good evening, sir," Sophie greeted him.

"I cannot discuss finances now," he replied brusquely.

"I've got more on my mind than a few shillings for play-bills."

"I imagine you do," she said, taking some satisfaction that he had no idea she was the author of the evening's fare. "I understand Edward Capell joins us tonight . . . with a manuscript in his grasp. Why is that, do you suppose?"

"The little sod did not appreciate being overruled by Lord Hertford on *The School for Scandal* . . . so I suppose he's here to see that we perform exactly what he has approved."

"And are you?" she asked quietly. "Performing *exactly* what he approved?"

Sheridan took a long draught on his glass.

"I inserted a line or two from the original version," he replied, affecting nonchalance. "That Ganwick is a witty chap and his work deserves to be presented as written. And since no one but Garrick knows who Sydney Ganwick really is, Capell can't do much."

"Until the unfortunate Mr. Ganwick submits his *next* work to the government censors," Sophie retorted. "And I rather imagine Edward Capell can try to close you down."

"Let him try!" Sheridan said angrily, finishing his drink. "Someone has to challenge that nickninny!"

Sophie spent the rest of the evening staring through the peephole at Capell, her stomach tied in knots. One moment her spirits soared when the audience fell into gales of laughter at the bumbling antics of foot soldiers in *Battle Royal.* The next instant, her hopes were dashed by the scowl darkening the mottled countenance of the Deputy Examiner of Plays.

The audience was still clapping and shouting its approval when the final curtain closed, but Sophie took no comfort from such an outpouring of enthusiasm. Capell leapt from his seat, exited the gallery door, and within moments, was storming backstage and into the Greenroom, where Richard Sheridan, his partners, and some of the principal players were awaiting well wishers from the audience. Sophie edged into the room, wondering what further disaster could befall her.

"Act One!" brayed Capell, as he pointed a shaking finger

at a passage boldly crossed out in his censored manuscript. "I marked these two lines *out* and you have restored them!"

Sheridan merely stared at the enraged functionary while sipping yet another glass of brandy. His fellow manager, Dr. Ford, and Roderick Darnly leaned against the opposite wall, watching in silence.

"Act Two!" Capell snapped. "An entire scene I ordered omitted is back *in* the work! Furthermore," he continued, seething with indignation, "I specifically demanded that you replace the words *damn stuff* to *hang snuff* . . . I shall *not* allow you to use such blasphemy upon the king's stage!"

"Have you discussed this hair splitting with my Lord Hertford, the Lord Chamberlain?" Sheridan challenged rudely.

Capell's eyes glittered dangerously, and he closed his copy of *Battle Royal* with an angry snap.

"You, Mr. Sheridan, may possess the requisite connections to persuade the Lord Chamberlain to overrule my judgment regarding your own work," he said in a menacing voice, "but this Sydney Ganwick, whoever he is, certainly does *not!*"

"David Garrick has forever been Ganwick's champion," Sheridan said mildly. "Has that no weight with you, sir? After all, our former manager has been generous regarding the use of his library for your work on restoring Shakespeare's texts. What if Sydney Ganwick turns out to be a mere pen name for your benefactor? Wouldn't that be a rip?"

For a moment, Capell's steely expression wavered. Then he shook his head, scowling.

"Ganwick is no Garrick," he declared stoutly. "There's a rebellious edge to this man's work I find offensive, even if he *is* a clever chap." He glanced around the Greenroom, suddenly aware that an audience larger than simply Drury Lane's managers was hanging on his every word. "You are fortunate that I shall not order you closed down, but each and every word excised by me is to be eliminated before the next performance, is that *understood?*"

Richard Sheridan stared insolently at Capell, refusing him the courtesy of a civil answer. The Deputy Examiner of

Plays flushed so deeply at this insult, his blotchy complexion took on the hue of rotting eggplant.

"Furthermore," he added in a menacing voice, "there were *additional* passages in the piece tonight that I also found objectionable, now that I see the way in which the players gesture on stage. I shall order further cuts. Good night, Mr. Sheridan."

The Lord Chamberlain's deputy rose to his fullest height and departed with as much dignity as he could muster, leaving absolute silence in his wake.

Chapter 36

The newly ordered cuts to *Battle Royal* eviscerated the piece to such an extent that it lasted only three nights and played to poor houses.

"After all the tumult, how much did the piece gain us?" Hunter asked despondently when Sophie called at Newgate to recount the latest developments at Drury Lane.

"Forty-two pounds," she admitted reluctantly.

"I've been in this dungeon *two years* and we've earned *forty-two pounds*?" he exploded. "'Tis barely enough to keep you and Rory from being tossed out on Half Moon Passage next winter. Oh, God, Sophie! 'Tis hopeless!"

"No 'tis *not*!" she replied fiercely, throwing her arms around his broad shoulders and pulling him against her smaller frame.

Hunter held himself stiffly, unresponsive to her entreaties to be of good cheer.

"This is no life," he said in a low voice. "Because of me, you've lived in a kind of suspended animation for years now. I can't let you do this to yourself or Rory any longer."

"Don't be ridiculous!" Sophie snapped. "So . . . *Battle Royal* was turned into mincemeat by that idiot Capell. So . . . we'll write something else . . . use *another* pseudonym. We can't let them win!"

"They *have* won," Hunter replied dully. "I'd rather die than stay cooped up in this rat hole . . . or see you running yourself ragged—a woman trying to earn the impossible sum of seven hundred pounds."

"*The School for Scandal*'s earned thousands! Why do you doubt I can do as well?" Sophie demanded.

"Because the world at large finds it . . . *unsuitable* for women to write for the public's amusement!" he said angrily. "Why fight it, Sophie? Why fight any of it?" He stared out his window, his face suddenly expressionless. His shoulders sagged and his hands reached up to his face and covered his eyes. Long minutes of silence widened the emotional gulf between them. "I hope you will understand," he said at length. "I would appreciate it if you left me now . . . I mean no offense, but I wish to be alone."

Sophie stared at him, a feeling of helplessness invading her every fiber. It almost seemed as if Hunter's spirit had departed the stone chamber which imprisoned him, and only his physical shell remained, indifferent even to her. She called softly for the turnkey to release her from the cell and slowly walked home.

❦

As the weeks dragged on following the failure of *Battle Royal*, Hunter remained polite but distant during Sophie's visits. Often he informed the warden that he wished to see no one, including her.

"You're not to blame for this predicament we're in!" she exclaimed one day in frustration, having stooped to bribing the turnkey to gain access to Hunter's cell. "I willingly sought your bed! I willingly had your son! I shall put every ounce of strength I own toward writing a play that will earn us your freedom! Hunter! Are you listening to me?" she pleaded, banging her fists on the small table. But he merely stared listlessly out his barred window and did not respond to her entreaties.

It was soon after this encounter that Sophie determined to seek the only remedy left to her, that of pleading with her estranged husband to withdraw the charges against Hunter.

"God's bones, Sophie," Mary Ann Skene exclaimed, observing her flat mate applying paint to her face as if she were an actress—or a whore. "Don't tell me things go so ill for you, you're joining *my* ranks tonight?"

"No . . ." Sophie replied grimly. "But I wish people to *think* I am. I must find Peter. I *must*!"

"Why in the world would you want to find that wastrel? Seems to me he's the *last* person to help you and that Hunter fellow."

"I'm sure that's what it seems," Sophie agreed, tight-lipped, applying more rouge to highlight her cheeks.

Within a few minutes, Mary Ann departed for her nightly chores at the bagnio run by the infamous Mother Griffith. Assured by Rory's steady breathing that he was fast asleep, Sophie threw a shawl over her provocative gown and slipped down the outside stairs, remaining close to the buildings that paralleled Bedford Street. Turning right on King Street, she paused at entrances along the road, inquiring if anyone had encountered the dark-haired Peter Lindsay of late.

"Saw him face down in Martlet Court, less than a fort-night ago, lovey," one blowsy whore cackled, revealing black gaps between her rotted teeth. "I wouldn't count on him for a tumble in the feathers or even a tippling of ale, if I were you."

"Thank you," Sophie murmured, moving on.

The Great Piazza was bathed with the golden light of a harvest moon as she crossed the square, looking for Peter at the most likely places. She studiously ignored the rude re-marks from sedan chair bearers and the invitations from young bucks emerging from Mother Douglas's house of il-licit pleasure. Turning left on Russell Street and left again on Bow Street, she soon arrived at the narrow lane called Mart-let Court.

"Hello, sweetheart," a hawk-nosed man called to her from the entrance to the Turk's Head on the corner. "You're a lovely little pigeon, aren't you, dearie? Want a soft bed to ply your trade? Come love . . . we'll split our winnings and—"

"Sod off!" Sophie snarled in her best imitation of Mary Ann Skene when in high dungeon.

She peered down Martlet's Court and proceeded cau-tiously along the darkened alley, praying that it led to Drury

Lane, as she expected it should. She could just discern the silhouettes of men pressing their attentions on whores who dispensed their favors standing upright. The twosomes glanced furtively at her, but none turned out to be Peter Lindsay. Shaken by the sight of such loathsome coupling, Sophie ran breathlessly past the Drury Lane Theater itself, and across Tavistock Street, near Mr. Jackson's costume shop. By traversing through several back alleys where rats and stray dogs were burrowing in the garbage, she emerged into Henrietta Street, the road that ran next to St. Paul's Churchyard.

"Another night of this?" she muttered to herself, still shivering from her glimpse of the underbelly of Covent Garden. 'Tis nothing but a wild-goose chase, she thought.

She paused to catch her breath, leaning against the wrought-iron fence that sheltered the churchyard from the road. Moonlight illuminated the familiar sight of her daughter's headstone, one of many standing as mute testimony to the trials of this world. Then, Sophie clutched at the cold metal bars. A sound like that of a rustling animal drew her glance to a rounded shape crumpled beside Danielle's grave. A feeling of dread crept over her, prompting her to retrace her steps. She passed through the high black gate that led to the churchyard itself, feeling her shoes sink into the soft grassy area stippled with the grave markers. She cautiously approached a figure curled up against the small granite tomb stone that read *Danielle McGann Lindsay 3 mos. died 1766.*

"Peter?" she murmured, staring down on a bruised and battered face bathed in moonlight. "Oh, God . . . Peter!"

The husband she had married thirteen years earlier gazed at her with unseeing eyes, dried blood congealed on his forehead.

"Sophie?" he whispered hoarsely, startling her. She thought him already dead.

"Yes," she cried as she sank to her knees and attempted to cradle his head in her lap. "Jesu . . . Peter? What has happened? Did you fall?"

"Hit . . . hit head . . ." he murmured. "Everything's dark . . ."

"Hit? How?" she demanded. "Where were you . . . ?"

"Coming out of the White . . ."

His words trailed off and his breathing became labored. Sophie frantically glanced at her surroundings. A hundred feet beyond the gateway to the cemetery she could see candles still flickering inside the White Horse Tavern, a rough public house situated across from Southampton Street where the Garricks had once lived.

"Were you in a fight?" she asked, feeling a rising wave of panic. "In the tavern? Who *did* this to you?"

"Don't know . . . hit . . . came here . . . our daughter . . ."

She stared down in horror at his swollen face and matted black hair.

"You were hit with something slender?" she repeated, perplexed. She glanced at Danielle's narrow headstone. "Did you fall against the stone marker . . . Peter, what *happened*?"

The once-handsome countenance was twisted with pain, distorting his features into a grotesque mask. A low moan escaped his lips. Then, his breathing simply stopped. Peter Lindsay had died a dog's death.

Sophie persuaded Mrs. Phillips to convince Bob Derry at the Cider House to report to the authorities that a corpse lay atop the grass in St. Paul's Churchyard. With all the troubles besetting her, the last thing she needed was to be accused of murdering the very husband who had caused her such grief. She learned from Derry that Peter would find what peace was to be had in a pauper's grave. His demise had been duly registered as having been caused by falling drunk against a gravestone and hitting his head.

With the death certificate in hand, she then petitioned to have the prisoner released from Newgate, citing the fact that the man to whom he owed seven hundred pounds had recently expired.

"I'm afraid nothing can be done," Mr. Lasley announced in his law chambers one chilly October afternoon, "that is, until 'tis been duly proved Peter Lindsay had no heirs who would claim title to such a debt. 'Tis a matter for the courts."

"I have heard Peter's grandfather died in '75 and Peter himself has no legitimate heirs," Sophie said, attempting to keep her temper under control. "And as women are so abused by British justice, I doubt Peter's *mother* can press a claim against Hunter cuckolding her son, if she still lives!"

"Lord Mansfield has said he would look into the matter," Hunter's barrister declared with rising irritation. "That is all I can do . . . and now, if you will settle the accounts owing," he added pointedly.

Sophie reluctantly handed him a guinea for his efforts.

In the frustrating weeks that followed, Sophie gave up her campaign to shake Hunter from his debilitating depression. She concentrated, instead, on earning money by printing broadsheets, placards, and tradesmen's cards and by working secretly again on *School for Fools*—everything and anything that would garner them a few shillings to pay the lease on their lodgings and keep them all alive. Garrick had been away from London most of the autumn, visiting noblemen and gentry who clamored for his company, including Lord Palmerston, who lured him to Broadlands, his estate in Hampshire. Sophie called at Adelphi Terrace only to learn from Hannah More that the Garricks had not yet returned.

"They've asked me to keep an eye out for them here," she explained self-importantly. Pressing Hannah for recent news of her friends, Sophie was distressed to hear that David had recently suffered a violent bilious attack that had left him very weak. "He also passed several gallstones while at Broadlands," Hannah added, shaking her head dolefully. "Dreadfully painful, they were, Mrs. G. wrote me. They'd hoped to spend Christmas at Althorp with Lord and Lady Spencer, but I expect them to come home first, as soon as Mr. G. is fit to travel."

Sophie nodded her thanks for the information imparted, however reluctantly, by Miss More, and retreated down the steps with a sense of foreboding.

Icy bursts of wind whipped at the edges of her cloak as

she passed by St. Paul's on her way home. There was a hint of snow in the air and Christmas was approaching, but there was little about her life to cause Sophie to feel festive. She reminded herself that she was, at last, making progress with her comedy that was set in London's madhouse, but she doubted she would have the funds to furnish any grand holiday fare for either Rory or poor Hunter.

She glanced up at the columns of St. Paul's. What could she possibly provide Hunter for Christmas that would make him believe there was a future for them . . . that all was not hopeless? Suddenly, she smiled, and, with a determined step, marched into the large cavern known as the Actors' Church.

"This arrived for you, Mr. Robertson," the turnkey said with a sly wink. He handed Hunter a bundle tied with string. "My instructions are that you are to don the fresh linen provided and clean yourself up."

"And whose instructions are these?" Hunter growled sullenly.

"One who should be obeyed," the turnkey pronounced solemnly. He reached for a tray held by an associate. "Here's a blade and a sliver of soap and a bowl of water. Shave yourself, my man! You'll have visitors anon."

As promised, within the hour Hunter heard the jingle of keys and the clatter of footsteps. The door to his cell swung open and a cleric in a black suit and white linen collar entered, followed by Hunter's seven-year-old son Rory, Mrs. Phillips, and Lorna Blount, the women cloaked in silks and furs. Lastly Sophie appeared, wearing a gown of wine-red velvet, cut alluringly low so as to reveal a great deal of her small but rounded bosom. Staring openmouthed at the group, Hunter silently wagered that every scrap of their finery had been secured from Drury Lane's extensive costume holdings, courtesy of Lorna Blount.

"I expect you'll be wanting to sign the forms first," the cleric said nervously.

"What forms?" Hunter demanded. The mother of his only child had a sweet but determined look on her face.

"The special license required to marry at a location other

than in a Church of England," she said calmly. "I've already signed them . . . see . . . you just need to put your name right . . . *there,*" she said, pointing at a line on the official-looking document.

He stared at her for a moment, and then accepted the quill held out to him by the turnkey. The jailor's smug smile revealed he had been Sophie McGann's willing accomplice.

"Is this legal?" Hunter asked the cleric gruffly.

"W-why y-yes," the rector stuttered. "At least Mr. Garrick's letter posted from Broadlands maintained that it was. He swore that to the best of his knowledge, you remain a bachelor. Your bride, here, has shown me the certificate that she is a widow and that there is some urgency to the formalities. Hence, I have agreed that this ceremony may be performed in . . . uh . . . a *prison.*"

"Refresh my memory," Hunter said, casting an unbelieving stare in Sophie's direction, "what is the *urgency* prompting these 'formalities,' as you call them?"

"I explained to the good rector," Sophie intervened, with a glance in Rory's direction, "that you wished to recognize your son and that I . . . ah . . ." she cast her eyes coquettishly downward and patted her abdomen, ". . . I believed myself to be—"

"Of course," Hunter interrupted hastily, marveling at Sophie's powers of imagination, since he had not touched her in three months.

"You *are* willing to make me your wife, aren't you?" Sophie demanded, uncertainty suddenly flooding her amber eyes.

Mrs. Phillips took a step forward.

"My advice to you, young man—"

"No need for entreaties, Mrs. Phillips," he assured her, raising both hands in front of his face as if to ward off a blow.

Lorna laid her palms on Rory's small shoulders.

"Your son wishes to stand as best man for you, and you can't disappoint him!"

He glanced at the little boy staring at him solemnly and slowly nodded his head.

"I'd quite like that," he murmured. "Come over here and

let me lean on you, lad." Rory looked up and grinned at his father. Then, Hunter extended his hand toward Sophie and waited patiently for her to clasp it. "This may be the daftest wedding ever in Christendom, but will you do me the honor, Sophie McGann, of becoming my wife?"

"Yes . . ." she replied softly, her eyes shining. She stood on tiptoe in order to whisper in his ear. "Happy Christmas, darling."

Following the brief ceremony, the chattering crowd, except for Sophie, filed out of Hunter's cell and the turnkey locked them inside with a lascivious chuckle. When the jailor's footsteps had faded into the distance, Hunter pulled Sophie against his chest and inhaled her fragrant hair.

"You always had a penchant for risking your lovely neck for your beliefs," he said ruefully. "I hope you haven't made one last, dreadful mistake marrying me."

"I've made no mistake, as long as you don't say 'tis hopeless, my trying to get you out of here," she said urgently. "If you give in to your melancholy as you have, we are *both* lost . . . for I cannot imagine my life without you. I've tried to write our life's script with other endings and I simply cannot. 'Tis we . . . together . . . for good or ill. And that's the end of it."

Hunter held her tightly against his chest. The crown of her head fit perfectly beneath his chin.

"I truly wonder how such a wee thing can turn a man's life upside down," he murmured into her hair. Then he pulled away from her, a mischievous smile turning up the corners of his mouth. "Now what is this the good rector said about the *urgency* prompting the wedding formalities . . . and you believing yourself to be—?"

"'Twas merely a ruse to prompt the cleric to perform the rite in prison," Sophie replied defensively. "He was rather reluctant when first I proposed the idea to him. My hinting I was with child, plus Garrick's letter, in the end prompted him to—"

"Ah . . . I see," Hunter chuckled. "You little deceiver." He gently strafed his fingers along the mounds of her bosom forced as high as humanly possible by the gown's tight bodice. "Well . . . we can't have you lying to a man of the cloth, can we now?" he said, bending forward to kiss the valley between her breasts. "We'll just have to make an honest woman of you . . ."

"We dare not make another baby, though," she whispered softly as she tenderly stroked his hair. "Not yet. But, have faith, laddie!" She reached into a wicker hamper filled with celebratory wine and cheese and retrieved a sheathlike object made of the thinnest sheepskin membrane he had ever seen. "'Tis Mrs. Phillips' finest," Sophie announced with a throaty laugh, "guaranteed not to cause blisters or feel like flannel sock!"

"Well, my dear Mrs. Robertson!" David Garrick greeted Sophie, as she entered his study on the second floor of his London residence on a wintery December afternoon. "Congratulations are certainly in order!"

Despite Garrick's hearty welcome, Sophie was dismayed to discover that his skin had taken on an unhealthy yellow tinge and his ankles and wrists were more swollen than ever, owing to his latest attack of gallstones. Nevertheless, Garrick remained buoyant in Sophie's presence.

"I have every expectation that *School for Fools* will provide the means to buy the release of your groom," he said, "especially now that we've managed to get it past Capell."

"He's granted it a license?" Sophie asked with astonishment.

"Sherry had the devil's own time getting him to, but we gave a bit of push through Lord Hertford." Garrick chuckled and then winced with pain as he leaned forward conspiratorially. "I even stooped to hinting that *I*, myself, might have chosen the pseudonym Sydney Ganwick for certain of my writing efforts. Capell didn't dare question the Lord Chamberlain after *that*!"

"Has he ordered major changes in the piece?" Sophie asked apprehensively.

"As I expected, cuts and deletions abound. You may have heard, our sovereign had a strange siege of brain fever briefly in his youth," he explained. "Nothing's tipped up since, fortunately, but who can predict whether the malady will strike

King George the Third again? 'Twas years ago, however, so Hertford overruled his deputy's objections to the comedy being set in a madhouse." He smiled reassuringly. "However, there *is* one aspect of your play that may still prove troublesome."

"Yes?" Sophie asked, her spirits sinking.

"Your character, Dr. Mudley, the director of the madhouse? Capell mentioned to Lord Hertford that Dr. Monro at Bedlam might raise some objection to the work. Lord Hertford waved it aside, saying that a number of men in the medical profession have publicly taken issue with Monro. However, I say remove the sinister elements to the Mudley character and keep the silly ones."

"I shall mull it over when I make the corrections," Sophie replied politely, trying to disguise her dismay both at Capell's numerous black *X*'s disfiguring her manuscript and at the prospect that Dr. Monro might create trouble again. Not wishing to tire Garrick further, Sophie rose to make her departure. "Do take care of yourself," she urged.

He smiled wanly. "I expect I shall not be in London for the debut of *School for Fools* in January, but I'm sure all will go well. You have much ability, my dear . . . and I'm sorry you've been thwarted so often, merely because of your gender."

Touched by his empathy, Sophie impulsively seized his gnarled hand and gently kissed it.

"Thank you for everything you have ever done for me," she murmured humbly.

"Now, now, my dear," he responded, resting his palm on the top of her head as he had when he offered his benediction to the three actresses playing his daughters in *King Lear*. "Your own formidable talents would have won out somehow, even without my help."

Sophie raised her head and felt tears filling her eyes. She had sought David Garrick's blessing for virtually everything she had ever attempted during the years she had lived in London—even her latest effort to wed Hunter Robertson.

"I will never forget your many kindnesses," she said in a voice choked with emotion.

"*You* are very kind," he replied, his eyes misting over.

"And please offer my best regards to that new husband of yours," he added, recovering his composure. "If through some bad luck, you don't make your blunt on your play, remember my offer of assistance."

"I will," Sophie whispered, barely able to talk. "Thank you."

She stumbled downstairs, blinking back tears she was determined to conceal from Eva-Maria.

"Thank you for not staying too long." Mrs. Garrick smiled gravely, joining Sophie in the foyer. "He so enjoys seeing young people like yourself, but I think he's in more pain than he's willing to admit. 'Tis such a comfort to have Hannah with us at this time," she confided, ushering Sophie to the door. "She's been kindness itself through all of Davy's difficulties."

Sophie smiled bleakly as Eva-Maria kissed her farewell, and suddenly found herself wondering what the ambitious Miss More might do if she ever learned the identity of Sydney Ganwick. Would she see that Edward Capell found out?

"Good-bye . . . and Happy Christmas if I shouldn't see you until the New Year," Sophie offered.

"Thank you and God bless you, my dear," Eva-Maria replied sadly. And, strangely, Sophie did feel blessed.

Mindful of Edward Capell's proscriptions, Sophie set to work on the required corrections of her manuscript. The pompous, menacing Dr. Monro whom Sophie had so feared when she was incarcerated in Bedlam with Aunt Harriet was depicted in *School for Fools* as an outlandish, laughable buffoon. He was full of self-importance, employing macabre devices and "methodology" that he ludicrously claimed would provide a cure for the "dear, demented souls" in his care.

Rereading the final version of her work in the early hours of Christmas day, Sophie became completely caught up in a world where the inmates were the rational beings, and the keepers of the asylum, the insane ones. Turnkeys took bribes in businesslike fashion, technicians brandished feeding tubes as if they were ministering angels, and the crowds invading

Bedlam for their Sunday amusement were mocked in wicked asides by inmates who appeared as lucid as the judges presiding at King's Bench.

Heaving an enormous sigh, Sophie scratched the word *finis* at the bottom of the last page. At that moment, an exhausted Mary Ann Skene stumbled through the door, her nose scarlet from the frigid December morn. She headed directly for the cheerful coal fire burning in the grate and unceremoniously lifted her skirts to warm her backside. Sophie hastily gathered the pages scattered on her desk and whisked them into a drawer.

"Working so early?" Mary Ann commented with an inquisitive glance in the direction of the desk.

"Totting up figures on some of my printing accounts," Sophie replied with a shrug. "I'd like to collect all monies owing by the new year and I thought to tackle the chore while Rory slumbers," she added quietly, nodding at her son, still blissfully asleep.

"Will you visit Newgate today?" the strumpet inquired. "It must be a gloomy place on Christmas."

No one but the Garricks and those attending the wedding ceremony knew that Sophie and Hunter had officially wed. She had taken this precaution to forestall the possibility that some busybody might question the propriety of her taking a new husband so soon after Peter's death. Besides, she had envisioned a proper wedding at St. Paul's, once Hunter was released from prison.

"I rather think I might go 'round there today," Sophie responded casually. "Bring the poor blighter a bit of that plum pudding Mrs. Phillips is so proud of."

"Me . . . I just want to sleep," Mary Ann yawned, scratching herself in the most unladylike fashion.

The Garricks departed for Althorp, the home of Lord and Lady Spencer, December 30, and so did not witness the phenomenally successful debut and run of *School for Fools* in early January. By the twelfth day of the new year, 1779, Sophie calculated her author's fees to be upward of three hundred pounds. Unfortunately, she couldn't collect the money until Garrick returned to London and pressed Sheridan, on Sydney Ganwick's behalf, for a full accounting.

"Sophie, you are a clever, clever lass!" Hunter crowed when she told him the news and showed him the journal articles.

Newspaper editorials trumpeted the play's call for reform, and rumors of another Parliamentary inquiry into practices at the nation's asylums began circulating.

"I just pray Dr. Monro isn't summoned before Parliament again. What if he learns that Sydney Ganwick is really Sophie McGann—"

"Sophie McGann *Robertson*," Hunter chided her teasingly.

". . . that Ganwick is *me*," Sophie continued anxiously. "All this talk of calling another inquiry to examine conditions at Bedlam could prompt Monro to cry 'libel' against me again. I merely wrote an amusing farce . . ."

Hunter smiled, drawing her into his arms. "Be honest, Sophie, your little comedy has achieved exactly what you intended. But dinna worry, lass," he bantered in an echo of his Scottish brogue, "there are many in the medical profession who agree with you . . . let *them* shoulder the call for reform from now on. For us, your play means that we can soon afford to hire the best barrister in the city to persuade Lord Mansfield that I should be set free!"

"Oh, Hunter, I pray that will be so."

Sophie and Hannah More sat side by side in the Garricks' box as the audience's laughter rang in their ears. Like a proud parent, Sophie had witnessed the production of her tragicomedy each night from this prized vantage point overlooking the pit. She had assumed that at some point Hannah would exercise her right of proprietorship as the Garricks' constant houseguest and claim a seat to determine what all the fuss was about—and tonight, here she was.

Drury Lane was packed to the rafters on this fourteenth day of January, and it seemed as if everyone was either doubled over in mirth or sitting with tears running down their faces. Sophie noticed that even Hannah looked as though she'd been moved by the play. Furthermore, Sheridan had slyly replaced a few lines ordered cut by the censor back into the dialogue. Fortunately, on this particular night, Edward Capell was nowhere to be seen.

As the final curtain closed and loud, appreciative clapping resounded from the audience, Sophie felt a hand clutch her wrist.

"You've written an *extraordinary* play!" Hannah exclaimed, her eyes shining. "'Tis amusing and poignant and sends a message as well. You should be so proud!"

Sophie stared openmouthed at her theater companion, dumbfounded and alarmed. This woman whom she so disliked was privy to one of the most crucial secrets in her life! Eva-Maria Garrick—certainly not David—must have trusted Hannah More absolutely to have revealed that Sophie was the genuine author of Sydney Ganwick's plays. Either that, or the woman had finally managed to gain complete control over the household at Adelphi Terrace. Before Sophie could recover from her shock, however, Lord Darnly suddenly entered their box.

"Good evening . . . Miss More . . . Miss McGann," announced the Earl of Llewelyn. "'Twas most gratifying to witness two such accomplished young women gracing this celebrated box tonight. Is your patron still absent from London?"

"Yes," Hannah answered, pleased to be the object of such flattering attention from a premier aristocrat of the realm. "However, I have word they are returning from Althorp late tonight or on the morrow. I fear Mr. G. has been particularly unwell."

"How unfortunate," Lord Darnly murmured, casting Sophie an appraising glance.

In early autumn, Darnly had decamped for Wales again to attend to his estates. Rumors abounded that he and Mavis Piggott had parted company during his absence, and the proof of such hearsay could be seen directly opposite from where the three were now standing. The actress was staring at them from a box presided over by one of Darnly's fellow club members, Viscount Wick.

"And you, Sophie?" Darnly inquired genially, ignoring

Mavis's stony glares. "Does not witnessing such brilliant theater make you nostalgic for your quill?"

Sophie stiffened. She refused to glance at Hannah, for fear the woman would say something foolish to the earl.

"Not at all," she said quickly, forcing a smile, "the play's success has been good for my printing business. Extra performances mean extra playbills!"

"Ah . . . how fortunate for you," he commented dryly.

"Well . . . I fear I must beg your leave," Hannah said, donning her cloak. "I must hasten to Adelphi Terrace in case the Garricks have returned." Garrick's self-appointed nurse quickly extended her farewells.

"Please convey my hopes for Mr. Garrick's recovery," Sophie said earnestly, doubtful any such message would ever be passed on.

Then, as Hannah left the box, Sophie, too, gathered her cloak from the back of her chair and prepared to depart. On stage and within the auditorium itself, candle snuffers were going about the business of extinguishing the hundreds of tapers that lit the playhouse each performance. A pungent odor of tallow and sulfur hung heavily in the air.

"Sophie," Lord Darnly said suddenly. "I need to have a word with you. May I offer you refreshments at my home?"

"I think not, m'lord," Sophie said slowly. "Our last conversation, you will recall, did not conclude on the friendliest of terms, and I fear—"

"I understand," he interjected smoothly. "Then we can speak here, if you like. Please take a seat."

Helpless to do anything else, Sophie reclaimed the chair she had just vacated. A clatter behind the closed curtains indicated that a stage servant had dropped something heavy.

"I hope they don't break the new scenery I purchased," Darnly noted mildly.

"You invested in *School for Fools*?" Sophie asked, startled.

"Let us say I provided one of the partners some financial assistance, and have been well recompensed for my trouble," he replied with a satisfied air. "I find it amusing to wager a bit of blunt on the works of playwrights I deem worthy . . ."

"Fascinating," Sophie murmured.

"That it is . . . and inspiring, wouldn't you say?"

"To sit in the audience at such a play? Yes, I would say so," she answered, wondering where the conversation was heading.

"We have so many amusements in common, do we not?" Lord Darnly ventured pleasantly. "Enjoying the cleverness of Sydney Ganwick is one of them, I would imagine."

Sophie felt her stomach muscles tighten. Once again she began to worry that Darnly had guessed her secret.

"While I was in Wales, I had an opportunity to ponder many subjects, including the subject of you, my dear."

"Oh?" Sophie replied warily.

"This sojourn provided an occasion to think on the course of my life . . . my youthful mistakes . . . the harm they may have caused certain people," he added somberly. "Perhaps Peter Lindsay's death filled my head with gloomy musings, but I now realize that I desire something more in my life . . ."

A yearning to be a respected author, perhaps? Sophie speculated silently.

"Such thoughts, I fear to say, come with our advancing age," she replied with false cheer.

"I have decided that it is an auspicious time for me to select a . . . life partner," he continued, gazing at her steadily. "Someone who shares my interests and amusements."

Sophie was surprised, but relieved. The man was once more without a mistress and simply wished to remedy his loss—perhaps to appear more like his fellows. She had dealt with this before.

"I am aware that on several previous occasions I merely offered to make you my paramour," he said quietly, taking her hand. "Now . . . I wish to make you my wife."

Sophie stared at him, speechless for several seconds.

"Your *wife*?" she gasped at length. "Why, that's preposterous!"

"Why, preposterous?" he answered sharply. "I am an earl, with sizable estates. I sit in the House of Lords. I am not *unknown* to possess some wit. I as good as have an interest in this theater! I may soon *own* this establishment, if certain other managers aren't careful! I—"

"'Tis not a preposterous proposal because of *you*," she interjected quickly. "'Tis preposterous because of *me* . . ."

"You think it absurd that an earl should offer for the hand of a publisher's daughter?"

"A mere bookseller, m'lord," Sophie corrected him. "No . . . that's not the reason either." Judging it prudent to leave his dignity intact, she added formally, "I am honored that you should consider me a suitable choice for a bride, m'lord."

"*Roderick* . . . please," he murmured. "We were once friends, Sophie, you'll remember . . ."

"Aye, Roderick," she amended.

She gazed at him across the gloomy theater box, reminding herself of the times they had greatly enjoyed each others' company, especially during the early weeks of their sojourn to his homeland. Perhaps, now that he had assumed the earldom, his family was increasingly anxious that he should marry and sire an heir. With Hunter conveniently in prison, was Darnly turning to her, a proven breeder, as the least objectionable candidate?

"Roderick," she repeated gently, "there are several reasons why I fear I cannot marry you."

"Certainly we can wed!"

"No, we cannot . . . because I am *already* married."

"Peter is *dead*," Lord Darnly said flatly.

Sophie studied him closely. His demeanor revealed not a shred of compassion for his former companion.

"That is correct . . . Peter Lindsay is dead," she echoed. "Therefore, I was free to marry and, during your absence, I did."

"*Married?*" Darnly exclaimed, stunned. "How could you be married and I not *know* of it?"

"Because 'twas a private matter between Hunter Robertson and me," she replied, standing to depart.

"You married that scoundrel, Robertson?" he exploded. "But he's in prison!"

"That's where I married him," Sophie retorted. "I obtained a special license and the rector from St. Paul's was persuaded to perform the ceremony in Newgate in front of four witnesses, thanks to the assistance of certain influential people," she pronounced.

An eerie silence filled the empty auditorium. The house servants had performed their tasks and departed. Near darkness enveloped the hall. A single taper burning inside its glass lamp attached to a nearby wall illuminated the earl's face. Roderick's eyes narrowed with barely contained fury.

"Why you little gutter slut!" he exclaimed scathingly. "You scribbling little strumpet! You—"

The earl seemed paralyzed by this sudden rush of ire. Sophie stared, astonished that his apparent show of tenderness should be transformed so swiftly into seething rage. He glared at her, speechless. But Sophie finally found her tongue.

"'Tis most curious, m'lord," she countered in a low voice, "that in one breath you claim your greatest desire is to put your bachelor ways behind you and make me your countess—and in the next, you call me a whore!" Slinging her cloak about her shoulders, she lashed out, "Since first I met you long ago in Bath, I've always thought there was something secretive . . . something odd . . . And after your brother's death—" She brought herself up short as he glowered at her within the close confines of David Garrick's theater box. "May I assume from the tenor of our present conversation that your offer of marriage is summarily withdrawn?" she inquired acidly.

"Yes!" hissed the Earl of Llewelyn.

"Then, m'lord"—she flung the words at him—"I bid you good night."

Chapter 37

The following morning, Sophie left Rory busily setting type for a tradesman's card and called at Newgate jail as soon as the keeper's gate was unlocked. Ignoring her unnerving encounter with the Earl of Llewelyn, she thought to cheer her new husband with news of another packed house and word that Garrick was due in London this day and could perhaps pry her author's fees from Sheridan. She also wanted Hunter's advice on measures to take, now that Hannah More had learned the identity of Sydney Ganwick.

"Sorry, but I have my orders," the warden announced gruffly. "No visitors."

"But I have a right to see my husband!" Sophie protested.

"Husband is it? I'm told the magistrates are looking into that, miss."

"Ask the turnkey!" Sophie cried. "He stood witness. The rector of St. Paul's performed the service. We're as *married* as any two people could be!"

"Says here you and Robertson cuckolded one Peter Lindsay," the jail keeper noted, reading from a sheet of parchment on his desk. "We can't be aiding and abetting adultery, miss."

"You aid and abet adultery every day of the week, bringing whores in here," she exploded, "and turn a fine profit doing it!"

"Watch that Scottish temper of yours, missy," the keeper

said menacingly, "or I'll have you arrested for disturbing the peace!"

※

Sophie was in a frenzy of worry by the time she rounded the corner near Number 5 Adelphi Terrace. A coach and four was just pulling up in front of Garrick's house. The driver and a footman leapt down and attempted to assist a stooped figure emerging from the carriage. Nearby, Mrs. Garrick and Hannah More fluttered around the invalid to no real purpose.

"Oh, Sophie . . . it took us all night to travel from Althorp. Every bump in the road was agony for him. He's terribly ill. We must send for the doctor," Eva-Maria declared distractedly.

David Garrick raised his head, his features ravaged with pain. Sophie tried to smile encouragingly.

"So glad you're back," she said soothingly, her own troubles forgotten for the moment. "Here . . . Hannah . . . let us go ahead and prepare his chamber . . ." She directed the butler, who had just appeared, to fetch the physician.

Garrick's manservant prepared him for bed while the women sat vigil downstairs sipping the strong tea Sophie had ordered the housekeeper to brew. Mercifully, the doctor soon arrived and was shown upstairs. Within a quarter hour, he entered the sitting room. Eva-Maria jumped up from her chair, wringing her hands in anticipation of the worst.

"He has a high fever and pain. I fear the gallbladder may have ruptured . . ." the doctor began.

"What will happen now?" Mrs. Garrick asked anxiously.

The doctor shook his head sadly.

"His pulse grows weaker and . . . there's very little we can do, dear lady," the physician said gently. "We shall administer more laudanum if the pain becomes too—"

Mrs. Garrick began to cry softly and Hannah was quick to put an arm around her, easing her back into a chair.

"Which of you is Sophie?" the doctor inquired.

"I-I am," Sophie faltered.

"He was asking for you."

Sophie glanced uncertainly at Mrs. Garrick, who urged

her to proceed upstairs. She entered the darkened bedchamber on the second floor where David Garrick lay as still as a corpse in the large canopied bed that reminded Sophie of the others in which the celebrated actor had played dramatic death scenes.

"You had come to see me?" Garrick said, barely above a whisper. His skin had taken on a deep, yellow hue.

"That's not important now," Sophie replied, swallowing a lump in her throat.

"Tell me why you've come," he commanded, looking at her strangely.

"I've suddenly been forbidden entrance to Newgate . . . the jailor claims the authorities are looking into the legality of my marriage to Hunter," she said, the horror of her own situation sweeping over her with full force. "I fear it may be Darnly's doing . . . he asked for my hand last night and was enraged at hearing—"

"Find me quill and paper," Garrick said hoarsely. "We must put an end to this incessant meddling by Roderick Darnly . . . over there . . . by the window . . . on the desk."

Sophie sprang to do his bidding. With supreme effort, he dictated to her a short letter asking Sheridan that all fees earned by Sydney Ganwick to date be committed to the care of Sophie McGann forthwith and forever from this date.

"Another . . . we must write another," he croaked.

"Oh, sir . . . are you certain you're able—"

"Quickly, my girl!" he snapped with a modicum of his former authority. "To the Honorable Lord Mansfield, King's Bench," he began, and then dictated a missive that recounted the recent, unhappy demise of the bogus baronet, Peter Lindsay. Garrick charged that from the beginning, the suit for Criminal Conversation had been instigated at the behest of the Earl of Llewelyn, both to satisfy a debt owed him by Lindsay and to seek revenge on Hunter Robertson for having proven the nobleman a cheat in the matter of finances at Sadler's Wells. Garrick's last paragraph to the judge attested to Hunter's good character and urged in the strongest possible terms that the defendant be released, paying only a token fine of ten pounds or so for the court's trouble.

"Here," he said, gasping for breath. "I must sign both letters. Ask Hannah to see the one addressed to Lord Mansfield is delivered by my servant, or he might think it a forgery."

Tears obscured Sophie's vision as she extended the papers and quill to the invalid who scrawled "D. Garrick" across the bottom of each page.

"Now," he directed weakly, "go into my study next door and select one of the finest Shakespeares . . . a morocco leather-bound edition, if you can find one."

Sophie quickly retreated to the adjacent chamber and did as she was ordered.

"Edward Capell is not a man I would consider an amiable friend any longer, but I admire his restoration of Shakespeare's texts," Garrick said, breathing with difficulty. "We have had many interests in common over the years, and perhaps if . . . here . . . let me write on the flyleaf . . ."

Sophie opened the book, holding it steady while Garrick scratched something with his quill.

" 'With all my admiration, D. Garrick,' " Sophie read in a breath.

"This is really for you. Give it to Capell *only* if you must and say . . . 'tis my last wish to see *School for Fools* continue." Garrick's face suddenly contorted with pain. "Oh, God!" he cried out suddenly. "Oh . . . please . . . *please*, Sophie! Fetch me something for the pain . . . Ohh!" he groaned.

Sophie ran to the landing and was about to call for help when Hannah More, together with the doctor and Mrs. Garrick, appeared at the bottom of the staircase, drawn by the sound of David's cries.

"He's in great distress!" Sophie rasped.

"You've exhausted him!" Hannah snapped, brushing past.

Stricken by her censure, Sophie exchanged glances with Eva-Maria.

"He's so very fond of you both," she murmured, gently squeezing her hand. "I must not leave him again."

The door shut and Sophie was left standing alone at the top of the landing clutching a copy of *The Tempest* and the two letters that she had taken down in dictation. Shaken, she grasped the banister and slowly made her way downstairs, feeling as if her heart were made out of lead. She waited several minutes in the sitting room, and when no one returned, she prepared to depart the silent house.

"I pray forgiveness for my shortness of temper," Hannah declared, entering the chamber suddenly as Sophie was donning her cloak. "But he is very bad."

"I know . . ." Sophie said, mortified by the tears running freely down her face. She fumbled to extract the letter to Lord Mansfield from the other items clutched in her hand. "He asked that you should send his liveried servant to deliver this to Lord Mansfield at King's Bench immediately."

"And the book?" Hannah inquired sharply, her gaze fastening on the burgundy and gold binding.

"A gift . . ." Sophie replied, certain that such generosity did not please Garrick's ubiquitous houseguest.

For an instant, Sophie took pleasure at Hannah's look of envy as she tucked the precious volume beneath her cloak. But then she was ashamed, recalling her own discomfort when her rival had been given the honored placed next to Garrick in the Greenroom when their mentor announced his retirement to his loyal company.

Thou shalt not covet!

She could almost hear the clerics of St. Giles thundering from the pulpit. Well, they were correct in such admonitions, Sophie thought ruefully. Envy was truly a despicable emotion. It made life miserable for everyone concerned and she hated it when she saw it in herself. Hadn't envy been the root of much of Roderick Darnly's unhappiness within his family circle? Suddenly, she wished to make amends. Impulsively, she reached out and seized Hannah's hand.

"I know how difficult all this must be for you," she said tentatively. "You've been a great source of strength to everyone. Please give my love to Eva-Maria . . ." she added, backing out of the sitting room.

"I will tell Mrs. Garrick of your concern," Hannah said briskly. "Good day."

Sophie set off at a dead run down the few short blocks to Drury Lane and sought out Sheridan.

"He's dying," she announced with an anguished cry, shutting the door to the manager's office behind her. Richard Brinsley Sheridan was seated at the desk where Garrick and Sophie had held so many conferences. As she took her customary chair facing the bookshelves crammed with playscripts, the full impact of the tragedy unfolding at Adelphi Terrace overwhelmed her and she began to sob. When her tears finally subsided, she gratefully accepted Richard's handkerchief and dabbed her eyes. "And something else . . . he wrote this to you, barely a half hour ago," she added, handing him the letter requesting Sheridan to release all of author Sydney Ganwick's fees to her.

"Were you his mistress or his favorite scribe?" Sheridan inquired calmly, studying the letter from Garrick.

Stung by his accusation, she blurted, "A *dramatist*, of course! He adores Eva-Maria!"

"Ah-ha! So *you* were Sydney Ganwick all along! Darnly had his suspicions, he said, but I honestly believed it was Garrick himself! By God, girl . . . you're *good*! But if Edward Capell ever discovers Sydney Ganwick is a woman, he'll scream like a banshee!"

"Well, you're *not* going to tell him, are you?" Sophie demanded, angrily brushing the tears from her eyes, "or anyone else, for that matter. Especially not now, when I— when so much is in a tumult," she finished lamely, thinking how dangerous it would be for her if Dr. Monro—to say nothing of Darnly—should confirm the true identity of the author of *School for Fools.*

"Never fear . . . I won't reveal your secret," Richard assured her, amused by it all. But Sophie wondered if a man of such a gregarious nature could resist dispensing this intriguing gossip.

"I'm afraid I must now request my fees . . ." she said, taking a deep breath to steady her nerves.

"Well . . ." Richard replied, eyeing her appraisingly, "I suppose with such a champion as David Garrick, I'd better pay his protégé, eh, Sophie?" He retreated into the Treasure Room and brought out a strong box. "Four author's night benefits thus far, comes to . . . let's see . . . four hundred and twenty-two pounds. God's Bones! Haven't paid *that* much blunt to a *woman* in ages!" he teased.

"And seven pounds for the playbills you owe me in arrears!" she retorted, declining to laugh at his jest.

Sheridan cast her a pained look and counted out the money—£429. Within the hour, the cash was secreted behind a panel in Aunt Harriet's old trunk.

Within a few days, all of Covent Garden knew that David Garrick had slipped into a coma, and soon a vigil began among the legions of friends and theater folk to whom he was, indeed, a kind of God.

On the evening of Tuesday, January 19, *School for Fools* was scheduled to be paired with *The Merchant of Venice*. To date, Sophie had no idea whether Hannah More had forwarded Garrick's letter to Lord Mansfield. Adding to her despair, the jail keeper had once again refused her admittance to Newgate.

By the time Drury Lane had opened its doors at five thirty, Sophie was beside herself with anxiety on all counts. She couldn't bear to sit in the Garricks' theater box as David lay dying less than half a mile away at Adelphi Terrace. Thus she remained in the Greenroom. During the orchestra's interlude, she wandered aimlessly among the wings with Lorna Blount. In an attempt to raise her spirits, she peered through the peephole at the packed theater.

"Oh *no*!" she wailed.

"What is it?" Lorna asked with alarm.

"Capell . . . sitting in the box on the left! He's got a manuscript in his lap! And Dr. Monro is sitting *next* to him."

"Bloody hell! Let me see," Lorna replied, elbowing Sophie out of her way to gain a clear view through the peephole. "Jesu! Dr. Monro . . . What's *he* doing here, do you suppose?"

"I can only guess," Sophie said grimly.

Throughout the performance of *School for Fools,* Sophie tortured herself by keeping an unwavering eye on Capell. The Deputy Examiner of Plays sat poised, pen in hand, waiting to pounce on the smallest deviation from the text he had approved. There were four times when Sophie saw him scribble something on the manuscript resting in his lap. Occasionally he was nudged in the elbow by Dr. Monro, who stared at the stage, stone-faced. By the time the final curtain closed, Sophie was faint with apprehension.

The audience was still clapping when Edward Capell stormed backstage and demanded in a strident voice that he wished to see the managers. Dr. Monro was nowhere in sight.

"You are up to your old tricks, Sheridan!" he said, lips pursed as he strode imperiously into the Greenroom.

"Gods wounds, Capell," Sheridan said genially. "I defy you to find two lines that have been altered since opening night."

"That's exactly the problem!" he snapped. "Two lines *have* been altered."

"And you are going to close us down over that?" Sheridan said incredulously.

"The actors have added stage business that wasn't present in the stage directions noted by the author," Capell said defensively. "Bannister renders the asylum director a fool, with all his facial tics and grimaces."

"Aren't you the Deputy *Examiner* of Plays?" Sheridan asked pointedly. "Didn't you *examine* this work line by line? What in the *written text* can you find fault with, besides those two lines to which you object and which we agree to cut forthwith?"

Capell's lips compressed in a thin, tight line. His hands, which clasped Sophie's manuscript, shook perceptibly.

"I have received information that Sydney Ganwick may be the pseudonym of a *female* scribe," he spat. "I am much displeased to have been deceived in this for so long!"

"I can't imagine what would have led you to that conclusion," Sheridan said blandly. "For years, most have believed Sydney Ganwick to be the pen name of some nobleman who fears the notoriety that sometimes comes with fame. 'Tis even been whispered that Lord Darnly, over there, might be he." The Earl of Llewelyn, who had slipped quietly into the Greenroom, shot a poisonous glance at Sheridan. "As I've said, I suspect 'tis Garrick himself who writes as Sydney Ganwick for amusement. Even so, I don't know of any law that says 'tis *forbidden* that a woman should use a pen to earn her pin money."

"Perhaps no law, but *custom* finds it most distasteful," Capell retorted.

"When you present proof of law breaking, good sir," Sheridan shrugged, "then I shall have a care. But for now, our playhouse is well patronized and there seems little disapproval from other quarters regarding our Mr. Ganwick's efforts. And now, if you'll excuse me—"

"I *demand* you identify Sydney Ganwick on pain of perjury!" Capell shrieked, refusing to be dismissed so ignominiously. "If not, I shall seek a summons for such intelligence sworn out in the name of the king!"

"I have a bona fide license to present this play!" Sheridan protested. "Signed by your hand!"

"I *rescind* it!" Capell shouted. "And I shall give you until tomorrow to reveal the true identity of Sydney Ganwick. If you do not, I have every assurance my informant will give me the name and a catalog of her transgressions against the law. And, in addition, sir," Capell continued, his voice shaking with anger, "there is a gentleman who finds certain characterizations in this work libelous in the extreme. No doubt, you shall be hearing from him as well!" He glared menacingly at the manager. "You, Mr. Sheridan, shall be *added* to this warrant for obstructing the office of the Lord Chamberlain if you do not reveal the true name of this odious Sydney Ganwick. Good night!"

Sheridan stared at the retreating back of Edward Capell, a look of astonishment and concern playing across his features. Sophie could almost see the calculations of lost revenues whirling in his brain, not to mention the cost of defending a personal lawsuit.

"You *mustn't* reveal I am Sydney Ganwick!" Sophie pleaded a few minutes later behind closed doors in Sheridan's upstairs chambers.

"What can I do, Sophie?" Sheridan replied worriedly. "Jeopardize the entire playhouse over this? Frankly, I cannot afford to."

"I will pay the losses if you must close down a day or two . . . just, pray, *don't* reveal my identity," she begged.

"Will you put that in writing?" he asked sharply.

"Hand me your quill," she replied.

"Capell's fury is hard to fathom," he said, shaking his head in disbelief as he tucked Sophie's pledge in his coat pocket. "And he claims to champion someone who finds the play libelous . . . why does not the person step forth himself?"

"I'll wager Capell's angry with himself for being fooled for so many years by a mere woman writer he thought was a man," she speculated. "As an expert in comparing bogus and genuine Shakespeare texts, he fancied he could tell the difference. And as for the person claiming libel . . ." Sophie shrugged, affecting a nonchalance she certainly didn't feel, "'tis probably all bluster."

Bidding Sheridan a somber farewell, she slipped out the stage entrance and made her way to Adelphi Terrace. Despite the late hour, candles glowed in every window. The vigil continued.

"I think it best if Mrs. Garrick not have any more visitors," Hannah More said crisply when the footman informed her that Miss McGann had called to receive word of Garrick's condition. "I'm sure you understand her wish for privacy at this time."

"*Your* wish, I'll wager," Sophie muttered, wondering for the hundredth time if the schoolmistress from Bristol had ever forwarded Garrick's letter to Lord Mansfield asking for Hunter's release.

"I'm only doing what I think best," Hannah replied defensively. "You've just come from the theater? How goes your play? Did it continue to find favor tonight?"

"How curious you should ask . . . at *this* particular moment!" Sophie retorted to the woman she deemed her fiercest competitor for the Garricks' affections. "Did you forward that letter to King's Bench, as requested?" she blurted angrily. "And have you tattled to anyone that *I* am Sydney Ganwick?"

Hannah stared at her blankly, obviously rattled by the rancor underlying the visitor's inquisition. During the awkward moment that ensued, Sophie gathered her cloak more tightly around her shoulders and simply turned on her heel and fled.

Speeding toward Half Moon Passage across the frigid darkness shrouding the Great Piazza, she could only rail silently against the insensitivity of Hannah More and the injustice of Edward Capell.

Now, the question was, who had told the woman-hating censor that Sydney Ganwick was a female—and who wanted her silenced?

The loud battering on Sophie's door the following morning roused her before she was fully awake. Her heart pounded as she stumbled toward the threshold. Fumbling to unfasten the latch, she could hear a woman's voice urgently calling her name. Lorna Blount, looking distraught, faced her on the landing.

"Oh, Sophie," Lorna whispered hoarsely, ". . . 'tis happened. Garrick has died."

"When?" Sophie breathed, clinging to the door for support.

"Early this morning. The funeral's to be a grand affair at Westminster Abbey on February first. Sheridan's taken charge."

But Sophie was hardly listening. She turned and slumped against Aunt Harriet's trunk at the bottom of her rumpled bedstead. Garrick *gone!* All night long, as she tossed in her bed, she had been acutely aware that the end would come soon. Now that it had, the loss was nonetheless devastating.

"And I'm afraid I have more bad news," Lorna said with trepidation. "There are rumors everywhere that an arrest warrant for libel has been issued for the author of *School for Fools.*"

"*Why?*" Sophie gasped, sensing that storm clouds were gathering on every front.

"No one knows for certain," Lorna said, closing the door behind her. "Sheridan's already notified the Lord Chamberlain's office he will not present the play again. Drury Lane will be closed tonight in honor of Garrick's passing, so that should save him a fine. But Sophie," Lorna added slowly, "gossips are saying 'tis Dr. Monro of Bedlam who claims to have been libeled by your play."

Sophie paced the gloomy chamber. "If Capell cannot legally threaten me beyond ordering cuts on a play he unwittingly approved, perhaps Monro *can*? Is that it?"

Lorna nodded sympathetically. "If somehow Capell learned of your identity and passed that information on to Dr. Monro . . . both men would have their satisfaction."

Suddenly, another sharp knock at Sophie's door rent the air. Both women froze. Then, with lightning speed, Sophie scrambled inside Aunt Harriet's trunk and pulled down the lid.

"Where is Sophie?" Mrs. Phillips demanded as soon as Lorna had cracked open the door. "Bob Derry tells me someone was asking questions about her at his Cider House late last night . . . wanting to know if Miss McGann still dwelled next to the Green Canister. What's ado? She's not in trouble, is she? The poor lass has had more than her share of woes . . ."

"Aye, Mrs. Phillips . . . I *am* in a bit of a fix," Sophie said, poking her head out of the trunk.

"God's eyeballs, lass!" Mrs. Phillips exclaimed. "Whatever are you crouched in there for?"

"There may be a libel warrant issued for my arrest. We hear the director of Bedlam's displeased with *School for Fools* and there are rumors circulating that I wrote as Sydney Ganwick."

"You do find the devil's own mischief, m'girl," Mrs. Phillips replied, shaking her mobcap. She peered around the room until her eyes fastened on Rory's little cot where the lad was sleeping peacefully. "Lorna," the older woman said emphatically, "take Rory to your lodgings for a few days. We can make Sophie a pallet in my back storeroom. Perhaps if the authorities think you've fled, 'twill blow by quickly."

Sophie hesitated, then nodded her agreement to the plan.

She had no alternative but to accept her neighbor's protection. With a heavy heart, she gently woke her son and sent him on his way.

As a precaution, Sophie spent the next fortnight shut up in the Green Canister's storeroom among the vials of mercury, oils and essences, washballs, potions, pills, and the packets of sheepskin condoms manufactured in France. Just outside the large cupboard where Sophie had fashioned a makeshift bed stood Aunt Harriet's leather-bound trunk packed with Sophie's belongings: her manuscripts, quills and half-empty ink pots, a few items of clothing, several books—including Garrick's inscribed copy of *The Tempest*—and Rory's playthings. Beneath this pile was hidden a pouch with nearly five hundred pounds in gold and silver coins, most of it thanks to the largesse produced by the successful run of *School for Fools.*

As each day passed uneventfully, she grew more hopeful that the rumors of Sydney Ganwick's imminent arrest had been exaggerated. Mrs. Phillips told her that Mary Ann Skene had never returned to her shared lodgings on the morning of Garrick's death, and Sophie was grateful, for it avoided the necessity of explaining to the strumpet why she, her son, and their belongings had suddenly disappeared.

"Mary Ann must at last have found a more permanent patron," Sophie remarked to Mrs. Phillips when the apothecary closed the shop one afternoon to partake of their midday meal.

"With *that* face?" Mrs. Phillips retorted scornfully. "He must be a wealthy blind man."

Suddenly, a loud pounding on the door at the front of the Green Canister echoed through the shop. Mrs. Phillips ran to the threshold that provided a view out the window facing the road.

"Quickly! Hide in the cupboard!" she cried, her ample bosom heaving with anxiety as she trundled back into the storeroom. "They've just gone up the outside stairway . . . probably searching your chambers!"

"Who?" Sophie exclaimed.

"Kings Guards, from the look of it! Get in here! *Hurry!*"

Sophie wedged herself into a corner of a small storage cupboard and pulled a length of linen over her head. Mrs. Phillips swiftly shut the door and retreated to the front of her establishment. Sophie could faintly discern the sound of furniture being moved overhead. The guards were evidently making a thorough search of her lodgings. After a half hour or so, she could hear the tread of heavy boots descending the steps that separated the staymaker's shop from the Green Canister. Then: silence.

"They've gone," a voice said ten minutes later.

The wooden boxes were hauled to one side and the cupboard door was opened. Sophie smiled gamely at Mrs. Phillips who had been joined by Lorna, the latter having arrived in the midst of the excitement taking place next door.

"They assume you've fled," Mrs. Phillips said, mopping her brow. The older woman was clearly shaken by her encounter with the King's officers. "The guardsmen eyed me all suspicious-like when I told 'em you'd left with your trunk and belongings a fortnight ago. They'll be watching the shop, to be sure," she added.

"Pray, where is Rory?" Sophie asked Lorna anxiously.

"Helping the man with the performing monkey in the Piazza," Lorna soothed. "I left him happy as a lark. I feared bringing him here in case the guards were still posted across the road . . ."

"How right you were," Sophie smiled nervously.

"Well, I suppose you won't need this," her friend sighed, handing Sophie a black-bordered card. The missive was an engraved invitation to Garrick's funeral, February first. "This was delivered, care of Drury Lane. Few women are allowed to attend tomorrow," she informed them, "and the actresses who didn't receive invitations are up in arms."

"Will Mrs. Garrick be there?" Sophie asked in a somber voice, a sense of bereavement sweeping over her anew.

"They say she's prostrate with grief. Hannah More and a few favorites have been granted permission by the Dean of Westminster to watch from a secluded gallery in Poet's Corner immediately above the grave," Lorna reported as Sophie read a note that accompanied her invitation.

"This says I'm invited to join Hannah and Lady Spencer in the second-story gallery," Sophie exclaimed, staring at the missive signed by Hannah herself.

"The procession will start from Adelphi Terrace," Lorna explained, "and will proceed the four miles to Westminster Abbey. From everything I've heard, 'tis to be a grandiose affair, with Sheridan playing chief mourner, accompanied by fourteen pages. A production worthy of an opening night at Drury Lane," she added with a tinge of sarcasm.

"What part is assigned to Lord Darnly in this gloomy pageant?" Sophie asked, wondering if she dared execute a plan that had just sprung to mind.

"Oh, he's in the thick of the preparations, to be sure," Lorna replied scornfully. "How can they ignore him? Young Lacy confided in me the other day that the earl had enticed him and his father to take on a mountain of debt with some scheme to discover a fortune of coal on their estate in Isleworth. The man holds mortgages on so many of their Drury Lane shares, he might as well be the Patentee himself!"

The following day, Mrs. Phillips stood in her storeroom among the boxes of apothecary supplies, pleading with Sophie not to attend Garrick's funeral.

"'Tis bloody folly for you to go!" Mrs. Phillips pleaded. "There's no one to save you this time, if you get caught!"

"I *must* go," Sophie replied. "I owe him this, at least."

There was no way she could express to this plainspoken woman the enormous debt of gratitude she felt toward David Garrick. From the very first, he had believed in her ability as a dramatist and had spared no effort to bring her talents to the stage. Recalling, suddenly, the lonely field outside Edinburgh where she'd laid her father in unhallowed ground, she was more determined than ever to bid a proper farewell to the man who had proven such a steadfast friend.

"Someone's bound to catch you out!" she exclaimed.

"They'll never recognize me," Sophie said as she stepped into a pair of breeches, part of an elegant satin page's uniform that Lorna, in her customary fashion, had spirited out of the Drury Lane wardrobe chamber late the previous night. "Everyone thinks I've fled London. Sheridan's clothed the attendants accompanying the funeral cortege in these same costumes from last year's Christmas panto-mime!" She pulled on the crimson cuffed coat and adjusted the ruffles at her cuffs. "Here, help me adjust this periwig."

"Well, pray, do sit in the gallery—away from the crowds," Mrs. Phillips urged, absently adjusting the hairpiece and centering the lace attached to the collar of Sophie's linen shirt.

"I think it may be safer simply to remain with the other pages," Sophie replied, tucking into an inside pocket the engraved invitation with Hannah's accompanying note requesting her to sit beside her. She threw her arms around Mrs. Phillips ample girth. "But when I return, I shall make plans for removing myself—not to mention sparing you, dear friend, from the danger of my discovery. Perhaps I'll repair to Bath, as I did once before!" She grinned wickedly, eager to escape her storeroom prison and see the London sky once more.

Poor Hunter, she thought with a sharp pang of longing. How ghastly these last two and a half years must have been for him, locked up in Newgate. And now, if she and Rory were compelled to flee to Bath, or if the authorities should somehow discover her disguise . . .

Ducking out the storeroom's back door into the alley behind Half Moon Passage, Sophie forced herself not to think of the dangers that lay ahead.

Chapter 38

The roads near Westminster Abbey were jammed with on-lookers straining for a glimpse of the great man's cortege. The line of David Garrick's public mourners, plus a string of fifty carriages transporting the elite of both the nobility and the arts, stretched across the city for some four miles. Mounted troops kept a path open for the official procession and the assembled dignitaries funneled at a stately pace toward the entrance to the largest church in the kingdom.

The Garrick family coach, devoid of passengers, rolled in its place of honor past the crowds lining the road. The vehicle was flanked by pages clothed in precisely the attire selected by Lorna for Sophie's disguise. Behind the empty carriage was the hearse containing Garrick's body, lying in a casket covered with crimson velvet. Mounted horsemen followed, garbed head to foot in black livery, and behind them were scores more coaches carrying the principal actors from both royal theaters, led by London's literary lions Richard Sheridan, Edmund Burke, and Samuel Johnson. How strange, Sophie thought, that Dr. Johnson appeared so distraught by Garrick's death when he had once withheld support from his friend's efforts to celebrate the Shakespeare Jubilee in Stratford. As for Dr. Johnson's shadow, James Boswell, Sophie had heard he was home in Scotland.

Many disjointed memories of her nearly two decades in London replayed themselves in Sophie's mind as she slipped into line with her fellow pages marching alongside Garrick's carriage.

Can it be possible I'll be thirty-five years old next year? she mused. The astounding realization startled her as the cortege drew in front of the double-towered Abbey. Her eyes returned to Garrick's casket, which was now being lifted from the hearse by a group of distinguished pallbearers: a duke, two earls, a viscount, and several legends of the theater.

The Abbey's carillon began to toll dolefully, echoing the church bells now ringing the melancholy tidings throughout the city. With every chime, the lump in her throat seemed to grow larger. Blinking back her tears, she continued in line with similarly clad companions who mounted the steps leading through the arched doors into the cathedral.

A one-eyed beggar crouching near the entrance suddenly extended a wooden alms bowl in brazen fashion toward Sophie's chest.

"A penny sir!" he rasped. "Just a penny!"

"Be gone with you!" Sophie snapped, realizing too late that she had forgotten to lower her voice to a masculine growl.

The ragged street dweller peered at her with both his good eye and the pulpy mass where his other orb had once been.

Ignoring the poor wretch, she quickly made her way past the west entrance and into the nave amid the surging crowd.

Inside, the frigid air echoed with the shuffling footsteps of hundreds of guests moving toward the spot where Garrick would be interred beneath a granite slab. To Sophie's dismay, Roderick Darnly was one of the first dignitaries she spied as the pallbearers solemnly bore their burden toward the freshly dug grave in the Abbey floor. Accompanied by his ubiquitous hireling, Trevor Bedloe, the two men—one tall and imposing, the other slender and at least a foot shorter than his employer—headed through the throng in the direction of the notables' assigned seats. As Sophie took up her post among the line of pages flanking the site, she did her best to ignore the presence of the two men.

Sophie glanced at the ceiling capped by three dizzying

tiers of lacy stone arches that soared over her head. Purcell's grand funeral service, blending choir and organ, created a powerful dirge that echoed throughout the enormous church.

The mourners from Drury Lane huddled near an area dedicated to St. Edward, the Confessor. This group included Mr. Collins, the doorman, and Mr. Hopkins, the prompter who had allowed Sophie to serve as copyist for Kitty Clive. Next to them stood the men's wardrobe keeper, the boxkeepers, and the humblest stage servants—all there to mourn their departed leader.

David's brother, George, pale and trembling, was hastily provided a chair. Sophie thought the poor man looked near death himself. Politicians, artists, merchants, and noblemen jostled for position as the casket neared Poets' Corner where Great Britain's literary lights and artists were laid to rest in pomp and glory. Chaucer was buried here, along with Coleridge and Dryden. Oliver Goldsmith had joined them not many years ago, and now . . .

Blinking hard, Sophie glanced toward the rear of the Abbey. She thought she discerned Mavis Piggott and several other ladies of the stage outfitted in mannish attire. Their garments appeared suspiciously like the costumes worn by Joseph Surface, Sir Peter Teazle, and the other familiar fops peopling Sheridan's *The School for Scandal.*

Suddenly, Sophie's gaze was riveted on one of the few mourners dressed in female garb. There, partially hidden behind a pillar, stood a sumptuously gowned figure with a ripe, voluptuous body and an astonishingly homely face. The woman was clad in somber gray silk of the most luxurious quality and sported a hat decorated with gray and black plumes.

Mary Ann Skene, late of Half Moon Passage, was adorned as fashionably as if *she* were the grieving widow! Where on earth, Sophie marveled, could the habitué of back streets and London brothels have acquired such expensive finery in so short a time?

Puzzled, Sophie returned her gaze to the honored guests stationed near the grave site in Poets' Corner. She found herself staring at the self-satisfied visage of Roderick Darnly,

Earl of Llewelyn. Trevor Bedloe was consigned to an area near the choir stalls, awaiting his master's bidding. On the nobleman's left sat Sophie's nemesis, Edward Capell. And on Darnly's right, Dr. John Monro, the director of Bethlehem Hospital—the infamous Bedlam!

Sophie felt as if she might faint. Quickly, she averted her eyes from the trio as Garrick's coffin, borne by the eight elegant escorts recruited by Richard Sheridan, was gently placed next to the opening in the floor. Sheridan and Dr. Johnson stood forlornly at the foot of Shakespeare's monument, weeping openly, and above them, peering down from the Dean's gallery was Hannah More, her eyes brimming with tears.

The Bishop of Rochester began to intone prayers for David Garrick's dead soul.

I am the resurrection and the life, saith the Lord,
he that believeth in me, though he were dead,
yet shall live; and whosoever liveth and believeth
in me shall never die . . .

Sophie's eyes were inexorably drawn back to the figure of Roderick Darnly. Not twenty paces from where she stood, the Earl of Llewelyn was staring at her steadily, attracted, it appeared, by the sight of a lock of reddish brown hair that had escaped from her white periwig and was tickling her cheek. Self-consciously, she tucked away the telltale strand. Immediately, Roderick's scrutiny turned into a look of recognition. With glazed eyes, she watched him lean to his right and whisper to Dr. Monro, then to his left, to say something to Edward Capell. Slowly, he pointed a finger in her direction.

With a bolt of sudden insight, Sophie knew, at last, why Edward Capell had declared Sydney Ganwick to be a woman scribe, and why Dr. John Monro had recently learned that Sophie McGann *was* Sydney Ganwick, author of the scathing *School for Fools*!

The fashionably attired Mary Ann Skene!

Sophie felt her breath coming in ragged gulps. Christmas Day! Mary Ann must have scanned the draft of *School for*

Fools that Sophie had quickly transferred to a drawer when the harlot came home from her nightly labors, inquiring if her flat mate intended to visit Hunter in Newgate Prison later that day. For a price, no doubt, the chit had confirmed this worthwhile intelligence to Darnly.

What else had she told him? Sophie wondered, her heart beginning to thud in her chest. Mary Ann Skene had probably kept him apprised of her every move! And not just in recent months! What of the time, years ago, when Darnly himself had paid for Mary Ann to lodge with her?

Frantic thoughts whirled through Sophie's brain. Staring straight ahead at Garrick's crimson-covered coffin, she tried to steady herself and think clearly while the bishop and mourners began to recite the Twenty-Third Psalm.

A female Trojan Horse!

During the time the strumpet had lived under her roof, Sophie had experienced nothing but difficulties with the Lord Chamberlain's office! Mary Ann Skene, the slattern who appeared to sleep all day and practice harlotry at night, had been a paid *spy*! But *why*? Why would Lord Darnly have a care for the literary efforts of a writer of plays— woman or no woman? And who else had he enlisted over the years in his attempts to control her and her dramatic work? Mavis? Peter? Hannah More?

A sudden vision of Peter's bruised and battered countenance appeared before her eyes. Mary Ann had watched Sophie paint her face like a tart the evening she set out, dressed in a provocative gown, to attempt to locate her estranged husband. But Peter had died before Sophie could even implore him to tell Lord Mansfield the truth about being coerced by Darnly to sue Hunter.

Hit . . . our daughter . . . Peter had mumbled that terrible night as he lay dying in St. Paul's churchyard beside Danielle's grave. The authorities had assumed he'd struck his head on a granite marker nearby. Had something—or someone—attacked him?

Despite her best efforts to remain calm, Sophie began to tremble. Roderick Darnly continued to gaze at her like a serpent poised to strike. As Garrick's coffin was slowly lowered below the level of the chapel's floor, the bishop solemnly cast a clod of earth on its polished wooden lid.

> *In sure and certain hope of the resurrection to eternal life through our Lord Jesus Christ, we commend to Almighty God our brother, David, and we commit his body to the ground . . .*

Like a thunderclap, a more violent emotion subdued all others raging in Sophie's breast—that of pure, unadulterated *fear*. She suddenly bolted from the tidy honor guard of pages flanking Poets' Corner and quickly threaded her way through the throng. Begging pardon for banging elbows and stepping on toes, she slipped through a door behind the choir stalls and darted into the ancient cloisters where monks had once dwelled in the days before King Henry VIII severed his church from Roman authority.

She entered the chilly passageway and hurried toward what she hoped would be an exit from the grounds of the enormous cathedral. Her upper lip was laced with perspiration, despite the cold blast of February air sweeping through the opened arched windows on her right. Struggling for breath, she halted abruptly, confused by the labyrinth of passageways branching off in several directions. She whirled around and retraced her steps for several yards. Then, without warning, a hand grabbed her arm and spun her around. Assuming that one of the King's Guards had stepped from some hidden portico to apprehend her, Sophie stared, openmouthed, at the slender figure of Trevor Bedloe, who smiled at her with grim satisfaction.

"You're to wait right here, Miss McGann," he said in a low voice, his grip on her forearm surprisingly firm for a man of such slight physique.

"Let me go, villain!" Sophie exclaimed, attempting to free herself from his grasp.

"Ah . . . the celebrated *Sydney Ganwick*!" a familiar voice exclaimed as Lord Darnly rounded the corner. He, too, took hold of her arm, pulling her into a recessed area adjacent to the Chapel of the Pyx, a stone chamber that once stored royal treasure. "Thank you, Trevor," the earl said pleasantly, as Bedloe released his grip. "'Pon my word, don't you reckon Sophie, here, should have tidied her hair before playing a breeches part?" he mocked, pulling her white periwig off her head and tossing it aside.

"So, you've deduced who I was," Sophie retorted, breathing raggedly. "And that I was writing as Sydney Ganwick. 'Tis no cause for this ambush. Let go of my arm, please."

"I've suspected your little ruse for quite some time," Roderick said, tightening his grip. "However, 'twas most gratifying to have Mary Ann prove it to my satisfaction."

"And so you betrayed me to Edward Capell and Dr. Monro," she said quietly. "Pray . . . why? What could it possible gain you?"

"What I am so desirous of having," he smiled affably. "You . . . and your quill . . . and your silence. I'll wager you'll prefer answering to me, rather than to the authorities. I revealed your identity to my fellow club member, Edward, only recently, when he found he could do nothing legally to thwart such female impudence."

"Could that be the secretive club I've heard about where members don monks' robes and kill defenseless animals for their amusement?" Sophie inquired with a withering stare.

Darnly paused, grim-faced, and then apparently chose to ignore her remark.

"'Twas Capell himself who informed the good doctor that his complaints against *School for Fools* filed at the Lord Chamberlain's office had merit," he said icily. "How fitting that the scandal-mongering author of the play was, in truth, a former *inmate* of the institution." He gave her arm a warning squeeze. "Sophie, my dear, if you will simply agree to be my anonymous scribe as well as my wife, I will put an end to all this unpleasantness about seditious libel."

"Your *wife*!" she exclaimed, dumbfounded. "Why do you persist in this nonsense when you know perfectly well that my marriage to Hunter Robertson is legal," she exclaimed, her jaw clenched. "Even you can't change the official registry."

"Ah . . . but what if you . . . sadly . . . were widowed once again?" he asked coolly. "You've produced two

live births. Why not an heir to an earldom? 'Twould be ever
so convenient for me, don't you see?"

Sophie stared up at her erstwhile benefactor, as certain
truths began to dawn on her.

"W-wouldn't Mavis Piggott serve your purposes just as
well?" Sophie temporized, frantically seeking a means of escape back into the sanctuary where the sounds of Purcell's
music soared toward the Gothic arches overhead.

"The strumpet aborted a babe once, it appears, and can
no longer become enceinte. And she's not as able a playwright as you, I discovered," he laughed. "Furthermore, she
doesn't know me as well as you do, does she, Trevor?" he
added cryptically. There was no reply from the slender
young man who had apparently retired to the shadowy arch
several feet from where they stood. "No . . . Sophie, my
dear . . . I wish *you* to be my silent and obedient spouse
and my amanuensis. You are the perfect choice to carry my
child and to take my ideas for plays and give them form and
substance."

"For what purpose?" Sophie demanded, wondering silently if Roderick planned a *ménage à trois* in the wilds of
Wales in order to succeed in bringing forth the necessary
heir.

"For my amusement, profit, and renown," the earl replied mildly. "There's little about the life I was born to that
I do not find tedious in the extreme. And gambling at faro or
whist bores me rigid. But gambling in the *theater* . . . now
that is a capital sport!"

"If that is so," Sophie retorted, "why not employ your
own efforts at play writing? Why appropriate someone else's
work?"

"Why not?" Darnly shrugged. "'Tis so much more pleasant to gain influence and accolades without soiling one's fingers with ink. With your pen and my connections, we can
gain the patent from those buffoons and—"

"*We?*" Sophie scoffed. "My business dealings with you at
Sadler's Wells are all too fresh in my memory. I was in the
cupboard in Rosoman's Treasure Room, Roderick. I saw the
ledgers. You didn't think twice about cheating me of my
due!"

"If you have any sense, my dear, you would be grateful for what generosity I do extend," Lord Darnly retorted, ignoring this revelation. "I suggest you accept my proposal to be my resident playwright and avoid what could be a very dicey situation for you with the authorities."

"Ever the dilettante, never the drudge . . . is that it, m'lord?" Sophie observed scathingly.

"What do you mean?" he demanded, stung.

"Your ambitions extended beyond merely acquiring a few mortgages on theater shares, didn't they?" she said mockingly.

"My work has been accorded some worth!" he retorted.

"By *whom*?" she responded ruthlessly. "The members of your 'club' who applaud your little playlets? You and your ilk were bred to assume that someone else would do the work! Well, I can tell you this"—she glared at him—"art can only be evoked by *artists*. You've shown neither the talent nor the perseverance it requires to be a dramatist in the way that Garrick was a dramatist, or Sheridan or Goldsmith or Colman or—yes! —women like Aphra Behn, whom you so abhor!" she shouted, nearly out of breath.

"'Tis unlikely that you *female* scribblers will be remembered day after tomorrow!" he retorted.

"Not if men like you have anything to do with it!" Sophie replied furiously. "But *you*, Roderick . . . you are merely a charlatan, posing as a man of wit and sensibility! No one will know your name a hundred years from now either! Your entire existence, since the moment you had the misfortune to be born two minutes after your brother, Vaughn, has been one consisting of nothing but *envy*! It consumed you before your brother died . . . and has obsessed you ever since. You, my dear earl, have become a covetous scoundrel—and the worst kind of *fraud*!"

"And you, a rebellious, seditious, libelous, contumacious Scottish polecat!" Darnly replied, practically shouting. He pushed her against the crenelated stone wall, its sharp edges painfully pressing her spine. "In the beginning, I admired both your pluck and your plays, but you never seemed to appreciate what I had done for you."

"*Done* for me?" Sophie echoed, astounded. "What have

you *ever* done for me lately, other than attempt to control my life?"

"Once I'd begun to lend Lacy money for his coal mining schemes, secured by his Drury Lane shares, I enjoyed complete access to the theater's inner sanctums," Darnly noted more calmly. The hand pressing against her shoulder eased a bit, giving Sophie some hope of making a dash for the door that led back into the nave. "If I liked one of your plays, my dear, I used my influence with Capell to have it licensed."

"You persuaded Capell to license my work?" Sophie asked in a pained voice.

"Both as Sophie McGann and under your pseudonym, once I was fairly certain who Sydney Ganwick was," he chuckled. "'Twas great sport and I even showed a profit with my selections! Sometimes I actually bribed Edward . . . not with money, mind you . . . but with an invitation to dine here, a rare book there. . . . And when your work became tiresome, I employed the same tactics to have it squelched."

"*A Maid Most Modestly Made* . . ." Sophie murmured, recalling Capell's refusal to license her first adaptation of Aphra Behn's play. As she was reflecting on Darnly's latest revelation, she noticed that Trevor was maintaining his silence in the shadows. If she succeeded in escaping Darnly's clutches, could she also dart beyond Bedloe's grasp? She made a sudden move to free herself, only to feel Darnly's fingers dig deeper into her flesh.

"Oh, you proved just how clever you can be, didn't you?" Roderick growled. "You slipped *Strife for a Wife* past the censor after I'd gotten Capell to reject that earlier version. And, of course, when you said you had given up the quill, I believed you for a time . . . until you wrote *The Rattecatchers.*" He stared at her somberly. "Your depiction of Peter and my little peccadillos at our club were too true for the author to be anyone but you. So I mounted a claque and had it shouted down."

"And were you involved in the theft of *Parsimonious Parson*?" Sophie asked quietly, painfully remembering how she had accused Hunter and Mavis of such perfidy.

"Indirectly. I had Peter copy it and then submitted it to Covent Garden through an intermediary."

"Peter copied it?" Sophie repeated faintly.

"Right out of your desk drawer at Cleveland Row . . . his labors satisfied yet another of his gambling debts to me," Darnly replied with a malevolent smile, "and at the same time, granted me the entré into Covent Garden I desired. 'Twas capital fun to invest in competing plays and wager which might be the winner . . ."

"But Garrick understood full well your plot to pass yourself off as a nobleman-dramatist—*and* to garner shares through illegal mortgages," Sophie mused. "For years he did what he could to frustrate your efforts, didn't he?"

"Yes," replied Darnly. "But now he's dead."

"Aye . . ." Sophie said. "But aren't you concerned that there are those who know for certain how you've circumvented the law in a number of ways?"

For an instant, Darnly's gaze wavered. Then, he seemed to regain his confidence.

"Ah . . . but we can deal with that, can't we, Trevor?" he said over his shoulder. "You see . . . despite your cleverness and your marriage to that rogue, Robertson, you will soon accompany me to Wales. Once that cur becomes the victim of some tawdry skirmish with another knife-wielding inmate, I shall make you my countess and there you will spend the rest of your days. 'Twill all be so convenient, don't you see? You'll bear my child . . . write my plays . . . and keep my secrets."

"I can't imagine why you find me worthy of such an honor," she responded sarcastically, and immediately regretted her outburst. Darnly yanked on her arm even harder this time, pulling her roughly against his chest. "Are you certain you can stomach the conjugal duties of a husband, Roderick?"

"You thankless jade!" he spat, color staining his cheeks. "Your value now, despite what you or Trevor believe, is that —as my bride—you solve a number of problems."

Sophie wrestled with a feeling of rising panic.

"Problems?" she echoed, trying not to show the fear that had taken possession of her and set her knees to trembling.

"It sat most ill with me, my dear, that you spurned all my attempts to accomplish in a civilized manner what needed to be done. But no . . . you would not reside in the rooms I had designed for you in my London house. And then, you were determined to persuade that wastrel Peter Lindsay to turn evidence against me in the matter of his suit of Criminal Conversation." Darnly's eyes glittered with malice. "You were correct in your presumption that Lord Mansfield would find such overt manipulation, even by a peer of the realm, *distasteful*. I couldn't allow that to happen."

"So you murdered Peter to guarantee he'd not recant to the court!"

"*I?* Never!" Darnly exclaimed, looking at her disdainfully.

"You ordered it done, then," she said, her mouth going dry. She was acutely aware of the proximity of Trevor Bedloe—slender Trevor Bedloe. The assailant who had hit him in the head that Peter had tried to describe as he lay dying?

"As I said to you in Wales," Darnly responded in a low voice while declining to confirm or deny her accusations, "I believe we might have made a go of it in some fashion, you and I. You severely tried my patience when you married that Scottish rascal."

"Your *spy*, Mary Ann, knew nothing of the ceremony at Newgate . . ." Sophie recalled softly. "And you'd remained in your homeland for Christmas."

"Yes," Darnly replied. "I was quite provoked at her for a time. Then she brought me proof *after* Christmas day that you were, indeed, Sydney Ganwick, and she was given silks and satins as her reward." He continued to stare down at her with a measuring glance while tightening his grip on her arm once again. "You, too, could be rewarded, you know. Even now."

"W-what do you mean?" she stammered.

"If you give me an heir. If you never reveal to anyone what you saw in the hay byre the morning the mine caved in."

"The *hay byre*?" she choked, almost laughing with relief. "You knew I saw the three of you—"

"You see? She *knows*, Roddy!" Trevor burst out, suddenly emerging from the shadows. "The dogs woke me! I heard her open the barn door, I tell you! She was standing there, taking it all in." He looked beseechingly at Sophie's captor. "Jesu, don't wed the chit, man! At any moment she could ruin you! She could—"

"I promise you, Roderick, on my father's grave," Sophie interrupted fervently, ignoring Trevor, ". . . I couldn't care *less* what you and Trevor and that housemaid were doing in the hay byre!" She stared up at him, making a desperate attempt to petition the Roderick Darnly who had shown he was capable of kindness when little Danielle died. "I realize what a wretched family yours must have been . . . and how difficult it can be to be the second son. I, too, have some inkling how envy can rankle one's soul. Believe me, Roderick . . . your private life is *your* affair," she pleaded earnestly. "As Trevor says, surely there must be some other woman you could press into service to be your countess? In the name of the association we *have* shared all these years, I swear I would never gossip about you!"

"She *knows*, Roddy! She's too clever by half!" Trevor exclaimed shrilly. He plucked at his employer's sleeve and looked as if he were about to weep. "Don't be tricked by the tart! She mustn't escape! If you're too faint of heart to silence the strumpet, then I'll do it for you, as I did that sod Lindsay!"

"Stand back, Trevor!" Darnly growled.

"For God's sake, Roddy . . . what's she to you?" Trevor cried. "*Nothing!* She'll ruin us, I tell you! I've said from the first, get rid of her!"

Sophie stared at her captors, and with awful certainty, realized that these two men had previously weighed the risks and advantages of dispatching her in the same manner they had Peter Lindsay.

"Why do you hesitate?" Trevor demanded. "'Tis merely a matter of time till she uses what she knows against you. Why, we'd scarce brushed the coal dust from our skin that night when she found us—"

For a moment, the only sounds heard in the cloisters

were the high, sweet voices of the all-boy choir singing the "Te Deum" inside the cathedral.

"Oh, no . . ." Sophie whispered, locking glances with Trevor. Then her eyes slowly returned to Lord Darnly's face, which had frozen into an expressionless mask. His vicelike grip on her arm hurt excruciatingly. "Oh, dear God! The mine accident!" she gasped. "After the performance of my play . . . when the old earl banished you both from Evansmor. You two went to the mine that night, didn't you?"

"Yes," Darnly answered in a monotone. "We'd been in the library for hours after everyone left . . . drowning our sorrows with drink, of course. 'Twas Trevor's notion to loosen the timbers supporting the shaft. Eventually I agreed to the scheme. It seemed the only thing left to do. . . . Even Glynnis lent a hand . . ."

"And when your brother's mechanical pump began to pour out water the next morning, the walls caved in . . . ?" Sophie added faintly, shuddering at the memory of Roderick, tears bathing his cheeks, carrying the crushed body of his dead twin out of the mine. "Poor Vaughn! Oh, God, Roderick! He was your *brother*!" she wailed, shaking her head. "I *didn't* know! It never occurred to me—"

"Blast you, Trevor!" the earl swore, roused at last from his trancelike state. With his free hand, he gave his accomplice a violent shove. "You damned idiot—"

Suddenly, Sophie saw the misshapen figure of the hunchbacked one-eyed beggar who had pestered her at the entrance of the Abbey. The ragged creature was stealthily advancing toward Roderick and Trevor, whose backs were turned. Without warning, he lunged, and in one fluid gesture, hit the earl soundly on the back of the head with his stout wooden alms bowl. Roderick crumpled to the stone floor, his white, uncalloused fingers splayed against the paving stone at the spot where the worn, seventeenth-century engraving marked the unheralded resting place of the playwright Aphra Behn. Then, the filthy wretch whirled around and dispatched Trevor Bedloe in similar fashion with a right fist to the jaw.

"Alms, m'lady?" the beggar inquired, thrusting the bowl

under Sophie's nose. "A penny, at least, for a bloomin' rescue!"

Ignoring the ruffian's demands, Sophie bolted beyond his grasp and ran blindly down the passageway toward a patch of daylight that beckoned her at the end of the cloisters. Pounding footsteps reverberated behind her. Once more, a powerful hand gripped her arm, and she was spun around to face the hideous one-eyed beggar, his empty socket peering down at her.

Sophie screamed. The detestable brute clamped a grimy hand over her mouth and dragged her toward the end of the passageway that led into a courtyard where a coach was waiting. Its four horses snorted steam out of their flared nostrils in the chill February air. The beggar thrust open the door and shoved Sophie inside, leaping in beside her. The vehicle lurched forward, nearly tossing her into the lap of her repugnant abductor.

Sophie pulled herself into a sitting position. Her eyes followed the curve denoting the man's hunched back which protruded in an unsightly mound beneath his ragged coat. Repulsed, she reached for the coach door handle, but her gesture was instantly arrested by her fellow passenger.

"I beg of you! Let me out of this coach!" she panted. "I've plenty of troubles of my own, and now you've gone and crowned an *earl*!"

"Ye've troubles, to be sure," the beggar retorted, also attempting to catch his breath. "But did you *have* to insult Lord Darnly to such an extent?" he demanded. "No one enjoys being labeled a covetous scoundrel *and* a fraud!"

Sophie's jaw went slack and she stared with astonishment at the figure clothed in wretched rags who appeared to be the poorest beggar in Christendom.

"*Hunter?*" she gasped, dumbfounded by the sight of his disguise.

"Aye . . . so *now* you finally recognize me!" he exclaimed irritably. "I all but flung my arms around your shapely thighs to slow you down going into the Abbey . . . but *no* . . . you marched right past with the rest of those counterfeit pages!" He pulled at a sticky mass of paste that covered his right eye. "You never were much of an actress, you know," he chuckled. "I immediately recognized your voice, not to mention that strand of auburn hair peeping out from under your white wig . . ."

"Jesu . . . is it truly you?" she whispered, grasping his ragged arm and feeling faint with relief.

"Aye, my lady scribe," Hunter replied. "Garrick's letter to Lord Mansfield finally gained my release this morning without so much as a fine . . . *only* my promise to remain mute about the embarrassment of Darnly's extorting Peter Lindsay to file suit against me."

"So Hannah had Garrick's letter delivered, as promised," Sophie murmured, recalling the young woman's red-rimmed eyes staring down from the gallery at David's open grave.

"I am now a free man while you're a condemned woman, charged with libeling the benevolent Dr. Monro," Hunter declared. "There's only one remedy."

"An escape to Bath," Sophie replied, knowing that solution was, at best, risky. She was now privy to the secret that Trevor and Darnly had committed murder. They would try to silence her wherever in Britain she fled.

"My Lord Mansfield had another suggestion," Hunter replied.

"What?" Sophie asked anxiously.

"Leave the country. He's arranged passage on a privateer sailing within the week from Plymouth for the West Indies. He thinks 'tis a way of avoiding embarrassment to all concerned."

"The West Indies!" Sophie said, horrified. "What playhouses have they there?"

"'Tis as close as we can get to the Colonies until the *real* battle royal is finally decided. However, once peace is declared, I think we should head for Annapolis. I know it well and 'tis a city that appreciates its players and playhouses."

Sophie threw her arms around Hunter's filthy neck and held him close. Then she pulled away to look at him earnestly. "Are you absolutely *sure* you wish to leave everything here? You must be certain 'tis what you truly want, or I fear—"

"What *I* fear, darling girl, is remaining in London!" Hunter replied with alacrity. "Lord Mansfield released me from Newgate on the condition that you and I make ourselves scarce. Let us not forget, I've given Darnly a broken jaw, a blackened eye, and now, a good crack on his noggin," he added, tossing his alms bowl out the window, "I believe a swift exit is called for."

"Aye," she replied, suddenly starting to tremble as the full impact of Roderick and Trevor's revelations began to penetrate her consciousness. "The shorter chap you flattened with your fist killed Peter on Darnly's orders, I believe. And Roderick . . ." Sophie hesitated, feeling both revulsion and an overwhelming sense of pity for her sometimes-benefactor. "Roderick caused the mine accident that ultimately gained him the title of Earl of Llewelyn."

"Yes . . . I know," Hunter replied soberly. "Thank God I saw you dart out the door to the cloisters, followed by those two scoundrels. I bided my time behind a pillar and heard most of what transpired between you three."

"But there's not a shred of proof for any of it," Sophie sighed, "so, on *both* our accounts, 'tis probably best if we— Oh!" she exclaimed suddenly, entirely changing the subject. "What about Rory? And my trunk? I've more than four hundred pounds in it! We must go back to—"

"Look out the window, lass, and calm yourself!" Hunter laughed, pointing at familiar landmarks near the outskirts of the Covent Garden district. "Mrs. Phillips told me this morning that Rory was with Lorna. I sent word by messenger for her to bring the lad to the alley behind the Green Canister, along with your trunk."

Sophie sank against the coach's upholstered interior and sighed with relief. Then she cast Hunter a sideways glance.

"You *knew* I would be foolhardy enough to pay Garrick my last respects, did you not?"

"Say farewell to your champion? That I did," Hunter replied smugly. "I even guessed you'd dress like a man . . . but not like one of fourteen matched footmen!" His fingers tweaked an auburn curl from her disheveled coiffure. "Thank God, Mrs. Phillips could describe your disguise. So, off I went to Covent Garden's wardrobe chamber, assumed *my* disguise and—"

"Your wounded eye was ghastly," she interrupted. "I truly thought you were the filthiest of beggars."

"And when I heard you defend us theater folk to Darnly," he smiled, "I thought you truly the bravest, most loyal, wee lad I'd ever cast one good eye upon."

They rode along in silence, hand in hand.

"What a long journey we've made together," Sophie said, thinking wistfully of the first day she had ever laid eyes on Hunter Robertson when he'd flung gaily colored juggling pins high into the Edinburgh sky.

"Why, we're not old crones—yet," Hunter protested mockingly. "We've a long journey ahead of us, my lass."

The swaying carriage turned into the narrow alley known as Bedford Court. Sophie peered out the window, relieved to see Rory bundled up to his eyebrows in coat and muffler. He stood expectantly between Lorna and Mrs. Phillips. Aunt Harriet's leather trunk rested nearby on the icy cobblestones.

"Driver!" Hunter called up through the window to the coachman. "Pray, turn 'round the horses. We'll set off again directly."

"A guardsman is still posted in front of the Cider House," Mrs. Phillips said nervously, "and there's another at Maiden Lane."

"Oh, Sophie!" exclaimed Lorna, throwing her arms around her friend as she descended from the coach. "I was so worried!"

"So was I," Sophie agreed, bending down to kiss her son.

Rory, glancing first at her and then at Hunter, appeared bewildered by the sight of his parents' odd attire.

"A beggar and a boy!" the lad exclaimed, pointing at their absurd apparel.

"Your mother and I make a fine pair, do we not, laddie?" Hunter laughed, hugging his son with abandon and then flinging his arm around Sophie's shoulders, pulling her against his chest. With his other hand he drew her mouth close to his and kissed her slowly on the lips. "A playwright and a player," he murmured softly. "What a fine pair, indeed."

"You'd best be off, you three!" Mrs. Phillips declared, glancing uneasily at the door leading to her back storeroom.

Reluctantly, Sophie pulled away from her husband's embrace. Bending over her trunk, she opened its lid and retrieved several items, including a simple wool dress and her cloak.

"We can't have Lorna charged for the price of this costume," she smiled. "I'll just step inside and change."

"I've my clothes beneath this disguise," Hunter volunteered as he doffed his ragged garments, "but I'll need help ridding m'self of this hump."

The couple swiftly repaired to the storeroom, changing their attire with dispatch.

"Hunter?" Sophie said softly, pulling a fat pouch of coins and a leather-bound book from beneath the cloak she had draped over her arm. "I have two gifts for you . . ."

"Gifts?" he repeated.

"To celebrate your release from Newgate and this journey we're about to embark on together. 'Tis from David Garrick . . . and me."

Hunter first peered into the coin pouch and grinned. Then he slowly opened the book's morocco leather cover and gazed at the title page, scanning the inscription written in Garrick's own hand.

"*The Tempest . . .*" he said in a breath, his fingers tracing the bold letters printed many years before.

"An early quarto . . . from his library. He gave it to me as an offering for Edward Capell if I thought it would cool the censor's ire. But he really wanted us to have it."

Hunter reached for her cloak and settled it on her shoulders. Then he clasped her hand and pressed it softly against his lips.

"You are kind, and generous, and a very bad liar," he smiled at her tenderly, handing her the rare copy of Shakespeare's play. "The inscription reads 'With great admiration.' Garrick meant this for you, my darling. You are his fellow playwright and 'tis to you his tribute was intended. However"—he grinned at her—"I shall enjoy perusing these pages from time to time when we finally reach America. I don't want either of us ever to forget how to play Prospero and Ariel."

Sophie stood on tiptoe so that her lips grazed his ear.

" 'All hail, great master, grave sir, hail I come,' " she whispered, " 'to answer thy best pleasure, be it to fly, to swim, to dive into the fire—' "

" '—to ride on curled clouds, to thy strong bidding task,' " Hunter continued, repeating the airy sprite's opening speech from *The Tempest,* just as he had that night in their darkened bedchamber in Stratford's White Lion Inn.

". . . to ride on curled clouds," Sophie murmured, tenderly pushing a stray strand of blond hair off Hunter's forehead.

"Now we are to ride across an ocean," he said, smiling ruefully. "Come, my Ariel," he commanded, taking her hand and leading her out the door toward the coach, where their trunk was now lashed on the roof and their son Rory waited excitedly to depart on their promised adventure.

"Good-bye . . . good-bye . . . safe journey!" Lorna and Mrs. Phillips cried as Hunter helped Sophie and Rory into the carriage.

"Driver!" he shouted up to the coachman joyfully. "To the Plymouth docks! Quickly, man! Let us be gone!"

Acknowledgments

A proper list of thank-yous to the scores of people who made significant contributions to this novel would comprise a book in itself. To everyone who helped me during this two-and-a-half-year odyssey into the world of eighteenth-century British and American theater, I offer my sincere appreciation.

Since 1983, I have held a Readership in eighteenth-century Scottish-American History at the Henry E. Huntington Library and Art Gallery in San Marino, California, where I have been given a desk in the magnificent Main Reading Room and limitless kindness and assistance from the staff and administration. Foremost among the Readers' Services stalwarts are Virginia Renner, Doris Smedes, Leona Schonfeld, Mary Jones, and rare book watchdog, Mary Wright. Assistant Curator of Rare Books, Susan Naulty, and I enjoyed many conversations as we browsed through booksellers' tradesmen's cards or chatted about the admirable David Garrick or debated the date when actresses first played the male sprite Ariel in Shakespeare's *The Tempest*. Assistant Curator of Early Printed Books, Thomas V. Lange, advised me on the intricacies of the smaller English wooden printing press. Cheerful support for this project also came from Robert Skotheim, President of the Huntington Library; William Moffett, Director of the Library; Martin Ridge, former Director of Research and Education; and Linda Zoeckler, Art Reference Librarian. I received invaluable guidance and encouragement from Huntington staff members Evie Cutting and Lee Devereux, as well as my fellow researchers and authors, among them Suzanne Hull, Grace Ioppolo, Harriet Koch, Karen Langlois, Karen Lystra, Barry Menikoff, Linda Micheli, Robert Middlekauff, Susan Morgan, Jeanne Perkins, Elizabeth Talbot-Martin, Midge Sherwood, and Paul Zall. Shakespeare and theater historian Helene Wickham Koon was enormously helpful. A one-woman show, "The Incomparable Aphra," part of Leia Morning's series *Literary Ladies . . . Working Women,* was presented at the Huntington in 1988 and provided inspiration for this effort, as did playwright, screenwriter, and novelist Catherine Turney—to whom this book is dedicated. For nearly a decade, Cathy has shared with me her wisdom and good humor concerning the hurdles facing woman writers in any century.

I also extend special thanks to Ellen Donkin, Associate Professor in the Theatre Program, Hampshire College. Her wonderful monograph "The Paper War of Hannah Cowley and Hannah More," in the book *Curtain Calls* (see page 694) made me realize I would be wise to make a pilgrimage to Amherst, Massachusetts, to discuss the entire subject of eighteenth-century women dramatists. Dr. Donkin was as extraordinarily knowledgeable, generous-spirited, and witty as any of the eighteenth-century dramatists we both admire.

In Edinburgh, as elsewhere, my research traveling companion, Gayle Van Dyck, showed as much pluck as my heroine, Sophie McGann, indulging my desire to walk and photograph virtually every inch of the Royal Mile. She even stood patiently in the rain as dusk enveloped Holyrood Palace, watching with a puzzled look as I reenacted James Boswell's celebrated farewell to the city of his birth as described in *Boswell's London Journal 1762–1763.* Also, a Harvard classmate and friend, actor Kenneth Tigar, who has created a one-man show on James Boswell, drew my attention to a number of intriguing insights concerning this brilliant scamp.

In addition, I would like to thank Robert Bearman, Senior Archivist, and Eileen Alberti, Archivist, at the Shakespeare Birthplace Trust in Stratford-Upon-Avon. Ms.

Alberti and I shared a wonderful moment when, attempting to determine the precise location of the White Lion Inn in 1769, we discovered we were *standing* in it! That same plot of land now forms part of the library and garden at the rear of Shakespeare's birthplace on Henley Street. Also in Stratford, actress and B&B hostess Mary Henry kept me fortified with a comfy bed, scones, and strong tea while I researched Garrick's 1769 Shakespeare Jubilee in that former market town.

At Bath's Reference Library on Queen's Square, the librarians and photocopyists were enormously helpful in chasing down the small details I sought regarding the Orchard Street Theater. Thanks, too, to guides at Bath Abbey, the Pump Room, the Assembly Rooms, the Roman Baths and Museum, Number One Royal Crescent House; to the proprietors of Sally Lunn's bun shop; and to Andrew Byrne and the staff at the Royal Crescent Hotel where I was pampered to excess in the Sir Percy Blakeney Suite. Also, in regard to the section of the novel dealing with the spa itself, Whittier College Associate Professor of Art History, Paula Radisich generously shared her marvelous lecture "Taking the Body to Bath."

In London, I owe a great debt of thanks to actress Helen Mirren who provided elegant digs while I prowled Covent Garden from Half Moon Passage to Martlet Court. Archivist and former manager George Hoare at Theatre Royal Drury Lane led me on a tour of the bowels of the building to the catwalk eighty feet above the stage, dispensing wonderful historical notes and information on items of interest. I enjoyed a similarly happy experience, thanks to Ewen Balfour, Director of Public Affairs, at the Royal Opera House, Covent Garden, the location of the original Covent Garden Theater. The Theatre Museum and Library on nearby Tavistock Street provided a wealth of information and engravings. Rare-book expert John Dreyfus was my host at a wonderful luncheon at the venerable Garrick Club and provided entré to the Garrick Library and the club's collection of portraiture and Garrick memorabilia.

I am grateful to internist Dr. Wilbur Schwartz, who advised me on the progressive nature of David Garrick's gall-bladder disease.

It is impossible to credit the many admirable scholarly works that provide the historical underpinnings of this novel. However, several books were crucial: first among them is *Curtain Calls: British and American Women and the Theater 1660–1820* edited by Macheski and Schofield (Ohio University Press, 1990). Central to my thesis that modern women writers have inherited a literary tradition from women in the eighteenth century was *Mothers of the Novel* by Dale Spender (Pandora Press, 1986). Other invaluable texts included *A Dictionary of British and American Women Writers 1660–1800* edited by Janet Todd (Rowman & Allanheld, 1985), *The Plays of Frances Sheridan* edited by Hogan and Beasley (University of Delaware Press, 1985), *The Great Shakespeare Jubilee* by Christian Dellman (Michael Joseph Publishers, 1964), *Eros Revived: Erotica of the Enlightenment in England and America* by Peter Wagner (Paladin Press, 1990), *David Garrick: A Critical Biography* by George Winchester Stone, Jr., and George M. Kahrl (Southern Illinois University Press, 1979), *Wits, Wenches and Wantons: London's Low Life—Covent Garden in the Eighteenth Century* by E. J. Burford (Robert Hall Publisher, 1986), *The Censorship of English Drama 1737–1824* by L. W. Connolly (The Huntington Library, 1976); *Drury Lane Calendar* by Dougald MacMillan (Clarendon Press, 1938), *Catalogue of the Larpent Plays in the Huntington Library* by Dougald MacMillan, *The London Stage: 1660–1800* (Part 4) by George Winchester Stone, Jr. (Southern Illinois University Press, 1962); *A Treatise on Madness* by William Battie, M.D. (1758) and *Remarks on Dr. Battie's Treatise on Madness* by John Monro, M.D. (1758).

Thanks to Scotland-lover, Ann Skipper, for reading early drafts, my map maker Marilyn McCracken, my fellow historical novelists and friends, Elda Minger and Cynthia Wright, and the Los Angeles Women Writers' Computer Group. Edmund and Mary Fry, proprietors of the tea emporium Rose Tree Cottage in Pasadena, obtained many British publications for me and allowed me to make their establishment my after-hours "club." I am also indebted to my brother-in-law, actor Christopher Cass, for posing for the portrait of Hunter Robertson on the cover of this novel.

And finally, my thanks to Bantam editor and friend Beverly Lewis for holding me to her high standards and to her assistant, Joe Pittman, a most reliable gent. My son, Jamie Ware Billett, deserves enormous credit for getting himself admitted to Harvard University while his mother's mind was elsewhere. My dearest husband, journalist-screenwriter Anthony Cook, knows how much he's contributed to this novel and how very much I appreciate his love and support. Without doubt, some of Sophie and Hunter's debates about life and literature may sound awfully familiar to him.

Ciji Ware

CIJI WARE enjoys hearing from her readers. You can write to her at P.O. Box 15133, Beverly Hills, California 90209.

"An enthralling tale of a splendid era and an amazing woman."—Judith McNaught, author of *Something Wonderful*

ISLAND
OF THE SWANS

Ciji Ware

Jane Maxwell can remember no time when Thomas Fraser was not at her side. Their wild childhood pranks through Edinburgh's cobbled streets scandalized the city, and when Jane grows to radiant womanhood, Thomas is the only man she wants. Then Thomas is reported killed in the American colonies, and a distraught Jane hesitantly responds to handsome, enigmatic Alexander, Duke of Gordon.

Both a lyrical love story and the glorious portrait of an era, this unforgettable novel moves from Edinburgh's candlelit balls to the London court of half-mad King George III...from Jane Maxwell's famed salon, where politicians and poets meet, to a remote castle on the lushly green Island of the Swans. And it is here that Jane and Thomas meet again, and a passionate but principled woman, must make her choice.

FANFARE

The Very Best in Historical Women's Fiction

Rosanne Bittner

_____ 28599-8 EMBERS OF THE HEART $4.50/5.50 in Canada
_____ 28319-7 MONTANA WOMAN $4.99/5.99
_____ 29033-9 IN THE SHADOW OF THE MOUNTAINS $5.50/6.99
_____ 29014-2 SONG OF THE WOLF......................... $4.99/5.99
_____ 29015-0 THUNDER ON THE PLAINS $5.99/6.99

Kay Hooper

_____ 29256-0 THE MATCHMAKER $4.50/5.50

Iris Johansen

_____ 28855-5 THE WIND DANCER $4.95/5.95
_____ 29032-0 STORM WINDS $4.99/5.99
_____ 29244-7 REAP THE WIND $4.99/5.99
_____ 29604-3 THE GOLDEN BARBARIAN $4.99/5.99

Teresa Medeiros

_____ 29047-5 HEATHER AND VELVET $4.99/5.99

Patricia Potter

_____ 29070-3 LIGHTNING $4.99/ 5.99
_____ 29071-1 LAWLESS $4.99/5.99
_____ 29069-X RAINBOW $4.99/ 5.99

Fayrene Preston

_____ 29332-X THE SWANSEA DESTINY $4.50/5.50

Amanda Quick

_____ 29325-7 RENDEZVOUS $4.99/5.99
_____ 28354-5 SEDUCTION $4.99/5.99
_____ 28932-2 SCANDAL $4.95/5.95
_____ 28594-7 SURRENDER $4.50/5.50

Deborah Smith

_____ 28759-1 THE BELOVED WOMAN $4.50/ 5.50

Ask for these titles at your bookstore or use this page to order.

Please send me the books I have checked above. I am enclosing $ _____ (add $2.50 to
cover postage and handling). Send check or money order, no cash or C. O. D.'s please.

Mr./ Ms. _____

Address _____

City/ State/ Zip _____

Send order to: Bantam Books, Dept. FN 17, 2451 S. Wolf Road, Des Plaines, IL 60018

Please allow four to six weeks for delivery.

Prices and availability subject to change without notice.   FN 17 - 8/92